To John B. Bryans

Contents

Preface

If you disregard for a moment the picture of two frightened little Jersey Boys traveling back and forth to LBI through the Pine Barrens with their families every summer, passing by the 'Painted Rock' while listening to tales of the Jersey Devil and other local lore, then this series began at the dawn of the new millennium, quite by accident.

The plan initially called for a three-day boat ride over Memorial Day Weekend starting at Barnegat, down the Intracoastal to the Delaware Bay, and up the Delaware River to the Falls at Trenton, our hometown. But Mother Nature had other ideas. The night before our scheduled departure a grinding Nor'easter blew in, scuttling plans for the lengthy nautical journey.

Happily, serendipity intervened. The Tuckerton Seaport was poised to have its grand opening that very weekend. When the weather cleared, an informative and engaging introductory visit to the newly recreated maritime village (which includes a replica of the original Tucker's Island Lighthouse doubling as a museum) eventually led to a pleasant and insightful drive out along the narrow connected wooden bridges of Great Bay Boulevard, culminating in a shorter boat trip from Toms River to Atlantic City. The improvised adventure resulted in the recording of a song, "Spirit of the Bay," and the writing of a screenplay entitled "The Treasure of Tucker's Island."

The screenplay was read by a big-time Hollywood producer and former Trenton-area resident with Disney connections who gave us some sage advice: "This would make an entertaining book." Needless to say we took his advice to heart and the rest, as they say, is history. More than a decade later we are still writing … books!

While most of these stories have appeared in print previously, their availability has been limited. With this new compilation the "adventures" have undergone rigorous updating and re-editing, and are for the first time collected in a single volume, which includes an entirely new story—*Storm Warnings*—written especially for this publication. We truly hope you will enjoy the adventurous romp with us through the mysterious Pine Barrens and along the ageless Jersey Shore.

Onward and upward!

Acknowledgments

Words alone cannot express the sincere gratitude we have for our friend and mentor, John B. Bryans, the tireless Editor-in-Chief and Publisher at Plexus Publishing Inc. His faith in us and his dedication to enhancing our craft, along with his relentless determination to help our series reach a wider audience, are the reasons our adventures continue. His insights and candor are only matched by his skills and pure passion for the writing. We are forever in his debt.

Adventures Along the Jersey Shore would not have been possible without the efforts and support of Peg Papp, Norma Neimeister, Nancy Ellor, Victoria Ford, Mike Pippin, Janie Hermann, Shelly Hawk, Linda and Jim Stanton, Randy Russell, Rich Klupp, Tim and Paul Hart, Jaclyn Wood, Joan Ruddiman, Brandi Scardilli, Jenny Bryans, Barbara Solem, Rob Colding, Tiffany Chamenko, Chris Stopero, Denise Erickson, Dorothy Pike, Jackie Crawford, Bernie Flynn, Marty Nicholson, Ralph Siegel, and Joe Weinbrecht.

We would also like to express our heartfelt thanks to our family, friends, and faithful readers.

Thank you one and all.

The Treasure of Tucker's Island

1

Storm Warnings

The storm had been brewing for nearly an hour. Strong, gale force winds blowing in from the southwest had come up suddenly and caught them by surprise. They had left Trump's Atlantic City Marina later in the afternoon than they had planned. Hard rain pummeled their sleek new boat. High seas and wind threatened to swamp her on this, her maiden voyage. Audrey and Dick Hanson struggled to keep their retirement investment afloat and maintain a straight course for safety through the narrow Beach Haven Inlet.

By his own reckoning Dick considered himself an experienced seaman. He did have a few seasons of sailing under his belt. But the sturdy canvas sails he was used to handled quite differently under these circumstances than this new, high-powered toy, and he was only now finding out.

For her part Audrey Hanson knew very little about boats or the moods of the sea. She had been busy fondly recalling the more pleasant points of their A.C. junket, the scrumptious buffet luncheon and the entertaining lounge act, in a vain attempt to forget Dick's more than trivial losses at the blackjack table when the storm's fury broke upon them. At first Dick Hanson thought it would blow over. Then he felt sure their new high-speed water rocket could outrun the storm. By the time he realized that neither would happen it was too late to put back into the marina.

He fought the weather bravely and thought he had at last gained the upper hand, getting them nearly through the wave-tossed inlet, when their boat, the *Naughty Tails*, struck something hard and unseen. The boat scraped and skidded noisily along a hidden shoal.

"What was that?" Audrey called up to her husband from the cabin.

"I don't know," answered a worried Dick.

Audrey shrieked as seawater began pouring in through a hole in the hull.

Dick reached for the radio. "Mayday! Mayday!" he repeated into the crackling air.

Before he could raise a response, a bright light came in through the port window catching their attention.

"Oh, thank God!" Audrey exclaimed. "That was quick."

Dick and Audrey went aloft. A small motorboat seemed to have appeared out of nowhere and came up alongside their wounded craft. A dark, solitary figure in hooded rain gear motioned for the panic-stricken couple to climb aboard his boat. His face remained shrouded in shadow, as he offered them a hand and helped them onto his swaying launch.

"What about our boat?" Dick pleaded. "We can't just leave it."

"Wait here," the stranger ordered. "I'll tend to her."

The hooded figure stepped onto the *Naughty Tails* and disappeared below deck. The cabin was awash in seawater. Debris was floating on the surface as the boat pitched back and forth. The stranger searched around, going through drawers and cabinets, pocketing valuables and other items of interest that he could easily conceal.

Stepping into the engine compartment, the stranger inspected the leaking hull. He yanked a fan belt from its post and kicked away at the floorboards until they splintered, letting even more water rush in.

Satisfied with his work he re-emerged on deck and climbed back aboard his own boat.

"You saved us," gushed Audrey huddled beneath her rain soaked shawl.

"Can you tow her?" questioned Dick.

"Too far gone," replied the stranger. "She'd slow us down, maybe even drag us under with her. I did all I could."

The hooded stranger untethered his boat, the *Mooncusser*, from the *Naughty Tails*, now listing heavily to one side, and sped off.

"What did we hit?" asked Dick. "It wasn't on the charts."

Looking back in the direction of their helpless boat, the hooded figure spied the sandy shoal of a small, newly forming island, spiking up into the Inlet.

"That's old man Tucker's Island, rising up from a dream," the hooded figure replied in a far off voice.

2
Wick and Wisdom

Kelly Martin shivered as she removed her sweatshirt in the brisk wind. Several other teens around her, already stripped down to their swimsuits, were running in place and blowing into their hands to keep warm. It was late June and school had been out for almost a week, but it didn't feel much like summer. Remnants of last night's storm had left the day gray and overcast. A stiff breeze was blowing off the agitated Atlantic Ocean, making the beach in the early morning hour unseasonably chilly and uncomfortably cold.

Kelly was one of only two female contestants trying out for the Long Beach Island Life Saving Squad (Ship Bottom Boro branch). The others were boys who, along with the leering and cheering returning veterans from the squad and a handful of curious onlookers, eyed the two young female recruits with a mixture of fascination and disdain.

She was no stranger to such stares. At sixteen, her form was lithe and lean. Tall for her age at nearly 5'7", her long auburn hair fluttered in the breeze as she retied her ponytail.

A fierce competitor, Kelly loved a challenge. Many a boy had felt threatened by her athleticism and then bowed to her competitive abilities. But there was no competition with her brother, Geoffrey. Younger by a year, Geoffrey enjoyed a good cerebral challenge and left the sporting events to his sister.

Next up was the beach flag race. A fifty-yard sprint across the soft sand to retrieve a stick with a brightly colored pennant attached to it. Speed mattered in this event. The flags represented injured swimmers in trouble on the shoreline. Time was precious. A few seconds could be the difference between a breath and death.

Kelly lined up with dozens of other aspiring lifeguards. Only six new recruits would be chosen for the Long Beach Island (LBI) Lifesaving Squad following the conclusion of the two-day tryouts.

She was ready. She had been training for this moment since she first learned she and Geoffrey would be spending their summer vacation with their favorite aunt, Sarah Bishop.

Kelly offered a friendly smile to Abby, the other female trainee, as she took up a position next to her. Moss Greenberg, the self-proclaimed "oldest lifeguard on the East Coast" fired the starter's gun. Kelly was off and running at the sound of the shot. She was the first to grab a flag, just edging out a well-muscled boy named Curtis Wick, who sported a fresh buzz cut.

"Time!" called Moss, and a handsome, blond beach boy and returning squad member named Danny Windsor called out Kelly's time. Several of the veteran lifeguards applauded and cheered when they heard her score.

"That was great, sis!" said Geoffrey rushing over with a blanket. "You beat everybody."

"That's the idea," she replied confidently, wrapping herself in the blanket.

The paddleboard event came next. Each trainee had to paddle out 100 yards on a full size surfboard, turn around a buoy marker, and paddle back in. Speed and endurance were tested here, and with today's surf being exceptionally rough, anything could happen.

Danny Windsor called for the group to follow him down to the water's edge. "It's time to get wet," he said with relish.

Kelly tossed the blanket to her brother.

"Good luck, sis. I'll keep these warm for you," he said clutching her sweatshirt and wrapping the blanket around himself to beat back the chill.

"Don't get too comfortable, Geoffrey," she said confidently. "I won't be that long."

As she hurried to join up with the others, Danny was already going over the last-minute instructions.

"Grab a board and brace yourself," he said with a grin. "Today's water temperature is a balmy 54 degrees!"

"Okay, guppies," continued Moss. "This is where we separate the bluefish from the blowhards. Anybody can talk a good game, now let's see what you've got. Speed without endurance and I've got two swimmers in trouble."

Moss raised the starter's gun again. "Once around the buoy and get back in quick. The last ones in are the first to go. Are you ready, Danny?"

"Ready when you are," Danny waved his hand.

"On your mark, get set ..." Bang!

In her excitement Kelly lost her footing and stumbled momentarily as she dashed board in hand for the ocean. She dove onto the board belly first. The icy water stung her face and hands. As expected, Curtis Wick was out in front of the pack paddling furiously.

Several of the riders ahead of her got tangled up going around the buoy, so Kelly had to take the turn wider than she wanted. Curtis still held the lead. Heading in, he was treading calm waters and expecting an easy ride in with the tide.

Kelly put everything she had into it but Curtis seemed to have a comfortable lead. The wide turn around the buoy had thrown her slightly off course and she had lost some precious time. But the angle had also pushed her out into a large rapidly forming wave. The huge wave crested beneath her, lifting her high atop it. Kelly saw her chance instantly and in a sudden, bold maneuver she stood upright on her board.

The wave curled, flinging her forward. As it broke, it caught Curtis in a torrent of whitewash. Kelly surfed on ahead into the beach, first again. A bedraggled Curtis Wick took second with a three-way tie for third. Abby, one of several bunched up at the buoy, finished a disappointing ninth.

Geoffrey was the first to greet her. "That was awesome, Kelly! When did you learn to surf?"

"Just now," she replied dropping her board and slipping into her sweats.

"Creative finish," added Danny approvingly. "But what about your victim?"

Kelly glanced over her shoulder at Curtis. "He'll get over it."

"She cheated! She cheated!" whined Curtis as he waded in.

The crowd waited in silence as Danny conferred with Moss.

"The rule simply states the guard's got to come in with the board." Moss pronounced at length. Smiling, he added, "Martin's the winner."

A rousing round of applause went up as the crowd rushed over to congratulate Kelly. Curtis flung his board down and kicked sand in her direction. All Danny Windsor could do was smile.

***

"I swear. It was right over there," said a befuddled Dick Hanson, pointing to a vast expanse of open water beyond the inlet breakers.

"The stranger who rescued us last night called it 'Tucker's Island,'" added Audrey Hanson.

State Police Captain Jim Davis let out a low laugh. Looking over at his snickering sergeant, Wally Parker, he added, "It sounds like this stranger was having some fun with you."

"What do you mean?" questioned Audrey. "He saved our lives."

Captain Davis removed the binoculars from his eyes. "Well, that may be true ma'am, but Tucker's Island sank into the sea a long time ago."

"But what did we hit and what about our boat?" asked Dick.

"Can't say for certain, since we can't seem to find her, but I hope you have insurance," said Captain Davis, as the police launch headed back to Atlantic City.

***

The annual beach party was in full swing. Overhead, a glowing new moon blazed brightly as if competing for attention with the roaring bonfire below. About sixty kids, some still in bathing suits, were crammed up against the stage where Danny Windsor was leading his band, Driftwood, through a rollicking rendition of Life House's recent hit "Hanging by a Moment." Kelly and Geoffrey Martin were grooving to the music and enjoying the whole scene. They had never experienced anything quite like this in their hometown of Teaneck. The freedom felt wonderful.

The song ended abruptly when the keyboard player, a carrot-haired boy named Tommy Sanders, stumbled off the stage. He ducked behind a sand dune and dropped to his knees. Kelly could hear him barfing up his guts before he passed out.

"Nice ending," she offered as Danny jumped from the stage in disgust. "But shouldn't someone see what's wrong with him?"

"That's what you get when you mix keyboards with vodka and Red Bull," Danny replied slowly with a distracted smile.

Turning his head he tuned in to the first tentative chords of "Jump" by Van Halen wafting through the sound system. He looked up to see Geoffrey Martin noodling Tommy's vacant keyboard. The pace picked up suddenly as the drummer and the bassist joined in.

"Hey, isn't that your brother up there?" Danny asked Kelly.

"Yes, and he's strung out on Snickers and Snapple so you better sign him up quick."

Danny hopped back on stage, strapped on his guitar and joined in the jam. Much to the crowd's delight, the band ran through a medley of current hits in an impromptu audition of Geoffrey Martin. The young rock 'n' rollers loved it and pleaded for more when the tunes finally ended.

"Sorry folks," said Danny apologetically. "Tomorrow's a big day. Finals for the Life Saving Trials start at 8:00AM sharp." Then looking directly at Kelly he added, "Make sure you trainees get your rest. You're gonna need it!"

The crowd grumbled but began to disperse. Moss Greenberg and the other squad members doused the bonfire with large buckets of sand. The band packed up its gear.

As he was leaving, Danny pulled Geoffrey aside. "You free on Tuesday nights for rehearsals?"

"Heck yeah!" exclaimed Geoffrey enthusiastically.

An over-sexed young blonde named Wendy Barnes emerged from the shadows. She snuck up behind Danny and covered his eyes with her hands. "Guess who?" she giggled.

Without peeking, Danny put his arm around Wendy and led her away from the crowd, disappearing behind the sand dune where Tommy Sanders lay sacked out.

***

Kelly sat on the beach with her head and arms resting on her knees. She was exhausted. Unlike yesterday, today's Life Guard events were strenuous, made all the more difficult by the blazing sun and lack of shade. On top of that she had forgotten her Gatorade and was feeling a little lightheaded. She and the other guard trainees were whooped. But there was still one more event to go: A simulated life saving.

For this trial every trainee needed a buddy, someone to swim out 25 to 30 yards and pretend to be drowning. All the trainees but Kelly had paired up with someone. The day before, Geoffrey had volunteered to be her victim, but so far today he was a no-show.

Moss called out Kelly's name a second time as everyone looked at her. She lifted her head slowly. Her eyes were puffy and almost tearing. She stood up and began to collect her things to leave.

Danny Windsor walked over to her. "So that's it? You're quitting now?—with one event to go?"

"I don't have a partner." she said dejectedly. "I guess Geoffrey had to work late. He was supposed to be here."

Danny handed his whistle to another guard and peeled off his T-shirt.

"Okay, I'll be your victim," he said to Kelly. "Save me."

Before she could protest, he was in the water and wading out into the ocean. About 25 yards out he turned to face the shore. Splashing and thrashing with exaggerated movements he yelled for help.

Moss called out Kelly's name again and, looking at her, blew his shrill whistle.

Kelly wasted no time dashing into the crashing waves. Danny went under and she had to wait until he surfaced again to make sure she was heading out in the right direction. She began to cut into the waves with long, efficient strokes.

Danny disappeared under the murky green water a second time. It seemed like he was out of sight longer this time, making it a little more difficult for her to keep him in view. When he resurfaced his movements seemed less active. No more flailing about. "He's really hamming it up," she thought.

She came up alongside him, but instead of finding the big, blue-eyed smile and the patronizing wink she'd expected, she saw that his eyes were closed and his body limp. He was going under for a third time. She reached out her right arm and placed it under his chest. She raised his head above water the way she was taught and began swimming slowly, gracefully with one arm back to shore. She was so intent on her technique that she didn't notice the slimy creature that had attached itself to Danny's thigh moments earlier. She didn't see it slide off and slip away, narrowly missing her as it bobbed past.

As Kelly swam, Danny didn't move a muscle to help her. His six-foot frame felt like a sack of hardened concrete. She treaded water more slowly now as the fatigue and dizziness she had felt earlier returned to her aching body. Even with the tide Danny's dead weight was a handful.

With her victim wrapped in one arm and treading water with the other, Kelly struggled to keep them both afloat. She kicked harder and felt the strain snake up her spine to her neck. She considered asking him to doggie paddle or kick lightly to help her, as she had noticed some of the others doing to help their partners. But she decided against it. If he was going to play it to the hilt, so was she.

As her toes finally touched the sandy bottom, Kelly was so exhausted that she floated motionless in the surf for a long moment, waiting for one last wave to roll them in closer to shore. Finally, she hoisted Danny up and dragged him onto the beach. The two teenagers fell together in a heap, side by side. Danny still wasn't moving. She rolled him over onto his back.

"Had enough?" she asked, straddling Danny and pounding on his chest.

Eyes closed, Danny offered no reaction. He lay perfectly still.

"Okay, buster, if you insist, but there are better ways to get a kiss," joked Kelly.

She bent down, pinched his nose, parted his lips and began blowing into his mouth.

Suddenly, his eyes flew open, a wild and crazed look in them. She pulled away quickly as he sputtered and stammered until at last seawater gushed out through his mouth and nose. He coughed and choked and heaved again.

"Help!" she screamed realizing he was in trouble. "Something's wrong!"

Immediately Moss and the other lifeguards came running over. Danny tried to sit up only to slump back down. Kelly lifted his head. Danny retched again.

As Moss applied additional CPR, Danny tried to wave him off weakly. Then Moss noticed the purplish-red marks on the young man's thigh. "Jellyfish," he said, pointing. He called for a stretcher and some Benadryl. They hoisted Danny on it and carried him way.

Spent and depleted, Kelly collapsed face down into an impression in the sand left by Danny's prostrate body. Her cheek struck something hard and metallic. Opening one eye she spied a coin-like object on a chain embedded in the outline made by Danny's head. Thinking it must belong to him, she picked it up, brushed it off, and turned to show it to the others. But everyone had moved up the beach to the guard house, where a crowd was now hovering over Danny like so many attentive midwives. An EMT arrived and whisked him away.

Kelly stuffed the medallion into her swimsuit and fell back onto the moist sand, giving her body a chance to recover from the drama of the day. She shuddered at the thought of Danny nearly drowning, and how silly she had been to think he was play-acting for her benefit. She began crying softly to herself.

After a few minutes she got up and waded out into the surf to rinse herself off. As she did, she looked around carefully for jellyfish. Seeing none she dunked under a wave and, trying to clear her mind, held out the medallion she'd found and went to work rubbing and scraping off the encrusted barnacles until it gleamed like a sparkling jewel.

3
Bishop of Crab Cove

Kelly was sitting at her desk reading a postcard from her mom and dad when she heard a knock on her bedroom door. "It's open."

The door swung open lazily. Geoffrey stood in the doorway in an ill-fitting waiter's uniform.

"Sorry I missed all the action today," he offered apologetically. "Manny stuck me with a double shift at the Quarterdeck. I heard you had to play lifeguard for real."

She looked up at her brother and he saw tears well up in her eyes. "Yeah," she said remotely. "Danny Windsor got stung by a man o' war and I acted so stupid. I thought he was just fooling around."

Geoffrey stepped into the room and sat on the edge of the bed. He looked tired and worn out. "Well then we're both lucky I wasn't there. I can't see you giving *me* mouth-to-mouth, although you must be pretty good at it. I just left Danny and he wasn't complaining."

"Is that supposed to cheer me up?"

"No," answered Geoffrey, "but this might. His doctor says he'll be fine. He never knew he was allergic to jellyfish—I guess he could have died."

She put her face in her hands and shook her head.

"Moss said the man o' war must have been a rogue because the water is way too cold for them right now. Did you say anything to Aunt Sarah?"

"No," said Kelly. "She's out with Mr. Parsons again. And don't you say anything to her, either," she added sternly. "She worries too much about us already."

"Don't worry, I can keep a secret."

Kelly studied her brother's face. Except for the round-rimmed glasses, frizzy hair, and a few more freckles, it occurred to her that Geoffrey was a carbon copy of her in appearance, only shorter.

"Can you really?" she prodded.

He crossed his heart and sealed his lips together with his fingers.

"Good. Then I've got something to show you," she said eagerly. She reached into the top drawer of her desk and pulled out the medallion she'd found on the beach. She dangled it from the chain in front of him.

He sprang off the bed. "Where did you get that?"

She placed the medallion in her brother's hand. "I found it on the beach near Danny after I rolled him over."

Geoffrey smiled. "Boy, you were all over the guy."

"Yeah, I guess so, but you have to admit, he does leave an impression."

Geoffrey whacked his sister with a pillow playfully.

"Do you think it's his?" he asked.

"Do you? Have you ever seen him wear it?"

11

Geoffrey shook his head. "From what I can tell Danny's not into jewelry. Besides, it looks pretty old."

"It does, doesn't it? I wonder what it is."

"I wonder what it's worth. Hey, maybe Aunt Sarah will know."

Kelly put the medallion back in the drawer and yawned. The day's events were catching up with her. She switched off the desk lamp. "We'll ask her in the morning," she said sliding past Geoffrey and into her bed. "Goodnight."

"Goodnight, sis," said Geoffrey stepping into the hallway and closing her door.

***

Sarah Bishop sat at the kitchen table in the cluttered apartment above the Crab Cove Gift Shop sipping a piping hot mug of black coffee. She let the steam fill her nostrils and deeply inhaled the rich aroma. "Ah," she sighed aloud recalling the splendid but late evening she'd spent with Noah Parsons last night. She smiled to herself and took another sip.

For Sarah, life these days was as simple as a good cup of morning coffee. After twenty years of devoted service in the Jersey City school system, she had retired from teaching to follow her lifelong dream of owning a small gift shop on Long Beach Island. As a child her family had regularly vacationed on Ocean County's magnificent 18-mile-long barrier island. Every summer she and her younger sister, Margaret, looked forward to the idle hours of swimming, sunbathing, and shopping with their mom at the quaint Beach Haven village shops. In the evening, after an outdoor barbecue consisting of steamed clams, fresh Jersey corn, and whatever fish their dad landed from the surf, the family would walk down to the bay and watch the sun go down at Sunset Park. Invariably, the stroll home would include a stop for hand made ice cream or salt water taffy. On special occasions the family played miniature golf at one of the numerous seasonal courses.

Like many who have visited this resort jewel along the Jersey shore, the hot summer days and long summer nights took root under Sarah's skin. She vowed that one day, if she ever got the chance, she would make "LBI" her permanent home. When the opportunity for early retirement came up a few years ago she jumped at the chance and purchased Crab Cove with her savings.

Widowed young in life, and without children of her own, Sarah was extremely close to her niece and nephew. So, when Margaret and her pharmacist husband, Robert Martin, decided to circumnavigate the globe this summer in search of natural cures for modern diseases, Sarah seized the opportunity to share her passion for LBI with her sister's two children. She was the one who suggested that Kelly and Geoffrey stay with her and find summer jobs on the island.

"Yum, bagels," said Kelly shuffling into the kitchen dressed for the beach. "Aunt Sarah, you're the best!" She bent down and gave Sarah a peck on the cheek.

"You mean thank God for Bageleddies," Sarah smiled. "You know I can't cook."

Kelly grabbed a honey oat bagel and plopped down in the chair beside her aunt. She poured herself a glass of juice. "Who needs to cook when you go out every night!"

"I don't comment on your social life, do I?" Aunt Sarah replied passing Kelly the cream cheese. "Where's your brother?"

"Still sleeping," she said biting into her bagel. "He did a double at the Quarterdeck."

Sarah folded the copy of the *Sandpaper* she had been fussing with and rested it on her lap. "Did they post the final grades yet?"

"This isn't Jersey City Central, Aunt Sarah," said Kelly chewing loudly. "The Beach Patrol doesn't post grades. You either make it or you don't."

Sarah buttered a bagel for herself. "We use to call that pass/fail."

Kelly took a sip of her grapefruit juice and smiled affectionately at her aunt.

"In beach lingo it's known as sink or swim, and right now I guess I'm still treading water."

Sarah smiled back and refilled Kelly's juice glass.

"Coffee … I need coffee," said Geoffrey in a dirge-like monotone as he dragged himself into the kitchen.

"Since when did you start drinking coffee?" Kelly said.

"If I keep doing double shifts, you'll see me mainlining mocha lattes before the summer's over."

"How will I ever tell your parents?" said Aunt Sarah jokingly. She poured Geoffrey half a cup of coffee into which he promptly added three sugars filling the rest with 2 percent milk.

"By the way, have you talked to them lately?" Sarah inquired.

"Yeah. Mom called last night. They're on their way to Madagascar," said Kelly slapping Geoffrey's hand as he grabbed for the other half of her bagel. "She's got a shopping spree planned while Dad attends another boring convention." She stuck her tongue out at her brother.

"There's nothing boring about botanical research," protested Geoffrey. "Where do you think modern medicine would be without guys like Dad?"

"Okay, Geoffrey, calm down. I love Daddy, too, and I miss both of them."

Aunt Sarah slid a plate with a freshly creamed everything bagel over to Geoffrey and rose to clear away her breakfast dishes. "Well, this summer will be over before you know it and you'll both be on your way home, leaving me all alone."

Kelly elbowed Geoffrey. "All alone with Mr. Parsons, you mean."

Sarah made a face as she took Kelly's dish and glass from her. "That's enough prying into my personal life. What are you two up to today?"

Geoffrey nudged his sister. "Did you ask her?"

"Not yet. Let me go get it." Kelly raced out of the room.

"Get what?" Aunt Sarah called out. She looked back at Geoffrey.

"You've got to see this," he said excitedly.

Kelly reentered the kitchen wearing the medallion around her neck. She took it off and laid it on the table.

"Where did you find this?" Sarah asked reaching for her reading glasses.

"On the beach at 17th Street. Have you ever seen anything like it?"

Sarah picked it up and examined it closely. "Only in a museum … if it's real."

"How do we find out?" asked Geoffrey.

"I think we need to talk to Libby Ashcroft," Sarah said handing the medallion back to Kelly. "She's the curator at the Seaport Museum. Noah says she knows her stuff." She let out a soft giggle. "When you meet her, you might think she was around when they minted this baby!"

***

The Manahawkin Causeway is the only road on and off Long Beach Island. A continuation of Route 72, the four-lane highway spans the shallow Manahawkin Bay from Stafford Township on the mainland to the Borough of Ship Bottom on the Island, where it becomes Ninth Street. During the height of the summer season, traffic is often backed up for miles; eastbound on Saturday mornings as the eager weekly renters arrive, and westbound on Sunday evenings, when the sunbaked day trippers and assorted weekend guests leave, are the worst times to cross.

Kelly's earliest memory of the causeway was the magnificent view at night. Arched between the pitch black sky above and the dark, narrow bay below, and lit in either direction by two endless rows of luminous white lights, it gave her the impression that she was riding across a starlit bridge forming a stairway to heaven. Many work-weary vacationers have expressed similar thoughts about the crossing. Some say the change of pace and mood is palpable as soon as you get over the causeway.

A sudden gust of wind blew through Danny Windsor's open Jeep Wrangler, sending dozens of papers from the back seat beside a sleeping Geoffrey into the air.

"Geoffrey, the flyers!" yelled Danny pulling over to the far right westbound lane and stopping abruptly. Several cars honked as they pulled around to pass.

Danny and Geoffrey hopped out of the Jeep and began running after the loose band flyers as they blew across the roadway. A large white seagull squawked from his perch on the bridge railing then flew off into the sun-filled morning sky. In the passenger seat, Kelly ran a comb through her hair and watched the boys through the rearview mirror as they scampered about the highway, darting in and out of passing cars, bending here and there to retrieve the fluttering leaflets.

"Hey, lifeguard, pitch in!" shouted Danny. "Let's go, cutie. Out of the car. You're part of my patrol now," he said pointing to the LBI Lifeguard monogram stenciled on his shirt. Kelly ran her hand proudly across the same logo on her own shirt.

"When you told me I made the squad I didn't know it included working as a roadie for your band, too," she replied feigning annoyance.

Opening the passenger door, Kelly paused at the railing overlooking the bay. The water was calm and sparkled in the sunlight. A group of brightly colored catamarans emerged from under the causeway. Off in the distance, just beyond the light blue domes of the Surf City and Harvey Cedar water towers she saw Old Barney, the lighthouse, standing in silent watch over the northern end of the island. Everywhere in between there were cottages, shacks, apartment buildings, churches, and stores as far as the eye could see, leaving her to wonder if one day the island might sink under the weight of all those people.

Danny came up behind her and stirred her from her musings. "This is how it works: You help me and I help you," he said smiling. "You did want a ride to the Seaport, right? It's a really long walk to Tuckerton so I suggest you help us pick up the rest of the flyers."

Typical Danny, thought Kelly. After the scare he gave her the other day, she was certainly glad to have him back to normal, bark and all.

"Yes, sir," she saluted and ran off to join Geoffrey.

4

'Nice Bumping Into You'

The idea for the Tuckerton Seaport grew out of a project spearheaded by the Barnegat Bay Decoy and Baymen's Museum. It was a simple idea really: preserve the past for future generations to enjoy. For decades the old timers, like their fathers before them, eked out a living from the bounty of the bay and the surrounding marshland. Their work was cyclical and followed the seasons of nature. In the springs and summers they engaged in clamming, crabbing, fishing, and harvesting salt hay. During the autumns and winters they got by with hunting, trapping, and boat building.

But the old baymen feared that with each succeeding generation their fulfilling though arduous way of life was dying out and would soon be forgotten. It wasn't good enough to follow the seasonal ebb and flow of nature any longer. The bay was changing. Housing developments and sprawling strip malls were springing up everywhere, encroaching on the baymen's simple way of life and degrading the very source of their livelihood. They watched each year as more of their children and grandchildren grew up and moved away, following the job market in search of a better quality of life.

Once known as Clamtown, the sleepy, backwater town of Tuckerton was renowned for its tasty oysters and its sumptuous clams in the early 20th century. Tuckerton shellfish was served in some of the finest New York restaurants.

Tuckerton lay nestled on the mainland directly across Great Bay from the southern tip of Long Beach Island to the east and along the fringes of the Pine Barrens to the west. To keep its history and heritage alive, the town hosted an annual event designed to attract area sportsmen. This also gave the locals a chance to share their stories and show off their crafts, which included the work of some of the finest decoy duck carvers on the East Coast. Soon sportsmen from all over the mid-Atlantic region were making the annual trek to this quiet little hamlet.

Over time, the old baymen realized they needed larger accommodations and thus plans were made to recreate the old time village just off Route 9, where Tuckerton Creek flows into the bay. Here the local craftsmen and volunteer docents could display their skills and tell their stories firsthand to a new and appreciative audience. The crowning stroke was the decision to build a replica of the fabled Tucker's Island Lighthouse to use as a museum and focal point for the working seaport. The attraction guaranteed scores of summer visitors to Long Beach Island.

***

Ryder Hayes was considered by many to be one of Tuckerton's Old Guard. Although shrouded in mystery, his family roots could be traced back to the 1700s, to the time of Reuben Tucker, the namesake of both the present day town of Tuckerton and the lost resort once briefly called Sea Haven but best remembered as Tucker's Island.

Among the local townsfolk, it was widely accepted as fact that the original Tucker's Island Lighthouse Keeper, Captain Eber Rider, was in some way connected by blood or marriage to Ryder Hayes. Thus, despite the odd spelling of his first name, it was commonly believed that Ryder was named after the good captain, who served with distinction as lighthouse keeper from 1865 to 1904 before passing the duty on to his son, Arthur. Ryder Hayes did not dispute these familial associations and often fostered them through his own vague recollections. But his reclusive lifestyle gave rise to other rumors as well.

Hayes no longer derived his living from the bay in the traditional ways of the baymen, but he was still indebted to the water for his livelihood. He was the owner and sole employee of a local salvage and antique business. To hear Libby Ashcroft, curator of the Tuckerton Seaport Museum, tell it, however, it seemed Hayes's business placed a far greater emphasis on salvaging the sea's refuse than digging up its treasured antiques.

So it was that Libby and Hayes were at it again, haggling over some cheap imitation of maritime scrimshaw that he was trying to pawn off on her as genuine, while Kelly, Geoffrey, and Danny were in the seaport's parking lot having a minor run-in of their own with Noah Parsons, a retired U.S Coast Guard lieutenant who was Aunt Sarah's current and nearly constant companion.

Their unscheduled rendezvous got off on the wrong foot when the usually mild-mannered middle-aged naturalist observed Danny tacking up band posters, announcing an upcoming gig, on utility poles in the parking lot. Their ill-timed meeting went something like this:

"Excuse me. What do you think you are doing?" said Noah sounding more like a school administrator than the liberal minded, cardigan sweater-wearing, college professor-type his looks and nature normally conveyed. "You can't hang that there."

"Why not, man? It's a pole," replied Danny defiantly.

Noah folded his arms and gave Danny a stern look.

"This is public property and you're advertising a private event."

"No, man, the public's welcome," Danny answered back.

Noah unfolded his arms and placed them behind his back. He rocked back and forth between the balls and heels of his feet.

"What I mean is that your flyer has nothing to do with the Seaport."

"Hey, lighten up. It's okay." Danny tore the flyer from the pole. "I'll find someplace else to put them."

The growing antagonism between the two was averted when Kelly and Geoffrey approached from another part of the parking lot.

"Hi, Mr. Parsons," greeted Kelly warmly.

Noah greeted Kelly and Geoffrey, calling each by name.

"You know this guy?" Danny asked in disbelief.

"Mr. Parsons and our Aunt Sarah are frequent dinner partners," Kelly said diplomatically.

Noah cleared his throat.

"I was just explaining to your friend that it's not appropriate to post personal solicitations at the Seaport."

Kelly and Geoffrey quickly hid the pastel-colored flyers they were carrying behind their backs.

"Danny, I have to agree with Mr. Parsons," said Kelly with mild sarcasm. "I've heard your music. And this peaceful seaport is no place to advertise loud rock 'n' roll."

"I have nothing against your music," interrupted Noah. "But, if we let you put up flyers, who takes them down? How do we stop others from doing the same thing? It becomes more than an eyesore. It spirals into mounting trash. Eventually it's bound to have a negative impact on the fragile environment that the Seaport is dedicated to preserving."

"Sounds cool to me," offered Geoffrey, dumping his handful of flyers into a nearby trashcan. Danny hurried over to the trash bin and retrieved those copies not already soiled with catsup and other condiments.

"So other than rock 'n' roll promotions, what brings you here?" Noah asked Kelly.

"Actually, we're here to see Mrs. Ashcroft. Do you know where we can find her?"

Noah made a face. "She's most likely in the chart room, cataloging artifacts. First door on your left," he said pointing.

"Well, thank you, kind sir. I'll let Aunt Sarah know how helpful you were."

"My pleasure," answered Noah, obviously pleased with himself. "So maybe I'll see you three at the little presentation I'm giving in the Oyster House. It starts in twenty minutes ... and by the way," he added, leaning in closer and whispering, "if it had been bluegrass ..." he smiled at Danny and winked at Kelly, "I might have been tempted to look the other way."

A volunteer at the Seaport, Noah had been on his way to prepare for a lecture about the bay area marine life but he enjoyed taking time out to give the kids a discourse on the virtues of bluegrass music relative to rock 'n' roll. Besides, he thought back to his own teen years, smiling, they had managed to escape a lengthy *private* lecture by agreeing to stop by the Oyster House to hear his public presentation on "The Fate of the Horseshoe Crab."

***

Geoffrey and Danny were still clowning around and making fun of Noah Parson's preference for "hillbilly" music when Geoffrey opened the door on a surprised and flustered Ryder Hayes, knocking his cheap trinket to the floor where it broke in half.

"Do you hoodlums have any idea what a piece like that is worth?" scowled Hayes staring at the shattered scrimshaw.

"We're sorry, mister," Kelly apologized for the group. "Maybe it can be fixed?"

"Yeah, you know, a little Crazy Glue and it's good as new," added Danny with a sheepish grin.

Kelly bent down to pick up the two halves. As she did, the medallion she had placed in the breast pocket of her Beach Patrol polo shirt tumbled out onto the floor.

She froze.

"My, my, what have we here?" said Hayes with a noticeable change of tone. He bent down and scooped up the medallion before Kelly had a chance to react. "Pirate booty from the pocket of a pretty lass?"

She stood and handed Hayes's broken scrimshaw to Geoffrey. "Then you know what it is?" she asked, unable to control the excitement in her voice.

Hayes smiled. It was not a warm, inviting smile. It was a sly, sinister smirk and it made the teens feel even more ill at ease.

"I might have some idea, yes," he replied, slowly pushing the brim of his seaman's cap back off his forehead. His eyes were small, beady, and gunwale gray. He flipped the coin over in his palm and studied the writing intently. "Spanish, I'd say." He placed it between his yellowed teeth and bit down hard. "And solid gold, I'd wager."

"Here, now, what's all this commotion," exclaimed Libby Ashcroft, running out from behind the museum's information counter at the mention of the word "gold."

She stood on her toes to add stature as she addressed Hayes good-naturedly. Her silver-blue, bonnet-like hair shone in the reflected overhead lighting. Aunt Sarah was right, thought Geoffrey; Libby Ashcroft was 90 years old if she was a day.

"Ryder, you scoundrel. I thought I told you to go peddle your junk someplace else. Leave these nice kids alone."

As Libby distracted Hayes, Kelly snatched the medallion back from his outstretched hand. She wiped the coin off on her shorts and placed it in her hip pocket.

Hayes turned away from Libby and looked straight at Kelly. He smiled that devilish grin again and slipped something out of his sleeve. "My card, Miss, if you want to know more about your little piece of history." He placed the card in her hand.

"Ryder Hayes: Salvage and Antiques," she read aloud.

Hayes bowed his head. As he did, he noticed the LBI Beach Patrol logo on Kelly's shirt. He raised his eyes and, trying not to be too obvious, directed his next question to all three teens. "So do you live on the island year round or are you just staying for the summer?"

"Enough!" exclaimed Libby, shooing Hayes to the door. "Isn't there a boat bottom somewhere you need to scrub?"

Geoffrey handed Hayes his broken faux scrimshaw.

"It was sure nice bumping into you kids," Hayes said sweetly as he reached the door. "Too bad about this carving though," he said, playing with the pieces. "Give me a call. I'm sure we can work something out." He tipped his cap to Libby. "Don't let this old sea cow steer you wrong," he said as he exited.

Libby closed the door and waited until Hayes was a safe distance away before she spoke. Rubbing her hands together she turned her attention back to the kids.

"Now then, what's all this nonsense about pirates and Spanish gold?" she asked, barely able to contain her excitement.

Kelly held out the medallion for Libby to inspect. Libby reached for the necklace then thought better of it and withdrew her wrinkled hand. She forced all expression from her face. "Spanish, I'd say. 16th century. That's the Great Seal of Philip II. Where did you say you got it?"

Kelly glanced at Danny. "17th Street. Ship Bottom. I found it on the beach during a … a rescue the other day."

Danny smiled warmly.

"So how much is it worth?" gushed Geoffrey.

Kelly shot her brother a stern look. Geoffrey just shrugged.

"Well, let's not be too hasty," Libby said slowly. "It *looks* Spanish, all right, but authentic? … now there's the question. First we have to prove that it is what it appears to be. It looks like a Spanish doubloon, a coin of the realm that's been fashioned into a fancy necklace, probably for some very important lady. That's what makes the piece a bit odd and maybe more valuable. We need to find out who she was and where it came from. Something we in the business call provenance," she said peering down at them over her half-moon spectacles. That means you've got to trace it to a ship. To do that you need to check through all the old ship registers and find out how it got here."

"But you said yourself that was the Great Seal of Philip II," offered Danny impatiently.

"Yes, indeed it is. But it could have been copied. Forgeries are common, especially with old Spanish coins. There's no record I can recall of a 16th century Spanish shipwreck this far north."

"But it's gold!" shouted Geoffrey. "You heard what Mr. Hayes said."

"Gold plated, possibly." Libby removed her glasses slowly, purposefully. Her cold blue eyes burned into his. He took an awkward step back.

"And pay no attention to that old wooden plank Ryder Hayes. He may come from a local seafaring family, but that doesn't make him the expert he thinks he is. You saw the junk he was peddling."

Libby turned to Kelly and forced a smile. "You don't suppose I could borrow that for awhile, do you honey? I'd be more than happy to run through the old shipping records myself for you."

"For how long?"

"Oh, a couple of days, I'd say."

"Well, I don't know," Kelly said hesitantly. She slipped Ryder Hayes's card into her back pocket.

"Oh, I understand," said the old woman, backing off. "That's all right. You're the Martin kids, right? Sarah Bishop's your aunt?"

Kelly and Geoffrey nodded.

"Tell you what. You hold onto it. I'll check around and see what I can find. In the meantime, I'd keep your little discovery under wraps if I were you. Pirate treasure has been rumored around the island for ages. Nothing worthwhile has ever turned up, but modern day pirates and treasure hunters are everywhere. You can't trust anyone," added Libby with a knowing little twinkle in her eye.

5

The Fate of the Horseshoe Crab

"**W**hat's the oldest creature you can name?"

"A dinosaur," replied an enthusiastic little boy in the front row. His father smiled proudly.

"Good," replied Noah Parsons standing behind a wide oblong display case.

"Dinosaurs lived three hundred and fifty million years ago. Now what would you say if I told you that one of the species on this table was around at the same time as the dinosaurs?"

The small crowd of mostly school-aged children and their parents who had packed themselves inside the cramped Oyster House stood in silence. Keeping a promise they had made to Noah earlier, Kelly, Geoffrey, and Danny squeezed in through the narrow doorway. They hung out in the rear and listened.

"Which one?" shouted several youngsters pressing up against the display case.

Noah reached in and picked up a spindly-legged, olive colored, helmet-like specimen. He held it up for everyone to see.

"A horseshoe crab?" the same little boy asked in a voice dripping with disappointment.

Noah nodded his head. "Right. That's what you call him. But what if I told you this ugly creature was not really a crab?"

"I know this one," Geoffrey whispered into Danny's ear. "It's an arachnid."

"Isn't that a spider?" Danny asked Geoffrey in a surprised voice loud enough for the entire room to hear.

Recognizing the voice Noah Parson scanned the back of the room until he spotted Danny, Kelly, and Geoffrey. He smiled to himself, delighted to see they had taken him up on his offer.

"In a way that's right. The horseshoe crab is actually a member of the same family as the spider."

Danny and Geoffrey gave high-fives to each other in the back of the room, embarrassing Kelly with their childish "guy thing" antics. She turned away and hid her face.

"Aren't they extinct?" asked the father of the little boy in the front.

"For the sake of the red knot I certainly *hope* not," said Noah in poetic response.

Several of the adults in the room chuckled at Noah's quip.

Noah set the crab down gingerly and stepped aside. Staring into the faces of his audience he used a hand-held device to switch on a computer monitor hidden beneath the table. It projected an image on the wall directly behind him, showing untold numbers of horseshoe crabs on a nearby beach with thousands of shorebirds walking and feeding among them.

"Red knots, sandpipers, and other migratory birds that winter in South America depend on the horseshoe crab for their return flight. They feed on the millions of crab eggs deposited on Mid-Atlantic beaches, refueling, as it were, in order to complete their trip north to their breeding grounds in the Arctic. It's their only stop. Without this food source they wouldn't make it."

The images on the wall changed from a bird-crowded beach to an offshore commercial fishing fleet. The camera lens zoomed in on a handful of men in yellow rain slickers on one of the boats. The fishermen stood over a bloodied table, using sharp cutting knives to scrape out chunks of chum from the embattled horseshoe crabs. A mound of empty shells lay piled up on the deck.

"Unfortunately, the horseshoe crab is also in demand as bait for such new-found delicacies as conch and eel. So commercial harvesting has taken its toll on their population."

Nervous coughs and whispers could be heard as Noah's presentation shifted to the next slide, which showed several homes under construction along the ocean and on the bay. It was a familiar scene to most islanders and local townspeople.

Noah paused to let the images sink in. His target audience was no longer limited to the children.

"Not to mention the loss of habitat due to over-development along the shoreline, and the impact it has on marine life."

Noah stopped the projector and flicked on the lights.

"So, what do you suggest?" asked a neatly dressed father standing beside his two well-groomed kids and suntanned wife. "We stop enjoying the beaches and cut back on sushi?"

The resentment in his voice was not lost on Noah or on some of the others in the room, as many chimed in on the man's comment.

"All I want you to do," Noah began in a calm, measured cadence, "is recognize that this creature, like many others, is of great value to mankind. In the case of the horseshoe crab, it comes down to a substance known as LAL."

"My dad told me about this," said Geoffrey stepping forward boldly. "Isn't that where they use the blood of the horseshoe crab to test for impurities in vaccines?"

Noah clapped his hands together in appreciation and relief.

"Exactly. After researchers extract the blood from the horseshoe crab they use it to make a substance called LAL, which stands for limulus amebocyte lysate. LAL enables lab technicians to test injectable drugs and biomedical devices for the presence of harmful toxins. So, in essence, horseshoe crabs save human lives."

"Do we hurt them in the process?" whispered Kelly from the doorway.

Noah's admiring wink made Kelly blush.

"No. Once their blood is drawn in the medical lab, they are released unharmed."

"That sure sounds better than being cut up for bait," Danny added with a cocky swagger.

Mild laughter erupted around the room.

Noah smiled approvingly. "I see someone may have learned something today. Thank you all for coming to the Seaport. I hope you enjoy the museum. Don't forget to visit the gift shop. Remember to tell a friend about us, and come back soon."

Noah waved goodbye to the kids as they exited with the rest of the crowd.

After the crowd had dispersed, Libby Ashcroft cornered Noah as he was rearranging the crab cage for the next lecture.

"Nice crowd. You keep pullin' 'em in like this and we're gonna need a bigger room."

Noah looked up at Libby for a long moment. It was not like her to leave the inner sanctum of the air-conditioned museum.

"It's not me, it's the creatures of the sea," he said shifting the crabs around in the display case.

"Yes, well, speaking of creatures, Ryder Hayes was here earlier."

The mention of Hayes's name brought an abrupt halt to Noah's activity.

"What was he trying to sell us this time? The anchor from the Titanic?"

Libby cracked a wrinkled smile. "Nah, something much smaller and probably worthless."

"He's not easily discouraged, is he?" said Noah raising his eyebrows.

"Well, that's what I came over to talk to you about," Libby said in a slightly conspiratorial voice. "He had a little run-in earlier with Sarah Bishop's niece and nephew. They seem like nice kids. Maybe you could do us all a favor and keep an eye on them. I'm afraid he might try to take advantage of them somehow."

***

"Hey, Kelly," said Danny, applying sunscreen to his face and arms. "Maybe if you sit down we can both see."

"I was just checking the surf for jellyfish," replied Kelly as she looked out over the water from the lifeguard stand she and Danny were sharing.

"Good one, but you haven't sat down since we got here," he said adding a thin layer of zinc oxide to his lips. "Want some?" he offered the tube to Kelly.

"I screened before I left this morning," she said sitting down beside him. "And I've got ChapStick on my lips," she said. "Wild Cherry," she added, licking her lips flirtatiously.

"I hadn't noticed," he said turning away. "Hey, keep your eye on that big guy in the Hawaiian shorts. His name is Fred Barnes. He's not too good in the water."

She followed Danny's gaze. "I think he'll float."

"You better hope so, Rookie, because you've got the first rescue."

She smiled. "From where I sit you still owe me one."

Kelly stood abruptly. She blew her whistle repeatedly and gestured to a couple of kids to get off the jetty. Reluctantly they obeyed.

Danny pulled her back down by her shorts. "Relax," he said. "Everything's under control." At that very moment he spotted a group of old timers combing the beach with metal detectors.

"Looks like that group missed the bus to Atlantic City," he said pointing them out to her. They were huddled around the very area where she had found the medallion the other day. The place where she'd pulled Danny to safety.

Even though she was disguised under the bug netting of her wide straw hat, Kelly recognized the diminutive features and purposeful posture of Libby Ashcroft.

"Maybe they think the odds are better here," she said jumping down from the guard tower. "I'll be right back."

Danny watched as she ran off toward the senior citizens.

"Keep them away from the flagpoles and fishermen," he shouted after her. "We don't want to set off any pacemakers."

"Well, hello, dear," said Libby as Kelly reached her. "What a nice surprise!"

Kelly smiled back. "Nice to see you, too, Mrs. Ashcroft." Staring at the metal detector in Libby's hand she added, "Looking for anything in particular?"

Libby lowered her head and moved away from the other women. "No, honey, just doing my part to clean up around here." She busied herself shoveling scoops of sand. When her unit chirped, Libby scooped up a rusted soda can and tossed it into her empty mesh bag.

Kelly was not fooled by the old biddy's feeble attempt to cover up her treasure-seeking motives. She decided to press the antiquarian by revealing some of the things her own research had turned up. She followed Libby up the beach, nearly jogging to keep up with her brisk pace. It occurred to her that Libby might be trying to shake her. She was undeterred.

"Speaking of buried treasure, did you know that Captain Kidd was rumored to have anchored near the mouth of the Brigantine Inlet and may have hidden a fortune nearby?"

Libby slowed her pace. "That's an old tale, honey, and the truth is Kidd was after young tail. Her name was Amanda. She was a local girl and she was the only treasure he left behind."

Kelly's thoughts were interrupted by the ear-piercing screams of a little girl in trouble. Fear gripped her as she turned toward the shoreline. Two older boys were brandishing a horseshoe crab like a weapon and teasing the girl with it. Kelly scanned the lifeguard stand for Danny to see if he was going to handle the situation. But Danny was preoccupied. He had a different situation on his hands. Her name was Wendy Barnes, the amorous blonde from the night of the bonfire. Her weapons were dimples and a skimpy bikini, and she was hanging around the foot railing of the lifeguard stand, giving Danny a good view of both.

"Gotta run," Kelly said to Libby. "Duty calls," she offered by way of explanation as she took off to put out a couple of fires.

6

Ryder Hayes

During the summer tourist season, the best way to get around LBI is by pedal power. This mode of transportation suited Geoffrey and Kelly just fine, especially since she was still a year away from the legal driving age in New Jersey. So it was on a gorgeous Saturday morning around 6:00 AM that the kids said goodbye to their Aunt Sarah at the door of Crab Cove just as dawn was breaking.

"See you later, Aunt Sarah," Kelly shouted. "We'll be back before ten."

Kelly and Geoffrey hopped on their twin Schwinn Roadsters and pedaled off for the mainland.

"Last one across the causeway is a rotten egg," she challenged him.

As the Martins pedaled along the bay they were impressed with how sleepy and peaceful the scenery was. Best of all, there was absolutely no automobile traffic. Gulls were soaring and singing overhead, calling the kids to join them in celebration of the new day.

Now that they both worked, early morning rides like this were a treat. They took their time to admire the scenery, occasionally pointing out things of interest to each other. A solitary man was kayaking in the morning mist across the bay. A pair of anchored sailboats lapped lazily in the channel, while an older couple fished off a creaky, wooden dock. They passed various nautical signs advertising Ralph's Bait and Tackle Shop, Island Boat Rentals, and one that read "No Vacancies" in front of the Sea Crest Cottages. What a wonderful way to start the day amid the sights and sounds of an early summer's morning on LBI, they each silently and smilingly agreed.

Once across the causeway, the kids followed Route 9 south toward Tuckerton. The seven-mile route included brief stretches along the eastern rim of the rumored-to-be-haunted "Jersey Pines." As the kids rode along they passed several quaint little hamlets with names like Cedar Run, Eagleswood, and West Creek, each featuring a variety of campsites and roadside produce stands just starting to stir. When they got into Tuckerton their nostrils were treated to the smell of bacon frying, eggs, toast, and freshly-brewed coffee from the Dynasty Diner on the corner of Main and Green Streets. The temptation to stop and chow down was nearly overwhelming, but they had a single destination in mind and couldn't afford to lose sight of their mission.

The teens hung a left at the light before the Seaport and headed east for Skinner's Marina. They stopped to get their bearings then followed a narrow gravel road to the end of the lane and a place called Skinner's Dock. At the end of the dock they saw a dingy looking houseboat across from a small cedar-shingled shack. The property in between was littered with pieces of old scrap metal, a rusted anchor, and a broken-down boat hull turned upside down with weeds sprouting from holes in its bottom. The kids checked the business card Ryder Hayes had given to them. It had no street address, except: "At the end of Skinner's Dock."

"Now I know what they mean by the 'boondocks,'" said Geoffrey.

"I can hardly wait to see Skinner's yacht," replied Kelly.

The two left their bikes alongside a broken picket fence, walked up to the shack, and knocked. There was a busted sign hanging from above the doorway that almost fell on them when they rapped on the door. The floorboards creaked and the siding even seemed to yawn in the early morning breeze, but no one answered. They backed away cautiously, recrossing the dirt path onto the pier that led to the houseboat. They noticed a peeling letterbox with the faded name "Hayes" barely visible on it. They knocked on the door and waited. No answer. Curiosity got the best of both kids as they peered through smoke-yellowed windows on opposite sides of the door.

Geoffrey exhaled on the window and rubbed his moist breath with the sleeve of his sweatshirt, hoping to get a better look inside. "I can't see a thing," he whispered.

"Neither can I," Kelly said.

"Well, now, that depends on what you're looking for," a deep voice boomed, scaring the bejesus out of both of them.

Startled, the kids wheeled around. Geoffrey fell off the bait box he had used to boost himself up to the window. Ryder Hayes stood motionless on the deck behind them. He was unshaven and dressed in coveralls over a gray flannel shirt. His drab appearance would have been complete if it weren't for the bright red kerchief he wore like a scarf around his leathery neck. A set of crab traps was slung over one shoulder. He held a large white pail in his hand.

"We came to pay you for the broken carving," Kelly said with all the confidence she could muster.

Hayes eyed the kids with a mixture of curiosity and suspicion. They waited for what seemed like a long time for him to speak.

Hayes set his traps down. "Had yer breakfast yet?" he asked brushing past them on his way into the house. The kids followed him cautiously.

The house was cramped, but cleaner than the outside conditions would have led them to believe. It was just an open room with a kitchenette off to one side and a cot-like bed on the other. The room was rustic and musty, but orderly. In the middle stood a wooden-plank table set for one. On the small gas range, a large pot was steaming over. Geoffrey looked around for a bathroom, expecting any minute to pee himself. Seeing none he bit his lip and tried to force the thought from his mind.

Hayes eased over to the steaming pot and proceeded to dump the contents of the white pail into the boiling water. About a dozen fresh crabs slid to their certain death. One scrawny fighter bounced off the rim of the pot and landed on the floor, right side up.

The dazed crab scurried around looking for an escape route. With cat-like agility Hayes stepped on him lightly, holding him fast. Then he bent down and deftly lifted the crab from under his rubber boot, barehanded. The crab pinched and clawed to no avail. In an instant he was in the pot with the rest of the catch.

"Slippery little devils," exclaimed Hayes wiping his hands on a soiled dishtowel. "Now, what can I git ya?"

"Nothing for me," Kelly stammered. "Me, either," echoed Geoffrey, shaking his head.

"What do we owe you?" asked Kelly nervously.

"I see," mused Hayes, lighting his pipe. He pulled a chair away from the table and sat down. "So, it's right to business, then?"

The kids sat down together on the cot and waited for Hayes to speak. He sat across from them blowing smoke rings that curled like clouds throughout the room.

Hayes studied their faces. The kids grew anxious and began to squirm. He appeared to be deep in thought. "You didn't happen to bring that medallion with you, did you?"

"No," replied Kelly.

"Too bad," said Hayes.

"Why?" she asked.

Hayes rested his pipe in the ashtray on the table. He rose slowly and stepped over to the nightstand next to the cot. Instinctively, the kids huddled closer together, protectively. The old man opened the top drawer and pulled out a small leather pouch. He loosened the drawstrings.

"Because now we can't match it against these," he said, dumping the contents of the pouch onto the cot between Kelly and her brother. The startled teens stared down at three old silver coins bearing what looked like the seal of Philip II of Spain.

"So that's it," exclaimed Geoffrey. "You're after Captain Kidd's treasure!"

"Kidd? Hah!" said Hayes in a deep laughing voice, his eyes flashing. "Is that what that old biddy Ashcroft told you? I suppose she gave you the old yarn about Blackbeard, too?"

Brother and sister looked at each other, but said nothing.

"Did she also happen to tell you about the cutlass in the glass case at the LBI Museum?"

They gazed at Hayes with blank expressions.

"I thought not," said Hayes. He picked up the silver coins, put them back into the leather pouch. He placed the pouch back in the drawer, then returned to his chair and sat down.

"Do you know what that is?" Hayes inquired, pointing to a picture on the wall behind them.

The kids turned and looked over their shoulders. In an old dark frame was a large, grainy, black and white photograph of a big white clapboard building. The building looked like a house with a square glass tower on top. It was tilted sideways at a forty-five degree angle, leaning out over the sea like it was about to fall into it, or so it appeared. It was the only picture in the house. In fact, it was the only decoration of any kind as far as they could tell. Kelly and Geoffrey turned back to Hayes in disbelief.

"That … that looks like the museum building at the Tuckerton Seaport," offered Kelly.

"You are an observant young lady," Hayes said admiringly. "Actually, that's the old Tucker's Island Lighthouse being swallowed by the sea. The photo was taken in 1927. For nearly sixty years before that, members of my family tended to the lighthouse. The building at the Seaport is a replica of the original."

"But where is Tucker's Island?" asked Geoffrey. "I don't remember seeing it on any of the souvenir maps."

"And you won't," replied Hayes. "It's gone. The sea took the whole island back. Just like in the fable about the lost continent of Atlantis. But this island was real. The lighthouse was one of the last buildings to go."

"Where was it?" asked Geoffrey curiously. "I mean, before it disappeared."

"Tucker's Island was a small, leg bone-shaped tract of land that lay between what is now Beach Haven and Little Egg Harbor Inlets. Long before Ship Bottom, Surf City, and all the other touristy towns on LBI today, Tucker's Island was a thriving community that boasted one of the finest hotels around. It even had it's own Life Saving Squad—a little historical tidbit you may be particularly interested in, Miss."

Kelly smiled. "And you think Tuckers Island is where Captain Kidd buried his treasure?"

"Not William Kidd. Not even Blackbeard," whispered Hayes, glancing around cautiously. "They didn't come this far north. They weren't that crazy. These waters were too treacherous for those experienced gentlemen. But other lesser-known pirates may have ventured a bit too near."

"But if Tucker's Island sank what chance does anyone have of finding any buried treasure on it?" asked Geoffrey, now fully engrossed in the story.

Hayes stood to check on his crabs, taking time to scratch his crotch as he stood. He turned off the boiling pot and poured the hot water down the sink, careful not to let the crabs slide out. His face was lost momentarily in the steam that hissed from the pot. From out of the haze he turned again to face the kids.

"Yes, that would seem to be a problem now, wouldn't it?" agreed Hayes. "But every now and then Tucker's Island makes an unexpected appearance, rising out of Neptune's depths to take in a little sun perhaps, or to tease would-be treasure hunters like our Ms. Libby."

Kelly glanced sideways at her brother. "I told you," her thoughts seemed to say.

"Ah, yes, the story is well known by Madame Curator and others affiliated with the Seaport," continued Hayes. "And oftentimes when winter and spring storms wreak havoc on the barrier island inlet, as they have done very recently, some of the loosely buried artifacts might just suddenly wash up in the surf of a nearby beach."

Hayes paused to gather them in even closer.

"Sometimes the tip of Tucker's Island may reappear. First as little more than a sandbar, but who knows, maybe eventually, if the tides are right, enough of the old island may rise up, high and dry, so that one could finally get a good look at what she left behind."

"But where would one begin to look?" asked Kelly. "You'd need a treasure map."

"Not just a map," said Hayes with growing enthusiasm. "The location is well known, a little *too* well known. 'Under the two cedar trees, near the lighthouse,'" he recited in a hypnotic voice.

"But the lighthouse is gone," exclaimed Geoffrey. "How would someone find the exact spot without it?"

"With charts," answered Hayes with a gleam in his eyes. "The government has charts on these islands and waters going back a century or more. Given the way old Tucker's Island is resurfacing, a person would only need to overlay a map of the island as it existed in the 1800s, with the longitude and latitude of the lighthouse, and he might just be able to pinpoint the exact place where the treasure, if it is real at all, might still lay buried."

"If it's that easy why hasn't someone already done it?" Kelly asked skeptically.

"Two reasons," Hayes replied. "First, the sea has to cough up enough of the island for somebody to stand on, unless very expensive submersible equipment is available. And secondly, while most of the recent government records and charts are public information, the charts needed for this kind of operation are classified and only someone who has the proper credentials, like U.S. Navy or Coast Guard personnel, can access them."

"We know someone who was in the Coast Guard," Geoffrey blurted out. "Noah Parsons. And he's dating our Aunt Sarah."

Kelly shot her brother a piercing look.

"Is that a fact?" replied Hayes pretending to be surprised.

"We couldn't possibly ask him," added Kelly hurriedly. "We don't know him all that well. Besides, how do we know he wouldn't just look up the old charts and search for the treasure himself?"

"You've got a point there, Miss," admitted Hayes. "I know Noah Parsons. He works at the Seaport part-time. And that means he probably knows as much about the treasure as Libby Ashcroft does. Still, you say he's dating your Aunt Sarah? Well, maybe if you two tell him you're doing a little summer project for school he might be willing to lend you some guidance."

"I don't know …" said Kelly hesitantly. "That sounds a little devious to me."

"Oh, c'mon, Kelly," urged Geoffrey. "Wouldn't Dad be shocked if we could discover something valuable? It's perfect. I'm really interested in this. We could probably get Danny to help us, too."

At the mention of Danny's name, and the possibility of him joining in their little summer adventure, Kelly softened.

"I guess it wouldn't hurt to ask," she said.

"Good. Then it's settled," said Hayes.

"But what about you, Mr. Hayes, what do you get out of this? And what about the piece we broke? You still haven't told us how much we owe you."

Ryder Hayes stood and smiled like a gracious host. "Tell you what," he said, "How much do you have with you?"

Kelly pulled the money from her pocket. "I've got a hundred dollars."

"That should cover it, shouldn't it?" asked Geoffrey hopefully.

Hayes took the cash from Kelly's outstretched hand.

"How about I just hold this for safe keeping. If you two happen to find any pirate treasure around old Tucker's Island, say a coin or two, like the ones I showed you, I'll give your money back. I see no reason why we can't all be happy. Sound fair?"

"Sure does," agreed Geoffrey.

"Okay, it's a deal," added Kelly with some reluctance.

"Good," said Hayes with an air of finality.

He showed the kids to the door and watched through the torn screen as they sped off on their bikes.

As Kelly and Geoffrey left Skinners Dock, a blue pickup truck that had been idling out of sight down the lane while they were inside with Hayes crept along the roadway after them, following at a discreet distance. At the intersection of Route 9, the kids turned right and pedaled for home. Had they taken the time to stop and look back they would have noticed the blue pickup go straight through the light and pull into the parking lot of the diner. Presently, Noah Parsons got out of the driver's seat and went inside to use the pay phone.

***

"You're late, Rookie," Danny said as Kelly climbed up onto the guard tower. "I had to set up the stand, drag out the boat, and put up the flags all by myself. Just for that you're buying lunch."

When she didn't answer he added, "Why the long face?"

"I'm broke," she said.

"You just got paid yesterday! What'd ya do? Hit the casinos?"

"It's a long story," she moaned.

"We've got all day together, sweetheart. Let's hear it."

"Remember that guy at the Seaport?" she asked.

"The one with the poster hang-up, or the coin biter?"

Kelly chuckled at his sense of humor.

"Ryder Hayes, the salvage and antiques dealer."

"Yeah, the coin biter. What about him?"

"Well, we either just paid him a hundred dollars for his broken carving or we bought ourselves a ticket to a treasure hunt."

"I don't know if I trust that guy," offered Danny slowly.

She stretched, drinking in the day and the soothing, calm ocean. The sky was cloudless and blue, the surf docile, and the crowd small and well behaved. A few youngsters were boogie boarding. Others were dipping in or just getting their toes wet.

"I felt that way at first, too. But Danny, he knows his stuff. He's got coins just like the medallion, only silver. And he knows where we might find more.

"Keep talking," said Danny waiting for the hook.

"We're gonna need a boat," she said without looking at him.

He watched in silence as the big guy in the Hawaiian shorts, now beet red from a bad sunburn, set himself up in a sand chair under the shade of a tri-colored beach umbrella. His daughter, Wendy, handed him a melting vanilla ice cream cone.

"I know where we can get a boat," Danny added at length.

Kelly looked into his shades trying to see through them to catch a glimpse of his beautiful blue eyes. She couldn't see them but smiled anyway.

"So what's the plan, Rookie? Get sweet old Aunt Sarah to charm Mr. Bluegrass into helping you?"

"Exactly."

***

Sarah set the covered casserole dish down in front of Noah and re-filled his wine glass. She put her oven mitt aside and joined him at the table. They were seated in her rarely used kitchen enjoying a quiet candlelit dinner for two.

"What a treat it is to have a real home cooked meal," said Noah putting down his wine glass. "Have you been taking culinary lessons behind my back?"

She blushed and took a swallow of wine.

"I know that must be the wine talking because we've dined in far finer places," she said, playing with her glass.

He reached across the table and gently took her hand.

"It's the personal touches that make a meal worth sharing," he added with a sincere smile.

"Say that after you've had my meatloaf," said Sarah half seriously.

"So this must be a very special occasion. To what do I owe the honor?"

"Actually, it was the kids' idea. They've got this silly notion that the way to a man's heart is through his stomach."

Noah emptied his wine glass with a nervous gulp.

7
Treasure Hunting!

Geoffrey sat between Noah and Kelly in the front seat of Noah's blue Dodge pickup. They were traveling over Great Bay Boulevard heading east toward the old U.S. Coast Guard Station on a beautiful sunny morning. Bluegrass music was playing faintly on the truck radio.

"So, your Aunt Sarah tells me you two are working on a school project about the shrinking habitat of the great sea osprey," offered Noah conversationally.

"That's right," Kelly acknowledged looking out the passenger window.

"They're an endangered species," added Geoffrey decidedly.

"I'm impressed," said Noah. "Was this an assignment or did you choose the topic?"

"We chose," replied Geoffrey.

"An assignment," said Kelly at the same time.

"It's an assignment we chose," she clarified giving Geoffrey a sideways glance.

Both kids were a little apprehensive about the story they had concocted to enlist Noah's help.

"You don't know much about kids, do you Mr. Parsons?" Kelly asked changing the subject.

"Only from what I encounter at the Seaport," admitted Noah. "I don't have any children of my own, if that's what you mean. I've never been married."

Kelly chuckled. "Kids are full of surprises."

"I don't doubt that," agreed Noah, "but what surprises me is your interest in the nesting habits of the great sea osprey. I didn't think teenagers had the time or the inclination ..."

"That's lesson number one," interjected Geoffrey, looking at Kelly. "Never underestimate the power of kids to challenge adult conventions." It was something he'd read in a child psychology book.

Noah let the truck idle as he stopped to talk to an old salt who was fishing from one of the several narrow, single-lane wooden bridges that stretched out into the Great Bay, connecting the mainland to the former Coast Guard Station.

"Top of the morning, Clem. How they biting today?"

"Near got my limit already," the old man replied.

"Doris ought to be real pleased 'bout that," grinned Noah. "You'll be back home in time to paint the fence."

The old man gave Noah a wrinkled smile. Noah put the truck in gear and drove on.

"Clem Baker gets his limit every day," confided Noah as they went along. "He's been fishing that same spot since I stood knee high in the eel grass. That reminds me, the first time I ever saw a snowy egret was right over there," he said pointing out the window.

The kids followed the direction of his finger to an open field of sedge grass along the roadside. A snowy egret had waded on pencil-like legs into the center of a watery bog. It dipped its long neck to drink.

"Egrets and herons have been feeding here as long as anyone can remember," Noah said remotely.

"Now, if I understand what your aunt was telling me, you think it might be the same for the osprey?" he continued after a moment, picking up the conversation with the kids where he had left off. "And you're hoping to prove that osprey were nesting on LBI before they started nesting in the channel markers out in the bay. Is that right?"

"We feel it makes sense," answered Kelly tentatively. "Osprey are people-shy by nature. We think they were on the island until the trees were cut down and the buildings went up. That's when they moved offshore."

Noah stopped and idled his truck at another light to allow a car to come across the bridge from the other direction. When the light turned green he crossed the narrow bridge, waving to a group of kids who were crabbing from it. They had to practically lean over the bridge to let the pickup pass.

"That's probably true," he continued again. "But I'm still not quite sure how poring over the old maritime charts and reports filed by the U.S. Army Corps of Engineers during the early nineteenth century fits in. What exactly is it you expect to learn from them?"

"I … we … believe the birds were once indigenous to Tucker's Island, not just LBI. The tall cedars on the island would have provided perfect nesting places," Geoffrey found himself saying.

Kelly jumped in. "If we can find support for our theory from the old logs we might be able to graphically illustrate a more complete history of the bird's plight."

"And what will you do with that information if you are able to get it?"

Kelly stared out the window. Another snowy egret was wading in a bog rimmed with sedge grass. "Petition the government to set aside a section of Holgate as an osprey sanctuary and plant new cedars there for them to nest in," she said in a moment of inspiration.

"Or maybe convince the government to build up the sandbar of old Tucker's Island for the same purpose," Geoffrey blurted out.

Kelly poked him sharply in the ribs.

Noah chuckled to himself. "Pretty lofty plans. Your Aunt Sarah is right about you two. She thinks you're pretty smart. That's why I've asked a friend of mine to meet us at the station. He's still with the Coast Guard so he has clearance for the archives you want to research. My access was terminated when I retired two years ago. I think you might learn a lot from him. His name is Johnny Longfeather."

He waited until the smirks died away from the kids' faces following the mention of Johnny's Indian-sounding surname.

"He's half Lenape and half Jamaican, and no one knows more about these waters or how to read those old charts than Johnny does."

Noah parked his truck on the side of the dirt road. The kids jumped out, then followed him past the open gate and up along the boardwalk leading to the former

Coast Guard building. A thirty-something light-skinned black man with dreadlocks greeted them at the door. He and Noah embraced one another.

After brief introductions, Johnny Longfeather handed them each visitors badges and ushered them into a modernized room full of stainless steel filing cabinets and new computer terminals. Noah excused himself and went to get a cup of coffee.

"This is no longer a functioning Coast Guard station," explained Johnny leading the kids on a brief tour of the facility. He pointed through a glass partition to a group of students huddled around several fish tanks and glass beakers. "I'm here on loan to Rutgers University which runs a marine biology lab. They're doing some fascinating experiments here. Are you familiar with the studies involving the horseshoe crab?"

"Yes, yes," the kids answered quickly, in unison.

"We've heard *all* about them," finished Kelly.

Johnny smiled broadly and knowingly.

"So I see Noah can still captivate an audience ..." he added approvingly.

"We got the message," said Geoffrey.

"He obviously cares a lot about it," added Kelly.

"It is a wise man who knows the value of his own environment," Johnny said sagely.

He sat down at the computer terminal. "So how can I help you?"

Kelly and Geoffrey sat down beside him.

Geoffrey spoke up first. "We're interested in seeing the U.S. Army Corps of Engineers' reports filed for the region just south of Long Beach Island during the early 1800s," he said sounding rehearsed.

Kelly recited her part next. "In particular we are interested in seeing if they mapped and tracked the gradual disintegration of Tucker's Island."

She passed the ball back to Geoffrey with a glance.

"That's right, we believe the few great sea osprey that remain around here are descended from a huge indigenous community of shore birds. If we can recreate the location and size of the island and demonstrate the feasibility of an osprey habitat from the records before Tucker's Island sank, we think we might be able to start a grass roots movement to reinstate the island as their natural home."

Johnny looked at the two kids incredulously. "You guys serious?"

"Of course," replied Kelly with a straight face.

He pushed himself away from the terminal so he could address both kids at the same time.

"Then I'm afraid you're wasting your time," he sighed. "Osprey are not native to this area. They migrated from up north, chased by the spreading human development. It won't be too much longer before the same thing happens here. Surely you didn't come all the way out here to research such an implausible topic? Noah could have told you what I just did. It sounds to me more like you two are—"

"Treasure hunting!" finished Noah as he re-entered the room unnoticed from behind them.

The blood drained from the faces of Kelly and Geoffrey Martin. They knew they were caught and had no choice but to own up to their charade. They did so quickly and apologetically while still keeping a few morsels of information—like their arrangement with Ryder Hayes—to themselves.

"All right!" exclaimed Johnny with a clap of his hands. "Now you're talking. This beats tagging fish and reading soil samples."

He slid back to the terminal and began tapping at the keys.

"How much time do we have?" he asked as the computer began accessing the old records.

"About an hour," replied Noah looking at his watch. "I promised Sarah I'd get Kelly to the beach before her shift started."

"No problem," said Johnny as the colorful graphs flashed on his computer screen.

The kids moved in to get a better look.

Noah drained his coffee cup and walked over to the printer to collect the charts and maps it was spitting out in rapid-fire succession.

***

An hour later, Geoffrey tucked the rolled charts under his arm. He and Kelly couldn't stop thanking Johnny enough for all his help as he escorted them outside. Noah and Johnny clasped hands tightly and smiled warmly at each other.

"You do realize that there is still one problem," said Noah.

"What's that?" asked Johnny.

"Tucker's Island is still submerged."

"Not for long," smiled Johnny. "According to the navigational satellite more and more of the old island is becoming exposed every day. At low tide, the Coast Guard has been responding to a non-stop stream of "maydays" coming from inexperienced seaman running aground on her widening shoals. At this rate, by mid-summer boaters may have a permanent new land mass to contend with."

Noah turned to Kelly and Geoffrey. "I suppose you two will be wanting a boat next."

"Got that covered," replied Kelly with a sly smile.

8

The Mooncusser's Tale

Danny guided the motorboat across the bay like a pro, skimming high, barely touching the surface of the water. Geoffrey was hanging onto his seat for dear life. Kelly was losing the battle to keep her windswept hair out of her face, so she could watch Danny.

"Where did you say you got this boat?" Kelly shouted over the din of splashing waves and motor hum.

"From a guy I know," Danny shouted back. "Pretty cool, isn't it?"

"Do you need a license to drive one of these things?" asked Geoffrey. He was sitting across from Danny in the co-pilot's seat.

"I sure hope not," replied Danny with a grin.

It was early evening, but the sky was darkening quickly.

"Do you have to go so fast?" yelled Kelly adjusting her life jacket and pulling a baseball cap down over her hair.

"We don't have a lot of time. Besides, I don't like the looks of the sky," Danny said looking behind to the west.

Turning around, Kelly could see a curtain of dark, slanting rain coming toward them in a hurry.

"According to the charts we should head straight for the Inlet then turn ten degrees north," shouted Geoffrey trying to read the charts while bouncing along with the waves slapping against the boat.

Suddenly, there was a sharp crack of lightning and loud, rolling thunder as rain began to pelt them hard.

"Danny, should we turn back?" Kelly pleaded in a frightened voice.

"We can't. We're too far out," shouted Danny. "We'd never make it."

Lightning crackled again. A jagged bolt shot through the sky and sliced toward the water.

That was enough for Danny. He couldn't afford to be reckless and he knew it.

"We've got to get off the water," he called to Geoffrey and Kelly. "We're sitting ducks out here."

"What's that?" shouted Geoffrey pointing straight ahead to the crumbling hulk of a large brick building looming 500 yards away.

"That's the old fish factory," replied Danny, straining to see through the driving rain. "Stink Island. It's been abandoned for years, but it might just give us some shelter until the storm blows over. I'll make a dash for it."

He gunned the motor and the boat lunged forward in the direction of the small island. The rain was coming down harder now. The sky was totally black. As the boat approached the outer shoals, he cut the engine and climbed out, guiding the boat toward shore in waist-deep water.

36

"This is as far as the boat can go without getting stuck. If the prop gets bent we'll be stranded for sure. You'll have to climb out and wade the rest of the way. It's not deep. Grab the gear. Let's go."

Kelly and Geoffrey grabbed what they could and followed Danny's lead by jumping into the water. Danny dropped the anchor and the boat came to rest about ten yards from the shore. He ran back to give Kelly a hand with the backpacks.

Geoffrey tucked the charts and binoculars inside his sweatshirt to keep them dry.

Danny led them through the missing doorway of the rundown factory. He found a place that still had enough of a roof overhead to keep most of the rain off them. There they collapsed against the wall and slid down to the bare floor. They huddled together for warmth. Danny threw a poncho over them and they all squeezed closer together.

"What's that smell?" asked Geoffrey sniffing the air around them. "Kelly, was that you?" he asked accusingly.

Danny let out a loud laugh just as another thunderclap rolled overhead.

"Now you know why they call it Stink Island. You'll get used to it. This used to be a fish processing plant. It's been closed since the 1960s."

Geoffrey shivered. "How long do you think the storm will last? I'm drenched to the bone."

Danny pondered the question. "It's hard to say. The prevailing winds are usually out of the west. This storm blew in from the southwest. If it's a nor'easter it could hang around for a while. They can get nasty and grind for days. Nor'easters are the primary cause of beach erosion on LBI."

Kelly managed a smile. "You sound like a weatherman."

"Lifeguard 101, Rookie," he replied returning her smile. "When you're swimming against the tide, you'd better know which way the wind is blowing."

***

Sarah stopped pacing the kitchen floor and reached for the telephone on the wall. She'd been sitting alone in the dark for hours. Morbid thoughts filled her head. Dreadful thoughts. If something happened to the kids she would never forgive herself. Slowly, she dialed the number she knew so well and waited for the line to connect on the other end. A sleepy Noah Parsons yawned into the receiver.

"Hello?"

"Noah, I'm worried. It's after midnight and the kids aren't home. It's not like them to stay out this late and not even call."

She paused as he moved the phone to his other ear to hear more clearly. "The Windsor boy picked them up after dinner. I thought maybe his band was playing tonight, but I don't know that for sure."

"Now, Sarah, don't panic. I'm sure there's a logical explanation," Noah said in a reassuring tone. "Try not to worry. Danny Windsor may never be mistaken for a member of the Vienna Boys Choir, but I think he's a fairly responsible person. They need to get cell phones all of them, and so do you."

"Noah, they're good kids. Do you think I should call the police?"

"Just sit tight and leave everything to me. The island's a close-knit community. I'll find them."

***

"I'm hungry," said Geoffrey disturbing the silence of the last hour that the trio had spent listening to the sound of the rain whipping against the building.

"So what else is new?" mumbled Kelly opening her eyes. Her chin was resting on her arms folded across her knees.

Danny stirred from his slumber and yawned.

"What did you bring along for food?" Danny asked Geoffrey.

"Nothing. I didn't think we'd be out here this long."

"You?" inquired Danny looking at Kelly.

She shrugged.

"Well, there's some Wheat Thins and spring water I saved from lunch," offered Danny. "Anybody grab the cooler?"

Kelly and Geoffrey looked at each other and shook their heads.

"All right, then. It looks like a run to the boat is in order. Any volunteers?" Danny paused awaiting a response. "Don't everybody jump at once," he said getting to his feet. He lifted the poncho and checked the weather. It was still raining but with less intensity than before. Through the gaps in the roof he could see that the sky was still dark, but a bit less threatening.

He stepped outside and sprinted around the building in the direction of where he had moored the boat. As he approached their landing place he stopped suddenly. Turning around he rechecked the direction he came from. He rubbed his eyes and took a few steps forward wading into the water. Their boat was gone!

Suddenly he heard the sputter of an engine cough to life. Straining his eyes to see, he could make out the silhouette of a hooded figure draped over the controls of a boat. An eerie bow light illuminated the name of the boat through the encroaching darkness and light drizzle: *Mooncusser.*

The boat was moving away from the island and was nearly out of his range of vision. "Hey!" he yelled aloud. He waded out toward the boat splashing and waving his arms. Suddenly the bow light blinked out and the boat was enveloped in total darkness. As it turned west in the direction of the mainland, Danny heard her throttle open up and she was gone.

He came back on shore sopping wet. He ran back around the old fish factory to rejoin Geoffrey and Kelly. They were still sheltered under the poncho and didn't hear him approach.He lifted the tarp, startling them until they realized he'd returned.

"Forget something?" joked Kelly noticing he was empty-handed.

"Our boat's gone," he said with exasperation.

"Gone?" they echoed. "Oh, that's a good one, Danny," added Geoffrey with a slight chuckle.

Danny dropped down beside them. His face was serious. "I'm not kidding. It's vanished."

"That's not funny, Danny," cried Kelly punching him in the shoulder.

He didn't flinch. It took a moment but Kelly and Geoffrey soon realized he was serious.

"Maybe it drifted and floated down a little ways," consoled Geoffrey.

"It didn't drift away," replied Danny.

"Are you sure the anchor was secure?" questioned Kelly.

"The anchor caught. I double checked."

"Then where did it go? Boats don't just vanish!" She snapped her fingers.

"This one did." Danny closed his eyes and shivered violently. "I think it was sunk on purpose, or stolen."

"Why do you say that?" asked Kelly reaching for his hand.

"I … I saw something out on the water … another boat," he said speaking slowly, in a trance-like voice. "A mooncusser."

A drum roll of thunder pounded off in the distance.

"A what?"

"A mooncusser." He switched on the flashlight illuminating the frightened faces of Kelly and Geoffrey. "That's what the old-timers down at the station call them. Got the name from cussing out loud on moonlit nights. Stopped them from doing their devilry."

He looked around … "A night like tonight would be perfect for …"

"For … for what?" stammered Geoffrey.

"Pirates," Danny continued in a hushed tone. "Land Pirates, to be precise. They're the worst kind. According to the old-timers, most of the stories about them come from New York and the Carolinas. But some swear to this day that mooncussers operated around these parts."

Instinctively, Kelly and Geoffrey drew in closer to Danny as he continued.

"On dark and stormy nights, the bastards would walk the beach with a lantern strapped to a mule-drawn cart. To a ship offshore, the moving lantern looked like the light from another ship in closer to shore. It gave them a false sense of security. Then, *bam!*"

Kelly and Geoffrey jumped in their seats. "It would happen," Danny continued. "Their boat would bust up on the shoals. People were thrown overboard. If they couldn't swim, they drowned. Some say they were the lucky ones."

Kelly punched him in the arm, again. "You're making this up. How could drowning be lucky?"

"A worse fate awaited them on shore."

"Mooncussers?" whispered Geoffrey, blinking and swallowing hard.

Danny nodded his head. "Yeah. Those that washed up were picked clean. All jewelry and money—gone! And worse. Some were found without fingers or hands."

"But that was a long time ago, right?" Kelly asked hopefully.

He looked deeply into her sad eyes. "Yeah. Sure. But no one really knows. Strange things still happen around here. Boats are found abandoned—stripped clean, if you know what I mean."

"Do you think that's what happened to our boat?" asked Geoffrey, near tears.

"I don't know. Maybe. I hope so." Danny struggled with his thoughts.

"Why do you say it like that?" asked Kelly.

Danny lowered his head then raised it up slowly. "Because I don't care if a mooncusser did take our boat, as long as he leaves us alone!"

"I wish Mom and Dad weren't so far way," sighed Geoffrey reaching for his sister.

"We're gonna be fine," consoled Kelly, gently stroking her brother's back. She turned to Danny. "Aren't we?"

He gave her a reassuring smile.

"I'm scared, Danny," she whispered.

She leaned up against him, letting down all her defenses. He put his arm around her and held her tight.

Leaving Kelly and Danny to their tender moment, Geoffrey sat up and pulled the charts out of his sweatshirt. He rolled them up and stuffed them down his pant leg. Stretching out on the cold floor he was suddenly overcome with sleep.

***

Daylight broke fresh and new. The rain had stopped. Birds could be heard playfully singing. There was a kind of cleanliness in the air that only comes after a severe storm like the one the night before. All three kids were asleep on the floor. Kelly lay snuggled up against Danny. Geoffrey was off to one side, wrapped in the poncho and snoring softly.

"You said these kids were full of surprises," a hooded Johnny Longfeather called over his shoulder as he stood over the sleeping kids.

Geoffrey was the first to stir. "Don't cut off my hand. You can have my watch," he said tossing his Timex at Johnny's feet.

Danny sprang to his feet and put up his fists ready to fight. He stepped in between Johnny and Geoffrey.

"You'll have to go through me first," he said taking a swing.

Johnny blocked the punch with a martial arts counter move. He grabbed Danny and pinned his arm behind his back.

"Easy, cowboy, I've already got a watch," laughed Johnny.

"Don't hurt him," cried Kelly jumping to her feet. "He's with us."

"I won't," Johnny and Danny said together thinking Kelly's comment was intended for each of them.

Johnny released Danny's arm and removed his hood. The two stared at each other then smiled at their awkward bravado. Relieved they would not have to beat each other up, Kelly introduced Johnny to Danny. The two shook hands.

"Warm blankets and hot chocolate, anyone?" Noah announced walking in through the doorway.

Elated at the sight of Noah Parsons, Kelly and Geoffrey ran over and hugged him like a father. Noah draped the blankets over them.

"And a dozen bagels from you know who."

Noah handed the bag to Danny and then dialed his cell phone.

"The kids are safe," he said into the phone as he watched Geoffrey attack his bagel. "A little hungry is all." He paused to listen to someone speaking on the other end. "Looks like they decided to make it a camping trip," he said shaking his head. "Yeah, in the rain. Must be some kind of teenage ritual," he laughed. "I'll have them back shortly. Oh, you're welcome."

"How did you ever find us?" Kelly inquired turning to Noah.

"I brought along my Eagle Scout. I told you Johnny knows every inch of these waters. Besides, we knew where you were heading."

"We just didn't think you would pick such a lousy night to try it," added Johnny. He turned to Danny. "Next time you might want to try listening to the weather forecast first."

The five of them began walking back to Johnny's boat. Danny paused at the sight of the name painted on the side: *Clewless*. He turned to Noah Parsons.

"Clueless. That's exactly how I feel."

"We found Fred Barnes's boat adrift near the old Coast Guard Station. It was pretty beat up. Anything you want to tell us?"

Danny shook his head, no. Kelly glared at him.

"Fred Barnes! The big guy with the Hawaiian shorts and bad sunburn? That was *his* boat? Does this have anything to do with his daughter, the little blonde slut you've been hanging out with?"

"It's not what you think," Danny fired back.

"You don't know what I think," Kelly said in a huff climbing onto the boat. She took a seat as far away from him as she could find.

9

Troubled Waters

The door chimes tinkled as Libby Ashcroft entered the Crab Cove Gift Shop. Stepping in out of the bright sunlight, she removed her sunglasses.

"Hello! Anybody here?" she called out as her eyes adjusted to the interior darkness.

Sarah rose slowly from behind the counter where she had been sitting, reading the *National Enquirer*.

"Libby! How nice to see you," she said with polite surprise.

"Hello, Sarah. How have you been?"

"Fine Libby, just fine." Sarah smiled warmly.

"Oh, I can see that. And isn't it strange. You and Noah Parsons have that same peculiar smile."

The two ladies giggled like schoolgirls. Sarah put the newspaper away under the counter and came out to greet Libby.

"Now, Libby, I'm sure you didn't come all the way across the causeway this morning just to see the smile on my face."

"No, you're right, Sarah honey. I didn't. Actually I came to have a chat with the kids. Are they home?"

"No, not yet. I guess you haven't heard. They were on a little unplanned overnight adventure. Had us scared to death. Anyway, they're safe. Noah tracked them down and I expect them back here shortly. Can I fix us some tea while we wait?"

"No telling what kind of things kids will get into in their teens, is there? Wish I could stay, but I'm in a bit of a rush. I'm expecting some very important people at the Seaport. That's what I've come to see your little adventurers about."

Sarah inclined her head indicating she didn't fully understand.

"The kids came to the museum a couple of weeks ago to see me. Seems they found an old Spanish trinket on the beach and wanted my opinion of its worth. Naturally, since I knew they were related to you I told them I'd do the research for free."

Sarah smiled patiently and waited for Libby to continue.

"Well, I've got some exciting news for them. I've spoken with Mel Fisher Jr. and he has agreed to come up all the way from Florida to examine the medallion."

Sarah shrugged, and Libby said, "Do you know who he is?"

"Hum," pondered Sarah. "Mel Fisher. Now, let me see," she said with a glance toward the *Enquirer*. "Is he the one they called the singing frog or the one who married Elizabeth Taylor?"

Libby Ashcroft exploded in a fit of laughter. "Neither, honey," she said with a wave of her hand. "I think you're mixing Mel Torme with Eddie Fisher. Mel Fisher is a world-renowned treasure hunter. Mel Fisher Junior is his son and he's taken over the family business."

"Oh," Sarah said still not fully comprehending.

"The point is, based on what I described to him, Mel Fisher Jr. may be interested in purchasing the medallion they found."

Libby stared at Sarah expectantly. Sarah smiled demurely.

"If it's authentic, as I believe it is, and the kids are willing to part with it, Mel Fisher Jr. may be willing to make a substantial donation to the Seaport," Libby added. "We like to think of it as a finder's fee for bringing the two parties together."

"I see," said Sarah. "That certainly does sound exciting. Kelly and Geoffrey should be back any time. Are you sure you can't stay a little longer?"

"No, honey," replied Libby turning to leave. "He's coming in this afternoon and I've got to get things ready. Can you give the kids the message?"

"Of course."

Sarah walked with Libby to the door. Libby stopped and reached for her hand.

"He can only stay a day or two. It sure would mean a lot to the Seaport."

"I understand," Sarah reassured her. "I'll tell them as soon as they get in."

***

Fred Barnes was waiting at the dock when the *Clewless*, her crew, and the fatigued passengers motored into the marina. The State Police had hoisted Fred's damaged boat out of the water. A man in a skinny striped tie and cheap short sleeve Dacron shirt was inspecting the boat and filling out a form attached to a clipboard. He said something to Fred, tore off and handed him a copy of the form, and walked away. Fred folded the paper, stuffed it into his pocket, and sauntered over to the *Clewless's* berth. Fred's daughter Wendy followed behind him.

The small gawking crowd that had assembled on the dock slowly began to disperse. Ryder Hayes was among them. However, unlike the others, Hayes decided to linger. He shuffled over toward the incoming *Clewless* to get a better view.

"Ahoy!" called Noah from the deck of the *Clewless*.

He let out the bumpers and threw Fred a dock line. Fred took the line and secured it to a piling, then ran to the bow and repeated the action. Johnny Longfeather throttled the engine into neutral and switched off the ignition.

"Thanks for the hand, Fred. Sorry about your boat," offered Noah looking over at it. "What did Ray Miller have to say?"

"My friendly neighborhood insurance agent says the boat is totaled," responded Fred bitterly.

"That's the way it looks from here," acknowledged Johnny as he helped the kids off the boat. "How much are you out?"

"That boat cost me twelve grand brand new, but apparently I have one of those Actual Cash Value policies, where they depreciate the crap out of it. Seems I'll end up with a little more than half—about seven thousand dollars," said Fred, directing the last comment to Danny as he stepped onto the dock.

"I'll make up the difference, Mr. Barnes," Danny said.

"You bet your sweet ass, you will. Where the hell am I going to get another boat like the *B n' B* for seven grand?"

"You'll get your money," repeated Danny.

"Hi, Danny," said Wendy sashaying over to him. She had on a halter-top with no bra and a pair of tight-fitting jeans. She glanced over at Kelly and gave her a forced smile.

Geoffrey grabbed hold of his sister's arm to restrain her. She glared at Wendy in disgust.

"And that doesn't change our deal," scowled Fred Barnes pulling his daughter away from Danny. "Keep that in mind. I'll be watching you."

"Go easy, Fred," interrupted Noah. "The boy said he would pay you back."

"He'd better," said Barnes. "Come along, Wendy." He pushed his daughter roughly toward the parking lot.

Noah turned to Danny. "Son, if you need help—"

Danny cut him off. "I can handle it. Thanks for the lift." He turned brusquely and walked away.

Kelly hurried to catch up with him.

"What was that all about?" she asked.

"Nothing," said Danny trying to blow her off. "You wouldn't understand."

She grabbed him by the arm and spun him around to face her.

"What's not to understand? Daddy hires his own private beach boy to keep the other sharks away from his little girl. That's how you got the boat, isn't it? But does he know how you really feel about her?"

"No! And neither do you!" Danny was fuming.

"Well, then tell me, Danny. What's going on?" she pleaded.

"What's it to you? It's my problem. I'll work it out."

He stormed off again leaving her standing alone. Noah and Geoffrey caught up with her and Geoffrey put his arm around her. There were tears in her eyes.

"C'mon, sis, let's go home. It's been a long night. We're all a little fried."

"Geoffrey's right," consoled Noah. "Danny will come around. He just needs a little time to work things out."

As Noah, Kelly, and Geoffrey walked over to Noah's truck, Johnny stayed behind to have a closer look at Fred's boat. He pointed out something he noticed to the head police investigator. The cop nodded his head and made a note in his pad.

Kelly looked up one last time before she slid into the passenger seat beside Geoffrey. Noah closed the door behind her and looked off in the direction of her gaze. Danny was standing, head bowed, at the end of the pier. But he wasn't alone. Noah climbed into the driver's seat and pulled away, leaving a trail of dust as stones kicked up behind them.

10

Crossroads

Danny Windsor stood brooding at the end of the pier. He felt like jumping in and drifting out with the tide. Who would know? Who would care? It was a solution to his problem. Where was he going to come up with the cash to pay off Fred Barnes for his boat? All the money he expected to make during the summer whether from the beach patrol or the band would not get him out of this jam. He felt trapped and alone.

"I couldn't help overhearing all the commotion down at the dock," someone behind him said in a faintly familiar voice.

Danny wheeled around to confront Ryder Hayes. "Too bad about the boat," Hayes added slowly. "You get caught in that storm last night?"

"It's none of your damn business," Danny snapped angrily turning his back on him.

"Got that right, you do. Ain't none of my damn business. Still, it's a shame 'bout that boat and the way that feller Barnes talked to you. Why, anyone could see his anger was misplaced. Should have been all over that fool insurance man of his. Instead he blames a boy for what nature done. Weren't your fault."

Danny said nothing. He just wanted to be left alone but there was something soothing in Hayes's voice. So he remained silent and let the old man continue.

"Yeah, that was a mighty wicked storm last night. Not safe for man nor beast out on the water. Why, even an experienced seaman can get caught up in a big brew like that once in awhile. Nothing you can do but find shelter and wait it out."

"That's what I did," Danny exclaimed turning to face Hayes. "I put in for Stink Island and we waited for the rain to stop."

"Then you did good." Hayes's voice was soft, comforting. "That was smart. You did the right thing and you all came away all right. You all survived."

"That's right, we survived. We made it. No one got hurt," Danny boasted proudly.

Hayes was thoughtful. "And they have you to thank, I would imagine. Bet you were the captain, right?"

"That's right. I was the captain," admitted Danny.

"Well captain, it was a mighty strange night to be out on the bay if I do say so myself. Must've been a pretty important reason to bring you kids out in that kind of weather. Where were you heading in such a hurry ... if you don't mind me asking?"

"No place special," sighed Danny sitting down on the pier. He let his legs dangle over the water.

"Now that is mighty strange," said Hayes. "You kids bust up an expensive boat, nearly get yourself killed with lightning, risk drowning, and yet you say you weren't going nowhere. Yes, that's mighty strange, it is."

Hayes eased himself down beside Danny, careful not to sit too close. "You know what *I* say?"

Danny tossed a stone into the water and watched the waves ripple out from the center. "No. What do you say?"

"I say everywhere is somewhere. Don't matter where you're bound—Tuckerton, Stink Island, hell—even that old scab of sand Tucker's Island is someplace special," Hayes guessed.

Danny's dangling legs suddenly stopped swinging.

"Yessir, Tucker's Island. Now if you told me you were headed for Tucker's Island, I'd say I understand. No kind of storm would keep me from old man Tucker's Island if I had reason to be going. If I had maps or charts, that is …"

"We had charts," Danny answered almost unconsciously. "With maps overlaid on top of them."

"Did you, now," said Hayes pretending to be surprised. "Do tell. Treasure maps, I'll wager. Good ones?"

"We'll never know now," sighed Danny.

"Ah, don't tell me you lost them overboard when the boat capsized?" Hayes probed skillfully.

"The boat didn't capsize. It … it just drifted away after we made for the beach," moaned Danny, not willing to reveal what he saw, at the risk of sounding silly or childish in his defense.

"You mean you didn't anchor her down snug, captain?"

"I did. I swear I did," said Danny in a pleading voice. "But something happened."

"What happened?" asked Hayes, warily.

"I don't know. I must have been seeing things. Maybe I wasn't thinking clearly, either. Maybe I *didn't* secure the anchor. I just don't know anymore."

"And the charts? Are they safe?" continued Hayes.

"Yeah, they're safe. Geoffrey slept with them tucked down his pants," chuckled Danny.

"Well now, that's one heck of a tale, young man."

"Danny, Danny Windsor. You're Ryder Hayes—we met at the Seaport a couple weeks ago. Geoffrey was the klutz who bumped into you and broke your statue or whatever that thing was."

"Yeah, I remember. I knew you weren't the klutz. You seem too smart, too cool to be that clumsy," Hayes added slyly.

Danny chuckled again. A small fishing boat idled past them on its way toward the inlet. Waves lapped up against the bulkhead. Danny felt more relaxed now. He felt an easy calm. The words of Ryder Hayes were soothing, and very comforting.

Hayes could tell he had Danny right where he wanted him—guard down and vulnerable. "And the truth is, I believe you. I think you did everything you could under the circumstances. So you lost the boat, but, hey, you saved your friends. What's more important?"

"Yeah!" agreed Danny enthusiastically.

"And because I believe you and I think you are smart and honest I'm going to help you, Danny Windsor—even though you are right this is none of my damn business."

Hayes pressed on.

An alarm went off in Danny's mind. He said cynically, "Help me? How can you help me?"

"I know an easy way for you to get the money you owe on that boat," offered Hayes, going in for the kill.

"Easy? What do you mean by 'easy'? I don't rob banks."

Hayes let out a harsh cackle. "My dear boy, I'm offended. I would never suggest such a thing. Why, it's against the law!"

Danny cocked his head slightly toward Hayes. "What *are* you suggesting, then?"

"It's rather simple, really. You said it yourself … what good are they now? You'll probably never get another chance to use them. After all, who's gonna lend you a boat?"

"I don't follow."

"The charts, Danny boy. The maps and charts!"

"What about them?"

"Can you get your hands on them?"

Danny shrugged his shoulders. "Maybe."

"Oh, now that won't do. We can't very well make a deal if you can't be more certain than 'maybe.' Let me ask you again, can you get your hands on the charts and maps of Tucker's Island?"

Danny suddenly felt like he was being challenged, and he was curious.

"Yeah. I guess so. Why?"

"Why, Danny boy? I'll tell you why," said Hayes, becoming extremely excited. "Because I just might happen to know someone who may be in the market for those charts—that is, of course, assuming they are what you say they are—charts and maps of old man Tucker's Island as it was in the days before it went under. Is that what they are?"

"Yeah, that's what they are."

"How do I know for sure?"

"Because Noah Parsons and Johnny Longfellow helped put them together for us from the U.S. Coast Guard files," Danny said loudly and somewhat defensively.

"Then we have a deal, Danny Windsor. You bring me those documents and your debt to Fred Barnes will be wiped clean. I guarantee it." Hayes put out his hand for Danny to shake on it.

"Do we have a deal?" Hayes asked enthusiastically.

"Deal," answered Danny shaking Hayes's hand.

***

"I don't believe it," said Kelly climbing into the guard tower on 17th street.

It was only 10:15 in the morning but already the beach was crowded and the sun was getting hot.

"I couldn't believe it either," said Moss Greenberg climbing up and sitting beside her. "This is the first sick day he's ever taken. They don't come any more reliable than Danny Windsor. Even after all that poor kid has been through."

"What do you mean?" asked Kelly turning to face Moss. He was wearing a weathered Australian bush hat to protect his balding pate from the sun.

Moss shifted uneasily. "Maybe I shouldn't be talking about his personal life, but Danny's mom and dad divorced when he was fifteen, and neither of them was ready to keep him. After his mother split for Spokane with a guy she met in a chat room the court appointed me legal guardian."

"Danny lives with you?" she asked with surprise. The truth was she didn't know much of anything about Danny Windsor's personal life.

"He used to," said Moss mopping his forehead with a handkerchief. "Since graduation he's been on his own."

"I never knew any of this," she sighed.

"Danny doesn't talk much about himself," admitted Moss. "He's at a crossroads in his life. On the one hand he loves the Beach Patrol and on the other hand, he's got his music. I just wish he'd go to college either way. I offered to help him."

"And?" she prompted.

Moss folded his arms across his chest and stared straight ahead.

"Danny's his own man. He wants to prove he can take care of himself."

Kelly let that last comment from Moss linger in her thoughts. She reached into her duffle bag and pulled out a tube of zinc oxide Danny had given her. She applied it to her lips and nose, all the while thinking back to her first day on the job and how much she had learned from Danny Windsor.

11

Treasure Chess

Geoffrey and Danny sat in Danny's Jeep, talking. Geoffrey was in his dorky waiter's outfit.

"I appreciate your picking me up at work, Danny. My bike's got a flat and I thought for sure I was going to miss band practice tonight."

"Hey, no problemo, man. Like I told you, anytime," replied Danny. "You'd do the same for me ... if you drove."

Danny smiled that award-winning smile of his. It made Geoffrey feel like a million bucks just to be in Danny's company. But to have Danny Windsor chauffeur him around ... well ... the kids in Teaneck were not going to believe how cool nerdy fifteen-year-old Geoffrey Martin had become. What a wonderful summer this was turning out to be, he thought.

They pulled up in front of Crab Cove. Geoffrey tried to hop out without opening the door, unsuccessfully. He recovered quickly in an attempt to look as cool as he could.

"It will only take me a minute to change," he said leaning on the roll bar.

"Take your time," replied Danny, amused by Geoffrey's antics. Changing the subject he asked nervously, "Say, Geoffrey, is your sister home?"

"No, she and Aunt Sarah went out." Geoffrey leaned back inside the Jeep. "I think they're looking for a new keyboard for me. They were very secretive about where they were going."

"She isn't still mad at me about the other day is she?" asked Danny.

"Didn't you see her at work?"

"No, I had the day off," Danny lied.

"Don't worry. She'll get over it. She couldn't stay mad at you. I think she digs you. I've never seen her get as close to anybody as she did with you the other night."

"Yeah, that was pretty cool," said Danny and he meant it. He had felt something, too, but since then he hadn't had much time to dwell on it.

"Hey, you're the King of Cool if you ask me, Danny."

"Thanks, man."

"You know, Geoffrey," Danny continued, "that reminds me, the other night I got to thinking ... what would have happened if we lost those charts. You know—if they fell in the water or something."

Geoffrey grew animated. "No way. I was holding onto them for dear life."

"Yeah, I noticed. You even shoved them down your pants for safe keeping."

"Hey, it was raining. Give me a break."

"That's my point. If anything ever happened to those charts we'd be totally screwed, right?" Danny slammed his hand against the steering wheel for emphasis.

"Yeah, sure. But nothing's gonna happen to them. I keep them locked up."

"I'm sure you do and that's great, but I think we should have a backup copy just in case. Don't you agree?"

Geoffrey was hesitant. "Well, sure … maybe, but who can we trust to do it?"

"I know this guy at work who could do it for us, he's cool, I trust him. Besides, he owes me a favor."

"Okay, if you say so, Danny. I'll grab them while I'm inside. Do you want to come in?"

"No, I'll wait out here. And hurry up. We don't wanna be late."

As Geoffrey dashed off into the shop Danny looked in the rearview mirror and ran his hand through his thick hair. "That was easy," he thought, pleased with himself yet uncomfortable at the same time.

***

"This is a wonderful thing you're doing for the Tuckerton Seaport," said Libby peering over her half-moon spectacles at Kelly and Sarah as they stood in front of her at the counter of the museum office. The gold medallion lay polished in a fancy case on the counter.

"Mel Fisher Jr. has given us permission to display it here for the rest of the summer," Libby gushed, obviously excited and proud.

"I'm just happy to get rid of this thing. It's brought me nothing but trouble."

Libby handed Kelly a check. "Well, then here's five thousand dollars for your troubles, as promised."

"So what are you going to do with the money?" asked Libby. She looked at Sarah.

"I'll think of something," Kelly answered cryptically.

Aunt Sarah smiled her approval.

Kelly and Sarah exchanged goodbyes with Libby and started to exit the museum. At the door Kelly hesitated. She turned back and addressed the curator.

"Mrs. Ashcroft?"

"Yes, dear?"

"I'm curious. Is Mel Fisher Junior coming here to search for the rest of Captain Kidd's buried treasure?"

Libby let out a low laugh. "Oh, didn't I tell you?"

Kelly and Sarah looked at each other with the same blank expression. "Tell us what?" asked Sarah.

"Well," she began tapping the glass lightly, "as it turns out this piece you found isn't part of Captain Kidd's fabled bounty after all."

"It's not?" Kelly could not hide the disappointment in her voice.

The flustered curator continued. "When Mr. Fisher was here … we," she corrected herself, "he … was able to trace the provenance of the medallion to Margulies Andragna, the wife of Captain Luigi Andragna."

"I know that name," said Sarah in amazement. "Wasn't he the captain of the *Fortuna*?" I remember reading his name on the plaque in front of the Ship Bottom Municipal Building."

"The same. According to the ship's manifest the medallion was one of several heirlooms the family reported as missing in the shipwreck. Presumed lost at sea."

"From a pirate attack?" asked Kelly hopefully.

"Heavens, no, from a winter storm. The *Fortuna* was in route to New York from Barbados with a crew of thirteen plus the captain and his family. She went down in heavy seas off the point near Ship Bottom on January 18, 1910. The anchor in front of the town hall is all that remains of the ship. Bits and pieces of the boat have turned up in the surf over the years, but nothing of any value like what you found."

"You mean all this talk about pirates and buried treasure is just a lot of nonsense?" asked Kelly incredulously.

Libby Ashcroft shook her head. "Afraid, so … at least in this case. But who knows, someday a lucky treasure hunter may stumble upon the real thing."

"Are you going to tell Geoffrey and Danny?" asked Aunt Sarah.

"I suppose so," Kelly sighed. "Maybe then things can get back to normal."

Outside, Kelly paused to look at the check.

"Kelly, are you sure about this? I know it's your decision, but you can do an awful lot with five thousand dollars."

Kelly folded the check in half and stuffed it into her pocket.

"Some treasures are worth more than others," she said.

***

It was early, just past sunup the next day when Danny pulled his Jeep up to Skinner's Dock and parked. He had spent a sleepless night fighting with himself about what he should do. Even now he still wasn't sure he could go through with it.

Ryder Hayes was waiting for him on the front porch of his houseboat.

"Right on time," Hayes said in a friendly voice. "I like a business partner who is punctual. Did you bring the charts?"

Danny reached into the window of his Jeep and pulled out a long tube.

"Excellent," exclaimed Hayes, obviously pleased.

"What about you? Got the cash?" Danny asked nervously.

Hayes reached into his overalls. "Will a check do?" He held it up for Danny to see. It flapped stiffly in the breeze that blew in off the bay.

Danny made a face. "How do I know it won't bounce?"

Hayes smiled broadly. "It's a company check."

"So?" said Danny trying to sound confident and self-assured.

"So, if it bounces," Hayes made a wide sweeping gesture toward his dilapidated work shed, "all this is yours."

Danny looked around. The whole scene had a surreal feel to it already. Looking around at the rundown property only made it feel more unreal, like a bad dream.

"Not good enough," replied Danny stiffening. "I'll need something more."

"More?" asked Hayes, caught off guard.

"Yeah. You've got something that doesn't belong to you." Danny's voice rose.

"I do?" Hayes asked inquisitively.

"The $100 you took from Kelly Martin. I want that, too," Danny demanded.

"They told you about that, did they? They owed me that. For the broken piece."

Danny planted his feet. "That's not the way I see it."

"No?" Hayes cocked his head. "How do you see it?"

"The way I see it is if I give you these charts, you get the coins and whatever other treasure you dig up. It's all yours. They don't owe you anything. So they get their deposit back now."

"That wasn't part of our bargain," Hayes snarled.

"It is now. Think of it as collateral in case your check bounces," said Danny with a cocky grin.

A wry smile formed on Hayes's lips. "I always knew you were the smart one, Danny Windsor. That's what I like about you."

Hayes disappeared into his houseboat and reappeared minutes later carrying a coffee can. He pulled out the $100 and tossed the can aside.

"You drive a hard bargain, young man." Hayes stepped down off the porch and ambled over toward Danny.

Danny felt his resolve begin to weaken. He started walking cautiously toward Hayes. They looked like two gunslingers about to duel in the street. As he got closer to the houseboat a strong gust of wind blew and Danny heard the low moan of a boat straining against its dock lines. Danny glanced up and noticed a small craft moored alongside the houseboat. There was something familiar about it. It was a Garvey, the traditional shallow-hulled boat of the old-time baymen. He changed his direction and went to get a better look. Hayes followed him to the boat, walking parallel with him.

"Something wrong?" Hayes asked nervously.

A boat engine droned off in the distance.

"That your boat?" Danny asked, nodding his head toward the one moored beside the houseboat.

"Ain't she a beauty?" Hayes acknowledged proudly.

Hayes placed the check and cash in Danny's hand. Danny pocketed the cash and studied the check. In old style calligraphy it read, "Pay to the Order of Danny Windsor. $5,000.00." It was signed "Ryder Hayes, Proprietor." Danny handed over the rolled up charts. Hayes unraveled one of the charts and muttered, "At last." He re-rolled the scrolls and extended his hand to Danny. "Done."

Another sudden gust rustled over the water, pushing Hayes's boat out away from the pier. The frayed stern line snapped and the boat drifted out of its berth exposing the name emblazoned on it. Danny spied the name that had haunted his sleep since the night of the storm: *Mooncusser*! He turned his head repeatedly between the boat and Hayes. The wheels of recognition were in motion. The look in Danny's eyes told Hayes all he needed to know and what he feared.

Suddenly Danny erupted. "That was you out there the night of the storm! I saw you! You did something to our boat, didn't you?"

Hayes smiled back devilishly, knowingly.

"Gimme back those maps!" Danny screamed, lunging at Hayes.

Hayes was ready for him.

"Too late, Danny boy. A deal's a deal," Hayes said whacking Danny on the side of the head with a pipe wrench he had hidden in the back pocket of his coveralls.

The check fell from Danny's hand as he dropped to the ground like a sack of flour.

Hayes heard the drone of a boat engine coming up the lagoon. He chucked the wrench into the water.

Hayes hurriedly tucked the maps into his coveralls. He grabbed Danny by the feet and began dragging him to his boat. Suddenly, from around the bend of the lagoon the *Clewless* appeared in full throttle.

"Danny!" screamed Kelly recognizing the body in Hayes's clutches.

Hayes let go of Danny and made a run for it. The *Clewless* reached the drifting *Mooncusser*, ramming into it. Johnny Longfeather leaped onto the dock while his boat was still moving. He broke into a full run, chasing Hayes across the littered junkyard. Johnny tackled him in mid-stride and wrestled him to the ground. Kelly and Geoffrey rushed over to Danny. He was unconscious, with a deep gash on his forehead, but was breathing. Kelly used Geoffrey's handkerchief to apply pressure to the wound.

Noah Parsons secured the *Clewless* and punched in the number for the Tuckerton police on his cell phone.

"We're at Skinner's Dock. You better hurry."

Noah went to check on Danny first. As he started to come around, Noah bent over to pick up the check that was lying on the ground nearby. Holding it in his hands, he walked over to where Johnny had Hayes pinned to the ground.

"Get this half-breed off me, Parsons," barked Hayes, "or I swear I'll sue both your asses. You ain't got nothin' on me!"

"Nothin'?" mimicked Noah looking at the bogus check. "Try assaulting a minor, operating an unregistered boat, and passing bad checks. And that's just for starters."

With sirens blaring, two patrol cars came wailing up the lane.

12
Spirit of the Bay

Danny reclined in the cushioned stern of the *Clewless*, his bandaged head resting on Kelly's lap. Noah wanted to take him to South Ocean County Hospital but Danny insisted he was fine. He made a remarkable recovery as soon as he heard that Sarah was waiting for them back at Crab Cove with Chef Moss Greenberg, fixing a hearty breakfast for all of them. There was no time to lose and, at this time of the day on a Saturday morning, the quickest way across the bay was by boat.

"How many times am I going to have to save you before you realize you need me?" asked Kelly, gently stroking Danny's hair.

"Okay. I admit it. I need you. But you don't have to hit me over the head with it." Danny reached up and pulled Kelly to him. He kissed her tenderly.

"How'd ya find me?" he asked, wincing as he sat up.

"Johnny had a hunch," said Noah walking back to check on the patient. He gave Nurse Kelly a knowing wink.

"We weren't actually looking for you," explained Noah. "Kelly and Geoffrey told me the whole story, including your run-in with the *Mooncusser* the night of the storm. I told you Johnny knows these waters like no one else. He'd seen the boat around."

"And we came to get Kelly's money back," Geoffrey added, joining them.

Danny grinned. "That's funny, would you believe I did, too? Here." He reached into his pocket and handed Kelly the money. She kissed him lightly on the cheek.

"There's more," Noah continued. "When they pulled Fred Barnes's boat out of the water, Johnny was able to show that it had been scuttled and set adrift. You had nothing to do with the damage."

"We were being set up all along," added Kelly. "All of us."

"And it worked. He conned me big-time," winced Danny.

"Not quite," Geoffrey chimed in. "We got the charts back."

"I'm sorry I lied to you, Geoffrey. It was wrong."

"Yeah, well, I'm afraid we've all gone a little overboard with this treasure stuff," replied Geoffrey. He looked at Kelly and Danny and shrugged. "I don't know about you guys, but I'm beginning to think that the best thing to do with buried treasure is to leave it buried. What d'ya say?"

Danny and Kelly agreed. Geoffrey crumpled the charts up in a ball and dropped them into a metal bucket. Noah Parsons handed him a book of matches. Geoffrey lit one and set the contents on fire. The maps disappeared into smoke curling up into the sky.

It was another beautiful clear morning. The sun was up bright and high. There was a warm gentle, westerly breeze. Sea gulls soared overhead.

The *Clewless* and her party passed clammers raking their clam beds and scores of fisherman in bobbing boats with poles aloft, drifting aimlessly in the channel. They all stopped and waved as the *Clewless* chugged by. The Whaler's crew waved back.

A sleek new cigarette boat pulled astern and blared its horn as it idled alongside them. Danny raised his head to see who it was. Fred Barnes was at the wheel of a brand new boat appropriately named the *B n' B II*. Wendy Barnes stood on the bow, decked out in a teeny bikini, arm in arm with a shirtless Curtis Wick.

"Gotta hand it to ya, Danny," shouted Fred between the boats. "I don't know how you came up with the cash so fast, but I'm mighty grateful. This baby's even better than her predecessor. You can take her out any time." As if to prove his point Fred gunned her full throttle and sped off in a showy display of power, pollution, and poor seamanship.

"He'd better be talking about the boat," Kelly kidded giving Danny a fearsome look.

"Where did I come up with the cash so fast, Rookie?"

"Don't change the subject," sparred Kelly.

"Does this have anything to do with a gold medallion?" Danny asked inquisitively.

She looked him straight in the eyes. "I'll make you a deal, Danny Windsor. I won't ask you about your interest in that blonde bimbo, if you don't ask me about that gold medallion."

He stood shakily and put his arm around her. They smiled at each other.

Kelly and Danny went up to join Noah and Geoffrey who were standing near the cabin next to Johnny, enjoying the sights.

A light wooden sailboat glided by them silently in full sail. Dick Hanson was running up his colors. He stopped and said something to his wife, Audrey, who was reading a trashy novel out on the deck. She put her book down and waved to the *Clewless*.

Noah turned to Kelly. "So tell me something, Kelly … all that talk about saving the osprey was just BS, right?"

She nodded. "I read something about them in the *Sandpaper*. Geoffrey and I made up the rest."

"Have you ever seen one up close in the wild?" Noah asked.

"No. I've never even seen one on TV," she admitted.

"Then maybe you should take a look at Channel Marker 52," he said, pointing off the starboard side.

The kids followed the line of Noah's arm about twenty yards out and looked up at the pole. A mother osprey had made a nest in the basket that cradles the channel marker's light and was busy feeding her young.

"Wow!" Kelly exclaimed, "I never realized this place was so alive."

"The Lenape had a name for it," Johnny said with a broad smile. "*Mesingwa*. The Spirit of the Bay."

Mystery of the Jersey Devil

1

Lost!
(Summer 1964)

Twelve-year old Tommy Banks and his father, Sam, were late. Worse than that, they were lost: lost in one of the last great wooded expanses north of Virginia, known as the New Jersey Pine Barrens.

Sam had promised his wife, Martha, that he and Tommy would be home from their annual Tuckerton fishing trip before dark. But Sam and his brother-in-law, Nate, celebrating the latter's recent divorce and reveling in their morning success with rod and reel, had one too many beers before lunch. In the lull of the afternoon the two soon nodded off, leaving poor Tommy to cope with navigating the shallows around Little Egg Harbor alone.

After a morning of boredom Tommy wasn't quite up to the challenge. Pulling the classic comic *The Creature from the Black Lagoon* out of his back pocket, he quickly forgot about fishing, channel buoys, and landmarks. As low tide rolled in the drifting *Lay-Z-Sues-N* ran aground on a small scab of sand just inside the Beach Haven Inlet. The small shoal was all that remained of the once splendid summer retreat known as Tucker's Island.

By the time the two men awoke from their afternoon siesta and managed to free their craft from the sandbar, they had barely enough time to return to the dock, clean their catch, and scrub down the boat before the hazy afternoon passed into early evening.

Knowing his sister did not tolerate tardiness well, especially when the day's catch was to be the family's intended dinner, Nate hurriedly scratched down directions for Sam, taking him on a shortcut through the Pines. It was a route that Nate himself was given one night several years back at a local bar, by an old piney who was in a similar predicament with his wife at the time. Nate had never actually taken the shortcut himself, which is not to say that he might still be married if he had, but that he might have given it a little more thought before passing it on.

Sam was more than willing to take a chance, if it meant he might be able to avoid Martha's wrath. So he packed up Tommy and their gear and set off in their well-traveled '59 Ford Country Squire station wagon, headed for Trenton just as the light was beginning to fade.

At the crossroads where Rt. 539 intersects with Rt. 72, Sam made a left onto 72 instead of going straight and staying on 539. Nate had told him that 72 would take him to Rt. 532. West on Route 532 would take Sam and Tommy through the sleepy little town of Chatsworth and eventually lead them to Route 206. That would help them avoid Saturday night beach traffic, Nate said. They could follow Route 206 north and get into Trenton from the south instead of having to make their way in from the congested northeast. It sounded great, but in reality it was terrible advice.

Four miles out from the intersection Sam took a forked left onto Rt. 532. Not more than a mile down the narrow, unlit county road, his Ford wagon began to lurch and buck as if it was low on fuel. Sam pounded the gas gauge. It read just above half. He pressed the gas pedal to the floor. The car coughed again and coasted to a stop on the soft, sandy shoulder. Steam rose up from under the hood.

The gentle rolling stop woke Tommy from his sleep.

"What's wrong, Dad?" Tommy asked yawning.

"I'm not sure," answered Sam stepping out from the car. He leaned his head back inside the window and added sternly, "Stay put."

As Tommy watched, his dad walked around to the front of the car and raised the hood. In the falling darkness, a cloud of smoke enveloped his dad obscuring him momentarily from Tommy's view.

"Dad!" yelled Tommy opening the passenger door and leaping out.

It wasn't until he stepped outside that Tommy noticed just how eerily dark the night had become. Then suddenly they heard a low howl off in the distance.

Father and son stared at the mute pitch pine trees, then at each other.

"I thought I told you to stay put," snapped the elder Banks.

"What *was* that?" asked Tommy nervously.

"That was nothin'," replied Sam.

"But you heard it, didn't you?"

The moan came again, louder and closer than before. It sounded like an animal in trouble.

"Get in the car, Tommy."

"No, I'm staying with you," protested Tommy moving closer to his father.

Suddenly, from the woods to their left, a rustling sound followed by snapping twigs and crunching pine needles caught their attention.

Sam grabbed Tommy by the collar and threw him into the station wagon. He climbed in beside him and locked the doors.

"What is it, Dad? Is it the Jersey Devil?" said Tommy excitedly.

Tommy's head began swimming with visions of the incredible stories he had heard his father and Uncle Nate tell during their trips through the Pines about the horrible creature—half man, half horse, with bat wings and a spiked tail—that roamed these woods among the peaceful evergreens.

"Nonsense, boy, I told you before there ain't no such thing."

"But Uncle Nate saw him. He was green and flew low over the lagoon."

"Swamp gas, Tommy. That's what your Uncle Nate saw. Swamp gas."

"Then what was that we heard?"

"A wolf, maybe, or a coyote."

"But I heard footsteps, Dad ... and you said we can't hear a wolf or a coyote walking."

There was a loud thump on the back of the wagon. Father and son ducked down under the front seat.

Sam raised his head slowly and looked out the rear of the car. He saw nothing but darkness.

"Whatever it is, it's after the fish. It can smell them, I bet. They're in the back."

Tommy's hands covered his eyes and his face was buried in the front seat. He raised his head slowly.

"Did you see him, Dad?" asked Tommy through his criss-crossed fingers.

"No."

Sam tried the ignition again. The car cranked and cranked but wouldn't turn over.

Tommy glanced out the side window and thought he saw a large blur rush by into the trees. He turned around for a look. He stared right, then left into the darkness and saw nothing.

There was another heavy thump, on the back door this time. It was a dull, dead sound like a fist pounding on the fender.

Sam reeled around in his seat.

Tommy hid his face in his hands again. He spread his fingers slowly and stared up into the rearview mirror. He let out a gasp. Was his mind playing tricks on him? He could have sworn he saw a pair of red glowing eyes staring back at him, but when he blinked to clear his eyes, he saw nothing!

Tommy whispered, "I'm scared, Dad."

"It'll be all right, Tommy," the older Banks consoled. He stroked his son's hair reassuringly.

"What are we gonna do?"

"Give 'em the fish," replied Sam. He climbed into the back of the wagon.

Tommy sat up. "What's that?" It sounded like chalk scraping against a blackboard.

Sam Banks bolted back into the front seat. His elbow hit the steering wheel. The car horn blared.

Suddenly, the scratching stopped. All was quiet again. Sam looked around through every window, but couldn't see a thing.

For several minutes father and son sat motionless in the chilling silence. Not another sound was heard. Not a single car had come past.

Their nervous breath had steamed up the windows while the pungent stench of fish filled the air around them. Sam Banks cracked the driver's side window ever so slightly to draw in some fresh air.

He tried the engine again. It still wouldn't turn over.

"Tommy," he said at last. "It's no use. She won't start. The way I see it we have two choices. We can wait here until someone happens along or we can start walking and try to get some help. Uncle Nate said this road was seldom used, except by the locals. That must mean there are some homes nearby. I think it's worth a try. Grab the flashlight from the glove compartment."

Reluctantly Tommy did as he was told, sticking close to his dad's side.

The night was dark but clear, with a pale light coming from a new rising moon. There were no streetlights on this lonely stretch of road. Tommy stared into the darkness of the trees. A creepy feeling came over him, like he was being watched.

Together father and son stepped slowly down the deserted road, crouching and walking side-by-side straight down the center of the lane.

About a half mile down the road Sam's flashlight went out. The batteries had died. Now they were in near total darkness. They stood there alone in the eerie silence and listened. An orchestra of cicadas serenaded them, but it was of little comfort. Every rustle of the wind, every hoot from an owl brought them to a dead stop. Cautiously onward they trekked into the night, too petrified to speak and too far down the road to turn back.

Suddenly Sam and Tommy saw headlights coming at them. The car was speeding and swerving from side to side, seemingly out of control. They had to run for cover into the woods or they would surely have been run down.

As the car sped by them one of the teenagers packed inside tossed a beer bottle out the window. It smashed into a zillion fragments when it hit the blacktop.

Dejected, father and son trudged forward until at last they saw a light through the thick trees off in the woods and smoke rising from a chimney. Encouraged by the sight, they sprinted the last 50 yards to the front steps of a rundown tar-papered shack. Sam checked the time on his watch under a hanging lantern that lit the porch. Nine thirty. Martha was going to skin him alive.

Before Sam could even knock, the rickety old screen door creaked open and he found himself staring down the twin muzzles of a double-barreled shotgun. Behind the gun stood a big black mountain of a man in frayed suspenders and a ragged T-shirt. He sported a dark unkempt beard with matching thick eyebrows. His deep-set eyes were dark and menacing.

The big man sighted the shotgun between Sam's eyes and said in a deep, husky voice, "State your business."

"My name is Sam Banks and this here is my son, Tommy."

At the sight of the gun Tommy slipped behind his father. He peered around cautiously.

"Our car broke down a few miles from here and we were wondering if we could use your phone."

"Ain't got no phone," said the big man dryly.

Sam looked over at a beat up red '48 Ford pickup parked in the yard alongside the house. Various discarded car parts were strewn about near the truck.

"How about a lift, then?"

"Ain't got much gas."

Sam reached around for his wallet. As he did, the big man cocked back the hammers to his gun.

Sam removed a five-dollar bill and gingerly laid it across the twin barrels of the gun. "Will this cover it ... er ... Mister ...?"

"Morris. Freeman Morris," said the big man, reaching for the bill with one hand while keeping the gun trained on Sam Banks with the other. "Maybe."

"How far is it to town anyway?" asked Sam.

Freeman Morris let out a good laugh. He returned the hammers to their resting position and lowered his gun.

"What's so funny?" Tommy blurted out.

Sam pushed his son gently back behind him.

"I can see you two ain't from around these parts."

"No," admitted Sam, "we're lost. Can you help us?"

"That all depends," said Freeman with a sly smile.

"Depends on what?" asked Sam slowly, afraid of what the response might be.

"On what you expect to find in town. This here's Chatsworth, the heart of the Pines. Ain't much out here but cranberry bogs and scrub pines."

"You mean you don't have a gas station?"

"Nope. Nearest one is in Tabernacle, about fifteen miles west."

Sam Banks took another five from his wallet. "Well then, can you take us there?"

"Not anymore," said Freeman, pushing away the bill. He hoisted the gun over his shoulder and started walking toward his truck.

"Why not?"

"'Cause it's Saturday night and Fred Brown's Esso is closed. Fred and the boys are over in Waretown a pickin' and a playin' at the old music hall. Heck, I'd be there myself if I wasn't fixin' a tonic for a nasty flare-up of the Widow Walker's gout. "

Sam and Tommy hustled after Morris as he opened the door to his truck and slid into the driver's seat. He rested his gun on the rack above the rear window.

"Is that where you're going? To get him?"

"Nope." Freeman started his truck. There was a loud bang. It sounded like a gunshot as the truck backfired, piercing the quiet night and silencing the song of the cicadas. "I'm gonna have me a little look at your automobile. You comin'?"

Sam and Tommy climbed in.

"You a mechanic?" asked Sam Banks hesitantly, sitting by the window of the passenger seat. Tommy, sandwiched between the two men, sat dwarfed beside Freeman Morris who reeked of ripe onions and cheap whiskey.

Morris let out a loud laugh the force of which seemed to come from his rather ample mid-section.

"I've been known to do a little tinkering here and there."

Sam tried not to let his disappointment show. But at the moment he saw no way out of letting this hayseed have a crack at his disabled car.

Tommy turned to his dad. "Do you think the Jersey Devil might still be lurking around our car?"

"Seen 'im, have ya?" asked Morris nonchalantly.

"Heard noises, that's all," replied Sam. "I'm sure you hear them all the time out here."

Morris gave Tommy a sideways glance. Tommy's eyes told him a different story.

Morris veered his truck across to the wrong side of road and parked facing the Banks's crippled station wagon. He left his headlights on, flooding the front of the wagon with light. He walked over to the raised hood.

"Start her up," he shouted to Sam.

Sam did as he was told.

After a moment of grinding Morris signaled him to stop. "That's enough."

Morris lifted the cap off the radiator. It gave a little 'pop' and 'hiss' then quieted down. "Yup."

"You got anything to drink?" he said to Sam as he walked around to the rear of the car.

"No," replied Sam with a disgusted look. "I'm with my son."

Morris opened the rear hatch to the wagon. He seemed unflustered by the strong odor of ripening fish. "This'll do," said Morris lifting the fish cooler from the back of the car. He laid the bag containing the fish along the side of the road and carried the cooler to the front of the wagon.

Tommy and Sam watched in amazement as Morris tilted the cooler and poured what remained of the long since melted ice into the radiator of the Country Squire.

"This ought to get you to Tabernacle," he said tightening down the cap. "There's a half dozen gas stations along 206 from there on up to Trenton. Start her up."

Sam did as he was told and after a moment of hesitation the wagon sparked to life. He left the motor running and followed Freeman to the rear of the car as he returned the empty cooler.

Morris picked up the bag of sea bass and fluke. "Better get these home quick, before they spoil."

"How did you know we were from Trenton?" asked Sam.

Freeman Morris closed the hatch to the station wagon. He pointed to the rear bumper. "It says so, on your license plate holder: *Haldeman Ford, Trenton NJ*. Right below those large claw marks."

2

Cepaea Memoralis
(Summer 2004)

Danny Windsor smiled. "Found any lucky beach trinkets lately?" Shielding her eyes from the glare of the sun, Kelly Martin felt herself instantly transported back in time a year ago to this very same beach where she, Danny, and her younger brother Geoffrey found themselves knee-deep in a summer adventure involving buried treasure, real-life pirates, and an island lost to the sea.

Kelly hugged Danny so hard he began to feel faint.

"Easy darlin' or you might have to give me mouth-to-mouth all over again."

Suddenly, Kelly began pummeling him with her fists. "You creep. You said you would call. Why didn't you call?"

Danny wrestled Kelly to the ground. "Hold on, Kelly. Give a guy a chance."

"You had your chance, buster, and you blew it."

Kelly pounced on Danny. They toppled over into the sand.

The roar of the ocean could be heard in the background as a small group of 17th Street beach enthusiasts began to gather around them. The whole scene felt a bit like deja vu to Kelly.

"You all right, Kelly?" said an aging lifeguard coming to her aid. He was wearing a well-worn leather Australian bush hat.

"Moss … Moss, it's me," said Danny sheepishly lying pinned under Kelly.

Moss Greenberg threw his hat onto the sand.

"Well, I'll be damned. If it isn't the prodigal son, come back home at last."

Danny recognized Curtis Wick, the muscle-bound lifeguard with a shaved head who assisted Moss in lifting Kelly off Danny. They glared at each other icily.

"Let me have a crack at him when you're through, Kelly," said Moss holding back the small crowd that had gathered.

When the gawkers started to disperse Moss continued, "I'll let you two have a moment to get reacquainted." Curtis scowled at Danny as he climbed back atop the lifeguard stand he had been sharing with Kelly.

"I see not much has changed at good old Ship Bottom beach since last year," said Danny with all the charm he was capable of mustering at the moment. At one time that was quite a lot of charm in Kelly's eyes. "You still pack a mean punch, Rookie."

"I'm not a rookie anymore," Kelly tossed back at him.

It was a statement that perhaps said more than she had intended. Kelly shook out her auburn hair, and although to the casual eye she was still waif-like thin and tomboyish in appearance, she had matured over the past year and Danny didn't fail to take notice.

Danny looked over at Curtis who was trying not to be obvious as he kept his eyes on them.

"No, I can see there's a new rookie in camp. Guess after I left the beach patrol they had to scrape from the bottom of the barrel for new recruits."

"At least *he* didn't forget me."

"I didn't forget you, Kelly. I wanted to call you a million times over the winter but …"

"But what? No time?"

"Exactly. School has been a bear. You know I've never been what you would call a model student, but at Stockton State I've really made an effort to hit the books. I'm even taking a class this summer. It's a course on New Jersey Folklore. It sounded interesting and I can use the credits."

Kelly folded her arms and stared into Danny Windsor's sky blue eyes. They twinkled in the reflection of the sparkling ocean water. "Is that supposed to make a girl swoon, the fact that you're a serious college boy now?"

"And a serious musician. I'm in a real group with a bunch of professional shitkickers. We've got a gig over at the Albert Music Hall in Waretown this Saturday night. That's why I came by, to see if you and Geoffrey wanted to come see us this weekend."

Kelly eyed Danny with suspicion, looking for some sign that this sudden invitation from her first serious crush was as innocent as it appeared. Maybe it was just a case of puppy love, as Kelly's Aunt Sarah had suggested at the time. Or maybe it was just the excitement of the times. But those were some great times.

Last summer the threesome was inseparable, sharing as they did an adventure of a lifetime. Following Kelly's chance discovery of an antique Spanish medallion on the beach during a life-saving lesson performed on veteran lifeguard Danny Windsor— an impromptu action that actually *did* save his life—the three set off in pursuit of the fabled Tucker's Island buried treasure, all the while being pursued by a real life twenty-first century scoundrel named Ryder Hayes.

The kids never did find Captain Kidd's buried fortune, but they did discover something they treasured in one another along with a sincere appreciation for the beauty of the bay and the saltwater marsh ecosystem it supports.

Still, despite their adventure and how close they had become, when summer ended the three kids drifted apart. Danny and Kelly hadn't spoken to each other since last September when their summer of fun and adventure at the Jersey shore came to an abrupt end. They went their separate ways, vowing to stay in touch but failing to do so.

Kelly and Geoffrey went back home to Teaneck where Kelly started her senior year of high school, while Geoffrey, younger by a year, entered his junior year at Teaneck High. Danny, a native of Long Beach Island, remained behind and began his long-awaited college career at Richard Stockton State College in Pomona.

"By the way, how is that freckled-faced kid brother of yours? Is he back busing tables at the Quarterdeck?"

"Noah Parsons got him a job at the Seaport," replied Kelly excitedly. "Can you believe it? Geoffrey Martin is a Tuckerton docent."

"No kidding. So Mr. Bluegrass actually came through. You know, I've seen him a couple of times at the Albert Music Hall with your Aunt Sarah. They make quite a pair out on the dance floor."

Kelly hit Danny again.

"You mean to tell me you've seen my Aunt Sarah and Mr. Parsons and you never asked about me or Geoffrey?"

"Easy, Kelly. How do you think I knew where to find you?"

"Liar. That bump on the head Ryder Hayes gave you sure didn't knock any sense into you."

Danny reached up and rubbed the old wound, the one Kelly had nursed after she'd sold the medallion to pay off Danny's debt, and just before he nearly made a deal with that old devil, Ryder Hayes.

Suddenly Danny felt a little foolish and regretful. He had wanted to call and had actually picked up the phone and dialed her number a couple of times. But when her mother or father would answer—the parents he had never met—he would suddenly lose his nerve and hang up.

"C'mon, Kelly, how about it? New summer, new start? Will I see you Saturday night?"

Curtis Wick vaulted off the guard stand and landed between Kelly and Danny. "She's busy Saturday night."

Danny looked around Curtis at Kelly. She nodded her head. "It's the annual beach party. I told Curtis I'd meet him there."

"Hear that, Windsor? She's going out with me on Saturday night. Now, unless you have a beach badge or would care to purchase one, I would suggest you take your sorry ass and go somewhere you're wanted. If there is such a place."

Kelly turned away. She could not bear to see the hurt on Danny's face, knowing it would be the same look she'd seen in her mirror a million lonely nights during a long fall, winter, and spring.

Curtis clenched his fists and braced himself for a fight.

Danny gave Kelly a sharp look. She looked away, afraid to have their eyes meet; afraid to let her feelings show. "Fine," said Danny. He turned and lumbered off.

***

Little Larry Fishman tapped on the side glass of the terrarium. Two tiny antennae popped out from one end of the zebra-striped, round shelled creature.

"Look, Brandon," Larry motioned to his younger brother. "They really are alien snails."

Six-year old Brandon Fishman let go of his father's hand and ran over to join his brother at the specimen table. "Wow!" exclaimed Brandon as the snail began to slide along the glass leaving a trail of slime in its wake.

"*Cepaea memoralis*, to be exact," said a red-haired young man leaning over the display case across from them. Geoffrey Martin adjusted his horn-rimmed glasses. "Not to be confused with the Cuban *Polymita*. They are a totally different species."

Little Larry tapped on the glass again. Several other snails appeared to be provoked into movement by the disturbance.

"Where did you find them?" Brandon asked excitedly.

"On the beach in Ship Bottom. But the *Cepaea memoralis* originally came from Europe. So I guess you could say they are foreigners here in America, or aliens, if you prefer."

"How'd they get here? Swim?" asked Brandon running his hand on the glass and following the slow-moving snail around the table. The snail disappeared under the cover of a long, slender *ti* leaf.

"Heavens, no," said an older man with salt and pepper hair who had joined the kids around the display case. His plastic nametag identified him as Noah Parsons.

Noah grabbed little Larry's hand just as the curious boy was about to tap the glass again. Big Larry came over and pulled his eldest son aside. He gave Brandon a stern look and the younger boy backed away from the terrarium, bumping into Geoffrey.

"They hitchhike on plants," added Noah. "The garden variety kind that are flown over by jet."

"And they're quite harmless," added Geoffrey sensing a hint of trepidation on the face of big Larry.

"They're everywhere and nothing but a nuisance," said the elder Fishman, taking his two boys by the hand and heading for the door. "We pour salt on them and watch them shrivel up. Stops them dead in their tracks. C'mon boys, let's go watch how they make those cool sneak boats."

"Well, I'd say that went over well," sighed Noah after the Fishman family had left the small marine life cottage.

"Kids that age are into video games and other interactive stuff, Mr. Parsons. Sometimes you've gotta let them touch."

"The Seaport is a *learning* center, Geoffrey. Not an arcade. If they want to play let them go to Fantasy Island. The old man is worse than his kids. He's showing them how to be pompous assholes when they grow up."

Geoffrey grinned as he retrieved a cloth and began wiping the handprints and smudges from the display case.

"Speaking of learning, Mr. Parsons, is there any chance of joining you on a field trip sometime soon?"

Noah Parsons placed his hand gently on Geoffrey's shoulder.

"Patience, Geoffrey. This is only your second week on the job. You have all summer to go traipsing through the woods. I told Mrs. Ashcroft when I hired you that you would help me gather specimens from time to time. But as you can see the Seaport is a little shorthanded right now."

"It isn't fair," said Geoffrey tossing the dirty rag into the corner. "The other kids get to help haul in clams and hunt for horseshoe crabs while I'm stuck here sweeping floors and cleaning display cases."

"Like I said, have patience. Your time will come. I promised you and your Aunt Sarah that this would be a memorable summer experience but I never said it would happen all at once."

"Mr. Parsons, you know I'm not afraid to work. I'm just bored, that's all."

"Would you rather be back busing tables and washing dishes at the Quarterdeck?"

"No, you know I wouldn't. But I wouldn't mind a little excitement either."

Noah cracked a smile, a rarity for him or so it seemed to Geoffrey. Sometimes he wondered what his widowed Aunt Sarah saw in this "by the book" former Coast Guardsman turned conservationist.

"You mean like that little treasure hunting expedition you and your sister went on last summer with the Windsor boy?"

Geoffrey's eyes lit up at the memory of it.

Noah handed Geoffrey a broom.

"Well, I can assure you that the field trips you'll be taking in the Pines will seem like a walk in the park compared to your escapades with that Hayes character last summer. There isn't any danger lurking in those woods like what you three fell into. Not while I'm around, anyway. Now, let's get back to work. Mr. Grainger's scout troop is on its way over."

3

Camp White Eagle

The bucolic, pastoral setting of the White Eagle Campground was barely visible as Kelly and Geoffrey made their way down the narrow, serpentine lane that led to the entrance of the complex. Nestled in the central, wooded Brookville section of Barnegat Township, the camp was only a stone's throw from the bay, yet, surrounded on all sides by tall pines and graceful white cedars, it seemed much more secluded. By the time the Martin kids arrived, the campground lay in the cool shade of twilight's evening shroud, further limiting their view of the park's natural beauty.

Kelly pulled her black and white Mini Cooper into an open space in the crowded parking lot. The kids stopped to ask a young Eagle Scout for directions. He pointed toward a giant wooden archway at the far end of the gravel lot.

Kelly and Geoffrey thanked the boy and made their way toward the imposing structure. Affixed to the high totem-like posts on either side of the archway were two huge murals. On the left was a soaring white eagle, an obvious rendering of the bird from which the camp took its name. On the pole to the right was a hideously horned, blood red creature that made the kids shudder as they drew nearer.

"Tell me again why we're here?" questioned Kelly.

"Because I promised Mr. Grainger's scout troop I'd come to the jamboree."

"Okay, but why am I dressed like some refugee from a sandlot baseball game?" asked Kelly tugging on the sleeves of her Derek Jeter jersey and adjusting her Yankee cap.

Geoffrey stopped and glanced around. "Because this is a *Boy* Scout camp. Girls aren't allowed."

Kelly threw down her arms. "So why am *I* here, Geoffrey?

"Because I needed a ride?" he replied sheepishly.

Geoffrey grabbed his sister by the arm. "Whatever you do, *don't* take off your hat!"

Suddenly Kelly was aware that people were staring at them as they walked by. She lowered her voice.

"Okay, Okay. I'll play along. But this means you're coming with me on Sunday to Chatsworth to get those fresh fruit preserves for Aunt Sarah."

"Agreed," said Geoffrey, greatly relieved.

When Kelly and Geoffrey reached the archway they stopped momentarily to observe the people who were passing through the entrance. At one point Geoffrey picked out all three Fishman boys walking toward the gateway. He quickly ducked behind a tree to avoid being seen by the little hell-raisers.

A slight man with a deeply tanned and weathered face, sporting a salt and pepper ponytail greeted each person who stepped up to the gate. The man had on a brown "Camp Director" T-shirt and wore faded blue jeans rolled up at the cuffs, Fifties style.

Kelly and Geoffrey watched in silence for a few minutes as the Fishman boys were turned away. Big Larry made a fuss, ranting and raving at the unimpressed gatekeeper while his two kids looked on. Eventually the trio skulked away nearly bumping into Kelly and Geoffrey. Geoffrey hid behind Kelly as they hurried by. "I told you, you should have worn your scout uniform," Big Larry chastised little Larry with a slap to his head.

"Whew, that was close," sighed Geoffrey once the coast was clear. The last thing he needed was to run into the Fishman firestorm tonight.

"Do you know that horrible family?" asked Kelly. She could only shake her head at her younger brother's antics. He had gotten her here on false pretenses so she felt she had the right to make him squirm a little.

"Don't ask," replied Geoffrey hastily.

"Well, here goes." He grabbed Kelly by the hand and led her to the gate.

"Howdy," gushed Geoffrey smiling nervously at the trim pony-tailed gatekeeper.

Without smiling back the man held out his hand and grabbed Geoffrey's left elbow in some form of greeting. Geoffrey mimicked the gesture. The man turned toward Kelly and repeated the greeting. His gray-green eyes narrowed as he fixed them on Kelly. Feeling suddenly self-conscious, Kelly lowered her eyes trying to avoid the man's piercing gaze and gripped his arm firmly.

"All who enter the gateway to witness the sacred rite must be acquainted with the ways of the Lenape," he said in a gentle yet commanding voice while his eyes remained fixed on Kelly. "What is the name of the spirit-guide who brings you here tonight?"

"*Mesing*!" Geoffrey blurted out.

The camp director waved his arm.

"You are welcome here, my brothers," he said with a slight bow of the head.

"Follow the torchlit trail down to the lake. The Algonquin campsite is on the left."

The camp director motioned them through the gate. Neither Kelly nor Geoffrey spoke as they hurried past.

"What was that all about?" asked Kelly when she had regained her composure.

"Beats me," replied Geoffrey keeping his eyes on the trail.

Kelly followed close behind him. "But what was that you said to him?

"*Mesing*? That was the password Mr. Grainger told me to give the gatekeeper."

"What does it mean?"

Geoffrey quickened his pace. "I think he said it means something like 'solid-face spirit' in Lenape lingo."

Kelly struggled to keep up with her brother. "Huh?"

"It has to do with an Indian ritual called the Order of the Arrow they're going to perform tonight."

Kelly grabbed her brother by the back of his pants. Geoffrey stopped and reeled around.

"I thought you said we were going to a dance," she scolded. "Now I find out it's an Indian ritual and no girls are allowed. What else haven't you told me, Geoffrey?"

Geoffrey screwed up his face. "Did I happen to mention that there was going to be a lecture about the Jersey Devil?"

Kelly's eyes bulged. "The *what*?" She grabbed her brother by the shoulders and shook him.

"You know the local legend about the monster that eats babies and sours milk with its hot breath."

Kelly released her brother. "That's it, I'm out of here." She turned and started back up the path.

"Wait," shouted Geoffrey. "Isn't that Danny Windsor over there?"

Kelly froze.

"Danny!" yelled Geoffrey running off in his direction.

Danny Windsor looked over and waved. He was standing alone in the clearing of the Algonquin campsite. The full moon sparkled off the dark shimmering lake behind him. All around, scouts and fathers were laying blankets on the ground and picking out places to sit near the blazing campfire. The scent of burning cedar and sage filled the cool night air.

Everywhere there were kids and grown-ups in animated conversation. Some were dressed in their scout outfits. Others were in shorts and T-shirts. Many had painted faces and wore feathers in their hair. A spirited few wore devil masks and green or red long johns trailed by long spiked tails.

Shaking her head and muttering under her breath, Kelly took off after her brother and Danny.

"Geoffrey?" greeted Danny with a look of surprise when Geoffrey reached him.

"Hi, Danny. Long time, no see."

When Kelly caught up with the two boys she was noticeably out of breath from her run.

Danny was taken aback at the sight of her. "Kelly? Is that you under that … that get-up? What are you doing here?"

"What are *you* doing here?" Kelly shot back.

"I asked you first," said Danny looking around anxiously.

"Geoffrey needed a ride."

"Oh, now I get it. And that's your chauffeur's uniform?"

Kelly made a face. "Very funny."

Danny stood on his toes and strained his neck.

"Who are you looking for?" asked Geoffrey.

"Just making sure Bulldog Wick isn't lurking nearby."

"Don't worry, I left him on his leash at home," Kelly slipped in slyly.

Geoffrey raised his eyebrows. "You and Curtis Wick?" he asked incredulously.

"It's a long story," Kelly shrugged.

"I can make it short," Danny chimed in. "Your sister is dating Bulldog Wick."

"I am not," Kelly shot back. "I just agreed to meet him at the annual lifeguard beach party."

"Sure sounds like a date to me," answered Danny. "What's it sound like to you, Geoffrey?"

"Sounds like a mistake if you ask me," Geoffrey said eyeing Kelly disapprovingly.

"Damn right," said Danny looking right at Kelly.

"You still haven't answered my question," Kelly persisted. "What are you doing here?"

"Getting extra credit," replied Danny with a smirk.

"For what? Charm school?" Kelly fired back.

"No, for class. It's for that college course I told you about the other day."

Now it was Kelly's turn to smirk. "Since when do they offer college credits to students who roast marshmallows and sing campfire songs dressed in war paint?"

"Hey, what do you think folklore is all about?" Danny said with a half-serious face. "The speaker tonight is my professor, Payton Tippett. That's him over there in the rumpled suit."

Three men were huddled in conversation illuminated by the campfire. Geoffrey recognized the burly, mustachioed man as Cletus Grainger, the scoutmaster, and said so. Kelly and Geoffrey both recognized the slim man with the salt and pepper ponytail as the camp director who had grilled them at the gateway entrance. The third man was short, stout, and distinctively professorial. He was bald except on the sides and had a neatly trimmed goatee. He was dressed in a white linen suit in need of a good pressing. His tie was loose and his collar unbuttoned. The kids guessed his age at about fifty. The three men seemed to be arguing about something. The professor was shaking a stubby finger at the camp director as he spoke. The camp director stood with his arms folded and just listened.

As they watched, the professor removed his jacket. At first it seemed to Geoffrey and Kelly like he was getting ready to take a swing at the camp director. Instead, he handed his jacket to a young scout who had stood silently alongside Mr. Grainger the entire time. Kelly thought the boy seemed nervous when the scoutmaster grabbed the professor's notes from the jacket, but she didn't give it any more thought after Mr. Grainger handed the notes back to the professor.

Danny moved in closer to Kelly and whispered, "If you're nice to me maybe I'll introduce you to Professor Tippett."

Kelly frowned. The thought of meeting one of Danny's professors did not appeal to her at the moment and neither did Danny's smug, condescending manner.

"Then again, maybe I won't," added Danny changing his tune. He looked Kelly up and down. Dressed as she was, without makeup and sans earrings, with her thick lustrous auburn mane tucked away under a dirty baseball cap and wearing a loose, unflattering jersey, he suddenly seemed to lose interest in the prospect of introducing her to a teacher he admired. Or perhaps Curtis Wick had reentered his thinking. At any rate, his mood had changed as he continued, "You know Kelly, your get-up doesn't fool anyone. Frankly, I'm surprised the camp director let you in dressed like that. He must be blind … or off his rocker. That's what people say about him, that he's a weirdo. Spends too much time alone in the woods."

Danny picked up his blanket. "I gotta go." He looked directly at Kelly. "I hope you and Bulldog Wick have a nice game of catch on Saturday."

Kelly shot her brother a sharp glance.

"I'll catch *you* around, Geoffrey," said Danny as he walked away.

"Yeah, later."

Kelly could feel the tears welling up in her eyes. She buried her face in her hands momentarily to hide the hurt.

"Wow," exclaimed Geoffrey, "either Danny has changed a lot since the last time we saw him or you did something to piss him off big-time."

Kelly wiped away a tear with the back of her hand. "I punched him a couple of times … hard … but he deserved it."

"I'd say it's more like you're into a sticky *Wick*-et and he ain't liking it."

Kelly shook her head. "Ugh, we're just friends."

The night had now fully closed in around them. Except for a canopy of twinkling stars beyond the moon overhead, and the occasional flicker of a lantern among the semicircle of campers, the only visible light emanated from the roaring campfire located in the center of the clearing.

Danny had disappeared into the crowd. Try as she might, in the darkness Kelly could not find him among the faceless, shapeless crowd. Kelly and Geoffrey decided to stay where they were and plopped down onto the soft ground.

From behind the campfire the outline of three figures re-emerged. A hush fell over the crowd as all eyes were trained on the campfire. Professor Tippett and Mr. Grainger stepped into the light. The third figure, the camp director with the rolled up jeans and ponytail, tossed a couple of logs onto the fire and stood by its perimeter.

Mr. Grainger stepped forward.

"May I have your attention please? Thank you all for coming out tonight. I know you're all anxious to get started with the program, but first let us begin by showing our appreciation to Mr. Tom Banks for allowing us to have the run of his facility this weekend."

The camp director bowed his head graciously then slipped back into the shadows beyond the fire's glow.

Mr. Grainger waited for the applause to die down before he continued.

"Next, it gives me great pleasure … indeed, it is a privilege to introduce our keynote speaker, a gifted writer and lecturer, an associate professor of cultural studies at the Richard Stockton State College, and one of the world's foremost authorities on folklore, legends, and myths. Scouts, friends, brothers … I give you Professor Payton J. Tippett, III. Dr. Tippett …"

The applause was thunderous. Many rose to their feet. Although neither Kelly nor Geoffrey had any idea who this man was, despite Mr. Grainger's splendid introduction, they both felt themselves swept up in the moment and stood up, applauding vigorously.

The professor drew himself forward and began speaking into a wireless microphone. His robust baritone resonated throughout the camp in the still night air.

"Tonight I am going to talk to you about a phenomenon. Some people refer to it as a legend. Some call it a myth. I like to think of it as a phenomenon; a natural and heretofore inexplicable phenomenon.

"You have all heard the stories. There have been countless sightings; thousands of documented first hand encounters. Perhaps some of you have even had experiences of your own or know someone who has. Nearly every New Jersey citizen has grown up hearing the stories. Sometimes they portend calamitous events. Such accounts have been reported for nearly 300 hundred years. And all of it started right here in these woods."

For more than an hour Professor Tippett entertained his audience, young and old, with colorful tales and amusing anecdotes about the infamous phantom of the Pines. He began his oration at the beginning in 1735 with the oft-told tale of how an overwrought woman known to history only as Mother Leeds cursed her unwanted 13th child, entreating, "it might just as well be a devil as a child." That being her wish, Tippett recounted how at birth the creature sprouted wings and flew up through the chimney, causing a certain frightened midwife in attendance to shriek, "There goes the neighborhood!" Naturally, this casual quip immediately brought peels of laughter from the mixed crowd.

Tippett continued his commentary with the unprecedented rash of weeklong sightings during the panic of January 1909, which stretched beyond New Jersey's borders—and beyond the borders of rational thought, he added—eliciting some chortles from the audience.

Tippett then recited some names of doctors, lawyers, politicians, priests and other famous people—including Joseph Bonaparte, Napoleon's brother and an avid sportsman who once lived in Bordentown, and Stephen Decatur, the naval hero of Barbary Coast pirates fame—who had all claimed to have encountered the beast at one time or another. As the story goes, Commodore Decatur winged the creature with a cannonball forged at the nearby Hanover Iron Works foundry, though it was not enough to halt the Devil's flight.

The distinguished lecturer held his captive audience spellbound and in awe with stories of the fabled creature, which he vaguely described as half man and half beast, in some accounts resembling a flying kangaroo, that has long haunted the woods known as the New Jersey Pine Barrens.

Against the backdrop of the pitch black night and the warm crackling fire, boy scouts huddled closer to their fathers and to other scouts, occasionally looking toward the lake, the trees, and beyond for an expected glimpse of Diablo Ceasara, the Jersey Devil.

"Now, I know what each one of you is thinking," Professor Tippett concluded. "Could such a creature really exist?"

He paused for dramatic effect and looked out into the crowd. As if on cue, a rogue flame crackled and leapt from the campfire behind Professor Tippett, illuminating the meditative face of Tom Banks who was standing arms folded in the shadows. Kelly watched closely as Tom's light green eyes seemed to flicker momentarily with the memory of some distant thought.

"Well, I can tell you this, the secret lies somewhere in these woods."

He paused again to let the murmur among his audience settle down.

"So, if I were you, I would say an extra prayer when you go to sleep tonight, and stay close to your fathers and brother scouts. For no one knows if and when the Jersey Devil will decide to show himself again."

Kelly reached for her brother's arm and squeezed it tight. Geoffrey let his gaze follow a rising plume of thick gray smoke as it drifted up, slowly blanketing the bright new summer's moon. Suddenly he stiffened. There, against the backdrop of the silvery moon, he saw a shadow … a shadow with wings spread and talons open … lingering in the hazy moonlight before disappearing into the thin wisps of passing clouds. He shivered as he held Kelly, saying nothing about what he thought he'd just seen.

4

'Sweet Chin Music'

Geoffrey Martin reached in front of his Aunt Sarah to lower the volume on the bluegrass music blaring from the truck radio. Sarah Bishop gave her nephew a gentle slap on the wrist and a mild "ask first" look. The Dodge pickup belonged to Noah Parsons, who was taking them to Waretown for an old fashioned hoedown.

Sitting between Noah and Geoffrey, Sarah was a little nervous. It was unusual for the young widow to be out with Noah in the company of her favorite nephew, or anyone else for that matter. However, just as she had last year when younger sister Margaret's kids came to stay with her on LBI for the summer, Sarah was adjusting to having them around again. She loved Kelly and Geoffrey dearly and they returned the feelings.

"I was surprised when your Aunt Sarah told me you wanted to come with us tonight," said Noah, making conversation. "I didn't know you were into Country & Western music."

"I'm not," replied Geoffrey. "I just didn't feel like sitting home alone tonight."

"Why didn't you go with Kelly to the beach party?" asked Noah inquisitively. "I thought you two were inseparable."

"She has a date," answered Geoffrey without hiding his feelings of disgust.

"A date?" exclaimed Aunt Sarah, genuinely surprised.

Geoffrey immediately realized his gaffe and tried to backpedal.

"It's not really a date. She's just meeting someone there."

"Well, I hope it's not that Windsor boy."

"Now, Sarah, Danny's got some good qualities," defended Noah.

"I'm sure he does. It's just that trouble always seems to find him. Like last summer when he got the kids mixed up with that Ryder Hayes character."

"We were all taken in by Ryder Hayes. He had a way about him," muttered Geoffrey.

Noah rounded a corner sharply and his passengers leaned his way in what he might have termed an "opportunity corner" had he and Sarah Bishop been alone.

"We all make mistakes," said Noah picking up the conversation. "Imagine what you would be like if both your parents walked out on you and, and rather than become a ward of the State, you ran off to stay with a sixty-something hippie from Down Under who had found a way to live out his endless summer by lifeguarding on LBI."

"I like Moss Greenberg," said Geoffrey. "And I like Danny, too. He's cool. Once you get to know him. But Danny doesn't live with Moss any more. He's on his own, now that he's in college."

Sarah smiled and patted Geoffrey on the knee. "Oh, Geoffrey, you like everybody. So, who is Kelly meeting tonight?"

"I promised I wouldn't tell. She's already mad at me about last night."

"I take it the jamboree wasn't quite what she expected?" queried Noah.

"You could say that," Geoffrey admitted vaguely. "She had a big dustup with Danny and freaked out when the scout's guest speaker talked about the Jersey Devil. We left before the Order of the Arrow's ceremonial dance."

Noah tilted back the brim of his cowboy hat. Dressed in jeans and a plaid shirt for the evening's festivities, the normally conservative Noah seemed a little out of character to Geoffrey, and more in line with the "Mr. Bluegrass" title Danny had dubbed him with after their inauspicious first encounter in the parking lot at the Tuckerton Seaport a year ago. Danny, Geoffrey, and Kelly had been illegally hanging posters for Danny's rock band's gig. The introduction ended with a stern lecture from Noah Parsons on the dangers confronting the fragile ecological balance of the bay area in the face of growing suburban sprawl. As an aside, Noah also let it be known that a bluegrass concert would be more to his liking.

"Don't tell me you believe all that stuff about the Jersey Devil?" asked Noah incredulously.

"You don't?" inquired Geoffrey, sidestepping the question. Actually, he wasn't sure what he believed after last night, and rather than spout off something half-cocked he thought he might gain some perspective from Noah Parson's personal view. It seemed to Geoffrey that anyone who lived his entire life in and around the Pine Barrens, as Noah Parsons had, must have an informed opinion on New Jersey's most famous legend.

"Geoffrey, I've seen a lot of strange things in my time in these woods. But I can honestly say that I have never seen or heard anything remotely resembling this legendary creature people have come to describe as the Jersey Devil. In fact, I'm not really sure I can tell you what he's supposed to look like. The descriptions I've heard are so varied it's mind-boggling. Depending on which accounts you read, he stands anywhere from four feet to eight feet in height, has a face at times like a deer or a horse or a dog, and is either wingless or flies around on short, bat-like wings. Sometimes he breathes fire and leaves cloven-hoofed tracks. If I didn't know better I'd say he was one confused, mixed-up beast, whatever he is."

"Sounds like a composite of many things," added Sarah.

"That's the conundrum, the mystery," Noah pointed out. "Around here, the Jersey Devil is the explanation for anything unusual that happens."

"But can you explain what these people happen to be seeing?" Sarah demanded.

Noah ignored the skeptical tone in her voice. "The most plausible explanation I've heard is that the Devil some have spotted may be a Sandhill Crane. They're rare around these parts, but an adult Sandhill can reach a height of four feet with a wingspan equal in length. I'm sure that in flight a Sandhill Crane is a frightening sight."

"Didn't you once spend a week alone in the Pines? Surely you would have seen something then?"

"That's right, Sarah. It was part of my survival training back when I was with the Coast Guard. I spent a week on my own in the wilds of the Wharton Tract. Luckily, I remembered a few things from my scouting days that proved useful. Important stuff like moss grows on the north side of the tree and the sun sets in the west. If you ever find yourself lost in the woods, knowing north from south and east from west is sure handy. But I didn't see a thing. No Bigfoot, no Sasquatch, no Yeti. Nothing that couldn't be explained rationally."

"Miss Maggie over at Colson's says that most Devil stories are made up by superstitious parents as a way of keeping their kids in line and getting them in the house before dark," offered Sarah as she winked at Geoffrey.

"What about your friend Johnny Longfeather?" asked Geoffrey recalling his admiration for Noah's amiable former Coast Guard buddy.

"Geoffrey, you've got to remember that Johnny is part Indian. His people believe in a Great Spirit. They accept all things in this world as a manifestation of some spirit, good or evil."

"You mean like a *boggart*?" asked Geoffrey.

"A what?"

"A *boggart*. From Harry Potter. A *boggart* is a shape-shifter that takes on the likeness of a person's worst fear," stated Geoffrey as if it were fact. "In the Harry Potter books the boggart is a frightening, unseen creature that has to be kept locked up in an armoire until a wizard learns to control him with a special *patronus*, or charm."

"Charming," added Sarah sarcastically.

"Um, that's interesting," mused Noah braking for a red light.

"What is?" asked Sarah turning around to look at the line of cars stopping behind them.

"The choice of the word *boggart* in the Potter books. It's similar to the Cherokee word *booger*, which means spirit, if I'm not mistaken."

Geoffrey giggled. "Do you suppose that's where the term *boogieman* comes from?" he asked expectantly.

"I suppose it could be," laughed Noah accelerating into traffic again. "It does seem oddly coincidental that all three words have similar meanings within their own cultural context."

"Well, I think the whole Jersey Devil legend is just mass hysteria at work," exclaimed Sarah twisting uncomfortably in her seat. "Like the little green men in those pictures you see in supermarket tabloids. If the Jersey Devil really exists, why hasn't anyone ever run into him while shopping at Walmart?"

Noah chuckled. "Yeah, most of those stories are more likely the result of bad booze."

"That reminds me of the Thelma Dobbs story," Sarah said with a smirk.

Noah let out a moan. "Oh, no."

"Who's Thelma Dobbs?" asked Geoffrey.

"She was an elderly neighbor of Noah's. Claimed she saw the Jersey Devil leaning up against her backyard fence. Said he looked like a goat with glowing red eyes."

"Knowing Thelma, it *was* a goat," laughed Noah. "And those glowing, bloodshot eyes were her own."

Noah made a left hand turn. When the truck was going straight again he looked over at Sarah.

"Well, you know there is a medical term for the condition when people hallucinate."

"Yeah, it's called 'being stoned,'" said Sarah with a little laugh.

Geoffrey smiled at his aunt.

"No, I'm serious," protested Noah. "There really is. It's called *scotoma*."

Geoffrey and Sarah both frowned, not really sure if Noah was serious or not.

"*Scotoma*," Noah repeated undeterred. "It's a term psychologists use to describe the condition where people with diminished sight see what they *expect* to see instead of what is really there."

"You mean like a mirage?" Geoffrey ventured.

Sarah stifled a laugh.

"Kind of. It's more like a figment of someone's imagination. The image seen is the result of an individual's belief system. It's determined by cultural and social parameters, which also explains why others sometimes claim to see the same thing."

"But it's not real?" inquired Sarah.

Noah shook his head.

"Professor Tippett thinks the Jersey Devil is real," said Geoffrey remotely. His mind was far away as he recalled the image the passing clouds had formed in front of the moon during the Boy Scout jamboree. Is that what Noah had meant by *scotoma*? Had his mind simply played a trick on him?

"Does he, now?" Noah probed.

"Well, sort of." Geoffrey seemed unsure. "He didn't say it in so many words."

Geoffrey looked out the passenger window. "He said the secret to the Jersey Devil is hidden in these woods."

"There are many secrets hidden in the Pine Barrens," replied Noah.

"Including Jimmy Hoffa," Sarah cackled.

Noah's expression was bemused. "Wow! You're really on a roll tonight, Sarah. What's gotten into you?"

Sarah hooked two fingers over her head like horns. "Wait 'til ya see this little devil dance!"

***

Spanning a tradition that has endured some seven decades, Albert Music Hall started as an old hunting cabin owned by two brothers, Joe and George Albert. Through the years, in one form or another, at one location or another, Albert Music Hall has evolved into the Nashville of the North. For good, down-home country music every Saturday night it is *the* place for residents of the eastern New Jersey Pinelands.

Currently located in a new double A-frame building located on Wells Mills Road in Waretown, Ocean County, the joint was already jumping when Noah pulled into the parking lot at just after 7:00 PM. Even though the doors didn't open until 7:30 the music had already begun as players sat outside tuning up and jamming with each other. Summer nights in particular were a big draw and this steamy Saturday evening was no exception as regulars and curious newcomers—many of them vacationing at the Jersey shore—mixed it up.

It was standing room only as Noah led Sarah and Geoffrey through the door. Noah paid the modest admissions fee for the three of them.

A number of people greeted Noah and Sarah as they made their way around the large, wood-paneled dance hall. Sarah and Noah introduced Geoffrey to various friends and acquaintances. Geoffrey was cordial and polite, dutifully exchanging pleasantries and engaging in casual small talk.

Although the live music was generally acoustic—or "unplugged," in the vernacular of today's youth—Geoffrey had to cup his ear now and again to hear what the people were saying. It was a lively, noisy scene.

The trio made their way toward the stage, which resembled the front porch of an old log cabin. Perched atop the roof facade was a pint-sized version of the Pines' most celebrated citizen. Make no mistake about it, lest anyone should forget, the house—his house—was packed, and it was as much for his sake as for the music that many people made the trek to this holy place. The Jersey Devil and Piney music were integral parts of the same whole.

A hot female fiddle player was on stage leading her popular group, Midwife Crisis, through a countrified number that Geoffrey recognized instantly as the cult hit *Sell Me Your Dreams*. The raven-haired beauty stood between a bearded, grizzled piano player and a tall, angular man playing an upright bass. Geoffrey could not take his eyes off the fiddle player.

"Shawna James," said Noah nonchalantly, standing beside Geoffrey and looking up at the stage. "Watch her fingers. They fly like lightning over the strings. And the rest of her ain't bad, either."

Aunt Sarah gave Noah a sharp elbow to the ribs.

Whatever her fingers were doing, Geoffrey didn't care, but he couldn't have agreed more with Noah's assessment of Shawna James. Her rhinestone-studded blouse, unbuttoned at the neck, shimmered under the glare of the soft spotlights.

When the group had finished, Geoffrey excused himself and retreated to the rear of the room for refreshments, following Shawna James who coincidently was headed in the same direction. Noah and Sarah seized the opportunity to hit the dance floor.

Geoffrey was busy observing Shawna sip coffee and fork through a slice of blueberry pie when he heard a familiar voice call out his name.

"Danny!" exclaimed Geoffrey, startled as the older boy made his way toward him.

"Hey, buddy," greeted Danny. "Is Kelly with you?"

Danny rested his battered guitar case against the wall.

"No, why?" said Geoffrey sounding surprised.

"I was hoping she would change her mind and come out to see my new band."

Geoffrey wanted to say something about the shabby way Danny had treated Kelly at the jamboree, but decided better of it.

"So who are you here with?" asked Danny.

"Noah Parsons and my Aunt Sarah."

"Lucky you," replied Danny sarcastically. "Hey, why don't you see if you can hang out for awhile and catch my band, The Pine Ridge Rockers …? We go on at ten."

Danny leaned in and added, "It's not really rock and roll but it gets the crowd stomping."

Before Geoffrey could reply, Danny paid for a bottle of spring water and moved off to talk to Shawna James. Geoffrey watched as Danny wedged himself between Shawna and her banjo player, joining in their conversation.

"There you are," exclaimed Aunt Sarah coming from the dance floor. She was linked arm in arm with Noah and another man. Geoffrey recognized the man immediately.

"Geoffrey," Noah began, "there's someone I want you to meet."

The trim man smiled slyly at Geoffrey and waited for Noah to continue.

"Tom Banks, meet Geoffrey Martin. Geoffrey is Sarah's nephew and my understudy at the Seaport."

Tom and Geoffrey clasped each other's arms firmly in the ritual shake they'd used the night before. Geoffrey blushed, remembering. Tom grinned his approval.

"Tom is the White Eagle Camp Director and a 'woodjin'—what the locals call a guide," finished Noah.

"We've met," Tom responded for both of them.

Noah continued with the introductions. "Tom also teaches survival training in the Pines to the servicemen stationed at Fort Dix and McGuire Air Force Base. You could say he spends a lot of time in these woods."

"Are you interested in survival training, Geoffrey?" The Camp Director's tone seemed genuine and unchallenging and his friendly manner put Geoffrey at ease.

"Heck no, Tom," Aunt Sarah answered quickly. "He's interested in the local lore like everybody else. Some high-sounding Stockton professor's gone and loaded his head full of wild notions about strange things being kept secret back in the Pines." She gave Tom an overly obvious wink.

Geoffrey's cheeks turned ashen as the blood drained from his face. "Oh, Aunt Sarah," he started to protest.

"Nonsense," replied Tom.

"That's what I tried to tell them," interjected Noah.

"No, no," Tom corrected himself. "The young man is right to want to know more about the Pine Barrens and all the creatures that inhabit it. The Pines are like a microcosm of the Earth. The health of one mirrors the health of the other."

"A symbiotic relationship as with all things," added Noah.

"That's right," said Tom.

"But is it safe?" asked Aunt Sarah. She looked at Noah for encouragement. "I mean, nothing terrible lives there, right?"

Tom grew thoughtful as he studied Geoffrey's ghost-white face.

"Safe?" He repeated Aunt Sarah's word. "Here's what I can tell you. There is a place in the Pines called 'Hell' where nothing ever grows, and there's a place in the Pines called 'Spirit Hill' where things are alive with the past. People have gone into the Pines alone and never come out."

***

The flames licked high into the night sky. Loud rock music could be heard over the roar of the cascading ocean surf. Half-naked young men and women danced around the bonfire. Bottles and cans littered the darkened beach.

Kelly Martin was frantic. This was certainly not what she had expected. The annual beach party, sponsored by the LBI Life Saving Service to recognize the completion of the arduous life-saving training course by the new recruits, had, over the course of the evening, degraded into a Roman-style orgy. Without Moss Greenberg who was uncharacteristically down with the flu, Danny Windsor, or any of the other veteran beach guards on hand to keep the peace and maintain order, all hell had broken loose.

Kelly expected the police at any moment. Surely *someone* staying in one of the palatial vacation homes just over the dunes would have complained about the ruckus by now. Several adult residents had, in fact, taken it upon themselves to check things out, and Kelly noticed that many left in outrage at what they saw.

At the moment, Kelly was searching for Curtis Wick. She and Curtis had been together earlier in the evening until a fight broke out between two new guards over a bottle of tequila. Curtis leapt into the fray on the side of one of the combatants, who ultimately became the victor, then disappeared down the beach with several other partygoers to celebrate the victory.

Kelly wanted no part of the fight or its spoils, and told Curtis as much. She had not seen him since.

Now, expecting the police to arrive and break up the party, Kelly just wanted to let Curtis know she was heading home.

She found him half-drunk sitting with his back propped up against a yellow trashcan. The can was spilling over with debris and it smelled hideous.

The winner of the fight over the contested bottle, Lester Jackson, lay sprawled out on his back a few feet away. No one else seemed to be around.

When Curtis spied Kelly he waved her over. She stood before him in disgust. He lit a joint.

"Where did you get that?" Kelly demanded.

"From my friend, Jacko," replied Curtis, thick tongued and gesturing toward the sleeping boy.

"You better get rid of it before the cops get here."

"How about a kiss first?" slurred Curtis, reaching up to pull Kelly down to him.

"How about some sweet chin music?" countered Kelly as she gave him a swift karate kick to the chops.

Curtis slumped over. Kelly retrieved the marijuana joint from his hand and buried it in the sand. Working rapidly, she dragged Bulldog Wick a safe distance away from the trashcan, the other boy, and the empty bottles. She laid him against the sand dune fence, out of harm's way.

As police sirens began blaring one street over, Kelly made a dash for her car.

5
A Little Magic

Geoffrey could see that his sister was in a sullen and ugly mood. She hadn't spoken a word since they got in the car at Crab Cove. When he asked her if she'd enjoyed the beach party last night, she replied with a shrug.

Undaunted, Geoffrey attempted to tell Kelly about his evening at the Albert Music Hall with Aunt Sarah and Noah Parsons. At best she listened with half an ear; grunts and sighs were her only signs of acknowledgment.

When Geoffrey mentioned running into Danny there, Kelly seemed to perk up. But since Geoffrey had left with Aunt Sarah and Noah Parsons before The Pine Ridge Rockers took the stage, his sister returned to tuning him out. Nevertheless, Geoffrey continued talking, content to let his own voice break the otherwise uncomfortable silence.

Kelly made a left off Route 72 West onto 532. Looking out his window during a prolonged lapse in the conversation, Geoffrey marveled at the row upon row of neatly spaced young pine trees. The effect reminded him of the bristles of a hairbrush as they sped by in the car.

At the "T" where Routes 532 and 563 meet, Kelly stopped the car at the stop sign. This was the center of the town of Chatsworth and there wasn't a soul in sight. Looking directly across the street, she and Geoffrey spotted a multi-story, clapboard building with a sign identifying it as Colson's General Store.

Kelly remembered her Aunt Sarah trying to describe the place to her. She said it was old in an antique sort of way, yet new insofar as it always appeared to be spruced up. According to Aunt Sarah, no one really knew the age of the building. That is to say that while it appeared to have been restored over the years, the restoration had not been done in a conventional way. Sure, it had received an electrical upgrade and a fresh coat of paint, but structurally nothing of consequence had been done to the store as far back as anyone could recall. The Colson family had owned the property for generations and, just like its present owner, the building simply defied age.

A well-known Pine Barrens oddity and tourist attraction, gone were the canned goods, dry goods, and livestock feed that were at one time the quaint corner store's staples. The penny candy counter was still intact, however, as was the functioning outhouse where it was rumored a local boy once successfully hid from the Jersey Devil—it being common knowledge that an outhouse was a truly safe haven when one is being stalked by the menace of the Pines.

Kelly turned left and pulled her Mini Cooper up along the curb just past the building. An elderly woman in a straw sun hat and wrap-around sunglasses was on her knees in a garden of lush sunflowers, turning the soil with a small hand rake.

"Excuse me …?" said Kelly, rolling down the car window and shouting past Geoffrey. They were the first words Geoffrey had heard her utter in nearly an hour.

The woman stopped what she was doing, looked up, and smiled cheerfully.

"Is it okay to park here for the General Store?" Kelly asked.

"Why, of course, my dear," replied the woman with a pleasant lilt in her voice. "The front door is open. Mind your step," she cautioned.

Kelly and Geoffrey hopped out of the car and bounded up the short flight of steps to the landing of the store. The door opened on an angle facing the main street. A tiny bell tinkled as they walked over the threshold.

The store's ambiance was bright and cheery. Large plate glass windows at the front washed the large main room with brilliant rays of sunshine. An antique ceiling fan whirled silently overhead.

The room was filled with gifts and collectibles, all made by local artists and craftspeople. Mason jars of jam and preserves lined one wall. Colorful rugs and stone earthenware lined another.

Adding to the coziness and charm, a fluffy pillow with the words "John McPhee sat here" embroidered on it lay propped against an old steamer trunk that rested under the storefront window. A chubby, sandy colored tabby startled the kids. She purred and wrapped herself around their feet, then moved on into the room. The kids followed.

"May I help you?" said a warm, friendly voice coming from behind the counter at the far end of the store.

Geoffrey and Kelly did a double take when they realized that the voice belonged to the same elderly woman they had just met in the garden outside. She had removed her straw hat and sunglasses, revealing a full round face with rosy red cheeks and keen, sparkling blue eyes. Her garden gloves and smock were replaced with a clean white apron.

"You're the store clerk, too?" Geoffrey asked incredulously, unable to control his surprise.

"And I take out the trash and drive the tour bus during the cranberry festival," the woman answered in the same sweet voice. "I'm Margaret Colson, the proprietor of this establishment. Most people just call me Miss Maggie. Now, how can I help you?"

Kelly handed Miss Maggie a list of things Aunt Sarah had asked them to pick up for Crab Cove, Sarah's nautical gift shop in Ship Bottom.

"Oh, my," exclaimed Miss Maggie, "*You* must be the Martin children. Your Aunt Sarah's my best customer for strawberry-rhubarb jam. It's made from an old family recipe," she added with a surreptitious smile.

Kelly gave her an amused half smile of her own.

Miss Maggie invited the kids to browse around the store while she filled Aunt Sarah's order.

"Make sure you have a look-see in the Resource Room," she added. "I think you each might find something that will tickle your fancy. We have quite an extensive selection, you know. It's right through there." She pointed to a narrow doorway across the room. "Just follow Jinx."

The kids turned around and followed the furry feline into the back room.

The room was smaller than the main room, but just as quaint. It was light and airy and covered from shelf to shelf with books and literature about the New Jersey Pines. A detailed map had been left spread out on a child's school table in the middle of the room.

Geoffrey and Kelly perused the book titles but didn't recognize a single one.

"I think you might find something of interest on the shelf," a charming, pleasing voice called from the corner.

Startled, Kelly and Geoffrey both looked up.

Miss Maggie was now standing behind the resource desk. She set a grocery bag down on the table. Her apron was gone, replaced by a green T-shirt with the store's logo on it. Over her curly silver-white hair she wore a cap with a green eyeshade visor. Neither Kelly nor Geoffrey had heard her enter the room.

"How does she do that?" Geoffrey whispered to Kelly.

"Why, with a little magic, of course, dearie," replied Miss Maggie suddenly standing beside them.

Miss Maggie took Geoffrey by the arm and led him to a bookshelf. A book on Pinelands flora and fauna lay open to a page that featured a picture of a tiny emerald green tree frog trimmed in lavender and white.

"*Hyla andersonii*," said the old woman with a smile. "Cute little critter, isn't he?"

Geoffrey frowned, but found himself attracted to the frog nonetheless.

Left alone, Kelly surveyed the room. Her attention was drawn to a poster in the corner of a creature somewhat similar to the one she'd seen on the gateway at the jamboree, but less demonic looking. It's appearance was dragon-like, with arched wings spread wide. Oddly, the beast was not fearsome to behold, but appeared rather stately, almost regal. The artist had depicted this "Devil" as green, not red.

"Sir Cedric is a big seller for us," said Miss Maggie walking toward Kelly.

"Cedric?" asked Kelly skeptically. "That thing's got a name?"

"Oh, quite a few," replied Miss Maggie, "but I know him as Sir Cedric, the Protector."

Kelly was astonished. "You know him?"

"Why, of course, my dear. And it's a rather good likeness of him, if I do say so myself."

"What does Sir Cedric protect?" asked Geoffrey joining the conversation.

"Why, the Leeds secret of course."

Geoffrey was nonplussed. "You mean the birth of Mother Leeds's 13th child? That's no secret. Everybody knows that story."

Miss Maggie smiled demurely, eyes twinkling.

"Wait a minute," interrupted Kelly, standing with her hands on her hips. "Isn't … ah … Sir Cedric, as you call him …" she pointed to the poster, "the Jersey Devil?"

"Oh, come now, children," replied Miss Maggie, blushing slightly, "Does Cedric the Protector sound like the name of a devil to you?"

***

"There's something very strange about that old woman," said Kelly when they were back in the car.

"Yeah, too much applejack," replied Geoffrey, "or whatever it is these Pineys call their hooch. Noah calls it Jersey Lightning. Potent stuff, too, the way I hear it. And if you ask me, Miss Maggie has been doing a little too much nipping from the local still."

"Did you notice she didn't charge us for the jam?"

"Yeah, but I did see her write something down in an old ledger. Aunt Sarah probably worked out some sort of credit plan with her. Hey, but what was she trying to prove by showing me those tree frogs?"

"Beats me," shrugged Kelly. "Like I said, she sure is odd."

"Anyway, I'm glad you're talking to me again."

"I wasn't mad at you, Geoffrey. I just wish I'd gone with you and Aunt Sarah instead of going to the beach party. It sounds like you guys really had fun. Besides, I might have been able to patch things up with Danny."

"He asked about you," said Geoffrey.

"He did?"

"Sure, right before he ran off with a hot girl fiddle player."

***

Redmond Franks took a seat at the counter in the corner of the Toms River Diner, near the cash register. He glanced absently at an open menu.

Numar Zoltanski, the diner's proprietor, finished ringing up old Mrs. Mayer's check, removed a nub of a pencil from behind his ear, and reached into his back pocket for his order pad.

"What'll it be?" said Zoltanski in a gravelly voice that betrayed his two pack a day, forty-year habit.

"What's the special today?" Franks asked calmly without looking up.

"The usual," replied Zoltanski impatiently.

"What's in it?"

"You on some kind of diet?"

Franks folded the menu and set it down on the counter. His cold, unflinching eyes looked up at the proprietor. "I like to know what I'm eating."

"A little of this, a little of that. You get what you pay for," replied Zoltanski with a slight grin.

"How's that working out for you?" said Franks coolly. He reached into his wrinkled shirt pocket and pulled out a crumpled pack of Marlboros. He took one from the pack and tapped it lightly on the counter.

"Today, not so great," answered Zoltanski studying his patron's movements. The guy was a local. That was all he knew about him. He'd seen his pock-marked face in the diner a couple of times before. Instinctively, Zoltanski looked toward the cash register where he kept his own stash of cigarettes.

"Why not?" Franks toyed with his cigarette twirling it across his fingers like a baton.

"Simple economics," Zoltanski said uncomfortably. "I'm low on stock."

Franks put the cigarette between his lips. "So, you'll get more."

"That's not as easy as it sounds. My supplier's run into a little, ah … trouble."

Zoltanski glanced around the room nervously. It was mid-afternoon. The lunchtime rush was over and the dinner crowd hadn't begun to collect so the booths and tables were nearly empty.

"Look, what's with all the questions? You gonna order or what?"

Redmond Franks lit his cigarette, taking a long, deep drag before he exhaled. Smoke streamed out of both nostrils like jet exhaust. "What if I told you I could help you out with your supplier issue?"

Zoltanski inhaled the burning sulfur from the lit match lingering in the air. It was a smell he craved every time. "Fresh. It's got to be fresh. Nothin' frozen, nothing old."

"How's same day fresh? Killed in the morning, you're serving it for lunch."

"When?" asked Zoltanski eyeing the man's cigarette pack.

"How soon do you need it?" puffed Franks.

"I'm out. How's the end of the week sound?"

"The end of the week it is. I want $2 a pound."

"All meat. No bone, no fat, no filler."

"One hundred percent Grade A Bambi," said Franks through a smoke ring.

"Done," Zoltanski said looking over at Franks.

Zoltanski reached behind the cash register for his cigarettes. An elderly gentleman approached him holding out a soup cup in his shaking, withered hands. "Can I have the rest of this to go?" he asked meekly.

Redmond Franks stood to leave. As he did he put his cigarette out in the old man's cup.

"You really should keep ashtrays on the tables," Franks said walking past the register.

"Hey," the old man protested weakly.

Franks snarled and the elderly gentleman turned away.

"I'll get you a fresh cup, Mr. Linowicz," Zoltanski offered while lighting his own cigarette. For just a few seconds, he stared at Redmond Franks as he walked out into the sunlit street.

***

The kitchen at Crab Cove was cozy but seldom used, especially for cooking.

For a makeshift family on the run, working the long, irregular hours that come with the summer tourist season at the New Jersey shore, breakfast was the only meal they had together. And at Crab Cove, breakfast meant Bageleddies takeout since it was just down the block.

This Monday morning started that way for two out of the three of them. Kelly was already out the door and at her post on the 17th Street Beach. Aunt Sarah was at the kitchen table, coffee cup in hand when Geoffrey glided in, guided by the pungent aroma of perked coffee and toasted bagels. Honey oat was his preference this week and he helped himself to one.

"So what do you think of Maggie Colson?" asked Sarah as she poured Geoffrey a cup of coffee.

Geoffrey bit into his bagel. "She's quite a character. How does she get around like she does? It's creepy."

"She *is* pretty spry for her age," answered Aunt Sarah.

"Which is?"

"Well, heavens," exclaimed Sarah. "I don't actually know."

"She's probably thirty and prematurely wrinkled," said Geoffrey. "She slinks around as quiet as that cat of hers." He gulped down a whole glass of milk.

"Thirty isn't old, Geoffrey. Better watch what you say, you'll be thirty one day."

"I wish I was now," sighed Geoffrey. "Then maybe Mr. Parsons would let me go out on a field trip with him. If I have to stay cooped up in that cramped docent shack all summer I'll die of boredom."

Sarah leaned over the table toward Geoffrey.

"He'd kill me if he knew I told you this, so act surprised when he tells you," she whispered in a low voice. "Apparently the Pinelands Preservation Alliance reached out to Libby Ashcroft and the Board of Directors about their interest in opening up a new exhibit at the Seaport focusing on endangered Pine Barrens species. The Board thinks Noah would be the right person to lead the research party. He was thinking of asking Libby to have you assigned to the project."

"All right!" shouted Geoffrey, unable to control his excitement. "Finally! Mom and Dad will be so pleased. Where will they be tonight?"

"New Guinea, tracking down a wild orchid known as the pink lady's slipper. Although I don't know why they have to traipse halfway around the world to find one. Noah says the Pine Barrens has the same variety here. The locals call it the 'moccasin flower.' Anyway, their number at the hotel is on the pad."

Geoffrey didn't hear a word she was saying. He stood and danced a little jig around the kitchen table before bending over to plant a loud kiss on his Aunt Sarah's cheek. As he did, his eyes fell on the front page headline of that morning's *Times-Beacon*:

MAN FOUND DEAD IN SECLUDED PINES,
JERSEY DEVIL SUSPECTED IN SLAYING

6

Cletus Grainger

"This doesn't make sense," Noah Parsons said to Sarah and Geoffrey as he stood at the sales counter of the Crab Cove Gift Shop. He had arrived only minutes earlier to pick up Geoffrey and drive him to work. He was unaware of the news until Sarah handed him the morning newspaper.

Noah picked up the paper and read aloud. "Two fishermen found the body early Sunday morning, face down in a cedar bog. His clothes were ripped to shreds. Blood was everywhere. The body looked liked it had been mauled by a bear, one source was quoted as saying."

"But what was Mr. Grainger doing out in such a remote area of the Bass River Preserve by himself?" asked Geoffrey.

"His wife said he left the jamboree around mid-morning on Saturday, apparently to survey the area for a scout expedition he was planning for later in the summer," said Sarah pointing to a section in the article. "She couldn't say for certain if he had gone alone or not, but remembers him mentioning that he had contacted a guide named Tom Banks about his plan. Authorities are looking for Banks to bring him in for questioning. Calls to his home late Sunday night went unanswered. A complete investigation is underway, involving state and local police. Since the death occurred on a federal preserve, the FBI is expected on the scene shortly."

"Tom and Cletus both know their way around in the Pines. Either one of them could handle trouble in these woods better than anybody else I can think of," added Noah.

"Maybe they ran into something they didn't expect," suggested Geoffrey.

"Something supernatural, you mean?" replied Noah. "Not likely, although that would be easier for me to accept than the alternative the authorities are pushing."

"What's that?" Geoffrey asked.

"That Tom Banks had anything to do with Cletus Grainger's death," Sarah answered for him.

***

The offshore breeze blew gently against Kelly's face and the morning sun warmed her neck as she strained her back and arms to row against the tide. Curtis Wick panned the horizon for signs of trouble, the gray, triangular dorsal fin kind. Out beyond the sandbar the ocean lapped lazily against the rowboat as they watched and waited.

Word had come twenty minutes earlier by radio that a shark sighting had been made near Brant Beach, just a few miles to the south of Ship Bottom. Now, as the unsuspecting sunbathers began to arrive on the beach, Kelly and Curtis patrolled the waterline.

At last a Coast Guard helicopter flew low overhead. The pilot gave the lifeguards the "all clear" sign.

The two turned their boat around and headed back to shore. They hadn't spoken a word since their shift started.

"Okay, it was stupid, I admit it. So I promise it won't happen again," said Curtis, leaning over his oars and breaking the silence. He was still feeling the effects of his hangover.

"You got that right," answered Kelly as she continued to row.

"So, what, you're gonna hold a couple of drinks against me for the rest of my life? Gimme a break."

"Let's face it, Curtis, we're not right for each other."

Curtis let go of his oars. He lay back against the bow and folded his arms.

"What's that supposed to mean? I ain't good enough for you, Miss Sunday School?"

Kelly didn't answer. She kept rowing toward the shore.

"You know, Danny Windsor doesn't give a rat's ass about you. He's a skirt chaser. The only reason he hasn't tried to make it with you is because he's afraid you'll clean his clock when he's through with you."

Kelly drove an oar hard into the surf, splashing seawater all over him.

"And what, you don't think *Windsor* drinks and smokes pot?" he said, wiping the water from his eyes. "What planet are you from, anyway?"

"Keep it up, Wick, and *you'll* be shark bait," Kelly said angrily.

Curtis snapped. He grabbed an oar and pushed it up against Kelly's throat, menacingly.

"Keep it up and they'll find you in some sand pit in the Pines, just like Cletus Grainger." He spat the words, his face red with rage. The large veins in his neck and biceps bulged.

Kelly struggled to pull the oar out of his grasp, but he held fast. He was too strong. Then she saw something else in his eyes. Fear? Despite his anger and his strength, she suddenly knew there was something he was more afraid of than she was.

The breeze stopped. The day had become surreal and still. Their rowboat floated on the water, directionless, riding up and down with each rolling wave. Voices of children at play on the beach were barely audible but growing louder.

Wick dropped the oar and fell back into the boat. He turned his face away from Kelly, hiding his shame.

Kelly sat up and rubbed her throat, then grabbed her oars and started rowing for shore again.

"Did you know him?" she asked in a low voice. "Did you know the man they found in the woods?"

His silence told her more than she wanted to know.

***

"Professor, what do you think about the latest incident attributed to the Jersey Devil?" asked Danny Windsor from a seat at the center of the auditorium. He'd voiced the question that was on the mind of every one of Professor Payton Tippett's students as they entered the classroom that morning.

The professor ignored Danny's question momentarily and flicked on an overhead projector. The lecture hall screen behind him was filled with a collage of images passed down through time, some strikingly grotesque, some surprisingly silly, of the creature in question. The student assembly, numbering about twenty, waited with bated breath.

"It would be a first," Professor Tippett said at last, looking out over the hall.

A young Chinese girl in the front row raised her hand. The professor pointed to her and she stood up. She had jet-black, shoulder length hair with straight bangs. She was wearing a T-shirt and cut-off shorts, typical attire for students taking summer courses at Stockton State College.

"What exactly do you mean, professor?" the girl inquired.

Tippett clutched the lapels of his suit jacket. "Ms. Li-Lung, if you and your fellow students had been paying attention in class you would know that other than the alleged murder of Mother Leeds and a hapless midwife on duty at his birth, this would be the first account of the Jersey Devil committing violence against a human being. Has he been known to frighten the hell out of people? Yes, plenty of times. As to maiming or killing anyone—no. But don't take my word for it. Read the reports."

A student in thick glasses and curly brown hair raised his hand. He stood up when the professor pointed to him.

Professor Tippett called out his name. "Mr. Blackwell."

"But what about the animals?" the boy asked.

The professor released his lapels and rocked back and forth on his feet.

"Poultry, yes. Livestock and dogs, possibly. If you've read the scholarly research of Messrs McCloy and Miller, who have published two fine books on the subject, or read any of the voluminous police reports and newspaper accounts, you would know this."

Tippett paused for dramatic effect, knowing he held the rapt attention of every student in the room.

"No, ladies and gentlemen. My take on this most recent event is that it is not the work of the so-called Jersey Devil."

Danny didn't wait to be recognized by Tippett. He stood and shouted up to the professor, "But how can you be so sure?"

Professor Tippet looked out again over the lecture hall. All eyes were riveted on him save one. A student sat alone, slouched in his seat in the back of the auditorium. A black cowboy hat covered his face. He appeared to be asleep.

The professor took a sip of water from a glass on his podium and adjusted his microphone. He looked directly at Danny as he spoke.

"Because, Mr. Windsor, I have concluded that the beast known as the Jersey Devil, if it still lives and breathes, is actually a benign creature. And that the frightening stories associated with it are part of an elaborate cover-up."

The reaction was loud and instantaneous as students started talking among themselves. Amidst the hubbub, several students stood and up and began firing questions at the professor.

"Professor, what about the Shourds connection?" Damian Blackwell asked above the clamor.

"A convenient contrivance, Mr. Blackwell," Tippett shot back. "A proud pioneer family and a spooky old house in Leeds Point … need I say more?"

Danny turned to the student sitting next to him. "Is he for real?" he asked incredulously.

The boy shrugged holding out his hands. His face mirrored Danny's own bewildered look.

"Settle down now, class," the professor shouted, motioning with his arms. As the room returned to order, he continued.

"There have been many well-known stories handed down to us through the centuries from various cultures about spirits and strange creatures, some fearsome to behold but benign by nature, whose job it was to protect some precious secret or treasure. The great sphinx of Egypt is said to be a monument to one such creature. Grendel of *Beowulf* fame is perhaps another."

Kim Li-Lung raised her hand again.

"But Professor Tippett, what would such a creature have to protect in the New Jersey Pines? There's nothing here but trees and sand. What's so important?"

Tippett walked to the edge of the stage.

"Ah, Ms. Li-Lung, that is the $64,000 question. And you of all people should know the answer."

Taken aback by the professor's comment, the young lady sat down with a puzzled look on her face.

Professor Tippett placed his hands behind his back and rocked on the balls of his feet again.

"Would anyone happen to know the answer to Ms. Li-Lung's question?"

As he waited for a response, the professor looked around the room, from face to face. The auditorium was dead silent.

"Water," came the assured response in a male voice from the back of the hall, loud enough for everyone to hear. All the students turned their heads in the direction of the individual who had appeared to be sleeping just moments earlier.

Tippett strained his eyes in the direction of the speaker, who remained seated with the brim of his hat pulled down low over his face. No matter—Tippett had recognized the voice. His appearance here had caught the professor off guard, but only briefly.

Danny Windsor recognized him, too.

"Ah, how refreshing," Tippett said finally. "At least one of you is familiar with the ecological importance of New Jersey's great wasteland."

He reached for his water glass and took a slow sip. He spent a brief moment appraising the contents of the glass before setting it back down.

"Yes, class, the answer is indeed the water. Mythical or real, find the creature that guards the Kirkwood-Cohansey Aquifer—the great natural reservoir that lies buried beneath the sandy Pine Barrens soil—and you will hold the key to the identity of our Jersey Devil. That is your assignment for next time."

"I guess he *is* for real," said the student sitting next to Danny. "But look on the bright side—at least he didn't try to get us to buy into the space aliens angle."

Professor Tippett had turned his attention back to the images projected on the screen. Now, as he turned to face his class again, the person who had correctly answered his question was gone.

7

Leapers and Creepers

Geoffrey put the horseshoe crabs back in their tank and finished tidying up the Oyster Shack. He hung his apron on a hook behind the door and switched off the lights.

It had been a brutal day, starting with the news of Mr. Grainger's death followed by relentless droves of visitors to the Seaport. All of them wanted to learn the "Fate of the Horseshoe Crab."

It was a lecture Geoffrey himself had reluctantly first attended over a year ago. The lesson given by Noah Parsons fascinated Geoffrey then and now. When asked, he was only too happy to carry on the tradition started by Noah of educating visitors about the delicate ecological balance of the bay area, the importance of the ancient, armor-plated, crab-like spider in the food chain of migratory birds and, most importantly, the value of this often maligned creature in saving human lives through the clinical use of an enzyme it produces. While the twenty-minute lecture could be a grind when given a dozen times daily, for Geoffrey it beat working the snail pit any day.

Geoffrey found Noah waiting for him in the parking lot. Noah's face was solemn when Geoffrey slid into the passenger seat of the blue Dodge pickup.

"Remember that little discussion you had this morning with your Aunt Sarah about the field assignment?" Noah began as he put the truck in gear and drove away. "Well, I'm sorry to have to tell you this, Geoffrey—and your Aunt Sarah should not have told you about it until after I finalized the arrangements with Libby and the Board—but the field trip has been postponed, indefinitely."

"No way," Geoffrey protested.

"I'm afraid so, Geoffrey. With all the hysteria surrounding Cletus Grainger's death and the Jersey Devil rumors, the Board has decided this isn't the right time to be collecting tree frog specimens in the Pinelands."

"Tree frogs?" repeated Geoffrey, his disappointment turning into surprise. "I didn't know we were going after tree frogs." He thought back to his visit with Miss Maggie Colson, and her insistence on showing him the book on the top shelf.

"Sarah didn't tell you?" Noah asked. "Well, maybe I forgot to give her all the details," said Noah, slightly amused with himself.

"*Hyla andersonii* is the scientific name for the Pine Barrens Tree Frog," he continued. "They're tiny little things, only one to two inches long, fully grown. They're the Lilliputians of frogs.

"And they make a hell of a racket, which is how you find them. You don't actually see them sitting in the sphagnum moss or floating around the cedar bog—their honking leads you to them. There isn't another sound quite like it in the world, Geoffrey. Trust me. You get a chorus of them going and it sounds like a traffic jam on the parkway."

"How long do we have to wait to go out after them?" asked Geoffrey, his interest piqued by Noah's description of the remarkable little critters. He wished he had paid more attention to batty Miss Maggie when he was in the Resource Room at Colson's.

Noah looked out his window into the woods. "Hard to say, but I hope it isn't a long wait because they stop vocalizing by July. This is the best time to find them—a delay of just a few weeks will make all the difference. I'm sure you know they're an endangered species. Their numbers are nowhere near what they used to be, and not because of natural predators, but due to human development. They require a more acidic environment for breeding than most frogs, and agriculture and other human activities tend to drive up the pH and lower the water table. Fragmentation of the Pinelands threatens their survival, too."

Geoffrey was listening intently as Noah pulled up in front of Crab Cove. The lot was empty, which Noah expected on Monday nights when Sarah closed the shop early to attend her yoga class. The class was held in Beach Haven at the Engleside Hotel, just across the street from the LBI Museum where Noah hosted a lecture series on Monday nights featuring significant storms that had ravaged the 18-mile long island. The two usually met up for dinner afterwards at either the Engleside or Tucker's on the bay.

"Looks like Kelly isn't home yet," said Noah letting the truck idle. "You want to come on down to the Museum with me? Tonight's storm is Gloria. She was a doozy."

Geoffrey opened the passenger door. "Thanks, Mr. Parsons, but I'm beat. I think I'll wait for Kelly and see if I can talk her into takeout from the Wheelhouse."

"Okay, Geoffrey, I'll pick you up in the morning."

Geoffrey hesitated. "Actually, there's something I have to do tomorrow. I may not get another opportunity for some time. Do you think Miss Ashcroft will blow a gasket if I miss work for one day?"

Noah Parsons studied his young protégé. In just a few short weeks he had become keenly aware of Geoffrey's work ethic, which was similar to his own. While this was a sudden and unexpected request, Noah didn't think Geoffrey would have asked if it wasn't important.

"Okay by me," he acknowledged. "I'll cover for you." He slapped Geoffrey lightly on the shoulder. "Just don't make a habit of it."

"Thank you, Mr. Parsons, you won't regret it."

***

When Kelly arrived at Crab Cove, she had Curtis Wick in tow. Geoffrey was upstairs watching television in the two-bedroom apartment Sarah Bishop maintained for summer renters. The past two seasons the apartment had been occupied by her niece and nephew while their parents, Robert and Margaret Martin, circumnavigated the globe in the course of Robert's work, attending pharmaceutical conferences and doing field research. Robert Martin was a scientist who used his summer sabbaticals to lecture and search for exotic plants with the potential for yielding new drugs.

For the past two summers Margaret had entrusted the care of her two children to her widowed older sister, Sarah, a retired schoolteacher turned gift shop proprietor. While Kelly was the athletic one, Geoffrey hoped to one day follow in the footsteps of his father. Both kids worked summer jobs on LBI—in Geoffrey's case this year, on the mainland—to help defray their aunt's expenses and save for their college education. It was an arrangement that was working out well for all parties, so far.

Geoffrey knew Bulldog Wick from the LBI Beach Patrol training course last summer, and from stories Danny had told him of Wick's well-known shortcomings. Geoffrey had attended a number of the training sessions to support his sister in her successful attempt to become a lifeguard. It was during this time that he saw first-hand what everyone else knew: Curtis was all brawn and no brains.

Ultimately, Kelly made the squad last year but Curtis did not, a result that did not sit well with "Bulldog." He held Danny Windsor, as one of the judges, personally responsible for his failure to make the team. Now, with Danny off the squad and in college, it seemed to Geoffrey like sweet revenge for Curtis to make the squad and muscle in on Danny's girl. At least that's the way Geoffrey saw it, and seeing his pretty sister Kelly with Curtis Wick reminded him of the fairy tale, "Beauty and the Beast."

"What's he doing here?" asked Geoffrey without a greeting.

"Hello to you too, Red," Curtis replied with a half sneer as he dropped into a chair.

Red was a reference to Geoffrey's colorful hair and freckles. It was a name he detested and Curtis knew it.

"Curtis is a little upset over Cletus Grainger's death, so I thought you and I would try to cheer him up."

Geoffrey had guessed right. His sister was trying to turn the beast into some kind of prince. *With that frog face, no way*, thought Geoffrey.

"You knew Mr. Grainger?" Geoffrey asked suspiciously.

"Yeah, I knew him, but I didn't like him much," Curtis replied with more than he had really wanted to share.

"Mr. Grainger was his former scoutmaster," added Kelly. "Curtis is having some trouble dealing with his feelings, so I thought it might be better if he wasn't alone for the next couple of days."

"Yeah, it's strange. I've got nothin' against the guy, but I can't say I'm sorry he's dead, either," said Curtis, again uncharacteristically open with his thoughts.

Geoffrey wasn't buying it. Had his sister lost her mind? After what happened at the beach party, he thought Kelly would rather date a sewer rat than Bulldog Wick. Come to think of it, in Geoffrey's mind they were one and the same thing. Curtis reminded Geoffrey of a sewer rat and Geoffrey wanted no part of his garbage.

"So," Kelly said, "we thought we'd go grab a couple of hoagies at the Subway. You up for that?"

"You two go ahead, I've already eaten," Geoffrey lied.

"You did?" asked Kelly, surprised.

"Yeah, I grabbed a quick bite before I left the Seaport."

"Well, do you want to come along anyway?" She seemed eager to coax Geoffrey into joining them.

But Geoffrey didn't want any part of a scene with Curtis. If his sister wanted to play Nurse Kelly, that was one thing, but he refused to hang out with the likes of Bulldog Wick if he could avoid it.

Kelly glanced at Curtis and he stood to leave.

"All right, then," said Kelly. "I won't be out late. I promised Curtis I'd run him over to the funeral service in the morning before work. His car is in the shop for repairs."

"Have fun," Geoffrey said and turned back to his television program, an early Munsters rerun.

Curtis grunted goodbye as he followed Kelly down the stairs.

***

The library on the Richard Stockton State College campus was set diagonally across the main quadrangle from the multipurpose center where Professor Tippett conducted his New Jersey Folklore class. A modern, two-story brick and glass building, the library lay at the geographic center of the campus on the northeast shore of Lake Fred.

Danny sat at a table on the second floor surrounded by books. He and a handful of other diehards from the professor's class had ensconced themselves inside the library the moment the class let out. Each hoped to solve the riddle posed by the professor in class: *Mythical or real, find the creature that guards the Kirkwood-Cohansey Aquifer ... and you will hold the key to the identity of the Jersey Devil.*

Danny didn't really have a clue what he was looking for. His head ached from facts he had spent the last three hours absorbing about the New Jersey Pine Barrens and the abundant supply of potable water beneath its sandy soil that he never imagined he would be interested in.

From his research, Danny was amazed to learn that the Pinelands National Reserve stretched across 1.1 million acres in southern New Jersey, encompassing roughly 22 percent of the state. The Pines included vast expanses of contiguous forest and wetlands that provided habitat for hundreds of rare, threatened, and endangered species of plants and animals.

The New Jersey Pine Barrens is something of an ecological marvel. The fact that such a large undeveloped forest area exists in one of the country's most urbanized states defies logic. Underscoring the importance of it all is the Kirkwood-Cohansey Aquifer, one of the largest freshwater aquifers in the country, and also one of the most vulnerable.

According to what Danny had read, the aquifer was said to contain some 17 trillion gallons of pure water, enough to supply the demanding populations of the

New York–Philadelphia megalopolis through this century. And the water is readily replenishable. The Pine Barrens receives, on average, 45 inches of rainfall annually, and while the soil is too sandy and acidic to sustain typical farm crops the porous soil acts like a giant sieve, allowing rainwater to pass through and become purified. The resulting underground lake continually feeds the streams and bogs that flow throughout the preserve.

In 1978, the Congress of the United States passed the Pinelands Preservation Act to protect much of the Pinelands from urban and industrial sprawl. However, over time it became evident that even this landmark legislation was flawed; widespread environmental abuses continued, threatening the future of the acquifer.

Page after page of detailed information about this extensive water resource left Danny deeply concerned, but no farther along on his quest than before he'd begun his fact-finding mission.

Next, he worked on developing a list of creatures that might be seen as guarding the acquifer. Beginning with water buffalos and hippopotamuses (river horses), Danny soon found himself in the nether regions of rational thought, exploring through his reading the myths and legends of creatures as diverse and perverse as river rats, water faeries, and sea nymphs. He'd been at it for hours by now, but nothing was clicking.

Danny was thinking of packing it in when Kim Li-Lung, his co-inquisitor from Tippett's class, stopped by his table.

Seeing her up close for the first time, Danny thought Kim was even more beautiful, in a mysterious and exotic way, than he'd expected from seeing her across the room during class.

She tilted her head sideways to study the titles of the books that were piled around Danny, seeming to wall him off from the rest of the world. He looked up and gave her that boyish killer smile of his. She smiled back.

Danny noticed she was clutching a single book, entitled, *Place Names of Ocean County of New Jersey.*

"What did the professor mean when he said that you of all people should know the answer to his question?" he asked without hesitation, as curious about this young woman as he was about the question.

"Buy a girl dinner and I'll let you in on an ancient Chinese secret," she said. The statement was delivered in a direct, matter-of-fact way with just enough duplicity and intrigue to make it impossible for Danny Windsor to resist. Even though it was late and he was exhausted from his day of unresolved research, he suddenly felt up for a new challenge. He glanced at his watch and gathered his notes. "You're on."

"They're after someone," a student yelled looking out the window.

Several students in the Stockton State College library bolted out of their seats and joined the excited student at the window looking out over the quadrangle.

"Look! They're chasing him across campus," said another student, pointing to the scene unfolding below them. As if watching a ping-pong match, the students turned and raced across the room to the west window. Danny and Kim ran to the window to see what all the commotion was about.

Outside, campus security was engaged in a high-speed chase with a late model Ford Explorer. It had started at the security checkpoint near Pomona Road, when the Explorer suddenly pulled out of traffic and doubled back along College Drive toward Jimmie Leeds Road. As it neared the athletic fields the Explorer's path was blocked by two campus cruisers angled perpendicular to the road.

The driver at the wheel of the Explorer made a sharp right and cut across the narrow grassy knoll between the tennis courts and outdoor track. He then cut across parking lot #5 and shot into the quadrangle, where the students in the library had caught their first glimpse of him.

With three cruisers in hot pursuit, the driver of the Explorer cut between the Arts and Sciences Building and pulled onto the access road that ran along the northeastern bank of Lake Fred. A maintenance truck suddenly appeared from out of nowhere and blocked his path as he tried to continue east along the access road behind the library. Veering to the right to avoid a collision, the Explorer plunged into Lake Fred.

As sirens wailed, campus security supported by a contingent of local police pulled a short man with a salt and pepper ponytail out of the Explorer.

"That's the student who answered the $64,000 question!" Kim exclaimed.

"You're right," said Danny Windsor. "But he's not a student here. His name is Tom Banks and I'd say he's in deep shit."

8

Field Trips

Geoffrey had never played hooky in his life. Even now he didn't actually consider what he was doing playing hooky. It felt too right. He had to do something. Besides, Noah had given him the green light to take the day off.

He had hoped that Kelly would come along with him, at least as far as Colson's General Store. After that, even Geoffrey wasn't sure what he was going to do. But Kelly seemed hell bent on comforting Curtis Wick in his hour of need so Geoffrey decided to go it alone, without telling her where he was going. It would take him a little longer by bicycle, but he could use the exercise after all the time spent cooped up at the Seaport.

Geoffrey left Crab Cove before 6 AM. He left a note for Aunt Sarah explaining that he had something important to do and was taking the day off from work. He added that Mr. Parsons had okayed it.

As he approached Colson's General Store, Geoffrey saw Miss Maggie out front helping an ageless black man unload boxes from the back of his beat-up '48 Ford pickup truck. Although appearing old, with a shock of curly gray hair and an unruly gray beard, the big man looked strong as an ox to Geoffrey as he shouldered the packages up the front steps and into the General Store. Geoffrey thought he recognized him as Shawna James's piano player from the Albert Music Hall gig. He was dressed in faded overalls held up by frayed suspenders hooked over a dark undershirt.

Miss Maggie smiled broadly at the sight of Geoffrey coming up the road.

Geoffrey pedaled up to the sidewalk and hopped off his bike. He greeted Maggie with an enthusiastic "Good morning!" She responded just as warmly.

Maggie politely introduced Geoffrey to Freeman Morris.

"You sure play a mean honky-tonk piano, Mr. Morris," Geoffrey enthused. "I caught your act with Shawna James at the Albert Music Hall Saturday night."

"Why, thank you, son. I've been known to tickle the ivories a bit," Morris replied modestly. "No doubt you noticed Shawna too. Now there's a gal who can fiddle," he said looking at Maggie.

"I noticed," admitted Geoffrey. "It was hard not to," he added blushing.

"Such a nice young man," Maggie said in a stage whisper to Morris. "Sarah Bishop tells me he's a born naturalist, just like his father."

"Is that right?" exclaimed Freeman lifting a carton full of mason jars containing ointments and salves, according to the handwritten label on the side of the box. "Let's see how he can handle the load, then," he added, turning to pass the heavy box to Geoffrey.

"Most people refer to Freeman as our local witch doctor," explained Miss Maggie with a hint of mischief in her voice. "I like to think of him as a healer. He knows the purpose of every plant in these woods and has a potion for whatever ails you."

"Oh, go on with you, Maggie."

"And he's modest, too."

Geoffrey followed Miss Maggie into the store, weighted down by the bundle. Strangely, she had not seemed the least bit surprised to see him. In fact, if he didn't know better he could have sworn she was expecting him.

"This ought to get us through another season of greenhead and chigger bites," said Miss Maggie when the last of the cartons came off the truck. "Can't keep enough of it on hand with all the birdwatchers and boy scouts that stop in. Freeman, I can't thank you enough."

Freeman Morris slammed the tailgate closed.

"Just holler if you need anything else, Miss Maggie," he said wiping his brow.

"Oh, this will do just fine, Freeman," she said patting him on the back.

"I'll be by sometime later with a batch of tonic … as soon as it's had a chance to ferment some," he added with a sly wink.

Maggie Colson cooed excitedly.

"You a Devils fan, Mr. Morris?" asked Geoffrey pointing to the "GO NJ DEVILS" license plate holder on the rear of his dust covered old truck.

Freeman Morris shot Maggie Colson a sly grin.

"You could say that," Morris replied rounding his truck and opening the driver side door.

"I'll bet you are, too," added Morris as he climbed into his truck.

"I sure am. How'd you know that?"

"Lucky guess," replied Freeman Morris waving and driving away.

Geoffrey turned back to Miss Maggie. She was calling to him from the porch.

"You'd better get a move on, young man. You've still got a lot of work to do."

Jinx let out a warm meow as he came through the door and ascended the porch steps.

"What is it you want me to do?" Geoffrey asked quizzically. He shook his head.

Miss Maggie's bright eyes sparkled with delight.

"Oh now, Geoffrey, really, that shouldn't be too hard for a gifted young scientist like you to figure out."

Maggie Colson took Geoffrey by the hand and led him into the store.

"Now, I've laid out the things you'll need," she said. "Net, wicker basket, compass, and a flashlight."

Miss Maggie led Geoffrey through the door and into the Resource Room. A hand-drawn map lay open on the little school table next to a knapsack and a brown bag. An index card was stapled to the brown bag. In sweeping, undulating script the name "Geoffrey" was handwritten in blue magic marker on the card. "Oh, and I packed you a lunch," Miss Maggie added blushing. "I hope you like tuna fish. It's Jinx's favorite."

Jinx purred at the sound of his name and eyed the brown lunch bag hungrily.

"I should be at the Seaport working," said Geoffrey looking over the equipment.

"Oh, don't you worry about that, my dear," Miss Maggie said with a smile. "Libby Ashcroft and I go way back. We are charter members of the same old biddy's club," she added lightheartedly. "Besides, this is like working for the Seaport. Isn't it?"

The genial old shopkeeper spun him around facing toward the front door. "Now, the best place for you to begin is over near the old Eagle Hotel ruins," she said pointing to the map. "You take the Speedwell Road to Friendship. Follow the dirt road about 1.5 miles. You'll come to an old cranberry bog. That's a good place to start. On a good day you can hear tree frogs crooning from here to Hog Wallow."

Geoffrey folded the map and stuffed it into his pants pocket.

"You'd better get started if you want to be back before dark," she said helping Geoffrey on with the backpack. "If you get lost, make for the fire tower at Apple Pie Hill. It's one of the few places you can count on being found." She smiled slyly, adding, "Even if it's just a couple of sweethearts parking."

When Geoffrey left Crab Cove that morning his intention had been to pick up a book or two on endangered tree frogs to inform his research. He hadn't seriously expected to embark on a field trip alone. But Miss Maggie's uncanny preparations and the note of urgency conveyed in Noah's comments about the survival of the species yesterday spelled out clearly what he had to do. The time to act was now.

Geoffrey bade farewell to Miss Maggie and sped off on his bike, on his very own field trip. He smiled as he imagined the surprise on Noah Parson's face when he returned to the Seaport with a basket full of green and plum colored amphibians. The accolades would come rolling in ... and a certain fiddle player would surely come to learn of his exploits.

***

Kelly sat silently in a pew beside Curtis Wick at the Tabernacle United Methodist Church. The old church was small, but sturdy for a one hundred and twenty-four year-old building. The size of the congregation struck Kelly as a surprisingly sparse send-off to the afterlife for Mr. Grainger, considering the number of boys he must have influenced through his lifelong dedication to the Boy Scouts.

There were only a handful of scouts on hand in full uniform. Kelly recognized a few of them from the night of the jamboree, including the boy who had stood next to Mr. Grainger during the bonfire. Apparently Curtis knew him, too, because the two immediately struck up a conversation, in low voices but still within her earshot.. Kelly heard Curtis call the young man "Forbes," and assumed he must have been in Curtis's troop.

"I'm sorry I didn't believe you before," she heard Curtis say. "But it looks like the old dog finally got his due."

"You got that right," agreed Forbes in a caustic tone. "Seems he had a devil of a time getting out of this one."

The two boys looked in the direction of the deceased with obvious contempt.

Professor Payton J. Tippett, III, pompous as ever, gave the eulogy for his friend, whom he described as "one of the truly charitable men of our time."

Mrs. Audra Grainger, dressed in black, occasionally dabbed a cheek with her handkerchief throughout the service as the Reverend Joseph Mathis offered his prayers and condolences to the mourners. At the end of the service, Mrs. Grainger draped the dampened handkerchief over her husband's casket before departing.

Filing out of the church with the rest of the congregants, Kelly found it odd that while a crowd of old-timers, friends, and relatives swarmed around Audra Grainger in the reception line to extend their sympathy, none of the scouts approached the widow. In fact, it almost seemed they were avoiding her. Even Curtis steered clear of the reception line, hastily dragging Kelly away with him and Forbes boy.

"Don't you want to offer the widow your condolences?" Kelly asked as they walked swiftly toward her car.

"The two of them weren't getting along near the end," Curtis said without stopping.

"That's for sure," said Forbes. "Mrs. Grainger always felt slighted by the time and energy Mr. Grainger gave to his scouts."

How terrible, thought Kelly. Judging from the remarks of Reverend Mathis and Professor Tippett, it was obvious this man had devoted his life to a good cause. What a shame Mrs. Grainger felt cheated by his devotion.

In that instant, Kelly felt a deep sense of sorrow for Audra Grainger and the part of her life she evidently didn't share with her husband. At the door of the car Kelly looked up to pray for someone she didn't know and for the woman who apparently didn't know the husband she had just lost. She watched as a small procession of family and friends led by Reverend Mathis made their way to the cemetery behind the church. Mrs. Grainger, head bowed, was leaning on Professor Tippett's arm for support.

***

Danny Windsor didn't know what time it was. Alarm bells were going off in his head big-time, clanging louder than St. Mary's. He thought it must be Tuesday morning, but that's about all the reality his mind could process at the moment.

Laying there in that drowsy state between wakefulness and sleep, Danny's mind became suddenly alert as it raced back over the events of the day before. It had started out normally enough with Professor Tippett's New Jersey Folklore class, but after that things got a little crazy.

Danny could vividly recall following up the class with several painful hours in the library, cramming his largely under-taxed brain full of facts and useless information about the New Jersey Pinelands in search of an answer to the professor's challenge. He had asked his class to solve a two-hundred and seventy year-old mystery about the identity of a creature known as the Jersey Devil.

What puzzled Danny was why it mattered to him. Until the summer folklore course began a week ago, he could honestly say he'd never given the Jersey Devil a second thought. But somehow Professor Tippett's knowledge of the subject had gotten under his skin. What if it was all one big hoax, he wondered—no more than teacher's trick to get his students interested in an arcane topic when they would rather be on the beach tossing Frisbees and bagging rays?

Danny rolled over in bed, his mind wrestling with the possibilities. *Yeah, maybe the professor was just jerking everyone around, messing with our heads.* He certainly wasn't alone. At least a dozen of his fellow classmates that he knew of were equally hooked; convinced the professor was letting them in on some secret knowledge, some inside information that had escaped serious study and consideration over the centuries until now.

Was the idea really so ludicrous? Danny had thought so, but then along came Kim Li-Lung, another one of Professor Tippett's challenged seekers, and his curiosity was suddenly an obsession. While the arrest of Tom Banks, White Eagle's Camp Director, provided an unexpected distraction that he still didn't quite understand, the incident had intensified the mystery surrounding this course he was taking.

What was Tom Banks doing on the Stockton campus? Was there a connection to Professor Tippett's lecture? Tippett and Banks knew each other, that much was certain; Danny had seen them talking at the Boy Scout Jamboree on Friday night.

Tom may have been at the lecture incognito, but Danny was sure he wasn't there for the benefit of his own education. It seemed more likely he already knew the answers to the professor's questions—and not just the one about what made the Pine Barrens worth protecting.

But what about the chase and the arrest? What was that all about? What had Tom done to force him to run from the law, if in fact that's what he was doing? Just more unanswered questions, thought Danny, and the pile was growing.

Enter Kim Li-Lung, his enigmatic fellow student with her strange proposition. Dinner, much to Danny's surprise and pleasure, turned out to be that and quite a bit more. At her suggestion they ate at a quaint little place in Stafford called The Golden Palace. It was a charming Mandarin-style Chinese restaurant located in a strip mall on Route 72. As he learned soon enough, it also happened to be owned and operated by Kim's family. So they had dinner with the whole Li-Lung clan: grandfather, grandmother, mother, father, brother, and sister, alternating between eating with them and serving them. So much for a quiet romantic dinner for two! And the surprises hadn't stopped there.

What developed over the course of the evening, between the egg rolls, appetizers, and an entree called Kung Pao Shrimp, only served to heighten Danny's intellectual hunger while stimulating his culinary curiosity and setting the stage for all that happened next.

The dinner was fabulous, to be sure, and Danny listened all night as Kim and her family regaled him with tales of the old country, of ancient China and the wondrous mysteries of the Far East.

While Danny and Kim ate, her grandfather, Zhao Li-Lung, sat with the couple and recounted the family history, with some translation assistance from his willing granddaughter.

Descended from Chinese royalty, the family coat of arms—the blue and gold five-clawed dragon—graced the restaurant's marquee, menus, and placemats. The name Li-Lung itself, Danny was told, meant "hornless dragon" and the restaurant's specialty was a hot, spicy shrimp and chicken dish they called "The Dragon and the Phoenix."

According to Zhao, in contrast to the view held by westerners, dragons in Chinese mythology are revered as the creatures responsible for carving out the rivers of the world. Chinese legend has it that instead of spitting out fire, dragons exhale the heavy mists that create the rains of the earth. Alas, lamented Zhao, the time of dragons and such legends was past.

Throughout the evening Danny found Zhao Li-Lung's tales fascinating and provocative. They certainly made for unusual dinner conversation. As the evening concluded Danny graciously thanked his hosts for the delicious meal and pleasant company.

It was only when Kim walked Danny to his car that the two of them finally had a moment alone.

"You have a wonderful family," Danny said to Kim looking up at the stars. A full canopy of constellations he couldn't name twinkled overhead. "Your grandfather is quite a storyteller. He really had me going with that dragon stuff."

Kim moved closer to Danny, pinning him up against his car. Her body was soft and warm.

"You're a good listener," she whispered, draping his arms around her shoulders and wrapping hers around his waist. "My grandfather tells the same stories to anyone who will listen. One night he kept poor Professor Tippett here until after closing."

That's when Kim leaned up and gave Danny a passionate kiss and he lost all memory of the evening … until now.

He took out his cell and dialed Kim's number.

***

The Pomona police officer opened the door to the jail cell. He removed the handcuffs from Tom Banks's wrists and tossed them on the desk behind him.

"You're free to go," Officer Bowman said dryly. "But not too far," he added. Tom rubbed his wrists.

"Why the sudden change of heart, officer?"

"Believe me, it wasn't my idea," Officer Bowman replied. "You made bail."

"I did?" Tom was taken by surprise. "Where did I come up with fifty grand?"

"From him," the officer said pointing to Noah Parsons as they stepped out into the anteroom.

"Well, not exactly from me," Noah corrected. "The camp took up a collection for the bond."

"Why?"

Noah Parsons shot a glance at Officer Bowman. He was in conversation with Lieutenant Walter Shipley who was busy signing the release papers.

"Let's just say there are those of us who believe you are more valuable in the woods than you are in jail."

9
Bogged Down

The midday sun was brutal. Geoffrey had dressed as if he was going to work at the Seaport, in shorts, a T-shirt, and sneakers. The shorts suited the long bicycle ride through the Pines in the afternoon sun, but the heat and humidity were still oppressive. There was literally no breeze blowing and once Geoffrey stopped pedaling his only source of coolness abated. Then the insects found him; the gnats, the mosquitos, and the nasty greenhead flies.

He left his Schwinn 12-speed at the ruins of the old furnace works. The abandoned iron factory was but a ghostly memory of what was once a proud and thriving Pine Barrens industry that had helped supply the American colonial army with cannonballs during its struggle for independence against England.

Geoffrey fought his way through the thick vegetation and the endless army of swarming bugs down to the old cranberry bog that had been flooded and made into a small pond. He unpacked his net, and waited. He listened carefully, turning in all directions hoping to catch the slightest sound that might suggest he was close to his quarry.

The summer air was still. There were no sounds at all coming from the dark water or elsewhere in the woods. It was a far cry from the cacophony of croaking and honking Geoffrey had expected.

He paced the rim of the bog, stopping every now and then to listen. Except for the occasional call of a bird or the buzzing of a bee there was little noise to disturb the summer silence.

Thinking perhaps he was making too much noise himself and scaring the shy little frogs, Geoffrey settled down into the tall reeds and waited.

Feeling hungry, he pulled out the sandwich Miss Maggie had made for him and ate lunch. Soon, his early morning rise, the long bike ride, and the sun's warmth got the better of him and he drifted off to sleep.

Geoffrey awoke about an hour later to a peculiar sound, one he had never heard before. He raised his head slowly and listened.

When the sound stopped he dared not move. He felt a strange sensation, as though he was being watched, not from any one direction but all directions at once, and from above.

Then the sound started again. It was an extremely high-pitched sound, one that strained the limits of the human ear's capacity to hear. Like a dog whistle, he thought, only audible. Just barely.

Geoffrey rose to his knees and looked out over the water. There, standing in a clearing on the far side, was a graceful young doe munching on the leaves of a berry bush. When the deer whistle blew again, the doe stood stone still as if in a trance, staring straight ahead, ears erect. She seemed to be looking across the water at him, although he was certain that he remained quite hidden behind the tall grass on the embankment.

Boom! A sudden, loud gun blast just to his left caught Geoffrey off guard. Startled, he felt his heart leap in his chest.

The doe went down on her forelegs. Another shot rang out.

Geoffrey glanced to his left. The poacher lowered his gun and for the first time caught sight of Geoffrey. Their eyes locked. Even at a distance of some thirty yards Geoffrey could see the look of surprise turn to anger in those cold, dark eyes. The poacher raised his gun and pointed it at Geoffrey.

Geoffrey's mind screamed. *He's going to shoot me. Run!*

But where to go? The poacher stood between him and the road. The path to the right led to a wooded area about ten yards away. Surely the poacher would drop him before he made five.

His mind racing, Geoffrey dove just as the gun went off, plunging into the cold water of a deep cedar bog.

***

Kelly pulled her Mini Cooper into a vacant spot alongside the curb in front of Colson's General Store.

"What are we doing here?" asked Curtis, surprised at the unscheduled stop.

"There's something I forgot to get when we were here the other day."

"What, a soda pop?" Curtis said staring at the store window.

"No, bayberry candles—my mom's favorite," replied Kelly.

Looking up at the sign, Curtis hesitated, then followed Kelly quickly around to the front of the store, up the steps, and through the door.

Jinx greeted Kelly with a warm purr and a soft leg rub but kept her distance from Curtis.

"Why, hello, dearie," Miss Maggie looked up from behind the counter. "I'm just finishing a rhubarb pie recipe for my new cookbook. Would you like a taste?"

Kelly stepped into the back of the store and greeted Miss Maggie. Curtis followed close at her heels.

"No, thank you, Miss Colson," Kelly declined politely.

"How about your friend?" Miss Maggie asked cordially.

Kelly introduced Curtis, who also declined a slice of pie. He slumped into a chair near the door.

"We're just coming back from Cletus Grainger's funeral over in Tabernacle. Curtis was in Mr. Grainger's scout troop years ago. We wanted to pay our respects."

"Hmm, is that so?" pondered Miss Maggie curiously.

"I thought while we were out this way I might pick up some of the candles you keep in those fancy crafted soap dishes. For my mom. She loves the smell of bayberry."

"And here I thought you were stopping by to help your brother!"

"Geoffrey?"

"Oh, dear me," stammered Miss Maggie. "You mean you didn't know? He should have been back by now."

"Back? Back from where?" asked Kelly.

"He went on a little errand a few hours ago."

"Geoffrey was here? He took off from work? He didn't tell me …"

"Seems he didn't tell anyone," Miss Maggie interrupted. "That's what I'm afraid of. And I haven't heard any quonks all day."

"Quonks?" Curtis repeated.

"My pet name for our rare Pine Barrens tree frogs," explained Miss Maggie. "Geoffrey went into the woods to collect a few specimens for the Seaport."

"Without Noah Parsons?"

"No, he's all by himself. And it will be dark soon."

"Which way did he go?"

"Take the Speedwell Road to Friendship. There's an old furnace works and hotel ruins on the right. Follow the path down to the flooded cranberry bog and pray he didn't go into the woods alone."

"Because the Jersey Devil's out there?" asked Curtis.

"Because the Pines are no place for anyone alone after dark, without special training."

Kelly grabbed her car keys. "If we're not back in an hour call the police. And please call my Aunt Sarah, too."

Kelly turned to Curtis. "Let's go."

The big man took his time getting up. It wasn't until Miss Maggie shooed him with her broom that he reluctantly took off after Kelly.

***

"Danny, this is crazy," said Kim Li-Lung hurrying to keep pace with him as he strode across the campus.

"Is it? I don't know …" replied Danny.

"Danny, my grandfather is an old man. They're just stories he likes to tell, fantasies. He loves the attention."

"Maybe, but Professor Tippett seems to think there's something to them. C'mon, Kim, the professor spelled it out for us. He even said that 'you of all people should know.' Kim, your family's last name means *dragon*!"

"Maybe he's crazy, too," she said.

When they reached Tippett's office door Danny finally stopped. "Look, I know it sounds crazy, I mean, dragons are like dinosaurs, right? Nobody's ever seen one and yet people believe they once existed."

"No, Danny, dragons are like unicorns. They *never* existed. Dinosaurs are extinct. They left bones … fossils to be discovered, studied, and pieced back together. Dragons are the stuff of fairy tales, like my grandfather's."

Danny knocked on the door.

"Did you see your grandfather's face? He believes in them."

"Okay, but I still don't understand why this couldn't wait until the next class."

"That's not until next week. I have to know now. Don't you? The suspense is killing me!"

"Avanti," a deep baritone voice boomed from behind the office door.

Professor Tippett loved to tantalize and confuse people, especially his students. He had a reputation among teachers as a trickster and a player of practical jokes.

Danny and Kim hesitated. "Are you *sure* this is a good idea?' she said.

The door swung open. "Come in, come in," waved Professor Tippett. "Oh, I thought you were Mary Ellen Cassini, the new linguistics professor. We have a luncheon engagement."

The professor could see that Danny and Kim were puzzled.

"It's our little joke," he added to clear up the confusion. "*Avanti* means, hello, and, goodbye, in Italian."

"Oh," said Danny nodding to Kim. "I get it."

Professor Tippett led them into his basement office in the J-wing. Every square inch of wall and ceiling space seemed to be covered with mementos; African tribal masks, a Lakota eagle feather dream catcher, an aboriginal boomerang. Everywhere else there were books. Books lined the shelves. Books sat in piles on the floor. Books covered the two side chairs.

"Watch your step," advised the professor dancing through a gauntlet of books on the floor. He carefully removed the books from the side chairs so Danny and Kim could sit. The students mimicked his movements through the maze to the chairs.

"The Internet is a wonderful tool, you know," said the professor as he took his seat behind a big wooden desk, "but I like the feel of a good book." He picked up a book and balanced it in his hands to demonstrate. "You can take it with you anywhere. You don't need cables or a phone jack. Besides, you have to be careful with the material you pull off the Internet. It's not always reliable. Most of it isn't edited or even monitored by a reputable organization. A lot of disinformation gets posted as truth, and a lot of fiction gets digested as fact."

"That's why we're here, professor," Danny began. "We think we have the answer to your riddle … about who or what the Jersey Devil is."

"Well now, Mr. Windsor, it surprises me to hear that from you. However, I am not surprised that Ms. Li-Lung has an idea or two. Let's have it."

After all the rushing around, Danny didn't know where to begin. His mind went blank. Luckily, Kim came to his rescue.

"Professor, you said that the key to the identity of the Jersey Devil lies in the discovery of the creature that protects the water … the Kirkwood-Cohansey Aquifer, to be exact, is that right?" she asked.

"That's right, and the wetlands and marshes—the entire hydrologic system of the New Jersey Pine Barrens."

"And that creature may be mythical?" questioned Danny.

"This is a folklore class, Mr. Windsor. Legends rule the day. You have the free reign of your imagination."

"Well, sir, I don't mean to be rude, but are you asking us to suspend disbelief and accept fairy tales or do you really believe the Jersey Devil is a dragon?"

Professor Tippett sat back in his chair. "A fair question, Mr. Windsor, but I think the more accurate question is do I expect *you* to believe the Jersey Devil is a dragon?"

Kim and Danny looked at each other.

"No," said Danny with a shake of his head.

"No," Kim added.

"Then the case is closed," concluded Professor Tippett. "My compliments on your resourcefulness. You selected the dragon, one of four possible mythical creatures from universal legends, the others being a turtle, a unicorn, and a phoenix. What led you to conclude the dragon is the water guardian?"

Before they could answer, the professor smiled at Kim Li-Lung and said, "Of course, I expected that if you knew anything about your ancestral name you would arrive at this logical conclusion, but tell me: how is it that you two now discard the possibility so readily?"

"Because, professor, " Danny began, "I have to believe, legend or not, that we are dealing with a real being, a creature of flesh, bone, and blood—not a mythological symbol. This creature has been seen many times. He leaves tracks. He attacks livestock. He is real. Therefore, logically in our search we can only accept a known life form."

"It's true that nobody has ever captured a dragon, or photographed one, or found any fossil remains," admitted Professor Tippett. "So I concede that the actual proof of dragons is nonexistent as far as the empirical sciences go."

"So is it all a big joke?" asked Danny. "Were you just trying to make the point that a fertile imagination is a prerequisite for the serious study of folklore?"

"It's not a joke, I assure you, but I must admit that having a lively, searching imagination does help."

Tippett picked up one of the numerous books lying on his desk. "Let me ask you both this. You have seen the many illustrations, the paintings, the drawings, the woodcarvings we have shown in class, but would either of you know a real dragon if you saw one? Now think about it. What comes to your mind when we say the word *dragon*?"

He faced the coffee-table book he held in both hands toward Danny and Kim and turned the pages as he spoke.

"Which one more closely resembles a dragon to you? The serpent? The lizard? The alligator? Or the kangaroo with bat wings? The truth is, no one knows. So is it any wonder that what we end up with is a kind of composite creature in the reported accounts of sightings?"

Professor Tippett picked up another book and opened it.

"Perhaps the closest thing we have to a real live dragon is a lizard, the Komodo Dragon. Yet the length of an adult male is about eight feet, with a maximum weight of 200 pounds. It walks on four legs. It is cold blooded, doesn't breathe fire, and doesn't fly. It doesn't even have wings. Yet as the name implies, for some this may be the best dragon model we have."

Tippett opened a third book and came around and sat on the edge of his desk facing the kids. He showed them the illustrations as he spoke.

"Now let your imaginations run a little and read into the literature. There is a lizard dragon in Polynesian mythology called the *Taniwha*. The legends tell us this dragon is imbued with chameleon-like abilities and is able to adapt to its environment, camouflage itself, and make itself invisible!"

Tippett tossed the book aside and picked up another.

"Other dragon folklore tells us that dragons can live for a thousand years—that certainly covers the nearly three hundred years of Jersey Devil sightings doesn't it? And even some educated naysayers would argue that the fire breath of a dragon is really a type of gas that when exhaled can feel hot to the touch. It is actually this gas in the lungs of a dragon that makes him lighter than air to give him flight, rather than his inadequate wings."

It became increasingly apparent to both Kim Li-Lung and Danny Windsor that the professor knew the material in each of his books intimately and that every one had expanded his body of knowledge on the subject. It was quite impressive. But did he really believe it?

"There are various Native American legends that tell of a creature that is able to shape shift, and of learned *brujos*—medicine men who can adapt to the body of another creature. 'Skinwalkers' they are sometimes called. What do you suppose they look like to the untrained eye? Is one of these creatures our Bigfoot or Sasquatch?"

"What about the Leeds curse?" Danny blurted out.

"A convenient cover story given eighteenth century morality, wouldn't you say?" Professor Tippett replied in stride.

"You almost make it sound as if someone was protecting him," interjected Danny thoughtfully.

"Hmm," Professor Tippett pondered bemusedly. "The thought did cross my mind."

"But where would someone hide an eight-foot dragon?" questioned Danny.

"My guess is more like four to six feet when his wings are not expanded, and, over thousands and thousands of acres—with a little help—almost anywhere!"

"So then you do believe the Jersey Devil is some sort of dragon-like creature?" Kim asked excitedly.

"Is it really so hard to believe? Dragons have long been associated with the role of protector or guardian of something we humans hold dear, whether that precious thing is buried treasure, secret knowledge, or a beautiful princess."

The professor closed the last book and flung it into the pile on the desk. He frowned and rubbed his eyes.

"Like everyone else, what I believe and what I can prove are two different things. And that is why the Jersey Devil remains at large."

Danny and Kim looked at each other dumbfounded.

Tippett read their disbelieving faces.

"Let me put it to you another way. It really all depends on your frame of reference."

The students looked even more confused. Tippett continued undaunted.

"In western literature we're taught that dragons are ferocious beasts that terrorize villages, devour maidens, and battle knights."

"See, Danny, fairy tales—like I tried to tell you," Kim blurted out.

"Yes, that's right, Ms. Li-Lung, but if you think in mythological terms the dragon is a substitute for nature—something larger than all of us, something inexplicable and feared that we mere mortals must slay to control. If we allow ourselves to think this way, then a dragon is transformed into a natural disaster such as a hurricane, a flood, or an earthquake. It consumes the maiden—thereby becoming one with Mother Earth, while providing the males in our society with a true purpose in life—to rescue and protect the maiden."

"Okay," said Danny a bit uncertainly, "but how does that tie in with the Jersey Devil?"

"And why does he appear differently to different people?" Kim threw in. "If the Jersey Devil represents an archetype—I think that's the word you used in class—why isn't he the same for all people?"

Both Tippett and Danny were impressed by the question.

"Very good point, Ms. Li-Lung. But remember that the same thing can be said about dragons, can it not?" Tippett used explanatory hand gestures as he rattled off the characteristics: "Some fly, some don't. Some spit fire, others don't. Some look like lizards, some like snakes. It's all based on one's cultural associations, for instance your grandfather's. I'm sure he could explain that better than I just did."

Kim smiled at the compliment.

"In western cultures, dragons are beasts—the embodiment of evil, even demonic, thanks to the church. But in eastern cultures and some Native American traditions dragons are sacred, revered as gods—beings with supernatural powers over the heavens, the Earth, the waters. They are here to help man by protecting all things sacred to life on this planet."

Danny summarized for the group. "So what you're saying is that the Jersey Devil is actually a dragon of some sort, the likeness and demeanor of which is in the eye of the beholder."

"Is that so strange as to be beyond belief?" asked Tippett.

"But it all comes back to the same question. If dragons are real, if they really do or did exist, why is there no hard evidence? How come no one has seen one?" asked Kim.

"How do we know someone hasn't? Have you heard of the Loch Ness Monster?"

"It's just a myth," exclaimed Kim Li-Lung.

"Or some poor, long lost, land-locked sea serpent," Danny offered.

"Aha! But which is it? And how would you rationally explain Leviathan in the Old Testament?"

"You wouldn't. It's just a story, a parable. You can't take it literally," said Kim.

"Ah, but I do, Ms. Li-Lung. Which brings us back to my initial point—these things, these creatures, whatever they are, whatever you care to call them ... it simply depends on whether your view of reality is based upon what you see or what you *think you see*. In my view, which you may or may not share, my young friends, all myths have their basis in fact."

10

Covering the Tracks

"I didn't do it," said Tom Banks.

He was sitting across from Noah Parsons in a booth at the Dynasty Diner in Tuckerton. The early bird dinner crowd was just beginning to amble into the restored chrome and glass diner on the corner of Main and Route 539.

"Everybody knows you didn't do it," replied Noah, "the police are just doing their job."

"They're a bunch of fools," Tom said. "They want a lynching."

"No one wants anything but justice," counseled Noah.

"Justice? That's not what the press is saying. What are the police going to believe? That some legendary creature killed their respectable scoutmaster, a pillar of society, or that it was someone who knew him … some weirdo *woodjin* who spends way too much time alone in the woods?"

"But what would be your motive, Tom? You were friends, weren't you?"

A pretty young blonde waitress approached their booth to take their order. Noah ordered coffee for the two of them.

Tom Banks waited until the waitress hurried off before he continued. He turned to face Noah, staring into his eyes so intensely it made the older man uncomfortable.

"He was no friend of mine. Noah, there were rumors about him for years, but we all chose not to believe them and to look the other way."

"What kind of rumors?" Noah asked reluctantly.

Tom took a deep breath before he launched into it. "Years ago, somebody accused him of being inappropriate with one of his scouts, but it never came down to a charge. The kid and his family moved on and everybody wrote it off to problems they were having. Grainger survived that, but it still left doubts in my mind. He also used to hang out with a distant cousin who was a convicted poacher. I heard the two of them bought booze for a few older scouts one time and took them on a shooting party out of season. There was a new story about him every year or so. None of the rumors ever survived daylight and nobody ever came forward, but I could never help but wonder if some poor kids weren't getting a bad dose of abuse from a role model in a position of authority."

Noah Parsons fell back against the booth. This frank discussion of Cletus Grainger's past was a revelation to him. Tom observed Noah's reaction for a moment before leaning in and saying in a low voice, "Noah, if I had known those rumors to be true I would have killed him myself, and now I think he just might have gotten what he deserved. But it was no imaginary monster that killed him. It was only a matter of time before somebody caught up with him."

Noah regained his composure. "That would be consistent with the coroner's report," he said. "The 'claw marks' were superficial. Like from a hand rake. An animal didn't kill him. His neck was broken. That was the actual cause of death."

Now it was Noah's turn to watch for a reaction. Tom did not appear surprised by the coroner's findings.

Noah rested his coffee cup on the saucer. "So why were you hiding out at the Stockton State campus?"

"I wasn't hiding. I went to see Tippett."

"Payton Tippett?"

"That's right."

"Why?" questioned Noah.

Tom took a sip of his black coffee. Staring into the cup he said, "Because he and Cletus Grainger were up to something."

Noah stared blankly at Tom while measuring the significance of this last remark. He knew there was more to it. Like a priest in a confessional he waited patiently for the rest to come out.

"Grainger wanted me to take him into the Bass River Preserve to look for a good, unblemished future campsite for his scout troop. He knew I wouldn't have any trouble getting permission from the Park Service."

"And did you?"

"You know I always do my part for the Scouts, no matter what I think of their leader. Sure, I got the permit. But then at the jamboree he told me Tippett would be coming along, too."

"Why would Professor Tippett want to go into the Pines on a scouting expedition?" asked Noah.

"That's what I wanted to know. Tippett is a pompous ass. He's full of himself. He tried to give me this cockamamie crap about knowing where to find the Jersey Devil. He said that if we found him, it would make us all rich men."

"What did you tell him?"

"I told him he was full of shit. What else could I say?"

"Is that all?" prodded Noah.

"We argued. I backed out. So apparently did Tippett at the last moment."

"And that's what you went to see Tippett about at the college?"

"More or less, but he had a class in session. So I sat in and heard all I needed to about this crazy theory of his."

"Did you tell any of this to the police?"

Tom shook his head. "I can't prove anything. They'd just laugh at me."

"Then I hope you know a good lawyer," Noah said.

Tom leaned across the table and whispered softly. "For Christ's sake, Noah, Tippett really believes that the Jersey Devil exists, that it's some sort of creature that protects the Pinelands water supply. Like a dragon. And he's teaching this crap to his students, stretching the truth and spreading his propaganda. Hell, he's got them all convinced he's really on to something."

Noah couldn't believe his ears. A respected scholar like Payton Tippett believing in something as preposterous as a living, breathing dragon, and in the 21st century? Maybe Tom was right not to say anything to the cops.

"Tom, is that why Tippett wanted to go with you and Grainger into the woods? To find the Jersey Devil?" Noah asked slowly.

"That's how he laid it out to me," Tom answered directly.

"You spoke to him then?"

"No, he left the campus immediately after class, before I could see him."

"And Grainger accepted Tippett's hypothesis?"

Tom sighed. "I think so. But Grainger had his own agenda."

"So why don't you just tell the police where you were Saturday night and be done with it?"

Tom drained his coffee and set the cup down.

"I can't."

"Why not?"

"Because I tracked him. I followed Grainger into the woods."

"You were with him?"

"No. I saw him, but he didn't see me."

"He was still alive when you saw him?"

"Sure, but he wasn't alone. The Forbes kid was with him. I didn't stick around."

***

Redmond Franks stopped to check his kill. He knew the difference between hunting out of season to put meat on the table for his family and killing for a living. As a professional poacher he chose the latter. He had an ongoing business arrangement with a greasy spoon in Toms River that liked to supplement their meatloaf special with a dash of fresh venison. No questions asked. It stretched the expensive beef and most people couldn't tell the difference.

But Franks had to be careful. Game wardens in the Pines were not on the take. They didn't have to be. The Pineys monitored it themselves and their justice was far harsher than any fine the game keepers could levy.

That's why he couldn't afford any slip-ups. His reputation and his meal ticket were both on the line. The boy saw him shoot a deer out of season. That was one thing. That he saw him shoot a doe was something else entirely. The boy could identify him. Franks could not let that happen.

Franks bent over the deer. It was dead. He couldn't just leave it there while he chased after the boy. It would spoil and all his efforts would be in vain.

The boy had dived into the flooded bog and emerged several yards away, pulling himself out and scampering into the safety of the woods. But time was on Franks's side. The sun was going down quickly in the west. Soon it would be twilight, then dark. The boy wouldn't be foolish enough to stay in the Pines at night. He would double back when he felt the coast was clear and Franks would be waiting when he came out.

Redmond Franks removed his hunting knife from a sheath looped through his belt and slit open the doe's belly. Blood and guts poured out in a steaming froth. He had never gotten used to the smell and he turned his face away quickly.

Next he dragged the carcass back to his maroon cargo van. He strung the deer on a line attached to a scaffold in the back of the van. He covered the carcass with a canvas drop cloth then drove his van around to the back of the old iron works, out of sight of the road. He picked up the kid's bicycle and submerged it in the bog.

Franks went back to the kill site. He scooped up the entrails and dumped them into the water. He had just finished washing off his hands when he heard a car coming up the Speedwell Road. Change in plans. With gun in hand, he scurried into the forest in the same direction the boy had gone, just as the Mini Cooper pulled up and stopped in front of the furnace ruins.

***

Although Danny hadn't spoken to either Kelly or Geoffrey since the blowout at the jamboree last Friday night, he was so charged up by the provocative theories Professor Tippett had expounded about the identity of the Jersey Devil that he simply had to share his enthusiasm for the deepening mystery with them. If anyone could appreciate it, they would, and it would give him a chance to make amends with Kelly and show her how seriously he was taking his studies.

Arriving at Crab Cove with Kim in tow, Danny was disappointed to learn from Sarah Parsons that neither Kelly nor Geoffrey were home. Sarah surprised Danny by confiding in him that she was a little concerned. Margaret Colson had called her from Chatsworth to say that Geoffrey had not yet returned from a field trip and now Kelly and her friend Curtis had gone to look for him. Maggie was not worried, she said, she just thought Sarah should know.

Sarah, however, was more than a little worried. First, she was annoyed because Geoffrey skipped work at the Seaport that day and she had to learn about it from a note he wrote her before leaving the house at dawn. Her annoyance was compounded by the fact that, according to the note, Noah had approved Geoffrey's plan and she'd been unable to reach Noah all day. According to Libby Ashcroft, he, too, had somewhere he had to dash off to. When Sarah learned it was to spring Tom Banks from jail she felt totally out of the loop, and embarrassed that none of the people she cared about most in the world had bothered to let her in on their plans.

She was also concerned that Kelly was truant at work today, although in Kelly's case Moss Greenberg had apparently excused her and Curtis Wick so they could attend Cletus Grainger's funeral in Tabernacle. And that brought her to what bothered her most about Kelly's day: the company she was keeping. While she was not enamored with Danny Windsor, as her niece and nephew obviously were—or even as Noah was, for that matter—Sarah was even less thrilled with the idea of a boy like Curtis Wick hanging around her niece. To her credit, Sarah had held her tongue around Kelly, making her thoughts on the subject known only to Noah.

Still, it was disturbing, no matter how pleasant Miss Maggie could be on the phone, not to have her sister's kids back at home at the end of such a long day. And Miss Maggie could not completely allay Sarah's fear, despite her charming manner, that something was amiss in Chatsworth.

When the dinner hour came and went and she still hadn't heard from the children, Sarah made a desperate call to Noah. Reaching him on his cell phone at the Dynasty Diner, where he was having coffee with Tom Banks, she made her concerns very clear. Noah said the situation struck him as odd, too, and he assured her that he and Tom would go to Colson's right away to find out exactly what was going on.

All of this came out of Sarah in a rush of words at Danny when he and Kim arrived at Crab Cove, and she told the story with more than enough conviction to worry him, too, especially with Curtis Wick involved. By the time Danny and Kim pulled away from the gift shop, his excitement over the whole Jersey Devil thing was completely forgotten.

***

Payton Tippett wondered whether he had said too much to the two young students who had come to visit him at his office earlier. It was true they had solved the riddle he posed in class. That was commendable. But did they believe in it as he did? Probably not.

They were young, impressionable, gullible kids. Too bad. He could use a couple of sharp assistants right now to do some grunt work. His very short list of prospective candidates was decidedly shorter now that Cletus Grainger was gone and Tom Banks was taking the rap for his death. That was a foolish thing Banks did trying to avoid arrest on the college campus, but there was no time to think about that. Now was the time to capitalize on Grainger's unfortunate death.

Tippett had not revealed all the pieces of the puzzle he was working on to anyone yet. He still held a few cards up his sleeve; aces he thought, like Ong's Hat. What he needed were people he could trust. He needed people who would do as he directed without any fuss. Cletus Grainger had been one such person until Tippett could no longer stomach the man's clandestine behavior. So when the opportunity arose, Grainger was dealt with, and the good old Jersey Devil was taking part of the blame as expected.

For her part, Audra Grainger had come through and now the spotlight had shifted unexpectedly on Banks. *Mr. Banks will regret not buying into my idea,* Tippett thought.

"You seem distracted tonight, Payton," said the nubile Mary Ellen Cassini. She was dressed in a sleeveless white cotton blouse and a tight blue denim skirt.

She and Professor Tippett were seated at a romantic candlelit table at Tucker's in Beach Haven, overlooking the bay.

Tippett had almost forgotten where he was and whom he was with. But now, looking across the table, he recalled he had agreed to have drinks and dinner with this vivacious, recently divorced brunette who just also happened to be the interim semester linguistics professor at Richard Stockton State College.

The thought had not escaped him that Ms. Cassini would make an enjoyable conquest this evening. His attention, however, was drawn away, focused on a greater quest, one he had pursued most of his adult life. And he felt now more than ever that the treasure was within his reach.

"I'm sorry, my dear," he said apologetically. "Care for another drink?"

Tippett downed his scotch and waved the waiter over to their table.

"Two more of the same," he said holding up two fingers.

"Would this distraction have anything to do with the students I saw leaving your office earlier?" asked Mary Ellen, trying desperately to open up a conversation.

"Students?" replied Tippett amused, obviously still lost in his own thoughts.

"That's what I thought," sighed Mary Ellen. "I didn't recognize the boy, but I've had Miss Li-Lung in class before. She's very bright. Did you know that she can speak several different languages fluently, including Mandarin Chinese?"

Mary Ellen pressed on. "Her family owns the Golden Palace restaurant on Route 72 in Stafford."

"Can she be trusted?" asked Tippett, seemingly from a foggy distance.

"If you mean for grading student papers, I think so. She's pretty much a loner. That's the first time I ever saw her with another student."

Tippett's cell phone rang just as the waiter arrived with their second round of drinks. He recognized the number and hesitated. It belonged to Audra Grainger and that could only mean trouble.

Several of their fellow diners stared at the couple as Tippett continued to let the phone ring.

"Aren't you going to answer it?" asked Mary Ellen, glancing around uncomfortably.

He switched off the phone without answering it.

"I'm sorry, Mary Ellen, but I have to leave," he said, rising. "May I drop you off somewhere?"

She threw her napkin on the table in dismay.

"No, I have my own car, remember? You were going to follow me back to my place after …" her voice trailed off when she saw Tippett wasn't really listening.

"Oh, yes, quite right," he said, flustered. He tossed a fifty-dollar bill on the table.

"Stay. Order anything you like. I'll call you tomorrow."

Mary Ellen Cassini folded her arms and fell back in her seat. Before she could respond to his offer, her date left the dining room.

11
The Game's Afoot

The faster Geoffrey ran the farther he went, deeper and deeper into the dark, impenetrable Wharton State Forest. He was wet, soaked to the skin from his impromptu swim across the old cranberry bog. And he was cold and scared, but at least he was alive.

Somewhere behind him was a man with a gun. He saw the man shoot the deer. Then he saw the man point the gun at him and fire. That was all he could remember. The images were running through his mind pushing his legs forward, carrying him farther into the dreaded New Jersey Pines as night was closing in around him.

How much farther could he run? Where was he exactly? Was he still being chased? All questions Geoffrey could not answer.

He stopped to catch his breath and listen. The sounds of the night woods were all around him. He was tired and hungry but in the back of his mind he knew he could not stay still for long.

As he ran, his mind raced. *What was I thinking? This was supposed to be a 'walk in the park.' Go to Chatsworth, grab a few books, scope out the local tree frog population, and be back home in time for dinner. I shouldn't have gone into the woods on my own. I should have waited for Mr. Parsons.* His father would be so disappointed in him. But, it was too late for regrets. He just had to stay alive.

Who knew where Geoffrey was? Maggie Colson knew and by now maybe others. Perhaps they'll send out a search party ... Yes, at some point Maggie will call the police and they'll come looking for him. But then again maybe they'll wait until morning. *That means I'll have to spend the night alone in the Pines.* He shivered with fear and kept running, swatting at the mosquitoes that were attacking his tender flesh, as images of the Jersey Devil danced in his head.

Stumbling now in the darkness, he could not see his own feet in front of him. He fished into his backpack for the flashlight, then wondered if he should risk turning it on. Would it give his position away? Maybe the poacher had stopped chasing him. *Maybe he was smart enough not to go into the woods at night ... or maybe he didn't care because he had a gun ...* More questions that he had no way of answering.

Geoffrey tripped and fell. The flashlight flew from his hand and was lost in the dark woods. He lay on the damp ground, too tired, too scared to move. He buried his face in his hands and cried.

And in the silence his cries were answered. For in the distance he heard the lone quonking of a tree frog soloing, soon followed by another, then another until a chorus filled the night woods and brought it back to life, with a nearly deafening but welcome noise. Noah had compared it to the sound of the Garden State Parkway at rush hour, and now Geoffrey knew what he meant.

He got to his feet slowly, made a vain attempt to look for the flashlight, then followed the quonking sound. It was guiding him like a beacon to *somewhere*. He didn't care to where. He followed it gratefully.

The tree frog symphony led him to the edge of another small pond. He put a foot into the water before he realized it was there. Then he saw the moon illuminated on the surface of the water, and, in the dark, he gave thanks for that rippling little light.

Geoffrey bent down and scooped some water into his cupped hands. In spite of a faint metallic taste, like iron, he drank until his belly was full.

In the pale moonlight his eyes spied a fallen tree with a space beneath it large enough for him to crawl under. He took off his backpack and fluffed it like a pillow for his head. He lay down completely covered by the broken pine and rested. Soon the frog serenade died away and he fell into a deep, soothing sleep.

***

Kelly and Curtis parked the car in front of the ruins and walked down the path to the flooded cranberry bog. They called out Geoffrey's name repeatedly but there was no response.

They split up. Each began walking around the pond in opposite directions.

Curtis spotted a bicycle pedal sticking up out of the bog. He sloshed into the water and pulled the bike out. He called out to Kelly.

Kelly came running over. The bike was covered with weeds and mud. Curtis rinsed the mud off and she recognized it as Geoffrey's. A look of anxiety betrayed her otherwise determined appearance.

The two walked the rest of the way around the flooded bog together. What they saw next made their hearts sink. Dark red stains splattered on the ground. Blood.

Kelly grew faint at the sight. Curtis caught her as she staggered backward. He sat her down gently on the grass. She put her head between her legs and closed her eyes, fighting back the tears.

"It doesn't prove anything," he said sitting down beside her.

"We've got to call the police," she said through her hands.

"You ain't callin' no one," said a gruff voice from behind them.

When they turned around, Redmond Franks had his rifle trained on them.

***

"You must remain calm, Audra," said Professor Tippett patting her hand. They were in Tippett's Audi driving on Route 72 West heading for Ong's Hat.

"But Tom Banks is free. He made bail," Audra Grainger replied. "And he called twice."

"What did you tell him?" asked Tippett sharply.

"Nothing. He wanted to know if anyone went with my husband on Saturday. I told him what I told the police, that I thought *he* went with Cletus."

"And?" pushed Tippett.

"Of course he denies going with Cletus."

"Does he know about Forbes?" asked Tippett nervously.

"I don't know. But I saw Forbes at the service talking to another young man. We better give him the rest of his money, before he blabbers about it to somebody else."

"We must remain discreet, Audra. He'll get the rest of it when we get the Devil."

"Devil, devil, devil, that's all you talk about, Payton. You're obsessed."

"No, my dear, we're close."

"Is that why we're going to Ong's Hat?"

Tippett took his eyes off the road for a moment and studied the widow Grainger closely. Lust had its moments, but this wasn't one of them.

"Yes, I've got a new lead on his possible whereabouts. This could mean pay dirt."

"But why Ong's Hat?" asked Audra Grainger with surprise and mild interest. "It's such a strange name … even for a hick town."

"That's because it's a derivative of an old Indian name: *Ongath.* It means 'place where he sleeps.' The *he* in this case is none other than the Jersey Devil. The early Swedish settlers misinterpreted the Indian meaning. They took it to mean, 'Place where he hangs his hat,' and bastardized the name to fit the expression. Thus we get Ong's Hat."

***

"Tell me honestly, Tom," said Noah Parsons. They were in Noah's Dodge pickup heading north on Route 9, just outside Eagleswood. "Do you believe this Jersey Devil theory of Tippett's?"

Tom was thoughtful. He looked over at Noah then returned his gaze out the window to the rows of passing pines, cedars, and white oaks—sacred trees he'd spent his entire life since the age of twelve trying to learn secrets and stories from.

"Yes … and no," came his measured reply.

He took a breath and continued. "Tippett believes the Jersey Devil is an actual living, breathing dragon like those written about in fables and ancient legends."

"And you?" asked Noah. "It almost sounds like you do, too."

"I know what this is going to sound like, Noah, but I trust you and I'm going tell you something I've never told anyone before."

Noah was listening intently.

"When I was twelve I had an experience with my dad not far from here. Our car broke down one night in the middle of nowhere. We eventually got help from an old black woodsman whom I have since come to know very well. He's someone you and I both admire."

Noah nodded in agreement. The image fit what little he knew of the enigmatic "Doctor" Freeman Morris.

"The experience marked me for life. I believe it helped me to find my true calling, even if to some it seems a bit unconventional. It is from that experience and the many happy, meditative hours I've spent alone in these woods since that I have come to a conclusion."

Noah had known Tom Banks most of his adult life. The two had gone fishing together and had many a good conversation in between the music at Albert Hall. In all of their time together Noah could not recall a single incident where Tom had been anything less than genuine or sincere. The man's integrity was what Noah respected most about him. Like it or not, he always shot straight. Noah was a good man in his own right, and at this moment he felt honored to share something held in such secret, profound regard by a man like Tom.

When Tom continued he didn't look at Noah; he didn't have to. He knew that Noah had an open mind and a heart willing to take a leap of faith.

"The Jersey Devil is more a creature of the mind ... a spirit, summoned when needed, or, as sometimes occurs, when expected to be seen."

Noah's heart skipped a beat.

"People of ancient times, like the Celts, followed what we call pagan religions today, but these were religions of the earth, not of idols. They understood the concepts of earthly and heavenly spirits and embraced them without reservation. So did the Native Americans. In fact, many Native Americans still believe in them today, although they are in a minority, vastly outnumbered by so-called educated, God-fearing people."

Noah remained speechless, numbed by the simplicity with which Tom spoke about such an incredible topic.

"This is what I have come to know and accept as the Jersey Devil, and I suppose that to a certain extent, the Leeds Curse is a fabrication, a myth created to conceal the truth. A truth that an ever-expanding Puritanical America would never be willing to accept."

Tom continued, "You see, Noah, the Lenape held onto their truth and, to their credit, realized the importance of the Pine Barrens and its precious water supply long ago. They were more than willing to let the plundering white men have their superstitions, even feeding into them at times in order to keep the intruders from destroying this great and beautiful ecological wonder. The Indians contributed to the vernacular of the white man's fears in the hope of keeping him out of the Pinelands forever. Did you know, for example, that one suggested Indian translation of the name Manasquan means 'place of the evil god'?"

"No, Tom, I didn't know that," offered Noah, engrossed in the revelations.

"Unfortunately for us, Noah, their efforts were only successful so long as man was stuck in an eighteenth century mindset, believing the Pines to be an inhospitable wasteland. It defies logic how the Pines Barrens have survived this far into the 21st century relatively unscathed. But it seems time and technology is finally catching up. The population is exploding and every square inch of land is in danger of being overrun. So, I wouldn't be surprised if the Jersey Devil were to make another appearance very soon."

Noah shook his head. "I'm afraid you lost me, Tom. You talk as though a sighting of the Jersey Devil is a good omen, a necessary thing. Is that what you mean?"

A faint trace of a smile formed on Tom's face for the first time since the whole Grainger affair started.

"It's all about our primal fears, Noah. I think Peter Benchley said it best: 'We love our monsters. They help us to survive as a species.'"

"How so, Tom?"

"Are you familiar with the trickster archetype?"

Noah thought for a long moment. "That's a psychological reference … Carl Jung, I believe. And if I'm not mistaken it has its roots in Greek mythology. From the antics of Hermes, the messenger of the gods."

"Right. And there are any number of parallels in tribal African traditions and in Native American lore—the coyote, for example."

"Why is that important?"

"Well, as you know from these accounts, in mythological terms the trickster is an abstract constellation of characteristics that is usually identified with a person or an animal. One that is clever, informative, and deceptive. The trickster flourishes in chaos and during times of societal change; dwelling in those liminal places, those in-between states where boundaries are blurred."

"Go on."

"But the concept," Tom continued, barely able to conceal his excitement, "is gaining acceptability among the mainstream scientific community thanks in large part to the notion of Quantum Mechanics and the Uncertainty Principle—the idea that matter as a form is always changing; defying, eluding, and confounding empirical measurement."

"What are you getting at, Tom?"

"Don't you see? The Virgin Mary sightings, angels, demons, UFOs … everything that is unexplained … it all ties in. The Jersey Devil is a manifestation of this trickster consciousness. The phenomenon is real—the creature isn't. And that's what Tippett doesn't get."

***

"There's just one thing I have to ask you," said Danny as he and Kim headed over the causeway in his jeep.

"What's that?" asked Kim.

"With your family ancestry, how could you not know instantly that the Jersey Devil was the dragon of Tippett's dreams?"

"Do you want the truth, Danny?" she asked, finally lowering her steadfast coy veneer.

"That would be why I asked."

"Not just *any* dragon, Danny. According to Professor Tippett, the Jersey Devil may be the *last* dragon of its kind. That's why the professor believes there is a secret sect of people living in the Pines pledged to look after him. They hide him and feed him. Things like that. But every now and then, he gets loose from their care and scares the living daylights out of someone."

"You mean all the shit your grandfather laid on him and me was *not* a lot of bull?"

"Oh it was, Danny," said Kim stifling a laugh. "My grandfather pretty much told Professor Tippett what he wanted to hear. Professor Tippett put it all together and pointed it out to me after meeting my grandfather. The professor had a hunch that the dragon has been around here a long time. Certainly the Indians knew about him. According to Indian legend, Ong's Hat in Burlington County is where he dwells."

She giggled.

"What's so funny?"

"I found that little gem for Tippett nosing around the library and fed it to him."

"Was that crap, too?" Danny asked.

"Yep. That's when I realized how obsessed he was with the whole thing. And so now I'm starting to get scared."

"Scared? You helped him. You fed his ego."

"Yeah, I know. But now I think he has to prove his theory or be made a complete fool, and I'm afraid he'll stop at nothing to get what he wants."

"Even if it doesn't exist?"

"That's my point, Danny. It *doesn't* exist. But he's so blinded by the desire to make a name for himself that I don't think he knows the difference between reality and fantasy anymore."

"But Kim, you gave him his fantasy. And now he's going to be the laughing stock of Stockton State College."

"I know, I know. It's gotten out of hand. That's why I decided to enlist your help."

"You dragged me into this by design?"

"I'm sorry. But you seemed pretty willing."

"So why tell me all this now?" he asked.

"Because, Danny, it's happening all over again. People want to believe so badly that the Jersey Devil is real, they'll believe just about anything."

"People? You mean like me?"

"Like you, Danny. I don't want to see you get hurt. And now I can't help thinking that this girl, your friend Kelly Martin, is somehow involved."

"What?"

"I don't know, call it intuition; call it psychic or whatever, but I can feel it."

"It's called psychotic. You're delusional, Kim. You need help."

"That may be, Danny, but right now I think it's Kelly who needs your help, so why don't you just drop me off at the restaurant."

12
Fire in the Pines

Redmond Franks marched Kelly Martin and Curtis Wick at gunpoint back to his parked van, being certain to keep to the woods and not be seen. One kid who could identify his illegal poaching was bad enough, but three? This was an unacceptable risk.

Initially, he intended to leave these two alone or maybe just scare them. But when they found the other boy's bicycle and the blood from the carcass he knew they would be back with the authorities. He had to act quickly.

Franks left the Mini Cooper parked where it was. It would be some time before anyone discovered it, and by then he would be long gone.

Kelly and Curtis were appalled when Franks opened the door to his van. The sight and stench of the hanging dead deer nearly made them vomit. When Franks leered at Kelly, Curtis turned and lunged at him, but the poacher was expecting it and whacked the lifeguard hard on the side of the head with the butt of his gun.

"Where are you taking us and what have you done with my brother?" demanded Kelly.

"I can see the resemblance now," Franks said. "You and your brother have seen too much for your own good. He ran off into the woods, but he won't get far. As for you two … well, let's just say we're going for a little ride." A devilish grin revealed a mouthful of rotten and missing teeth.

Franks hog-tied and gagged Curtis and Kelly then secured them below the hanging deer carcass. Kelly was terrified, but the gag prevented her from screaming.

Franks closed the panel door, leaving the teens awash in total darkness, scared out of their wits and fearing for their lives.

Their abductor grabbed a spare can of gasoline from the cab. With two hostages he could no longer wait for the kid to come out of the woods. He could survive a night in the Pines alone, but not if there was no place for him to hide, Franks decided.

He poured the gasoline along the tree line leading into the Wharton Forest. He regretted that the fire would damage some of his prime hunting area before it burned out, but the woods would come back in a few years. It always did. In the meantime he would hunt elsewhere for his game and the authorities would blame the kids for starting the fire. Firefighters would find the Mini Cooper but no sign of the young couple, and it would appear they'd perished in the flames.

Night had fallen, and Franks knew that in the darkness it wouldn't take long for the fire to be noticed. With flames licking up along the dry, brittle timber, he made a hasty departure sticking to the back roads, satisfied that he had removed all evidence of his presence.

As he drove south along a deserted stretch of Route 563, something suddenly flew in front of the van, startling Franks and momentarily blinding him. A dark, hulking mass with glowing red eyes covered the entire front windshield, obscuring his view. Franks's last terrifying percept before his van swerved off the road and plowed into a big white oak was of a loud screech and a tangle of claws, fangs, and wings.

***

Geoffrey Martin awoke in a sweat amidst a growing clamor. Although it was still night, the sky to the southeast was aglow so brightly it looked like morning. And the heat from the glow was intensifying. *Fire!* His mind screamed as he realized it was headed his way.

The clamor was the otherworldly shrieking of hundreds if not thousands of frightened tree frogs filling their voice sacs with air as they leaped about in panic. Most appeared to be heading for the water. Many were climbing over Geoffrey as they sought a haven from the approaching fire.

Observing the frogs, Geoffrey had an *aha* moment. He opened his backpack and carefully guided a few frogs inside. A parade of frogs soon followed, leaping and hopping frantically into the bag. Dozens of them clung to his shirt and pants.

Geoffrey put the backpack over his shoulders and went down to the water's edge, intending to swim to the other side. Brushing aside some tall reeds, he saw a small rotting, wooden boat in the bright light cast by the fire. Would it float? He wondered.

There was little time to debate. The fire was raging closer and closer and Geoffrey gauged his choices as float or swim. He knew he couldn't outrun the fire on foot and he couldn't even be sure the fire would stop at the water.

As Geoffrey reached the boat, he was surprised to find a host of tiny amphibians jumping aboard as if it was Noah's ark. He pushed the battered craft out into the flooded bog and stepped in. There was an inch or more of water in the bottom but she floated low. Geoffrey grabbed the one good oar and paddled for the far bank.

***

Redmond Franks lay unconscious against the wheel of his van. In the back, Kelly and Curtis were bumped, bruised, and shaken up but otherwise unhurt.

Noah Parsons peered in with a flashlight then quickly moved in to remove their gags and binds.

Kelly threw her arms around Noah and hugged him for all she was worth. "How did you find us?" she asked, tears running down her cheeks.

"I didn't. Your aunt sent us to Colson's to find out what mischief you and Geoffrey had gotten yourselves into. We were on the road from Tuckerton heading towards Chatsworth when we saw the van. Where's Geoffrey?"

"Oh, my God, you haven't found him?" Kelly said frantically. She nodded toward the front of the van. "All I know is what he told us—that Geoffrey ran into the woods."

"Noah, you'd better come take a look at this," said Tom Banks walking up behind him.

Noah stepped back out of the van. Kelly and a dazed Curtis Wick followed slowly.

"There's a big blaze a mile north of here and it's sweeping fast over the Wharton Tract," Tom said pointing to the sky in the northwest. "I called it in. But it'll take the Rangers a good twenty minutes to get to it."

"Geoffrey!" screamed Kelly, putting her hands up to her face. She turned to the older men. "He could still be in there!"

"I can reach the perimeter in less than five minutes," Tom said to Noah. "Starting another fire will cut off the oxygen feeding the big blaze. I think I can keep it from reaching this area while you search for Geoffrey. But we'd better hurry."

"What about this guy?" Noah asked, looking toward the unconscious driver.

"I don't think it's wise for us to move him. His leg is broken and there may be some internal bleeding. The rescue squad and police are on their way—let them take care of him."

"You can't leave him with us!" cried Kelly. "He was going to kill us!"

"He's in no position to hurt anyone now," said Tom. "You have nothing to worry about."

Noah tossed Tom his truck keys. "I'll look for the boy."

Tom gave Noah a determined grin, and was off.

***

Geoffrey was exhausted by the time he reached the far side of the pond. He checked on his small green charges and they looked fine. *What do I do now?* he wondered. *I don't know where I am or which way to go other than away from the fire.* Unfortunately, that meant deeper into the woods.

He thought back to Maggie Colson's words just before he left on his mission, a mission that had gone woefully astray. "If you get lost, make for the fire tower at Apple Pie Hill," she had said.

But at night, from deep in the Pines, Geoffrey couldn't see the fire tower. All he could do was hope he was walking in the right direction. In the thick of the woods he was reminded of his earlier vision of the great New Jersey Pine Barrens the day he and Kelly drove to Colson's for the first time. Passing by the rows and rows of thick but orderly trees brought back that image of the bristles of a hairbrush. Only now he felt like a tiny flea caught in the thick of those bristles.

Fatigue was beginning to get the best of him, but he trudged onward. The fire was well behind him now, but that only meant the woods were darker than ever, and he was bone tired. Without being able to see clearly, he found himself repeatedly tripping, stumbling, and falling. As he lost his footing again for what seemed the 100th time, he tumbled to the ground, this time stepping on his glasses as they fell from his face. Adding blindness to the darkness, he remained on the ground as he tried to put the cracked lenses back into the frames.

Through the haze of thick smoke, blurred further by his acute nearsightedness, Geoffrey saw a dark hulking figure rushing toward him. He blacked out as Freeman Morris bent down, pulled him to a standing position, and hoisted him over his shoulder.

***

Tom Banks took a little-known fire access road into the heart of the Wharton State Forest. There wasn't a moment to spare. The fire was raging toward the center of the reserve with nothing to stand in its way unless he could reach it in time.

He parked Noah's pickup and ran around the fire's left flank toward the old flooded bog that he knew so well. When he got there he found the fire roaring straight for him. He removed his shirt and ignited it. Using it as a torch he lit a stretch of underbrush well ahead of the oncoming flames, hoping to steal the bigger fire's oxygen and kindling and thus stop it at the water line. He was fully aware that if it didn't work, and the fire vaulted over the bog, he would fail and likely die.

The backdraft roared to life and burned straight up. There was no breeze pushing the bigger fire so when the two met they were like a couple of wrestlers locked in a death grip. It was working! The bigger fire had nothing to burn as it reached the area scorched by the one Tom had started.

Tom couldn't afford to stay and admire his handiwork. The left flank he had driven past to reach this spot was closing fast. He'd have to hurry to get around the fire line in order to go out the same way he came in.

Despite all his training, Tom felt himself becoming increasingly disoriented as dust and ash filled his eyes and lungs. Thick smoke obscured his view of the trees, the wind, and the night sky, and challenged his sense of direction.

Which way? his mind screamed. *Which way out?*

At that moment, Tom felt an eerie presence, as though he was being watched. Looking over his shoulder he couldn't see a thing through the smoke and haze, but he felt it strongly. It was the same feeling he'd had forty years ago, as a twelve-year-old in his dad's Ford station wagon—on the night Freeman Morris had fixed their car on the road somewhere near Chatsworth.

Just then, behind a row of trees he caught a glimpse of sudden movement. Fluttering. Something darting through the woods. A shadow cast pale gray against the deep forest. Then, in the moonlight filtered through the smoking pines, he saw the glowing red eyes that had filled his dreams for so many years. No longer fraught with fear, he sensed an urgent warning by its presence.

Tom stood motionless, transfixed, gazing toward the wavering apparition. *So we meet again at last, old friend,* Tom silently affirmed. And then it was gone.

Ashes rained down on Tom like glowing gemstones. Flames closed in around him seemingly from all sides. He covered his mouth with a wet handkerchief and fell to his knees coughing, then began to crawl in the direction in which the phantom spirit had fled.

13

The Devil Gets His Due

Maggie Colson hung up the phone.

"That was Freeman Morris," she announced to the crowd standing around in her corner store. It was 2:00 AM Wednesday morning, but with all the lights on and the curious crowd huddled around having coffee and sandwiches, buzzing over the events of the evening, it seemed more like midday.

"He's at Apple Pie Hill. The fire's been stopped, it's under control," she shared happily.

Maggie turned and put her arms around Kelly and Curtis but directed her words to Sarah Bishop, who had driven up from LBI to see for herself what was going on.

"Freeman tells me he has a hungry young adventurer named Geoffrey Martin with him. Lucky for us that Freeman was on watch tonight."

There was a boisterous round of applause.

Sarah was so happy she cried. She hugged Kelly for a long time before falling into Noah's arms.

Miss Maggie looked at Noah. "I'm sorry, Noah, there's no word yet on Tom Banks. The Rangers found what's left of your pickup truck, but Tom wasn't in it.

"But wait! There's more," she added excitedly. "It seems our young adventurer may have singlehandedly saved what remains of our very own *Hyla andersonii* from perishing in that fire. Freeman tells me the fire tower is being overrun by Pine Barrens tree frogs!"

Another loud cheer and more applause went up from the assorted firemen, police, forest rangers, and townsfolk packed inside Colson's General Store.

"I'm sorry if I was a little hard on you, Master Wick," admitted Miss Maggie, "but now we know you have the courage to help others in need."

She smiled her whimsical smile as Bulldog Wick blushed. Kelly gave Curtis a big hug and his face reddened even more.

"The poacher's name is Redmond Franks," the federal game warden said, addressing Noah and Sarah. "He's over at Southern Ocean County Hospital with a busted leg. That's the least of his worries. He's going to be behind bars for a long time. We've got him on four Federal counts: Trespassing, illegal hunting, discharging a firearm near a federal reserve, and starting a forest fire."

"You'll have to fight us for him," replied one of Chatsworth's finest. "I think with kidnapping and assault we can double his time to life behind bars."

"Boys, boys—let's not fight over Redmond Franks," Miss Maggie lightly chastised. "We still have one mystery remaining … the death of Cletus Grainger."

"Miss Maggie's right," Lieutenant Shipley agreed. "With Tom Banks missing and presumed dead in the fire we've lost our prime suspect."

"Why, Lieutenant," said Miss Maggie slyly, "does that mean you're letting Sir Cedric off the hook?"

The cop scratched his head, confused. *"Who?"* he inquired.

"The Jersey Devil," replied Kelly, pointing to the poster Miss Maggie had described as a true likeness of the famed creature.

"Hogwash!" Officer Bowman spit out. "The press printed that on their own. We had nothing to do with that angle of the story."

"I think perhaps we can blame that one on the imagination of the fishermen who found him," Noah threw into the conversation.

"I know who killed Mr. Grainger," mumbled Curtis, looking at the floor.

The room fell silent.

"What did you say?" asked Lieutenant Shipley.

Curtis looked first at Miss Maggie then at Kelly.

"Curtis, what are you saying?" Kelly said coming to his side.

He looked Kelly in the eyes and held her by the arms. "I learned something very important today, Kelly. Some people *really* do care about people. I think it's time I started being honest with myself ... and with others."

He let go of Kelly's arms and faced Lieutenant Shipley. "Chris Forbes told me at the funeral," Curtis said dryly. "We all knew Grainger had abused him years ago, but none of us knew what to do about it, so we pretended it never happened. Eventually we just stopped believing it had happened at all."

"Now you hold on just one cockamamie moment, young fellow," the lieutenant said sharply. "Cletus Grainger was a pillar of society."

"He was a lecherous old man," interjected Miss Maggie. "If you had opened your eyes you would have seen it a long time ago. It was just that kind of attitude that protected him all these years." She smiled sadly at Curtis.

"But he was mauled. He had claw marks all over his body," Officer Bowman said.

"His neck was broken," said Noah. "It's in the coroner's report."

"From the struggle he put up with the Devil," Bowman added.

"Shut up, Lance," Shipley said.

"The claw marks were made by a gardening tool—a hand rake," Curtis explained. "That was the idea of a man named Tippett."

"Professor Payton J. Tippett, III?" exclaimed Miss Maggie in disbelief. "Why, I've got some of his books on my shelf."

"Yeah, that's him," answered Curtis.

Kelly looked at Noah and Aunt Sarah. "That's the name of Danny's folklore professor."

"Who's Danny and where can we find this Professor Tippett?" asked Lieutenant Shipley.

Just then Danny Windsor burst through the door of the store.

"If I heard your question correctly, I believe you'll find Professor Tippett at a place called Ong's Hat," he blurted.

"Danny!" Kelly ran over and wrapped her arms around him.

"Are you all right?" Danny asked stroking her hair.

"I'm fine, now," Kelly said and meant it.

Danny patted Curtis on the shoulder and nodded. Curtis smiled back.

"By the way," added Danny, "I found that guy you know named Banks hitchhiking up the road."

"Tom!" exclaimed Noah.

"Careful. He's quite a sight. It looks like someone tried to make toast out of him. Smells like it, too. I wanted to take him to the hospital but he insisted on coming here. He's in my Jeep, coughing and hacking up a storm."

Noah headed for the door.

"Noah, stay. Finish up here. I'll bring him some water and a blanket," offered Sarah. "You two follow me," she said calling to two paramedics before rushing out of the store.

Officer Bowman stopped scribbling in his notepad. "Payton Tippett murdered Cletus Grainger? Preposterous!" he said. He pointed to Curtis. "I don't think this young man knows what he's talking about."

"How can you take anyone seriously who teaches impressionable students that the Jersey Devil is real?" Noah added to the discussion.

Maggie Colson gave Kelly a sly smile then covered her mouth.

"Tippett didn't do it himself," Curtis continued. "He just put up the money—well, half of it according to Forbes, and that pissed him off. Tippett's partner was stalling on the other half."

"His partner?" asked Lieutenant Shipley.

"Grainger's wife," responded Curtis coldly.

"But where does Tippett fit in?" inquired Officer Bowman.

"Forbes thinks he was having an affair with Mrs. Grainger."

"So the two of them were in on it? Why did Forbes tell you all this?"

"Because he never stopped believing what had happened. Remember, it had *happened* to him. He couldn't wait to tell us he had finally gotten back at that monster."

"There you have it, gentlemen," Noah said as Kelly moved to console Curtis. "The Jersey Devil was none other than Cletus Grainger." Tears welled up in Wick's eyes.

"We can all rest easy now," added Maggie Colson with a slight twinkle in her eye. "Looks like the devil finally got his due."

හඬ

Secret of the Painted Rock

1

Graduation Night
(1965)

Peter Miller sat behind the wheel of a brand new 1965 Ford Mustang convertible and smiled. The car was a graduation present from his grandparents, with whom he had lived his entire eighteen years following the untimely death of his parents in an electrical house fire when he was just an infant. The money used to buy the candy apple red roadster came from an annuity that his father, the former proprietor of Clark's General Store in West Creek, had had the foresight to purchase when Peter was born. Although originally intended to fund his college education, it was no longer needed for that purpose. How proud Abraham and Emily Miller would have been to learn that their only son had won a full scholarship to attend the world-renowned *Academie des Beaux Arts de Paris* in France.

Their job finished, now that he had reached the age of maturity, Peter's maternal grandparents had put their little bungalow in Leeds Point up for sale and, with his imminent departure for art school overseas, decided to move back to their native Albuquerque, New Mexico. While art school would be a new beginning for Peter, the timeless desert figured prominently in the sunset years of his aging grandparents.

Peter was figuratively and literally moving down a different road tonight and much to the delight of his two traveling companions, he clowned around, leaning out over the driver's side door of his fast moving vehicle and yelling his fool head off at every passing car that happened to breeze by. They were in a celebratory mood, having just left their graduation ceremony at Pineland High School.

Struggling to keep her hair from flailing in the wind, Sally Parker snuggled up closer to Peter in the front seat of his car. Sitting atop the open back seat, her sandy-haired twin brother, Andy, was singing the "Star-Spangled Banner," hopelessly off key and at the top of his lungs.

"Enjoy your last night of freedom, Andy," Peter shouted over his shoulder. "Tomorrow your butt belongs to Uncle Sam."

"O'er the Land of the Free … and the Home of the Brave," Andy sang, ignoring the comment and saluting the stars that twinkled in the night sky. He let out a series of wild whoops and hollers, cheering his own performance.

"I wish he weren't going," sighed Sally softly. "Vietnam sounds so far away. I hope he'll be all right."

"He'll be fine," replied Peter. "The Army will be good for him. It'll make a man out of him," he offered with mock maturity.

"That's what our dad keeps telling him," said Sally, the doubt evident in her voice. Peter laughed.

"What's so funny?" asked Sally.

"I have no doubt that your father knows how you pulled Andy and me through high school. He probably feels it's about time Andy made his own choices, lived his own life."

"I'm serious, Peter. War is a little more challenging than memorizing formulas for chemistry class."

Peter studied his friend in the rearview mirror. Andy Parker, for the moment at least, seemed oblivious to the horrors of the escalating conflict being waged in the rice paddies of Southeast Asia and to the battles being fought in many living rooms around the country—thanks to the wizardry of live television and the evening news—for the hearts and minds of America's youth. Tonight Peter could see that there was nothing but duty and adventure on Andy's mind.

Peter exhaled slowly. "Yeah, that's why I don't want any part of it."

Sally sat up straight. "So … what does that mean? Do you intend to hide out in art school for the rest of the war? That could take a long time, Mr. Miller!"

"Now, Sally, we talked about this. It isn't every day a kid from the Jersey Pines gets a chance to study impressionist art abroad in the land of the masters. Besides, you get to look after my baby," Peter threw in, caressing the Mustang's sleek black vinyl dashboard.

"It just isn't fair," protested Sally. "While you're off painting your masterpiece and Andy's busy making the world safe for democracy, I'm stuck here driving around the swamps of Stafford."

"Driving in style," Peter added, hitting the gas pedal for emphasis.

"Humph," scowled Sally, folding her arms. "It just isn't fair."

Peter whizzed by another car.

"That's why I've decided to leave you a little something to remember me by," Peter shouted above the din of the passing wind.

Sally held on tightly to the armrest.

"Wherever it is we're going and whatever it is you have to show me, do you have to drive so fast?"

"We have to get there before they do!"

"Who?"

"The stags."

Sally's eyes scanned the periphery of the rambling pine forest. "You're trying to outrun a herd of deer?"

"No, silly. The Lacey High Stags. Tonight's their graduation, too, in case you've forgotten. I don't want them to beat us to, uh, my surprise. It would spoil everything."

"Oh, Peter, you're so thoughtful. What's the surprise?"

"If I told you," he replied, looking at Sally with a devilish schoolboy grin, "then it wouldn't be a surprise."

Sally shot him a girlish pout and Peter could feel himself starting to give in. She stared admiringly at his dark, handsome face, lit by a pair of blazingly bright blue eyes.

"Let's just say it's a little artistic tribute from me to you, memorializing that special place of ours. You *do* remember the night we—"

Sally poked Peter in the arm. "Stop it. Andy will hear you," she added, blushing and glancing back at her brother.

"Hear what?" asked Andy, leaning forward and nearly losing his balance as Peter negotiated a sharp bend along a deserted section of Route 539.

"Nothing," Peter and Sally replied together.

Andy took it in stride and carried on with a torturous rendition of "God Bless America."

From the vantage point of a slight rise on a long sloping hill, Peter could see the headlights of a vehicle looming in his rearview mirror. In the opposite lane, it was approaching them from behind at a terrific rate of speed.

Before Peter could blink, a late model pickup truck packed with partying teenagers came up alongside them. Except for its antler rack as a hood ornament, the once faded green pickup was practically unrecognizable. The entire truck—doors, bed panels, and windows—was lavishly spray-painted with white lettering paying homage to the graduating Lacey High "Stags," Class of '65.

"That's Donny Connelly's truck," Andy shouted up to Peter. "And look, isn't that Eddie Farley and his girlfriend, what's-her-name, sucking face in the back?"

"Nina Kaszanski," replied Sally, grabbing at the loose strands of her knotted auburn hair.

"The slut?" inquired Andy, a little too loudly for propriety's sake.

The remark seemed to part the entwined pair lounging in the bed of the truck as a bleached blonde in a pleated cheerleading skirt and a crew cut kid in shirtless overalls came up for air. The full figured young girl made an obscene hand gesture while her companion stood and dropped his drawers, giving Peter, Sally, and Andy a rather healthy view of his better end. The half dozen kids crammed into the back of the pickup roared their approval.

"That's gross!" exclaimed Sally, turning her head away.

"Pigs!" shouted Andy from the back seat, igniting a volley of obscenities between the two vehicles.

"*Oink, oink!*" Eddie Farley fired back. Nina Kaszanski stood up beside her man and popped an enormous bubble with her gum. She passed the bubble gum between her teeth onto Eddie's wagging tongue.

Peter pulled his car away as the two vehicles started to drift into each other's side of the median strip.

A dark-haired, freckle-faced boy riding "shotgun" in the pickup leaned out of the passenger window shaking a can of spray paint. He sent a blast into the night air. A faint mist of white speckles struck the windshield of the Mustang, sticking to the glass like frosty snowflakes.

"Nice shot, Bailey," Eddie Farley encouraged the freckled boy.

"They're headed for the rock!" shouted Peter in dismay.

Andy stood up in the back, rocking and hooting like a cowboy on an untamed mount as the pickup truck sped away.

"Let them *go*," pleaded Sally.

"No way," replied Peter, flooring the Ford in pursuit.

Locked in a drag race, the two vehicles barreled side by side down the narrow, dark country road, neither one gaining on the other for more than a few feet, with each determined not to give an inch before the other did.

"Look!" shouted Sally with growing alarm. She pointed straight ahead at a pair of oncoming headlights breaking the darkness over the low ridge in front of them.

"Pull over, Peter. Let Connelly in," she implored.

Peter looked over at the pickup. Apparently, Connelly hadn't noticed the headlights or, if he had, he was hoping Peter would turn chicken first. There was no letup in his speed. It was a game of nerves and neither one wanted to break off first. Peter gripped the wheel tighter.

"Peter, please!" Sally's voice was quivering. The oncoming car was flashing its high beams to get their attention.

Peter looked over at Sally. Her face was ghostly white, her teeth clenched and her eyes fixed straight ahead on the approaching car.

Peter glanced in his rearview mirror and saw Andy jumping up and down and pumping his fists at the pickup. He was engaged in a heated shouting match with several of the rowdies in the rear of the truck.

"Sit down, Andy," Peter ordered, but his friend ignored him.

The oncoming car was now less than a hundred yards away and showing no signs of slowing down. Neither was the pickup.

Suddenly, Bailey threw an object out of the pickup's passenger-side window. Reflexively, Peter leaned back in his seat as the paint can went flying past his face. It caught Sally squarely in the left temple. She slumped against the car door.

"Sally!" cried Peter, taking his eyes off the road. He released his foot from the gas pedal and reached across the seat to catch her.

In a split-second maneuver, Donny Connelly slipped his truck neatly in front of Peter's Mustang and just narrowly missed being sideswiped by the oncoming VW bus. The bearded, wild-eyed driver in the van let up on his horn, which he'd been hammering for about the last fifty yards. He shook his fist and cursed repeatedly as he drove on by.

Peter struggled to keep his Ford on the road and off the soft sandy shoulder. Inexplicably, Donny Connelly abruptly stopped short, prompting Peter to apply his brakes but too late to avoid ramming into the rear of the pickup truck.

The sudden, unexpected ferocity of the crash sent Andy aloft. He flew out of the backseat of the Mustang and into a shallow clearing of woods along the roadside, where his body smashed against a large, singular boulder. The impact instantly severed Andy's neck and spine.

Unconscious, Sally lay pinned on the floor of the front seat, wedged under the crumpled dashboard of the Ford. The entire front end of Peter's new car had buckled. Steam hissed from the ruptured radiator into the warm night air. Oil dripped onto the gritty road.

Peter had banged his head against the steering wheel, snapping the wheel in two. A huge gash opened on his forehead, oozing blood like a plump ripe tomato, but he did not lose consciousness. He shut off the ignition and flung the key ring into the woods in angry desperation, as if he intended to throw away all that had just happened with it.

Dazed, Peter looked up to see the truckload of stunned Stags fleeing the scene in a panic. No one in the pickup was hurt, but they were plenty spooked. Peter tried calling out to them for help but they were long gone.

Slowly, painfully, Peter freed himself from the wreckage and dragged himself around what remained of his graduation present to attend to Sally. He managed to disentangle her, and, lifting her gently in his arms, he carried her to the safety of the nearby woods.

He set her down on a bed of soft pine needles. He tore off a piece of his shirt and gingerly wiped the blood that trickled from an open cut and ran down the side of her head.

When the bleeding stopped, Peter staggered over to Andy's body. He was overcome by the horror of what he found. Andy Parker, his best friend, the future GI, lay splattered on top of the immovable stone monolith. His limp, lifeless body lay across it, as dead as the rock itself. Rivulets of blood spread out like tentacles, obscenely obscuring the simple message Peter had painstakingly put there for Sally Parker to see.

2

Tour de Pines
(2005)

"It's a rock, Geoffrey, like your head," said Danny Windsor sarcastically as he removed his cycling helmet and mopped his wet brow with a sweaty forearm. He stretched out across the giant bolder and scratched his back on its jutting bow-like peak. His matted hair glistened in the morning sun.

"I can see that," replied Geoffrey Martin impatiently as he struggled to set his bike's kickstand in the soft sandy shoulder along the roadside. "But who painted the American flag on it?"

"Nobody knows," said Moss Greenberg, gliding to a stop beside them. He hopped off his bike and massaged the kinks in his aging but taut quadriceps. "It's just another one of those endearing mysteries you hear about in the Pines," he added casually in his warm, infectious Aussie accent.

"Probably someone from Fort Dix," offered Kelly Martin, Geoffrey's older sister, who had pulled into the shade of the pine trees and sat straddling her bike. "Isn't the Army base somewhere around here?"

"Just up the road a piece," replied Moss. "And you may be right, Kelly. This paint job is a bit more patriotic than the others."

"Others?" inquired Geoffrey.

Danny sprang up and eyed his two friends as if for the first time, although the truth was they had been inseparable—and at times insufferable, as Kelly would say—over the last two summers. "You mean to tell me that, in all the trips you two have made to your Aunt Sarah's place on LBI, you have never seen the Painted Rock before?"

Geoffrey shrugged. "We never came this way."

"We've always taken the Parkway from Teaneck," Kelly added defensively.

"Route 539 is out of the way."

"Wonders never cease," mumbled Danny. He tipped back his water bottle and drained it dry. "Well, time to take care of a little urgent business," he added as he sauntered off into the thicket to relieve himself.

"Very little," Kelly giggled under her breath at her former heartthrob's expense. *Some things never change.* "Don't call us if you need a hand," she shouted after him.

"Or if you run into the Jersey Devil," added Moss with a knowing wink at the Martin teens.

Danny waved off the comments and continued down the well-worn path until he was out of sight.

Moss Greenberg sat down on a pile of pine needles in the shade and rubbed his tired, sixty-something's legs. "Must've forgotten to take my Geritol this morning," he said, wincing.

Geoffrey and Kelly went over to examine the rock more closely.

"Are we on government property?" asked Geoffrey, gently feeling his way around the smooth surface of the curious monolith.

A car drove by and honked its horn. Without looking up Moss Greenberg cocked his arm in a mock salute. "Sort of," he replied, continuing to rub his aching muscles. "This area is part of a state preserve known as Greenwood Forest."

"Oh, I get it," chuckled Kelly, "like Sherwood Forest."

Moss smiled broadly. "If you like." His newly added white-blond fu-man-chu, which matched his wispy strands of hair, formed a neat perimeter around his perfect teeth.

"But why spruce up this rock?" inquired Geoffrey, standing back to admire the work. "I mean, it's a nice paint job, but why not just put a sign on it saying, 'Welcome to Greenwood Forest'? Wouldn't that serve a more useful purpose?"

"Useful? Perhaps," mused Moss. "But I doubt it would deter the tons of graffiti that finds its way onto the rock."

"You mean like 'Johnny and Mary forever,' blah, blah, blah?" asked Kelly, gesturing like she was gagging herself.

"That's mild compared to what's been written on this rock over the years." Moss Greenberg stood and rejoined the teens around the rock.

"You see, the Painted Rock has become a landmark to travelers headed for Long Beach Island. Nobody wants to see trash strewn along the road on their way to the beach, whether that garbage is manmade litter or trashy print. You know—the stuff kids write, immature high school junk, obscenities and such."

"Uh, huh," both Kelly and Geoffrey agreed, looking at each other.

Moss Greenberg reached for his bike and began adjusting the chain links absentmindedly.

"Well, anyway, it seems this Greenwood Forest, much like the fabled Sherwood Forest, has its own Robin Hood looking after it. But instead of 'stealing from the rich and giving to the poor' with a sword, this Robin Hood wields a paintbrush and dresses up the trashy transgressions others have left with scenic pictures for the passersby to enjoy on their long ride to the Jersey Shore. The American Flag has been emblazoned on the rock since the 9/11 terrorist attacks. An act of solidarity and support for the thousands who lost their lives, I suppose. But before that, dating back as long as anyone 'round here can remember, there have been flowers, pumpkins, snowflakes, shamrocks—you name it—all gracing the stone at one time or another."

"And no one knows who is responsible for the colorful artwork?" asked Kelly incredulously. "It's really good."

"People have tried to find out. It's kind of like those crop circles you read about. One day the rock is covered with vulgar obscenities, and then the next day, damned if it isn't adorned with sunflowers and roses. Why, I even heard some local kids camped out a few times in the nearby woods attempting to 'catch' the anonymous painter, but he—*or she*—" Moss nodded at Kelly, "slipped in and out without ever being seen."

"Are you still talking about this stupid rock?"

Geoffrey and Kelly had been so enthralled with Moss's history of the Painted Rock that they failed to notice when Danny quietly returned from "doing his business."

"You don't think it's fascinating?" asked Geoffrey, crawling around the rock hoping to gain some additional perspective into its past. "Judging by the splattered paint there must be layers and layers caked on it," he added as he bent down to examine the base.

"Like I said, Geoffrey, it's a rock. Solid and hard, like your head," Danny said, putting on his helmet.

Moss continued to fiddle with his brake pads and checked the air pressure in his tires.

"No, wait, Danny, Geoffrey's got a point," said Kelly, coming to his aid and siding with her younger brother, as was her nature. Danny had seen that combative stance before: jaw set, back erect, head up. Unfortunately, Danny didn't always know when to back off, either.

"Look around you, Danny," she said with a wave of her arm. "This rock is an anomaly. There isn't another one like it anywhere. I mean, how did it get here in the first place?"

"It fell out of the sky. Who cares?" said Danny, mounting his bike.

"Is that your final answer?" goaded Geoffrey.

"Or just an educated guess, from a sophisticated college man?" Kelly chimed in.

"All right, all right. Time to saddle up," urged Moss, trying to diffuse the tensions that had been escalating between the old friends all day. One would have thought that after a whole school year apart, and all that they had been through together on previous summer adventures—running from modern day pirates and dodging ghostly devils—that the old chums would be ready to play nice. At least that was what Moss Greenberg had thought when he invited the threesome on a preparatory ride to help raise awareness for the Pinelands Preservation Alliance. Now all he could do was shake his head.

"We've still got a bit of a ride ahead of us, if any of you plan to get in shape in time for the Tour de Pines. So save your energy for the open road," he said as he pedaled off.

"Yeah," added Danny emphatically. "And this time, try and keep up." He was about to set off after Moss, but he threw a stern look in Kelly's direction first, chiding, "How do you two expect to ride in the Tour on those old Schwinn Classics, anyway?"

"We don't," said Kelly, holding her brother's bicycle for him while he adjusted the chinstrap on his helmet. "The road isn't wide enough for Danny Windsor and anybody else," she shouted, but he was already out of earshot.

3
Wedding Song

Geoffrey Martin sat on the edge of his bed in a white dress shirt, pale blue silk tie and paisley boxer shorts. He was putting on a pair of dark dress socks when Kelly came into his room nonchalantly. She was dressed in a fashionable light peach cotton dress that accentuated her tan and made her green eyes sparkle.

"I've never seen Noah so nervous," said Kelly, wrapping her long auburn hair up in a bun that would eventually be accented with a splash of colorful yellow and brown marigolds cut fresh from her aunt's garden. "We better get a move on, before he wears a hole in the shop floor with all that pacing back and forth."

Geoffrey turned and faced the wall with modesty as he slipped on his pants. He adjusted his thick tortoise shell glasses and tousled his soft curls, barely glancing in the mirror. "You'd be nervous, too, if you were an aging bachelor about to tie the knot for the first time."

"Especially if you were tying the knot with *our* Aunt Sarah," Kelly added, straightening Geoffrey's tie when he turned to face her again.

"You mean our *mother's* sister," he added playfully.

"Our *father's* favorite in-law," Kelly persisted.

"Okay, you win," said Geoffrey resignedly, "but do you always have to top everybody? No wonder Danny gets so nuts around you. He can't win but he's crazy enough to keep trying."

Kelly put her hands on her hips and stiffened. She blushed angrily. "I'll ignore your petty little comments today. This is Aunt Sarah's day, and Mom and Dad have never even met Noah before. I hope they like him."

"What's not to like? He's witty, he's charming …"

"… and he likes *bluegrass*," Kelly finished with a flourish.

"Well, two out of three ain't bad."

Geoffrey slipped on his blue blazer.

A man's impatient voice hurried up the stairs, cutting their merriment short. "Let's go, kids. We're gonna be late. And we don't want your Aunt Sarah to send out a search party now, do we?"

"Why did Aunt Sarah insist that we go to the wedding with Noah instead of with Mom and Dad?" Kelly wondered out loud.

"I guess she wanted us to make him look like he's already family," Geoffrey suggested insightfully.

"Aww! You're so sweet for a bratty little brother." Kelly messed up his hair on their way down the stairs.

***

Danny Windsor knew Cedar Bonnet Island was more than just a small scrap of marshland that lay between Long Beach Island and the mainland. Barely noticed by seasonal commuters, it nonetheless boasted some of the finest clamming beds and crabbing spots around. Recently it had garnered more attention when a real estate development group chose to build an expensive, luxurious banquet hall complete with a serviceable chapel barn and a flower garden that overlooked the beautiful bay on the north side of the island.

The property known as the Bonnet Island Estate was clearly like nothing the area had seen before. Ostensibly a large dining facility and an elegant bed and breakfast accommodating up to 24 overnight guests, the Estate resembled an exclusive country club without the golf course. It provided a breathtaking and somewhat glamorous setting for important social functions.

Danny and most of the locals referred to the upscale mansion as the "Gatsby House," partly because of its classic Hamptons look but also because it was something they felt was out of their reach.

The price tag was beyond what Noah Parsons, a retired Coast Guard serviceman, could afford, and his soon-to-be spouse, Sarah Bishop, was herself a widow and retired school teacher now operating the Crab Cove Gift Shop and struggling to balance her own modest budget. But good fortune decided to smile on them. Noah's coworker at the Tuckerton Seaport was the well-connected curator, Libby Ashcroft, whose pedigree came from New York's high society and who had managed to make her way onto the Bonnet Island Estate's board of directors. Applying an off-season rate and a members-only discount, Libby was able to work out a deal that even the frugal newlyweds could almost handle. When Sarah's sister Margaret and her husband Robert Martin sprang for the balance to show their appreciation to Sarah for taking Kelly and Geoffrey under her wing each of the last two summers, the plan was set.

Danny wheeled his Jeep Wrangler around the horseshoe entranceway, pulling to a stop in front of the large gray and white mansion's main doors. A lovely young Hispanic girl dressed in a casual pale blue business suit greeted him warmly.

"Good day, sir. You are here for the wedding, no?" She inquired politely in a delicate accent.

"I'm with the band," Danny replied, trying out his most devilishly handsome grin.

The young woman's smile vanished. "The staff entrance is around the back," she offered, pointing to a gravel road. "Drive slowly please, and try not to kick up dust on the guests."

Danny pointed toward the curving roadway. "This way?" he asked flirtatiously, still trying to charm her.

"*Sí, sí,*" the obviously unimpressed young woman insisted, while waving him toward the road. She closed the big double doors and disappeared inside.

Danny rounded the corner, narrowly missing a graying maintenance man in coveralls who was clipping the hedges that encircled the drive.

The man jumped back dropping his shears under Danny's Jeep.

"Sorry," Danny apologized, waiting for the man to retrieve his clippers. The man seemed to be in no particular hurry. He gave nothing more than a vacant stare, his dull, rheumy eyes focused on some distant, obscure point beyond Danny.

"That's the trouble with youth," the groundskeeper said, straightening up slowly, "always in such a damned hurry to git somewhere." His white, stubbly face glistened with sweat as he approached the Jeep. Deep lines, like lashes delivered from an unkind whip, cut into his dark, leathery face.

"I said I was sorry," Danny repeated, growing annoyed.

"So am I," the man almost shouted, waving the shears under Danny's nose. "So am I," he repeated over and over, mumbling and shaking his head as he turned away.

A car horn honked behind Danny's Jeep.

"Hey there," an impatient young woman in a rose-colored, rhinestone-studded, low-cut blouse called out the window. It was Shawna James, the band's stunning lead singer.

"Stop your chit-chattin', Windsor. We've got a gig to play."

Danny put the Jeep in gear and followed the gravel road around to the rear of the mansion. By the time he looked into his rearview mirror, the groundskeeper had returned to trimming the hedges.

***

Reverend Jones wasn't really a reverend, but he didn't fight that impression. He was more like a lay deacon once removed, on loan from the Lutheran Church in Barnegat Light, where he claimed to be granted a wide range of authority over issues both secular and ecclesiastic.

In truth, McAllister Jones was an acting Justice of the Peace for Southern Ocean County. That gave him the civil authority to marry people, collar or no. He had acquired the title "Reverend" because it was rumored he had attended St. Regis' seminary school outside of Boston until a pretty young Irish lass from the Back Bay docks won his heart and stole him away from the service of the Lord. The girl, Mildred O'Hara, went on to become his wife and bore Reverend Jones four sons, one of whom became a professional surfer; two others ran local businesses on LBI, a local marina and a jet-ski rental shop; and the fourth son, the black sheep of the family, was apparently now a young woman living in relative seclusion in Santa Cruz, California.

Everyone on the island knew Reverend Jones. He made sure of it. He was a big man who commanded attention. His social climbing wife usually took care of any introductions that escaped his attention, especially if they could add to his stature on the island. That's why it was a surprise for him to meet Kelly and Geoffrey Martin, along with their parents, Robert and Margaret, for the first time at Sarah Bishop and Noah Parsons's wedding. It might also explain why the Reverend Jones had been so eager to officiate when asked to do so by another friend and admirer, Libby Ashcroft.

He had heard about the teens' summer adventures secondhand from some of the cronies he bellied up with at Wida's bar. Indeed, he had counted Ryder Hayes and

Professor Payton J. Tippett among his many "acquaintances" until they both ended up dishonored and behind bars for crimes and misdemeanors the kids had helped to unravel.

For their part, Jones's grandstanding did not impress Kelly and Geoffrey. They were anxious to get the ceremony over with so they could hit the chow line. Jones's pontificating made the whole affair seem more like an evangelical TV show than an old-fashioned wedding.

Dressed in an eggshell chiffon evening gown that she had borrowed from her sister, Sarah Bishop made an angelic bride while the usually staid Noah Parsons fell into the role of nervous bridegroom. Serving as the best man was Noah's longtime pal, the half-Native American, half-Rastafarian mystic Johnny Longfellow. Donning a rented black tuxedo for perhaps the first time in his life, mutual friend and renowned local woodsman Tom Banks gave the beautiful bride away.

The sun was just beginning to set over the scenic Barnegat Bay as the wedding party exited the chapel barn, winding its way to the English garden where an open bar cocktail reception awaited. Like being released from Sunday school, the sixty-plus people who had suffered through Reverend Jones's service were grateful for the fresh air and the breathtaking view of the bay afforded by the garden setting. All the guests crowded around the newlyweds for the ceremonial toast on the boat landing.

"To the newlyweds, Sarah and Noah," Johnny Longfellow began, raising his glass of chilled Moet Chandon. "May their union be long and fruitful!" (This raised a few eyebrows.) "May they find comfort and pleasure in each other arms." (This drew a few *ooh*'s and *aah*'s.) "And, in between all that fun stuff, may they always find time for their friends."

"Here, here!" The crowd applauded, joining in the frivolity and downing their drinks.

Framed against the warm orange glow of the setting sun beside the rippling water, the happy couple kissed, as the house photographer snapped what would become the wedding album's cover picture. The crowd responded with thunderous applause.

Right on cue, the band, Midwife Crisis, with Danny Windsor on guitar and featuring Shawna James on fiddle and lead vocals, broke into a countryfied rendition of Paul Stookey's "The Wedding Song."

The sight of Danny hamming it up onstage with Shawna gave Kelly a little twinge of jealousy. Danny noticed Kelly and gave her a familiar wink.

"So that's the Windsor boy we've heard so much about?" asked Robert Martin, eyeing the stage suspiciously.

"In the flesh," Kelly answered with a sigh.

"I must say, he's a handsome young man," the stylish Margaret Martin added cautiously.

"And he plays a mean guitar," Geoffrey chimed in, pantomiming on air guitar as Danny went into a little Chuck Berry duck walk routine.

"He seems pretty sure of himself," said Kelly's dad, watching Danny and Shawna trading solos.

"More like *full* of himself," Kelly replied, shaking her head at Danny's stage antics.

"I, for one, have always admired a man with a confident manner," offered Margaret Martin, squeezing her self-assured husband's arm affectionately. "Although, I'm sure someone else might find his self-assurance egotistical, even …"

"Mom," Kelly interrupted, "when it comes to being cocky, Danny Windsor is king."

"Yeah," agreed Geoffrey, studying Danny as he imitated The Who's Peter Townsend's signature windmill chops. "He's over the top, man."

"Oh, puh-*lease*!" exclaimed Kelly.

"Hi, y'all," greeted Tom Banks, introducing himself to Kelly and Geoffrey's parents.

"Having a good time?" Tom asked the kids with genuine interest.

"Of course they are," Reverend Jones answered, making his way toward them, drink in hand. "With their Aunt Sarah moving into Noah Parsons's flat, they'll have the run of the shop. There's no telling what new adventures they've got planned for this summer, is there?"

"Adventures? What adventures?" asked Margaret Martin. "Do you know about any adventures, Robert?" she asked, turning to her husband.

"Now, see here, Jones …" Robert Martin started.

"Not to worry, Mr. Martin," Tom said, coming to their aid. "They've just been having a little harmless teenage fun."

"'Fun'?" aped Jones. "I guess you call outwitting a junkyard pirate and bagging a nasty poacher 'fun'?"

Margaret Martin looked aghast. "Sarah never said a word …"

"Because it was nothing, Mother," said Kelly, looking to Geoffrey and Tom for help.

"Really, Mrs. Martin," Tom jumped in. "The Reverend here has it all out of proportion. Trumped up gossip, not the actual facts. I was there."

"Gossip?" Having made his point, the Reverend decided to change the subject. "That reminds me: Did you hear that someone has covered over the American flag on the Painted Rock with peace signs and flower power? Sounds like the '60s all over again, doesn't it?"

4

Two Left Feet

"**I**s it true, Tom?" an excited Noah Parsons inquired, joining the conversation. He was linked arm in arm with his new bride. "Has someone defaced the flag?"

"I'm afraid so, Noah," Tom Banks sighed.

"That's an outrage!" exclaimed Noah.

"Indeed, my sentiments exactly," said Reverend Jones, though rather unconvincingly.

"Who would do such a thing?" asked Sarah.

"Kids, more than likely," answered Jones, looking down his nose at the teenage Martins.

"I don't think so …" Tom replied slowly.

"Noah, aren't you going to introduce me to your guests?" interrupted a charming woman in her mid-fifties who looked much younger than her age. Even with a shock of gray that streaked the front of her perfectly coiffed hair, she appeared to Kelly and Geoffrey to be a striking, ageless beauty.

"Of course, Sally," Noah apologized. "Where are my manners? Ms. Sally Parker Lawson, may I introduce the Martin family."

"The new outlaws," Reverend Jones threw in jokingly.

"How do you do?" said Robert and Margaret, exchanging greetings.

"Sally is Noah's first cousin," offered Sarah.

"She's more like a big sister," Noah said, affectionately giving Sally a gentle hug.

"And you must be Kelly and Geoffrey," Sally said grabbing each teen by a hand. "Noah has told me so much about you. Your escapades are legendary." She leaned in closer and whispered, "They remind me of another group of adventure seekers I knew in my youth."

Margaret shot her sister Sarah a sharp glance. "That reminds me … we need to talk later."

"Do you mind if we move away from the loud music?" asked Sally Lawson. "My hearing is not what it used to be."

"Yes, come, everyone. I believe it's time we went inside," said Sarah with relief spying the lovely young hostess, Luz, beckoning for her in the doorway.

Luz rang a tiny silver bell. "Dinner is served," she announced.

The newlyweds led their guests through the garden and into the main hall of the mansion. The design of the great hall resembled an inverted ship's hull, with a vaulted 30-foot-high ceiling. Inside the elegant dining hall, the wedding guests were treated to a royal feast. Pressed white linen tablecloths topped by crystal vases filled with dozens of long stemmed red roses adorned each table.

Libby Ashcroft had personally seen to all the details of the meal herself. For appetizers, she selected bruschetta à la Tuscany, baby lamb chops, and artichoke hearts with sun-dried tomatoes *en croute*. The pasta course followed. Here, Libby selected penne à la vodka and broccoli garlic farfalle. From the carving station, guests had a choice between grilled London broil with sautéed portabella mushrooms and glazed pork tenderloin stuffed with spinach and Edam cheese.

Libby saved her best selections for last. For dessert, guests were treated to cheesecake lollipops and chocolate fantasy cake. Kelly and Geoffrey had never seen so much food in their entire lives—nor could they resist the temptation to try everything.

Over the course of the evening, whenever Kelly wasn't gorging herself on one of Libby Ashcroft's sinful selections, she couldn't help but notice how Danny shuffled back and forth between Shawna and Luz, engaging in lighthearted laughter and conversation. The fact that Danny never once sought her out annoyed Kelly to the point of distraction.

At one point during dinner, Kelly's mom leaned in casually and said to her daughter, "That Windsor boy has quite a way with the women."

"Really?" Kelly replied curtly. "I hadn't noticed. More potatoes?" she said, passing a family style platter of pasta to her mother.

After dinner, the wedding guests, most of them part of Noah and Sarah's Saturday night Albert Music Hall crowd, took to the dance floor.

When Geoffrey was summoned to the stage to join the band on keyboards for a few numbers, Kelly sat alone at the head table, sulking. She was lost in her thoughts when Sally Lawson came and sat down beside her.

"How is it that a pretty young thing like you is not out on the dance floor, my dear?" She asked sweetly.

"Two left feet," Kelly lied. Not wanting to talk about herself in her present mood, Kelly was quick to add, "And you?"

"Oh, dear me! I haven't been on a dance floor since my husband passed away. That was almost a year ago."

"I'm sorry," Kelly apologized sincerely. "I didn't know."

"That's all right, my dear, I'm used to it by now. Jack was quite a dancer, though … whenever he wasn't out fishing, that is." She laughed softly as she said it.

Kelly took the bait. "Don't tell me a stunning woman like you was stuck on shore waiting for her fisherman to come back to port?"

"Not just any old fisherman, my dear. He was a boat captain, the best around. He commanded the tuna fleet out of Barnegat Light. I begged him to give it up. At his age, I told him, he should not have been working those long, hard hours. But he loved the sea. It was his life."

"What happened?" asked Kelly delicately.

"He had a heart attack during a tuna run one night out beyond the Klondike. Never saw it coming."

"I don't know what to say. I'm so sorry."

"Oh, don't be. We had so many wonderful years. Plus, he left me a house in Barnegat Light and a sizable life insurance policy, so I'm pretty well set for life. Although I do get bored once in a while," Sally admitted guilelessly.

Kelly shared her gentle laughter and enjoyed this lovely woman's perspective. "Perhaps you could stop by for tea some time?" Sally asked hopefully.

"Yes, I'd like that," Kelly replied sincerely. She'd allowed herself to feel comfortable with this gentle stranger and had momentarily forgotten all about Danny Windsor, but when the band struck up another number, she looked wistfully at her handsome young guitar hero. Her new companion couldn't help but notice.

Sally sighed. "Yes, Jack Lawson and I had a pretty good life, considering."

Kelly could not mistake the trace of sadness in her voice. Tears welled in the woman's kind eyes. Kelly looked at her, slightly puzzled. *Considering?*

"Oh, well, that's a story for another time, perhaps. Right now it's well past my bedtime and I wonder if you would be a dear and walk me to my car?"

Kelly jumped at the chance. She was ready to do just about anything other than sit there sulking by herself.

"Certainly," she agreed, without the need for any additional prompting.

With Kelly accompanying her, Sally Lawson made her way slowly, gracefully across the room to say goodnight to the bride and groom.

"That's sweet of you to see her out," Noah said to Kelly.

"Don't forget to take a piece of the wedding cake, Sally," reminded Sarah. "I had Luz put it aside for you in the kitchen."

"Thank you. We'll get it on the way out." She hugged and kissed Noah and Sarah tenderly and bid goodnight to the Martins and other nearby guests.

Kelly and Sally cut across the back of the main hall, heading for the kitchen. Kelly held the door open for her new friend. As Sally stepped into the kitchen, she came face-to-face with the rheumy-eyed groundskeeper in soiled coveralls as he was collecting the trash. She let out a piercing shriek just before she fainted. Alarmed, the rumpled man dropped the garbage bags he had been holding and ran out the back door just as Kelly entered the room.

Johnny Longfeather and Tom Banks were the first guests to reach the kitchen, followed closely by Noah Parsons, Sarah Bishop, the Martins, Libby Ashcroft, Reverend Jones and his plump wife, Mildred, Geoffrey Martin, Danny Windsor and his band mates. They all crowded into the service kitchen to find Sally lying on the cold tile floor, her head propped up on Kelly's lap. Luz Sanchez, the Bonnet Island Estate's young hostess, was gently applying a damp cloth to Sally's ashen forehead. She was visibly shaken but conscious.

"What happened?" Noah demanded.

"I don't know," replied Kelly, clearly unnerved. "We came in here to get a slice of wedding cake for Sally to take home. There was a strange man in here collecting the trash. They saw each other, and the next thing I know, Sally screamed and passed out, and the man ran out the back door.

"Was he trying to steal something?" inquired Libby Ashcroft with alarm. "Silverware, perhaps?"

"I don't think so," replied Kelly. She pointed toward the door. "Those are the bags he dropped on his way out."

Johnny Longfellow stepped over Sally adroitly and checked the bags. "Nothing here but trash," he announced to the anxious group.

"Then why did he run?" asked Robert Martin.

"She must have spooked him," offered Reverend Jones, pulling on his lapels. His wife nodded in agreement.

"I'd say it looks like they spooked each other," Tom concluded.

"Luz, do you know who the man was?" Libby Ashcroft demanded.

"*Sí, señora*, he is the … how do you say, *el jardinero*?"

"The gardener," Geoffrey translated.

"Yes, he keep the grounds and do the maintenance, too." Luz smiled at Geoffrey, "But I do not know his name."

Sally Lawson stirred, trying to find her voice.

Noah bent down to comfort her. "Take it easy, Sally. Let Doc have a look at you." Freeman Morris grabbed her wrist to check her pulse. "Danny, hand me that water bottle," he directed, and Danny obliged, opening a bottle of Evian and handing it over.

Sally took a sip and cleared her throat.

"I'm all right, Freeman. Thank you."

"Did he hurt you?" Sarah inquired with concern in her voice.

"No, no," Sally protested. "It was like Tom said, I—I think we just startled each other."

"Do you know him?" Libby asked incredulously.

"I thought I recognized him as someone from my past, someone I knew a long time ago." Sally's voice was thin, her eyes distant. "But …" She looked into Kelly's eyes.

"But …?" Kelly encouraged.

"I must have been mistaken," Sally replied distractedly.

5

Fish Outta Water

Moss Greenberg took the news in stride, but Danny could not hide his disappointment. "Was it something I said?" he asked Kelly and Geoffrey with an exaggerated pout. The four of them were huddled around the cash register inside Crab Cove, their Aunt Sarah's cluttered but cozy nautical themed gift shop on 25th Street in Ship Bottom. Moss and Danny sported stylish Gore-Tex cycling gear in preparation for their morning ride.

"Sorry, Danny, this had nothing to do with you," Kelly deadpanned. "We talked it over with Aunt Sarah and Noah before they left on their honeymoon."

"Where did they end up going?" Moss wondered aloud.

"Atlantic City," Geoffrey replied, "Can you believe they have never been there before?"

"That's not quite true. They had both been there years ago, but they had never been there together," explained Kelly.

"*Any*way," Geoffrey continued with mock exasperation, "our parents gave them a wedding gift of four nights at the Trump Hotel and Casino."

"So you offered to watch the shop while they were gone, right?" asked Moss.

"Not exactly," Kelly said quietly before slowly continuing. "You see, it's not just the bike tour we'll be skipping this year. I won't be back on lifeguard duty either, boss. With Aunt Sarah and Noah setting up house across the causeway and my needing some extra pocket money before I head off to college in the fall, we all figured it was a perfect fit to have me run the shop this summer. I can make a lot more money here and help Aunt Sarah out at the same time."

"Besides," Geoffrey added, "after our parents heard about last summer's adventures, they wanted to keep a closer eye on us this year."

"So are you still going to work at the Seaport, or will you be working here, too?" Danny asked Geoffrey.

"Neither," Geoffrey replied. "Tom Banks offered me a job at his camp."

"Babysitting a bunch of spoiled brats in the woods," chuckled Danny. "He tried to get me to do that one year, too."

"I think facilitating the development of survival skills in a world-renowned outdoor education program will look better on your college applications," offered Moss.

"Especially if I want to get into Princeton," countered Geoffrey, smiling.

"So that's it, huh? No bike ride, no lifeguarding, no summer adventure. Am I the only one who feels like I've lost a friend, or two?" Danny revealed his thoughts, looking back and forth at Kelly and Geoffrey.

"You know I'm going to come out to see the band," Geoffrey said, shaking Danny's hand.

"And we don't have any plans for the fourth of July," added Kelly.

"Speak for yourself," muttered Geoffrey, "I might have plans."

"Then might I suggest a romantic boat ride accompanied by fireworks?" Moss beamed a little too obviously at Danny and Kelly as he put on his helmet and made his way to the door.

"I *definitely* have to make other plans!" exclaimed Geoffrey, as Kelly blushed at Danny's warm and direct gaze.

***

"Noah, what's wrong?" asked his new bride, Sarah. She was having fun pumping quarters into a gold and gleaming slot machine in the lobby of the hotel and casino. Noah was quietly surveying the crowded, noisy, smoke-filled room.

"Oh, it's nothing," he replied unconvincingly.

Sarah could tell he was uncomfortable, and even though she was temporarily enjoying the whole adult carnival atmosphere, she didn't mind leaving it either.

"Let's take a walk on the boardwalk. It's getting a little stuffy in here." She made a funny face for his benefit and waved her hand at the smoke lingering in the air. Then she gently placed her hand on his arm and led him outside.

"You're awfully quiet, mister. Cat got your tongue," she inquired once they had gotten away from the crowd.

"I feel like a fish outta water," he replied apologetically.

"Yeah, I didn't have the heart to tell my sister that Atlantic City wasn't on the top of our list of places to go," Sarah blurted out.

"Oh Honey, don't get me wrong," said Noah. "This was wonderful of them and the hotel is beautiful, plus I love the chance to get away from everybody else and spend time alone with you."

"But?" Sarah quizzed her husband of nearly forty-eight hours.

"Can I talk to you about something?" Noah asked as he ushered Sarah over to an empty bench facing the ocean.

"Of course you can, what's on your mind?" she responded.

"This is gonna sound silly, and maybe I am making a mountain out of a molehill, but I just can't get my mind off of what's happened to the flag on the Painted Rock."

"Is *that* what's been bothering you?" Sarah asked incredulously.

"Hear me out," Noah answered quickly. "You know I'm not one of those 'my country, love it or leave it' kind of guys, but on 9/11 when we were attacked on our home soil and that rock was painted with the flag of our nation within a matter of days, I felt a renewed sense of pride for the time I had spent in the Coast Guard. I believe in this country, and I hate to see people take their freedoms for granted. It really irritates me that young men fight and die to protect some idiot's right to trash the very symbol of our freedom."

"I never knew you felt so strongly about it," responded Sarah, slightly confused, "but if you don't mind my asking, what brought this on tonight? Here? On our honeymoon?"

"God, I must really seem like a nutcase," Noah laughed out loud and hugged her. "I've always equated protecting my country with taking care of my loved ones. I never had anybody to protect before who meant so much to me. I guess I just want you to know that I'm a decent man and that I stand for something. It hurts when somebody makes a mockery of what I believe in, and I won't put up with it."

"Noah, I knew you were a decent man when I agreed to marry you, and I really do admire your patriotism, but I think it's a little misplaced," answered Sarah, the former schoolteacher. "After all, it's not your rock."

"Don't you think it's disrespectful?" Noah asked somewhat emotionally.

"Yes, I do," Sarah replied, "but like you said, that's one of the freedoms you swore to defend—the right to paint your own slogans in this world."

"I think the flag belongs on that rock as a symbol of our appreciation for what others have sacrificed for our freedom," Noah pronounced.

"Okay, but I have a question: What was the first thing ever painted on that rock?" Sarah wanted to know.

"I'm not sure," Noah replied. "It was probably graffiti, a declaration of high school love, something like that, and over the years it's been used to honor holidays, rites of passage and all kinds of things, but I thought we had finally all agreed on something worthwhile to paint on it, and I don't want to let that be destroyed."

"If we had all agreed on it," mused Sarah, "Then no one would have tried to destroy it. I'll tell you what I think."

"That I am nuts?" asked Noah.

"No. I think the only way to decide what really belongs on that rock is to find out who painted it first."

"It might be easier for me to learn to shut up and enjoy Atlantic City," Noah admitted.

"That'll do for now," smiled Sarah as she kissed him on the cheek.

6

The Key

"**I** want to thank you for coming out on such short notice," greeted McAllister Jones, extending his hand to Tom Banks. "I see you brought the volunteers I asked for."

They were standing along the side of Route 539 about a quarter-mile south of the Painted Rock. Six young boy scouts tumbled out of the back of Tom's Chevy Suburban carrying large plastic trash bags and long pointed sticks. Geoffrey Martin climbed out of the front passenger seat and yawned.

"Your message said it was urgent," said Tom as they started walking up the road toward the rock. The scouts followed in single file with Geoffrey in the lead, a metal detector slung over his shoulders like a rifle.

"Did I say urgent?" replied Reverend Jones, somewhat bemused. "Well, uh … what I meant was that it is *extremely* important to have the site cleaned up before the 4th. We wouldn't want the tourists to see this eyesore on their way to boosting our economy, now would we? By the way, why did the Martin boy bring along a metal detector?"

Tom chuckled as he looked over his shoulder at Geoffrey. "It was Libby Ashcroft's idea. Seems to be she's always prospecting for something."

"Like a husband, perhaps?" Jones said with a devilish grin.

"Don't look at me, Reverend," Tom said defensively. "You're barking up the wrong tree on that score."

"Well, I'll be damned …" said Reverend Jones, caught off guard by what was right in front of them. "I mean, w-what do you think of *that*?" he stammered.

The roadside procession stopped dead in its tracks. Everyone stared in disbelief at the freshly painted rock, once again draped in an American flag, done in bold yet meticulous brush strokes.

The scouts dropped their tools, took out their digital pocket cameras and scurried about, taking photographs of the controversial and ever-changing monument.

Tom gave Reverend Jones a severe look. "Did you know about this?" he demanded.

"I had no idea," replied Jones.

Tom walked over and examined the rock. It was about the size of a small table, only lumpy and curved. It was obviously solid and looked heavy. The side of the rock facing the road came to a point like a ship's prow, with the blue field of white stars occupying a place of prominence on the top. Thirteen alternating red and white stripes undulated horizontally around the rock on all sides. Tom counted the fifty delicately painted white stars.

"Pretty professional job," he said, running his hand along the boulder's smooth spine.

"So it is," replied Reverend Jones, viewing it from the road, obviously impressed.

Several cars whizzed by and honked. The reverend responded to each with an exaggerated wave and toothy smile.

Tom divided the scouts into two teams of three and he and Geoffrey each supervised a team. They fanned out in opposite directions, collecting and bagging the assorted litter, paper, bottles, cans and other debris as they went along.

"Don't wander off too far," Tom cautioned the group.

Reverend Jones removed two yellow ribbons from his bible. They were cut in the shape of a cross. He hung them on the pine tree nearest the road, to the left of the rock.

"What's that for?" inquired Tom, not hiding his disapproval.

"Always looking for any opportunity to do a little work for the Lord," Reverend Jones replied with a sheepish grin.

"Nature is its own divinity," Tom said, annoyed. "The trees have no need of human symbols to achieve grace."

"The symbols are not for them," argued Jones.

Tom was about to say something else when one of the scouts in Geoffrey's troop let out a scream. Geoffrey was standing about twenty feet away from the scout, in a deep hollow, sweeping the ground with the metal detector. With the headset on, he had not heard the scream.

Geoffrey caught sight of Tom in flight. He put down his equipment and hustled over to see what was going on.

Tom and McAllister Jones were huddled together with the scouts. The screaming scout, the youngest in the group, was pointing to something on the sandy ground. All the kids were talking excitedly amongst themselves.

Tom's keen eye studied the small mound of bones. He looked around for tracks. Slowly he bent down to examine more closely.

"Chicken bones," he pronounced. "About three weeks old."

Tom jumped up and sprinted over to a nearby hedgerow, while the scouts watched with their mouths wide open. He reached into the thicket and pulled out a discarded Colonel Sanders Kentucky Fried Chicken bucket.

"Looks like somebody had a picnic," he said, stuffing the bucket into the youngster's garbage bag. "Okay, excitement's over. Let's get back to work." He gave Geoffrey a stern look.

"Sorry," Geoffrey mouthed.

Tom shook his head. "Try to be more observant, Geoffrey," he chided, winking.

"So what do you know about this rock, Tom?" Jones asked casually as Tom buried the bones in the sand.

Tom shrugged. "Same as everyone else," he said. "No one knows how long it's been here or how it got here. There are rumors that two adulterous lovers committed suicide on this spot and that a great Indian chief is buried under it."

"Or maybe Jimmy Hoffa," Jones snickered. "But you don't buy any of it?"

Tom wiped the dirt from his hands on the back of his jeans as they started walking back to the rock. He stood for a long moment collecting his thoughts.

"When I was a kid I used to come this way every year with my dad. We'd pass the Painted Rock on our way to Tuckerton, where we would fish for fluke and snapper blues. Geez, even the blowfish were still around in those days. The Painted Rock was always a landmark for us. It meant we were getting closer to our destination. It was a thrill and a surprise to see what was painted on it. There was always something different.

"I remember one summer when we went by it: the rock had the most beautiful bouquet of red roses covering it. They looked so real I thought they were, but my dad insisted it was just paint. He told me he had read about an auto accident only a week or two earlier, right here on this spot. Some teenagers were out joyriding in a convertible and they crashed into something—presumably another car, although that was never verified. One kid died. One or two others were injured. My dad didn't recall the names."

"Yeah, I've heard that story, too" admitted Jones. "But I thought it was just another one of those legends of the Pines."

Tom took a moment to survey the surrounding woods and drink in the gloriously bright June day. He watched quietly as the kids picked up the scattered trash that had been tossed out of passing cars.

"There actually is also an old Lenape legend," he began thoughtfully, "that was told to me by one of the tribal elders one night awhile back as we sat rocking in our chairs and smoking pipes outside of Albert Music Hall. He told me that the Painted Rock guards the gateway to a very special place in the woods beyond: a spiritual place where the Lenape once held sacred ceremonies in tribute to nature and to the abundance of game, fish, and fowl that fed their families and allowed the tribe to survive. There would be chanting and drumming and feasting. The medicine man or shaman would ritually summon their animal brothers and sisters to join them in celebration. According to the elder who told me this story, during the ceremony animals transformed themselves into humans and vice versa."

Jones could not restrain his laughter. "What a load of rubbish, Banks!" he exclaimed.

"You think so?" Tom countered.

"What, you believe that primitive crap? Animals shape-shifting into humans?" Jones asked incredulously.

"Is that any harder to accept than a virgin birth or a body's resurrection from the dead?"

"Those beliefs are a matter of faith, Tom. What you're suggesting is nothing more than pagan superstition. Next you'll ask me to believe this rock has a *soul*," Jones added dismissively.

Just then a giant Ocean County Waste Management garbage truck arrived with a noisy hiss of hydraulic brakes. Black-gray exhaust from an enormous pipe belched high into the air.

"I see you've thought of everything, Reverend," said Tom.

Tom blew his whistle, signaling the troops to cease work for the day. All the kids came running, bags and spears in hand.

Tom put his arm around Geoffrey Martin's shoulder. He was still lugging the metal detector and looking rather dejected.

"So what treasures did you scoop up for Madame Curator?" Banks asked Geoffrey as they made their way back to the Suburban.

"Thirty cents," said Geoffrey, "and this." He produced an old rusty key and linked chain from his pocket.

"Hmm," mused Tom, turning the piece over in his hand. "Now that's interesting."

"What's interesting?" inquired Geoffrey curiously.

"The initials on the metal cap that's attached to this key chain." Tom scraped away some of the dirt and handed it back to Geoffrey.

Geoffrey read the inscription aloud: "It looks like 'To P. M. from S ... uh ... F'? Do you know whose initials they are?" Geoffrey asked hopefully.

"Nope," replied Tom. "But that's a key from an old Ford, I can tell you that. I know because my father owned a 1959 Ford Country Squire. Same kinda key. See the Ford insignia?"

"And the little cap?" asked Geoffrey with growing interest.

"I'll betcha there was once a lucky rabbit foot dangling from it," said Tom.

7

English Tea and Scones

Kelly Martin traveled Long Beach Boulevard often. It was the main road that ran the full length of the island, but she couldn't remember the last time she had driven the stretch that crossed over the causeway from Ship Bottom into Surf City and beyond to the north.

It was a scenic route, Kelly noted, as the mixed residential-commercial landscape of Surf City, with its freshly painted gray-blue water tower, gave way to the sparsely populated North Beach environs. North Beach was one of the narrowest points on the island, where it was said that a person could stand in the middle of the boulevard and view the ocean on one side and the bay on the other, simply by turning his head.

Noah Parsons had told Kelly and Geoffrey that the farther north one traveled on the island, the more affluent and expensive the homes became. Harvey Cedars, the next little hamlet that Kelly drove through, boasted some of the most exclusive homes as did its tiny neighbor, Loveladies. Many were hidden from view by strategically overgrown vegetation and gated, winding private lanes. The most expensive was an 8,000-square-foot, 8-bedroom estate that carried a $10 million price tag. Kelly had no idea what a $10 million home looked like, but Danny assured her it made the Gatsby House look like a broom closet.

At last Kelly reached her destination, Barnegat Light at the northern tip of LBI. Here she noted the homes were more humble and conventional than the eclectic styles she had glimpsed on the ride through North Beach, Harvey Cedars, and Loveladies. She pulled her Mini Cooper up to the address Sally Lawson had given her. The beachfront home was a large gabled Victorian with weathered cedar shakes and a round portico porch.

Kelly parked in front of the house and bounded up the high wooden steps leading to the porch. The day was bright and sunny, and her cheerful mood matched the weather perfectly. She was excited by the prospect of chatting with Sally, a woman she'd felt strangely drawn to ever since the older woman first extended an invitation to her at Aunt Sarah's wedding. With Sarah and Noah recently back from their brief honeymoon in A.C., Kelly had the opportunity to leave the gift shop for the first time in nearly a week. Sally was delighted when Kelly called, saying she couldn't wait to see her again.

Porch chimes tinkled sweetly in the cool ocean breeze as Kelly rang the doorbell. After a slight pause, Sally appeared behind the screen door and led Kelly into the foyer.

"So nice of you to visit," said Sally with genuine warmth. She was dressed in a pair of khakis and leather sandals, with a navy crew neck T-shirt covered by a wrinkled white smock that hung open. Her delicate hair was swept up in the back and tucked under a frayed straw sun hat. She was a study in casual sophistication, but she had obviously been working at something.

"I hope I'm not interrupting anything," Kelly said.

"Not at all, my dear. It's such a lovely day. I've been out on the back deck painting. Come have a look?"

She took Kelly by the arm and led her through the living room.

"Have you recovered from the excitement at wedding reception, Ms. Lawson?" Kelly asked.

"Please call me Sally, and yes, I'm feeling much better. I don't know what came over me."

"That man, the maintenance man?" Kelly began. "It was like you'd seen a ghost."

Sally slowed her pace but kept moving. "Yes, it did seem like that, didn't it? I guess I was just … startled."

"Mrs. Ashcroft told Noah that the man hasn't reported back to work since that night," said Kelly, looking for a reaction.

If Sally was surprised by that news, she didn't show it. "Did Noah happen to mention his name?"

"No," Kelly admitted. "I didn't ask." She stopped suddenly and stared at a model boat resting on the fireplace mantel.

"Recognize that boat?" asked Sally with a mischievous smile. "It's a longliner."

"I think I've seen it before," Kelly said.

"It's my late husband's flagship, the, *Lorelei*," Sally said proudly. "Ever see the movie, 'The Perfect Storm'?"

"Yes!" exclaimed Kelly. "That's it!"

"The *Lorelei* was used in the film," added Sally. "The producers presented Jack with this scale model as a token of their appreciation. John Jr. pilots her these days."

"You have children?" Kelly asked, surprised.

"Two. Stepsons. They're actually men now," she was quick to add. "Billy is the younger," she motioned to a picture on the mantel. "He manages the fish market in Viking Village at Barnegat Light. Almost every restaurant on the island gets their fresh fish from him."

The two women made their way through the dark, cool house to the rear terrace. The large redwood stained deck opened out onto a crested dune, providing Kelly with a sparkling panorama of the beach. An easel, brushes soaking in a jar, and scattered paint tubes were off to one side. "May I?" inquired Kelly, taking a peek at the work in progress.

"Certainly," said Sally, smiling. "I don't often get to show off my artwork."

The picture was like a photograph of the seascape in front of them, with every detail captured perfectly.

"I'm no expert," admitted Kelly demurely, "but this is exquisite. Do you paint for a living?"

"Oh, heavens, no," said Sally blushing. "I used to paint a lot when I was your age. I had a wonderful instructor—a fellow student. He was the real master. I'm only now getting back into it."

"Well if you're this good and he's the master, I'd love to see *his* work," Kelly said enthusiastically. "Is he still painting?"

"I don't know," replied Sally sadly. "We lost touch after high school graduation." She beckoned Kelly to take a seat in one of the wide-backed Adirondack chairs. "Make yourself comfortable."

"Thank you," said Kelly, sliding back into one of the chairs facing the ocean.

"I was just about to have a snack," Sally said cordially. "Care to join me?"

Kelly admitted she was famished. She had skipped lunch to rush over for their visit.

Sally disappeared into the kitchen and returned shortly, carrying a serving tray laden with a steaming teapot, cups, and some biscuity looking things. Kelly didn't know what to make of them.

"Scones," said Sally. "In nineteen years of marriage, the only vacation Jack and I ever took was to Great Britain. I acquired a taste for proper English tea and scones." She poured Kelly a cup of Earl Grey and pointed to the plate. "Try one."

"How old were you, when you got married?"

"Can I just say that I was 'in my prime' and leave it at that?" Sally responded slowly and with mild amusement.

Fearing that she might have offended her hostess, Kelly was quick to explain, if a bit awkwardly. "I didn't mean to pry or offend you. It's just that I think I'm a lot like you for some reason and I was wondering what took you so long. I mean …" She continued to trip all over herself in a nervous effort to speak tactfully. "Was he your first love, or was he the love of your life … and can they be one and the same, or did you have to wait for him?"

"That's an odd way to put it," replied Sally with a gentle laugh. "But yes. I guess I had to wait for him."

"That's me: Odd," Kelly said with a self-deprecating shrug of her shoulders.

Sally sat down beside her.

"Sometimes, love comes when you least expect it, Kelly," Sally counseled her new friend. "I'm sure you won't have to wait too long. That is, if it hasn't already found you."

Kelly gulped her tea before asking sheepishly, "Why does it have to be so complicated?"

The two women chatted for more than an hour, enjoying the conversation and each other's company, pausing now and then to take in the view of the beach. With the sun starting to wane, Kelly thanked her hostess and got ready to leave.

"Oh, I almost forgot," she said, placing her teacup back on the tray. "Noah asked me to remind you about the 4th of July picnic. You're coming, right?"

"I wouldn't think of missing it."

"Good. I told Geoffrey and Danny that I wouldn't be going to the fireworks, if you came to the picnic."

"That's nonsense, Kelly," Sally said scolding her in fun. "You can do both. The picnic is during the day; the fireworks are at night. You should definitely go."

"You wouldn't mind?"

"Of course not," Sally chuckled. "You're young. Go … enjoy life."

They strolled along the neatly trimmed walkway in silence until they reached the front of the house, where Kelly's car was parked.

"By the way, how is that charming young brother of yours? I thought he might come by with you today."

"He went with Mr. Banks. Reverend Jones asked them to help tidy up the area around the Painted Rock for the tourists."

Sally's mood suddenly darkened. "Please tell Geoffrey to stay away from there. That rock is cursed!"

8
Coincidence?

Geoffrey closed his laptop and pushed it aside. He stared across the table at his sister, not quite certain he had heard her correctly. They were with their parents in a secluded booth at the Gateway Restaurant, near the causeway leading out of Ship Bottom.

"She actually said the rock was 'cursed'?" Geoffrey repeated incredulously. "Why would she say something like that?"

"Maybe she was referring to some other rock, dear?" offered Margaret Martin offhandedly.

Kelly made a face and stated matter-of-factly, "Mom, there is only one Painted Rock."

"That's not entirely true, Kelly," Robert Martin spoke up. He continued, while idly stirring his drink with a cocktail straw, "One of the best known rock art sites is in southern California at a place called the Carrizo Plain. The painted rock there dates back to 1876 and is perhaps one of the finest examples of Native American pictographs in existence. Chumash, if memory serves me."

"Don't you mean petroglyph, Dad?" corrected Geoffrey, stuffing a dinner roll into his mouth.

"No, son," admonished Mr. Martin. "Pictographs are images painted on rocks, as is the case with the one you and Tom Banks cleaned around today. Petroglyphs are symbols carved *into* the stone."

"I just don't understand it. This isn't one of your archeological wonders, Robert. Can anyone tell me what the attraction to this stupid rock is?" asked Mrs. Martin, exasperated by the subject. "Poor Sarah says Noah is obsessed with it."

"The rock is controversial right now, Mom," answered Geoffrey. "It's dividing people into two factions: those who oppose American involvement in Iraq and those who support it."

"Perhaps that's what Sally Lawson meant when she said the rock was cursed," his father suggested, as the waiter arrived with the soup and salad course.

"Mmm," enthused Mr. Martin, as he took a taste of the New England clam chowder. "*That's* what I call good soup," he said, diving in for another spoonful.

"Chow-dah," teased his wife. "According to Noah that's what they call it on the island and he did say this place has the best around. Mmm, that *is* good!" she concurred after tasting.

"Well, I don't know what anyone else thinks about it," Kelly said softly, picking at her chicken caesar salad. "But there's something very strange about that rock. I mean, where did it come from? What's it doing way out there on Route 539?"

Geoffrey spun his laptop back toward him and popped it open. "That's what I've been researching." He brushed the crumbs from his dinner roll off the keypad. "My guess is that the composition of the underlying rock—if you could see beneath all that paint—is pure granite."

"Granite because it is impervious to the long-term effects of salt water," their father added, nodding his head and enjoying the direction this dinner table conversation was taking, even if his wife had tuned it out while she concentrated on her meal.

"Exactly, Dad," replied Geoffrey, full of excitement. "Very durable. No fissures or fractures: solid through and through. I'm convinced that at one point in time our Painted Rock was bound for LBI to become part of a jetty."

"But how did it end up where it is?" demanded Kelly, forcefully spearing a leaf of lettuce.

Geoffrey and his dad looked at each other, waiting to see who would answer Kelly's question first.

"It fell off the truck," they blurted out together, father and son both laughing with glee.

"In fact," added Geoffrey, tapping at the keys on his notebook again, "based on a list of possible quarry sites within a 50-mile radius, I would have to say that this rock—if not all of the jetty rocks—most likely came from the stone quarry in Kingston, New Jersey."

"Sourland Mountains," acknowledged Mr. Martin thoughtfully. "But why not the New Hope quarry, son? It is closer and a quick trip down the Delaware by barge," quizzed his father.

"Because those are sandstone and limestone sites, Dad," responded Geoffrey confidently. "Soft rocks. They don't mine trap rock like granite there."

"Well said," agreed Mr. Martin, proudly.

"Ahem," Kelly cleared her throat. "Aren't you two forgetting something?"

Even Margaret put down her fork to listen to her daughter's next point. "Why there? Why did the rock fall off the truck—if that is your hypothesis—at that exact spot and not at an intersection, around a bend, or while making a turn somewhere? I've been to the spot. Remember, Geoffrey? I saw it. The road there is perfectly flat and straight. How do you account for the fact that the rock landed in such an unlikely spot, in an upright position facing the road?"

Her father and brother looked at her dumbfounded. Neither of them had considered these questions in their methodical approach to solving the riddle of the rock. Margaret Martin broke the silence as the waiter arrived with their entrées.

"Coincidence?" she smiled, winking at her daughter as if they shared the glory of stumping their own little scientific community.

***

The moldy old wooden door creaked open slowly, and from inside the dark recesses of the room, a man's coarse and unpleasant voice crept forward, strengthening to ward off an intruder: "Who goes there?"

"It's only me," the rheumy-eyed old maintenance man whispered his reply, stepping into the room cautiously and closing the door quietly behind him.

"I told you never to come here," the hoarse voice in the darkness replied sharply, then cracked while asking, "What do you want?"

"I saw her," the intruder said in a low voice.

"Saw who?"

"Sally ... Sally Parker."

The man in the darkness stirred. "Where?"

"At work," the groundskeeper said.

"Did she see you?" the voice in the darkness demanded.

The visitor hesitated.

"Did she see you?" the menacing voice repeated.

"Yes," said the man, sighing.

The man in the darkness coughed.

"Did she recognize you?" the hidden man hissed.

"I think so," the maintenance man said in a worried voice.

Dead silence spread out over the dank, mildewed room.

"Did you hear me?" asked the rheumy-eyed workman stepping further into the room, swiping cobwebs out of his way as he proceeded.

"Stay where you are," the unseen man's voice froze him in his place. The harsh dry tone gave way to another round of mild coughing. "What happens now?" he managed to spit out between the hacking.

The known but unwelcome visitor squinted into the darkness. "You can't hide out here forever," he argued, cautiously.

"Why not?" the angry reply reverberated off the empty walls.

"The place is up for public auction."

"So what? They tried that before. Nobody's interested."

"This time they have a buyer," the groundskeeper retorted.

"Who?" barked the aching voice in the darkness.

"The publisher of the *Island Sentinel*. And he's got the money. Says he wants to renovate the place and move in with his family."

"Then you know what to do."

The maintenance man grew flustered. "No, I won't. I ... I can't!" he stammered.

An empty bottle whizzed through the darkness and shattered at the man's feet. "You have no choice," the voice commanded.

The workman fidgeted, rubbing his hand on his leathery, whisker-stubbled face. "I don't care," he said softly. "I've had enough."

There was a scraping sound from the depths of this dark and eerie place. The shadowy man stood up uneasily. A wooden chair came hurtling across the room. The maintenance man ducked. The chair splintered in a half dozen jagged pieces against the wall.

"You can't frighten me anymore," said the old workman, summoning his courage. "It's over."

"It's over when *I* say it is!" the man in the darkness shouted angrily. He coughed and wheezed uncontrollably.

"For God's sake, man. Listen to you. You need help," the workman pleaded. "You're wasting your life."

"No!" bellowed the voice of a wounded animal in the darkness. "*You* wasted my life. And others that were even more important."

9

Fireworks

Noah Parsons stood behind the hot, smoky outdoor grill, spatula in hand, perspiring in the afternoon sun. Dressed in a red, white and blue cooking apron and a puffy white chef's hat, he looked like a cross between Wolfgang Puck and Uncle Sam. Robert Martin was his willing assistant with hands full of chicken and ribs, which he lined up meticulously for the perfect degree of exposure to the smoldering hickory flames.

"Why is it that men take charge of a barbecue, but when it comes to kitchen duty it's women's work?" asked Libby Ashcroft without expecting a response. She was supervising the festivities from her lawn chair, drink in hand, along with several other party guests on the private boat dock overlooking the bay behind the Crab Cove Gift Shop.

"It must be a guy thing," Sarah Bishop-Parsons observed, setting paper plates and plastic utensils down on the patriotically decorated, long redwood picnic table.

"Oh, I think it goes deeper than that," Margaret Martin chimed in handing Sally Lawson an iced tea. "I think it's a primitive ritual dating back to Neanderthal man's need to control the fire pit in the cave. Otherwise we might realize what helpless creatures they really are." She waved at her husband Robert, who was busy wiping the tears from his smoke-filled eyes.

All the women giggled.

"Pay no attention to these feminist theories, children," McAllister Jones pronounced in his best preacher's voice, as he sat beside his wife Mildred on the veranda. "They simply can't take the heat of an open fire."

"The hell we can't," muttered Libby Ashcroft under her breath.

Kelly, Danny, Geoffrey, and Luz Sanchez weren't paying any attention to the grownup battle of the sexes. They were engaged in a contest of their own as they ran along the waterfront, checking their crab traps.

Kelly hoisted up her wire basket. Two blue claws were climbing over each other trying to escape. "That makes an even dozen for me," she proclaimed.

"Keep 'em coming, Kelly," encouraged Geoffrey. "I can hear the pot a-steaming."

"You go, girl," echoed Luz, her accent hidden in a hip-hop phrase.

"Maybe we should trade places," suggested Danny tactlessly, pulling in his empty line. "You've been monopolizing the hot spot all day."

Luz pulled up her trap. A tiny crab was hanging by a claw on the outside of the basket. Geoffrey lunged for the net and lowered it under the trap just as the crab let go.

"Bravo, Geoffrey," said Luz clapping her encouragement.

"That's no keeper," said Danny. "I can tell that from here."

"Go back and get your *hermano grande*," Geoffrey smiled at Luz before turning the net upside down. "Did I say that right?" he asked her.

"Perfectly," Luz replied, gently taking his hand. They stood close together, watching the little crab plunge back into the bay with a loud plunk.

"Come and get it," announced Noah, removing his cap and carrying a sizzling tray to the table.

The teens left their traps and raced to the chow line.

Beer, wine, and flavored iced teas flowed freely as the party swung into high gear. After mooring his boat, the *Clewless*, dockside, Noah's friend Johnny Longfeather joined the happy group midway through the meal. Tom Banks was fashionably late but there was more than enough food to go around. Much to Danny's chagrin, Kelly's fresh catch seasoned with Old Bay by Aunt Sarah was the hit of the party.

"Where is that adorable Aussie Moss Greenberg keeping himself these days?" Libby Ashcroft asked Danny nonchalantly, helping herself to another serving of Margaret's potato salad.

"He's resting up for this week's ride," offered Danny. "It's pushing him to his limit."

"It's too bad Freeman Morris couldn't join us," added Sally Lawson with genuine disappointment.

"Yeah, it's a shame," replied Noah. "but it seems the widow Walker's gout has been acting up again. Doc had to whip her up a batch of rutabaga tonic on short notice to ease the pain."

"That poor man can't go anywhere without somebody needing him for something," Sally shook her head.

During dinner Reverend Jones and Libby Ashcroft regaled everyone with spirited stories and delightful anecdotes from some of the fabulous LBI 4th of July parties they had attended in the past.

Chief among them was the last fireworks display to be held at Harvey Cedars, in 1998. Reverend Jones recalled for all in vivid detail how an errant windblown ember had set off a chain reaction that resulted in fiery streamers exploding into the large crowd gathered at Sunset Park. Seven people had to be taken to Southern Ocean County Hospital, including two firefighters and two pyrotechnicians with leg injuries and missing fingers.

Johnny Longfeather was working with the EMT squad that night. He recounted how it took the rescue team nearly an hour to dodge and weave through the traffic jam along the Boulevard. He added that the evacuation of the injured would never have been possible if it weren't for the volunteers who walked up and down the bumper-to-bumper traffic, pleading with the alarmed and frazzled tourists to pull over and let the ambulances get through.

"That's why we go to the fireworks display in Beach Haven now," volunteered Mildred as Johnny and her husband concluded their story. She glanced at her husband for approval. When he smiled, she added, "And sometimes we'll go over to Tuckerton just for a change."

"Which do you like better?" Geoffrey quizzed her.

Jones spoke up. "Last year's Beach Haven event was very disappointing," he said. "The fireworks only lasted about ten minutes or so and the climax was a dud."

"I like the rainbow pinwheels, myself," slurred a slightly inebriated Libby Ashcroft to no one in particular. She finished her glass of wine in one swallow. "And those cork-screwy things that spiral 'round and 'round up there in the air. They remind me of spermatozoa," she added with a girlish giggle.

Danny howled as Kelly blushed.

Luz turned to Geoffrey and confessed, "I never knew she was so much fun."

"That's it, you're flagged," laughed Tom Banks, gently taking the glass from Libby's hand. "Time to switch to coffee, Madame Curator," he said passing her a cup he had just poured for himself.

"Speaking of flags," said Mildred with a slightly cautious lilt in her voice, "McAllister has some wonderful news. Don't you dear?"

"I don't know if this is the appropriate time, Mildred …" Jones responded, shifting uneasily in his seat.

"Of course it is," his wife encouraged.

"Come on, Reverend. Out with it!" exhorted Libby.

"Yes, yes, do tell," added Robert Martin.

Jones acquiesced, but gave a measured look across the table at Noah Parsons and Tom Banks before he continued speaking. "I believe I have the solution to our little rock problem," he announced at last.

Noah and Tom appeared unfazed, but the kids perked up and listened intently.

"We all know there are two factions, each claiming the right to display what they believe in on the face of the rock. And it's very divisive. This Hatfield-McCoy type of feud reminds people of the worst stories of the Pines and it is obviously not good for business, so I thought maybe the best thing for everyone would be simply to move the rock."

"Move the rock?" repeated Johnny Longfeather in disbelief.

"For safe keeping," added Mildred Jones.

"Move it where?" asked Tom with a slight edge to his voice.

"Well, that's the beauty of this whole thing," replied Jones slyly. "We can move it out of harm's way—but not far—and put it someplace where even more people can enjoy it than just those few who happen to drive by it now."

"Move it where?" Noah repeated Tom's question.

Jones fidgeted nervously. His wife gave him an encouraging look. "I have a contact—an entrepreneur, actually, from Philadelphia—who is willing to negotiate the rock's removal with the state authorities, shoulder the cost of hauling it away and putting it on display …" Jones hesitated. "On the boardwalk … in Atlantic City."

Noah jumped out of his seat. "Atlantic City!" he roared incredulously.

"Are you out of your mind?" added Tom.

"No way! That is out of the question," fumed Johnny.

"McAllister, you can't be serious!" admonished Sarah Bishop-Parsons.

"Now, wait a minute," said Jones motioning with his arms for calm. "Before anyone blows a gasket, hear me out."

The teens all looked at each other. They could hardly believe their ears.

"The rock is an irritating problem," Jones continued. He stared directly at Noah. "Noah, did you know the flag's been painted black and covered with peace signs and anti-Bush graffiti again?"

"On the 4th of July?" remarked Margaret sadly. Everyone else was thinking the same thing.

"We can end this thing," said Jones. "Arnold Tessler, this Philadelphia businessman I've been talking with, guarantees the rock's safety. He'll put it under bullet-proof glass, if he has to."

Noah sat down slowly. "What does he get out of it, McAllister?"

"The satisfaction of knowing the rock is safe … and a small admission fee."

"Outrageous!" Tom said angrily. "So this is why you wanted the area around the rock cleaned up." He looked at Geoffrey and shook his head.

"And the flag will be repainted on the rock?" Noah inquired.

"Yes, as soon as we can find the right artist," Jones replied without hesitation.

"Noah, you can't be taking this deal seriously!" cried Tom. "The rock belongs in the woods."

"And what do you get out of it, Reverend Jones?" asked Danny coyly.

Jones gave Danny a derisive smile. "The satisfaction of knowing there will be peace in the Pines again."

Sally Lawson had been sitting silently through much of the evening and all of the discussion until now. "Well, I approve of the plan, McAllister," she said at last. "That rock is a menace. It has brought nothing but hardship and bad luck to all who have come into contact with it."

"I second that opinion," hiccuped Libby. "Only Atlantic City is still too close. Reverend, do you think you could talk Tessler into taking it back to Philadelphia with him and putting it next to the Liberty Bell?"

"Well I, for one, disagree with the whole idea," said Kelly, looking carefully at Sally Lawson. "That rock has major significance right where it is. There's something very special about it. I don't know exactly what that is, but I know it's special."

"I agree with Kelly," said Geoffrey. "There is something special about that rock."

"You're both wrong," said Danny. "It's getting entirely too much attention. It's an eyesore. It takes away from the environment."

"Since when did you become an advocate for the environment?" Kelly shot back.

Margaret stared into her daughter's eyes. "Kelly, I'm sorry," she said apologetically. "But I happen to agree with Danny. That rock is getting far too much attention."

"It really is," admitted Aunt Sarah, meeting Noah's confused gaze. "Even here, among family and friends, we can't seem to come to a consensus. Imagine what it's doing to everyone else."

"So it's settled," said Reverend Jones hopefully.

But it wasn't. No one answered him because they were still busy arguing among themselves. No two people could agree on exactly what the right course of action should be. At one point, Robert suggested, "Bury the damn thing and be done with it."

Tom left in disgust after arguing with Noah for seeming to buy into Jones's scheme. Before he left, he reminded Geoffrey to be on time for camp the next day. Libby passed out and had to be carried to the upstairs loft to lie down. The Joneses made a hurried departure, alleging they had another party to attend. Robert and Margaret disappeared to pack for their trip to Samoa in the morning. Kelly and Danny had an unexpected blowout when Kelly learned that Shawna James was now a registered rider for the Tour de Pines. She accused Danny of purposefully withholding the information from her. Danny left in haste while Kelly stormed to her room to sulk.

That left Sally, Johnny, Geoffrey and Luz to help Noah and Sarah clean up. So that the entire evening was not lost, Johnny offered to take Geoffrey and Luz aboard the *Clewless* to view the Beach Haven fireworks. They jumped at the chance. Sally declined the invitation, deciding to stay behind and help mediate a truce between Sarah and Noah.

Despite Sally's attempts at playing peacemaker, Sarah blamed her new husband's obsession with the painted rock for the meltdown of their party. She remained cold and aloof as the night wore on. The party was supposed to have been a festive occasion in which family and friends could come together to celebrate America's independence. Instead, family and friends ended up splitting apart over a relatively petty but rather important issue: the right to self-expression. It seemed things had not changed all that much since 1776.

Sally made one last attempt to salvage the evening and console a new friend. She found Kelly alone in her room, listening to her iPod. Kelly removed her headphones respectfully when Sally knocked and entered her room.

"Want to talk about it?" Sally inquired discreetly.

"There's nothing to talk about," Kelly answered her coolly.

Sally sat down on the bed beside Kelly, taking her hand. "The ones we love the most can also hurt us the most," she began slowly, tears welling in her eyes. "I once loved a boy very much like Danny: impetuous, headstrong ..." She raised her eyebrows and gave Kelly a wry smile, "And *so* good looking. His name was Peter Miller."

Sally stared blankly into Kelly's caring eyes as she continued. "He was an artist, and yes, he was the one who taught me how to paint," she answered Kelly's unspoken question. "Oh, he was brilliant. He even had a full scholarship to study art in France. But then tragedy struck. There was a car accident and he was driving. My brother, Andy, was Peter's best friend, and he was killed."

"It happened at the Painted Rock, didn't it?" asked Kelly, already guessing the answer.

"Yes, it did," replied Sally. "That accident drove us apart. I never saw Peter again after that terrible night. I assumed he went away to art school and never came back. I suppose he just couldn't face me again."

"Does this have anything to do with the man you saw at the wedding reception?" asked Kelly, trying to read the older woman's mournful expression.

"Yes," replied Sally, wiping away a tear.

"Who was he?" pursued Kelly.

"Someone who reminded me of that horrible night. Someone who was in the other vehicle," Sally answered through her pain.

"Have you ever tried to contact Peter?" asked Kelly, gently probing deeper.

"His parents died when he was young. His maternal grandparents raised him, and they moved away when he entered art school."

"So you don't know where he is?" inquired Kelly politely.

"No, I don't even know if he's still alive," said Sally, raising her head and holding back another tear. "I don't think he is," she said at last.

"Why do you say that?" asked Kelly curiously.

"Because he left a message for me on that awful rock," Sally moaned softly. "A silly fantasy we shared. He painted a reminder of where I could find him when he returned from art school. I've gone there so many times over the years longing to see him, yearning for him, but he has never shown up."

"Maybe he doesn't know you got the message?"

"Perhaps," replied Sally thoughtfully. "It was my own brother's blood, smeared all over the rock that made it hard to grasp the message in its entirety. You have no idea how painful that was, but I still wanted to see him. I loved him and I knew he loved me. Somehow, I thought we could overcome anything, even that horrible night."

"Do you still look for him?" asked Kelly.

"Once every week, for the past forty years."

10

When It Rains...

Danny Windsor was annoyed, and the more agitated he became, the harder he pedaled his Cannondale titanium-frame road bike down Route 9. He was heading south from the Oyster Creek Power Plant near Forked River, where he and twenty-nine other riders had spent the night after completing the first leg of the Tour de Pines.

There were five planned legs to this ride, covering approximately 150 miles through three New Jersey counties and lasting a total of five days. Depending on training, individual readiness and time constraints, riders could sign up to cycle specific segments or the entire route. Danny had signed up for the whole trip. So had Johnny Longfeather, who was a perennial rider in the annual event. Shawna James, who had given in to Danny's persistence and charm, agreed to ride the first two junkets, covering about 75 miles. At sixty-four years old, Moss Greenberg, the self-proclaimed "oldest lifeguard on the East Coast," was simply looking to go as far as he could.

The first day of the ride was more ceremonial than grueling, covering only about 30 miles. The Pinelands Preservation Alliance sponsored the ride to raise awareness of the delicate ecological balance of the New Jersey Pine Barrens. It began at the Fort Dix military installation on Route 539 just outside of New Egypt. This specific starting point was chosen by the ride organizers to commemorate the site where a toxic (and until recently, covered up) plutonium spill had occurred in the 1970s.

The riders spent an uneventful night at the Oyster Creek Nuclear Power Plant, where they participated in a peaceful sit-in and handed out pamphlets warning about the potential dangers of a nuclear accident. It was here, while camping out under the stars, that Danny first learned his muscle-bound, mentally challenged old nemesis Curtis Wick was on the ride. In the spirit of the adventure, Danny decided he was okay with that, and everything would have been fine if the two alpha males had kept their distance from one another. But when Danny found Curtis hitting on Shawna, just like he had hit on Kelly the previous summer, tempers flared and sparks flew. Moss and Johnny had to intervene to make sure no blood was spilled.

That was the reason for Danny's foul mood, as Day 2 of the tour began. The main group was already on the road, riding in single file just before dawn. Their destination for that day was Atlantic City, about fifty, relatively flat miles away. There, the group planned an open protest in the mecca of greed and consumption before retiring to a quiet campsite along the Absecon Wetlands. Atlantic City was the end of the road for Shawna unless Danny was successful at persuading her otherwise. At the moment, however, he didn't care. Still reeling from the 4th of July argument he had had with Kelly, and even more annoyed by the events of the night before with Wick, Danny was of a mind to be female-free for the rest of the journey.

The remainder of the ride, as planned, would take the riders on Day 3 from Atlantic City west to Indian Mills in Burlington County, the site of one of the first Native American reservations in the United States. Many of the riders were looking forward to this 50-mile stretch, since it would take them directly through the popular Wharton State Forest. Day 4 would find the hardy riders making the 20-plus-mile junket northeast to Whitesbog, the home of the very first blueberry farm in the United States. Here, a victory celebration was planned to recognize the efforts of the Alliance and the generosity of the White family for recently setting aside a large portion of their former farm as a state-protected natural reserve. The conclusion of the trip, on Day 5, would take the riders back to the Fort Dix area for a barbecue at the Manchester Wildlife Preserve.

The weather added to Danny's irritable mood. Yesterday had been sunny and warm—almost too warm—but today's forecast called for showers, possibly heavy at times. If there was anything an experienced rider like Danny knew, it was to get out of the rain, especially if that rain included thunder and lightning. He wanted to put as much real estate between Oyster Creek and Atlantic City as he could, so he was hammering the pedals hard, leading a pack of riders that included few friends, as far as he was concerned at the moment. While Johnny had no trouble keeping up, Shawna and Moss were obviously struggling.

"Slow down, Danny," Johnny shouted, coming up alongside. "We're losing Moss."

"Please, wait up," added Shawna breathlessly.

Danny turned his head to look back at the group. He glanced up at the sky and indicated to Johnny that he should do the same. "We're in for some serious weather," he said to Johnny. "There's very little cover until we get to Stafford."

"Then you go on ahead, Danny," said Johnny. "I'll stay with the others. You're not going to outrun Mother Nature, and you might end up killing Moss."

Danny nodded and geared up, pulling out ahead of the draft line. Johnny dropped back and re-formed the draft line expertly in front of Shawna and Moss, breaking the headwind for them and creating a nice little pocket where his momentum could pull them along with less effort on their part.

No sooner had Danny broken away than his rear tire went over a shard of glass that, at his speed, he had failed to avoid. The thin racing tire ripped open. He had no choice now but to stop or risk causing damage to the entire wheel. Curtis flipped Danny the bird as he breezed by.

Danny returned the gesture and cursed his luck. This would slow him down despite all the headway he had been making. Stafford was in sight, but his tire needed immediate attention and he knew it would be time-consuming because it involved the back wheel, which meant dealing with greasy chains and gear sprockets.

Johnny Longfeather was all smiles as he and the others slowed to a halt beside Danny and his disabled bike along the side of the road.

"Reminds me of the fable of the tortoise and the hare," quipped Moss, taking a swig from his water bottle.

"Save it," said Danny, trying to control himself. Again he checked the skies. "Listen, this storm is coming in pretty fast. Why don't you guys go on ahead? With any luck

I'll get this puppy on the road in time to meet you in Tuckerton for lunch before it hits. That'll put us about halfway."

"Sounds like a plan," said Johnny. The others agreed.

"Do you need anything?" asked Shawna, wanting to be helpful.

Danny smiled for the first time all day. "We can talk about *that* later," he said with a flirtatious wink.

"Oh, he'll be just fine," said Moss, adjusting his helmet and pedaling away.

"See you at the diner," Johnny called back.

Danny watched as the trio made their way down busy Route 9 into Stafford. When they were out of sight, he turned his attention back to the bike.

Within a half-hour he was back on the road. The rain, which had begun lightly at first, was now steady and relentless. Then it happened. He heard his first roll of thunder followed by the whip-like crack of lightning. He was heading right into it.

Danny knew he was only a couple of miles outside of Tuckerton, but in a thunder and lightning storm a few miles might as well be fifty to a rider on a bike without any protection. The rain began to pummel the road in a torrential downpour. His visibility was bad. The intervals between thunder and lightning quickened, indicating the storm was growing closer and more intense. A car sped by, drenching Danny in its wake. He decided to stop pedaling and run for shelter.

He had a pretty good idea where he was, near the south end of Eagleswood in a tiny one-horse hamlet called West Creek. He thought he could make it to the Post Office, but that was on the opposite side of the road. A bolt of lightning in the trees behind his intended destination sent him scrambling for cover onto the front porch of a long-abandoned, dilapidated building he vaguely remembered as the once prosperous Clark's General Store.

He stood soaking wet and dripping on the porch of the old store when his cell phone rang. It was Moss. The trio had made it to the Dynasty Diner on Main Street in Tuckerton just as the heavens opened up. They were about to order but figured they would wait for Danny if he was close.

The cell phone signal faded in and out with the force of the storm. Danny managed to tell Moss that they should go ahead and order, that he was fine for the moment and that he was going to dry out and have a Powerbar while he waited out the storm, before the satellite connection gave way in a shudder of thunder and a zigzag streak of lightning.

He pulled his bike up onto the porch and out of harm's way, then hunted through his panniers until he found the fortified Powerbar. As he chewed, he stared out past the overgrown vegetation that partially hid the porch from view into a wall of cascading rain. The realization that he was totally and utterly alone turned into a full-body shiver and reminded him that he needed to relieve himself and get into some dry clothes.

Danny finished his snack and yanked his spare biking shirt from his pouch. He looked around the porch and the grounds for a place to pee and change. There was no place that wasn't in the middle of the downpour. He turned around and tried the front door. It wasn't locked, but something was barring it from opening on the inside. He threw his weight into it and the door flung open, ripping a hastily nailed two-by-four from the wall.

"Hello?" he called instinctively into the damp, dark storeroom.

He made his way deeper into the musty, cluttered store, stepping over piles of rubbish and bumping into upended debris. The walls were stocked with rusty cans and dusty packaged goods dating back to a happier time. Heavy cobwebs hung from the light fixtures and ceiling fans.

He walked toward the counter at the far end of the storeroom, hoping to locate an old restroom or some convenient place to urinate. He stopped at the counter and removed his shirt, drying himself with the clean shirt before he put it on. Suddenly he heard a scuffle coming from another room behind the counter.

"Hello? Is anybody there?" he called out nervously. His voice echoed around the empty room.

Danny donned his clean shirt, stuffing his wet one into the waistband behind his back like a tail. Cautiously, he proceeded around the counter toward the other room. The scraping sound came again.

Picking up a ball-peen hammer lying on the counter, Danny raised it up to his shoulder. A large rat scurried out from what turned out to be a stockroom, sliding on the dust and hurrying under the counter. The sudden unexpected movement froze him in place. He composed himself and started forward again. He was about to put the hammer down but thought better of it when another noise from inside the stockroom caught his attention. This time it sounded like a can rolling across the wooden floor.

Danny held the hammer high. He pushed away the cheap nylon curtain that separated the storeroom from the stockroom and entered. The room was almost pitch black, devoid of any windows to let the daylight in. He waited until his eyes adjusted to the light. The stockroom had high shelves on either side covered in the same cheap, faded plastic as the doorway. He spied another door at the end of the room. *Perhaps it leads to a bathroom, or an outhouse*, he thought.

A floorboard creaked as Danny stepped through the doorway. Before he took another step, a row of shelves came tumbling down, pelting him with heavy cans and powdered grains. He fell to the floor with the shelving resting on top of him. With startled eyes from underneath the plastic sheet, he looked up to see a figure looming over him, holding a baseball bat aloft in one hand.

"What's your business here?" the man's voice more bellowed than cracked. "This is private property," he wheezed.

"I needed to get out of the rain," Danny said in a frightened voice. He struggled to remove the dirty shelf.

The grimy man gave Danny a hand with the shelf and helped him to his feet. The man was dressed in a tattered, smelly hooded sweatshirt and soiled army fatigues.

His long scraggly black and gray hair was matted and dirty, matching an unkempt beard. His face was gaunt and hollow but his blue eyes blazed brightly out from behind sunken sockets imparting a feeling of intelligence and a sense of heightened alarm at the same time.

"I'm sorry. I didn't think anybody lived here," said Danny, shakily getting to his feet.

"Nobody does," said the bearded man. "I'm just visiting, same as you," he joked uneasily before entering into a coughing jag that doubled him over. The bat fell from his filthy hand.

How odd, thought Danny, *a bum with a sense of humor?* "Hey, are you all right?"

"I'm fine," the man wheezed, but he remained bent over.

The two men stood there for a moment in silence, listening to the rain pounding down on the roof overhead.

Danny pulled out his cell phone. "Do you want me to call someone for you?" he asked with genuine concern.

The bum did not answer.

"Do you want me to call someone?" Danny asked again, holding out the cell phone.

The man straightened up awkwardly. "Who ya gonna call?" he laughed loudly, parodying the famous Ghostbusters slogan.

"How about 911?"

"How about a name? You got a name, boy?" The voice was raspy and weak.

"Danny Windsor."

"Windsor, you say?" The bum coughed. "I know that name. You Buck Windsor's kid?"

"You knew my dad?" Danny said with a mixture of confusion and excitement.

The bum was swaying back and forth, his eyes fluttering as he struggled to stay conscious. "And your mom, too," he said as he collapsed on the floor.

11

Living Water

It wasn't easy for Tom to convince Noah and Sarah to let Geoffrey spend a week in the woods assisting in his summer program, but oddly enough he got help from the young teen's father. Mr. Martin, the scientist, recognized the value of learning basic survival skills and was intrigued by the notion that these skills would be taught from the perspective of an enlightened Lakota Sioux elder whom Tom referred to as "Grandfather." Tom himself was recognized as an expert local guide and the sponsor, the Children of the Earth Foundation, was a nonprofit organization whose expressed mission was to promote a personal connection between children and nature. Geoffrey had shown a keen interest in environmental science last summer, as a docent at the Tuckerton Seaport. Tom was sure he would make a very capable assistant and learn from the experience, as well. Mr. Martin saw no harm in allowing his son to participate in this adventure.

Another summer adventure was exactly what Mrs. Martin feared and her mind reeled. Last summer in these same woods, Geoffrey had been chased by an illegal poacher who, incidentally, had also kidnapped his sister Kelly and some boy named Curtis Wick before setting fire to a wooded area surrounding Geoffrey, who had only been there to try and save an endangered species of tree frog. So much for the safety of scientific pursuits.

In the end, Tom's reputation and his reassurance that he would keep a close eye on his apprentice had convinced the boy's guardians to let him go. Besides, this was one way to guarantee that the money he earned would go directly into his college fund, since Geoffrey wouldn't have anyplace to spend it in the woods.

Tom, Geoffrey, and half a dozen prepubescent young scouts he affectionately referred to as the "F-Troop" set up camp deep in the Greenwood Forest. It was only a few short miles from the Painted Rock but far enough from civilization that it seemed as if they were in a vast, limitless wilderness. For most of the kids, this was their first time away from home. For all of them, it was their first overnight experience in the woods.

The first day had been spent gathering and constructing the essentials for survival. In the morning, the young scouts paired up and took turns looking for potable drinking water, edible berries and nuts. In the afternoon, Geoffrey demonstrated how to start a fire by rubbing two sticks together, and with Tom's help he showed the scouts how to build an upright cocoon-like shelter out of dried leaves and branches even though this time they would be sleeping in tents.

After an evening meal of corn on the cob and stewed perch, the kids gathered around a huge campfire to drink hot chocolate and roast marshmallows. Tom took advantage of the quiet time to share some of Grandfather's spiritual wisdom with the kids. Later he and Geoffrey had the opportunity to delight them further with tall tales about the fabled Jersey Devil.

Geoffrey was already familiar with most of the stories Tom told, but there was one tale he had never heard before. It was a story Tom had learned from Grandfather about another phantom-like mystery that lived in the Jersey Pines. From time to time, this wonderful creature materialized in the form of a beautiful white stag in order to warn travelers of unexpected dangers that lay in their path.

One of the earliest known stories of the White Stag of Shamong dated back to 1772, when the great white buck had suddenly appeared on the road to warn a stagecoach driver that the bridge leading into town had been washed away by a storm. Startled by the ghostly apparition, the frightened team of horses pulling the stage reared to a sudden stop, throwing the driver to the ground. When he walked ahead to investigate what had spooked his horses, he saw that the bridge was out. Had the team continued, the stagecoach and all of its passengers would have been lost in the raging river.

The White Stag story Grandfather had relayed to Tom was from much more recent times. It involved an eighteen-wheeler and its drowsy driver barreling down a lonely stretch of Route 539 in a thunderstorm. The tractor-trailer was bound for Long Beach Island with a truckload of boulders for a jetty construction project. Had the sleepy driver not slowed and swerved to avoid what he later swore to the authorities was a ghostly white stag standing in the middle of the road, the big truck would have crashed head-on into a stranded disabled vehicle blocking the road a mere fifty yards ahead. As it turned out, the only casualty that night was a solitary rock that shook free and rolled off the truck.

Geoffrey went to sleep that night with visions of a gallant white stag prancing through the pine trees; a runaway stagecoach that morphed into a tractor-trailer weighed down by a big crane affixed to its bed; torrents of pure, clear rainwater with drops the size of gleaming pearls; and the Painted Rock encased in a block of concrete, all dancing in his head. In his dream, Geoffrey saw the rainwater streaming down upon the entombed rock, fine as sand, cleansing it, washing it clean of the caked layers of repressive, symbol-ridden mercury and lead based paint.

When Geoffrey awoke his mind was clear but the sky overhead was dark gray and ominous. When he first saw Tom that morning, he wanted to talk about his dream, but he knew by the threatening look of the sky that they had a lot to do in a very short period of time to be ready for the rain. He followed Tom's lead, taking charge of his troop as if he had done it a million times as he helped them cover their tents with waterproof tarps and plastic runoff sheets.

By mid-afternoon, the camp was drenched, but the campers were dry, thanks to their own hard work in the morning. Geoffrey took the opportunity while the kids slept or played cards—no electronic devices were permitted in the camp—to approach Tom's small, yet efficient hut.

Tom greeted Geoffrey as though he had been expecting him. The two sat Indian-style on deerskin rugs in the lodge while Geoffrey told Tom about his dream. As Geoffrey spoke, Tom crumbled sage leaves into a small fire that glowed before them in a pit, at the center of the hut. The sweet, pungent smoke began to fill the air.

Tom listened patiently, careful not to interrupt Geoffrey until he had finished.

"Well, what does it mean?" Geoffrey asked, unable to hide his excitement.

"What do you think it means?" inquired Tom calmly.

"I was hoping you could tell me," said Geoffrey, "like Grandfather told you."

Tom grew circumspect. "Grandfather taught me to interpret my *own* dreams." He paused thoughtfully. "Geoffrey, you are the only one who can know the meaning of what you saw."

"But it was the white stag," said Geoffrey animatedly. "You know what that means!"

"And so do you, Geoffrey," replied Tom evenly.

"I do?" said Geoffrey, confused and frowning.

"You do," answered Tom, nodding his head for emphasis.

Geoffrey looked around the lean-to. The small fire separating them glowed red as he stared into it. Tom sprinkled more sage leaves onto the embers and leaned back.

Geoffrey looked to Tom for help. His mentor's eyes were closed as he said, almost trance-like, "In traditional legends, white is often associated with purity, innocence, or hope. The form doesn't matter much."

Geoffrey straightened up. "Like the white knight?" he asked tentatively.

"Like the white knight," agreed Tom remotely.

"It's me, isn't it?" asked Geoffrey as if a light bulb in his head had been switched on. "Am I the White Stag in my dream?"

Tom smiled knowingly but said nothing.

"And the truck," Geoffrey added. "The stag is trying to warn the truck of some impending danger, just like in Grandfather's story," he finished quickly.

"Maybe the truck *is* the danger," Tom said.

"To what?" Geoffrey pondered. Then his eyes flew open wide as the answer to his own question came to him. "To the rock! The truck is a danger to the rock! It's going to crash into it!"

Tom leaned forward and smiled, taking it all in. He was clearly enjoying his role as mentor and knew intuitively what the role entailed. If the student was to learn anything he had to find the answers for himself.

Geoffrey stood up and paced, his excitement growing. "The water, what about the water?" he repeated out loud, searching for an answer, thrilled by the challenge and feeling wonderfully alive. He began listing all the forms of water he could think of off the top of his head. "Rainwater, flood water, waterfalls, showers, pools, rivers, oceans, lakes, streams, and seas." He repeated his list, this time pausing after each of the things he mentioned, reflecting on its intrinsic beauty. He was already feeling more in touch with nature and he liked it a lot.

His guide shared his enthusiasm. "Water is one of the sacred elements," said Tom unhurriedly, but with conviction. "Perhaps, it is the most sacred of all."

Tom stood up and took two water bottles out of his pack. He gave one to Geoffrey. "Come with me," said the teacher to his student.

They left the shelter of the hut unnoticed. Walking in the rain, they passed a narrow brook that ran behind the camp and emptied into a small freshwater pond. Tom talked as they walked. "Water is in the air we breathe, in the food we eat."

Tom stopped near the edge of the pool. He took a sip from the bottle. Geoffrey followed suit. "It nourishes us, even as it cleanses us."

Tom swept his arms over the pond and continued his soliloquy. "Water speaks to us and if we would only listen, we could learn from water. It connects us to all things and all things to us."

They drank again, together this time, reaching down into the pond to cup a handful of the cool liquid from the pool. Geoffrey closed his eyes and felt the water tingle and almost sing to him as it flowed through his body, down into his empty stomach, pulsing through his veins and arteries, even into the tiniest cells of his fingers, his toes and his hair. The sensation was electrifying.

"Water is life. Water is alive," Tom's faint voice was saying. "Bathe yourself in the purity—in the truth, in the knowledge—of living water."

Geoffrey opened his eyes and looked out into the pond, lingering on Tom Banks's words and letting his imagination run. He was stunned by what he saw and felt. He was no longer separate from nature. He was part of it. His eyes were the eyes of nature itself, seeing what they saw. Through them he watched the drops of rain fall from the heavens and splash into the pond. Each drop, when it hit the surface of the water, created a tiny wave that widened into a circle; then another circle formed inside the first, then another and another, the concentric circles spreading wider and wider until the outermost ring merged with another wave circle formed by a different drop, and so on and so on, until the pond was one vast pool rippling with life and reaching out to join other raindrops from other pools, lakes, streams, and rivers, meeting at last in one ever-expanding, distant ocean.

Geoffrey had witnessed all of this, unfolding like a slow motion film in front of him. He had not thought about what he was seeing, but somewhere deep inside, he had realized that we are all raindrops falling on this planet bonding with other raindrops forming families, communities, and civilizations. All working and moving together on the same journey toward some greater unknown.

The vision finally passed, and for a time Geoffrey found himself drifting in a state of semi-consciousness. When he became aware of himself and his surroundings again, he immediately thought back to his dream of the night before. "But how can water clean concrete?" he asked Tom with a puzzled expression, reaching back to something more familiar, if still unexplained.

Tom understood his young protégé's dilemma. He looked up at him with a smile and gently offered, "This is *your* vision, Geoffrey. You need to figure it out. Go to the rock and purify yourself with sacred water. Learn what it is you need to know."

12

Legion of Doom

Danny Windsor stood over the fallen derelict, uncertain as to what he should do. This bum wasn't his problem. The rain was slowing down. He should just empty his bladder, jump on his bike, and leave. If he pedaled hard enough, he could join the others and finish the ride like he planned.

But for some reason, that thought troubled him. Nothing about this ride was going right. First Kelly and Geoffrey bailed on him. And even though *he* was the one who had convinced Shawna to come along, she paid more attention to Curtis Wick's sorry-ass advances than she ever did to Danny's half-hearted efforts. *Maybe she knows they're half-hearted*, he thought in retrospect. It didn't matter. She was leaving the tour when it reached Atlantic City anyway, and good riddance.

The flat tire and drenching rain had done more than take the wind out of his sails. It had knocked him off his game, completely. But why did he seek refuge in this rundown general store of all places and not across the street at the Post Office? What unknown force had guided him here to this place, at this precise moment? It was downright unsettling.

And what about this man? He was obviously sick. Maybe even dying. But who was he and how did he know Danny's parents? He even knew their first names. Danny's mind seesawed back and forth as he played over the events leading up to this point. Had this guy tried to hurt him? No, he'd seemed as afraid of Danny as Danny was of him. He's s just some old kook, holed up in a boarded-up shack, trying to protect himself.

Danny bent down over the fallen figure lying motionless on the dirty, damp floor. As a one-time certified lifeguard, he was trained in CPR and other life-saving techniques. He checked the man's pulse. It was almost imperceptible. He needed help quickly.

Danny took out his cell phone and dialed 911. When the dispatcher came on, he gave her all the information he could. "Whatever you do, don't leave him," were the woman's last words. *Easy for you to say*, thought Danny.

Next, he dialed Moss Greenberg. They were already back on the road. He explained his situation.

"Do you need help?" asked Moss.

"No, the paramedics should be here shortly."

"Does he want us to ride back there?" he heard Johnny ask Moss. Moss repeated the question into the phone.

"No, you guys go on before it starts raining again," Danny said. "I'll be fine. I'll catch up with you in Atlantic City—if not before," he joked. "Thank God you guys ride as slow as you do." He was on the verge of asking to speak to Shawna but thought better of it. "I gotta go. I think the EMTs are here."

***

Kelly Martin analyzed the rusty key chain her brother had found the day he and the scouts had pulled cleanup duty at the Painted Rock. Geoffrey had showed it to her and shared Tom Banks's insight regarding the make of the car and the rabbit foot. She hadn't thought much about it until after her 4th of July conversation with Sally Lawson, when she started to make the connection. Eventually she realized that the inscription wasn't "To P.M. from S.F." but rather "To P.M. from S.P." *To Peter Miller from Sally Parker!*

Her mind screamed, realizing that part of the P had worn away, leaving an F behind. She laughed, remembering that Geoffrey called his scouts the "F" troop and they had found it near where Danny stopped to take a "P." Once she had it all figured out, she knew she had to go see Sally *Parker* Lawson.

Kelly rang the doorbell. At length, Sally came to the door and peered through the screen. "Kelly, what a pleasant surprise. Come in, come in. To what do I owe this honor?" she asked amiably, letting Kelly in. Once again, she was dressed for yard work.

"I think I have something that once belonged to you," said Kelly, holding the key and key chain out in front of her.

Sally's eyes widened. "Oh my!" she exclaimed, taking the key chain from Kelly and examining it closely. A mist formed over her eyes, a mist as faint as the glow from the memory of the last time she saw that key ring. "Won't you please come in," she managed to say, motioning Kelly toward the parlor.

"I haven't seen this in forty years," Sally said as they sat down on the sofa together. Tears began to fill her eyes. "Wherever did you find it?" she asked in a voice choked with emotion.

This time it was Kelly who reached for Sally's hand to console her. "Geoffrey found it near the Painted Rock, using Libby Ashcroft's metal detector. It was buried in the sand."

"I gave it to Peter as a high school graduation present to go along with the car his grandparents had just bought for him. That car was his 'baby'—a candy apple red Mustang convertible. He was going to leave it with me until he came back from France."

She pulled a tissue from her sleeve and dabbed at her eyes. Kelly had noticed that they were already red when she had first opened the door.

"You've been crying, haven't you?" asked Kelly without judgment.

"Yes." Sally blew her nose. "Foolish, isn't it? You would think a grown woman would have moved on, after all these years."

"He must have really been something," Kelly offered. "If he meant so much to you that you still think about him after all these years, then you had to mean something special to him, too. Why hasn't he come back for you?"

"I wish I knew the answer to that, my dear. But I'm afraid I'm in the dark as much as you are. After the accident he just disappeared, vanished off the face of the earth. I prayed for him to come back so I could tell him I still loved him, that I didn't blame him for what had happened, but he never gave me the chance."

"What about the maintenance man you ran into? Could he have stayed in contact with Peter?"

"Eddie Farley?" said Sally with a slightly haughty laugh. "I can't imagine why. Farley was a no-good hoodlum from our rival school, Lacey High. A real ladies' man, if you know what I mean. He did have a steady girlfriend at the time, Nina-something—I think it started with a K. Anyway, Nina must have wised up because they split up not too long after high school. That's all I know. I never really had much to do with that bunch."

***

"You?" exclaimed Danny, expecting to see a paramedic walk through the door.

"You?" snorted the rheumy-eyed maintenance man, shaking the rain from his wet clothes and definitely not expecting to see this young punk, with whom he'd had a run-in at Bonnet Island Estate, standing over his friend. "What have you done to Peter?"

Danny was dumbfounded. "You know this guy?

"Yeah. What's it to ya?" he said, glaring at Danny.

"Good, then you can stay with him until the paramedics arrive. I'm outta here."

"No. Wait a minute," said the maintenance man, nervously barring Danny's way. "I can't be seen here."

"Why not? He's your friend, isn't he? Well, he's sick."

"I never said he was my friend. I just come by to check on him from time to time."

Danny's look told the old man he wasn't buying it. Judging from the way both men were dressed, Danny figured they were two rummies hanging out together in this rundown store, sharing a bottle whenever they could get their hands on one.

"Look, man, here's how it is," said the rheumy-eyed man, softening his tone. "I know he don't look like much. But this fellah, Peter Miller," he said pointing to the unconscious man on the floor, "he's been through a lot. I mean, he's a decorated war veteran for Christ's sake."

"Yeah, from the Legion of Doom. Why the hell should I care?" asked Danny sarcastically.

"Yeah, you're right," said the man, changing his approach. "Why should a smart kid like you care about our kind? Hey, you don't owe us nothin'."

"Damn right," agreed Danny. "I don't owe you *or him* anything," he said, nodding to the heap on the floor. "Now get out of my way. I've got people waiting for me."

"Right, I forgot. Always in a hurry."

Danny braced for a fight. "You got a problem with that, old man?"

"Listen to me," the man said in a pleading voice. "I've been running from trouble all my life. If you don't want to end up like me, then do the right thing. Don't walk away now. He needs your help."

The rescue squad burst into the room, followed by a burly police sergeant named Herbert Fisk and two armed patrolmen.

The paramedics, an earring-laden young man and a muscular young woman sporting a severe butch-cut that tapered to a pointed V in the back, immediately went to work on Peter, starting to administer intravenous fluids.

"Nobody move," barked Sergeant Fisk. "You're all under arrest for vagrancy."

The two patrolmen cuffed the rheumy-eyed man as he tried to flee through the back room. Danny started to protest, but as beat-up, soaked, and filthy as he was from the day's events, he looked almost as bad as the other two, and the officer wasn't listening.

"Save it for the judge," huffed Fisk, "unless you want me to cite you for resisting arrest, too."

"But I was the one who called for help," argued Danny.

"That's your story, eh? We'll sort it out down at the station."

***

"Thank you for coming," said Danny, rising from his chair in the interrogation room at the Tuckerton Police Station. "I know it's early, but Moss isn't answering his cell phone and, at this hour, I didn't know who else to call." He crossed the room and gave his visitor a bear hug.

"Danny, what's going on?" asked Kelly Martin when he released her from his grateful embrace "You're shaking … and you look awful!" She handed him a cup of piping hot coffee that she'd somehow managed to hold onto.

Indeed, Danny looked terrible and felt worse. He was dirty, wet, and chilled from the air conditioning, and his feet hurt from standing for hours in his cleated cycling shoes. He'd had only one opportunity to relieve himself and just a few hours of sleep before Tuckerton's finest allowed him his one phone call and started in on him again with a barrage of questions and threatening gestures.

"Sergeant Fisk said you've been hanging out with winos," she said with a faint smirk. "Trading up? Shawna isn't good enough for you anymore?"

Danny rubbed his arms, attempting to get warm. "You gonna give me a chance to explain," he shivered, "or tune me out like that fat-head Fisk?" he said a little too loudly.

"All I can say is that you are one lucky son-of-a-bitch to have the likes of Noah Parsons vouching for you," scolded a flush-faced Sergeant Fisk as he entered the room, shadowed by his two deputies.

"I called Noah," explained Kelly in response to Danny's puzzled look.

"You want my advice, Windsor?" said the corpulent sergeant, holding the door open for them to leave. Danny didn't want the surly cop's advice but wisely held his tongue.

"You should thank your lucky stars for your girlfriend here, or else right now you'd be sharing a bunk in the same cell with your lowlife friend, Farley."

Kelly's jaw dropped at the mention of the name. "*Eddie* Farley?" she asked. "The maintenance guy at Bonnet Estate?"

"The ex-con is more like it, miss," said Fisk. "Farley's got a rap sheet the size of Rhode Island. Apparently he and his fellow freeloader, Peter Miller, have been calling the old Clark place home for some time now."

Kelly couldn't believe her ears. She turned to face Danny. "You found Peter Miller?"

Now it was Danny's turn to act surprised. "Yeah … I guess," he said sheepishly, ready to take credit for something if there was any credit due. "That's what I was trying to tell you both. I ducked into that old building to get out of the rain. The next thing I know, this guy Miller almost attacks me before he collapses. And I end up here."

Kelly grabbed Sergeant Fisk by the arm. "Where's Peter Miller now, Sergeant?" she demanded.

"He looked like he was in bad shape," replied Fisk. "The EMTs took him directly to the hospital."

"What's so important about this Peter Miller?" Danny asked Kelly as they were hurrying out of the police station.

"I'll tell you on the way. Get in," she urged, sliding into the driver's seat of her Mini Cooper.

"Wait a minute," cried Danny as he hopped in beside her. "What about the ride? And my bike?"

"Your plans have been officially changed, Mr. Windsor," announced Kelly as she peeled out of the parking lot, and headed north on Route 9.

13

The Living Dead

"That looks like pretty strange behavior for a scientist," Luz Sanchez laughed, watching Geoffrey try to communicate with the Painted Rock. "Are you sure you're doing it right?" He shrugged his shoulders, which made her smile tenderly.

It was just before sundown and getting dark fast. Luz had picked Geoffrey up at Tom Banks's camp, where he had spent a couple of incredible days traipsing through the woods with his young troops, living as one with Mother Nature. He was certain that the lessons he learned from Tom and through his communion with the natural world would last a lifetime, but as Tom reminded him before they broke camp, Geoffrey had one more challenge to face: He had to find out the full significance of the dream he had while in the woods and, according to Lakota teachings, the best way to do that was right here in front of him.

"I don't know," Geoffrey sighed, feeling his way around the rock in the encroaching darkness. He was more perplexed than his lovely companion. "I've never talked to a rock before."

"Maybe you should just try listening?" she suggested in all seriousness.

"Tom said I should go to the rock to find out what it is I need to know," Geoffrey repeated verbatim. "He said that only by learning something from the rock could I come to fully understand my vision. Here, why don't you give it a try?" he asked, passing his bottle of Poland Springs to Luz.

Luz imitated the meditative gestures she had seen Geoffrey perform moments earlier. First she took a long, slow sip of spring water. Next she closed her eyes and tried to clear her mind of everything except the mission at hand, engaging in a non-verbal conversation with the Painted Rock. She felt foolish as she walked around the rock, placing her hands on various points along its surface, as Geoffrey had done.

"Well?" he asked at last. "Did you get a sense of anything?" His expression was hopeful.

Luz shrugged. "I'm sorry, Geoffrey, I got nothing," she said. "Everywhere I touched it felt cold and hard and dead. Just like any old rock."

"Hmm, it felt warm to me," he said. "Maybe that was from the last bit of sunlight," he mused. "How about the surface?" he asked her expectantly. "What impressions did you get from the shape of the rock?"

"It was smooth and hard like I would expect a painted rock to be."

"I got the same impression, Luz, except along the back there—on the top. That part felt ridged ... sort of like the backbone of a skeleton."

"I certainly didn't hear any voices from beyond the grave," joked Luz. "Did you?"

"No," Geoffrey sighed. "I don't get it. Tom seemed so sure I would find the answer to what the White Stag, the truck, the water, and the cement-encased rock all meant. But I'm coming up blank."

"I think you could be trying too hard," said Luz, taking his arm and leading him back toward her car. "You're probably tired. You've been in the woods a long time. Maybe you need a hot shower and a soft bed. We can always try it again tomorrow."

Although he was disappointed to come away from the rock empty-handed after the startling insights he'd glimpsed while in the woods, it was difficult not to be persuaded to rejoin civilization and enjoy the pleasure that human contact offered—especially when the offer was being made by the warm and lovely creature now holding his arm. Geoffrey decided that the secret of the Painted Rock, if there really was one, would have to wait.

***

"So you think this wino is Sally Lawson's high school sweetheart?" Danny asked while taking the hospital steps two at a time in his slippery cycling shoes, trying to keep up with Kelly.

"Yes, I do," she said, waiting at the top step.

"Then why don't we just tell Sally and let her come see him," said Danny as they walked through the lobby toward the Information Station.

"Because Peter Miller is a pretty common name, and if it's not him she'll be disappointed," said Kelly, waiting for Danny to catch up with her. "And if it is him but he doesn't want to see her, she'll be crushed."

"Got it," said Danny, catching his breath.

"Peter Miller's room, please," Kelly said to the elderly hospital volunteer.

"Are you a relative?" asked the matron with no authority behind the counter.

"Yes," said Kelly without hesitation. "I'm his daughter. And this is my fiancé."

Suddenly a bit queasy, Danny averted his eyes.

"Sign here please," the woman said, pointing to the registry book and handing each of them a pass.

Danny watched silently as Kelly signed in as: Kelly Miller and Danny Parker.

"Third floor. Room 308. Elevator's on your right."

"Fiancé?" Danny questioned as they reached the elevator.

"It worked, didn't it?" she said as the elevator door closed.

"I hope you know what you're doing," he said as they ascended.

She smiled. *So do I,* she thought.

A young candy striper with a flower cart got into the elevator on the second floor and rode with them up to the third. Acting on impulse, when the girl's back was turned, Kelly helped herself to a single red rose.

Danny felt his stomach rumble. He was in the company of a liar and a thief, taking flowers to a man she didn't know, who, only a few short hours ago, had threatened him with a bat. *What's wrong with this picture?* he asked himself.

They walked hurriedly down the sterile hall, scanning the numbers on the doors for Room 308.

The hall reeked of a strong antiseptic that reminded Kelly of her grandmother's nursing home, which her parents had made her visit. The smell reminded Danny not to touch anything. He didn't like hospitals. Germs and sickness were everywhere.

Room 308 was just before the nursing station, on the same side. They slipped into the room unnoticed.

Peter Miller lay in a single bed propped up with pillows. The other bed was unoccupied. A tube ran from an IV stand into his left arm and he had an oxygen clip around his nose. He'd been cleaned up somewhat since Danny saw him earlier, but the sight of his unkempt beard, hollow cheeks, and blazing blue eyes startled Kelly.

Danny scanned his chart: "Dehydration, malnutrition and a mild case of pneumonia," read the doctor's notes. Miller's condition was not as bad as he'd expected.

Peter Miller recognized Danny immediately and sat upright in bed.

"Why is it you keep popping in on me, Mister …?"

"Windsor. Danny Windsor," he said, keeping an arm's length of distance between them.

"Ah, yes. Danny Windsor. Now I remember, Buck's boy. Couldn't you find something a little less conspicuous to wear for this visit?" joked Peter, noticing Danny still had his damp and clinging cycling clothes on. "I'm sure we could find one of these in your size," he said, tugging at his hospital gown. "White all right?"

"I see you didn't lose your sense of humor in that fall you took at Clark's," replied Danny. "Too bad, I liked it better when you were unconscious."

"*Touché*," nodded Miller. "I suppose I do owe you a debt of gratitude for calling the paramedics," he added, his voice dripping with sarcasm. "You'll excuse me if I don't get up and thank you personally. It seems I'm tethered to a saline pole for life support. Did I happen to mention that I detest hospitals?"

Kelly took a brave step forward, coming into Miller's view.

"And who might this lovely creature be?" he said, smiling up at Kelly. "At least she knows how to dress for the occasion."

"My name is Kelly Martin," she responded with a smile of her own, standing by the bed rail. She handed Peter the rose she had commandeered.

"How thoughtful. I do have a penchant for flowers, you know? But then, how would you know, when you have no idea who I am?"

"You're Peter Miller, right?" asked Kelly, trying to hide her excitement.

He studied Kelly for several seconds before answering. "Are you from the homeless shelter?"

"No, I'm from Teaneck," she answered in all sincerity.

"Oh, that explains it," said Peter mockingly. "You obviously want the Teaneck Peter Miller. So sorry, he's on the *second* floor."

Danny winced, but Kelly was undeterred.

"Does the name Sally Parker mean anything to you?" she blurted out.

Peter was suddenly silent. His eyes narrowed as he studied Kelly more intently.

"Should it?" he asked coyly.

Kelly looked to Danny for support.

"You're wasting your time, Kelly," said Danny, reading her face. "I tried to tell you, he and Farley are just a couple of drunks. I'll bet he doesn't know my parents, either."

Miller perked up. "Farley. You know about Eddie Farley?" he prodded.

"Yes," replied Kelly. "We met him, too, unfortunately. Right now he's safely behind bars at the Tuckerton Police Station. And if you know him, then I'm guessing you know Sally Parker, too. Don't you?"

Kelly placed the rusted key and keychain Geoffrey had found at the Painted Rock beside Miller on the white hospital bed sheet.

Miller glanced at it and then addressed Danny. "She your girlfriend, Danny?" he inquired, trying to appear nonchalant.

Danny and Kelly looked at each other for an awkward moment.

"No," replied Danny truthfully.

"That's too bad, Danny. This gal's pretty perceptive and she's got spunk."

"We know about the accident, Mr. Miller," Kelly said in a soothing tone. "Sally told me she never blamed you. She would tell you herself but she doesn't know if you're dead or alive."

"I am the living dead," said Peter Miller slowly and dramatically, tears welling up in both of his eyes. "Even if *she* doesn't, I blame myself. Do you know what it's been like, living with all this guilt for so many years?"

"Judging from the way you look, and how I found you today, I think we have some idea," added Danny, trying to rekindle some humor in the uncomfortable conversation.

"No!" shouted Miller. "You have no idea. And neither does Sally."

"All she knows is that you went away to art school in France and never came back," offered Kelly.

"Good! That's what I wanted her to believe," said Miller. "I thought it would help her forget me, if she thought I had skipped out on her. That way she could get on with her life, without any reminders of that terrible night."

"You mean you didn't go to France?" questioned Danny.

"Andy Parker was more than Sally's brother. He was my best friend and I loved him like he was my own brother. The three of us went everywhere together."

"That sounds familiar," said Danny.

"If you didn't go to art school, then what did you do?" asked Kelly innocently.

"The only thing I could do, under the circumstances," replied Peter. "I took Andy's place. I enlisted in the Army. I figured I owed him that much."

"What about Sally?" asked Kelly angrily. "You didn't think you owed her anything?"

Peter Miller took Kelly in his gaze, slowly. "I know this may be hard for you to understand, but I spent four years in Vietnam. It changed me forever. It took away whatever good I had left in me, after the accident had already turned me inside out."

"Farley said you got a purple heart," remembered Danny.

Miller laughed. "To replace the human heart I'd lost."

"What have you been doing all this time, since you got back from Vietnam?" asked Kelly, now more curious than angry.

"Painting," he answered without hesitation. "It started out simple enough. I painted a small bouquet of flowers as a memorial for Andy. But it felt good and the reaction from people who saw my work was positive. I've been trying to bring some joy into this world, some happiness to people, ever since. Using the old paint cans and brushes I scavenged from that abandoned store, I've been painting that big old rock out on Route 539."

"You? You're the mysterious Picasso of the Pines?" exclaimed Danny.

"Disappointed?"

"No," replied Danny, and Kelly agreed. "Relieved," conceded Danny.

"Relieved?" retorted Miller with a puzzled expression. "Why do you say it like that?"

"Haven't you heard?" asked Danny

"Your rock has become a battleground," Kelly jumped in. "People are using it to fight over what this country stands for."

"Yeah, and then there's another group trying to sell it to the highest bidder and move it someplace else," added Danny.

"We'll just have to see about that," said Peter Miller, ripping the tubing from his arm and nose. "Quick, Danny, get my clothes out of that closet over there."

"Don't you think you should wait until the doctor discharges you?" Danny asserted his reluctance.

"That might be too late," replied Miller as he climbed out of the bed

"Are you feeling well enough to travel?" asked Kelly worriedly.

"I'm feeling well enough to fight—and die, if I have to," said a determined Peter Miller, peeking around the door toward the nurse's station. "The coast is clear," he called back to his new recruits. "Let's roll!"

14

Rock Star

At the center of the storm, two groups stood separated by the infamous rock, each armed with spray cans as if they were pistols in the hands of gunfighters facing off at high noon near the O.K. Corral.

On one side, there was Noah Parsons accompanied by his bride Sarah Bishop and a platoon of flag waving recruits composed of veterans and their patriotically adorned family and friends. On the other side, the liberal Libby Ashcroft and her gaggle of free-speech activists had fortified their position with placards and signs calling for an end to U.S. militarism abroad.

Somewhere in between, in no man's land, stood the environmental naturalist Tom Banks flanked by his new disciple Geoffrey Martin and the lovely Luz Sanchez. Off in the periphery, like jackals readying themselves to feast on the spoils, were McAllister Jones, his docile wife Mildred, and Philadelphia businessman Arnold Tessler along with several of his henchmen in construction hats, patiently waiting by their equipment for the outcome of the showdown.

The feud had ripped the community apart, pitting brother against brother, friend against friend. Noah was still outraged by what he considered a desecration of the Stars and Stripes that had graced his revered rock, so he commissioned a young artist who happened to be the wife of a soldier stationed at Fort Dix to repaint the symbol of his beliefs. Libby was equally incensed that a declaration of a desire for peace could be so militantly opposed.

Tempers had escalated over the past few weeks as each group aired its views in the public arena at taverns, clubs, and churches, and in the editorial columns of the local newspapers. Recently, a local radio talk show had picked up the story, airing a debate that set the stage for a confrontation. The atmosphere was circus-like, befitting the star status the Painted Rock had achieved.

"I warned you it would come to this," said McAllister Jones, decked out in his Sunday finest, addressing Noah Parsons. "If you cannot reconcile your differences, I shall have no choice but to take matters into my own hands and remove this wicked instrument of division from our midst."

"Over my dead body," came a voice from the crowd. The gruff voice of a man burdened by years of torment and sacrifice was strengthened by the hope that his creation would not fall victim to mob rule.

The emaciated, bearded Peter Miller strode through the crowd, supported physically by Kelly Martin and Danny Windsor. Miller was wearing a bulky raincoat, which seemed suspect or at least highly irregular, even for a hermit, on such a hot and humid July day, noted Tom and the others.

"And who might you be?" interrogated Jones, not accustomed to having his authority challenged or his self-righteous harangues interrupted.

"Peter Miller," the bearded man said proudly. "The original painter of this rock."

Several people in the crowd gasped and others whispered heatedly among themselves.

"Original or not, this rock belongs to the people," announced Jones in his best pulpit preaching voice. "You have no claim on it."

"I beg to differ with you, sir," Miller said firmly but politely. "For better or worse, this rock has shaped my life. I have fought for this rock. My best friend died here and the love of my life was lost to this damned rock. I am willing to die and take it with me rather than see it destroy another soul because someone is determined to use it to sell tickets or cover it with their version of the truth."

Peter threw open his raincoat, revealing a jumble of wires and plastic packages taped to his body. "Stand back," he commanded, hurling himself onto the rock. "Or I'll blow us all to kingdom come!"

The crowd recoiled in horror, dispersing in all directions as fast as their feet would take them. Some jumped into cars and pickups parked nearby. Others ran for cover in the woods.

Tessler and his men loaded their crane and the front-end loader onto the bed of their tractor-trailer and high-tailed it down the road, leaving Jones and his sobbing wife stranded by the roadside.

"You're not serious?" asked Libby Ashcroft in disbelief, standing alone, deserted by her peace-loving minions.

"I assure you, I am deadly serious, madam," replied Miller, taking the detonator in his hand.

"Let's take him," said a few of the vets standing beside Noah, edging forward. Noah held them in check with an outstretched arm.

"Stand back, everyone," shouted Danny. "He means it. Can't you see this man is crazy?"

Miller held the detonator higher.

"Run, kids, run!" Sarah urged. But all four of them stood their ground.

Tom tried to step in front of Geoffrey and Luz to protect them.

"Stop!" Geoffrey shouted, stepping toward the rock. Tom could not restrain him. "I have something to say," he announced, addressing the remnants of the group. He turned back to face Peter Miller.

"Let's hear it, son," barked Miller.

"Last night I came out here hoping to learn something about this rock that might explain why you are all fighting over it. First, I tried to approach it like a research project, relying on logic and sensory observation to stimulate a quantifiable outcome. When that failed, I abandoned all scientific pretense and tried to delve into the consciousness of the rock itself by asking it to help us come to some kind of understanding."

A few of the veterans mumbled and scoffed.

"What are you trying to say, boy?" asked Reverend Jones. "That you talked to the rock?" he asked mockingly. Mildred Jones stifled a laugh.

"Let him finish," demanded Noah with a sideways glance at Tom. "Go ahead, Geoffrey, continue."

"I didn't get the message at first," Geoffrey said, taking a step toward Peter, "but now I do. May I?" he asked, moving closer to the Painted Rock. Peter stepped to the side.

Next, Geoffrey slowly reenacted a part of his ritual for the onlookers. "When I ran my hands over the spine, it was rough and ridged. It reminded me of the Rocky Mountains—the Continental Divide."

He gave Noah and Sarah a tender glance before continuing. "I think I'm starting to get what it really stands for. Just as the Rocky Mountains divide the United States, this rock has come to divide us, though it was never intended to."

Geoffrey pressed the side of his face against the rock, then stood back up to explain. "When I first went to feel the rock, like that—through the sensitivity of my face, I felt an unexpected warmth. Luz, who was with me, had just the opposite impression. She felt nothing. That confused me. How could two people have exactly the opposite impression of the same experience? Today, standing here, listening to all the rhetoric and posturing from both sides, it dawned on me that we had actually arrived at the same conclusion, only from different points of view. Whereas I felt the glowing warmth of energy and life coming from the rock, Luz felt the lifeless coldness that comes from having one's spirit buried, imprisoned and cemented under layer upon layer of somebody else's concepts and definitions. This rock is a living entity; it has a nature and a spirit all its own, and that spirit is trapped by the symbols, slogans, and graffiti we have placed upon it. Don't you see, *that* is the secret this rock needed us to know."

"Poppycock," snorted McAllister Jones.

"Oh, shut up, Jones!" snapped Aunt Sarah.

The small crowd applauded, causing Mildred to giggle.

"So what do you suggest we do about it, young man?" asked Peter Miller.

"I think we should do what is right for the rock and return it to its original state. We should sandblast away all the paint that has been covering up its natural beauty all these years. That way the rock can enjoy its true identity, without being saddled by our conflicting values."

"I can accept that," said Noah with growing admiration for Geoffrey's Solomon-like wisdom.

"Me, too," said Tom Banks, beaming proudly.

"I'll gladly initiate a fundraiser to pay for the cleaning," added Libby.

"Jones?" questioned Noah.

The reverend seemed to be brooding, mulling his options.

"We'll pass around the plate at church, won't we, dear?" Mildred answered for her husband.

"Oh, all right," he conceded with an exaggerated sigh.

"Whew!" said Peter Miller, pulling off the raincoat and stuffing the detonator into the pocket before tossing it to Danny. "I'm glad that's over with. I thought I was going to roast to death."

Sarah clutched Noah's arm with alarm.

"Be careful with that coat, Danny," cautioned Noah.

"You'd better let me have it," Tom Banks insisted, holding out his arms to accept the coat from Danny.

"Oh, the explosives aren't real," Danny said cheerfully.

"What?" the group echoed.

Kelly looked at Aunt Sarah and Noah lovingly. "You don't think we'd actually play with real explosives, do you? What kind of people do you think we are?"

Thunderous laughter and applause rang out all around.

Just then, Johnny and Moss came riding up the road. "Hey, what'd we miss?" Moss said with a worried look on his face.

Danny went over to greet his friends. "Moss, why didn't you answer my calls? I had to spend the night in the slammer until Kelly rescued me."

Johnny and Moss looked at each other sheepishly. Johnny spoke up. "During the ride, Moss made the mistake of lending his cell phone to Shawna. Curtis started calling her every few minutes, and that got old fast. She finally threw the phone at him and the front wheels of a pickup truck took care of the rest."

"I figured you guys would be halfway to Indian Mills by now," Danny said, enthusiastically hugging them one at a time and enjoying the camaraderie of the reunion. He was also secretly gloating over the news that Shawna had put Curtis in his place.

"Aw, shucks, Danny, it just wasn't that much fun anymore," admitted Moss. "So we pulled out of the ride and backtracked …"

"… until we found you," finished Johnny.

Moss picked up the story. "Yeah, we checked in with the Tuckerton Police …"

"… and a rather surly police sergeant named Fisk said he had no idea where you two had run off to, but he had gotten a call that there were big doings over at the Painted Rock …" Johnny chimed in.

"… so we figured we'd try here first," concluded Moss, grinning as Kelly, Geoffrey, and Luz sauntered over. "It sounded like something you kids would be involved with. You do have a certain reputation around here, you know."

15

Rumors

"That was a quite a heroic stand you took back there at the rock," Kelly said supportively to Peter Miller. They were riding in Kelly's checkered Mini Cooper, heading east on Route 72, returning to Clark's General Store to retrieve Danny's bicycle. "I can see why you earned your purple heart. How are you feeling, anyway?"

"I'm fine. A little tired, maybe," he replied from the compact back seat, stifling a cough.

"I'm just glad they didn't call our bluff," Danny said from the passenger seat.

"You got that right," Peter concurred. "And it's a good thing that smart kid was there. His timing, not to mention his idea, saved the day."

"That smart kid is my brother Geoffrey," said Kelly proudly.

"I could see the resemblance, especially intellectually," replied Peter Miller.

Kelly smiled at the compliment. "Do you want us to drop you back off at the hospital?" she asked over her shoulder.

"Hell, no," came the emphatic reply.

"Then where should we leave you?"

"I guess I should go try and help Eddie Farley out," Peter sighed. "But I could sure use a meal and a hot shower," he added, daydreaming.

"Why don't you come back with me to my aunt's gift shop on the island?" Kelly said. "It's just Geoffrey and me, now that Aunt Sarah has moved in with Noah. There's a spare bedroom in the loft. We can pick up some takeout from Ming Dynasty on the way."

Danny perked up. "Count me in, that's great Chinese. Just let me make a quick stop at my apartment to change my clothes."

Peter Miller gave his own tattered rags a good whiff. Kelly observed his embarrassment in the rearview mirror.

"Hey, Peter, Danny's about your size," she said, elbowing Danny in the ribs. "Maybe he can find you something to wear."

"I don't want you to go to any trouble," Peter objected politely.

"No trouble," Kelly answered before Danny could open his mouth, "Between him and Noah I'm sure we can find you something nice to wear for your reunion with Sally Parker—I mean Lawson."

"Who said anything about a reunion?" Peter grumbled, looking out the window.

"Haven't you kept her waiting long enough?" chided Kelly.

"It's a little more complicated than my simply popping in after a forty-year absence," replied Peter, raising his eyebrows.

"She doesn't think so," argued Kelly.

"How do you know that? I mean, I hear what you're saying, but it could be very awkward, the two of us alone together. What would we talk about?"

"The past forty years, for starters," volunteered Danny.

"I'd rather forget my past," mumbled the bearded man.

"Well then, how about asking her what *she's* been up to?" suggested Kelly, trying to keep things upbeat.

"I already know what she's been doing," Peter said mysteriously.

"You mean you've been following her?" Danny asked.

"You don't have to be polite, Danny. Have I been *stalking* her is what you meant to say, but it wasn't like that. I had Eddie to do most of the dirty work."

"What are Sally Parker and you to Farley anyway?" queried Danny.

"Guilt and blackmail provide some powerful persuasion," Peter replied unapologetically.

"Explain," Kelly challenged, annoyed by this revelation.

"Yeah, explain," seconded Danny.

Miller leaned forward and whispered into Danny's ear, "Are you really sure you want to know?"

"I think we'd both like to hear what really happened the night of the accident," answered Kelly. Danny nodded his head in agreement.

The older man took a deep breath, summoning the courage to journey back through his pain to the darkest moment of his life. To the moment when that unbearable pain began.

"We had just left our graduation ceremony," he began slowly. "Sally, Andy—her brother—and I were cruising in my new Mustang when Eddie and some of the other Lacey High rowdies caught up with us in Donny Connelly's pickup truck."

"Were you drinking?" Danny wanted to know.

"No," Peter said without hesitation. "But I can't be sure about Connelly. Eddie denies it, but Connelly isn't around to defend himself anymore. He got hit with a mortar shell in Vietnam during the Tet Offensive and came home in a body bag."

He paused a minute to reflect and gather his thoughts, then continued. "Bailey, the kid riding shotgun that night, was a real bed bug. The kind of kid who would probably be labeled as ADD today."

"Sounds like my kind of guy," joked Danny.

"I don't think so, Danny," Peter said seriously. "Bailey was institutionalized not long after the accident. I thought it was a scam so he could get out of being drafted. But I found out later that he hung himself."

"That left Eddie Farley," guessed Kelly.

"Yep," acknowledged Miller, "and Nina Kaszanski."

Danny turned around in his seat to face Peter Miller. "My mother?" he said with a puzzled look on his face. Kelly glanced over quickly but said nothing.

"I told you I knew her and your father." Miller said it as a matter of fact.

"What was she doing with them?" prodded Kelly.

"Nina was Farley's girlfriend at the time," Peter blurted out.

"You've got to be kidding me," said Danny, caught completely off guard.

Peter shook his head. "I take it she never told you this story or anything else about Eddie Farley?" he said sadly, not expecting an answer.

"No. Never."

"Are you sure you want me to go on?" he asked Danny, looking him squarely in the eye.

Danny looked to Kelly for support. She tried to focus on the road although she was obviously listening. She gave him a forced smile.

"Go on," said Danny, bracing himself for the whole story.

"Eddie and your mom were in the back of Connelly's pickup truck with some other kids, taunting us from the passing lane," Miller continued. "Andy was standing in the back of my convertible dishing it right back at 'em. We were drag racing on route 539. You know that stretch of the road. We just came from it.

"At that time the Painted Rock was known as 'graffiti' rock. That's where all the young lovers left their secret messages and the happy graduates left their marks for posterity. Or so we thought."

"So that's where you were racing Connelly to," surmised Kelly.

"You got it," Peter said.

"So what happened?" she asked.

"A Volkswagen van came up over the rise suddenly in Connelly's lane, heading straight for him. Sally begged me to slow down and let Connelly into the right lane. I refused to slow down, thinking he would chicken out and drop back in line behind me."

Danny jumped in, "But he didn't, right?"

Miller nodded. "The van kept coming and we kept racing, side by side. Then Bailey tossed a spray can out of the passenger window. I ducked and it knocked Sally out cold."

"And then?" asked Kelly urging him on.

"I slowed up. Connelly cut in front of me and slammed on his brakes. I had no time to react. I rear-ended him and Andy went flying out of the backseat. Sally was pinned under the dash. I was the only one who wasn't injured—physically, anyway. I think you can still see some other kind of scars."

"Wasn't anybody in Connelly's truck hurt? My mom, for instance?" Danny asked.

"No, and Connelly was able to drive away from it. He took off like a bat outta hell."

Kelly was stunned. "They never even stopped to help? Why?"

"I don't know," Peter said tentatively. "Farley says something scared the bejesus out of Connelly. He said he saw a ghostly white creature, an angel maybe—or maybe even the Jersey Devil, take your pick. Superstitions run rampant in the Pines, especially among scared high school kids."

"Maybe he was drunk, or maybe he was hallucinating. It could even have been an image projected on the road when the light beams from the oncoming van and Connelly's truck crossed each other," Danny theorized, now fully engrossed in the details.

Miller shrugged his shoulders. "Maybe, or it could have just been low-hanging fog on the road? I didn't see it. Farley thinks Connelly believed it was some kind of mystical warning. Obviously, it came too late." He drew a deep breath. Reliving the horror of that fateful night had drained him. He knew there was more to tell, but he was hoping he wouldn't have to. "You know the rest. Connelly and his crew bolted. Andy was pronounced dead at the scene, and I was the only one around to blame. What a mess."

"What about Sally?" asked Kelly.

"I left her beside her brother with a message on the rock telling her I was sorry and where she could find me if she ever wanted to see me again. Then I ran to get help and once I did I just kept running. Now you know why I can't face her."

"You said you blackmailed Eddie Farley into spying for you," said Danny thoughtfully. "Were you going to use him to finger Donny Connelly?"

"No. Connelly's family had a lot of money and nobody would be a witness against him, anyway. They all clammed up pretty fast."

"But you had Sally to corroborate your story," suggested Kelly.

"I honestly didn't know what she would say. She got knocked out before the crash. I had no way of knowing what she'd seen or how she felt about me, since she never responded to the message I left."

Peter began to sob softly. He wiped his damp eyes with his sleeve. "No, Farley was guilt-ridden. I guess they all were. But as long as I disappeared quietly, no one had to admit to anything. So I enlisted and dropped out of sight."

"What happened with Farley and my mother?" asked Danny tentatively.

"Well, Farley got himself into more trouble—big trouble. We're talking armed robbery, grand theft auto, forgery, you name it."

"I can't believe my mom would date such a scumbag," challenged Danny.

"Actually, Danny, she smartened up and left Farley just before he got caught and sent to Rahway."

"Good for her," cheered Kelly.

"Yeah, well, maybe," continued Miller. "Farley did his time—close to twenty years—and came back to look for your mother. By that time, of course, she'd married Buck Windsor. But Farley was persistent."

"What do you mean by persistent?" Danny probed.

Miller stared out the window, collecting his thoughts. "Look, Danny," he said at last. "I shouldn't be the one telling you this."

"Telling me what?" Danny insisted.

"About the rumors."

"What rumors?"

"Let me put it this way," he said, choosing his words carefully. "Buck and your mother had been married for twelve or thirteen years. Then Farley shows up and Nina is pregnant around the same time."

"So?" countered Danny defensively.

"So, he was seen around town … talking to her, you know?"

"No, I don't know," said Danny angrily.

"I think I do," interrupted Kelly. Turning to Danny she said, "Danny, I met you about a year or two after your mother and father divorced. Do you know why they split up?"

"Not really. They were having problems, always fighting. Dad said it was Mom's fault and Mom said it was his fault. Then she got mixed up with some guy in a chat room on the Internet and split."

The three of them were quiet as they considered what they knew or didn't know.

Miller finally said, "Danny, there are only two or three people who know for sure what the truth is."

"Yeah, and one of them lives in Spokane, Washington. I haven't spoken to her since the divorce."

"And Buck?"

"I don't know. He went to Florida to live with relatives, I think. After the court put me in Moss Greenberg's custody, I never tried to contact either one of them. I needed to move on with my life."

"I'm sure it still hurts," said Kelly, tears welling in her eyes.

"How would you feel, Kelly, if your parents split up and left you behind and you didn't know why? I used to blame myself for everything, but now I feel even worse. I just wish somebody could have told me the truth."

"Danny," Peter said abruptly, "someone who knows the truth is still right here in town."

16

The Light of Old Barney

Kelly and Sally were lounging on Sally's back deck, enjoying a cup of afternoon tea. Kelly declined Sally's offer for a second scone. The day was beautiful and sunny, just as it had been on Kelly's first visit to Barnegat Light, but beneath the surface, things weren't quite the same.

"You told me you didn't know what happened to Nina With-a-K," Kelly said accusingly. "That wasn't entirely true, was it?"

Sally held her teacup genteelly on her lap. "I told you that I had no contact with either her or Eddie Farley, and that was the truth," she answered calmly.

"But you knew Farley was Danny's father," Kelly pressed. "You knew it as soon as you met Danny at the wedding. Why didn't you say something?"

"It wasn't my place to say anything," countered Sally, taking a sip of her tea. "I heard the rumors, Kelly, like everyone else. That's all."

"Peter Miller thinks they were more than just rumors," said Kelly, trying a different tactic. "Farley even came to him for money, for his little 'problem.'"

"You know how happy I was to learn that Peter is still alive, but I have to admit, it worries me to hear that he's been associating with Eddie Farley in any way, shape, or form. Farley had lots of problems. Peter shouldn't have told Danny what he did. The poor boy must be beside himself."

"He's confused," admitted Kelly, realizing Sally was right. She agreed that Peter should not have been the one to tell Danny, but his own parents had left without a word and, eventually, he was bound to find out why. "But mostly he's hurt, really hurt," she confided.

"I know about hurt," offered Sally, putting down her cup and looking away.

"Well, at least there's a chance you can still salvage your relationship with Peter," Kelly suggested.

"It's a little more complicated than that," replied Sally in a tearful, whispery voice.

"That's exactly what Peter said," revealed Kelly.

"Then you know the difficulty," Sally said sadly.

"What I know is that two people once loved each other very much and that a horrible accident separated them. They've each suffered more than enough." Kelly walked over to Sally and knelt down beside her, taking the older woman's hand in own. "I also know that once a week for the past forty years, these two people have been waiting for each other, in the right place at the wrong time, missing each other because one of them misunderstood the message left by the other."

Sally Parker-Lawson lifted her head to stare directly into Kelly's caring gaze. Kelly was nodding her head and smiling broadly. Sally became wild-eyed with tears of joy, alternately hugging Kelly and shaking uncontrollably.

***

Three teenagers waited with uncharacteristic patience in the shadows of the Barnegat Lighthouse, talking quietly among themselves. Two hundred and seventeen winding steps above them, two people who thought life together had passed them by embraced passionately for the first time in forty years.

"I've gotta hand it to you, Geoffrey," said Danny, shaking his head from side to side. "How did you ever figure out that Sally hadn't gotten the whole message Peter left for her?"

"First off, you have to remember that Peter had painted his petroglyph for Sally *before* the terrible accident that night." Danny nodded and Geoffrey continued, "It was intended as a promise to return after art school. According to Peter, he painted Old Barney with its light beacon shaped like a big glowing heart and a brightly shining sun in the background above it."

"Then it became obvious," said Kelly picking up the story. "The message was clear and unchanged even by the consequences of the accident: If we both truly believe in our love, we will meet again in our special place, Old Barney's light tower."

"Right," Geoffrey added, "but after the accident, because her brother's blood had been splattered over a part of the picture, the glowing disk in the sky looked more like a crescent moon to Sally. She thought it was the moon above the lighthouse, not the sun. She understood Peter's message correctly but mistook the meeting day as Monday for the day of the moon, when Peter had actually painted the sun, representing Sunday."

"So, for forty years, they missed being together by one day," Kelly summarized.

"It's nice to know that some stories can still have a happy ending," said Danny Windsor, casting a long glance skyward.

"What are *you* going to do now, Danny?" asked Geoffrey with genuine concern.

Danny looked at him before turning to Kelly. "I was thinking of flying to Spokane."

"If that's what you need to do," Kelly said supportively. "Could you use some company?"

"Thanks," he said, hugging her tenderly. "But this is something I have to do on my own."

"Then I'll be waiting for you to get back," Kelly whispered tearfully as she kissed his cheek.

"In the shadow of Old Barney?" he said with a broad smile.

17

The Truth

Sergeant Fisk led Danny through the door to the jail. He selected a key from a heavy hooped ring and unlocked the cell door. The prisoner was lying on his cot, facing the wall. He did not stir.

"You've got five minutes, Windsor," challenged the sergeant.

Danny slid into the jail cell. He stood awkwardly in the middle of the cramped, eight-by-eight-foot room. For an agonizing moment, he considered turning around and walking out, but before he could make up his mind, Fisk locked the door behind him and left them alone.

"Peter told you, didn't he?" said the rheumy-eyed Eddie Farley with his back to Danny.

"Yes, and Sally Parker confirmed it."

"What did they tell you?"

"They told me you're my father," Danny said with clenched teeth.

"So what do you want from me?"

"I want to hear it from you."

Farley turned to face Danny. He sat on the edge of the cot and drew a heavy sigh. "What do you want to hear?"

"The truth," said Danny, folding his arms.

"What *truth?*" asked Farley in a cynical voice. "That the man you thought was your father, isn't? That your mother cheated on him? That you've been lied to? That you're a bastard and your father is a two-bit loser in an orange jump suit? Is that what you came to hear?"

Danny stood his ground, fighting back the hatred and the anger he was feeling. "Is that the truth?" he spat out.

Farley ran a hand through his few greasy strands of gray hair, carefully considering what he would say. He always figured he'd have this conversation someday, and it looked like today was the day.

Danny pushed hard. "Well, is it?"

"The truth is, I loved your mother very much," he began uncomfortably. "We dated all through high school. But I was always in trouble with the law. Eventually, she smartened up and dropped me. That was before I got sent away."

Danny listened intently but showed no emotion. He was fighting back the contempt he felt for this man and so far his story was really hard to swallow.

Farley looked down at his shoes as he continued. "When I finally got out of prison, I came back here and heard that Nina had gotten married. Buck Windsor was a good guy. They'd been married for awhile and she was having trouble conceiving. There was some friction."

"So you thought you would slip right back into her life like the scumbag you are and take care of business, didn't you?" accused Danny.

207

Farley slowly raised his head, taking in the full measure of the boy he had hoped to avoid confronting in this way. "Yeah, something like that," he said at length.

Danny threw his hands down and spun around. "Great. And this is supposed to make me feel better?"

"Look kid, this isn't easy for me, either," said Farley, raising his voice for the first time. "You said you wanted the truth, so now you're gonna have to deal with it."

Danny turned away. He was clearly upset but didn't want to give Farley the satisfaction of seeing it on his face.

Farley let out a heavy sigh. "The truth is, I'm not your father." He said it so fast that Danny wasn't sure he'd heard him correctly.

"What?" exclaimed Danny, not knowing whether to feel shock or relief.

"You heard me," Farley said evenly. "Nina and I never got back together. Oh, I tried plenty, but she refused me every time. She was loyal to Buck and there was nothing I could do to change that."

"But ... you said they couldn't conceive?"

"I said they were having trouble, kid. Apparently, they resolved those difficulties."

"But everyone says it was you."

"Sure, I even helped spread the rumor. It seemed like everyone bought into it, so I didn't bother to tell anybody anything different. Your mother pleaded with me, begged me. I think eventually Buck started to believe it, too. That's probably what led to them splitting up in the end."

"Why would you do such a despicable thing?"

"I guess I just hated the idea of them being happy," admitted Farley.

"I don't believe you," said Danny, pacing the room. "Peter Miller said you came to him for abortion money. Was that a lie, too?"

"Yeah." Farley chuckled. "It was more like extortion money."

Danny was puzzled. "What do you mean?"

"Look, I knew he would never give it to me and I didn't need it anyway, but I felt guilty about the accident that took Andy Parker's life. All of us did: me, Bailey, Connelly, even your mother. We were all there and none of us helped. We were too scared. We just left them there. I guess I went to Peter with the idea of abortion money just so he could feel like he had something on me, something he could use against me if he wanted to. Hell, I wanted him to use it. It helped ease the guilt."

"Seems like you screwed up a lot of things in your life ... and everybody else's."

"Hey, I ain't proud of the life I've led. But I'm glad the truth is finally out. If you ever see your mom again, apologize to her for me. Tell her Eddie Farley did the right thing for once in his life. I told the truth. And tell her you took my advice. You stayed around to help a guy out when he was down, instead of running away like everybody else did that dark night, a long time ago."

ಇಾಲ

The Lost Mission
of Captain Carranza

1

Descent of the Eagle
(July 12, 1928)

Using his teeth, Emilio Carranza removed a leather glove and tapped the foggy altimeter with a bare knuckle. The needle remained fixed at 3,500 feet. Outside the cramped cockpit, a driving rain raged against the windshield, obscuring his view of an already dim horizon. With a few glimpses provided by sharp cracks of lightning, the young aviator could tell from the dark treetops swaying before him that the instrument reading was wrong, horribly wrong.

Only hours earlier, with his Ryan B-1 monoplane safely hangared for the night following the severe storm warnings reported to him throughout the day by the U.S. Weather Service, the 22-year-old Mexican flying ace had been comfortably ensconced in New York City's famed Waldorf-Astoria Hotel, enjoying dinner with a close coterie of new friends and admirers. Expectations had been that he would attempt the flight again in the morning if the weather improved.

After his solo flight from Mexico City to Washington, D.C. in a bold and audacious tribute to Colonel Charles A. Lindbergh's goodwill flight to Central and Latin America, the handsome young aviator had quickly become the toast of two major U.S. cities. The accolades and fanfare that followed were, like his ambitious feat, nonstop.

Dubbed "the Lindbergh of Mexico" by an adoring press corps, upon his arrival in the nation's capital Carranza had been greeted by President Calvin Coolidge and an enthusiastic throng of well-wishers. One week later, his "friendship" tour had continued with a flight to New York City, where Mayor Jimmy Walker gave him the key to the city. All the while, in Mexico, a "welcome home" parade had awaited the triumphant hero's return.

Carranza had found the media's comparison of him to the "Lone Eagle," whom he met and befriended when he once passed through Mexico, very flattering. Carranza and his family had lived for a time in San Antonio and, later, in the small town of Eagle's Pass, Texas. He knew well that North Americans honored the bald eagle as their national symbol. He also knew that Mexicans had long considered the eagle a sacred symbol of spiritual flight and strength.

The stressed silver-gray craft rolled to the right as a thunderous boom echoed through the cabin. Fighting the fierce, gusting winds and straining against the constant barrage of pelting rain, Carranza wished his American friend and brother flyer were with him now. Employing all the skill and aeronautical knowledge he had acquired in his short career, which began when, as a brash young fighter pilot, his strafing raids had helped put down the Yaqui uprising, Carranza struggled to keep his laboring craft aloft.

He had been in trouble in the air before—many times. Once, when his plane had caught fire, he purposely flew through a nearby rainstorm to put it out. Only a few months ago while en route to San Diego to inspect the design of the famed *Excelsior* he now piloted, Carranza crash-landed in a remote section of the Arizona desert and was forced to complete his journey by train. It seemed like a joke now, but it had nearly cost him his life and the life of his trusted flight mechanic and older brother, Sebastian, who had accompanied him on that run.

In the dim cabin light, Carranza checked the time on his wristwatch. It read 9:10 PM. He had left New York from Long Island's Roosevelt Field at approximately 7:18 PM on the pre-charted southward trek along the Atlantic Coast, so he reasoned that in two hours of flight time he had covered approximately 80 miles, placing him somewhere very near to his next reference point. The well-lit streets and factories of Philadelphia, however, were nowhere to be found. His compass confirmed his course, but by the flashes of light emanating from the storm, all he could see was a thick blanket of primeval forest.

Carranza groped under his seat for the flashlight and, finding it, switched it on. Bracing the steering yoke between his knees, he waited until the plane leveled off, then hurriedly unfolded a hand-sketched map from his flight jacket pocket. He laid it open across his lap.

The return flight plan had been carefully designed to take Carranza back over his native Coahuila region, near Mexico's northeast border. His eyes narrowed as he traced the map's route, the one his mind had indelibly etched into memory: Long Island, NY–Philadelphia–Washington, DC–Greenville-Spartanburg, SC–New Orleans–Galveston–Tampico, Mexico, and finally on to Mexico City.

The sight of New York as his starting point on the map reminded Carranza that he hadn't said goodbye to his father before he departed. His heart sank. He regretted leaving for the airfield without telling him. An accountant working for the Mexican Consulate in New York and a shrewd survivor of post-Revolution unrest in Mexico, Sebastian Carranza Sr. knew all too well the dangers inherent in committing one's life and fate to a country and a cause. And yet, in a proud show of solidarity, the elder Carranza had been at his son's side from the very moment he touched down in the Big Apple. True to his generous nature and time-earned connections, it was the senior Carranza who introduced his increasingly famous son to the New York elite; the high society politicians and business tycoons who ran the city, the country and, indeed, as some claimed, the world. They could help Emilio's career. They could help with many things.

Carranza deliberately kept the last-minute flight decision from his father for fear that the senior Carranza, knowing the risks were great, the glory fleeting, would not approve. Although a proud and honorable man in his own way, his father would not understand his son's sudden compulsion to take to the air despite all warnings against it. Señor Carranza would have tried to persuade Carranza to postpone the anxiously anticipated return flight yet again.

But time was running out. New record-breaking flights were being attempted every day. There could be no more delays, no more excuses. His father had been in New York too long to realize that the pride of the Mexican people was at stake; that his son's success would guarantee worldwide recognition for the fledgling Mexican Air Force and maybe even put it on par with that of their great neighbor to the North. Carranza's commanding officer, General Joaquin Amaro, understood the importance of his mission and, while Carranza was having dinner at the Waldorf, his impatient superior had raised the stakes, issuing a highly confidential communiqué prodding the aviator into action.

Now, the fragile plane lunged forward in a heart-stopping drop as if the cushion of air on which it had been riding was suddenly sucked out from under it. Carranza stuffed the map into his jacket pocket. He pulled back hard on the joystick, but the engine failed to react. The throttle stayed shut.

A lightning bolt sizzled and danced off the left wing. Another shot down in a jagged pattern into the open space occupied only moments before by the *Excelsior*. Brilliant, hot, white flashes scattered everywhere. Carranza had entered the vortex of the storm.

For the first time in his life, utter terror swept over him, chilling him to the bone. His hands shook. His body trembled. Even in the thick, dense fog that had hampered his historic outbound flight to Washington, forcing him to land 300 miles shy of his intended mark, Carranza had been more disappointed than scared. This time was different. He launched a distress flare; he then set about unsuccessfully in search of his parachute. Panic gripped him. Never had he felt more helpless and alone than at that very moment. With tears welling in his eyes, he called out for his sainted mother. His dry, chapped lips softly repeated his wife's name, Maria Luisa, over and over. Then, quietly, he began to pray for the chance to see their unborn son.

Initially, the brave pilot had thought—perhaps foolishly—he could ride out the storm. But the length and severity of it proved to be a far greater challenge than he anticipated. The urgent cautions in the weather reports had been justified, after all. At one point he even considered climbing to an altitude above the storm's fury. However, with his altimeter malfunctioning, he really had no way of knowing how high that would be. At 6,000 feet, the air would thin out. Too high, and he could black out. And then there was the fuel to consider. He was carrying more than 400 gallons—enough for the 2,400-mile flight, but with precious little to spare. Climbing would expend fuel. He had never been above 10,000 feet with more than 300 gallons of gas. Whether or not the *Excelsior* could handle the added load at that height was an unknown, but it no longer mattered. His instincts told him his altitude was dangerously low.

Carranza looked down toward the ground, first right, then left, desperately trying to get his bearings. His only hope was to find a road or a flat field—anyplace he might reasonably be able to set the *Excelsior* down. He knew full well that even if he could find such a place, there wouldn't be much of a chance for a safe landing unless he could control the speed of his plummeting plane. He would have to glide her down blindly through the severe crosswinds and ease her between the treetops, which would be no easy feat, not even for the highly touted "Lindbergh of Mexico."

In the distance, illuminated by his dying flare and streaks of lightning, beyond the merciless, torrential rain, Carranza thought he spotted an opening in the sea of dense trees below. From his vantage point it looked like a slim trail laced with railroad tracks cut through a tangle of dark forest. His heart leapt with renewed hope.

He tugged again at the stick, hoping to open the throttle even a little. It was as if it had been frozen shut. Frantic, Carranza reached for the silver flashlight and whacked the steering yoke, hoping desperately to engage the throttle.

Suddenly, a jarring crack split the night sky, sending shock waves of searing white light into the cockpit. Carranza felt a sharp jolt lift him from his seat. A faint tingling sensation enveloped his entire body. The very last thing Captain Emilio Carranza thought to do before a deep, creeping, darkness overwhelmed him was to grab onto the flashlight … and turn off the light.

2

Lights, Camera, Action
(July 2007)

"*C**ut!*" barked the young director into a hand held megaphone. "Dante, Dante, Dante," he sighed in exasperation as he looked down at the handsome young man in the soiled jump suit and torn flight jacket sprawled out beside the set's twisted plane wreckage. "How many times do I have to tell you? This shot calls for you to lie face down in the dirt."

Danny Windsor stared up at the director, befuddled. "But then how will anyone know who I am?"

"Yeah, like your mother," a burly cameraman snickered from behind the lens.

A cute, pony-tailed production assistant named Megan Turner, who was standing next to the director, giggled. She quickly hid her face behind a clipboard.

The director removed his trademark Philadelphia Phillies cap, which he always wore with the peak backwards, Ken Griffey Jr.-style. He scratched his smooth, bald head anxiously. Wade Sawyer, the slender 26-year-old aspiring director, and Danny Windsor, the ne'er-do-well former LBI lifeguard and perennial student, had met one night at Baker's Port Hole on the Island. A late night spent commiserating over a few shots and beers about the mounting misfortunes of their favorite baseball team had given Danny an opportunity to showcase his nonexistent acting skills for the ambitious NYU film school graduate, who, in order to finish a few last-minute scenes, desperately needed a photogenic stand-in for the film's title character.

The two young men became fast friends, although they were complete opposites in looks and temperament. Danny had a full mane of sweeping, thick, dirty blond hair, which always caught young ladies' eyes, but he dyed it jet black without a second thought for the chance to play a small part in his new friend's first feature-length documentary. Wade was one of those guys who had shaved his head to beat the inevitability of genetics. He cultivated the Vin Diesel look to be intimidating, and it worked. With his chiseled jaw and steel gray eyes, the director managed, despite his youth, to command everyone's attention. He had unlimited aspirations and an ego to match.

"Dante," Wade seethed between clenched teeth, trying to keep his frustration in check, "you are the handsome, dashing Captain Carranza, and this movie is about *him*. In this particular scene, the famed Mexican aviator is *dead*, which means *you* are dead. If you had been following the script, you'd know that Emilio Carranza was found face down in the thick and tangled vegetation of the New Jersey Pine Barrens, his pretty-boy face scorched and unrecognizable after his plane crashed. *¿Comprende?*"

The pert production assistant leaned over and whispered something into the director's ear, interrupting his tirade. Megan pointed to a newcomer on the set. An attractive blonde news reporter in tight jeans was trying to hide behind designer glasses and a straw hat. She was standing off to the side, busily entering notes into a BlackBerry.

As the film crew waited, swatting at the greenhead flies and tiny gnats that were a constant annoyance on the live set near the actual location where Carranza's body had been found almost 80 years ago, Wade took a long, pleasurable moment to study the young reporter. When Feather Sparrow realized the entire crew was also staring at her, she stopped writing; then, slowly, she removed her hat and Oakleys, tousled her hair a bit and smiled, revealing a dazzling set of pearly whites that would have made Julia Roberts envious.

Wade checked his watch. "Okay everybody, that's a wrap," he announced. "Be back on the set tomorrow at 8 AM, sharp. Dante, make sure you study the script tonight."

Danny watched as the sexy reporter and Wade met and shook hands. After facilitating the brief introductions, Megan slipped away, exit stage left. The two proceeded to walk slowly toward the director's trailer, talking animatedly as they went.

"There's someone here to see you, too, Dante," Megan said, coming up so close to Danny that he could practically taste the sparkle in her shiny silver lip gloss. "But I wouldn't count on your seeing the same action," she added with a flirtatious wink as she sashayed away.

Danny turned to see a familiar redheaded nerd linked hand in hand with a slim Latina. The two were making their way through the dispersing crew.

"Hey, Geoffrey," Danny said, the surprise in his voice at seeing his old friend slightly dulled by lingering thoughts about Megan's moist lips and the sexy reporter's tight jeans. "Hey, Luz," he offered almost absently to Geoffrey Martin's companion.

"Danny?" Geoffrey began timidly. "Did that girl just call you … Dante?"

"Dante Reed," Danny replied, posing with his thumbs on the lapels of his flight jacket. "It's my stage name. Whaddya think?"

"Ooh, I like what you've done with your hair," Luz Sanchez gushed teasingly. "I think it's sexy. Grrrr!" she purred.

"Did everybody look like Rudolph Valentino back in the 1920s?" Geoffrey questioned Luz, after carefully inspecting Danny in his Carranza attire.

Danny ran his fingers through his hair. "Hey, if you've got it, flaunt it. That's what I always say. So how ya been, Geoffrey? Princeton Tigers treating you all right? I see you haven't lost any freckles. Are you shaving yet?"

Despite having just completed his freshman year at the prestigious university with honors, Geoffrey turned three shades of red.

"And where's that Looney Tunes sister of yours?" Danny added, looking around. "What's her cause this summer? Saving the whales?"

Geoffrey grinned. "I wondered how long it would take you to ask about Kelly. Actually, she's back here for the summer again, working at Maggie Colson's general store."

"You don't say," Danny replied, squashing a pesky mosquito against the back of his neck. He wiped the perspiration from his face with a handkerchief. "So then, what brings you two to lovely Tabernacle? Come to pay your respects to a wayward Mexican pilot?"

Geoffrey and Luz both hesitated, waiting for the other to speak first.

"We heard the scuttlebutt around the island that you were working with an independent filmmaker on a documentary about the life of Emilio Carranza," Geoffrey said slowly.

"More like his death," Danny said sarcastically, still smarting from Wade's reprimand. "I don't think this guy had much of a life. But yeah, we're making a film."

"Well, so are we!" Luz exclaimed with nervous excitement.

Danny cocked his head in confusion. "What do you mean, 'so are we'?"

"What she means," replied Geoffrey "is that Luz has been hired by a Mexican film producer to assist in *his* production of the Captain Carranza story."

Geoffrey smiled warmly at Luz. "Luz was also kind enough to get them to hire me so I could learn about filmmaking firsthand. I've got my own pet project in mind and I'm hoping to learn the ropes."

"Another Carranza movie? That's ridiculous. Who needs it?" At this, Danny struck a tacky pose: right hand to his heart, the other hand raised high like a Greek statue. "There is need for only one Emilio Carranza … and *I* am *he!*"

3

Golden Sombrero

The tiny antique silver bell over the heavy wooden front door of Colson's General Store tinkled lightly. Kelly Martin looked up from the pages of the latest Chuck Palahniuk novel she'd been reading, *Haunted*, which was a lot more enjoyable than facing Adam Smith's *Wealth of Nations*, the required reading for her economics class next semester at Georgetown.

"Finally, a customer," she almost blurted aloud. Kelly hadn't seen anyone all morning—not even a visit from Freeman Morris, the old piney witch doctor who, according to Maggie Colson, the store's ageless and amiable proprietor, usually made his rounds on Tuesdays to stock her shelves with his highly sought-after "skeeter balm" and assorted other natural concoctions. It had been just as quiet all day yesterday except when two bikers who had motored in from Bordentown had burst in looking to use the "loo." They were so grateful, they left with a few mementos: a poster of the Jersey Devil painted by reclusive local artist Lydia Lattimer, a copy of John McPhee's seminal bestseller *The Pine Barrens,* and a bag of penny candy each. Those were Kelly's only sales the whole day.

She was beginning to have serious second thoughts about having agreed to "look after things" while Miss Maggie headed off to the West Coast to attend to her ailing sister. Before she left, Maggie had confided to Kelly that she was taking along a jar of Freeman's rutabaga rub and a bottle of his "Jersey jack" tonic in the likely event that her sister Grace needed a more old-fashioned remedy. "Good for whatever ails ya," Maggie told Kelly with that trademark twinkle in her pale blue eyes.

Had it not been for her Aunt Sarah's encouragement, Kelly probably would have been back at her usual summer perch on the 18th Street beach with her fellow Ship Bottom lifeguards protecting unsuspecting tourists from the perils of the unpredictable Atlantic currents—and from their own stupidity. She had known this environment would be more conducive to her studies, but the silence was almost unbearable.

Kelly heard several voices near the door but couldn't see anyone. She had been sitting in the rear of the store, also known as the "Resource Room" because of its unique library-like arrangement of shelves and its tables piled high with hard-to-come-by books, maps, and other reference materials relating to the New Jersey Pinelands. For more than a century, Colson's General Store, (a.k.a. Buzby's) in Chatsworth—the heart of the Pines—was *the* central meeting place where all the locals gathered to chat, to get their news, and to pick up dry goods and sundries. While many things had gradually changed over the decades—curious tourists' faces, for example, had all but taken the place of local townspeople's familiar ones—the old store had changed very little, remaining in the capable hands of the Colson family.

Kelly slid Jinx's milk bowl to one side of the floor and nearly stepped on Miss Maggie's sandy-colored tabby as she stood and hurried out. Jinx didn't stir, choosing instead to stay snuggled, cozy, and carefree on the large area rug beneath the table.

The voices grew more animated as Kelly caught the tops of three heads beyond the shelves that were stocked with Mason jars and patchwork quilts. By the looks and sounds of it, there were two males and a young female. As Kelly approached the group she still couldn't make out what they were saying because, she realized, they were speaking in Spanish.

"Kelly!" An enthusiastic Luz rushed over and greeted her with a warm hug. She turned and introduced her companions. "Kelly, may I present Don Alejándro Reyes-Peña and Miguel Aguilar," she said excitedly. "Gentlemen, this is Kelly Martin."

"Charmed," Don Alejándro said with a slight but noticeable accent, bowing his head politely. He was a tall, thin, handsome man in his early forties with smooth olive skin and deep-set, dark brown eyes. Impeccably dressed in a cream-colored linen suit and pale blue silk shirt, Don Alejándro, like his name suggested, had a worldly air about him. He took Kelly's hand and kissed it gently, his eyes never leaving her face.

"You must be Geoffrey's sister," Miguel reasoned as he stepped forward, offering his outstretched hand. "I can see the family resemblance." Miguel was shorter, stockier, and younger than Don Alejándro, and not nearly as formal. He was dressed in a funky flowered Hawaiian shirt and pleated white Dockers. As she shook his hand, Kelly noticed his light hazel eyes, immediately sensing in them warmth and intelligence, set off as they were beneath a shock of unkempt raven hair.

"You know … my brother?" Kelly stammered, catching herself.

"Yes, of course," Don Alejándro offered confidently. "He is in our employ."

"These gentlemen are from Mexico," Luz explained. "They're filmmakers. Don Alejándro is producing a movie, part of which will be filmed right here. Miguel is the director, and … get this … they've hired me and Geoffrey to assist with …"

"… essentials," Don Alejándro finished for her. He smiled and added, "Sometimes, as visitors in another country, we find that we do not know enough about the local culture and customs to conduct ourselves in an efficient manner. Here in New Jersey, for example, the permissions and protocols required to visit the forests and even your wonderful beaches are foreign to us. And, alas, our time is limited. We have only the time our working visas permit to accomplish our goals. Hopefully, Luz and Geoffrey can help us to overcome certain … obstacles. Through her connections in food services, for example, Luz has already introduced us to caterers that will suit our purposes."

Don Alejándro paused and glanced at Miguel expectantly.

"Ahem, yes, and your brother Geoffrey claims to know a great deal about these woods," the young director continued, a look of mild amusement stealing across his face. "He and Luz have told us of your adventures, and we would very much like to avoid this fearsome *chupacabra*, this … 'Jersey Devil' of yours."

Kelly began to sense these men's comments were a little too rehearsed; she was neither amused nor taken by them. "That's great," she said, struggling to find the right words without sounding totally disinterested. "I'm sure Luz can open some doors for you while you are here, and my brother has definitely spent some time in these woods over the past few summers … with all manner of strange creatures"— she cast a sideways glance at Luz—"but honestly, what does any of this have to do with me?"

"We come to you in the hopes you can give us the golden sombrero," Don Alejándro proffered humbly and sincerely.

"But we don't sell hats," Kelly responded with amusement.

"Then we will throw one into the ring," Miguel added hopefully.

"*Sí*," Don Alejándro agreed, a little too quickly, "one that will bring us good fortune when we reach for it, no?"

Luz laughed. "I think they mean a brass ring."

"Yes, that's it!" Miguel replied diplomatically. "Only, much bigger: a ring the size of a *beeg* sombrero," he said with a giant sweep of his arm extending over his head.

Don Alejándro nodded.

Kelly shrugged. "I'm sorry, but I still don't get it."

Luz waited for the men to speak up, but their eyes told her this was one of those "essential" occasions she was hired for. She directed Kelly's attention to what was happening outside.

Through the large plate glass store window Kelly saw a bustle of activity. Cars were slowing down inquisitively, some even stopping, as men across the street, wearing cutoff shorts and equipped with cameras, were setting up tripods and light panels aimed at the entrance of the general store. Passersby eating at Hot Dog Hannah's roadside luncheonette took in the scene as they chowed down on their noontime meal. One of them was Geoffrey, a coil of cable wire wrapped around his shoulder. He and the rest of the film crew, standing and gazing in the direction of the store, all seemed to be waiting for something to happen. Geoffrey waved sheepishly when he saw Kelly looking back at him through the big store window.

"Hey, what's going on here?" asked Kelly suspiciously. "Is that Geoffrey?"

The men kept silent.

Luz winced. "Kelly, Geoffrey mentioned Miss Maggie would be away for awhile and that she left you in charge of the store."

"Oh, did he now?" Kelly felt uneasy. Her stomach rolled just a little. Even Jinx sensed that something was amiss. He came up alongside Kelly and purred insistently until she picked him up and stroked him in her arms.

The men, who only moments before had been so loquacious and eloquent, now busily walked about the store, examining various curios and such, all the while discussing shots, angles, and light.

Finally, when the men came to a halt a safe distance away, Luz blurted, "Kelly, would you mind if they took a couple quick shots of the interior and exterior of the store?"

Dumbfounded, Kelly didn't know what to say. She was still trying to piece it all together.

Sensing her confusion, Miguel sighed heavily and said, "Our research tells us that the body of Captain Emilio Carranza was brought here to Chatsworth, to this very store, in preparation for military transport back to Mexico, his beloved homeland … and ours."

Miguel flashed his hazel eyes, imploring Kelly, "It would mean a lot to us, and to his memory, if we could take just a few simple shots of this most honored place. We promise not to disturb a thing."

"Miss Maggie wouldn't even have to know," Luz added hopefully. "It's not like you're overrun by customers at the moment."

"Carranza, huh?" Kelly asked Luz. "Isn't that the flyer guy Geoffrey's been carrying on about lately?"

"We are all very excited about him, Kelly," Luz explained passionately. "It's time the whole world knew his story."

"*Sí*, that is our goal, Miss Martin," Don Alejándro offered. "And you would be of such great help to us that we would certainly mention your name in the credits."

"What do you think, Jinx?" Kelly asked, gently stroking the cat.

Jinx purred his approval, and then went back to licking his paws.

"Okay, I guess there's no harm in letting you toss a hat into Miss Maggie's ring," Kelly reasoned. "But if this is your 'golden sombrero,' what does that make Geoffrey?"

"Our big *enchilada*?" Miguel asked, looking at Don Alejándro.

"Consider him promoted to key grip," Don Alejándro suggested with a formal nod to Luz.

"Oh, perfect. As if his head wasn't already big enough," Kelly said with a laugh.

4

Junta

Noah Parsons fumbled with the top button on his dress shirt and tried to loosen his tie. His palms were sweating. A confirmed bachelor most of his life, Noah hadn't been this nervous since he married Sarah Bishop a year ago. *And that turned out all right*, the U.S. Coast Guard veteran reminded himself. Still, he would have preferred to be patrolling America's shores and assisting Sunday sailors in distress instead of addressing a large audience on matters of civic importance any day.

Sitting in the front row beside her husband, Sarah Bishop-Parsons, the former widowed schoolteacher and current LBI gift shop owner, gave her husband a reassuring smile.

The American Legion Post 11 meeting hall in Mount Holly was warm—very warm—but not because of the sweltering July heat outside. The big, spacious room was packed to capacity and then some, which forced the central air conditioning to work overtime, without much success.

"The whole town must be here," Noah said anxiously to Sarah, turning in his seat. "I haven't seen a crowd like this since they closed down the drive-in 30 years ago."

"Looks like the media is even taking notice of this meeting," Sarah replied, inclining her head toward the rear of the hall, where a news crew led by the well-known Feather Sparrow, gifted and tenacious reporter with the *Island Sentinel*, was interviewing several Legionnaires.

"Great," moaned Noah. "Just what I need."

"Maybe not you, dear, but it could be just what this town needs," Sarah mused.

It wasn't often that the American Legion allowed the public to join its members in the great hall, but Noah was glad this meeting was one of those rare exceptions and that his wife was with him. She patted his hand gently. Her mere presence was a comfort to him, considering what he had to do.

Although currently living in Ocean County, Noah had been born in Burlington County in a place called Pemberton, not far from Mount Holly. His father, Benjamin, was both a WWII veteran and a mason stationed at McGuire Air Force Base, and it came as no surprise when Noah one day followed in his father's footsteps and joined the same American Legion Post. At the core of the proud organization were veterans' descendants with military service records of their own.

Since its inception in 1919, as a veteran's organization dedicated to the needs of United States' servicemen returning home from combat in Europe at the end of WWI, American Legion Posts had sprung up in cities and towns from coast to coast. Supplemented by new generations of vets returning from tours in more recent wars, the Legion remained active in politics and lobbying efforts, especially those related to the interests of veterans. Traditionally, Legion posts nationwide sponsored commemorative events, parades, and volunteer activities.

Actually, the American Legion had its conceptual roots in ancient Rome. From about 104 B.C. onward, the triumphant, all-conquering Roman Legion adopted as its symbol the "aguila," or eagle. An officer even carried into battle the golden eagle mounted on a staff. Loss of its standard was considered an embarrassment to the regiment and, therefore, it was protected at all costs.

Except for the unfortunate legacy of a deadly airborne disease that surfaced in Philadelphia in 1976 during a Legionnaires convention and now bears its name, the organization had endured and thrived as an American institution.

Dressed in full regalia, with his mosaic of polished medals glistening on his lapel and his red, white, and blue sash pulled snug around his ample midsection, Fred Carlson, the septuagenarian American Legion Post 11 Commander, took the onstage podium and motioned for the nine Carranza Memorial Committee members to join him on the dais. Noah checked the buttons on his shirt and straightened his tie. Sarah gave him a peck on the cheek for luck. He adjusted his Legionnaire's cap and took his place of honor to the right of the Post Commander.

Fred tapped the microphone to make sure it was working; the resultant "thump" echoed so loudly around the room that it silenced the crowd, preempting the call to order.

"Brother Legionnaires, ladies and gentlemen, members of the media, friends and neighbors from near and far," he began slowly, consciously nodding his acknowledgement to select individuals of each group as he glanced around the room. "As most of you know—otherwise you wouldn't be here tonight—for generations, it has been this Post's most solemn pledge and privileged duty to keep alive the memory and accomplishments of a fallen comrade from our good neighbor to the south of our border."

He paused and waited for the cheers and catcalls to die down before continuing. "This we have done, faithfully and unfailingly, every year since that dark and tragic day, 79 years ago, when the remains of the fearless Captain Emilio Carranza and his American-built monoplane were found scattered in our cherished woods. While his crash was a grisly, horrible tragedy, the fact that it happened here, over New Jersey skies, was no accident. It was preordained!"

Again he waited for the crowd's response to die down. While Fred may have relished the applause, Noah began to shift uncomfortably from foot to foot. He couldn't pinpoint the reason for his discomfort, but something in the delivery, if not the meaning of Fred's message itself, was disconcerting. Perhaps it was only his nerves, the knowledge that he would soon be called upon to deliver his own remarks to this charged crowd. Noah glanced at Sarah and then stared out into the sea of faces, fixing on no one in particular and yet everyone at the same time.

Fred continued. "Through all kinds of weather, in storms and squalls, in heat, haze, and hell fury, there has always been a Legionnaire from this appointed Post present at that anointed place to commemorate the fate of one of Mexico's finest young aviation pioneers. Yes, Captain Carranza was a true hero in every sense of the word; a young man of great daring who showed the world tremendous courage and bravery in the face of insurmountable odds; a man whose actions told us not even the unbridled rage of Mother Nature herself would stand in the way of a military man's duty to bring glory to his homeland by completing his mission." He paused for effect before continuing.

"Now, as I reflect on the towering stone monument that stands in the hallowed clearing of sacred ground that witnessed his last breath on this earth, I see a grand and wonderful memorial, purchased with the hard earned pennies of admiring Mexican schoolchildren. I see neither a failed mission nor a man who died in vain. No, sir. What I see is a symbol, a symbol of sacrifice, a symbol of friendship and goodwill, and a symbol of our humanity and hope, which we of the American Legion Post 11 are rightfully proud to keep alive!"

The hall shook with thunderous applause as the crowd rose to their feet and cheered wildly. Women reached for tissues. Grown men fought back tears. Children stood up on their chairs. In the whole place, no eye was dry, no heart untouched by the Post Commander's moving tribute.

It was at this exact moment that Noah came to realize the source of his uneasiness. He took a step back and watched from behind as the Post Commander acknowledged his well-received performance. And that was precisely what bothered Noah. While the remarks may have been genuine, the delivery seemed overwrought compared to previous years. Words like "anointed" and "preordained" weighed heavily on Noah's mind. From his perspective, the aged commander came across more like a Sunday morning soapbox preacher than the amiable and humble commander he knew and respected. Was it the curious media circus atmosphere, the crowded hall, or the presence of the conspicuous pair of well-mannered Hispanic men Noah had just noticed standing near the doorway, applauding approvingly?

Before Noah could come to terms in his own mind with his trepidation over the Post Commander's uncharacteristic grandstanding, Fred was speaking again. "Thank you. Thank you. And now, dear brothers, friends, and neighbors, I ask your patience and support while I introduce the men standing up here on the dais with me. They are, starting on my left: Edgar Wilson, Paul Sloan, Lester Hatch, and his oldest boy, Leroy."

The men nodded and waved to modest applause.

"And to my right, at the far end, we have Amos Hurley, Wayne Nye, Harlan James, Lewis Brewer, and the Chairman of this year's Carranza Memorial Committee, Noah Parsons."

Sarah clapped the loudest and, much to the dismay and embarrassment of Noah, she placed her fingers to her lips and produced a shrill whistle, to boot.

Fred motioned with his hands for everyone to keep their applause down.

"These are the folks who have been charged with overseeing the preparations for the 79th memorial service. As I mentioned earlier, there have been times when we've had but a handful of attendees at the service, half of them vets from the 11th. Other times we've had the Sugar Sand Ramblers play and the magnificent Thunderbirds soar overhead. It varies based on the weather, but I can truly say that interest has certainly picked up in recent years. And that's why, for the past few weeks, these nine fine gentlemen of the Carranza Memorial Committee have found themselves in the middle of a dilemma. It seems this year, suddenly and unexpectedly, there is not one but two filmmakers vying to—you'll pardon the pun—memorialize our ceremonious event on film."

The individuals in the room nodded in acknowledgment as Fred called out their names. "They are Mr. Wade Sawyer, fresh from New York, and, representing the Carranza family, all the way from Mexico, Señor Don Alejándro Reyes-Peña and Miguel Aguilar."

Noah shifted his weight and glanced down at Sarah as Fred continued. "After careful review of the applications and credentials of both parties, the decision as to which one will get the approval falls to our own little *junta,*" he joked, misusing the Spanish term for a small ruling military group usually associated with having just overthrown the government.

There was a sporadic grunt of indulgent laughter from a handful of amused people.

Fred looked at Noah, then back at the audience. "Mr. Chairman, has the committee come to a decision?"

Noah took a deep breath and exhaled slowly. "We have, Commander," he replied dryly.

Fred stepped aside, yielding the podium to Noah, who adjusted the microphone to his height and looked out into the patiently waiting crowd. Seated with Wade Sawyer in the center row were Feather Sparrow, Megan Turner, and Danny Windsor, although, with his dyed-black hair parted down the middle, Noah did a double take before he realized who it was. Seated over in the far right corner, near the exit door where Don Alejándro and Miguel stood waiting anxiously with their arms folded, were Luz, Geoffrey, and Kelly. All three waved enthusiastically and called out to Noah when he looked in their direction. Sarah stood up and waved when she saw the kids seated in the Hispanic filmmakers' camp.

"Ladies and gentlemen," Noah began. "The committee is pleased to permit both of these film crews to capture this year's ceremony for posterity, each from their own unique perspective."

5

Dante's Inferno

As far as Fire Chief Arthur Adams could determine, the blaze had ended where it began, in the old barrel warehouse at Whitesbog Village. The fire essentially was contained in the large, oblong, barn-like building, thanks to the immediate action taken by Chester Potts, the onsite overseer, and his handy brigade of bucket-toting volunteers. Passing pails of water with assembly-line precision from the pumping station on the premises to the fire 100 yards away, the campsite volunteers had the blaze under control by the time the fire truck arrived. Unfortunately, the harm was already done, not so much from the fire or to the warehouse, but from the water damage to the cameras, tripods, props, and other movie equipment that was being temporarily housed in the building.

Known in its promotional literature as "the Birthplace of the Cultivated Blueberry," Historic Whitesbog Village was a restored turn-of-the-century town operated by the Whitesbog Preservation Trust. During the early 1900s, it had been a thriving community built around the largest cranberry farm in New Jersey. Founded by J.J. White, it had gone on to gain even greater prominence under the care of his eldest daughter, Elizabeth. A compassionate provider for the migrant worker community, she would be remembered fondly as the "Blueberry Queen," because it had been largely through her efforts, in collaboration with the USDA, that a ripened berry was first produced and brought to market, earning for the lowly blueberry official designation as New Jersey's state fruit.

Nestled in Lebanon State Forest, the rustic village boasted nearly 40 buildings in various stages of restoration. Including the abandoned cranberry bogs and the lush blueberry fields, the grounds covered nearly 3,000 acres on a tract of land just outside the rural town of Browns Mills in Burlington County.

Off the beaten path but accessible by car or bus from Route 530 along a winding, gravel drive, the village was just the kind of place where a small army of moviemakers from a foreign country could set up shop inconspicuously and work peacefully until their job was done. At least, that's what Noah thought when he enlisted the aid of his good friend Tom Banks, a naturalist and Preservation Trust member, to obtain the permits needed in order for Whitesbog Village to play host to the "Poco Loco Film Company," as the Mexican crew was being called around town. Evidently, not everyone agreed with the arrangements.

"It was definitely arson," Arthur pronounced to the small crowd assembled on the porch steps of the village's general store after the fire had been subdued. They were drinking sparkling apple cider and mineral water to soothe their parched throats. He pulled a stogie from his mouth and spit over the railing.

"How can you be so sure, Chief?" Feather shot back, her BlackBerry at the ready.

Arthur considered for a moment, through a haze of curling cigar smoke, both the question and the young blonde reporter herself. He lowered one eyelid to get a better look at her through his good eye. *Now what do we have here?* he thought. *She don't look like she just rolled out of bed and onto the news scene at this hour. No siree, Bob. She's all dolled up for business—monkey business, no doubt.*

"Because, Missy, that there was kerosene I smelt in the warehouse. And that building ain't seen a kerosene lamp inside her walls in over 60 years."

Feather was undeterred. "But aren't the 'campers' using lanterns in their tents? Maybe one of them dropped a lamp by accident."

"None of my people would have gone into the building at this late hour, Ms. Sparrow," Don Alejándro interjected formally. "We have an early shoot scheduled for tomorrow morning."

"And there was no broken glass," Miguel added, sweat showing on his face, which was blackened from fighting the blaze. "If someone had dropped a lantern, wouldn't there be shattered glass lying around? Or a broken lamp?"

"That still wouldn't explain the door being locked ... from the inside," Geoffrey said, leaning over the railing to get in on the conversation.

"Now hold on just a cotton pickin' minute," the fire chief stammered. "Are you tellin' me that door was locked the whole time the fire was burnin'?"

"Yeah," Chester groaned gloomily, "we had to break it down."

Arthur scratched his grizzled face. "Is there another way in?"

"The gangway doors are barred, Chief," the overseer explained. "Now that we don't do crate packin' no more, ain't no reason to open those doors. They're bolted shut."

Arthur kicked absently at the ground. "Now, that just don't make no sense. How could an arsonist get in and out with all the doors bolted and locked?"

Danny and Feather exchanged glances.

"He could climb down the side of the building from the rooftop," Danny tossed out.

Kelly, Geoffrey, and Luz looked at him in disbelief as he continued, "Slip in through the window, make his way down the stacked crates, and then back out the same way."

"In the dark?" Arthur questioned.

All eyes were now on Danny.

"Ever hear of a flashlight?" came Danny's sarcastic answer.

"That there's some theory, boy," Arthur said suspiciously. "Mind if I ask you where you were when the fire started?"

"He was with me," Kelly and Feather blurted out simultaneously.

The group was stunned into silence.

"Now, I do declare, son," said the fire chief, shaking his head. "Either you're one lucky son of a bitch, or one of these fine young ladies here is lying."

Kelly and Feather glared at each other.

"Perhaps I can explain," Don Alejándro jumped in.

"Oh, by all means, please do," Arthur replied. "I'm sure we'd all like to hear this."

"No, let me," Kelly pleaded. "I'm the one who dragged Danny into this."

Feather was nonplussed. She put her hands on her hips and waited.

"You see, sir, when Señor Reyes-Peña invited my brother Geoffrey, Luz, and me to hang out with them tonight for an old-fashioned Mexican barbecue, I didn't want to come alone, so Geoffrey talked Danny—that's him, there—into coming along.

"Danny—or Dante, if you prefer, take your pick, he goes by both these days—is working on the Wade Sawyer film. Maybe you've heard about it. It's been in all the newspapers." Kelly shot a hard glance at Feather, who acknowledged the plug with an approving smile. "Geoffrey and Luz thought it would be fun to have Danny mingle with the competition, so to speak, and I guess he agreed, because, well … here he is."

"Anyway, we had a nice meal of …" Kelly looked toward Miguel for help.

Miguel smiled warmly. "*Arróz con póllo.*"

"Chicken and rice," Luz translated for the baffled chief.

"And *churrasco*," Geoffrey chipped in.

"Fine Argentinean beef," Don Alejándro explained proudly.

"Yeah, that was my favorite," Danny said with a broad smile. "You don't get that kind of beef at Arby's."

Miguel picked up the story. "After dinner, we set up in the old barrel factory next to the warehouse to screen the dailies we shot at Colson's General Store the other day."

"That's where I fit in," Kelly said awkwardly. "I'm working there this summer, helping Miss Maggie out."

Arthur listened intently and did not interrupt, but the truth was he was somewhat lost.

"Following the screening, we had Paul Sloan, our story consultant, share some anecdotes about the amazing life of Emilio Carranza," Miguel continued.

"That would be me," Paul spoke up. The bearded and bespectacled middle-aged man in combat fatigues offered a casual wave of his hand. He had been perched quietly on the corner of the porch steps, nursing a cold beer and obviously enjoying the others' longwinded retelling of the night's tale.

"It was some really cool stuff," Danny remembered aloud. "I'll bet you didn't know that Carranza's great-uncle was the first president of Mexico?"

"Sadly, he died for his beliefs," an emotional Miguel added with a knowing glance toward Paul.

"Now, hold on, Baba Louie, I don't mean to be rude, but what's all this got to do with my fire investigation?"

"Probably nothing, Chief, but it does make for great copy," Feather said with a coy wink, scribbling in earnest.

"That's my point," Kelly snarled with a withering glance at Feather. "Everything was perfect until she showed up. That's when we lost Danny."

Feather smirked. "I didn't know he was yours to lose."

Danny rolled his eyes and frowned.

"Then you *were* with him, Miss?" Arthur asked conclusively, directing his question to Feather.

She looked at Don Alejándro and then at Danny. "Not exactly," she replied, discomfort showing on her photogenic face.

Don Alejándro rushed to her rescue. "After the screening, I gave Ms. Sparrow a guided tour of the White mansion," he offered, smiling through his obvious embarrassment.

Miguel and Chester each raised an eyebrow.

"We were there … uh, having refreshments … when we heard Mr. Potts raise the alarm."

"I see," Arthur replied, absentmindedly rubbing his facial stubble and studying the faces of the motley crew assembled before him. "Yes siree, I think we all get the picture."

The fire chief started to leave, then turned back and, crunching his cigar beneath his foot, addressed Danny. "A little piece of advice, son: You might want to consider getting yourself legal representation. The police may want to talk to you after I file my report."

6
What's in a Name?

"**D**ante!" Wade Sawyer exclaimed, feigning surprise at the intrusion. He was sipping a margarita in the sun-drenched study of his rented villa overlooking Manahawkin Bay at the very private end of Cedar Run Dock Road. "So? You've created quite a buzz, fraternizing with the enemy. What are we supposed to think?"

Danny didn't bother to answer. He stood there quietly, admiring the view. Through the large picture window, against the backdrop of a shimmering bay, his gaze lingered on Feather, lounging on the deck in a white string bikini barely hidden beneath a sheer muslin cover-up that showed off her golden tan and much more. Her long hair was pulled tightly into a bun and held in place by an antique silver and turquoise trident. He couldn't tear his eyes away.

"I was just about to mix Feather another drink. Care to join us?"

"Sure, I'll have whatever you're having." Danny made his way through the sliding glass door out onto the deck adorned by Feather, while Wade went into the kitchen.

Feather turned around slowly, giving Danny a close-up of her stunning beauty.

"I'm sorry I ran out on you the other night, Danny. I hope I didn't spoil things between you and your girlfriend."

"She's not my girlfriend."

"Tell that to her," Feather replied with her sexiest smile.

Danny tried not to show her the effect she had on him. It worked.

She tried a more direct approach. "So, was that your plan? To get me to rendezvous with you in the warehouse?"

"Hey, I thought that was your idea," he responded with all the casualness he could muster.

"Well, I did think it would be fun to see what was locked up in there," she offered suggestively.

"Yeah, well, nobody offered *me* the house tour," he said defensively.

Feather looked hurt. "Don Alejándro was a perfect gentleman."

"Right, and I'm Don Juan."

"Well you sure had the fire chief convinced."

"You mean old Deputy Dawg? I didn't think he was even listening to me. I saw the way he was staring at you. It's the way *all* men stare at you."

"It can be a burden sometimes," Feather said nonchalantly before unknotting her hair and giving it a melodramatic toss.

"When it's not opening doors?"

"Look, I didn't go through four years at Syracuse and earn a degree in journalism just to report on the number of potholes in Bumpkin County. Besides, there is a connection between the Carranza story and the media. The Mexican newspaper *Excelsior* sold subscriptions to finance the flight. Lindbergh himself donated $2,500."

"How do you know all that?" Danny asked. He was impressed but wary at the same time.

"An old writer's trick called *research*," Feather replied. "Geez, Danny, give a girl some credit, will ya?"

Danny felt a little foolish. Maybe Feather's approach to the job was more professional than he had realized.

"So what's with Sawyer? Is he research, too?"

"Maybe," Feather replied, toying with him.

"And what's your story? I mean, what's with the name, anyway? Was your father some sort of frustrated birdwatcher?" Danny tried to rattle her as he sat down beside her.

Feather leaned back in her lounge chair. "No, actually, he's a successful orthodontist. He and my mother met at Woodstock in the summer of 1969. She was one of those bewitched, mud-clad nymphets you see dancing naked in the movie. They were never sure whether it was the drugs or the music, but they fell in love and got married six years later when my dad finished up his studies at the University of Medicine and Dentistry in New Jersey."

"That explains everything," Danny said smugly. "Your mom and dad were a couple of spaced-out hippies intent on keeping their far-out counterculture ideals alive by giving their children unconventional names like Moon Unit Zappa and Barbara 'Seagull' Hershey."

Feather frowned. "I'm serious about my work," she protested.

Danny's grin widened. "So, do *you* like to dance naked to rock music?"

"Only when it's raining," Feather replied seductively, relaxing into the moment. "Actually, my name started out as kind of a family joke. I wasn't a very good eater when I was little. My grandmother would say that I 'ate like a bird.' One day after lifting me up on his shoulders, my father remarked that I was as 'light as a feather.' For some reason, the name just stuck. As you can imagine, the fact that our last name is Sparrow just added to the merriment."

Danny looked away, momentarily lost in his own thoughts. *Dante Reed, where the hell did I come up with that? Okay, so my parents separated when I was young and the oldest lifeguard in the world raised me. Then some scum named Eddie Farley claims to be my real father but my real mother makes him admit that he wasn't even in the running. Only by that time, my real dad wasn't so sure he was my real dad. That's not much of a family tree. No wonder I chose a stage name. If she can get away with Feather Sparrow, then I can get away with Dante Reed.*

Feather mistook Danny's long, brooding silence as a sign that he had processed, but didn't quite accept, what she had just shared with him, so she added, in a soft whisper while looking out onto the glorious bay: "It's Mildred."

"Huh?" Danny responded, his thoughts returning to the present.

"My real name; it's Mildred," Feather admitted, dropping all pretense. "I was named after my maternal grandmother," she added, catching Danny's blank stare. "Somehow the name silly 'Millie' doesn't quite cut it in the media."

Danny cracked a contented smile, and they exchanged their first genuinely tender look into each other's eyes.

"Showtime," announced Wade as he came out onto the deck with a fresh tray of drinks, chips, and salsa. "A Slow, Comfortable Screw for the lovely lady. Oh, yes, and a Molotov Cocktail for the boy arsonist. Sure is a damn shame all that equipment went up in smoke!"

7

¡Aye, Carrumba!

The sea spray splashed against Luz Sanchez's face and unprotected arms, sending a chill through her entire body. The blindfold she wore, which prevented her from seeing where she was going, only served to magnify the sensation.

"Are we there yet?" she shouted nervously above the sound of waves thumping against the hull of the chugging boat.

"How much farther?" Geoffrey asked, turning to address the squat, ruddy-looking man at the helm. With his round face, sparse hair, and squinty eyes, the man reminded Geoffrey of Popeye. All he needed was a corncob pipe and a can of spinach.

"Oh, not much farther," Ned Thompson replied calmly above the noisy torque of the outboard. "It all depends on the wind and tide. The best way is for us to make our approach from the north, but if the ocean's too choppy, we'll have to come back around from the west and shoot through Simkin's thoroughfare. The channel's only about four feet deep there and it kind of zigzags, so we'd have to be careful."

Luz wasn't comforted by what she could hear of the captain's description of their route over the sounds of the wind and water. Noah had convinced Geoffrey that Ned was the right man for the job, so Geoffrey and Luz had hired him. Now neither of them had much choice but to sit back and enjoy the ride. Although Geoffrey didn't want to spoil the surprise for Luz by removing the blindfold, he could tell her apprehension was building at the same rate as his excitement.

Geoffrey's fascination with Little Beach had begun several summers earlier, during his search for another of New Jersey's lost treasures, Tucker's Island. It had been a thrilling adventure Geoffrey shared with Kelly and their then-new friend, Danny. While Tucker's Island neither revealed all of her secrets nor coughed up the pirate booty rumored to have been buried on her, the teens did learn valuable lessons about the fragile ecosystem of the bay area, as well as a few insights into trust and friendship.

Geoffrey had learned most of what he knew about Little Beach from the old baymen who volunteered their time and talents working at the Tuckerton Seaport. He had worked there last summer, an experience—and what an experience it was!—that whetted his appetite for lost causes. Certainly, to the untrained eye, Little Beach was a lost cause.

In its mysterious and checkered history, Little Beach was sometimes referred to as Pullen Island and other times as Dog Island. The name Little Beach had probably stuck to distinguish it from its northerly neighbor, Long Beach Island. For a while in the late 19th century, unscrupulous real estate developers mounted a marketing campaign that rivaled the great Florida swampland scandal of the 1920s, shamelessly promoting Little Beach's tree-lined building lots, which didn't exist—and never would.

The cornerstone and fundamental selling feature of Little Beach had been its proposed pedestrian bridge to the mainland over an adjoining series of small sedge islands that skipped out into Great Bay. Seven wooden bridges would be linked together. When the stock market crashed in 1929, the final bridge to Little Beach was left unfinished. In no time, the cabins and other buildings constructed on Little Beach fell into rapid decline. The state had bought up and burned what remained of the island's development and turned it into a preserve to discourage vandals and squatters. Over time, Mother Nature gradually reclaimed one of her own, reducing Little Beach to a desolate patch of sand that made it a worthwhile habitat for various species of wildlife such as the endangered piping plover, but unfit for man.

In 1949, Ned, then a member of the Lifesaving Station, was one of the last people to leave Little Beach and the only one who still periodically returned, happy to reminisce for anyone who would listen. In Geoffrey, he found an enthusiastic audience.

The approach from the north didn't work. The waves were too intense. So Ned cranked up the engine on his 19-foot Boston Whaler and headed back into the bay. Geoffrey held his breath. Ten minutes later, Ned cut the engine, and Luz could feel the hull of the boat scrape against soft sand.

"You can look now," Geoffrey said as he removed her blindfold.

Luz adjusted her eyes and stared in disbelief. "This is it?"

Geoffrey waited for confirmation from Ned, who nodded.

"This is it," Geoffrey affirmed.

"*¡Aye, Carrumba!* What exactly am I looking at?" Luz exclaimed.

"You mean, what was it before this?" Ned asked. "Believe it or not, Little Beach used to be a lot bigger than what you see today. It was my home. Now, hold out your arms."

They looked puzzled but complied. Ned produced a spray can from his tackle box, with which he sprayed Geoffrey, and then attempted to spray Luz. "I'll pass," she said, pushing the can aside.

"Suit yourself."

Geoffrey gave her a stern look.

"That stuff stinks," she insisted.

"It's citronella mixed with beeswax," Ned explained, applying it generously to his own skin. "Doc Morris makes it. No finer stuff around."

He helped the kids out of the boat. Immediately, a swarm of greenhead flies, as thick as a cloud, attacked the unprotected Luz. They covered her from head to toe. "Get them off of me!" she screamed.

Ned gave the insects a shot of the bug repellant and the cloud dispersed. "They're attracted to the carbon dioxide you emit when you exhale—so, try not to breathe," he joked.

"I think I'll wait for you two in the boat," Luz said, climbing back aboard.

"There's a tarp in the back if you need to take cover," Ned said, laughing and revealing an upper gum missing a couple of front teeth.

Geoffrey gave Luz a dejected look and then quickly followed in Ned's tracks.

"Over there," Ned said, pointing. "That was the Guard Station. You can still see the electrical box on the utility pole." They strode over to inspect the rubble.

"What's that?" Geoffrey asked, looking further down the beach. "It looks like an outhouse—like the one behind Colson's General Store."

"Don't worry, this one's empty," Ned replied after checking the hole.

Geoffrey studied the cutout design on the door, which hung in place by a single rusty hinge. He had a puzzled look on his face. "Looks like a half moon."

"That it is," Ned confirmed with a slight chuckle. "Lets in the moonlight so you can see what you're doing in the dark."

"This is perfect," Geoffrey grinned, looking around at, essentially, nothing but sand and a derelict old building.

"What exactly are you trying to capture with this movie of yours?" Ned asked with genuine interest.

Geoffrey spoke without hesitation. "Civilization has always documented man's dominance over nature. But this little island represents a victory for nature over modern man. I know it's a small example, but it's an important one. And what better symbol of that triumph than an abandoned outhouse in the middle of nowhere, surrounded by water, where nobody can use this marvelous manmade contraption but the flies!"

"Well, did you find what you were looking for?" Luz asked, peeking out from under her tarp to greet the men when they returned.

"Absolutely," Geoffrey answered with a satisfied look on his face. He climbed in behind Ned and took a thoughtful look at his less-than-enthusiastic companion. "I'm sorry it wasn't your cup of tea," he added sheepishly. "Maybe next time we can visit that shrine you were telling me about."

"Padre Pio's shrine, near Vineland! Now, that would be exciting, but you'd still need a camera … and a crew," Luz added. "And *that*," she concluded, "would require a miracle."

Ned yanked on the pull cord. The outboard sputtered and coughed to life.

"I'm working on that," Geoffrey replied, taking a long last look over *his* island.

8

¡Aye, Carranza!

Everyone in the room was talking at once. What had begun as several murmurs grouped around sidebar conversations had grown into a dull rumble and then gradually became an outright roar. Noah found that he could no longer hear himself think, let alone make sense of the conversations whirling around him. His head throbbed, his pulse quickened, and his patience wore thin. The emergency meeting of the Carranza Memorial Committee had clearly gotten out of hand.

"Enough!" he bellowed, slamming the gavel down. "Order! Order! Let's have some order, please. Now, then. One at a time."

"As I was saying," Lester Hatch continued in his deep, rich baritone voice. The local cranberry farmer, seated directly across from Noah at a long rectangular table, peered through his Walmart eyeglasses at his fellow committeemen as he spoke. "With less than a week to go before our traditional Carranza service, I think it's clear that the show must go on. We cannot disappoint the community. Canceling or postponing the event is out of the question."

"I agree with Pop," Lester's son Leroy added. He was a chip off the old block in more than one way. "It's unfortunate that the Poco Loco Film Company had their equipment destroyed, but we still have the American crew. I say we let them go it alone."

"But we awarded the film rights to both groups," Noah replied, "in an open public forum and, thanks to the coverage of the *Island Sentinel*, the story's even been picked up nationally. Going back on our decision now would cause a public relations nightmare that could flare up into an international incident."

"Perhaps Mr. Sawyer would be willing to share his equipment and film time with Señor Aguilar?" came a suggestion from Edgar Wilson, the country lawyer.

"Oh, I can just imagine what kind of terms and conditions he would have for that," Wayne Nye, the Deputy Post Commander and retired Amtrak engineer, replied. "Wade Sawyer does not strike me as the type that would be interested in sharing the spotlight with anybody."

Lewis Brewster sighed audibly from behind his walrus-like mustache. "The problem is, the clock is ticking ... and for Poco Loco, time is running out."

"Yeah, it's not our fault their stuff got ruined. Maybe it's a sign," Amos Hurley added, drumming his fingers on the table. The tattooed auto mechanic was not one to mince words, which made it even harder for Noah to reconcile the secret obsession Amos had admitted to him: He collected cocktail stirrers. His most prized possession, he confessed, was a hot pink plastic stick bearing the likeness of Celine Dion. He had picked it up years ago in Atlantic City when the diva did a show at the Golden Nugget. Going on a month ago, he had shown it to Noah with a schoolgirl's glee and Noah still couldn't seem to shake the image.

Fred, the pontificating Post Commander, cleared his throat. "Gentlemen, gentlemen, I know I am not on the committee, and my vote doesn't count, but may I remind you that this is America, and these people are our guests, our neighbors? They've come here in good faith to keep alive the spirit of one of their own. But Captain Carranza belongs to us, too. Is he not one of our brothers? Did we not decide that long ago, when we committed ourselves to his legacy? Don't we have an obligation to help our 'friends' tell the world about what we at Post 11 have kept alive for so long?"

Noah drew a deep breath. "It's true. Carranza is a powerful symbol of hope and unity," he agreed, "and we owe it to his memory to try and find a way to help his fellow countrymen tell his story, so that his achievements might inspire others from his homeland."

"Can't Sawyer's film do that? Why do we need two films?" Harlan James asked. The committee could always count on the John Deere salesman to be straightforward in his thinking.

The veins in Noah's neck popped out. "We've been over this before, Harlan. We have no right to deny the Mexican people access to one of their greatest heroes. Lord knows they could use a hero today. That poor country has been in the throes of political unrest ever since last year's presidential elections."

"Isn't that really the point here, Noah?" Lester asked. "I mean, come on, you read the newspapers. Should we really be reaching our hand out across the border when it's obvious that most Americans would rather be putting up fences?"

"Immigration is a whole 'nother subject, Lester," Noah replied with obvious annoyance, "and one that has no place here."

"C'mon, Noah, 11 million illegal aliens," the younger Hatch threw out. "We all *know* where they're coming from."

"I can't believe you want to bring that up! Next thing you're going to tell me is that they're muscling in on your cranberry business!"

The room burst into heated debate all over again.

"*¡Aye, Carranza!*" exclaimed Noah, looking up at the ceiling. "There must be something we can do!"

"Maybe it's not up to us," Paul reasoned. The ex-military paratrooper had remained quiet throughout the intervening debate. Paul was a miscreant who, at times, talked much but said little. When aided by a little whiskey, he talked far too much about a great many things that seemed preposterous. Noah got the distinct impression that behind the trimmed gray beard and probing green eyes was a formidable, if peculiar, intellect. Paranoid and burnt out is how most of the others characterized him.

"Maybe Edgar's got the right idea," Paul continued, inclining his head toward Edgar, who was seated beside him. "Maybe we should simply stay out of it and let the two camps sit down and work it out between themselves. It ain't our fight."

"That sounds like good advice, Paul," the elder Hatch replied. Several others concurred around the table.

"But what if they can't come to terms?" Amos wondered. "I have my doubts."

"So do I," Wayne said, nodding vigorously. "We should have a backup plan—an outside source of equipment."

"All right, does anybody have any ideas?" Noah asked hopefully.

"Well, I do have a contact in Jersey City," Paul offered cautiously. "Joey Bonetti. Most people know him as 'Joey Bones' because of his fondness for horror flicks and for his uncanny ability to crush competition at whatever he does. He's the head of the film syndicate called Hollywood East. He's quite powerful and very well connected." He threw an unconscious glance over his shoulder and lowered his voice before continuing. "Rumor has it that Joey *made* his 'bones' by taking out the head of a Hollywood film company who refused to distribute his nephew's campy slasher film, *Whackin' Jersey Style.* The movie was so bad, nobody wanted it except the FBI!"

"Sounds like a nice guy, but can he get the Mexicans what they need in time to shoot the memorial?" Harlan asked.

"I've always heard he was the right man, for the right price, at the right time," Paul said, chuckling at his own words.

"Perhaps we could take up a collection for Poco Loco—just like the Mexican kids did for Captain Carranza's monument," Lewis offered enthusiastically. "Now wouldn't that be fitting?"

"With Joey Bones, it might be a little more expensive than you've bargained for," Paul cautioned.

"I say we approve this Bones character on a contingency basis," Fred advised. "There's no harm in our doing the neighborly thing by putting the Mexicans in touch with him, if necessary. But they'll have to pay their own way on whatever he can deliver."

There were nods of agreement all around the room. The Hatches said nothing. Paul leaned back in his chair, re-considering his proposal. Remembering that his last encounter with Joey Bones ended up in a street brawl outside a bar in Bayonne, he was having second thoughts about his own suggestion. But in deference to the show of solidarity he saw from the faces around the room, he kept those thoughts to himself.

Noah felt a deep sense of relief from the proposed plan. "Looks like we have a consensus," he said aloud to the group. "Okay," he said, exhaling deeply. "Wayne, show Mr. Sawyer and Señor Aguilar in."

9

Vibes

"They're gone!" Wayne shouted, bursting through the committee room door, his face flushed with disbelief in his own announcement.

"Who's gone?" Fred asked.

"The filmmakers, Sawyer and Aguilar."

"Where did they go?" Noah couldn't believe this.

"I don't know. But they're not in the hall," the Vice Commander said, pacing nervously. "The place is empty."

"They had an argument," Megan explained as she made a dramatic entrance into the male-dominated hall. Wade's sassy production assistant and gal Friday paused to catch her breath. "The Mexican director asked Sawyer to lend him a camera so he could shoot the memorial and complete his film. Wade told him to … well, I'd rather not say … "

The committee members looked at one another. Noah and Fred exchanged hesitant glances.

Megan coughed before she continued. "Then they got into a heated debate over who really had the right to do the film. I don't speak Spanish, but I'm pretty sure the Mexican director started cursing at Wade. Next thing I know, Wade takes my keys, jumps in my car, and drives away."

"And Miguel Aguilar?" Paul asked.

"He called someone on his cell phone and left."

Noah started for the door.

"Let them go," Edgar calmly advised. "If they need our help, they know where to find us."

Megan studied the utterly confused faces of the committee. No one seemed to know what to do next.

"Okay, so what so we do now, Mr. Chairman?" Lester asked Noah sarcastically.

"We wait," Noah replied, retaking his seat.

"Wait for what?" Leroy fumed. "World War III?" He went and stood beside his father.

"We wait until things settle down," Noah answered, holding his temper.

"And then?" pressed Harlan.

Noah looked up at the Commander and sighed heavily. "And then we do what we can to help."

"Well, I could sure use a lift home," Megan ventured timidly.

"My car's parked right outside," Fred offered. "Will a Lexus and a 70-year-old chauffeur do?" The Post Commander gallantly made for the door, adding, "Paul, you'd better get in touch with that Joey Bones character right away."

***

Kelly checked her watch. It was two minutes to five. Closing time was supposed to be 5 PM but the woman wearing ruby red lipstick couldn't seem to make up her mind about which fruit preserves to buy. She was the only customer in the store at the moment, and there had been only a handful all day. She'd been mulling over the decision for the last half hour, reading each label carefully, comparing the ingredients: strawberry-rhubarb or cranberry; blueberry, peach, or plum. Evidently she'd narrowed the choices down to two, weighing a jar in each hand.

"Why not buy them both?" Kelly found herself asking as she approached the middle-aged woman, who was dressed in a floral frock with a red hibiscus that matched the color of her lipstick.

The woman, startled out of her reverie, thrust the two jars at Kelly. "Which would you recommend?" she asked in a slow, deep voice while arching her painted eyebrows in an air of mystery. *Strange lady*, Kelly mused, also noticing she wore a knotted extension that looked like a rat's tail in her stringy, graying black hair.

"Strawberry-rhubarb is, hands-down, the local favorite," Kelly said quickly after examining the two labels.

"Hmm, yes, but I'm partial to blueberry, myself," the woman mulled.

"That's good, too," Kelly replied, reaching for the blueberry jar. "Shall I wrap it for you?"

The woman hesitated. "Well, I don't know," she said with mock exasperation. "Maybe I need a change." She stared into Kelly's eyes. "Have you ever felt like that?"

"Every day," Kelly said, trying to dodge the question. She glanced at her watch.

"Oh, I'm sorry," the woman apologized without meaning it. "Am I keeping you from something?"

"We close at five," Kelly replied. She didn't want to admit it, but she actually was in a bit of a hurry. She was supposed to meet Geoffrey and Danny after work. Kelly was anxious to find out if there had been any new developments in the Whitesbog fire investigation and whether the Poco Loco Film Company was going to be able to finish the Carranza film, now that she had a personal stake in it. In truth, she was really more worried that Danny might still be the fire marshal's chief suspect.

"If you're in a hurry, I can just leave now," the woman finished, as if she were offended.

"Whatever," Kelly replied impatiently. She looked around the store, making mental notes of what she had to do before she closed up and how long each step would take.

The woman put the jars back on the shelf. "Maggie Colson would never treat a customer this way."

The words cut Kelly deeply.

"Listen, I'm sorry, ma'am, but if it were any other night I'd stay open until midnight," Kelly lied.

"I see," the woman replied in her slow, plodding way. She took Kelly in for a full measure and probed further. "Meeting your boyfriend?"

Kelly began to squirm uncomfortably. "No, just friends … for dinner," she found herself saying hastily. *Maybe if I stick to the truth, I can get out of here quicker*, she thought to herself.

"Doesn't sound too important."

"Well, it is to me. Now, if you don't mind," Kelly said, moving toward the front door. "If you've been here before, then you know we'll be open again tomorrow morning at eight o' clock sharp."

"No, I think I'll buy this one now," the woman said, reaching for the strawberry-rhubarb preserve. Kelly kept walking toward the door. "And this one, too," the woman added, reaching for the jar of blueberry.

Kelly turned and stared the woman down.

"You see, young lady, life is about choices," the woman said behind her enigmatic smile. "I've made mine. Now it's time to make yours. You can sell me the preserves, or show me to the door." She held the two jars out in front of Kelly. "But I can tell you one thing: If I leave empty-handed tonight, I won't be back tomorrow, or ever again."

Kelly took the two jars from the woman without a word and walked over to the counter with them. The woman followed quietly.

"That'll be $9.50," Kelly said, ringing up the cash register. She bagged the items and waited as the woman rummaged through her purse.

"Good choice," the woman said wryly.

Kelly stuck out her hand for the money.

"Oh, dear!" the woman gasped, grabbing Kelly's hand.

"What's wrong?" Kelly asked, pulling it back.

"It's your lifeline," the woman replied.

Kelly examined her own palm. "What about my lifeline?"

"Oh, it's nothing, really," the woman said, toying with Kelly. "You don't want to know."

"Know what? Are you some kind of a psychic?"

The woman pulled a card from her purse and handed it to Kelly. She read the card aloud: "MADAME ZORA, LIFE ADVISOR: ASTROLOGY, PALM, TAROT & INTUITIVE READINGS. MEDIUM FOR ALL AGES. BY APPOINTMENT ONLY."

Kelly gave a skeptical smirk.

"I take it you don't believe in the power of seeing the future?" Madame Zora asked.

Kelly chuckled. *This is crazy*, she thought.

Madame Zora was undeterred. She had seen that look and heard that laugh many times before and knew just how to handle it. "Of course not, a smart college kid like you, what would you need a psychic for?"

"How did you know I'm in college?" Kelly heard herself ask.

"I can see lots of things others can't," Madame Zora replied, reeling her in.

"Oh, yeah? How?" There was no way she was falling for this phony.

Madame Zora smiled pleasantly. "I can feel the vibes; read auras; sense magnetic changes in the air."

"What kind of vibes?"

"Well, for one thing, I know your friends are worried about you … and you're about to get a phone call."

Before she even finished, Kelly's cell phone rang.

Kelly opened her phone cautiously and put it to her ear. It was her brother. "Hey," Kelly said, staring suspiciously at the fortune-teller. "No, everything's fine. I need to take inventory." Kelly looked to see if her little lie had registered with Madame Zora. The psychic remained impassive, listening intently and smiling knowingly.

"Sure, that's fine. You two go ahead. I'll catch up with you later. Oh, Geoffrey—any news on what happened the other night? … No? … Okay. Thanks."

Kelly snapped her phone closed and laid it on the counter. She held out her hand.

"What else does my lifeline say?" she demanded.

Madame Zora studied Kelly's palm, looking back and forth between Kelly's hand and the mix of doubt and intrigue evident in her eyes.

"I see flames … and a plane crash … and a dark-haired stranger. Do you know what this could possibly mean?"

"No. Do you?" Kelly was afraid this woman was a charlatan, but she wanted to believe. The phone call trick had been impressive, but she could have heard about the Carranza film from anybody in town and she still needed to be convinced this woman was legitimate.

Madame Zora closed her eyes and mumbled an incoherent incantation that Kelly couldn't understand. Then she opened her eyes and peered deeply into Kelly's as she replied. "Your path is cloudy and your future is uncertain. I can only tell you that this person desperately needs your help … now!"

10

Three Vultures

"I take it things didn't go too well," Fred Carlson remarked as he navigated his midnight blue, late-model Lexus into traffic.

"It got downright ugly," Megan replied, reapplying her sparkling lip gloss and puckering into her compact mirror. "They reminded me of two vultures fighting over a scrap of roadkill."

The elderly Post Commander chuckled at the analogy. "Where was the third vulture?"

"I heard that Don Alejándro is busy fighting his insurance company for a quick settlement on the claim so they can purchase new equipment. Apparently, the insurance policy lapsed."

Fred smiled to himself. "Do you think Sawyer suspects anything?"

Megan studied the old man's weather-lined face and proud nose, admiring his neatly pressed Garrison cap and chest of shiny medals. She wondered how many good soldiers the Colonel had commanded in battle during his tenure in the Vietnam conflict.

"I don't think so, Grandpa. Sawyer is so focused on getting to the awards ceremony at Sundance with a certain blonde reporter on his arm that he's oblivious to everything else."

Fred smiled again. "Good. Then let's stick to the script … and hope your mother plays her part just as well."

***

"I really appreciate you letting me tag along," Danny said to Geoffrey as the two motored down Route 206 toward Southampton in the black and white Mini Cooper they had borrowed from Kelly. "I'm hoping Mr. Sloan's knowledge of Emilio Carranza will give me deeper insights into his character that I can bring to life onscreen. You told him I was coming, right?"

"He knows *I'm* coming," Geoffrey replied. "With your reputation for wreaking havoc wherever you go, I thought it might be best to spring you on him when we get there."

"Ah, that's not fair, Geoffrey," Danny whined. "You don't really think I had anything to do with that warehouse fire, do you?"

Geoffrey ignored the hurt in Danny's voice and the downcast expression on his face. He kept driving as he answered. "Danny, with you, I never know what to expect. I remember the way that cagey old Ryder Hayes duped you into giving him the maps and charts of Tucker's Island—which, I might add, you had suckered *me* into giving to *you* in the first place. And I still haven't forgotten the time you put your faith in that pompous Professor Tippett's ridiculous theory about the Jersey Devil being some sort of ancient water guardian capable of camouflaging itself to avoid detection."

"Hey, I never said I actually believed that crap about the Jersey Devil," Danny protested vehemently. "I just thought it was an interesting hypothesis. It certainly made his class a little less boring."

"Bullshit," Geoffrey laughingly replied, pounding his fist on the steering wheel for emphasis. "You swallowed that garbage, hook, line, and sinker."

"At least I never pissed off a crackpot poacher bad enough to torch the woods with me in it. And no matter what people may say about me, at least nobody will ever accuse me of talking to a freaking rock. You've got to admit, there are some weird genes running loose in your family tree."

Geoffrey pretended to be indignant. "What exactly do you mean by that?"

"I don't know," Danny relaxed his attack, "but face it: Between you and your sister, something ain't right."

"You just can't get over the fact that Kelly saved your sorry ass after that jellyfish stung you."

Danny straightened up. "That doesn't mean I have to marry her!"

"Danny, look at you. You think you're some kind of prize? You don't have a real job, you're using a fake name, and you've got black shoe polish in your hair!"

"Maybe, but I'm not half-bad on guitar. And the chicks dig me."

"You mean 'chicks' as in, Lois Lane and Miss Lip Gloss? Well, I hate to break it to you, Danny boy, but Lois has her sights set on that egghead director ... who could pass for Lex Luther, come to think of it."

"Man, what is it that chicks dig about these cue ball dudes? What's the appeal? Think about it ... doesn't it make you wonder what his driver's license has down for hair color? I mean, is *bald* a color?"

Geoffrey considered the question.

"Anyway, at least the girls I date speak English."

Geoffrey pulled the car off the road and slammed on the brakes. "That's it. Get out!" he demanded, pushing Danny against the door.

"Okay, okay, I'm sorry. That was a cheap shot. I didn't mean it. I really like Luz. I just haven't been myself lately."

"Of course not. You're Captain Emilio Carranza, the Lindbergh of Mexico. But just remember, Danny, he crashed and burned at a young age without ever really knowing what his life meant."

"Yeah, but just look him now," Danny shrugged. "He's the subject of two movies ... revered by millions; he's got his own monument and a street named after him, and it's not even in his own country! And why? Because he was stupid enough to go up into a lightning storm—alone—and die? Makes you wonder where he would have ended up if he had lived."

Geoffrey made a right onto Pemberton Road and pulled the Mini Cooper into the gravel parking lot behind #17, the restored farmhouse that served as the Pinelands Preservation Alliance's Visitor Center. The well-manicured property had, at one time, been known as Willow Tree Farm, and the members of the PPA were determined to maintain the farmstead in the rich rural tradition to which it belonged. The grounds were in step with the organization's mission to keep all things in their natural state for future generations to enjoy.

The boys followed the sidewalk, under an arbor lush with ripening red grapevines, around to the front of the old two-story wood farmhouse. Inside, a kindly receptionist named Jean directed them back outside to a long, white, corrugated shed that doubled as office space and an assembly room for the PPA's frequent events. It was the only building on the property that was air-conditioned and equipped with modern technology.

They found Paul alone in the large empty room, sitting at a long folding table with his eyes half shut, running through a series of slides that were being projected onto a white screen. The shades were drawn to darken the room. Through the open door, just enough sunlight filtered in to expose a menacing-looking, six-foot-tall, plaster-of-Paris replica of the Jersey Devil standing behind him, seemingly ready to pounce. The replica was so realistic it gave the boys a start.

"Come on in, the Devil won't bother you," Paul said without looking up. "You get used to him. He's our best prop. We like to take him on the road with us when we lecture at the schools. The kids get a big kick out of him. Right now he's off for the summer, enjoying the air conditioning … and the solitude, I might add."

The boys stepped tentatively into the room and joined Paul at the far end of the rectangular table. "I've been going over this slide show we're planning for our Post's Carranza Memorial event. We're going to have it here at the Visitor's Center immediately following the annual service. We're expecting quite a crowd, you know, and some notable dignitaries." He motioned for the two boys to have a seat.

"I see you brought along a friend, Geoffrey," Paul said thoughtfully, stroking his beard. "Shall we check him for matches, a cigarette lighter, or anything else that might be flammable?" he asked with a friendly wink at Danny. "Now, what can I do for you two?"

"We'd like to know all you know about Captain Carranza and his last mission," Geoffrey volunteered cheerfully.

Paul took a quick swig from a Styrofoam cup. Ice cubes crackled as he placed it back down on the table. "I seem to recall that you were both at my lecture the other night. Don't tell me you forgot everything I said?"

"Not everything," Danny spoke up. "But that was just the standard take on Carranza, the same junk everybody knows. We want the real story; the stuff no one would dare print even if it was the truth."

Paul was amused. "Oh, you mean the conspiracy theories?"

Geoffrey's mouth fell open.

"Oh, don't look so surprised, Geoffrey. Political intrigue is not a contemporary invention, by any means."

Danny clapped his hands. "Hot damn, I knew there had to be more to it! Carranza would have had to be a damned fool to get up in an airplane on a night like that without a good reason, especially after he'd been warned."

"Not only warned," Geoffrey added, remembering Paul's lecture. "Didn't he actually have his plane put away for the night before he went off to dinner with friends? What possibly could have possessed him to change his mind?"

Paul tapped a key on his laptop and immediately a swirl of images splashed up on the blank screen.

"You have to keep in mind the tone of the times. This was the Roaring '20s. It came after the 'war to end all wars.' The world was overflowing with renewed optimism. Following Lindbergh's nonstop solo flight from New York to Paris in 1927, the world suddenly got a lot smaller. Aviation was the new frontier. There was a manic international thirst for adventure. The race was on to make or break any flight record. Ordinary men became heroes overnight."

New images appeared on the screen. Danny and Geoffrey recognized very few of the faces in the faded photographs aside from the one Danny had been made up to look like for the movie.

"Carranza's 2,400-mile return flight to Mexico was postponed and rescheduled repeatedly for over a week because of the weather, or so it was reported. But time was running out. If he didn't do it soon, somebody else would. One of his contemporaries, Major Roberto Fiérro, also a quality Mexican aviator, was just days away from embarking on the first nonstop goodwill flight from Mexico to Havana. There was rivalry and real pressure, not to mention national honor at stake. It was truly a 'you snooze, you lose' situation, to use today's vernacular."

Geoffrey and Danny appreciated Paul's humor, even if it was somewhat chemically induced. It made the presentation seem less like a lesson—more open and honest and, therefore, more believable.

"Then there was the growing fear that Emilio Carranza was getting a little too chummy with the New York hosts and too comfortable with his new lifestyle. His father, Sebastian, who was living in New York, had become an influential figure who traveled among the inner circles of the high-powered politicians and moneyed industrialists of the day. And now his son had met the United States' president, flown with Charles A. Lindbergh, and dined with Edsel Ford. It wasn't much of a stretch to imagine that the topics of cheap Mexican labor and new markets for American products were making the rounds at dinner conversations during Carranza's visit. In fact, Mayor Jimmy Walker's welcoming speech emphasized the economic opportunities growing between the two countries."

Danny couldn't disguise his excitement at what he was hearing. He could hardly believe this was the character he had been asked to portray. There was certainly more to the man than he had been conveying.

"Abroad, Captain Carranza was becoming very popular. He was the darling of the American press. They covered his every move. Everywhere he went, enthusiastic crowds and ticker tape parades greeted him. He kissed babies, attended banquets and presided over awards ceremonies; he was even honored at West Point—don't think *that* didn't raise a few eyebrows back in Mexico City.

"The welcome mat was rolled out. He was young, handsome, and courageous. Most important, he spoke English, having lived and attended school in Texas while his family was in exile, and that made it easier for him to win over the hearts and minds of the American public.

"But this caused suspicion at home. You have to remember, Mexico was still trying to establish its own brand of democracy after centuries of Spanish imperial rule and a long, drawn-out revolution that saw its popular leaders like Zapata and Páncho Villa become victims in the bloody and bitter civil wars that followed. Carranza's great-uncle, Venústiano Carranza, was also deeply involved. During the revolution, the United States actually supported the cause and Venústiano, directly, by giving him weapons, ammunition, and—get this—airplanes, too. However, after becoming the first president of the Mexican Republic in 1917, his victory was short-lived. He soon found himself outmaneuvered by several of his former revolutionary colleagues: men like Calles, Huerta, and Alváro Obregon. They eventually forced Carranza to flee Mexico City for Veracruz, where he was assassinated on Obregon's orders.

"That was in 1920. By 1928, the time of Emilio's daring flight, Calles was in power, with Obregon waiting in the wings as president-elect. Perhaps the dust hadn't yet settled on that old score. It's not unreasonable to suggest that among the Mexican ruling party, questions began to surface concerning the Carranza family loyalty, both father *and* son. The fact that Emilio Carranza had delayed his departure for home only further fueled this kind of speculation. The Carranza name was still respected by the common Mexican people, and a hero in the family, coupled with his American business connections, could make for quite a formidable foe in the confused political landscape of post-revolutionary Mexico."

"Wow!" Danny exclaimed. "I had no idea."

"Of course," Paul continued, his eyes twinkling mischievously at having a captive audience, "this is all pure conjecture. There is no hard evidence to support any of it."

"But you believe it, don't you, Mr. Sloan?" Geoffrey asked, almost pleading for it to be true.

Paul smiled smugly. He could see his little exposé had the young minds thinking, perhaps even hoping, that they could be the ones to discover the truth that had remained buried for nearly eight decades. But he wasn't done.

"Boys, I've seen enough in my time to know that anything is possible. One thing I know for certain is that things are not always what they seem." He finished his drink.

"Of course, there are other viewpoints to consider," he added slyly, "like the one that suggests not every American at the time was enamored with the prospect of a

The Lost Mission of Captain Carranza

foreigner getting so much publicity, or his accomplishments potentially eclipsing those of the great Colonel Lindbergh, or any other American, for that matter. Prejudice runs wild on both sides of the Rio Grande … then and now."

"Whew," Danny exhaled, amazed. "I had no idea all this was going on behind the scenes. How come none of this stuff is in Sawyer's script?"

"Good question," Paul replied. "I'm fairly certain it isn't in the Poco Loco script, either."

"What makes you say that?" Geoffrey asked.

"Because I believe the same person is responsible for both scripts."

11

Pot Roast

Sarah Bishop-Parsons placed a simmering pot roast on the dinner table between two hungry men and then sat down to join them.

"Well, what are you waiting for, boys? Dig in," she ordered.

Her husband didn't need any further prodding. After carving out a healthy portion for their guest, Noah helped himself to a heaping plateful.

"Sarah, this is heavenly," Tom Banks complimented the chef, savoring a mouthful as he spoke. "Noah, now I understand where those extra pounds come from. Married life certainly looks good on you," he said with a casual wink in Sarah's direction.

"Worth coming out of the woods for, eh, Tom?" Noah asked, grinning good-naturedly at the ponytailed man, a locally acclaimed survivalist. Noah couldn't help noticing that his close friend, though fit and trim, looked like he could use a good home-cooked meal.

"Yes, it was worth leaving *my home* for this," Tom conceded with a gentle laugh.

"Well, as they say, Tom, *mi casa es su casa*," Noah said, pouring his dinner companion a drink from a pitcher.

"Thanks, Noah. That's nice to hear. Besides, this last group was a real challenge." Tom sighed before sipping his iced tea. "I would much rather train a troop of green Cub Scouts any time. At least they listen. They want to learn. But cops—now they are the worst," he said, shaking his head in dismay. "They think they already know everything about the woods when they get there."

Noah gave his wife a knowing glance. "I feel a story coming on," he baited his guest. "What happened this time? Did one of New York's finest forget to bring his compass or lose his water bottle in the mud?"

Tom let out a hearty laugh. "No, that would be too easy. Some simpleton got separated from the rest of the group and ended up at Talley's Dump, where he had a run-in with a pack of wild dogs. They chased him up a tree for half a day. I had to go back in after him and almost got my leg chewed to shreds in the process."

"You need to go back to the camp, Tom," Sarah suggested politely. "I hear it from so many customers who come into the store. They say Camp White Eagle just isn't what it used to be without you there."

"That's sweet, Sarah," Tom replied warmly. "But after a summer there with Payton J. Tippett *the third* and his Jersey Devil delusions, I am much happier and far safer in the woods—even with macho cops and stray dogs. But, enough about me, Noah, how goes the Carranza plans? Everything set for the big day?"

"I sure hope so, Tom," Noah answered slowly. "I'm a little concerned about the filming, though."

"Yeah, I heard about the fire at the village. Some of the other trustees told me they were ready to revoke my membership card for letting you talk me into turning the place into the Alamo."

"I'm really sorry about that, Tom."

"Don't be. Chester Potts assured me there was minimal damage done to the warehouse. Besides, that's what insurance is for."

"Yeah, well, tell that to the Poco Loco Film Company. Unless they can come up with their insurance money quick enough to get some new equipment, they're going to be leaving town empty-handed."

Tom shook his head. "That's a shame. I hear Chief Adams swears the fire was set on purpose, although he still has no plausible suspects or motive."

"It seems some folks would like to pin it on the Mexicans. But that just doesn't make sense," Noah said. "Why would they sabotage their own film? It's nearly done."

"Then, how about the American film company?" Sarah offered casually. "They have everything to gain by knocking out the competition."

Noah swallowed a forkful of sautéed green beans before he replied. "Right, except that no one even remotely connected to their crew was anywhere near the village that night." Noah hesitated. "Unless, of course, you consider Danny Windsor part of that crowd."

"How's Danny Windsor connected to the American film company?" Tom asked curiously.

"Oh, don't listen to him, Tom," Sarah scoffed. "He's not, really. At least, that's what the kids, Kelly and Geoffrey, tell me. He sweet-talked himself onto the set and wangled a bit part. Apparently, he plays Emilio Carranza's corpse, dead on the ground for all of about 30 seconds in the film, and even that may end up on the cutting room floor."

She leaned across the table and whispered conspiratorially. "Besides, according to my 'source,' Danny and this Wade Sawyer fella, the American film director, are butting heads over that pretty reporter from the *Island Sentinel*. I think we know who's going to win *that* contest. Danny Windsor's days as a film star appear to be numbered."

"And that's if it's only a two-man race," acknowledged Tom, adding his two cents to the tabloid-like table talk. "According to our friendly neighborhood fire marshal, a certain Hispanic gentleman has also entertained Ms. Sparrow."

Noah frowned. He was impressed with this newsy tidbit and nodded his head as he pondered the implications.

Just then, the doorbell rang.

"I'll get that," Sarah volunteered. "You boys go ahead and help yourselves to seconds."

Sarah returned to the dining room a few minutes later with Luz and Miguel, whom she introduced to Tom. Both Sarah and Noah couldn't help noticing how nervous Luz seemed to be.

"We apologize for the intrusion, Mr. and Mrs. Parsons," Miguel began hesitantly, searching for the right words, "but we didn't know who else to turn to."

Noah stared at Luz, trying to read her expression. "Luz, has something happened to Geoffrey?" Noah inquired anxiously.

"Oh, no, nothing like that, Mr. Parsons," Luz assured him. "It's about Don Alejándro."

"The producer?" Noah asked, more for Tom's clarification.

"*Sí*," Miguel interjected. "He is gone."

"Gone?" Sarah echoed with a puzzled look.

"He's gone back to Mexico," Luz blurted out. "He's been deported."

"Please, sit down," Noah said, motioning to two unoccupied chairs at the table. "Have you eaten?"

"*Gracias*, you are very kind, but ..." Miguel began.

"... we wouldn't want to impose," Luz finished.

Noah waved them off. "Nonsense. Sarah, two more plates for our guests, *por favor*." Sarah disappeared into the kitchen.

"Okay, now. Start from the beginning," Noah gently urged.

Miguel brushed back his shaggy black hair. His hazel eyes glistened in the soft light from the chandelier hanging above the dining room table. He folded his hands in front of him piously. It was obvious to Noah and Tom that he was deeply troubled by what he was about to say.

Sarah returned with two clean plates and began loading them up as Miguel quietly spoke. "Don Alejándro's visa expired last week."

"Last week?" Noah groaned. "He told the committee he was here on a 90-day work visa."

"That's what we thought, too," Miguel admitted. "But he only had a tourist visa. Good for 30 days."

"He lied to you and to us," Luz confessed.

Noah and Tom exchanged confused glances.

"He lied to us about many things," Miguel continued. "There is no insurance policy. There is no money, period. Don Alejándro squandered it all ... or stole it."

Noah was dumbfounded. "But I thought he was hired by the Carranza family to make this film. Didn't they provide the funding?"

"Apparently, they put up some of the money," Miguel replied sadly. "Don Alejándro promised to use his connections to raise the rest."

"But he took what they gave him and spent it, without ever securing any more," Luz explained. "And now it's all gone."

"When did you first learn of this?" Tom asked. "Surely there must have been some indication of what he was doing."

"*Sí*," Miguel replied. Oddly, though the pain in his voice was obvious, he didn't seem angry—just demoralized. "Checks started to bounce with the catering bills. Don Alejándro said it was a currency problem and he would take care of it. He never did. Luz was kind enough to get the caterer to give us more time. Alas," Miguel sighed, "time has run out, and the film is unfinished. Without the memorial ceremony, there is no story."

"I don't get it," Sarah said. "What did Don Alejándro hope to gain by carrying on this charade?"

"Apparently he was a con man," Tom offered. "Plain and simple."

"*Sí*," Miguel agreed. "Even his title is a fake."

"But, surely, the Carranza family must have checked him out?" Noah reasoned. "How is it that he was able to dupe them into letting him run the show? And you, Miguel, you worked with him—what made you trust him?"

Miguel broke off a piece of fresh-baked bread as he pondered Noah's question. "Don Alejándro came to us with just one thing, and because of that one thing, we never thought to question anything else: He brought us the perfect script on the life of Captain Emilio Carranza."

"Well, where did he get the script?" Noah persisted.

"We don't know for sure. He told us a friend of his had acquired it on the open market from a reliable source, here in the states. The screenplay is credited to someone named M. Byrd, but I never met the screenwriter. Any changes—and there have been very few—I made myself with Don Alejándro's approval after he consulted with the family. To tell you the truth, now, I don't know if the family was ever consulted at all. I just accepted what Don Alejándro said. He was, after all, the film's producer. The rights and responsibilities were his to obtain and to control as he saw fit."

Noah exhaled at length. "Okay. Now we may be getting somewhere. This could help to explain what's been going on here."

"Do you think Don Alejándro had something to do with the fire?" Sarah blurted out.

"He could have used that to distract everyone from his embezzling," Noah mused.

"But the film is almost done," Miguel exclaimed. "Why disrupt things now with a finished product so close at hand?"

"Publicity?" Tom suggested. "Maybe he figured that the controversy would generate some momentum for its theatrical release."

"But we don't even have a distribution deal yet," Miguel said.

"All the more reason to create some buzz now," Sarah suggested.

Again, the doorbell sounded, giving everyone a start.

"Now who could that be?" Sarah cried, jumping up to get the door.

12

Lost ... and Found

"I'll get two more chairs," Noah offered when his wife returned to the dining room with Danny and Geoffrey in tow.

"I had no idea your home had become Grand Central Station," Tom joked.

"Neither did we," Sarah replied. "Pot roast, anyone?" she asked, placing settings down in front of the two boys.

"Mmm, you'll love it. It's great," Luz said, voicing her pleasure and her gratitude.

"Awesome," Danny sang, smacking his lips and sitting down. "I'm famished."

"You won't believe where we've been ..." Geoffrey announced with his mouth full.

"... or what we've found out," Danny added.

"Try us," Noah said. "This night can't get any stranger."

"Wait until you check out the slide show Paul Sloan has planned for the Carranza event," Geoffrey said excitedly.

"Yeah," Danny agreed. "I mean, this Carranza cat was one super cool dude."

"On this we are in agreement, my friend," Miguel said amiably.

"Right, I know you. You're the director of the other Carranza film, aren't you?"

Miguel nodded humbly. "I was."

"There still might be a way to get you what you need, Miguel," Noah said, sounding optimistic. "I can make a call to Fred Carlson. As Post Commander, he can authorize the release of certain miscellaneous funds without the consent of the full membership. How much do you think you'll need?"

Miguel thought for a moment. "I'll need two Sony or Panasonic digital cameras, a tripod, and a mobile sled. I could rent them in Mexico City for ... *veinte mil pesos* a day."

"That's about 3,500 U.S. dollars," Luz quickly calculated, "give or take." She shrugged her shoulders shyly and smiled at Geoffrey.

"Okay," Noah said. "Let's hope we can rent Japanese digital cameras for the same price here in the states."

"But the memorial is tomorrow," Luz reminded Noah. "Even if you can get the money, where can you get that kind of equipment overnight?"

Noah turned to Geoffrey and Danny. "Did Sloan happen to mention whether he was able to get in touch with his friend Joey Bones?"

"He was waiting for his call when we left," replied Geoffrey.

Danny turned to Miguel. "I was wondering," he asked nonchalantly, helping himself to the mashed potatoes, "does your film show how Carranza was murdered?"

"Murdered?" Miguel inquired politely. "What do you mean?"

"How does your film explain his untimely death?" Geoffrey asked.

"He died in the service of his country, in a terrible thunderstorm," said the Mexican director emphatically.

"You can call it a *bolt* of lightning if you like, or a *streak* of envy, or even a *flash* of misguided pride. Take your pick. But it's a pretty good bet that his death wasn't entirely accidental, at least not according to what we learned tonight, right, Geoffrey?"

"What exactly did Sloan tell you boys?" Noah asked skeptically.

"There was a conspiracy to knock him off," Geoffrey fired back.

"That's just silly," Miguel said. "Who would want to kill Emilio Carranza? He was a hero."

"Not to all Mexicans," Danny corrected him. "His family name was feared by those in power at the time."

"Nor to all Americans," Geoffrey added quickly. "No one really wanted to see him upstage Lindbergh or the good ole U. S. of A."

"You boys are talking nonsense," Noah interrupted them.

"Noah, he had no business being up in the air that night, and he knew it," Danny insisted. "He was warned about the weather conditions. But he went anyway."

"He was ordered by his commander to fly home," Miguel said with determination. "It was his duty to obey."

"He was ordered to his death," Geoffrey countered. "He was on a suicide mission."

Tom stirred. "I know I've been away in the woods for awhile, and I've missed a lot of this little soap opera, but this discussion reminds me of the Cherokee elder teaching his grandchildren about life," Tom waxed philosophical, reclining in his chair. "The elder said: 'A terrible fight rages inside of me, a fight between two wolves. One wolf represents fear, anger, jealousy, greed, resentment, false pride, lies, and guilt. The other wolf stands for peace, love, hope, joy, humility, truth, friendship, and brotherhood. The same fight is going on inside us all.' When his grandchildren asked him which wolf would win, the wise old Cherokee told them: 'The one you feed.'"

Although Tom's message had been intended to represent the two sides arguing over the Carranza controversy, Danny felt the impact of the words hit him like a ton of bricks. To Danny, they illustrated perfectly what was happening in his personal life. Inside himself, two wolves were engaged in a bitter struggle for dominance and control. Danny even had names for his wolves: the good-natured, happy-go-lucky, peaceful wolf was named Danny Windsor; the other—the fraud, subject to delusions of self-importance and fits of self-pity—was named Dante Reed.

Suddenly he realized, in pursuing an image on the silver screen, hanging out with social climbers, trying to be an insider, and lusting after the likes of Feather Sparrow, he was, in essence, feeding the wrong wolf.

"I believe it," Luz exclaimed, to everyone's surprise. She was ready to speak her mind about Carranza for the first time. "I believe in the Carranza conspiracy theory and the prejudice. It is an insult to the Mexican people that continues to this day."

"What are you saying, Luz?" Miguel asked with a bewildered look on his face.

"Think about it, Miguel. Don't you find it just a little ironic that the first 700-mile segment of President Bush's border fence—the one meant to stop illegal immigration—is starting in Eagle's Pass, Texas?"

"The American home of Carranza's exiled youth," Miguel muttered in disbelief.

Geoffrey looked at Luz with consoling eyes. "Well, I know an abandoned little island not far from here with bathroom privileges where today's exiles would be welcome."

Luz smiled appreciatively.

"It's just a shame we can't ask Captain Carranza what happened," Sarah said, bringing the conversation back to the original controversy.

Just then, Kelly appeared in the hallway, a set of keys dangling from her index finger. "Anybody want to go to a séance?" she asked excitedly.

13

Under Two Flags

The flickering candlelight, casting twisted shadows all around the grounds of the Pinelands Preservation Alliance farmhouse, made for an eerie beacon as the guests of the Parsons's expanded pot roast dinner party pulled up in three separate vehicles. The gypsy-like Madame Zora greeted the apprehensive party at the door, cloaked in a long black robe, her earlobes adorned with a pair of oversized silver hoops that matched the color, if not the texture, of her Medusa-like hair.

"Come in, do come in," she cooed as she ushered the group up the steps and into the foyer. "We've been waiting for you."

"We?" Noah asked, a queasy feeling growing in the pit of his stomach.

Madame Zora did not take time to explain. She didn't need to. As the group moved through the two-story farmhouse into the open study, Noah saw several familiar people were already there, enjoying light refreshments and engaging animatedly in conversation.

"Ah, good, Noah, you're here," Fred exclaimed, coming forward to greet him. "And I see you brought along the whole gang. Excellent!"

Madame Zora gave Kelly a wink of appreciation. "I knew you'd be able to convince the others to come," she said, smiling. "My, this looks like a fun group."

Besides Fred, Noah saw Paul, Edgar, and Megan. Together, with Madame Zora and his party of eight, the total head count present was a superstitious thirteen.

Noah confronted the Post Commander. "What's all this about a séance, Fred?" Noah demanded. "The committee was not informed—"

"Relax, Noah," Fred cut him off. "It was my idea. Last-minute kind of thing. I thought it might be stimulating on the eve of our memorial service to see if we could actually make contact with the famous Captain Carranza. You know Madame Zora, I presume?"

"Hello," Noah nodded cautiously to the new-age gypsy. Actually, he did remember her, from the Tuckerton Seaport. The museum's curator, Libby Ashcroft, had hired Madame Zora to rid the old Jamieson House of a vexing ghost. While that effort had not entirely succeeded, it did make for splendid promotional material in the Seaport's newsletter—so much so that the Jamieson House had become a Seaport attraction as well as a business office.

"Besides, the occasion might prove useful to our energetic filmmaker," Fred continued.

"Where *is* Count Cue Ball?" Danny asked, scanning the room, more for Feather than for the hotshot director.

"Why, I don't really know," Fred replied slowly, making sure to catch Megan's attention. "He was on our list, too, but ..."

"He's not answering his cell phone," Megan explained, coming up behind Fred. "I left him another message."

"No matter," Fred added, turning to Miguel. "We have our other filmmaker on hand."

"But I have no equipment," Miguel responded with resignation.

Megan handed him a camcorder. "See what you can capture with this."

"Listen, Fred, what are you trying to accomplish, here?" a frustrated Noah asked assertively, pulling him aside.

"Why, contact with the dead, of course," he replied cheerfully. "Where's your spirit of adventure?"

"That's the only spirit you're gonna conjure up with this circus act," Tom admonished.

"I see we have a doubting Thomas among us," Madame Zora said, apparently rising to the challenge.

Tom looked at her, unflinching. Himself an esthete, he was well acquainted with the power of the spirit world and was adept at communing with elements of nature and the supernatural. The present masquerade, however, under the guise of spiritualism, he found mildly offensive.

"Perhaps you would be more comfortable if the séance were conducted in a sweat lodge," Paul added, sidling up along side Tom and Noah, his trademark drink in hand. "I know I would." Sloan brandished a flask and spiked his own cup.

Tom let out a low groan as he ambled off in pursuit of what he hoped would be the unadulterated punch bowl.

"Oh, come on, dear," Sarah nudged her husband, linking her arm in his. "What have we got to lose?"

"Hey, this is what *you* asked for, not me," Noah reminded her.

Sarah giggled with delight.

"Be careful what you wish for," Paul added with a sly smile.

Madame Zora pulled up the voluminous sleeves of her robe and clapped her hands to get everyone's attention. "If each of you will take a candle and follow me, we can begin."

One by one, each of the guests lifted a lighted taper candle from a pewter cup on the sideboard table and followed Madame Zora's long, billowing robe out the back door of the farmhouse, down along the walkway to a spacious old barn.

While most of the participants paraded single-file, trying to maintain decorum in the face of the weird proceedings about to unfold, Kelly's skin crawled with excitement. She skipped along happily, glad that Danny had agreed to come without the usual fuss. When she caught up with him, Danny listened intently as Kelly rambled on about her strange meeting at Colson's with Madame Zora, but, inwardly, he regarded the procession with a skeptical eye.

Meanwhile, Geoffrey and Luz chattered enthusiastically, as they walked with Miguel, about what, if anything, he expected to shoot at the séance. Did he need special infrared lighting to capture apparitions? Would 'spook speak' be audible on a digital recording? Miguel admitted the whole experience was new to him, but, for the first time in more than a week, he felt like he might be in the right place at the right time.

Noah and Sarah argued mildly about the lunacy of the occasion while a still-doubtful Tom followed along without expectation. He was keenly aware, while en route, that the other members of the séance group—Fred, Megan, Edgar, and Paul—showed no reservations whatsoever about what might or might not happen.

The "chosen" thirteen silently climbed the steps to the second floor of the barn to find the huge hayloft entirely dark and empty. Madame Zora motioned for the group to gather in the middle of the room and place their candles on the hard wooden floor in a circle in front of them. Inside the circle, now illuminated by the lighted candles, was a pentagram that had been drawn in luminous white chalk. Several curious items had been carefully placed at the five points of the star, an ancient symbol of Wicca.

Two neatly folded flags—one of the United States, the other of Mexico—were strategically positioned at two opposing star points. The polarized placement read as a clear and unambiguous statement to the group.

At the point to the group's left lay a hand-drawn flight map of the cities over which Captain Carranza had intended to fly on his return trip; directly across from it, on the group's right, was a toy replica of Lindbergh's *Spirit of St. Louis,* the plane after which Carranza's own *Excelsior* had been modeled.

At the remaining point, two written documents lay side by side: One, typed in English, was a faded copy of the U.S weather service report Carranza had received less than 24 hours before his impromptu flight, warning the aviator of the protracted dangerous weather conditions that lay ahead. The other, in Spanish, was an open copy of the alleged telegram from Carranza's superior officer, General Joaquin Amaro, ordering the young, impetuous aviator to take flight without further delay.

Madame Zora bent down to pick up the cablegram. She held out her candle and handed the paper to Luz. "Ms. Sanchez, would you do us the honor of translating for the group?" Madame Zora intoned politely. Luz nodded and read the following in a chilling voice:

> Leave immediately without excuse or pretext,
> or the quality of your manhood will be in doubt.

Luz returned the note to Madame Zora, who placed it back in its spot on the floor, as silence fell over the group. Everyone took a moment to ponder the exact meaning of these implausible words and to consider their consequences.

From outside the open loft door, cicadas serenaded the otherwise still summer night. In the warm glow of the thirteen tiny dancing flames, shadows shimmered on the wooden walls and bare oaken beams of the vast open room. High above the solemn thirteen, the ceiling soared into a gaping black void. From somewhere in that inky darkness a barn owl hooted, making his presence known.

Madame Zora clapped her hands together forcefully, in an effort to call everyone's attention back to the present. Latching onto Fred and Sarah, she indicated the circle of participants should follow suit and all join hands.

"Each of the objects you see set out before you bears a particular significance in the final moments of Emilio Carranza's ill-fated flight. I believe, for the most part, their meanings will be obvious to you. The selected pieces represent the touch points of a death shrouded in mystery. It is only through the virtuous efforts of our noble Post 11 members that his memory has been kept alive."

Fred smiled proudly, as did Paul and Edgar. Of the American Legion members present, only Noah seemed to have misgivings as Madame Zora rattled on. "On this occasion, we remember a young, tender life, forever struck down from the lofty heights of the living and submerged into the world of shadows beyond the veil. But he left behind clues for us to follow, to solve the riddle, to unwrap the mystery of his last mission. What we shall attempt tonight is to contact the eternal soul of Emilio Carranza and petition him to reveal to us what happened in those final moments of his time on Earth. To do this, we must all focus our energy together on each object. It is only through our absolute concentration and undivided attention that his intention can become fully realized."

Standing between Kelly and Megan, Danny felt a sudden urge to snicker … and could not suppress it. Megan looked at him distantly, as if her mind were already somewhere else. Kelly squeezed Danny's hand hard enough to turn the end of his ill-timed snicker into a soft yelp.

In a soothing voice, Madame Zora asked the congregation to sit on the floor without uncoupling their hands. Paul, slightly inebriated, had to be helped to a sitting position by Edgar and Geoffrey. Madame Zora closed her eyes and appeared to go into a trance-like state. In English, she called for Carranza's spirit to show himself.

"This is ridiculous," Noah said after a few beats.

"Yeah, this is bogus," Danny agreed.

"It's unnecessary," Miguel added. "We all know Carranza's mission was to spread goodwill, brotherhood, and friendship between the countries of Mexico and the United States. What more do we need to know?"

"What about the flashlight?" Fred insisted.

"What flashlight?" Miguel asked.

"The one in the pentagram," Madame Zora muttered in a low voice.

All eyes came to rest on a single silver flashlight, which until then had gone un-noticed by the group, standing on its end in the center of the pentagram, its guiding light magically illuminated.

"Carranza died clutching a flashlight in his hand," Danny said, remembering the scene he was asked to reenact on film. "Well, at least, that's the way it is in the script."

"So what's the big deal about the flashlight?" Edgar asked Fred. "I seem to recall reading the light was busted, probably from the impact of the crash. What of it?"

Fred eyed him. "Do you know what happened to the flashlight?"

"Haven't a clue," Edgar snapped defensively.

"Or what was inside the flashlight?"

Edgar shrugged. "Four D-cell batteries, I would imagine?"

"Then why would he hold onto it until the bitter end, as if his very life depended on it?" Fred insisted with rising fervor.

"He needed it to see where he was going?" Geoffrey suggested.

Fred persisted. "It was *still* in his hand when they found him. He grabbed it for a reason when he bailed out."

"Instead of a parachute?" Danny offered, his expression puzzled.

"He didn't have a parachute," Fred replied angrily.

"And why do you think that was?" Paul inquired, fidgeting.

"Because he needed to keep the load light for the long flight," Miguel answered.

Fred stood his ground. "And you believe that?"

"He was carrying 430 gallons of gas in a plane designed with the gross vehicle weight of a Volkswagen," Edgar replied.

"As I recall, Lindbergh didn't carry a parachute on his transatlantic flight, either, for that very same reason," Noah added.

"We've all done our homework, Fred," Edgar reminded him. "What's your point?"

Fred harrumphed, unconvinced.

"Let's have it, Fred," Noah prodded. "What are you driving at?"

Again Fred stared directly at Edgar. "While he was in America, we know that Carranza met with President Coolidge, Mayor Jimmy Walker, and the Fords, along with other officials and powerful businessmen. His father was an expatriate living in New York since 1923, ostensibly working for the Mexican government, but who knows? Maybe he was just biding his time."

"For what?" Kelly entered the discussion.

"To make his move," Paul mumbled in his stupor.

Fred tried to ignore Paul's worsening condition. "He had no love for the people in power in his own country, nor they for him. To Sebastian Carranza, the people in charge were a band of ruthless cutthroats who outlawed the ringing of church bells and murdered members of *his* family. To men like Obregon and Calles, the most recent presidents of a fledgling Republic, the name Carranza was a real threat. His American connections and his son's international acclaim only made him all the more dangerous."

"Here, here," Paul said, his speech noticeably slurred but excited. "I do believe our Post Commander is onto something. It's obvious that young Captain Carranza left in quite a hurry. Why, I hear tell he was still wearing his bedroom slippers when he took off. Now, does anybody but me find that just a wee bit odd for a 27-hour flight?"

"Oh shut up, Paul," Fred barked.

"Pilots have to be concerned with comfort and circulation," Tom thought aloud.

The group stared through the eerie candlelight at Paul, wondering if the liquor had brought him to the point of totally impaired judgment, or ...

Paul let out a loud belch. "It's no more ridiculous than your flashlight theory. How do we even know for sure that it *was* Carranza in the plane?"

Fred pondered this unexpected conjecture. "His face *was* completely disfigured from the crash."

"As I recall, the authorities identified him from the maps he carried in his pockets and from the remains of the plane, of course," Noah volunteered.

"And from the money he was carrying," Edgar added.

"Both U.S. and Mexican currency," Fred offered coyly, "and lots of it."

"No," Miguel insisted. "You're all wrong. It *had* to be him. The height, the hair, the uniform ... who else could it have been, and why?"

"Yeah, get to the point, Fred," Edgar said with growing impatience. "Where are you going with all this?"

"If I'm following this discussion correctly," Tom interrupted, "he's suggesting that Carranza was on a mission, all right, but not the one he is remembered for."

"Exactly!" Fred exclaimed. "Carranza was an agent for change who supported the ideal of capitalism in his homeland with the aid of American involvement."

Paul applauded weakly, the effects of his spiked punch having clearly taken their toll on his faculties. "Bravo!"

Geoffrey and Danny exchanged a glance. They had heard some of this before from Paul. But Fred's heated pitch kicked it up a notch.

Noah remained unconvinced. "Now you sound just like Paul. Conspiracy theories make quaint barroom talk, Fred, but where's your proof? Where's the flashlight, and what was supposedly in it?"

"I don't know," Fred admitted. "Secret documents, covert plans, maybe? I thought Edgar might know, since he's related to the people who found Carranza after the crash."

"Sorry to disappoint you," Edgar Wilson said with an apologetic shrug.

"That's it?" Miguel uncharacteristically bellowed. "*That's* your proof? Your whole conspiracy theory hangs on the broken flashlight found in Carranza's hand? You don't know where it is or what it contained, if anything at all?"

Fred composed himself. "Where would *you* hide secret documents you didn't want found during a 2,400-mile journey in the air? What would you grab if you were about to crash in the middle of nowhere?"

"A parachute," Danny whispered.

"Or, if I didn't have one, something to cushion the fall," Geoffrey tossed out.

"There is more to the story," Fred said. "According to an account by the investigating officer, the altimeter in Carranza's craft registered 3,500 feet, even though he plummeted through acres of trees and skirted the ground before he crashed. And his throttle was found locked in a closed position."

"What does all that mean?" asked Kelly.

"It means, in his final moments, Carranza had no visibility and, apparently, no maneuverability, either," Noah explained. "He couldn't control the speed of his craft, and he didn't have any idea how high or low he was in the sky."

"It suggests his controls may have been tampered with," Tom summarized for everyone's benefit.

Confused and displeased by the unanticipated direction the evening was taking, Madame Zora tried to take advantage of the momentary pause to get the séance back on track.

"Why don't we ask Carranza himself to explain it to us," she said, waving her arms dramatically.

"Forget it, *Zora*. We're way past that point," Fred snapped.

Startled by his condescension, the medium shrank away, blending into the darkness of the room.

Tom's perceptive summary encouraged Fred not merely to carry on but to go straight for the jugular. "Hey, you don't have to take my word for it. Read for yourself. It's right here, in the quotes reported in the newspapers. What do *you* think was going on?"

He removed several news clippings from his shirt pocket and read aloud: "This one is from Carranaza, delivered in a speech soon after he triumphantly reached New York, three weeks before his death: *'I thank you for all your kindness, and I wish to stay* here *all my life!'* "

"See, I told you," Paul exclaimed, regaining control of his speech, "Carranza had no intention of ever leaving the U.S."

"He was only trying to convey his gratitude. Emotions are difficult to translate," Miguel countered.

Fred tossed the clipping aside and read from another: "President Calles issued this statement from Mexico upon hearing the news of Carranza's death: 'With all my heart, I lament Captain Carranza's tragedy, which I attribute to fate and to the fury of the elements.'

"He's pretty quick to identify the cause of death, and then, without skipping a beat, he goes on to sing the praises of the man who ultimately succeeds where Carranza has failed: 'The Mexican government, with absolute confidence in the skill of its aviator-pilots, has faith that Lieutenant Colonel Roberto Fiérro will successfully fly from Mexico City to Havana'—in other words, 'The mourning is over, folks. Let's move on.' No trouble translating his emotions there; he had none."

"A time for healing was in order," Miguel suggested calmly.

"Maybe. And maybe it's just a coincidence that Major Fiérro suddenly became *Lieutenant Colonel* Fiérro upon Carranza's death," Fred added indignantly.

"The promotion was to encourage young pilots to keep going after Carranza died," Geoffrey volunteered. Luz looked at him tenderly.

"Maybe the president was misquoted," Kelly reckoned.

"Or the American press translated it wrong," Luz added.

Fred dismissed both out of hand. "Then how do you explain the comments made by Manuel Tellez, the Mexican ambassador stationed in Washington, D.C., when he referred to Carranza's death, in English, as 'a sacrifice that has served the noblest and highest cause'?"

"That's easy," Luz said, brimming with pride. "He died in the service of his country. What greater cause is there?"

"You don't think that maybe he was 'sacrificed' to *save* his country from the designs of outsiders?"

"That's absurd," Noah argued. "You're taking their words out of context."

Fred plowed on, undeterred. "Am I? It was also Tellez who refused to allow a religious service and ordered that the special train carrying Carranza's body from New York to Mexico could not stop in the United States until it reached Laredo, Texas. What was he afraid of? And how about this one from the American Embassy in Mexico City, where it was reported that Ambassador Dwight Morrow was too 'grief-stricken' to make any comment to the press on Carranza's death?"

"Why is that so hard to understand?" Sarah asked with a puzzled look on her face.

"Read between the lines, my dear lady," Fred replied condescendingly. "Of course he was 'grief-stricken.' You might say he was traumatized. His dreams were shattered because the U.S. ambassador to Mexico was involved in the plot to turn Mexico over to his friends, the American industrialists. And so was Lindbergh. The Lone Eagle hid behind a convenient wall of silence. Carranza held the key. Their futures flew with him. One news account at the time reported that 'friends of Lindbergh declared that his high regard for the Mexican flyer made him feel that Carranza's death was too personal a matter for comment.'"

"That's speculative at best," Tom argued, shaking his head.

"Wait, I'm not finished." Fred tossed the remaining clippings to the floor. "Nothing can explain why Sebastian Carranza initially declined to accompany his son's body back to Mexico, claiming that he 'remembered his boy's face too well to see it in death' and therefore intended to 'stifle his sorrow in work.' What father would refuse to attend his son's funeral? He wasn't overcome with grief! Hell, no. He knew he was a marked man … just like his son. It all adds up!"

"Or maybe he knew it wasn't his son's body," Paul muttered. "Like I told you, what if it wasn't Carranza in the plane? He knew something was up, and he bailed out. Got someone to switch with him and go in his place."

"And then he disappeared off the face of the earth?" Noah asked incredulously. "Vanished? *Poof!* Just like that?"

"He was a celebrity," Edgar said. "Where could he go?"

"America is a big country. One could get lost easily. Especially one with money and contacts," Paul held out.

"But what fool would be stupid enough to take his place?" Danny asked.

Miguel stood to leave. "I have heard enough of your insults and lies!"

"We only seek the truth," Fred replied, extending his hands to all present. "It does us no good to continue to memorialize a falsehood, a lie, and a cover-up."

"Why reexamine his death," Miguel asserted, "when we can celebrate the meaning of his life?"

Fred wouldn't budge. "Wrong, *amigo.* I want to celebrate the message of the life he sacrificed. But was that message—of peace on Earth, goodwill to men of all nations— really the one he died for, or just the one we've come to accept in its place?"

There was a burst of commotion in the stable area below. Light suddenly flooded the loft as three intimidating-looking men barged in on the aborted séance.

14

Undivided Sky

"**J**oey! What a surprise," Paul said, lifting his head and squinting to focus on the figure in the poorly lit doorway. "You didn't have to bring the film equipment personally."

"Cut the crap," came the no-nonsense response from Joey Bones as he barged in, rousing Paul from his drowsy state and alarming the rest of the group.

The diminutive man stepped into the room, flanked by two super-sized bodyguards. Double-chinned and deeply tanned, the head of the Hollywood East Film Syndicate removed his fedora and wiped his brow. "I'm shutting down the Sawyer film," he announced. His gravelly voice resonated off the bare walls and reverberated around the room.

Fred bravely took a step toward him. "What for?"

"Violation of Section 619.7 of the New Jersey Screen Actors Guild."

"And what, exactly, is that?" Noah asked calmly, moving up alongside Fred.

Joey placed his hat back on his head, stuffed his hands into his pockets, and rocked back and forth on his heels like a wiseass penguin. "Engaging in the hiring of non-union actors."

The four members of the American Legion Post looked at each other quizzically.

"We don't follow you," Noah said at length.

"Your Mr. Sawyer hired someone named Dante Reed for a part in his film. Reed isn't a union member."

All eyes focused on Danny. He swallowed hard and bit his lip. This was the last straw. He had to ditch that stage name once and for all. It had brought him nothing but trouble.

"It's a bit part," Fred explained. "And, he's just a local kid."

"Besides," Noah added, showing off his newly acquired Hollywood vernacular, "it would be easy enough for Wade Sawyer to leave him on the cutting room floor."

Danny gave Noah a wounded glance.

Joey lifted his chins. "Too late." He was not one to waste words or time. "We've already sent Sawyer's crew packing. If he tries to shoot tomorrow, my people are instructed to force him to cease and desist by any means necessary," he said with a nod in the direction of his suited henchmen bookends.

"Joey, baby, be reasonable!" Paul implored him, realizing the gravity of the situation.

"Oh, yeah, thanks for the tip, Sloan. I owe you one. I'da had the A.C. union boys all over me for this one if it had gotten out. Good night, ladies," Joey said with a perfunctory tip of his hat. The two goons waited for their boss to exit and, with a cautious look back at the group, followed quickly behind him.

Edgar helped Paul to his feet. Paul moaned and clutched his head.

"We're screwed if we don't deliver a movie," Fred said to Noah, the anxiety evident in his voice. "This is all on your head. We'll be the laughingstock of this town."

"No," Tom corrected him, "what you and Madame Zora tried to pull tonight is reserved for that honor."

Fred stormed off to sulk alone.

"Wait a second," Noah exclaimed. "I have an idea." He turned to Miguel. "Is your crew still camped out at the village?"

"*Sí,*" Miguel answered excitedly, understanding where Noah was heading. "We are here until Monday."

Noah patted him on the shoulder. "Good. Round them up. We're not finished yet."

"Geoffrey, Luz, will you two come with me?" Miguel asked, grabbing the kids gently by the arms and pulling them toward the door.

Geoffrey already had his keys out.

Noah searched the room for Megan. She was huddled in the corner with a disconsolate Fred. "Megan, do you know how to reach Wade at this late hour?"

She shook her head. "I can try, but his cell phone's been turned off all night. And he doesn't have a landline."

Danny stepped into the mix. "I know someone who can reach him." He gave Kelly a furtive look and reached for his cell phone. She smiled approvingly.

Noah hesitated, and then it registered. "Okay. Have Feather tell Wade that if he still wants to film the memorial tomorrow, he should meet us at the monument at 8 AM, sharp."

"What do you want me to do?" Madame Zora asked, coming across the room to Noah.

"Why don't you try your hand at something constructive," Sarah replied, rescuing her husband and ushering him out the barn door, "like making yourself disappear."

***

Geoffrey, Luz, and Danny met up with Kelly at Colson's General Store for their early-morning drive. From Chatsworth they took Danny's Jeep east on Route 532 to Tabernacle, where they made a left onto a narrow, rural lane aptly named Carranza Memorial Road, so called for obvious reasons. They were only eight or nine miles below the Red Lion Circle, but the desolate, pitted road leading into the Wharton State Forest, with its scrub pines and sandy white wasteland, made it seem 100 miles from civilization.

To Kelly, the scenery was initially disappointing. She had been expecting something more exciting for the location where the body of this acclaimed Mexican aviator had been found. Hidden by the pine trees and lacking suitable roadside signage, the hallowed ground might easily have been missed, had Danny not been there before, while filming his singular movie scene nearby. He pulled his Jeep into the adjacent trail park's gravel lot.

Leaving his vehicle there, Danny, Kelly, Geoffrey, and Luz followed a narrow horse trail through the thick woods to where a solitary stone monument stood in the center of an open, sandy grove. Chiseled from granite mined from a quarry near Carranza's home and paid for by the donations of Mexican schoolchildren, each block represented a different Mexican state. They had been shipped to Chatsworth, where they were assembled and erected in 1933. Gray and weather-worn, the tapered block obelisk was framed around its base by an untended garden box containing nine symbolic, spindly yucca plants, reminiscent of Carranza's native Mexico but stunted by so many harsh New Jersey winters.

Although it was still an hour or so before the scheduled start of the formal festivities, a burgeoning crowd had already begun to mill about the memorial. The teens watched as men, women, and children of all ages and various nationalities placed lighted votive candles and pocket change—particularly U.S. quarters bearing their home state's emblem—around the base of the monolith. Using branches and twigs broken off nearby trees, several of these Carranza pilgrims etched messages for their fallen hero in the sand around the monument: *¡Viva Carranza! Jesus loves you!*

Having spent considerable time over the past few days in the company of knowledgeable and determined individuals who analyzed, criticized, and debated the relative meaning of Carranza's death, Danny, Kelly, Geoffrey, and Luz approached the monument with profound reverence.

Danny ran a hand down the carved relief of an arrow and a descending Aztec eagle, symbolic of flight and Carranza's plummet to the earth. It formed the focal point of the monument's stonework. Kelly traced the lines of the embedded footprints, which, according to the informational tableau, represented the famed aviator's final walk on the planet. On the two side panels, one in Spanish, the other in English, Luz and Geoffrey read the following inscription together: *The People of Mexico hope that your heartfelt ideals will be realized.*

"I feel like we know him," Kelly marveled, rubbing her arms to smooth the hair that had risen there.

"I feel like we *should* know him," was Geoffrey's reply.

"He is here with us," Luz offered solemnly.

"Shh. Listen," Danny whispered. "Can you hear that?"

All four stopped what they were doing. Despite the bustle of activity around them, they all tuned in to what Danny had heard: Silence. Dead. Still. Eerie. Silence. Even the breeze didn't stir on this gorgeous summer day as they stood poised beneath the shrine to a man about whom they had recently heard and learned so much.

"A *peso* for your thoughts." Though the female voice was friendly and familiar, all four of them jumped at once.

"Don't you ever do that again," Kelly pretended to reprimand her Aunt Sarah.

"You kids okay?" Noah asked, standing beside his blushing wife.

"Are *you*?" Geoffrey asked as Wade and Miguel strode up together behind them.

"Couldn't be better," Noah replied, observing the two directors as they discussed their plans.

"I got some great aerial shots right off the same kind of wing formation, coming in low over the Pines. Looks like they came from Andalusian Dogs, straight out of a Buñuel playbook," Wade was saying.

"You should see the footage we picked up at Colson's General Store. Makes it look like Shyamalan's *The Village*, ageless and authentic," Miguel shared proudly.

They were beaming at each other with newfound admiration and understanding. The others remained speechless as they continued.

"Look, Miguel. I may be a social-climbing Hollywood wannabe, and, yeah, I tried to make a deal with the devil himself to get distribution, but I never wanted you out of the way, and the bottom line is, I really love this script," Wade confessed with as much honesty as he could muster.

"Well, I'm no saint either, Wade, but I do have a full crew with me, if you can stand the idea of sharing the spotlight."

"What choice have I got? I may have a lot of equipment, but I can't run it all by myself, and I don't speak a word of Spanish," Wade said with a laugh.

"Don't worry. I'll make sure my crew follows both our leads." Miguel smiled.

"Then we really are working from the same script," Wade offered, extending his hand to shake. Miguel grabbed it and pulled him into a bear-like embrace.

Noah broke the celebratory mood. "What are we standing around for? We've got a movie to finish!"

"Danny," Wade said seriously. "I'm sorry to have to tell you, but we've got so much good footage that your big-screen debut probably won't make the final cut."

"Man, I'm really sorry I caused you so much trouble," Danny said.

He shot Danny an aw-shucks look. "Yeah, well, live and learn, I guess. Anyway, thanks to Miguel here, I think we're going to have one hell of a film."

"A lot better than the ones we each started out to make," Miguel added graciously.

"And, I am happy to report that Joey Bones can't touch us," Wade beamed.

"That's right," Miguel concurred. "Mr. Bonetti and his New Jersey Film cronies have no jurisdiction over my Mexican camera crew, or our right to film a public event with the sponsor's approval. We decided to bring Wade on board as associate director. He will be in charge of today's shoot of the memorial celebration."

"You sure these guys will follow my directions?" Wade asked uncertainly. "They don't understand a word I say."

"But I do," Miguel reassured him. "Now all we need is an editor who speaks both languages."

"I have a cousin in Austin who edits music videos for Univision," Luz gushed, running over and hugging Miguel.

Noah smiled like a proud papa. "I can't help thinking this may be just the kind of cooperation and international amity Carranza dreamed of when he attempted his momentous flight all those years ago."

"Yeah, mission accomplished, *amigo*." Wade acknowledged the stone monument with a tip of his baseball cap.

"But what about Fred?" Geoffrey wanted to know. "Is he going to cause any trouble today?"

"Oh, I wouldn't worry about Fred," Noah said confidently. "In fact, I expect our soon-to-be-*ex*-Post-Commander won't have the nerve to show his face anywhere near the memorial today or any time soon."

Sarah giggled. "Miguel, you didn't tell them?"

Miguel shrugged. "*Perdóneme*, it must have slipped my mind," he apologized with a sly smile.

"Tell us what?" Kelly prompted.

Sarah couldn't control herself. "You remember the camcorder Megan gave Miguel last night? Well, Miguel taped the whole scene: Fred, Madame Zora, Paul, even Joey Bones—every sordid detail. Fred would be humiliated if that tape were ever made public."

Miguel pulled the tape out of his satchel and tapped it against his hand.

"That's called blackmail," Geoffrey whispered.

"That's so cool," Danny commented.

"*Ay, Miguel te pasaste*," Luz said, throwing her arms around the director's neck. Danny, Geoffrey, and Kelly joined in the jolly melee without understanding or caring what Luz had just said. The two directors walked off together with their arms draped around each other like brothers.

"What did I miss?" Feather asked, catching up with the party around the inspiring monolith.

"Just a chance to witness what a real good-neighbor policy looks like in action," Kelly teased with obvious relish. "Even Emilio Carranza would have been impressed."

A confused Feather looked around at the happy faces, hoping for an explanation.

"There goes your scoop," Danny said, pointing her in the direction of Wade and Miguel. "If you hurry, they might even let you share the spotlight."

Feather held on to her sunhat. "Hey, wait for me," she said, whipping out her BlackBerry and dashing after the directors.

Just then Tom came running up to join the group. "Noah, you might want to get things started a little early. There's rain headed our way."

Sure enough, as Noah cocked his head skyward he could see the dark cumulus clouds rapidly rolling in. "Have all the Legionnaires arrived?"

"Everyone but Fred and Paul. I'm told Paul's a bit under the weather."

"Just as well," Noah sighed. "Saves me the trouble of telling him we've nixed his slide show."

Noah straightened his cap and took Sarah's arm in his. "Can you imagine it, Sarah? Back in 1928, Carranza's coffin was borne down Broadway on a horse-drawn gun caisson, draped with the American and Mexican flags, and followed by 10,000 U.S. soldiers."

"That must have been some sight," Sarah pondered.

"Well, at least we're doing our part to remember him," Noah offered humbly.

"Amen," Sarah said, kissing her husband's cheek.

Geoffrey gave the group a thoughtful look.

"What is it?" Kelly asked.

"I was thinking of something Paul said. Danny, do you remember when he told us that 40,000 Mexican workers were on hand to greet the body when it was returned to Mexican soil?"

"How can I forget?" Danny responded with conviction.

"Noah, with that of kind popular outpouring, don't you think the Mexican government had good reason to be concerned about Carranza's fame and success?" Geoffrey asked.

"In my opinion, they would have been foolish to ignore it."

Miguel and Wade took their positions amid the camera crew. "Relax, Wade, we already have the establishing shots."

"I know but I want to capture the ceremony from the two angles we talked about, and you need to be at one of them, so how do I talk to the other cameraman?"

"Luz!" both young filmmakers shouted at once.

An hour later, with the sounds of "Going Home" played by the Sugar Sand Ramblers wafting in the background, the 100 or so members of Mount Holly American Legion Post 11 made good on their unbroken, solemn pledge for yet another year. And as the Carranza Memorial Committee Honor Guard concluded their ceremony, retiring the national flags of the United States and Mexico, the heavens opened up with a violent thunderstorm—not unlike the one the courageous Captain Emilio Carranza had flown into some 79 years earlier.

As all eyes and two film cameras gazed upward, a lone eagle flew off into an undivided sky.

15

Hope

Kelly, Geoffrey, Danny, and Luz lounged comfortably on the rear deck of Sarah Bishop-Parsons's Crab Cove Gift Shop in Ship Bottom. After the events of the past few weeks, they were glad to be enjoying the pleasures of the peaceful bay and golden summer sunshine.

Maggie Colson had returned from her California mission of mercy to report that her sister, thanks to a well-measured Freeman Morris tonic, was on the mend after her bout with shingles. Kelly was grateful to have some downtime and was finishing the final pages of the Palahniuk novel with which she had started to fill up the hours of boredom that came with managing the out-of-the-way general store in Maggie's absence. She was ready to relax and enjoy the rest of her summer spending time between Crab Cove and the beach.

For his part, Geoffrey had decided to abandon his quest to film a documentary about Little Beach. Having visited the island, he was now content to leave it to the flies. He didn't want to bring that much attention to an unspoiled place when doing so could result in bringing an unending stream of eco-curious tourists to the wildlife preserve—which neither Mother Nature nor Ned "Popeye" Thompson would appreciate for very long.

After saying *adios* to the Poco Loco Film Company, Luz went back to her old job as hostess at the elite Bonnet Island Estate and even got Geoffrey a job interview for the position of groundskeeper for the balance of the summer.

Before leaving, Miguel promised to send invitations to everyone when *The Lost Mission of Captain Carranza* premiered in the spring. He and Wade were headed to Mexico City to edit their joint masterpiece, and a debate raged as to whether they would premiere, it in San Antonio, as a tribute to the Alamo, or in Austin, to take advantage of the growing music scene and Wade's connections there.

Danny, sporting dark shades but no longer content with hiding his feelings behind a dangerous stage name, was making good on a promise to hang out more often with his summer friends. Though currently unemployed, he had heard from Moss Greenberg about a lifeguard vacancy at his old 18th Street haunt. Apparently, the opening had been created when the current guard on duty, one Curtis Wick, got busted for underage drinking at Daddy O during his lunch break. The thought of taking his old nemesis's spot was tempting, but the new Danny found he derived enough pleasure from laughing at Curtis's troubles without feeling the need to add to them.

"I do like you better as a blond," Kelly said casually, tousling Danny's restored Beach Boy locks.

"I liked it better when you didn't mess up my hair," Danny answered with a toothy grin.

"You know, Danny, when Madame Zora told me that a 'dark-haired stranger' would need my help, I immediately thought of you in your Dante Reed disguise, rather than Emilio Carranza," Kelly said, now gently stroking his golden tresses.

"How could you make that mistake? I'm much taller than he was," Danny joked.

"Do you suppose she really had Carranza in mind when she said that to you?" Geoffrey asked, sipping lemonade through a straw.

"Of course," Luz said, joining the conversation. "Only, by my way of thinking, the dark-haired stranger turned out to be Miguel."

"Oh, that's a stretch," Danny disagreed. "I don't think we can give you or Madame Zora any credit for clairvoyance on that score."

Noah, followed by his wife and Tom, joined the kids on the deck. The kids were excited to see them and to get answers, finally, to their questions.

"Well, it's official," Noah announced to the group with a heavy sigh of relief. "I tendered my resignation as chairman of the Carranza Memorial Committee to Wayne Nye, Acting Commander of American Legion Post 11." He took a seat under the Cinzano beach umbrella.

"Boy, are *we* ever glad," Sarah said, handing him a glass of iced tea.

"Now, don't keep the kids in suspense, Noah," Tom goaded him, "tell them what we've learned."

"Right, but where to begin …?" Noah mused as he nursed his cold tea.

Danny piped up. "How about starting with the fire? Did old Deputy Dawg ever get to the bottom of that mess?"

"Funny you should ask, Danny—it is okay to call you Danny again?"

Danny just nodded while his friends exclaimed in unison, "Yes, please!"

Noah cleared his throat. "I met with Arthur Adams earlier today. In light of recent events, including several confessions from key people involved in the Carranza affair, the fire marshal is ready to bring his investigation of the Whitesbog Village fire to a close.

"Danny, you may be interested to know that you're not the only one who's been masquerading around town under a pseudonym. It seems that your lovely *Island Sentinel* reporter, Feather Sparrow, goes by the name Mildred Byrd in some of her more … creative professional work—the very same M. Byrd who is credited for writing not just Wade's script but also the one Poco Loco was using. They are, in fact, the same script, translated and sold separately to undisclosed buyers.

"Clever girl that she is, after seducing Wade and then getting to know Don Alejándro, she realized the two versions of her script were being made into a movie at the same time. Recognizing this would be disastrous if they hoped to get a decent distribution deal like the one Joey Bones had promised her, let alone how it would affect both films' theatrical life expectancy and profit-making potential, she decided to cast her lot with the American film. She just had to find a way to terminate the Mexican film and thought she'd found it with the fire that destroyed their equipment."

"But she didn't do it alone," Tom said, picking up the story while Noah paused to quench his thirst. "She had help, a willing accomplice, in the form of Chester Potts, who, as overseer of the village, had both the means and the access necessary to do the deed. Arthur had suspected Chester from the very beginning, simply because the fire had been so well-contained as to ruin the movie equipment completely while causing only slight damage to the historic building itself. The locked door was a giveaway, but, without a motive, he was at a loss to point an accusing finger. The big break came when he was following up on a separate lead and scrolled through the enrollment registry on the Minuteman Project website. There he discovered that, regrettably, Lester and Leroy Hatch were, in fact, gun-toting, anti-alien, border-watch members of this ruthless vigilante group. Applying a little subtle pressure to the Hatch boys, Arthur was able to learn that Chester was also a closet member. He now had his missing motive. When he cornered the overseer with the evidence—circumstantial though it may have seemed—he was able to secure Chester's plea-bargained confession. Naturally, he'll lose his job at the village and will have to compensate Poco Loco for the loss of their equipment. But in return for reimbursing them for their losses, he can avoid hard jail time, if Poco Loco agrees not to press charges."

"I'm sure Miguel will be willing to let bygones be bygones," Luz answered for the absent director. "He has his film, which is all he really cared about."

"Spoken in true Carranza spirit," Sarah commended her.

"What's going to happen to Feather?" Kelly asked with a heartfelt glance at Danny.

Noah smiled warmly. "She's been let go by the paper, but, knowing Feather's spunk and ambition, I don't think she'll be unemployed for long. In fact, it's rumored she's already working with two guys from Trenton who are the authors of a young adult book series. Feather is going to write the screenplays for an HBO television series based on their books."

"What about her role in the fire? It was her idea, even if she didn't set it. Won't she go to jail?" Geoffrey asked.

"Not likely," Noah replied. "She's got a sharp lawyer—Edgar Wilson—who has managed to convince the court to waive all criminal charges and all punitive damages against her, in return for her assigning all rights to the script to the Poco Loco Film Company of Mexico. The film company intends to use the royalties to start a film institute for children in Carranza's hometown of Ramos Arizpe. And, apparently, according to Miguel, who has been named the institute's interim director, one of the first films the institute plans to tackle will be the Spanish translation of an animated short based on a story by those same two writers from Trenton and directed by Wade."

"And what about Fred Carlson?" Sarah wanted to know. "Did you ever find out what he was really up to?"

Noah smiled approvingly at his wife. "Fred always believed something wasn't quite right about the accepted version of the Carranza story. When he became Post

Commander, he decided to use his position to dig for the truth—to discover the story behind the story, as it were. He made it his business to study all the archival material he could find from the stories printed in the *New York Times* and *Washington Post*, both before and after the crash. He contacted friends, relatives, and associates of anyone remotely connected to the incident. Fred was convinced something was going on behind the scenes, and he felt certain the key to unlocking that secret was hidden in the flashlight Carranza clutched so dearly when he died.

"When he found out that Edgar was a descendant of the Carr family, the blueberry pickers who first discovered the remains of Carranza's corpse and the wreckage of his plane, Fred invited him to join Post 11. As a former Navy Seal, the invitation seemed entirely appropriate. But Fred got nothing of substance about the plane crash or its aftermath from him.

"Later, when Fred was approached by Wade about the American film project, he orchestrated the hiring of his granddaughter, Megan, as the personal assistant to the director in order to keep tabs on the progress of the film and any leads that might provide him with information to satisfy his personal quest.

"Over time, Fred realized that neither Wade's film nor the Poco Loco film was going to be anything more than the accepted version of the events. He decided to push the envelope by talking his estranged daughter—a mostly two-bit, faux medium who eked out a meager living telling fortunes in Atlantic City and went by the stage name 'Madame Zora'—into conducting a séance on the eve of the memorial. Fred was hoping a night entertained by the spirit of Emilio Carranza might coax Edgar into a state of admission. As you know, that never came to pass, thanks in part to his loss of self-control and what happened to our filmmakers. If Edgar learned anything at all from his kin about secret, coded messages being smuggled into Mexico by Carranza inside his flashlight, it appears likely that such information will remain with Edgar and go with him to his grave."

"Well, I don't know about Fred's harebrained ideas," Danny said as Noah took a break to wet his lips with more iced tea and to munch on some chips and salsa, "but I sure was convinced that Paul was on the right track with his hypothesis."

"Yeah, he had me going, too," Geoffrey admitted.

"Paul is a character, all right," Noah agreed. "In fact, it turns out he was a former CIA military operative. According to him, his connection to Joey Bones began when he found out that Joey's people were backing Noriega in Panama, but he has a weakness for liquor and believes there's a government conspiracy lurking around every corner. Whether any of his assertions are true or not is anybody's guess. He's cried foul so often that no one really knows what to believe anymore. The line where fact ends and fantasy begins seems to be blurred, even to Paul himself."

"Ah, but Don Alejándro, now *there's* an enigma," Tom offered with a twinkle in his eye.

"What do you mean?" Kelly asked.

"What he means," Noah said, gladly jumping on his friend's lead-in, "is that Don Alejándro was not who he claimed to be, a movie producer hired by the Carranza family. The Carranza family *did* hire him, but his job was simply to see to it that the accepted version of the Carranza story got told. In other words, it was his job to make sure no surprises or embarrassments tarnished the Carranza myth."

"Apparently," Tom said, snatching back the story from Noah, "the Carranza family got wind of the inquiries Fred was making. The family, in fact, may have been contacted by him directly and may have hired Don Alejándro specifically to keep a lid on any conspiracy theories that might be percolating just below the surface—not Paul's, because most people wrote him off as a lunatic, but Fred's, because his position as Post Commander gave them real cause for concern. He had the power to accept or reject the Poco Loco application to film the memorial event. Wisely, Fred decided to delegate the authority to the committee, but not before cramming it full of people he thought were of the same opinion, like Paul, Lewis Brewster, Amos Hurley, and people he thought he could manipulate, like Edgar, the Hatches, and—sad to say—our boy Noah here."

"Boy, did he read you wrong, eh, dear?" Sarah said endearingly, hugging her husband.

Noah smiled shyly. "Unfortunately for Don Alejándro, Fred found out about his true mission with the film and discovered the glitch in his visa. It was Fred who notified the authorities, who then had Don Alejándro deported, but not before Don Alejándro paid Fred considerable hush money to allow Poco Loco to film the event and keep his flashlight theory under wraps until after the film's completion."

"That accounts for Poco Loco's empty treasury," Luz exclaimed.

"Not entirely," Tom said. "I'm afraid Don Alejándro's reputation for wine and women was not totally without merit. He did spend a little extra here and there. Oh, and there's one more thing you should know: It was Don Alejándro who tipped off Arthur Adams about the Minuteman Project, in the hope it might ultimately implicate Carlson, whom Don Alejándro suspected might also be a member."

"So, there you have it," Noah said, stretching out on a chaise lounge. "We may never know the truth about why Emilio Carranza climbed into the cockpit on that stormy July night back in 1928. What drove him toward his destiny? All we have are more questions. Had the plane been sabotaged? If so, by whom? Was it the paranoid Mexican government or misplaced American nationalistic pride? Indeed, did friend or foe betray Carranza—or was his death simply a matter of fate?"

"Fate!" The crowd cast their vote.

Noah smiled as he continued. "All we can say for sure is that Captain Emilio Carranza is more important today in death than he ever could have been had he succeeded in his flight or survived his crash. Mexican children idolize him and the U.S. Bureau of Tourism claims that the Carranza Memorial is the fourth most frequented Hispanic site in North America. You saw the faces yourself, shining with hope for a better world, a world drawn closer to that goal by the immense courage of Carranza and the solemn, unbroken pledge of American Legion Post 11. Isn't it ironic how a crash landing in the New Jersey Pines nearly 80 years ago spawned a legacy that survives his death and completes his mission in a way that he never, ever could have imagined?"

಼ಌ

Riddle in the Sand

1

Brielle, New Jersey
(1971)

Around the Brielle Marina, Jack Walker was known as a drunk, and that was just fine with him. The hardscrabble owner-operator of a 32-foot charter boat known as the *Sea Mist,* he was a self-sufficient man whose vast experiences on the open water included such diverse occupations as oil driller, deep sea diver, and tour boat operator.

After enlisting in the Merchant Marine at the age of 18, he saw action in the Korean conflict and was later called up to serve during the 1962 Cuban Missile Crisis. To anyone who asked, he would say the man he admired most was former Arizona senator Barry Goldwater and that his favorite actress was Maureen O'Hara, the flaming scarlet-haired beauty who played opposite John Wayne in many of his best Westerns. His favorite drink and best friend, as far as he was concerned, was Jim Beam—a double, straight up.

When he wasn't out to sea, the twice-divorced captain could usually be found camped on a barstool at the Outside Inn, a local watering hole frequented by service men from the Fort Monmouth Arsenal. There, for the price of a drink, he would tell his tales to any bleary-eyed, youthful admirer from the post's 754th disposal unit who would lend him an ear. Over time he became buddies with the disposal unit's commander, Major Ralph Richter. In a never-ending game of "Can you top this?" Jack and Ralph would swap stories, some fanciful and some more or less close to the truth.

On one particular occasion, a cold, bleak, and dreary night in early October, Jack was holding court as usual at the Outside Inn when Ralph came in for a nightcap. A career officer, he had just returned from a special duty out at sea and was scheduled to make a similar trip the following evening. He was cold, damp, and in foul humor from his moonlight exercise. He was in desperate need of something warm to eat and soothing spirits to take away the night's chill. For that, the genial atmosphere of the inn fit the bill.

The barkeeper and patrons in the pub proved to be the perfect remedy for Ralph's surly attitude. He found Jack perched on his barstool and primed for company. As time wore on and the two men pounded back drink after drink, Ralph's stony veneer gradually faded, and he told Jack about his special mission.

"Room is getting tight over at the Arsenal," he whispered. "Especially when a fresh new pile of munitions arrives every other day headed for Vietnam. I tell you, we're running out of space."

Ralph went on to describe his assignment in hushed tones to his new best friend. It was a trip the major had made many times before. His mission was to slip under the radar of the emerging watchful eyes of the Department of Environmental Protection

279

and to dump the old pre-WWI vintage munitions that had been collecting dust on the Arsenal shelves for decades into the depths of the Atlantic. But now, with the Whole Earth movement gaining in popularity following the aftermath of a medical waste wash-up on some New Jersey beaches, the DEP had begun to clamp down on all dumping in the ocean.

"It's all legal and everything, but the DEP boys are always on the lookout. I tell you, it's these damn liberal bureaucrats that ruin it," Ralph complained. "These tree huggers and whale lovers have got them chasing their own tails."

As he finished his story, Jack, being the good charter boat captain that he was, realized this military dumping of "harmless" unexploded ordnances—UXOs, to use Ralph's terminology—had, over time, probably built up into a pretty substantial natural reef on the ocean floor, much like those found among shipwrecks in which plankton and algae attach themselves to the boats, attracting schools of bait fish, which, in turn, attract boatloads of game fish for Jack's eager paying passengers. The best part about the whole thing was that, according to Ralph, the dumping ground was located just three miles off the Jersey coast—a mere half day's charter for the aging *Sea Mist* and her wily, well-lubricated captain.

This was back in the days before fancy global positioning systems were standard issue on recreational boats, so finding the exact spot where the munitions were being disposed of could be problematic even if Ralph were willing to share his navigational charts with Jack, which of course he was not. So Jack resolved to do the next best thing. The following evening, he decided to trail Ralph's garbage dumping detail out to the spot, being careful to stay out of sight and avoid being detected by the U.S. Navy, and to pinpoint the untapped fishing fields for himself. Unfortunately for Capt. Walker, the gods were in an angry mood that night and the seas were a lot rougher than desirable. Nevertheless, with a pint of Jim Beam already under his belt to steady his nerves and another one in his cabin for good measure, he untied the *Sea Mist* from the Brielle dock and shadowed the fleet out into the open sea.

Once he got out of the inlet and was still less than a mile from shore, the seas took a turn for the worse. Swells pummeled the *Sea Mist*'s hull relentlessly. He struggled to keep the bow straight and the boat on course. Under a darkening sky, he was beginning to have trouble keeping the fleet in sight.

About two miles out, Jack started to contemplate turning his boat around and making for port. He peered through his rain-soaked binoculars, trying to estimate the distance between his boat and Ralph's three-ship flotilla. For a brief instant, he thought the ships had stopped moving forward, but that just wasn't possible. They were far short of the three-mile legal limit Ralph had to reach. Still, with his visibility so poor, he could not be sure.

Jack polished off his second bottle of Jim Beam and tossed the dead soldier overboard. As if she were angry at his thoughtless littering, the sea slammed back against the *Sea Mist*'s wooden hull. A bit unsteady on his sea legs and feeling the effects of the alcohol, Jack was thrown against the cabin overhang and struck his head on the angled corner joint. A deep crimson gash opened on his forehead. He began to feel lightheaded and to sway uneasily. Groping for the side rail, he slipped and fell to one knee. As he tried to regain his footing, another wave rocked the *Sea Mist*, sending Captain Jack into the drink. A final wave washed over the pilotless boat, capsizing it.

Less than half a mile away, Ralph Richter had decided his detail had gone far enough. His head pounded with a nagging hangover. The raging storm had made the ocean far too rough for his liking. It didn't make any sense to continue the journey the entire distance to their usual destination. Whether it was three miles out or two and a half, what difference did it make anyway? He told himself it was all just one big ocean. Who would ever know? He signaled the captain to stop the engines and ordered the crew to begin dumping their unwanted cargo.

2

Full-Blown Obsession
(Present Day)

It started out as a good way to get exercise and lose weight. Libby Ashcroft had gained about 50 pounds after her husband of 14 years left her for a peroxide blonde working in his real estate office across from the Viking Village commercial docks in Barnegat Light.

Long walks beside the shifting Atlantic surf in the early morning sunshine and fresh salt air proved to be a tonic for the assiduous curator of the Tuckerton Seaport Museum. Her metal-detecting hobby soon blossomed into a full-blown obsession.

Dazzled by the many finds brought to her by an army of amateur treasure hunters and coaxed by a beachcombing corps of like-minded adventurers, Libby soon found herself forgetting Walter and immersing herself in the thrill of weekly scavenger hunts. They reminded her of the Easter egg hunts her mother had organized for the neighborhood kids every spring when she was a child. But instead of candied treats hidden in pastel-colored plastic eggs, Libby and the members of her beachcomber club were on the prowl for pirate booty—Spanish doubloons, silver crosses, and pieces of eight.

She would always remember her first big find: a rusty old oil lamp from a 19th-century whaling vessel that was rumored to lie shipwrecked just beyond the reef. She was hooked—and that was 22 years ago. Shined up and polished, that working lantern had adorned the fieldstone mantel over her fireplace ever since. Now blue-haired and slightly stooped, weathered but trimmer, and wearing her hat, at 68 Libby wouldn't dare miss a single day of beach action, especially the first good day after a weeklong nor'easter had churned up the coast.

She stopped her sweeping motion and adjusted the discrimination level that controlled her instrument's sensitivity for certain metals. Experience had taught her that the more you discriminate, the less depth you are going to have. That also means less digging. However, if she set the controls to tune out soda can pull tabs and discarded nails, she might also miss important objects like small coins and pinkie rings.

For Libby, discrimination was more of an art than a science. A practiced *detectorist*, as the diehards preferred to be called, had to feel one's way around a specific locale. She had picked this particular piece of the Division Street beach in Surf City because of its high volume of activity. She knew intuitively that detecting could be especially rewarding after a good soaking rain. Wet ground generated more conductivity.

The sound of screeching seagulls caught her attention for a moment. She watched as a convoy of the squawking gray-white feathered birds took flight and circled around a group of hardy surfers in wetsuits waiting on their boards out at sea. The surf was rough following the storm and provided perfect waves for the small contingent of four stout-hearted surfers who were trying to make the most of the Jersey Shore in late springtime, before the hordes of day-trippers landed there in the summer.

Libby adjusted her headset, tuning out the crashing waves, and honed in on her unit's faint but constant signals. She was using a Minelab Excalibur 1000 that she had bought used for $500 six months ago. It seemed like a lot of money at the time, but by now she was convinced it was the best investment she had ever made.

The Excalibur 1000 was not for beginners and she was still getting used to it. Equipped with waterproof coils and a VLF (very low frequency) meter, it was designed to detect in shallow water and to help differentiate between unwanted junk and precious metals. It was also very light, and Libby found that she could sweep an area with relative ease. Her arms almost never got tired or cramped up, as they had with her previous, less sophisticated detector.

She had already sorted through her fair share of junk for the day, but her trash pouch wasn't that full for a morning that followed a drenching rain. Unlike many of her cohorts who were sitting this gorgeous day out, she felt obliged to stand by the courteous detectorist's creed to "never re-bury your dug-up trash" and "always fill in your scoop holes" so people didn't trip and injure themselves.

A high-pitched tone resonated in Libby's earphones. She stopped and listened carefully, moving the arm of her instrument in a slow arc over the packed, wet sand. She glanced at the dials. Judging from the long blips emanating from the DISC meter, she was getting a strong reading for silver, maybe eight to ten inches down.

Her pulse quickened. Perhaps it was a brooch or a medallion, she thought, like the one that naïve niece of Sarah Bishop-Parsons found while lifeguarding a couple summers ago on the beach not far from here. As she recalled, the girl claimed it had simply washed up in the surf in Ship Bottom. It turned out to be a priceless gold medallion that was later bought by the son of renowned treasure hunter Mel Fisher, after validating it had come from the *Fortuna*, the wreck that gave Ship Bottom its name. From her position as curator at the museum, Libby had brokered the sale. It was indeed a very fortuitous find for the lucky young lady, she recalled with a twinge of jealousy.

The first sieve yielded nothing when she sank her pointed cup into the sand. She tried again with similar results. She took a short step to the left and swept. Suddenly her magnometer began to beep and click at strong, erratic intervals. The range on the meter was now registering something solid and iron-like. Libby grew confused. *Where did that antique brooch disappear to*, she wondered?

She stuck her scoop down deep. The point of the cup-like trowel struck something hard and metallic. Libby dropped to her knees. She began clawing the sand away from the pit with her hands. The tip of something hard and rusted poked through the sand. It had an oddly familiar shape to it—like an oversized penis. It made her think of her ex-husband, and she laughed. *An old relic ... like Walter*, she mused. She dug more furiously. *If I can clear around it, then I can yank it out the rest of the way*, she reasoned.

Despite the warning signals flashing from every neural center in her petite frame, Libby sank her pointed scoop into the hole once more. Hoping to slip around the projectile, she missed her mark and struck the partially exposed canister head on. A spark leaped from the contact of metal on metal. In one thunderous instant, the beach beneath Libby erupted into a fountain of shrapnel and blasted sand.

3

"Con-FUZE-ion"

From where Danny Windsor sat, atop his 8'6" longboard, the explosion on the beach looked like Old Faithful, but instead of spewing steam and scalding-hot water into the air, this blast sent an ungodly mix of sand and human flesh spraying skyward.

"Lesson's over," said a well-tanned Danny, shaking his shaggy blond surfer's hair and turning anxiously to Kelly Martin. She sat motionless on her board, her hands covering her ears. A look of total shock was etched upon her sun-freckled face.

Danny didn't bother to repeat his words. He motioned to the other two surfers, Johnny Longfeather, with his long Rasta braids, and Rodney Coles, the shaved-headed, muscular, tattooed surf bum, that he was heading in. He caught the next wave, leaving Kelly, dumbfounded, to paddle in on her own.

By the time Danny hit the beach, a small crowd had already gathered. A barrel-chested middle-aged man was talking animatedly into his cell phone while trying to keep his leashed twin terriers from sniffing and licking at the frayed and bloodied body parts scattered all around them.

Another man, wearing a crisp blue Mets cap and an unbuttoned floral-print shirt, came running, the binoculars draped around his neck lashing back and forth across his chest. He had watched the whole ordeal from the balcony of a big beach house that overlooked the dunes and was now prepared to videotape the carnage. He set his beer can down in the sand and flicked the camera's ON button, which immediately started glowing. "This is Six O'Clock News stuff," he exclaimed to no one in particular.

Danny knocked over the man's beer as he swept past. He bent down and picked up the deceased curator's distinctive straw sun hat. The embroidered Tuckerton Seaport Museum logo was speckled with fresh blood. A wave of nausea made him wretch as he recognized the hat. He swallowed hard and bit down on his lip until the feeling passed.

"*Sweet Jesus*," moaned Johnny at the site of the shredded face and bloodied corpse. The twin terriers were yapping incessantly and straining in opposite directions against their master's leash, adding to the surreal horror of the moment.

"What a fracking mess," sighed Rodney, paying homage to *Battlestar Galactica*. "I'd hate to have to be the one to clean this up."

"Keep back," Danny shouted to Kelly as she came up alongside the threesome. He held her back, pulling her away brusquely. She didn't appreciate being manhandled by Danny in front of the others and tried to resist. He showed her Libby's soiled hat.

"Oh my God!" she cried, gripping Danny's arm tightly. She, too, felt suddenly faint.

"Yes," acknowledged Danny, pointing to the remains, "That is ... er, *was* Libby Ashcroft."

More and more people poured onto the beach from over the dunes, curious to see what was going on. Some had heard the explosion from a distance. Others were simply drawn in by the excited crowd. Soon, with sirens wailing and lights flashing, two police cruisers and an emergency vehicle were speeding up the beach from Ship Bottom.

Johnny bent down and inspected the spent metal canister. It was eight inches long and four inches in diameter, and it was still warm. He scraped away the rust and embedded barnacles with a pocket knife. "Property of the U.S. Army" was partially legible in faded, chalky white letters.

He showed the charred cylinder to the others.

"I thought they cleared this beach of those things a couple of years ago," said Danny, turning it over in his hand.

"So did I," replied Johnny. "It cost a bundle to clean it up and it embarrassed the hell out of the Feds."

"Well, it looks like they missed one, dude," said Rodney.

"What is that thing, anyway?" asked Kelly curiously.

"It's called a DMM, in Army talk," said Johnny. "Discarded military munitions."

"A bomb?" asked Kelly.

"More like the detonating device that sets off a bomb," he explained, drawing on his Coast Guard training. "Sometimes the military refers to them as F-U-Z-E-S so as not to be confused with the F-U-S-E-S that you light with a match to set off fireworks."

"Same difference," shrugged Danny.

"Not really," said Johnny. "A DMM can be all sorts of things. An unexploded ordnance or UXO, a fuse booster, or an unfired projectile."

"Uh-huh," said Danny. "Sounds like bombs to me."

"It sounds like military mumbo-jumbo, if you ask me," said Kelly impatiently. "What I want to know is what's that thing doing here?"

"Obviously killing people," replied Rodney morosely. He began peeling off his wetsuit, hoping Kelly would take notice of his rock-solid tattooed pecs. She didn't seem to, but Danny did—and not with admiration.

"Hundreds of these things were inadvertently pumped up onto the beaches in Surf City and Ship Bottom, along with the sand fill during the Storm Damage Reduction Project back in 2006," Johnny said to Kelly, continuing his explanation. "The Army Corps of Engineers failed to realize that they had been dumped offshore decades earlier where the sand was being sucked in from."

"Yeah, it scared the hell out of everybody back then," Danny chimed in. "You and Geoffrey were away at school, Kelly. You missed all the fun. Nobody got hurt, but the beaches had to be closed until the area could be cleared. The money men were all worried it would be bad for business just when the summer tourist season was about to start."

"No one expected these suckers to be 'live' after all those years underwater, but … well, as you can see … they still are," said Rodney. "It's just one more government screw-up."

Kelly picked up her towel and started for the ramp. "We'd better let Aunt Sarah and Noah know," She told Danny. "They were about the closest thing to family Libby had."

"I think her ex-husband still lives in Barnegat Light," Johnny added encouragingly. "He should probably be notified, too."

"I'll take care of that little detail," said the long-limbed police chief, Raymond Butler, through his droopy, gunslinger-like mustache as he approached the group. "And if you don't mind, Johnny, I'll take that little piece of evidence you're holding."

Raymond turned to face the spectators.

"Listen up, people," he shouted through a bullhorn. "As of this moment, this here beach is closed, by order of Mayor Dillard C. Webb. And if you don't want to end up in a body bag, I'd suggest you clear out of here, pronto. We'll let you know when it's safe to return."

"Oh, no, not again," grumbled the man in the Mets cap. His sentiment was echoed throughout the dispersing throng.

4

"Safety Is Our First Priority"

Face squeeze. That's what Mayor Dillard Webb's former colleagues in the U.S. Congress had called it whenever they saw him rubbing his eyes and forehead repeatedly like he was trying to wipe away some painful thought or some petty annoyance. It was a sure sign that a significant provision in the legislation coming up for a vote was amiss. Like first-rate poker players, they could all read the silent clues this peculiar mannerism offered on his otherwise genial, ruddy, weathered face.

Sitting in the crowded, noisy assembly hall of the Surf City Municipal Building on Long Beach Boulevard, across from the Surf City Hotel, famous for its karaoke and prime rib Tuesdays, Dillard shut his fatigued, pale blue eyes tight to block out the circus-like atmosphere that surrounded him and slowly went into a prolonged face squeeze, wishing he were anywhere but where he was at that moment.

Having retired from Congress at the tender age of 58, after four successful terms on Capitol Hill, he anticipated settling into a life of leisure at his summer home on LBI to paint and write his memoirs. But his solitude didn't last very long, and he soon succumbed to the seductive and persistent urgings of family and friends to run for local office.

As if his twin brother Cornelius, an Ocean County businessman, wasn't convincing enough, his own young legislative aide Benjamin Leef agreed to act as his former boss's campaign manager—gratis. Running on his reputation and his platform of beach beautification, which he had championed in Congress, Dillard overwhelmed his octogenarian, fish-merchant opponent by a landslide.

Approved while Dillard was still a member of Congress, the Barnegat Inlet to Egg Harbor Storm Damage Reduction Project was a done deal by the time he was sworn in as Surf City's mayor. Initially pegged with a price tag of approximately $71 million, 65 percent of which would be shouldered by the federal government with state and municipal taxes kicking in the balance, the project was not a slam dunk with all LBI residents on the picturesque 18-mile barrier island. Many objected to the public parking, public beach access, and public restroom accommodations— terms that the federal subsidy foisted upon municipalities and, in turn, onto private citizens, some with very exclusive beachfront properties. For many residents in the more affluent areas like North Beach, Harvey Cedars and Loveladies, who paid a premium for privacy, preventing beach erosion was viewed as a pretext for more unwanted government intrusion into their lives. To them, the stench of "in-perpetuity easements" and "eminent domain" hung uneasily in the air.

That was when Dillard went to work. He stepped up to the plate and singlehandedly convinced the residents of his tourist-friendly town to become the first of LBI's famous beach communities to accept, if not embrace, the federal beach replenishment program. After all, what was a trifle more public annoyance in the end, if it guaranteed that their little piece of paradise would be better protected from the ravages of the great Atlantic storms? It might even lower flood insurance rates and raise property values, he hinted.

And so the citizens of Surf City signed on as guinea pigs, and work began in earnest in the fall of 2006 to siphon 886,000 cubic yards of sand from the supposedly pristine ocean floor approximately three miles offshore and dump it onto the roughly 1.5 miles of beach comprising all of Surf City and the northern tip of Ship Bottom.

But by the spring of 2007, it was evident that something had gone radically wrong. Beachcombers began finding a veritable depot of disposed WWI-era ordnances that had been dredged up from the ocean depths and deposited on their dunes. Characterized as hazardous if not handled properly, the U.S. Army Corps of Engineers was summoned to remediate the danger. What followed was an ill-conceived effort to satisfy the competing aims of protecting the public while avoiding any interruption of the shore town's economic life blood: summer tourism.

The results were, as expected with any quick fix, less than satisfactory. More munitions continued to turn up during the 2007 summer season and into the next, even as restrictions on sand digging depths and prohibitions on the use of metal detectors, metal shovels, and aluminum beach umbrella poles were put into place. The public outcry and angry protests were not muted by the roar of the cascading surf until, finally, in the spring of 2009, after nearly 2,000 discarded fuzes were found—measuring about four inches in diameter by eight inches in length—an all-out effort to sweep the beaches down to a depth of 12 feet was undertaken at a cost that approached $13 million. Crews worked around the clock to beat the calendar. A giant sigh of relief went up three weeks before Memorial Day, when the Army Corps of Engineers pronounced the beaches "all clear" of the dangerous debris.

During the entire two-year period of the cleanup effort, Dillard went into hiding and held his breath, hoping all would turn out well for his constituents, the visiting tourists, and the town. In all that time not a single casualty was reported. It was a miracle, and once again Dillard was able to show his face in public without being accosted or harassed.

And now, just when everyone felt it was safe to spread a blanket on the sand once more, Libby Ashcroft had turned up dead! Not just dead, but blown apart by an exploding ordnance. And so, despite the repeated promises and assurances, Surf City had its first munitions-related casualty, and it was a gruesome fatality involving a respected and well-liked neighbor.

Dillard felt a gentle tap on his shoulder that woke him from his musings. He abandoned his habitual face squeeze and opened his eyes.

"The people are waiting, Mr. Mayor," Benjamin whispered firmly. "It's time to call the meeting to order." The effeminate young man crossed his arms and took his station behind the mayor, reminiscent of a servant behind a Roman senator.

Dillard shielded his eyes from the glare coming off the bank of television lights positioned in the back of the packed and boisterous room. News reporters from the major networks stood poised with microphones and cameras ready to roll.

He took another moment to gain composure and studied the room. He was seated at the center of an oblong folding table set up in the front of the room and covered with a royal blue felt cloth bearing the municipal seal. He fiddled with the glass-enclosed, spent munitions canister that was on display in front of him. Town council members dressed in casual attire flanked him on either side. A small delegation from the state DEP was seated conspicuously in the front row. All waited for him to speak.

He banged the gavel on the wooden block, and immediately, the room fell silent. His gaze fell on the two bomb-sniffing dogs leashed tightly to their military attendants. The canines and their escorts were part of the EOD (Explosive Ordnance Detail) dispatched from the 754th Ordnance Company at Fort Monmouth.

"Thank you all for coming," he began slowly, adjusting his necktie and facing the cameras straight on. Ordinarily, he would have reveled in the attention and the chance to be on TV. Free media coverage was a politician's stock in trade. But he couldn't help feeling a little like Nixon must have felt before giving his famous "Checkers" speech. Dillard was certain his face was just as pasty under the glare of the flood lamps. The press conference was intended as a call to action for the supporters still in his camp. He needed to find a solution to the current dilemma quickly, or a scapegoat willing to take the fall. Memorial Day weekend was a mere two weeks away.

"By now, you all know the simple truth. Our worst nightmare has come true. The fear we have lived with for years, and thought we were rid of, has claimed the life of our own dear Libby Ashcroft. As terrible and tragic as her death is, at least the gregarious museum curator went out with a bang—pursuing that special passion she enjoyed in her all-too-brief life."

The mayor's nervous and feeble attempt at lowbrow humor amused no one.

"But you told us our beaches were safe," said a pert young mother Dillard recognized as Kathy Wollert, the local second-grade teacher. She was sitting in the third row, cradling her two small children, one in each arm. "If you ask me, our beach has become a minefield. Is that what you call safe?"

"I'll answer that, Mr. Mayor," said a smart-looking officer in a neatly pressed uniform moving to the dais. He had keen, sharp eyes; *eagle eyes*, thought Dillard when he was first introduced to Phillip "Skip" Landers, the project's chief engineer, at the beginning of the beach conservation project back in 2006. He wore a colonel's insignia pinned proudly to the heavily starched collar of his olive-colored shirt. Deep, furrowed ridges lined his brow, making him appear older than the 40-something he actually was. His closely cropped hair was a premature salt-and-pepper mix.

"Your beach *is* safe, ma'am," said Skip politely. "I am quite sure of that." He searched for the right words. "This detonation was an anomaly, a fluke." He glanced around the room. "I want you all to know that safety is our first priority."

"Yeah, we've heard *that* speech before," shouted Rodney Coles, dangling from his seat on the windowsill. "Your 'anomaly' is lying on a steel slab in the morgue with her face blown off."

Rodney's challenging remarks set off a cacophony of excited conversation around the crowded room. Voices became elevated and agitated. A shouting match ensued between various members of the council and several irate citizens seated in the large hall.

"Settle down, settle down," Dillard beseeched the crowd. He banged the gavel authoritatively. On Skip's command, the canines were hurriedly brought to the front of the room. The sight of the two German shepherds, teeth bared, quieted the noisy crowd.

"No one was supposed to get hurt, Dillard," said Noah Parsons, sitting beside his wife, Sarah. "What do you say to the merchants, the shopkeepers whose livelihoods depend on the bustling summer tourist trade?" He looked into his wife's deeply troubled eyes, knowing her concern for the future of Crab Cove, her island gift shop. "Most colleges are already out, and the other schools will finish up in a couple of weeks." Noah looked around the room at the reporters and video cameras. "You won't be able to keep this out of the news, Mayor."

Benjamin bent over and whispered something into Dillard's ear. The mayor shook his head affirmatively.

"I don't intend to," he replied, looking into the cameras sternly, "long as the news people report the truth. This one 'fluke' must have come in with the tide," he suggested lamely. "That's all. The beaches were cleared ... we all know that. But a spate of bad weather could have brought this single, errant ordnance in from offshore." He looked to Skip for support.

"That's entirely possible," Skip admitted hesitantly. "Yes, that would explain it. The beaches were 100 percent cleared. We swept 8,160 square feet of beach, including 150 feet into the surf. We dug down 12 feet below the surface. We went over every square inch with a fine-toothed rake. Nothing, I repeat, *nothing* was missed."

"Well, I don't know about anyone else, but I'm not buying it, dude," said Rodney, rising to his feet. Danny and Kelly stared at their surfing buddy from their seats beside Noah and Sarah. Although neither of them knew him well, they did know he was an avid environmentalist who distrusted the government to the point of occasional irrationality. His pet expression was that the only information the government gave out willingly was disinformation, as in the case of UFOs. He argued that the Feds' penchant for the use of acronyms was meant to confound and confuse the general public. Tonight, however, both Kelly and Danny felt his accusatory tone was particularly acid-tinged and inappropriate for this very public setting.

Rodney was aware that all eyes were glued to him. He was used to it. He knew a few were commenting under their breath about his appearance: his shaved head, his scruffy Van Dyke goatee, and his colorful Asian-style tattoos. Plus, dressed as he was, in cutoffs and a tie-dyed T-shirt of his own design that read, "LBI Is Dynamite," he was guaranteed to draw attention. He just hoped that a few of them were also listening to his words.

"By now, we all know that nothing the Army Corps of Engineers touches ever goes off as planned," he said, challenging Skip. "Just look at Barnegat Inlet. You've been working on solving that baby for decades, and you haven't done dick!"

Skip made a move toward him, then thought better of it and stopped short. Sensing the escalating tensions and fearing a confrontation between the military and civilians being caught on film, Dillard used the excuse of unacceptable language and diplomatically asked the two armed Surf City policemen positioned nearby to escort Rodney out the door, implying "bodily" if necessary. He motioned to Benjamin to go with the officers.

Relieved, if a little flustered, Skip turned first toward the council, then toward the waiting crowd.

"We said from the beginning that the fuzes are made up of 98 percent explosive material. These munitions, while old and in decayed casings, are unpredictable. We warned you all, if you came into contact with any DMM, to engage in restraint. Remember the three 'Rs': recognize, retreat, and report."

Several people in the room, Kathy and her two children among them, recited the three "Rs" along with the colonel.

A man named Mac Adams stood and cleared his throat. Dressed in suspenders and well-worn khakis, with his distinctive long, flowing white beard, many around the room recognized the old man as the Santa Claus who stood in front of the Surf City Five and Ten every Christmas.

"Colonel," he began in a steady voice for all to hear, "isn't it true that your best demolition experts have been stationed overseas in Afghanistan and Iraq during this project?"

The room fell silent. No one stirred and not a sound could be heard except for the ambient whirl of the air conditioning.

Skip hesitated.

"That's what the dogs are for," he replied, limply caught off-guard by the knowledge behind the question. "The Canine Command Force can sniff out explosives down to a level of eight feet."

"But you said the sand fill was as much as 12 feet in some places," Mac countered.

Skip took a deep breath and addressed the room. "We used a combination of man, beast, and machine. You may recall that the first cleanup we did, in 2007, was cleared down to a level of three feet with an estimated accuracy rating of 95 percent." He turned and glanced at the panel of council members, letting his eyes linger on Dillard. "For reasons of expediency we were compelled to stop there."

Several members of the council squirmed uncomfortably in their chairs.

"Last year," he continued, "we returned to finish the job. We brought in 50 pieces of heavy equipment, employed three crews working around the clock, and added the Canine Command Force. No expense was spared. As I said before, safety is our first priority."

"And in that you failed, Colonel, didn't you?" countered Mac empathetically. "The military is responsible for the beach debacle because they did not properly dispose of the munitions in the first place. And now civilians are made to suffer and die once again because of *your* incompetence," he blurted out with noticeable disdain in his voice before retaking his seat.

The cameras panned the stunned room slowly.

Sanjay Patel, a slightly unkempt, arrogant-looking senior member of the DEP delegation who was dressed in a rumpled pale-blue polyester suit, stood up before Skip could speak.

"We all know the story of how we got into this mess," he said with a thick accent. "Dumping discarded munitions off the coast was legal until 1973, but apparently those in charge of disposing of the munitions misjudged the distance." He paused. "Or else they were very eager to get back to the PX for a nightcap. In either case, they didn't go out far enough before dumping the stuff overboard. They simply weren't supposed to be there."

"It's possible that over time the ordnances drifted in closer to shore," offered Skip for the benefit of the military personnel in the room who, like himself, felt their sensibilities being called into question.

"Right," agreed the DEP senior representative unconvincingly. "Anyway, had the private salvage firm the army hired used one-and-a-quarter-inch screens instead of four-inch filters, the whole damned thing could have been avoided."

"Hey, that wasn't our idea," replied Skip. "You were the ones who insisted on the larger filters in order to allow the *sea turtles* to pass through unharmed."

Members of the DEP delegation rose to their feet and jumped to Sanjay's defense. The canines began snapping and barking. In an ugly instant the crowd became unruly and people started arguing among themselves again. The reporters were having a field day, scribbling down notes for their news stories. The mayor was powerless to restore order. The two Surf City cops who had escorted Rodney out returned to the hall, practically unnoticed, and joined in the fray, trying to restrain the groups from coming to blows. Dillard banged his gavel repeatedly to no effect. He looked helplessly around for Benjamin, but did not see him. He squeezed his face with renewed vigor.

Everyone was pointing a finger at everyone else, yelling and arguing vehemently, when a highly excited Hannah Newbury, Dillard's very pregnant young secretary, stepped into the room and slammed the door behind her. The ruckus came to a screeching halt. All eyes were fixed on her.

"Quick, Mayor Webb, you gotta see this," gasped Hannah, struggling to catch her breath. "Somebody's spray-painted 'SurfDogs Rule' all over the colonel's Hummer."

Then, suddenly, Hannah's face turned ghostly white as she placed both hands on her oversized belly. "Uh-oh," she added with a wince. "I think my water just broke."

5

Venturi Float

"**B**oy! Am I glad that's over with," said Kelly, stepping into Danny's Jeep Wrangler and kicking off her Birkenstocks. She felt uncomfortable in her old black dress and wondered whether anyone at the service had noticed it was about two sizes too small on her. She hadn't realized how much weight she had gained over the winter while looking for a job. Two years after her graduation from Georgetown with a degree in political science, and there was still no meaningful employment in sight for Kelly, a perennial Dean's List student. She had once dreamed of working at the United Nations or maybe even in Foreign Services, putting her knowledge of gamesmanship to proper use, but the recession had taken its toll on government jobs, and many corporations had to put their plans of expansion into global markets on hold. Only China seemed to afford any employment opportunities, but the threat of avian flu and lead paint contamination, combined with the image of a lone student confronting a tank in Tiananmen Square, made Kelly decide to stay on her side of the Great Wall.

Still, a lot can be said for being in the right place at the right time, and with Hannah Newbury suddenly out on maternity leave, following an impromptu introduction to Dillard Webb by Aunt Sarah after the calamitous town council meeting, Kelly wasted no time in offering her temporary clerical services to the beleaguered mayor. To her surprise, he accepted her offer on the spot.

"I'm glad it's over, too," agreed Danny, slipping in behind the wheel. "I can't get that image of her blowing up on the beach out of my mind. Maybe now that she's finally laid to rest, I'll be able to get some sleep."

Kelly nodded. She didn't let on how comforted she was to hear that Danny was having nightmares, too. It wasn't like him to admit things like that openly to her. They had known each other for years now and had been through many adventures together while she and her brother Geoffrey summered on LBI with their Aunt Sarah. But even after all that time, Danny Windsor was still the same stubborn chauvinist she had met when she was a naïve 16-year-old lifeguard-in-training who saved his life after he had been stung by a jellyfish during her tryout.

Danny pulled out of the parking lot of Saint Peter's at the Light Episcopal Church and into the traffic meandering south on Long Beach Boulevard. He *had* noticed, sitting next to her in church, how snug Kelly's black dress was and, although the sight of a little more Kelly Martin than usual didn't bother him, he knew it was the reason she insisted they go back to Crab Cove to change before they went anywhere else.

"That was some eulogy Noah gave," he said, trying to mask his thoughts with idle conversation. It had been nearly nine months since he and Kelly had spent any time together in close quarters. It was always awkward trying to reconnect during the summers after so much time apart. "I didn't realize there wasn't any next of kin, but Noah certainly made up for that."

"Aunt Sarah always said that Libby was pretty much an odd duck and a loner, but she did have a special connection with Noah, especially after her husband left her."

"Speaking of connections," Danny changed the subject, "that was some pretty quick thinking, having Aunt Sarah put in a good word for you with the mayor the other night."

"With the beaches closed, I just dreaded the thought of sitting around doing nothing all summer. I'm just grateful Mayor Webb gave me the time off to attend Libby's funeral service today."

"No argument here," Danny said, genuinely impressed at the way Kelly's extended family pulled for each other. "Now what's this I hear about Geoffrey getting an internship at Fort Dix? Isn't it gonna feel strange not to have your baby brother underfoot this summer?"

"That's why I decided to take up surfing," she replied with a sarcastic smile. "I needed something to make up for the loss of testosterone around me."

Danny broke into a hearty laugh, even though he realized Kelly's comment could be taken as a barb directed at him, too.

The talk of surfing made Kelly think about super-surfer Rodney's antics at the Surf City town meeting.

"Do you think Rodney is responsible for the graffiti on the colonel's Hummer?" she asked, turning toward Danny to catch his immediate reaction to her question.

"Does Mayor Webb think he is?"

"I think so, just like everyone else who was in the room. But that doesn't make him guilty."

"True," he agreed. "But SurfDogs *is* the name of his club, and he was pretty pissed off when they threw him out."

"You seem to forget that we are SurfDogs, too," Kelly reminded him. "Does that make us suspects?"

"No," said Danny slowly, "but then again, we never left the room."

"He was ushered out by those two robocops and Mayor Webb's assistant, Benjamin Leef."

"Leef? The gay guy?" interrupted Danny, pondering the odd name.

"Yeah, he was hustling after them. They probably waited until Rodney drove away before they came back inside, don't you think?"

"Maybe Rodney doubled back after the coast was clear. It was pretty dark by then, too, you know."

"I suppose you're right," sighed Kelly. "I guess I just don't *want* to believe it."

"Well," said Danny, making a U-turn at the Wawa convenience store and heading back to the causeway. "There's only one way to find out. Let's go ask him."

***

"I didn't see you at Libby's funeral service, Walter," said Noah, addressing a suave, silver-haired gentleman. The man was standing on the Barnegat Light dock with a clipboard in his hand, talking to a younger man wearing a construction hat. Walter Ashcroft riffled through the pages on his clipboard until he found the one he was looking for. He said something to the younger man and gestured to the heavily laden barge bobbing up and down at the marina. A small uprooted house sat incongruously atop the old wooden scow. The man in the hard hat nodded and walked off. Walter turned to face Noah.

"We all deal with grief in our own way," he told his old acquaintance. "You should know that."

"Yours is by working?" asked Noah.

"And yours is by intruding," snapped Walter, showing his annoyance. "So unless you're here to buy a house from me, I suggest you let me tend to my business."

"Say, I know that house," said Noah, looking at the colorful saltbox-style cottage sitting on the barge. To Noah's eyes it looked more like a big transistor radio than a house. "I recognize that large number nine on the door and the sailboat-shaped window on the side."

"It's a Venturi," Walter replied proudly. "Robert Venturi, the noted architect, built it here back in 1967. A couple from New York just bought it to use as a guest house for their property in Jamaica Estates. I'm having it shipped to them."

"Didn't you ship one last year?" Noah asked.

"Yes," answered Walter, beaming. "I found another one."

Noah let out a low whistle. "They must cost a pretty penny."

"About a hundred thousand for the tow; the house itself went for a song. But these people can afford it. Besides, it was scheduled for demolition. The new property owners here on the island were going to tear it down. Can you imagine that? A Robert Venturi original. And they were simply going to tear it down."

"The island's changing," offered Noah sympathetically.

"And not for the better," retorted Walter. "Which brings me back to my ex-wife; you know we hadn't spoken to each other in years. It was better that way."

Noah shook his head. "You don't mean that, Walter."

"Yes, I do. We were direct opposites, she and I. Like this old boat here. I can appreciate the beauty and the design of the house, while all Libby would be interested in is the barge. 'How old is it? Where'd it come from? What did it carry?' It took us 14 years to figure out we were wrong for each other."

Noah shuffled his feet. He had heard their story before, many times, mostly from Libby's point of view. If anything was different about them, it was Walter's philandering. His dalliances with women half his age were well-known around the island. Noah had even heard that Walter's sexual appetite was not limited to women. Although a successful realtor, Walter wasn't exactly the art-loving Boy Scout he made himself out to be, and he knew Noah knew the truth.

"Oh, don't get me wrong," he continued, guessing what Noah was thinking. "We had some good times, Libby and me. And no one deserves to go the way she did. Horrible, just horrible," he said with a slight quiver to his voice.

"Beachcombing was her passion. We all need something we can turn to when things get tough in life," Noah suggested.

"Mine is real estate," said Walter, as if he thought he had to defend himself. "And I've done pretty well for myself, if I may say so. I built up A Shore Thing Realty from nothing."

"No one will dispute that," said Noah sincerely. "But that doesn't explain why you didn't feel it necessary to attend Libby's funeral. After all, you said it yourself—you two shared 14 years together. If the situation were reversed, she would have been there to see you off."

"She would have been damned glad to see me go," said Walter with a sarcastic laugh. "She probably would have pissed on my grave and danced a jig around it."

Noah chuckled.

"Yeah, I know, I know," he said apologetically. "You're right, Noah, I should have gone. It's just that, well, you know … I never really cared for some of her … friends. Dillard Webb is an arrogant fool, if you ask me. He's more a bureaucrat than he is an islander. And now he's gone and let the Feds run roughshod over his town's prime real estate."

The man in the hard hat called out from the barge that they were ready to cast off. Walter signaled back with a wave of his hand.

"You mark my words," he said, poking a suntanned finger into Noah's chest. "This thing with the beaches isn't over yet." Then his mood lightened and he grinned slyly. "But when it is, it will be up to people like me to step in and pick up the pieces."

6

"Our Beaches Will Blow You Away"

For as long as Geoffrey Martin could remember, he'd had a strange and inexplicable fascination with Fort Dix. Perhaps it was simply a male thing that dated back to his prepubescent days, when he played with army figures like G.I. Joe while Kelly, older by one year, was "whupping" other boys their age on the basketball court and soccer field. Neither brother nor sister engaged in such adolescent activities any longer, but the competitive side of his sister's complex feminine makeup still struggled to dominate their mutual friend Danny's heart and mind. With those two, reflected Geoffrey after presenting his papers and passing through the Fort Dix gatehouse accompanied by his official escort, surfing was simply the latest contest of wills in their long line of love/hate war games.

Geoffrey's interest in Fort Dix intensified during the summers when he and Kelly began their annual treks to LBI. It all started in 2003 when he was an innocent 15-year-old, pimply-faced, curly-haired geek. Now, following his recent graduation from Princeton University, the biochemistry major was ready to make his mark on the world.

Initially, the Martins' summer journeys to the shore had always been via the New Jersey Turnpike from their Teaneck home, down the Garden State Parkway, then east on Route 72 across the causeway. But ever since their encounter with the famous Painted Rock and the people possessed by it, they opted for the more scenic, albeit circuitous, route, cutting out the Parkway altogether and hopping on Route 539 from the Turnpike just outside of Allentown for their ritual LBI pilgrimages.

The single lane, back-country road—so irksome and frustrating for many motorists speeding to reach the reward LBI afforded—was a marvel to the Martins' insatiable quest for all things Pinelands. The thought of U.S. military maneuvers being conducted on the Jersey Devil's home turf only further piqued Geoffrey's academic interest and natural curiosity. He didn't even mind occasionally being stuck behind a slow-moving military transport bound for the Central Jersey army base. It forced him to pay closer attention to the partially fenced-in perimeters, the mysterious unpaved sand roads that seemingly began and ended nowhere, and the thick, dense rows of limitless pine trees that lined the route.

So when a respected professor at Princeton learned of the camp's need for researchers to study the effects of a newly isolated toxin infiltrating the base, he suggested the internship to Robert Martin, Geoffrey's father and former Fort Dix researcher during the swine flu epidemic of 1976, who was now an executive in a Fortune 500 pharmaceutical firm. The elder Martin made a few phone calls, including the most important one, to his brother-in-law, Noah Parsons. The retired Coast Guard veteran in turn put in a call to his good buddy and noted local woodsman, Tom Banks, who served as best man at his wedding. Tom taught survival training to Fort Dix personnel. The base commander was a close personal friend. He, in turn, pulled a few strings and, ultimately, Geoffrey landed the job.

For his part, once the position was finalized, Geoffrey threw himself into an all-out online study of the history of Fort Dix. From his reading he learned that the Army base was named for Major General John Adams Dix, a veteran of the War of 1812 who later enjoyed a distinguished career as Secretary of the Treasury, minister to France, and governor of New York.

Construction on Camp Dix, as it was initially called, began in 1917. During World War I, it was a staging ground for the 78th, 87th, and 34th divisions. It quickly grew into the Army's largest facility in the Northeast. After the armistice, the camp became a demobilization center. In between wars, Fort Dix was a top training center for active Army, Army Reserve, and National Guard units undergoing summer exercises. By the start of World War II, it had become a permanent Army post and expanded rapidly. During the height of the Vietnam conflict, it was rumored that a complete Vietnamese village was built on the grounds of Fort Dix for special ops training. In 1990, combat troops bound for Desert Storm were deployed from Fort Dix.

No sooner had Geoffrey's first-night orientation been completed than an alarm sounded. Suddenly the sleepy complex was awash in a frenzy of organized commotion. Doors shut. Lights went out. Gates closed automatically and armed sentries manned the corridors.

"What's going on?" Geoffrey asked the sergeant-at-arms in charge of the processing center when he had set down the telephone he had answered.

"It's a lockdown," replied the stoic-faced sergeant.

"Are we under attack?" Geoffrey asked with audible panic in his voice, remembering the terrorist attempt on the base a few years back that he had read about. A group of Albanian nationals, hell-bent on making a political statement about U.S. imperialist aggression, had purloined a hand-drawn map of the compound's interior from the sympathetic son of a local pizza shop owner who made regular deliveries to the troops stationed at the base. The plot was thwarted thanks to an informant prior to the assault. All of the conspirators were caught, convicted, and sent to prison.

"No," said the sergeant. "Someone's broken into the containment center where some discarded munitions from the Surf City reclamation site were being stored for disposal. Several of the munitions are missing."

***

Every time Danny pulled into the parking lot of the large, iconic, robin's-egg-blue building with its giant arched windows trimmed in yellow-gold, he was reminded of the Ron Jon Surf Shop's humble beginnings. Opened in 1959 by a young New Jersey surfing enthusiast named Ron DiMenna, who had become hooked on the Hawaiian sport of kings that was all the craze in California at the time, the original single-story, white cinderblock store had since blossomed into a bustling East Coast enterprise, with shop locations in Cocoa Beach, Orlando, and Fort Myers, among others. But since its earliest days, "the original" Ron Jon Surf Shop had always been synonymous with teenage dreams of endless summers at the New Jersey shore. And even if the cold, murky waters of the mid-Atlantic didn't exactly offer the same long, roiling thrills as the rolling pipeline waves of the Pacific, the fashionable swimwear and fab beach gear sold at Ron Jon's more than made up for any perceived shortcomings.

Located at the eastern terminus of Route 72—still the only road on and off Long Beach Island—Ron Jon Surf Shop took up an entire block of choice real estate in the center of the causeway, providing easy access for both eastbound and westbound traffic, when traffic permitted, of course. Inside, the store was like the Virgin Records of beach shops, with its multiple levels of merchandise space replete with the world's largest rideable surfboard, a 24-foot, 200-pound beast that made for the perfect photo op to impress friends back home.

The store was having one of its customary sidewalk sales, and Kelly paused to peruse the assorted goods, which included a colorful array of Ron Jon low-rider bathing bottoms, multi-sized Wave Rebel bodyboards, and zinc tins full of Mr. Zog's Sex Wax. When Danny pressed her to sign up for the annual Ron Jon Wet T-shirt Contest, Kelly knew it was time to drop the outdoor bazaar shopping pretext and head inside to find Rodney Coles at his place of employment.

Both Danny and Kelly were surprised to see Trevor Moore, the store manager, working alone behind the counter.

"What can I do for you two chaps today?" the middle-aged Brit greeted them cordially. "No, wait. Let me guess. A thong for you, and a bong for you," he said, gaily pointing to Kelly and Danny in turn. He reminded Kelly of a suntanned Hugh Grant but with better teeth. He nauseated Danny with his English charm and boyish good looks. But he did have a pleasant accent. Danny turned and gazed about the interior.

"We were looking for Rodney," said Kelly. "This is his normal shift, isn't it?"

"Of course you are, and yes it is, but I'm afraid the Rod-man didn't report for work today," said Trevor with no hint of annoyance.

"Is he sick?" Danny asked curiously.

Trevor shook his head. "Oh, dear, I don't know. No, I don't think so. He just simply didn't show up."

The store was crowded with Saturday morning shoppers. Trevor watched each shopper closely, meticulously memorizing the merchandise being handled. He was enjoying the buzz that suggested the coming of another successful summer shopping season which, for him, invariably meant another fun-filled winter in Rio de Janeiro to look forward to.

"You don't seem upset," said Kelly. "Is this a normal thing for him?"

"Well, yes, that's our Rodney," he said with a toothy grin.

"And you're not mad that he stuck you?" asked Danny, incredulous.

"Oh, heaven's no," replied the officious store manager. "Have you seen his latest silkscreen design?" Trevor was giddy with excitement. "It's going to make a mint for us this summer." He tossed a T-shirt to each of them. "Here, they're complimentary for SurfDog Club members only."

Trevor held up one of the T-shirts for them to see: It was a typical beach scene, showing an open rainbow-paneled beach umbrella in the foreground, shading a little boy on a beautiful sunny day. The boy was digging feverishly in the sand with a tiny plastic shovel. Beside the boy was a little pastel beach bucket, and bulging out of the bucket was an oversized bomb with a warhead pointing upward. In the background, a second umbrella had been upended, tossing a pail, a shovel, and a toddler up in the air on a fountain of sand.

At the bottom of the shirt, the caption stenciled in scarlet letters read: "Our Beaches Will Blow You Away!"

7

Man With the Plan

"**H**ave they found any more?" the mayor asked. He was standing on the spacious balcony of the Sand Castle, which overlooked the Division Street beach, surveying the cordoned-off area through a borrowed pair of binoculars. The imposing, white stucco, three-story rental home was once again serving as headquarters for Easton Solutions, the contractor engaged in the latest cleanup effort. At a cost of nine grand a week, Dillard thought the accommodations were a bit extravagant, but he didn't think to ask how the government was going to pay for it.

"They found five more DMMs," replied Skip after some hesitation. "One here and two on each of the Third and Fifth Street beaches."

Dillard put down the binoculars and stared off into the pounding surf.

"Our most popular beaches," he mumbled remotely.

"They certainly are," agreed Benjamin from where he was leaning against the railing, watching the shirtless, muscled workers raking through the sand with their graters. He stepped back to rejoin his boss.

"There's more," added Skip, turning to face the mayor. "But I'm not sure you're going to like what I have to say." He gave a quick glance past Dillard to Benjamin, unsure if he should share what he had found while in earshot of the mayor's assistant.

"Let's have it, Landers. Get it all out," exhorted the flustered mayor.

"Well, sir, it's like this. So far, there have been six DMMs found on three beaches. When you called and told me that one had killed a woman, I was deeply troubled. Not because the woman was killed—that danger existed as long as *one* unexploded ordnance remained behind on any beach." Skip paused a moment to consider his next comment. "What surprised me most was that, even after our massive cleanup, there was still one device left behind. I was sure we'd gotten them all."

"But then, I'll bet you never figured you'd find over 2,000 discarded munitions when you first started, either, did you?" Benjamin reminded him.

"That's quite true," admitted the engineer. "But I would have bet my life that this time, nothing was left; that all the beaches were completely clean. We did it right. We went over every grain of sand."

"So, you missed some. What's your point?" asked Dillard impatiently.

"My point, Mr. Mayor," Skip began with controlled annoyance, learned through a long career in the military when speaking to so-called superiors, "is that something is not quite right with this new picture. If you include the blast that killed the woman beachcomber, this sweep has yielded *six* ordnances so far, two on each of Surf City's busiest beaches. But what's even more surprising is that each DMM has been found at a similar distance between the surf and the dunes. The chances of this being a coincidence are astronomical."

"Are you sure about this?" Benjamin asked skeptically.

Skip nodded. "I checked the readings myself. All the DMMs were found at nearly the same measurable point, just beyond the reach of high tide."

"So they wouldn't get washed out to sea," Benjamin surmised.

"Exactly. Or be discovered without at least some minimal digging," Skip added. "They were each buried in roughly eight to ten inches of sand."

"Wait a minute, Colonel," interrupted Dillard, shaking his head in disbelief. "Are you suggesting that these things were planted intentionally?"

"That's preposterous," added Benjamin with a look of astonishment. He shot the mayor a dubious glance.

"Nonetheless, the possibility must be considered," Skip replied adamantly.

"Who would do such a thing?" cried Dillard. "In God's name, what purpose would it serve?"

"Besides, how would anyone get their hands on those awful things?" added Benjamin. "They were all taken away by *your* men. And whatever wasn't taken away should still be somewhere out there in the middle of the ocean," he said, waving an index finger at the water.

"Not quite," Skip said reluctantly.

Dillard turned to confront Skip face to face. "What do you mean, 'not quite'?" asked the mayor, his face now fully flushed.

Skip stood his ground. "Mayor, do you have any enemies? Is there anyone you can think of who would want to … uh, embarrass … you or your administration?"

As instantly as it had risen, the blood suddenly drained from the mayor's weather-worn face as he considered the question. He reached for the back of his neck and grimaced.

"A man of Dillard Webb's stature does not get to be where he is without taking risks and making a few enemies," Benjamin said defensively. "Hazards of the job—you can't please all the people all the time."

"Thank you, Benjamin," said the mayor with a sigh. "Any politician worth his salt is bound to have enemies. You just hope that whenever you walk into a crowded room, you know who they are before the daggers come out."

Both men waited for the mayor to continue.

"I know there were some disgruntled property owners when this project first started, but, my God, the job is finally done and over with. Why on earth would anyone choose to make an issue of the work *now*, after things are finally getting back to normal?"

"What about that surfer?" asked Skip, "the one you tossed out of the council meeting the other night?"

"You mean the guy who left his calling card on your Hummer, Colonel?" added Benjamin with a shameless snicker.

"Rodney Coles?" Dillard asked.

"Yeah, that's the guy," said Skip, folding his arms across his chest. "I've done some checking on him. This is not the first time he's caused trouble for the Corps or the government. And he and his—*ahem*—associates are apparently having a field day poking fun at your town's misfortunes, Mayor … and they're making a couple of bucks in the process, I might add. Have you seen the T-shirts?"

"They're a bunch of harmless surfing fanatics," said Dillard, exhaling audibly. "They're just pissed off because their beaches are closed again, that's all."

"Sure, and Greenpeace is just a group of whale lovers. How do we know they don't have a political agenda?"

"This is nonsense, fellas," Dillard said after a moment. "Even if the SurfDogs have some sort of hidden agenda, like Benjamin said, how would they get their hands on the munitions?"

"This is the part I said you weren't going to like, Mayor," Skip said slowly. "It's been discovered that some of the reclaimed munitions were stolen from the storage facility at Fort Dix where they were awaiting disposal. They may have been missing for some time."

***

"How did you know where to find me?" asked Rodney flatly, without turning around, as Danny and Kelly approached him from behind. He was kneeling in the sand facing the sun-drenched ocean, half-dressed in his wetsuit, painstakingly waxing his surfboard.

"We were listening to Noah Parsons's police scanner," said Danny. "There was an anonymous complaint that someone had illegally parked a rusty old VW van on the beach at Holgate."

"Ah, so Moss Greenberg told you," guessed Rodney, smiling faintly.

"He told us this is where you come to think," admitted Kelly. "It made sense. Since you didn't show up for work at Ron Jon's and your local beach has been shut down *again*. This was the most logical place to find you."

"And so you have," he said, running a hand down his board and removing some sand that had collected. "What's on your mind?"

Danny and Kelly moved around to face Rodney as he worked on his board. His bald, suntanned pate glistened in the morning sunshine. The yin-yang tattoo on his bulging right bicep rippled with each circular sweep of his arm.

"Trevor showed us your latest design," said Kelly. "Thanks for the free T-shirts."

"You didn't come all this way to thank me for the rags Trevor is hawking." He motioned for Kelly to step out of his line of vision. When she complied, he shaded his eyes to check on the developing waves. "All right, the tide is going out," he remarked casually. "Swells are breaking in threes. It's almost time to fly."

Danny decided to come clean about why they wanted to talk. "You really laid into that engineer from the Corps the other night."

"He had it coming," said Rodney. "The guy's a moron."

"Is that why you tagged his ride?" asked Kelly.

Rodney stopped brushing and waxing. "Well, ain't that a pretty way to put it, Freckles," he replied sarcastically, staring at her.

"So it's true," said Danny. "You sprayed 'SurfDogs Rule' on the colonel's Hummer. You're not denying it?"

"I'll tell you what I told the cops when they came looking for me afterward," said Rodney, returning to his work. "I'm an artist. I don't do graffiti. That's kid stuff."

Kelly and Danny looked at each other, wondering what to say next and who would say it. They had assumed, like everyone else, that Rodney was guilty. However, his statement sounded more like a denial in typical Rodney Coles fashion, as they understood him. But if Rodney didn't do it, then who did? And why?

"My beef isn't with Skip Landers," continued Rodney as if eavesdropping on their thoughts. "The U.S. Army Corps of Engineers are just the hand puppets of a larger, more sinister force."

"The federal government, right?" volunteered Danny, looking to connect.

"Maybe," replied Rodney in that vague, noncommittal way of his that frustrated everyone who tried to understand him. No one really did, not very well, anyway, and maybe that was the way he liked it, Danny thought, trying to sort it out for himself.

"I don't follow you," said Kelly, verbalizing what Danny was thinking.

Rodney put his board aside with deliberate care. He stroked his diamond-shaped beard absentmindedly.

"It's simple, really," he answered slowly. "Take this beach for example. The tide rolls in. The tide rolls out. The sands shift. The beach erodes one year and comes back the next. Some days, where we are right now is covered in three feet of water. It's nature's way, man. Left alone, she knows what to do, and it's right for the birds, the fish, and all the plant life around here."

Kelly and Danny sensed this overture was an invitation from Rodney to sit, and they did so without being asked. Part eccentric, environmental guru, part hippie-beach-recluse, whenever he spoke seriously an important sermon of one sort or another invariably followed. The trick was getting him to open up.

"It's only man that wants it his way, and he will stop at nothing to get what he wants. Forget the shorebirds; forget the shellfish; forget the cedars. They mean nothing to him. Humanity wants more condos, more beaches for the kiddies to use as sandboxes, and more roads to provide access to it all."

"That's progress," said Kelly.

"That's bullshit," he disagreed.

"Yeah, but without these manicured beaches and paved roads, where would you go to surf?" Danny asked.

"Hey man, don't get me wrong; I'm a part of this humanity too. But there is a right way and a wrong way to do things. And this beach reclamation thing going down in Surf City is definitely the wrong way."

"Because it backfired," suggested Danny.

"Because it's bogus, man. Those comfy cats in their seaside McMansions can keep their private beaches. I don't mind, so long as I have my little strip of sand to bag some rays and ride my board. There's plenty to go around. But the way the bigwigs went about building up those beaches in Surf City and Ship Bottom is all wrong."

Now it was Danny's turn to show his ignorance. "Rodney, I'm sorry, but now you've lost me, too."

"All I'm saying, amigos, is that these humongous beach berms and the shit they coughed up from the sea could have all been avoided totally. There's a more natural way to replenish eroded beach sand, and the Army Corps of Engineers knows it. They just chose to ignore it."

Kelly and Danny sat transfixed as Rodney animatedly explained the process he had obviously taken the trouble to understand in depth.

"In environmental circles, they call it building a 'feeder beach,' and it works just the way nature does. Sand is pumped from the ocean floor, creating a J-like sandbar peninsula that runs perpendicular to the beach you're trying to save. And, dig this. That sand eventually washes ashore and acts like the natural drifting sand that builds up any beach. But here's the best part. This feeder beach forms a nice, gentle slope that has zero impact on the wave action. Is that cool or what?"

"It sounds like the perfect solution," exclaimed Kelly. "So why didn't they use it?"

"That's the 64-thousand-dollar question, sweet cheeks … why wasn't it used?"

"And?" asked Kelly and Danny in unison, hanging on Rodney's answer.

"Beats the hell out of me," he replied with a shrug. "A feeder beach was proposed for Long Branch recently at a cost of about a million bucks. That's peanuts, man. The jury's still out on that one. But it sounds like a no-brainer to me, considering what's been shelled out on LBI so far."

"I hear that," acknowledged Danny.

"And you know what else gets me?" Rodney went on. "The DEP needs to do their homework on this beach thing. No one really knows what kind of crap has been hauled up from the deep and dumped on the reinforced beaches. I mean, hey, the ocean's been polluted for years. So why drop all that accumulated dung onto the beaches where little Johnny and little Mary are playing? Leave it out there, man, and let Mother Nature do her thing and dilute all that nasty stuff."

Kelly and Danny were dumbfounded, and their expressions communicated as much to Rodney.

"What? You two don't read the papers?" he kidded them, measuring his audience's silent reaction. He didn't really think of the feeder beach concept as common knowledge, not like the New York Yankees' perennial place in the standings, but he enjoyed educating those who wanted to know.

"Rodney, how do you know all this stuff?" Danny asked, shaking his head. Frankly, he was impressed by Rodney's wealth of knowledge on the subject, although he thought he shouldn't have been. The surfer was full of surprises, but he knew his stuff when it came to his first love, the beach. Moss Greenberg and Johnny Longfeather had tried to warn Danny not to underestimate the head SurfDog simply because of his nonconformist lifestyle and menacing physical appearance. Danny was beginning to understand what they meant.

"Because I used to be in the business," confessed Rodney with a hint of shame rather than pride. "In my former life, I worked as a diver for Laval Marine Works, the outfit that was hired to pump the shit onto the beaches."

"What happened?" asked Kelly.

"I got smart," he replied in a dull, even tone.

"And so you think the Army Corps of Engineers is out of touch?" asked Danny, attempting to interpret Rodney's jaded response.

"More like out of the loop," said Rodney convincingly.

"But aren't they in charge of the project?"

"They were put in charge of managing it, after the plan was set into motion," corrected Rodney. "I think Dillard Webb is the man with the plan. He pushed the project through Congress, and then he convinced his constituents to buy into it when he became mayor. He got the DEP to look the other way, and he's the one getting all the publicity. Who knows what else he gets from it."

"But it's all negative publicity," Kelly protested.

"It's still publicity," replied Rodney with a shrug of his shoulders. "Keeps his name in the news."

He stood, stretched, and zipped his wetsuit up over his chest. The ocean was calling him. "Say, you two SurfDogs didn't happen to bring your boards along, did you?"

"It just so happens we did," said Danny, standing and helping Kelly to her feet. "They're in my Jeep." He brushed away the sand from her butt playfully. She smiled.

"Then what do you say we can the chatter and catch some waves? Surf's up, dudes," said Rodney, grabbing his board and rushing headlong into the surf.

8
Wolf in Fool's Clothing

"I've come to offer my services," declared Walter Ashcroft, settling into the soft leather armchair that was facing the mayor across his impressive desk. Walter was dressed in a pastel lilac, almost-purple seersucker suit with a wide red paisley tie and had a white carnation jutting out of his lapel. Dillard resisted the urge to laugh. His visitor's apparel reminded him of Craig Sager, the TNT sports commentator notorious for wearing a "Swinging Sixties" retro wardrobe during TV broadcasts. Walter's thick, silver-white, Elvis-style pompadour was parted to one side to complete the picture.

"What kind of services are we talking about?" asked Dillard with some reluctance.

"Well, Mayor, isn't it obvious?" Walter began smugly. "It seems this munitions thing is spinning out of *your* control. The borough has spent beaucoup bucks over a four-year period, and the problem still persists—and opening day is just around the corner."

Dillard shifted uncomfortably in his seat but decided to let Walter have his say. A good politician always needed to know what people were saying on the street. Even if Walter didn't represent his constituency, per se, he did have solid contacts and worked with the public daily. He reminded himself to consider the source of the information before he made any decisions about its content.

"Property values are down 20 percent," continued Walter. "Single-family homes and commercial buildings are both on the market for months without any offers. Your ratables are at critical levels. Pretty soon, basic services, which have already been drastically cut, may have to be shut down completely."

Dillard gave his face a quick hard rub, and stared directly into Walter's slate-gray eyes without blinking.

"I don't know where you get your information, but in case you haven't heard, the entire country's been in a recession. The economy tanked, and municipalities everywhere are struggling to make ends meet."

"That may be so, Mayor," said Walter politely, "but Surf City's outlook is particularly dismal. Look around you. Homes are shuttered, businesses are boarded up, rentals are down, and tourists are bypassing your little hamlet to vacation elsewhere." He leaned forward in his chair. "The exodus has begun. But I can help."

"What do you have in mind?" Dillard asked cautiously.

"Well, for one thing, you need a good PR person in your administration—somebody who knows how to handle the press. Somebody who has the trust of the people."

"And that's you, right?" Webb almost snickered, unimpressed.

"Why not me? I can put lipstick on this pig of yours, and I can sell it to the buying public like it was gourmet bacon."

Dillard had had very few prior dealings with Walter's successful real estate firm. A Shore Thing mostly catered to the upscale and moneyed clientele on the north end of the island, but the mayor was familiar with Walter's methods. It was rumored that he represented a syndicate of investors who bought up shore properties on speculation at pre-market prices, just before the properties actually hit the open market. When the market was right, the investors would turn around and resell the bargain-bought properties at a profit, oftentimes providing a little creative financing as part of the package.

When the real estate market went bust nationwide, signaling the beginning of the economic downturn, LBI wasn't spared its rancor. However, the impact on the island was mitigated by the time-proven law of supply and demand, especially for ocean or near-oceanfront properties. That's not to say that New Jersey shore properties were recession-proof, but even in the worst of times, by and large, properties on LBI held their value. Sales were slowed by the economy, but they hadn't stopped.

Surf City, however, had a new, unexpected wrinkle to deal with—a nagging nuisance that just wouldn't go away. And with that in mind, what Walter was saying was true. The public—tourists and residents alike—was losing confidence in the local government's ability to stop the bleeding. Better PR would certainly help … but frankly, Dillard, who was himself a master at PR, was at his wit's end with what to do about the latest round of beachfront bombshells. He had truly thought the problem was behind him. Worse, he had staked both his professional and personal reputations on the Storm Damage Reduction Project. Now all of it seemed to be spiraling out of his control.

Briefly, Dillard thought back to his conversation with Skip. Could someone really be trying to sabotage his beaches?

"Are you finished, Walter?" he asked, after a pause. "Because I think it's time for you to leave."

Walter sank back into his chair. "*Leave*? But you haven't even heard my proposition yet!"

"And I don't intend to," replied Dillard coldly. "I've heard enough to know that I'm not interested in anything you have to propose."

"Wait," exclaimed Walter. "Does this have anything to do with Libby?"

"What?"

"My ex-wife? Noah Parsons seemed pretty upset that I didn't attend her funeral. I'm guessing you're sore about it, too."

Dillard shook his head at the idea. "I can assure you that my lack of interest in your 'proposition' has nothing to do with your blatant disrespect for your ex-wife. Now if you don't mind, I've got work to do. Good day!"

He stood and began shuffling the papers on his desk.

Walter rose slowly. "What about Cornelius?" he asked, gauging the mayor's reaction carefully.

Dillard stopped shuffling the papers abruptly and took a hard look at the man in the preposterous suit standing across the desk from him. His eyes narrowed as he spoke slowly and cautiously. "What has my brother got to do with this discussion?"

Walter lowered his voice and leaned on the mayor's desk. "I don't think Cornelius would take it too kindly, to hear that you threw me out of your office before you even heard me out."

The thought of his entrepreneurial twin brother doing business with Walter somehow did not surprise Dillard. Cornelius was a self-made millionaire who had business dealings the mayor did not fully fathom flung up and down the Jersey coast, including possibly real estate on LBI. The idea, however, that he might be involved in an arrangement with this shyster in clown's clothing, right here in Dillard's own town, seemed patently out of character for the usually careful Cornelius.

"Speak plainly, Walter. Did Cornelius send you here?"

Walter backed away from the desk. "No. Not exactly," he said hesitantly.

Dillard scooped up a fistful of papers. "Then I reiterate: This discussion is over." He pressed the intercom on his phone.

"Yes?" said a pleasant, upbeat female voice Dillard was still trying to get used to. He allowed himself a slight smile.

"Ms. Martin," he said, leaning into the phone. "Mr. Ashcroft and I have finished. Would you mind showing him out?"

Before Dillard could count to three, his new temp was at the door and Benjamin was looming over her shoulder.

"This is far from over," sneered Walter, glancing at Benjamin as he went through the door Kelly held open.

"Trouble, Boss?" his assistant asked, stepping into Dillard's inner sanctum and closing the door behind him.

"Nothing I can't handle," Dillard replied with a thoughtful frown. "Get Cornelius on the phone for me."

9

St. Nick

"You must be the Martin boy," said the jovial white-bearded man in the stained kitchen apron heaping a helping of mashed potatoes onto Geoffrey's plate.

Geoffrey did a double take. Had the man been dressed in a fur-trimmed red suit, ringing a bell outside of Macy's or standing beside a Salvation Army donation pot, instead of slinging hash in the chow line at Fort Dix, Geoffrey would have actually believed he had come face to face with the mythical St. Nick.

"Yes," he replied, somewhat startled. "I'm Geoffrey Martin. This is my sister, Kelly, and our friend, Danny Windsor," he added, pointing to each as they stood gawking behind him with trays in hand.

"I just knew it," the kindly old gentleman said, beaming with joy. "I see the curious eyes of a scientist behind those thick, horn-rimmed glasses—and you do have your father's carrot-red hair."

The three kids moved aside, allowing several hungry servicemen to pass them in the chow line. The old man dished out potatoes and gravy with a friendly smile to each as they went by.

"You know our father?" Geoffrey nearly shouted back at the white-bearded man after a quick glance at Kelly.

"I do indeed, Geoffrey Martin," he replied with a gleeful smile. "I worked with him right here at Fort Dix over 30 years ago. Good man, Robert Martin. Full of integrity. And I hear he's done well for himself."

"Wait a minute," said Danny, stepping in front of Kelly and Geoffrey. "I know you. You're that dime-store Santa who accused the army lieutenant of lying down on the job at the Surf City Council meeting last week."

"Macarthur Adams, at your service," said the portly old man with a slight bow. "And, just for the record … he deserved it."

"What do you mean?" asked Kelly, stepping aside to allow another group of lean soldiers get in front of her. She brushed shoulders with one of them and followed him and the others with her eyes. She couldn't help but notice the handsome and trim young men with their clean, shaved heads in their freshly pressed fatigues smiling at her as they slipped by. Neither could Danny. It wasn't every day that a group of horny young soldiers so far away from home got to see an attractive girl in street clothes standing in line in their mess hall.

And that wasn't so easily arranged, either. Using his connections with Tom Banks, Geoffrey had wrangled weekend passes from the post commander for Kelly and Danny to help stave off the stifling boredom he was feeling ever since he had arrived at camp. For their part, Kelly and Danny weren't particularly excited about coming to the base until they found out they could take advantage of Geoffrey's PX privileges and buy all kinds of things at seriously discounted prices.

Mac put down his well-worn wooden spoon and wiped his hands on his apron. He looked up and down the line until the coast was clear of servicemen before he spoke.

"The government would have you believe that it is infallible," he said slowly, the twinkle suddenly vanishing from his bright blue eyes. "Nothing could be further from the truth. Every time Uncle Sam meddles with anything short of an all-out war, trouble follows. This beach munitions thing is just another prime example."

"That's terrible, I'm sure," offered Geoffrey impatiently, unsure where jolly old St. Nick was headed with his remarks, "but I'd like to hear more about our father's work here, at the base."

"Hey Mac, quit holding up the line," shouted a brutish drill sergeant named Whitmore upon entering the room. "Or you're gonna miss that bus of yours again," he added mockingly with a coarse laugh. Several mud-splattered reservists accompanying him snickered as they grabbed their trays and formed a not-so-quiet line behind Geoffrey, Kelly, and Danny.

Mac leaned across the counter. "Do you kids have a car?"

"I have a Jeep," Danny said.

"That'll do. If you'll give me a lift home, I'll tell you all about your father … and his work here for Uncle Sam," he said, winking slyly at Geoffrey.

Forty minutes later Danny, Kelly, and Geoffrey were driving out of the Fort Dix entrance onto Route 539, with Mac sitting in the front passenger seat beside Danny. Kelly and Geoffrey sat quietly in the back. Danny had the canvas top up in case of rain.

"Man, does it ever feel good to get off that base," exclaimed Geoffrey, looking back over his shoulder. "It's like a prison in there," he added.

"You should have been here in 2007, after the terrorist plot to attack the base was uncovered," said Mac. "Security is only now getting back to normal."

"This is normal?" said Geoffrey. "Did you hear those alarms the other night? It was deafening. I heard somebody broke into the munitions containment area."

"Probably just some initiation stunt pulled by a couple of greenhorns," Mac mused. "It happens all the time. Some of the vets like to make the new recruits do the damnedest things to prove their manhood."

"By the way, where do you live?" interrupted Danny, instinctively heading toward the Parkway.

"Lakewood," Mac replied. "They have a bus that runs a few of us back and forth to the base every day."

"You don't drive?" asked Kelly casually.

"Not anymore," he said evenly. "My doctor won't let me."

"Because of your eyesight?" Geoffrey had noticed Mac's somewhat squinty gaze.

"Because of my medication," he corrected. "Just as well. I can't afford a car nowadays anyway."

Geoffrey couldn't restrain himself any longer. He was teeming with a thousand and one questions for this strange old man and busting to get them all out before the ride was over. "So what can you tell us about our father?" he blurted out, poking his head in between the front seats.

"Like I said, I met him over 30 years ago, in 1976, right here at Fort Dix."

"When he was working on the swine flu epidemic?"

"That's right. Only I didn't sling hash back in those days. I was an enlisted man with a degree in biochemistry. I assisted your father in his research and experiments."

"You're a biochemical engineer?" asked Geoffrey in disbelief.

"I was," said the old man. "Caltech, Class of '61."

"And now you're a cook?" asked Danny with a touch of derision. "Go figure."

"That was a long time ago," replied Mac, nostalgic. "An awful lot has happened in between then and now."

"Well, I'd like to know what happened," said Kelly, joining the conversation.

"I was living on-base back then, with my wife and our young son, Tad, in a nice little house the government provided for us—carport, two bedrooms, little backyard for barbecues. Anyway, one of the men in our troop, guy by the name of Lewis, took ill suddenly and died. Tests revealed he had contracted a virus. No one knew where it came from. It tuned out to be a mutated strain of the swine flu virus, similar to the Spanish influenza of nearly a half-century earlier. That one had wiped out about 50 million people around the world, following the end of World War I."

"What happened next?" asked Danny.

"I think I know," said Geoffrey slowly. "I remember Dad talking about it and then reading about it later. Fort Dix was quarantined. About 500 servicemen were infected with the virus, but they all recovered."

"That's right, Geoffrey," Mac said uneasily. "Only Private Lewis died. But that didn't matter. The incident pushed everybody into panic mode. Fears ran high that a worldwide epidemic on the scale of the Spanish influenza was looming. So the United States government kicked its bureaucratic butt into high gear and pumped out enough vaccine for all 220 million Americans."

"I remember that from history class," said Kelly. "President Ford went on TV and urged every American to get inoculated."

"And so they did; some 40 million Americans were eventually vaccinated, including my wife, Annie, and our little boy. Like I said, we were living on the base, and almost everybody said they were particularly vulnerable, being so close to the source of the virus."

"But weren't there problems with the vaccine?" asked Geoffrey, adding what he had learned from his recent reading. "Some people got sick from the shot, didn't they?"

"Right again, Geoffrey," said Mac with an admiring grin. "You *are* your father's son."

He grew silent a minute before continuing. "In their haste to get the vaccine out, the government failed to take all the necessary precautions. They didn't test for all possible side effects. Several safeguards were omitted, including a warning that some people might be at risk of a very strong reaction to the vaccine. That's why, today, before doctors give people flu shots, they always ask if the person is allergic to eggs."

"What happens if you are?" asked Danny.

"If you're allergic to eggs or if you're pregnant you shouldn't get the shot," Kelly explained. "The vaccines are grown in egg whites."

"That's correct," confirmed Mac. "Some people are predisposed to becoming sick from certain vaccines. In the case of the miracle flu shots dispensed by the government in 1976, a lot of people developed Gullain-Barré syndrome from the inoculation. It's a very debilitating disease that attacks the central nervous system."

"Didn't some people actually die from those shots?" asked Geoffrey.

"Yes," Mac murmured. "About 30 people died from the inoculation … including my Annie."

He turned in his seat to face Geoffrey and Kelly. "Your father was one of the few scientists who tried to persuade the government to err on the side of caution—to delay the wholesale inoculation of American citizens until additional testing and safeguards could be developed.

"But it was too late. With the normal flu season rapidly approaching and the pharmaceutical wheels already in motion, to the tune of $135 million, the machine just couldn't be stopped. Your father's warning and those of a few others like him fell on deaf ears. Shortly after that, the evidence got too big to ignore. Only one fatality actually resulted from the killer influenza strain itself, Private Lewis, but over 500 people became seriously ill from the vaccine and at least 30 of them died. When the truth finally came out, the inoculation program was abruptly halted, but the damage was done after about a quarter of the American population had already been vaccinated."

An eerie silence fell over the four passengers inside Danny's Jeep that lingered on for several miles. Following the old man's directions, Danny eventually pulled his Jeep off Route 9 into a secluded wooded area on the outskirts of Lakewood. It was dark, but in a nearby clearing a single halogen lamp strung from a tree threw a surreal light onto an encampment of about 20-odd tents, a couple of teepees, and a rundown pop-up trailer. Unpenned chickens scattered in the glare of Danny's headlights.

"You can leave me off here," Mac said.

"In the middle of the woods?" asked Danny, incredulous. "Why on Earth would you want to get out here?"

"Because this is where I live," he said quietly sliding down out of the Jeep.

10

"Riot on Your Hands"

Even before Dillard heard the crackle of static on his two-way radio, somehow he knew what to expect.

"Mayor, you better get over to the Division Street beach right away," squawked the slow, nasal draw of Ray Butler over the airwaves. "Looks like you've got a riot on your hands."

Dillard picked up the radio and put it to his lips. "I'm en route, Chief," he said without emotion. "I should be there in a few minutes."

Benjamin took the next left off Long Beach Boulevard onto Division Street so sharply that the mayor almost tumbled out of the doorless Gemma and onto the road.

"Sorry, sir," he said, regaining control of the Mayor-mobile, a car that looked more like a golf cart and was perfect for a beach town. No sooner had the words left his lips than he hit the brakes hard.

"Uh oh, this doesn't look good," said Benjamin said as he recoiled from the sudden stop.

At the far end of the lane, an unruly crowd of about 200 people had gathered on the street in front of the yellow police tape that cordoned off the beach. Several of them held up placards, demanding, "We want our beaches back!" Some, with fists raised, were shouting obscenities at the municipal police, stationed in a tight line behind the tape.

"What do you expect?" exclaimed Dillard with a deep sigh. "This is the first time in Surf City history that the beaches have been closed on Memorial Day Weekend."

At the sight of the mayor's easily recognizable means of transportation, a small faction split off from the larger group and rushed the lightweight vehicle. Dillard nearly leaped from the car. "Call the state police. The National Guard. The Swiss Guard. Anybody! Get HELP!" he shouted, tossing the walkie-talkie onto his assistant's lap. Benjamin grabbed the radio, threw the cart in gear, and sped away.

Instantly, Dillard was enveloped by angry protesters and disappeared into their ranks. Several police officers, nightsticks drawn, broke from the line to come to his aid. One by one, they began to physically separate the crowd from their elected official before he was torn to pieces. The jostled and beleaguered mayor sought to calm the crowd with conciliatory words, but they were having none of it.

At the site of the colorfully painted Nardi's Party Bus rumbling toward them, the agitated crowd separated in two, leaving Dillard alone in the center of the street. The bus screeched to a halt just inches from where the stunned mayor stood. The rear exit door swung open and a dozen SurfDogs in matching "Our Beaches Will Blow You Away" T-shirts hopped out of the bus—Kelly, Danny, Moss Greenberg, Johnny Longfeather, and Trevor Moore among them. The team immediately began to offload the infamous 24-foot Ron Jon surfboard.

Rodney jumped out of the driver's seat to join the others at the head of the longboard.

"Where do you think you're going?" a dazed and concerned Dillard demanded.

"Surfing," replied Rodney, coolly leading the 'Dogs to the beach.

"And you?" Dillard asked Kelly, none too pleased to see his new gal Friday disobeying his prohibition edict and hanging out with beach riffraff.

"It's a holiday, sir," Kelly pointed out. "I believe you gave your office staff off until tomorrow."

Dillard scratched his head.

The stunned crowd gave way as the SurfDogs broke through the police tape and headed up the ramp to the dunes. Even the police stood aside, uncertain what to do.

"Stop them," shouted Dillard, running toward the beach entrance. "They're going to get themselves killed," he screamed at the cops. Perhaps it was his poor choice of words, but none of the policemen moved to respond to the mayor's orders. If the idea of explosives buried on the beach like land mines had not entered their minds before, it was certainly in their heads now. The men in blue did not budge.

The demonstrators-turned-spectators gathered at the top of the dunes, anxious to see if the surfers would make it to the water safely. Dillard could do nothing but look on helplessly. *Dear God*, he prayed. *I sure hope Skip's men have done their job right. Where's the damned National Guard when you need them?*

About 10 yards from the water's edge, the surfers stopped in their tracks. They were distracted by a man waving his arms and shouting wildly, running up the beach toward them. The man was stark naked.

"Oh my God," exclaimed Kelly, letting go of the big surfboard and putting her hands to her cheeks in an imitation of Edvard Munch's famous painting "The Scream." "Danny, I think that's St. Nick!"

"The cook from Tent City?" Danny focused on the man's long white beard. It was about a foot too short to cover his privates, or his ample stomach, for that matter. "I think you're right, Kelly," he said, dropping his end. The board fell in the sand as the SurfDogs stood and stared at the buck-naked old man running around flapping his arms and uttering nonsense.

***

"You have to let them go, Chief," pleaded Sarah. She was standing in front of Ray Butler's desk at the municipal jail accompanied by her husband, Noah. Kelly and Danny stood beside them, mute and submissive, their heads bowed and their hands cuffed behind their backs.

"Your behavior was deplorable. You could lose your summer job over this impetuous incident," Sarah had chided her niece earlier when they were alone. Now she took Kelly's side and defended her actions.

Hovering behind his desk, the tall, gangly police chief put his hands on his hips. His angular appearance always filled Aunt Sarah with the silly notion that his tailor had to add extra material to his uniform in order to make it stretch out to meet his long limbs.

"Just your gang, Sarah, or the whole lot of them?" he asked.

"All of them," she said firmly.

"Including Mac Adams," added Noah defiantly, giving his wife a tender look.

"That ain't so easy to do, Noah," Ray whined. "The SurfDogs were arrested for trespassing; Mac Adams was arrested for trespassing and public nudity."

"Is that your decision or Dillard's?" Noah asked pointedly.

"I only enforce the law, Noah, you know that."

"You can interpret it, too, Chief," offered Noah. "It was a peaceful demonstration. No one got hurt."

"They broke down a police barricade and accosted the mayor," argued Ray.

"That's not the way we heard it," replied Noah, coolly exchanging glances with Kelly and Danny. "We heard your boys just stood by and let the whole thing happen."

"Now wait just a damned minute, Noah." His face turned beet red. "My boys did everything they could under the circumstances."

"We all know that," said Noah reflectively. "And we all know that the SurfDogs were not part of the mob that circled the mayor—I read the report."

Ray stared evenly at Kelly and Danny. "They all could have been killed. Then we'd have a bloody mess on our hands, wouldn't we? Mayor Webb was just trying to protect them."

"We know that, too," replied Noah, reading the looks on Kelly and Danny's faces as they lifted their heads. "Tempers flared."

"And they're going to get hotter if the beaches don't open soon," volunteered Sarah. "Everybody's complaining."

Noah could tell that the police chief was wavering, weighing all the facts as he knew them and taking into account the mood of the townsfolk. The administration couldn't afford any more acrimony over the beach closings.

"I'll tell you what, Ray," Noah said calmly, "seeing how it's a first offense for them, what if each one promised not to let anything like this happen again. Would you let them go, give them all a second chance?"

"That's Dillard's call," he replied, dodging the decision.

"What about poor Mr. Adams?" Sarah reminded him. "The kids said he was pretty much incoherent, babbling on about his wife and son when he came up to them. He didn't even seem to know where he was, let alone what he was doing."

"I didn't know he had a family," admitted the chief.

"His wife passed away years ago," offered Kelly, recalling with a shudder the vivid story he had told them the night they drove him home in Danny's Jeep.

"He never told us what happened to his son, ah, Tad, I think he said his name was," added Danny.

"And we never asked," admitted Kelly sheepishly.

"He must have skipped his meds," suggested Noah. "C'mon Ray, release him to us and we'll see to it that he gets proper care."

"And you'll take responsibility for him?"

"Yes," Noah and Sarah agreed. "I even brought along some extra clothes for him," added Noah with an impish grin, "although my pants might be a bit snug around his waist."

Ray picked up the phone. "Let me clear it with the mayor."

11

King of the Castle

"**H**ello there, brother."

The sun had long since set in the west, and the light on the wide oval veranda of the Sand Castle was poor, lit only by the flicker of a citronella candle and a steadily glowing ash at the tip of a big fat Cuban Cohiba being smoked by the man, reclining on a hidden lounge chair. To Dillard Webb, however, the voice was unmistakable.

"Cornelius! What are you doing here?" he asked, trying not to appear more surprised than he was. "Where's Skip?"

"I sent him out for sushi," replied the mayor's identical twin, barely visible in the darkness, "I heard you had a bad day at the beach today."

"Nothing I can't handle," said the mayor, taking a seat beside the familiar form of his brother.

"Ah, but the natives are restless, Dill. If those beaches aren't open soon, you might find yourself out of a job. Hell, they might even string you up or run you out of town."

"Yeah, well, I've got me a doozy of a puzzle this time. Somebody's out to get me all right, but I don't know who and I don't know why."

"That doesn't sound like you," said Cornelius, stirring the ice in his drink with an index finger. "Ever since we were kids, you were always the one on top of things."

"Yeah, but you made all the money," replied Dillard with a broad smile.

"What can I say? You got the looks and I got the brains."

"Have you looked in the mirror lately, Cornelius? If you got all the brains, then I got shortchanged." They both laughed easily.

"Okay, Dill, but you did get the gift of gab." Cornelius balanced his cigar on the arm of the chaise and took a sip of his drink. The ice rattled in the nearly empty tumbler.

"Save it, Cornelius. We both know how you feel about public service."

"That's why God made two of us."

"And what do I get out of it?" demanded Dillard. "You encourage me to run for these damned offices, then you run for the hills."

"You know I like to keep a low profile." Cornelius threw his cigar over the nearby railing.

"Yeah, like a snake in the grass, or so I've been told." Dillard stood up and started to pace the deck.

"Ooh, you wound me," Cornelius mocked his brother, rising slowly to his feet. "I try to stay out of your affairs unless you need me."

"Unless I need your money, you mean." Dillard closed in on him.

"Whatever," he said, taking his time to light another cigar and puff a smoke ring into the night.

Dillard let out an exaggerated sigh and walked away from the smoke. "We've been over this a zillion times—I have to make my own way."

"And so you have, brother. I'm only here to help if you want me to."

"Not if your help includes the likes of Walter Ashcroft," said Dillard, turning to confront his brother again.

Cornelius picked up what was left of his drink. "I told you over the phone, Dill, I had nothing to do with his visit. That was his idea, whatever he had in mind."

"Well, I don't know what he had in mind, and I sure as hell don't want to find out."

"Fair enough, so what *do* you know? Are you any closer to solving this 'puzzle' of yours?"

"That's what I was hoping to learn from Colonel Landers. Which reminds me, how do you know him?"

"I just met him here, tonight. I had him going there for a minute. He thought I was you. Can't imagine why," Cornelius snickered.

Dillard folded his arms and frowned. "Right, and why are *you* here?"

"Benjamin asked me to come by. He thought I might be able to help in some way."

"Not unless you know who has it in for me."

"You mean besides all the Democrats you've ruined in your political career?"

Now it was Dillard's turn to look hurt. Cornelius didn't have to see his brother's face. He read it in the telltale silence. "All right, I'm kidding. Benjamin did tell me it looks like this latest round of 'beach bombs' appear to have been planted."

"They're not bombs, Cornelius; they're unexploded ordnances. Obsolete and old, but live and deadly nonetheless."

"Same shit as before, right?" He flicked his ash onto the patio floor.

"I think so, only this time, according to Skip, they weren't put there by accident."

"Greetings all," Benjamin said as he slipped through the sliding glass doors with Skip and an armful of takeout containers.

"Oh, good, the grub's here. Put it on the table," Cornelius directed Skip, who did a slow double take, seeing the twin brothers side by side. "And Benjamin, I'll have another bourbon and branch water when you get a minute. What can we get for you, Dill?"

Dillard laughed at his brother's host-like antics. "Make yourself at home, why don't you? I'm sure the owner won't mind, since he's never around and the government is footing the bill at, what, about nine grand a week to rent this castle, isn't it, Colonel?"

Skip nodded as he lit several citronella torches around the pool.

"I like this place, Dill." Cornelius smiled broadly. "I'm even considering spending the night. That's how *certain* I am that the owner won't mind."

"And how is that, Cornelius?"

"Because, dear brother; *I'm* the king of this castle."

***

"Ms. Martin told me I might find you here," said Benjamin, cautiously opening the wood-and-glass-plated door to the tax assessor's office. "She's relieved you decided not to fire her over the beach incident."

Startled, Dillard looked up from the filing cabinet he was rummaging through. He eyed his young protégé with a mixture of curiosity and annoyance. Time and time again, in a variety of roles, the slim and effeminate Mr. Leef had proven himself to be indispensable—motivated, highly knowledgeable, and immensely resourceful. Dillard decided it was time to put him to the test once more.

"She does seem to have a bit of a rebellious streak in her," he said. "But I dare say I've done far worse things in my youth."

"So you often remind me," Benjamin said politely with a half-smile.

Dillard acknowledged the sense of fealty his young aide's statement implied and began to feel more relaxed. "Well then, since you're here, does the name Henry Gladstone mean anything to you?" He fanned himself with a file.

"No, should it?" asked Benjamin, his eyebrows slightly raised.

"According to the tax records, Henry Gladstone is listed as the owner of the Sand Castle property." He pointed to the card he had found in the file.

"Yeah, so?" asked Benjamin, seemingly nonplussed.

Dillard stared at his assistant, bemused. "Last night, Cornelius claimed *he* was the owner ... remember?"

"I assumed he was just joking, didn't you?" Benjamin moved farther into the room. "You know how he likes to kid around."

Dillard set the card down on top of the filing cabinet and wiped his sweating brow with a handkerchief. "Benjamin, I know my twin brother better than anybody, and yet even to me he is an enigma wrapped inside a riddle."

Benjamin shifted uneasily but said nothing. He waited for Dillard to continue.

"In the corporate world, Cornelius is like a shark among guppies. He's shrewd and calculating. He uses humor, wit, and sarcasm to completely disarm his prey. Then he sinks his teeth into them and devours them, smiling, one bite at a time."

Benjamin rocked on his heels as the mayor stood and handed him the card.

"Take a look at the assessor's record for the Sand Castle. Built in 1999 by the Toms River Construction Company; sold to Henry Gladstone in 2000 for $10 million. There's no mortgagee shown, and the sales agent listed is A Shore Thing Realty."

Dillard could see he had his assistant's undivided attention.

"I had my new temp do a Google search on this guy Gladstone. She found zip, zilch, nada."

"So?" Benjamin was following his boss's thinking but knew from past experience that Dillard liked to tell you what was on his mind rather than let you guess. Besides, under the circumstances, it was the only thing he could think of to say.

Dillard gave his protégé a quizzical look. "So, a man pays $10 million cash for a home on LBI, and I can't find out anything about him? That doesn't make sense. He's got to be *somebody* important!"

"Perhaps he is. But he also sounds like a man who values his privacy and knows how to keep it."

"Hmmm," Dillard considered his assistant's remarks. "Maybe, but then there's the address listed on the tax record to consider: 100 Grand Street, Neptune, NJ."

Benjamin's eyes widened. He glanced at the card. "Okay …"

"So, I had Chief Butler do some checking. It turns out that address is a warehouse … owned by Laval Marine Works."

"Laval Marine Works," Benjamin caught himself repeating.

"That's right. The geological survey group hired to siphon the sand for the Storm Damage Reduction Project."

"Where are you going with this, Boss?" Benjamin asked, handing the card back to the mayor.

He looked at Benjamin completely dumbfounded. "Isn't it obvious?" he asked. "We've got a palatial home, one of the most expensive ones on LBI, built in boom times by a non-local construction company and sold by Walter Ashcroft's agency for $10 million cash to a man nobody has heard of, who lists his address as a warehouse that is owned by the firm that was hired by the government for a $71-million beach project. A house, might I remind you, which is subsequently rented to Easton Solutions, the contractors hired by Skip to do the cleanup at a cost of another $13 million. And you don't think anything smells fishy about the whole thing?"

It was Benjamin's turn to mimic his boss with an uncharacteristic face squeeze of his own. "What are you going to do about it?" he wondered out loud, exhaling forcefully.

Dillard thought a moment before he answered. "Me?" he laughed, shaking his head. "If Cornelius is involved, nothing. But I need you to investigate it thoroughly. Talk to Walter; see what he can tell you about Henry Gladstone. And get Ray to use all the resources at his disposal to find out where this trail begins … and hopefully ends!"

"Why not just ask Cornelius yourself?" offered Benjamin, tongue-in-cheek.

Dillard gave him a sudden look of suspicion. "Because he won't tell me the truth. Not that he would purposely deceive me, but this is how he protects me from his business dealings, by keeping me in the dark."

"Aren't you jumping to conclusions?"

Dillard's eyes narrowed. "Somebody's planting bombs on my beach, Benjamin," he said icily. "Somebody's out to destroy me, and you think I'm jumping to conclusions? I'm beginning to wonder whose side you're on."

"Yours, of course, Boss," stammered Benjamin. "I've always been there for you."

"Sometimes I wonder," replied the mayor. "Cornelius said it was you who asked him to come by last night to help me."

"Yes, I admit it was me."

"Well what did you expect Cornelius to do?"

Benjamin shuffled his feet. "I don't know," he said, stuffing his hands in his pockets and looking at the floor. "Talk to you. Help you sort things out. He's your brother, your *twin* brother!"

"My *rich* twin brother," Dillard corrected him. The suspicion in his voice turned up a notch. "For all I know he could be behind this whole thing."

"That's absurd."

"Is it?" Dillard shot back. "Then why would Ashcroft drop his name like that to me? And how did King Cornelius acquire ownership of the Sand Castle—if in fact he did—and just who the hell is Henry Gladstone?"

"I'll get right on it," vowed Benjamin with an affirmative nod to his boss.

12

"Unstable"

A weary Noah slid into the booth beside his wife at Ship Bottom Shellfish on Long Beach Boulevard. Across from them, Kelly and Danny were fighting over the last clam left in a bucket of steamers they had ordered while waiting for him to arrive. Danny won the tussle and graciously offered his catch to Noah, who declined.

The restaurant was a no-frills, gray clapboard building, famous for fresh seafood. Primarily a takeout joint, the limited seating was full as usual and a long waiting line extended out onto the front porch. The Parsonses and their two young guests, having decided to eat in, were lucky to find an available table.

"I ordered you the jumbo crab cake with French fries and coleslaw," said Sarah, taking note of the fatigue etched across her husband's face. "How did it go? What did Dr. Shelton say?"

"He confirmed what we suspected all along. Mac Adams is unstable," said Noah, taking a sip of his unsweetened iced tea. He added a packet of raw cane sugar.

"What kind of doctor is he?" asked Kelly, keenly interested.

"Alan Shelton is the camp psychiatrist at Fort Dix. It turns out Mac has been a patient of his for years," he replied in a slow and tired voice. "According to the good doctor, Mac is delusional and suffers fits of paranoia. He's been treating him, fairly successfully, with Prozac for depression and Ativan for extreme anxiety, but lately something must have exacerbated his normally controllable condition. Obviously, it hasn't helped that Mac has stopped taking his medication regularly."

"He's gonna be all right, isn't he?" Kelly asked hopefully.

"That depends. Dr. Shelton told me that Mac's paranoia is firmly rooted in his wife's death. He blames the government."

"He told us she died from that nationwide flu shot back in the '70s," volunteered Danny.

"Apparently, that's true," said Noah. "Mac was a promising biochemical engineer. He was recruited right out of Caltech by the Army to help them develop a chemical warfare program to use against the North Vietnamese. Agent Orange was one of the projects that came out of his research."

Danny let out a low whistle. "No kidding," he said, clearly impressed.

"I'll bet poor old Mac wishes he had never gotten involved in that project," said Noah.

"Because he feels like he was misled?" suggested Sarah.

"Not just misled. In his therapy sessions with Dr. Shelton, Mac claimed that he was used—not only by the government, but also by the chemical manufacturers who lined their pockets from the poison profits. When his wife Annie died, Mac said he could never forgive the government for killing her. Those were his exact words, according to Dr. Shelton."

"I could see why he wouldn't trust the government after that," said Kelly. "But I don't understand how he can still work for the Army."

"As a cook," Danny reminded her with a questioning shrug of his shoulders.

"Where he can't do anyone any harm," suggested Sarah. "He probably feels the government owes him some kind of living, don't you think?"

"Or maybe he just wants to keep his eye on them," Noah threw out shrewdly. "As if the death of his wife weren't bad enough, it seems he holds another grudge against Uncle Sam, this one over his son."

"Tad?" exclaimed Kelly. "What happened to Tad?"

"Dr. Shelton said he was born severely autistic. Mac blamed that on the government, too. Sarah, do you remember the radiation leak at Fort Dix in 1960?"

Aunt Sarah shook her head.

"I'm not surprised," said Noah. "The Army kept that one under wraps."

He paused to let the waitress set down their dinners. Sarah had ordered a small bowl of the seafood bisque with old-fashioned Trenton oyster crackers and the Chilean sea bass, while Danny and Kelly shared an order of twin Australian lobster tails. Noah tasted his delicious jumbo crab cake before continuing.

"Few people know that in the '60s, during the height of the Cold War, Fort Dix and McGuire Air Force Base were both used as staging areas for nuclear missiles. Forty-six missiles tipped with nuclear warheads were housed in above-ground concrete sheds with steel roofs at Fort Dix. One night in June 1960, a fire broke out in one of the missile bays and the authorities were scared to death of a meltdown. Local fire companies were called in to assist with putting out the fire. An official report was issued, claiming that any radioactive material that had leaked was minimal and well within acceptable levels. It went on to say that military personnel at Fort Dix were not in any danger from contamination, as the spill and fire had been contained within the concrete retention walls designed for just that purpose."

"How does that tie in to Mr. Adams's son?" Kelly asked, dipping her lobster tail into a cup of liquid butter. Danny had forgotten how attractive his dinner partner was. Watching Kelly savor the seafood, as if in slow motion, he was reminded of that sensuous scene from the movie *Flashdance* and he had to force himself to keep his libido in check, given the company and the seriousness of the matter being discussed at the table.

"Well, by that time, Mac had been transformed into the proverbial conspiracy theory nut. He swore that the government had lied and covered up the gravity of the situation. He maintained that the leak was far more serious than the government had initially reported. And while he didn't have any direct proof, it was Mac's contention that radioactive waste had actually leeched into the underground water tables and gotten into the drinking water around the base. As a consequence of that spill and the government whitewash of the incident that followed, Mac believes a genetic mutation occurred within his body or possibly his wife's that caused his son to be born with autism. He has never forgiven the government, or himself, for that matter."

"What actually happened to his son?" Kelly repeated.

Being involved in the conversation was helping Noah sort out his feelings, but he found it increasing difficult to concentrate on his food. "I'll have it to go," he said to the waitress who came by to check on them. Then he went on with his narrative, being sure to include everything he had learned from his visit with Dr. Shelton.

"The son has been institutionalized since the age of seven, someplace in Skillman, I think he said. Mac spent time in and out of the Trenton Psychiatric Hospital and couldn't care for his son alone after his wife passed away, so the boy has become a ward of the state."

"He must be a man by now," commented Danny.

"Probably close to my age," said Noah thoughtfully, "maybe a little younger."

"How did you ever get Dr. Shelton to tell you all of this, dear?" asked Sarah. "Whatever happened to doctor-patient privilege? Aren't these things supposed to be kept confidential?"

"Evidently, Dr. Shelton is really worried about his patient," replied Noah. "It also seems as if some of Mac's ideas may not be that far off-base. Decades after that missile fire, government documents were made public that showed much higher than normal levels of plutonium were found in various aquifers in and around the base. I'm guessing Dr. Shelton felt the need to share this information with somebody outside of his hospital or the military chain of command."

"What's going to happen to Mr. Adams now?" asked Kelly, not really sure if she wanted to know. "He can't go back to living alone in that dreadful Tent City, can he?"

"They found him a room at the base, temporarily," said Noah, moving on from his iced tea to a cup of coffee. "But he's been put on a leave of absence from his job in the mess hall."

"That poor man," sympathized Sarah. "It's so sad to think of all the kids he brought happiness to by playing Santa Claus at the Five and Ten during the holidays, all the while knowing that he couldn't bring any joy to his own son."

"It's such a shame," said Kelly, echoing her aunt's sentiments.

"It sure is," agreed Noah, "but at least there's a small silver lining to this latest development. Geoffrey's volunteered to take Mac's shift in the kitchen."

"How can he do that?" asked Sarah. "What about his internship?"

"The initial problem seems to have resolved itself, much to Geoffrey's dismay," said Noah. "Apparently the toxin that made the soldiers sick was a form of botulism that comes from spoiled food. Anyway, the solders are responding to treatments, and there have been no new outbreaks in several weeks. The experts are confident that it was simply a case of one or two bad chickens."

Kelly giggled. "You mean Cornish hens. That's what Geoffrey says the reservists call them. He said they squawk when you stick a fork in them."

"No wonder Geoffrey's been so bored," laughed Danny. "He was hoping to discover some violent new virus to follow in his father's footsteps and all he got was squeaky chickens."

"That still doesn't explain what's going to happen to Mr. Adams," said Kelly. "He needs people around him who can look after him."

"What are you suggesting?" asked Sarah.

"He could help you out in the gift shop," she said eagerly. "And we could put out a cot for him at night in the store."

"No way," Danny insisted. "You're not playing nursemaid to some crazy old coot without me around. How about if I take the couch?" he asked a truly surprised Sarah.

Kelly was touched by Danny's sudden show of concern for her and gave him a tender glance that told him so. This Sir Galahad act was new for Danny, and Kelly was starting to believe it just might be genuine.

"Just hold on, everyone," Noah said, reaching for the bill. "I know you all want to help out, but you should know the doctor's got Mac on suicide watch because he's so unstable. For now, he's got himself a place on the base. Let's leave well enough alone. That should do for a while."

"We can talk about it later," said Sarah, patting Kelly's hand. "That's awfully nice of you, though, and you too, Danny."

"Hmm," Noah murmured, looking up from the bill. "Unstable ... it just occurred to me, but that's the same term Colonel Landers used to describe the ordnance found on the beach. How odd to have it come up again this way."

"Which reminds me," said Danny, standing with the others to leave. "Rodney's got this unique take on the whole bomb cleanup thing."

"Yeah," said Kelly, smiling as she took Danny's hand, happy he remembered to bring it up. "He told us while we were in the jail, waiting for you guys to come bail us out."

"Oh, this ought to be good," remarked Noah as he held the door open for the others. "Let's have it."

"Well, Rodney used to work for Laval Marine, the contractors who dumped the artillery-tainted sand on the beach," said Danny, taking pleasure in relaying his little tidbit.

"Okay," said Noah, "so?"

"Well, last year when the crew was hustling to get the job done before Memorial Day ..."

"Lot of good that did us this year," groaned Sarah.

"Tell me about it," Kelly lamented. "My guard post has been put on hold indefinitely."

"Go on," Noah encouraged Danny, moving out of the way of the people waiting in line for a table.

"Rodney said he used to stop by the beach to watch the progress and chat with men from Easton cleaning up the mess," Danny continued. "He noticed that they worked day and night for weeks on end."

"To make the deadline," surmised Sarah.

"That's what he thought," replied Danny. "But Rodney says it's very unusual for that kind of work—dealing with potential explosives—to be done at night. They would have to get special permission to work in the dark like that, using nothing but generator-powered lights to see with."

The group stopped short of their cars. Danny had everybody's attention.

"Whose permission?" asked Noah, still tired but now fully alert.

"Well, the mayor, for one," replied Danny, "and some officials from the DEP, and maybe even the federal government. This led Rodney to his hypothesis. Want to hear it?"

"Yes!" everybody answered at once.

"Rodney heard about this guy who went online and used Google Earth to pinpoint the exact location off the coast of Texas where a Spanish ship laden with gold from the New World had sunk in the 17th century."

"I remember that story," said Noah excitedly. "I read about it in *U.S. News and World Report*. Because the Gulf coastline has shifted over the centuries, the location is now actually a dry gulch a few miles inland. It's somebody's private property and the owner has refused to give the Google guy permission to dig where the satellite indicates the wreck is entombed in the clay bed."

"Exactly," said Danny with equal excitement. "So Rodney said, what if somebody positioned the Google Earth satellite on the New Jersey Coast and verified through thermal photographs that a beach on LBI showed indications of buried treasure being present—the pirate treasure long rumored to be somewhere on the island? Couldn't somebody, armed with that information and given an opportunity for subterfuge, be willing and able to labor all through the night in secret to extract the treasure?"

"I'd say your friend Rodney has quite an imagination," exclaimed Sarah, grinning slightly as she caught her niece's eye and noticed the young couple holding hands.

Noah was slower to react. As a former Coast Guardsman, he was well aware of the spy photography capabilities of the hundreds of satellites orbiting Earth. His only skepticism was in the layman's ability to get his hands on that kind of data and to use it for what Danny, or rather Rodney, was suggesting.

"And your friend Rodney has someone in mind, I suppose, whom he suspects could carry out such an elaborate plan?" said Noah after a lengthy pause.

"Yeah," replied Danny with unabashed enthusiasm. "Mayor Webb!"

13

Chaos Theory

When Dillard cut the 235-horsepower Mercury engine on his 23-foot *Sea Ox*, the silence was a welcome relief; unbroken until he heard his own topsiders squeak as he made his way around the outside of the cabin to the bow. He paused to study his boat's position relative to Stink House Point before dropping the anchor. There was a slight breeze blowing in from the southwest at about seven knots; otherwise, the channel was calm and serene. The day was cloudless and flooded with brilliant sunshine. Several other fishing boats were lined up near the mouth of the inlet, gently bobbing up and down on the waves. Returning aft, Dillard reached into a built-in red and white ice chest and pulled out two frosty Miller Genuine Drafts. He twisted the cap off of one and handed the bottle to his companion. He opened the other one for himself and paused before taking a healthy swig.

"Well, Colonel, we've missed the opening of the summer season," he said, touching the bottle to his forehead in a mock salute. "It's almost mid-June, and I can't help but wonder if we're any closer to solving this riddle in the sand of ours."

"Benjamin told me you've been receiving death threats, Mayor," said the mild-mannered Skip formally. "I was really sorry to hear that, sir."

"Whoever is sending them is quite tenacious, I must say, and full of venom, I might add," said Dillard, taking a seat in the stern on the cushioned bench beside Skip. "It's getting to the point that I'm a little afraid to leave my house. That's why I asked you to come out here with me on my boat. It's the only place I truly feel safe anymore."

"We found a total of six DMMs," replied Skip after a swallow. "As I told you before, there's been nothing new since. Short of a complete sweep of the entire beach area like we did back in 2009, I can't say for certain whether we'll find any more buried munitions or not. My gut tells me it would be highly unlikely."

Dillard took some pleasure in hearing those words, but he'd been in this position before and reminded himself just how much stock he had put in the Army engineer's words back then. "What makes you say that?"

"Because I believe this latest round of DMMs were the ones that had gone missing from the bunker at Fort Dix," Skip said flatly.

"I'm listening."

"Five of the ones we found are of the old pre-World War I type, consisting of Mark I and II boosters and Mark II point detonating fuzes, including the one that killed the civilian beachcomber. We know they came from the pump site during the Storm Damage Reduction Project the first time around. All of those were supposed to be carted off for disposal, but some of them got sidetracked to Dix for detonation in order to observe the strength of the active explosive materials."

Dillard studied Skip's features carefully, taking in the full measure of the man in an effort to better understand the worth of his words.

"However, one of the buried munitions we found recently was a Mark IV projectile—a missile, not exactly your typical World-War-I-era ordnance," explained Skip.

"Where do you suppose that one came from?"

"I'm told that a few of them were apparently mixed in with the older types at Fort Dix by accident." Skip rubbed his beer bottle in his hands like a stick to make a fire. "Whoever stole the old stuff and planted them on the beach would also have taken the missile, perhaps by mistake."

"So what's your full assessment up to this point, Colonel? I want to make sure I understand you correctly."

"Well, it's your call, Mayor, whether to reopen the beaches or not, but I think our findings clearly indicate that the latest round of munitions are from Dix, meaning the ordnances are not a random appearance, like they were before, and therefore they are presumably limited." Skip took a sip of his beer. "I honestly believe we've found them all."

"Interesting," mused Dillard, stroking his chin. "That means that our 'beach bomber' had to have access to the military base."

"Agreed," said Skip with a nod of his head.

"But who, and why? Besides the people stationed at Fort Dix, there must be dozens of people on LBI—business leaders, government officials, and former servicemen like myself—with base privileges."

"This situation reminds me of something we in the military refer to as the chaos theory, Mayor. Cause enough commotion, generate enough confusion, and it makes it much more difficult to locate the source of it all."

Skip set his bottle down in a cup holder and looked directly at the mayor. "Is there anyone you know of who stands to profit from the beaches' continued closure?" he asked.

Immediately Dillard thought about his aborted business meeting with Walter Ashcroft and the syndicate he reputedly represented. *Was this his endgame?* Then he thought about Cornelius and the mysterious Mr. Gladstone. *Were they both mixed up in this bomb business somehow?*

Dillard was also keenly aware that the long-range beach enrichment project he had sponsored in Congress and fought so hard to secure funding for was in jeopardy of falling short of its mark. When he had initially drafted the bill, the cost was pegged at $71 million for the entire 18-mile stretch of Long Beach Island. Now, with the delays due to the discovery of the ordnances and the subsequent $13 million in cleanup costs, plus the added cost overruns, the price tag was approaching $100 million.

The continuation of the program to several other LBI municipal beaches hinged on the success of the Surf City segment, which had obviously not gone off without a hitch. In fact, he had heard from a variety of sources that Harvey Cedars and Beach Haven were both having difficulty securing all the necessary easements from their residents.

"Not that I know of," he answered truthfully. "Do you mind if I ask you something, Colonel?"

"Shoot," replied Skip.

"Who do you send your checks for the Sand Castle to?"

"A Shore Thing Realty is the rental agent for the property. I drop off a check to Walter Ashcroft monthly. Is that a problem?"

"No problem," replied Dillard, splashing the beer around in the bottle aimlessly.

Skip decided to press on with the more difficult question he'd been saving for the mayor. "Sir, is there anything you or anyone in your office may be responsible for or may be trying to cover up, that would give someone cause to mine the beach in order to bring it to the public's attention?"

This was a loaded question, of course, and one that Dillard could not give short shrift to or dismiss out of hand. He was impressed that the officer had the balls to ask it in the first place. But out here, in the middle of the bay, with no one around, all discussion was fair game.

Off in the distance, the roar of a motorboat momentarily interrupted the mayor's deep thoughts. He stood up to get a better view. The low-riding speedboat seemed to be at full throttle—an action prohibited by maritime law in the channel—and coming toward them.

"Of course not," Dillard answered eventually.

"Then we're left with only one possibility," said Skip, taking note of the reason for his host's distraction.

"What's that?" managed Dillard absently.

The speedboat was indeed at full throttle now and bearing down on Dillard's *Sea Ox*. He quickly considered his options. His boat was securely anchored. He wouldn't have time, even with Skip's help, to weigh anchor and start his engine before the speedboat would be upon them. At its present course and speed, it seemed that all they could do was brace for the broadside impact.

"We are dealing with someone who has an ax to grind," said Skip, closely observing Webb's unease. "This will make things more difficult for us, because," he grew frantic as he realized the impending danger they were in, "there are no rules or rational thoughts that govern this person's actions."

His eyes still trained on the oncoming boat, Dillard removed a small black plastic box from under his seat. Nimbly unfastening the clasp, he reached inside and put his hand around the butt of his service revolver.

Less than 20 yards away, the speedboat suddenly veered off, sending a wake that rocked the *Sea Ox* wildly. As the boat coasted away, Webb and Skip saw a shirtless young man with one arm draped around a bikini-clad babe and the other arm trying to hold on to a beer can and the steering wheel at the same time. The babe waved enthusiastically to the men, oblivious to the near collision.

Dillard snapped the lid closed on the black box and slid it back under the seat. "Ready to do some fishing, Colonel?" he asked, reaching for a rod and reel.

14

Unintended Consequences

Mac sat on the edge of a thin mattress in his T-shirt and boxer shorts, his prodigious belly overlapping the waistband in several folds. He glanced at the lamp on the nightstand and a glass of water shimmering in colors beneath its fake tiffany-shaded glow. In his hand, he held two pills. Outside his tiny bedroom window, morning's first light was at least another hour away.

His sleep had been restless and unsatisfying. He was haunted by dreams and nightmares both real and imagined. He tossed and turned until he could endure no more. At the tent city campsite in Lakewood, which had been home for the last few months, he might have taken a walk to feed the chickens or gazed up at the stars in order to relax a bit, but here in his government-issue sterile quarters there was no such natural relief available. The unforgiving memories flooded back into his shattered, fragile mind. Dreams die when illness arrives!

He was not a religious man. His scientific training and inherent skepticism of assumptions that couldn't be proven empirically prevented him from considering spirituality as anything more than wishful thinking. He was, however, a pragmatist rather than an atheist. He believed in God, more as a means to an end than as part of a grander purpose. Like many, he reasoned that if he believed in God when he died, he would be rewarded with eternal life as the Bible promised. If, on the other hand, after this earthly existence, he found out there was no God after all, he could rationalize his beliefs simply with the saying "nothing ventured, nothing gained."

But if he died without believing, only to find out there truly was a Supreme Being who loved us all, then he would have squandered his one opportunity for redemption. *Better to believe than not,* he reasoned.

He was tortured by thoughts of his life, or rather, the great unfulfilled promise that his life had become. He agonized privately over thoughts about his family—his wife and young son—and what might have been, had they not been so unfairly afflicted. Sadly, when he did speak up about what happened to them, he found that no one listened. When he cried out for them, no one cared.

The government defended their actions. It wasn't our fault, they said. Our intentions were good, they argued. But their greed had forced them to turn a deaf ear and a blind eye to the victims of their unintended consequences. Thus, Mac had no choice. He struck back at those he blamed—the rich power mongers and the bureaucratic whores who served them. Only this time, the innocent became the victim of *his* unintended consequences.

So now the weight of all these consequences, causes, effects, and grief dominated the landscape of his daily life; and in the loneliness of his dark dreams, a nightmarish reality of wakeful dread reigned without mercy.

Mac rose and walked slowly to the window, his only link to the outside world and perhaps to a world beyond. How beautiful and sad the new breaking dawn appeared, he thought as he drew the Venetian blind closed, yanking so hard on the cord that it came away in his fist. He threw the pills on the floor and wrapped the cord around his neck.

15

Webb of Lies

"That's your problem, not mine!" Walter sneered at Benjamin. It was nearly midnight and the two of them were standing toe-to-toe in the empty parking lot of the Barnegat Light Marina. "Dillard Webb may be a glad-handing politician, but he's nobody's fool. Sooner or later he's gonna figure it all out."

"I know, I know," moaned Benjamin, walking alongside Walter toward the dock. "Cornelius shouldn't have said what he did about the Sand Castle. It's all my fault for dragging him out there. But I was worried about Dillard."

"Do you hear yourself, Benjamin? You sound like a spoiled little school girl. I can't wait to see the mayor's face when he finds out you've been playing both sides of the fence, leading a double life as Benjamin Leef and Henry Gladstone, depending on which master you're serving at the time."

Benjamin grabbed Walter by the arm and spun him around. "He won't find out unless you tell him!"

"Oh, he won't find out from me, Benjamin," Walter laughed coldly, "you can be sure of that. But there's no telling what that police chief bloodhound, Butler, might turn up."

Walter turned and continued walking down the ramp toward his boat. Benjamin followed him like a puppy. Starlight danced on the harbor.

"Once you convinced Dillard that sponsoring the Storm Damage Reduction Project would enhance his cherished legacy, all I had to do was sit back and wait for my opportunity," continued Walter. "Of course, it didn't hurt that you were able to secure the bid for Laval Marine. But, hell, I don't even think Cornelius could have anticipated the windfall he got when Laval inadvertently pumped the replacement sand from that watery military munitions graveyard ..."

"Allowing Cornelius to bring Easton into the act for the cleanup," Benjamin finished the thought for him.

Ashcroft grinned. "Fortune favors the well-connected. What could be better than one Cornelius Webb enterprise sucking on a limitless federal teat?"

He answered his own question, thrusting two fingers forward. "Two! Until now, Cornelius has been able to keep his network of sheltered businesses safe from public scrutiny and even from his own brother, but it's only a matter of time before your involvement is discovered and the whole 'Webb of lies'—you'll pardon the pun—comes unraveled like a ball of yarn."

"We can't let that happen, Walter," said Benjamin, stepping over the gunwale and boarding the boat behind him. He surreptitiously removed a small clear bottle of liquid and a white monogrammed handkerchief from his breast pocket.

"Hey, I've got nothing to do with this," said Walter, unlocking the door and ducking down the steps into the spotless cabin. "I'm clean. I'm just waiting for the scraps to fall from the table in the real estate crash. I only wish I knew who this mad bomber was; I'd like to thank him for making my job a whole lot easier."

Walter stood with his back to Benjamin. He reached up into the cupboard for two glasses and dropped a single ice cube into each. He filled each glass with three fingers of Scotland's finest amber liquor.

"I never thought it was you, Walter, but I had to be sure," said Benjamin, sprinkling the contents of the vial onto the cloth, "It really doesn't matter now. You represent a connection between me and Cornelius that has become an unacceptable risk."

"What are you saying?" Walter turned to give Benjamin his drink. "We can't have our weekly trysts anymore?"

In one swift motion, Benjamin grabbed Walter's arm and pinned it behind his back, then he smothered his face in the chloroform-laced cloth. Walter's eyes rolled upward. He dropped the drinks and slumped to the floor.

"Actually, what I'm saying, Walter dear, is that we need to terminate our relationship *permanently*," he said, dragging Walter's limp body toward the cabin steps. "Now, let's see if the fish like the taste of you any better than I did."

***

By the time Geoffrey had finally convinced the two MPs to break down the door to Mac's room, they were too late. They found his cold body dangling at the end of a double-knotted cord that was strung around the ceiling fan in the center of the room. A wooden chair that had been kicked away lay on its side beneath the corpse.

"The Sarge ain't gonna like this," barked one of the MPs.

On the night table, beneath a half-empty glass of water, Geoffrey found a note stuffed inside an envelope along with a key. While the MPs struggled to take the body down, Geoffrey couldn't resist; he opened the unsealed envelope and read the brief handwritten note silently. It was addressed to Dr. Alan Shelton.

Dear Doctor Shelton:

I am truly sorry. I no longer have the strength to wage a war against the corruption and greed that permeates our society. I am afraid I have become the very thing I set out to destroy.

My intentions were good. I never wanted anyone to get hurt. I only hoped that I could make people aware of the pork barrel politics that were being passed off as sound public policy.

When that ordnance exploded—the ordnance I had buried in the Surf City sand to shed light on how taxpayers' money was lining the pockets of rich businessmen—I didn't plan for the unintended consequence of someone's death being caused by my own hand. I've become one of them. I am an instrument of destruction.

Please give Sgt. Whitmore back his key to the munitions facility with my apologies. I swiped it from him a while ago when he asked me to bring him a late night snack. He was kind enough to invite me to stay for a drink and even gave me a ride home. I wish I hadn't taken advantage of him that way.

I am sorry for a great many things, but please don't feel sorry for me. I leave this world eagerly to rejoin my wife in the next.

Think of me at Christmastime. The role of St. Nick was the best that was left of me; it allowed me to escape my pain during a difficult season for lonely people.

Mac

P.S. Don't let the men eat the Cornish hens.

16

Hanky Panky

"They found Walter Ashcroft's body in Barnegat Bay this morning," said Dillard, accompanied by that peculiar ritual he had of squeezing his face between both hands and massaging a little too vigorously. His face flushed bright red from the rub.

In contrast, Benjamin's face was pale, almost like porcelain. Sitting across from the man he once admired the most, the one behind whose back he had gone more times than he could count, the mayor's assistant suddenly felt ill at ease.

"The police searched his boat," Dillard continued, his eyes fixed unflinchingly on Benjamin's. "They found two empty drinking glasses lying on the floor of his cabin with good scotch spilled on the floor beside them. You like single malt, don't you Ben? Shame to see it go to waste, eh?"

Benjamin blinked out of reflex under his boss's penetrating stare. He couldn't think of a clever response and thought it best not to say anything until Dillard spit out everything he knew.

The mayor studied his young assistant's handsome, boyish face. Not an unshaven whisker could be detected, nor was a single strand of his wavy brown hair out of place. Years of faithful, loyal service, and there had never been an inkling of anything amiss. Now it seemed so obviously too good to be true.

"They also found a monogrammed handkerchief," said Dillard, leaning forward, "with the initials B.A.L. stitched in a rather bold magenta script."

He waited. Still Benjamin remained impassive, desperately trying to hold it together. *Don't crack now*, he told himself.

Dillard raised his eyebrows. "Is there anything you'd like to tell me, Benjamin?"

"All right, I went to see Walter," he admitted at length, clearing his throat with a nervous cough, "just like you asked me to." He crossed his legs to keep them still. "We had a drink, and he probably just forgot to clean up. It wasn't his first drink of the night, I can tell you that. He seemed pretty upset about something when I got there."

"What time was that?" asked Dillard, now truly sounding like the grand congressional inquisitor of old, someone capable of skillfully grilling even the most stoic of liars testifying before his committee hearings.

"Around 10 PM," Benjamin lied. "I remember it was hot and stuffy in his cabin, and I took out my hanky to wipe my face. I must have left it there."

Dillard sat back in his chair and folded his hands across his chest. "So, that's it?"

"Yes." A trickle of sweat ran down Benjamin's right temple.

Dillard stood and walked slowly around to the front of his desk.

"You'd never make a good criminal," he said, circling behind Benjamin. "Most killers clean up after themselves!"

"What are you suggesting?" Benjamin challenged him, whirling around in his seat. "That I killed Walter Ashcroft? Why would I do that?"

Dillard grabbed Benjamin's chair by the arms. "Traces of chloroform were found in your handkerchief."

"That's circumstantial. Anyone could have used my handkerchief. Walter had lots of enemies."

"Maybe," said Dillard, straightening up. "But whatever else could be said about Walter Ashcroft, he was a meticulous record keeper. It seems he kept a log of every business transaction he ever made since about the age of 16. Does that surprise you?" Dillard began, pacing around the room.

Benjamin tensed up. Several more beads of sweat formed at his temples and then left streaks as they ran down his ashen, pasty face.

"No, I was well aware of it," he lied as calmly as he could manage under the circumstances. He began to tap his foot nervously. "It was no secret that Walter also had a pretty high opinion of himself."

"Agreed," said Dillard, coming back around to face Benjamin straight on. "Walter Ashcroft was a vain and insensitive man, cocksure that he would *be* somebody in this world; hence the flamboyant clothes, the coiffed silver-white hair, and his taste for fine Scotch."

Benjamin looked up at the ceiling while the mayor once again took a seat behind his desk.

"But tell me, Benjamin, did you know that he also kept a daily diary, detailing things going on in his personal life?"

All the blood drained from Benjamin's face.

"The police found it inside the liquor cabinet on his boat."

Dillard pressed the intercom, and the police chief was in the mayor's office before he released his finger from the button. Ray carried in a nondescript leather-bound book, which he gave to Dillard. The mayor thumbed through a few soiled pages leisurely, pausing every now and then to utter a sound of shock or surprise and incline his head toward Benjamin.

Eventually, Benjamin couldn't take it anymore. He leaped to his feet. "It was all Cornelius's idea! Everything, including having me pose as Henry Gladstone, so *you* wouldn't find out. He treated me well. All I had to do was secure the bid contracts." Benjamin eyed the book with a mixture of desperation and loathing. "Taking up with Walter was a bad mistake. My mistake."

"You disappoint me, Benjamin," said Dillard, "after all we've been through, all the political battles we fought together. What did I do to lose your loyalty? How did I fail you? Was it just the money?"

"You never saw me for who I really was," cried Benjamin like a hurt child to an unforgiving father. "All I ever was to you was your *assistant*—someone to keep your appointments and make your excuses. Cornelius gave me a life, a real life."

"As someone else, Benjamin," said Dillard sadly, "as Henry Gladstone. He used you like he uses everybody to get what he wants."

Ray removed a pair of handcuffs from his belt.

Benjamin looked around the room for an escape route but found none. "I want to talk to my lawyer," he said meekly.

"You may be interested to know," said Dillard as Ray cuffed Benjamin roughly from behind, "that I plan on resigning as mayor of Surf City effective immediately. I'll ask for a new election to be held in the fall. Meanwhile, Chief Butler will work with the council to choose an interim mayor. That okay with you, Ray?"

Ray nodded. "Fine with me," he grunted.

"As for Cornelius, when the authorities finally do catch up with him, I'm sure he'll have the best lawyer money can buy ready to convince any jury of his innocence and your—or, should I say Henry Gladstone's—guilt. So, if I were either of you, I'd begin preparing my confession immediately … and leave nothing out."

As Ray hustled Benjamin out of the room, Skip appeared in the doorway. Dillard tossed him the book.

"Thanks for the use of your logbook, Colonel," said Dillard with a grin.

"I take it your little gambit worked," he replied with the erudite air of a man who was glad to take part in the charade.

"Like a charm." He pressed the intercom again. "Did you get all that on tape, Ms. Martin?"

"Every word," his temporary secretary replied over the speaker. "Are you really going to resign, Mayor?"

Dillard couldn't tell if that was shock or jubilation he heard in his young temp's voice. Maybe a little of both, he reasoned. "I have no choice, Kelly. My brother Cornelius is mixed up in this up to his eyeballs. I have to step down and let justice have a free hand."

He turned his attention to Skip. "Colonel, to begin with, I would recommend you send the Storm Damage Reduction Project back out for bid. And pull the plug on Laval and Easton immediately. As of today, they're through—off the project. I want those beaches back and I want them now!"

17
SurfDogs Rule ... Again

"It's great to be back on the beach again and feel the sand between my toes," said Sarah as she and Noah made their way across the crowded Division Street beach to where Geoffrey, Kelly, and Danny were sunbathing near the water. It was a cloudless, sunny day in June, the first official day of the summer season, according to the equinox.

Kathy Wollert, the second grade teacher so concerned about the beach closings a month ago, stood at the water's edge watching her two kids jumping into the waves and splashing each other. One of them picked up an empty Jim Beam bottle that had washed up on the beach and offered it to her. Kathy directed her son to place it in the recycling container near the beach exit, and he obliged.

Nearby, a dark-skinned man in a light-blue polyester suit was taking soil samples of the beach sand and handing them to a female assistant who stored the glass vials in a padded briefcase. Rodney, talking animatedly with his hands, shadowed Sanjay Patel and his DEP staffers as they made their way to another stop and bored into the sand.

"I hear your buddy Rodney Coles is thinking about running for mayor in the fall election," said Noah, setting up sand chairs for himself and Sarah under a brightly colored beach umbrella.

"Yeah, SurfDogs rule!" Danny exclaimed, pumping his fist in the air.

"What about the charges against him for defacing government property?" Kelly asked.

"According to Ray Butler, he's been completely exonerated," said Noah, liberally applying sunscreen to his face and legs. "Benjamin Leef confessed to spraying the graffiti on Colonel Landers's Hummer to draw attention to the SurfDogs and away from himself and Mayor Webb's crooked brother."

"It's what the military refers to as chaos theory," said Geoffrey, setting down the graphic novel he was reading.

"So you did learn *something* during your brief stay at Fort Dix," teased Danny.

"Sure, I learned that army life is not for me," he replied.

"You know," said Sarah with a frown, "I will never be able to think of the Christmas holiday at the Surf City Five and Ten the same way again."

"I know what you mean," Noah said. "Life sure is strange. This whole ordeal with Mac Adams was tragic and unfortunate. Same goes for Libby Ashcroft. They'll both be missed. And yet I'm sure neither one ever realized the kind of impact their lives would have on others. It kind of reminds me of a little piece of ancient wisdom I read somewhere: One does not leave footprints in the sand by standing still."

স০ও

Spirits of Cedar Bridge

1

Butcher of Barnegat
(April 2, 1783)

The heavy oak door crashed in upon the tavern floor and a thunderous volley of musket shot followed streaming shafts of blinding sunlight into the smoke-filled room. After a brief pause to reload, an armed team of New Jersey militia rushed through the splintered opening, their pointed bayonets fixed and ready.

"Find him!" the officer in charge bellowed, stepping over dead bodies.

Crouched behind an overturned table in a darkened corner of William Rose's "publick house," John Bacon knew he was trapped. It wasn't the first time the captain of the infamous whaling sloop, the *Black Joke,* had found himself in a tight fix. But this time it felt different. All around him was chaos, the mournful shouts and dying moans of his fearful and confused men swirling about the room. Their desperate cries mingled with the smell of gunpowder that hung in the morning air like a heavy funeral shroud.

Only hours earlier, the arrogant captain lay asleep on a warm straw mattress in an upstairs room, his head nestled contentedly upon the soft, ample bosom of a young serving wench with whom he'd spent the night. Try as he might, he could not remember the comely maiden's name, but neither could he easily forget the pleasures she had brought him. Clad in his rumpled nightshirt, she lay draped over the table like a dish rag … dead. Felled by a musket ball intended for him, crimson blood trickled from the corners of her mouth like so much red wine spilt in the revelry of the night before. Weary but now fully aware of his predicament, Bacon hid beneath her lifeless form as if it might protect him from the events that had led him to this fateful moment.

The evasive brigand had come to this once friendly tavern looking for a place to rest. For him and his roving band of Loyalist sympathizers, running had become a way of life. From the moment hostilities commenced and independence was declared—severing what tenuous ties existed between King George and his former colonies—Bacon and other likeminded Tories sought refuge in the vast, inhospitable wilderness of the New Jersey Pine Barrens. Considered refugees and outcasts in the War for Independence from Great Britain, they did not sit by idly. Relying on a practice known locally as "mooncussing," referring to a preference for moonless nights, wherein pirates on land could lure ships at sea into shallow waters to crash upon hidden shoals by cleverly deploying lanterns on the shore to appear as if they shone from other sailing ships, these scoundrels made their living plundering indiscriminately from neighbors and even friends, on land and sea.

By all accounts, Bacon had known for some time that the war was over for him and his British benefactors. Still, he remained unbidden and unbowed, a rogue to the last. Desperate for one final act of defiance that would enhance his already sullied reputation, he had gotten his chance six months earlier on October 25, 1782, when

343

a Belgian cutter under British sail ran aground off the Barnegat Inlet. When word reached him that a certain young lieutenant by the name of Andrew Steelman had enlisted the local inhabitants to help offload the stranded ship's valuable cargo, Bacon hatched a daring plan. Under cover of darkness, while Steelman's tired recruits bedded down for the night, Bacon and his crew crept up on the beach where they lay and slaughtered them in their sleep. In the morning, some thirty men, Lieutenant Steelman among them, were found butchered in the sand.

Within the sparsely populated wooded communities of southern New Jersey, where each cause had its supporters and fighting broke out frequently between the two factions, atrocities were committed on both sides. But after the Barnegat Massacre, all pretense of civility ceased, and the hunt for Captain Bacon intensified, taking on a bitter and personal tone that left him and his followers with no safe haven. Overnight, Bacon and his Pine Barrens bandits went from disreputable marauders to despicable murderers, with a bounty of fifty pounds sterling placed upon the captain's head. A detachment of local militia numbering some twenty men under the command of Captain Richard Shreve was dispatched from Burlington City with strict orders to bring Bacon to justice for his heinous crime.

On the 27th of December, Captain Bacon and a dozen raiders, including six of General John Burgoyne's British regulars, were headed for the comforts of Cedar Bridge Tavern in Stafford, seeking a warm fire and a stiff drink. To their dismay, Shreve's detail had beaten them to the tavern's beckoning hearth and cordial spirits that day.

Outnumbered, Bacon's men barricaded themselves on the north side of the rickety wooden bridge that spanned the slowly meandering Cedar Creek, barring the way for Shreve and his men to leave the premises. In a burst of bravado, Shreve's troops led by light horse cavalry rushed the refugees' position, not once but three times. Owing to the ferocity of the attacks, Bacon's stalwart line began to give way. In close combat Bacon took a glancing blow to the shoulder while three of his men were dislodged from the bridge and fell, wounded—one mortally so—into the shallow, muddy creek.

Shreve's contingent suffered light casualties but kept up the assault until, unexpectedly, out of a nearby thicket a mob of armed inhabitants emerged, some carrying only pitchforks and axes, and engaged Shreve's bewildered troops. Surprised by the sudden show of support for Bacon and hampered by their force of arms, Shreve's men fell back. With the militia distracted by the intervening locals, an opportunity for escape opened up and Bacon ordered his men to beat a quick retreat into the thick cover and safety of the forest. Apparently news of the Barnegat Massacre had not fully alienated Bacon from the populace. The unanticipated action taken by the local inhabitants remained a mystery even unto Bacon, albeit for him a fortunate one.

Now, nearly four months later, as he cowered in the darkened corner behind the overturned table, the nameless wench's limp, rag-doll body separating him from certain death, the "Butcher of Barnegat" readied himself for one final round.

"Show yourself, coward," the militia officer called into the dusty, smoke-filled room.

Casting the corpse aside, Bacon drew his cutlass in one hand and pulled out his pistol with the other. "You'll never take me alive," Bacon shouted.

"So much the better," the stiff-faced officer snarled, his men closing ranks around him. "Kill him."

Rising swiftly from his hiding place, Bacon fired blindly into the on-rushing soldiers until his rounds were spent. Then he threw the useless gun into the middle of the charging horde. It grazed the officer's left shoulder harmlessly.

With his cutlass Bacon hacked at empty air until he was less than a yard away from the lunging militia. The pointed tips of several bayonets found their mark, plunging deep into his chest, puncturing his black heart. A wave of searing pain engulfed him, followed by an incongruous rush of giddiness as the air compressed in his lungs, issuing forth the nefarious mooncusser's final breath.

2

Exile's End
(Present Day)

Rudolph Koenig sat on an old wooden bench, pulling off his worn rubber work boots in the rustic kitchen of a place he had called home for more than fifty years. The fact that, as one young female reporter recently pointed out, he shared his last name with the TV actor who played Ensign Chekhov in the 1960s hit series "Star Trek" was clearly unimportant to him. He didn't own a television—or telephone; for that matter. His only connection to the outside world was a beat-up RCA transistor radio that he kept in a planting shed behind the house, tuned to WPRB and turned up extra loud so he could hear it while tending to an expansive backyard garden.

The bench on which the wiry, white-haired, eighty-something, decorated World War II Navy veteran sat was a relic he had rescued from a suspicious fire that destroyed Clayton's Log Cabin Restaurant over a decade ago. Located on Route 72 about a quarter mile east of the junction with Route 539, the huge faded sign advertising the famous German-American restaurant still stood on an empty gravel lot—all that remained of the popular eatery which had served Barnegat Township and the surrounding communities since 1936.

Living as he did, behind a thicket of tall pines on a narrow, unpaved ribbon of road within spitting distance of the restaurant, Rudy, as he preferred to be called, in bygone days would sometimes take a meal at Clayton's to supplement his diet of fresh fruit and vegetables from his prolific garden. Sweet corn, Jersey tomatoes and plump huckleberries were a few of his staples.

The knotty pine table he leaned against was made from a section of highly polished flooring he had rescued from the local high school gymnasium when that building had to be rebuilt after yet another mysterious fire. It proved the perfect complement to the four-foot-long wood tavern bar that occupied the southwestern corner of his small dining room.

Before concluding the recent sale of his property to Ocean County in a deal that guaranteed the octogenarian life tenancy, in addition to making him a wealthy man, a local historian had advised him that his quaint dining room was very likely the oldest standing bar still in existence in New Jersey, dating back to the early 1800s, if not earlier. As soon as this little known fact leaked out, a rash of reporters and curiosity seekers began beating a path to the well-preserved private home to see the bar that had once been part of the celebrated colonial "publick house" known as the Cedar Bridge Tavern.

With the rediscovery of this state treasure, lovingly restored and maintained by Koenig without much thought for its historical significance, came the end to Rudy's five decades of hermit-like existence. An electrician by trade, living in Philadelphia at the time he purchased the property and surrounding acreage, his was a carefully

346

orchestrated, self-imposed exile, engineered in order to get away from his overbearing parents and his soon-to-be-ex–wife. Prior to his purchase, the building had fallen into terrible disrepair, having been used as a dormitory for migrant cranberry workers. Large enough to house a small army or raise a big family, Rudy reasoned it was probably a blessing that he and his wife had never started a family, as they would undoubtedly have shown up with the worst of both sides of the gene pool. The Lord indeed works in mysterious ways, he reminded himself gratefully over the years.

Alas, fate and age had finally caught up with Koenig. He knew it and accepted it as surely as he knew from his creaking bones and labored breathing that his days tending to his prized garden were numbered. But he had no regrets. And although it was an intrusion on his coveted privacy and an annoyance to his painstaking planting and weeding, he warmly greeted any and all visitors who popped in, particularly those guests bearing bottled gifts to be opened and shared at his now famous bar.

Besides the delightful old caretaker's lively tales and the cozy antiquity of the tavern walls, what visitors found most impressive upon arriving at Cedar Bridge Tavern was the startling history lesson to which they were treated. Here, under the soothing spell of imbibed spirits, one learned that long ago, on a cold December morning in 1782, a Revolutionary War battle took place; a deadly skirmish that pitted Loyalist sympathizers led by an infamous, blood-thirsty privateer against Patriot soldiers of the New Jersey militia; brother against brother, the tight-knit rural community had played an active and controversial part in the fight.

Many history books cite the minor incident as the last land battle in the War for Independence, but in actuality it had occurred *after* the British Army had already surrendered at Yorktown and while the peace treaty was being negotiated in Paris. Thus, the bloody fight need not have been fought at all; and yet, to many descendants of the local families who remained in the area, it was still being fought to this day.

There were other treasures this special place held, enchantments that sprang from the soil or blew in on the breeze, mysteries that only Rudy came to know and appreciate in the long and peaceful years he'd spent here in seclusion. Without likeminded kin to inherit the land, it saddened him to think these secrets would most likely go with him to the grave.

A sharp pain radiated across Rudy's chest. It made him wince as he struggled to straighten up. He hadn't seen a medical professional since he left the service, and he was not about to now. He had gotten as far as he did in this life by using home remedies made from roots and herbs grown in his garden, prescribed according to the time-proven recipes given to him by "Doc" Freeman Morris, the black witch doctor of the Pines, through connections with Maggie Colson, the owner of Colson's General Store (a.k.a Buzby's) in Chatsworth. That and a good snort of apple-jack whiskey once in a while was all a man in these woods ever needed. He closed his eyes and waited, willing the pain to pass.

3

Dress Rehearsal

"**O**ur daughter tells us you are quite the adventurer," said the short, heavyset man with a thick Spanish accent. He eyed his dinner guest cautiously as he expertly wielded a carving knife and fork to shred the roast beef his wife had placed in front of him alongside the home made tamales, rice and beans and fresh garden greens. "She says you are a tiger from T-neck?" he added as he proudly served his guest a healthy portion of each dish. "But this I do not understand. Perhaps you can explain?"

"Oh, *Papi*," blushed Luz Sanchez with embarrassment. "Geoffrey's from Teaneck, New Jersey, and the tiger is his college mascot." She gave the freckled young man in horned-rimmed glasses sitting beside her an apologetic look. "I'm sorry," she mouthed silently.

"*Sí*, Santiago," echoed Inez Sanchez with a stern look at her husband followed by a quick warm smile at Geoffrey. "You promised not to interrogate Luz's guest at the dinner table."

"It's quite all right, Mrs. Sanchez," said Geoffrey Martin, his face redder than his hair. He smiled nervously across the table at Luz's little brother and sister, who were giggling. "I'd be happy to explain." He had practiced his remarks for a full week now.

He turned his attention back to the man at the head of the table, a proud Guatemalan-American who had made his roots known early on. With his salt-and-pepper hair, bushy eyebrows, and matching moustache, Santiago Sanchez reminded Geoffrey of one of the Super Mario Brothers. The bright red suspenders he wore over his best white dress shirt made his appearance even more comical. His petite wife had a very pretty face with soft, kind brown eyes that glistened whenever she smiled, which was often, Geoffrey noted. He knew that meeting Luz's parents for the first time was going to be difficult, but now that he was living on Long Beach Island instead of just visiting for the summer, he insisted on it, despite her misgivings.

He spread his napkin across his lap. "As Luz mentioned, I was born in Teaneck, New Jersey, and I am a recent graduate of Princeton University, whose Mascot is the Tiger," he added, trying to sound casual if not clever. "My focus is in applied chemistry, and recently I've been doing field research here in the Pinelands on crop yield dynamics, using organic methodology based on established practice. My premise is that primitive farm techniques actually preserve the viability of the land while providing a healthy product. Of course it doesn't hurt that, in addition to being beautiful, Luz is a very talented chef who adheres to the 'eat local, drink global' philosophy." He gave Luz a tender glance. Her mother's eyes smiled. Mr. Sanchez wondered what exactly Geoffrey was explaining and how long he could go on, but since Luz had never brought a boyfriend home before, and this one had graduated from college, he decided to cut him some slack.

"My first memory of Long Beach Island is the day my father patiently explained that salt water taffy was cooked in copper kettles and pulled to add air to the corn syrup

348

and sugar confection. It could not be coaxed out of magical, striped seashells hidden on the ocean floor, no matter how much my five-year-old imagination wanted it to be that way. To this day, I cannot eat escargot without wishing for a hint of sweetness underneath the garlic and the butter. This roast beef is delicious, by the way."

Luz's father and her two siblings kept on eating. Luz and her mother sat transfixed as Geoffrey continued speeding through his overly rehearsed remarks.

"We visited Long Beach Island for a week every summer up until my fifteenth birthday. I remember it well, since I had just finished sophomore year with the first B I had ever received—in music appreciation, of all things. My mother bought me a Yamaha electric piano so I could sharpen my skills over the hiatus from class work, and my sixteen-year-old sister Kelly and I were unceremoniously shuffled off to our Aunt Sarah's gift shop here in Ship Bottom to spend the entire summer without further parental supervision. They were off to Europe for a pharmaceutical conference, and we were stuck with the greenhead flies and local surfers.

"Of course, Kelly, my sister, was living a young athletic girl's fantasy-come-true. She became a lifeguard and started hanging out with Danny Windsor, a quintessential surfer with enough confidence to fill an ocean. I, on the other hand, was not particularly suited to the beach scene. As you can imagine, I burn easily; I don't really enjoy the ocean that much and, as luck would have it, at fifteen I was a bit shy with members of my own sex, let alone the mysterious female of the species."

Geoffrey took a breath, stopping long enough to look for a reaction as Mr. Sanchez put down his cutlery and picked up his glass of wine. He took a sip and motioned with his free hand for Geoffrey to continue. He took another sip and resumed his meal.

"The only thing—or person, rather—that saved me that summer was my aunt's husband, Noah Parsons. He secured an internship for me at the Tuckerton Seaport. It is not an overstatement to say that he introduced me to my greatest passion and opened a channel for the studies that I pursue to this day. At the Seaport I was able to see firsthand the devastating impacts of environmental carelessness and decided to devote my energies to learning as much as I can about adopting a more positive stewardship of our planet's resources.

"As for my social life, it turned out that the piano lessons mother had insisted on served as my entrée into Danny Windsor's world. One fateful evening at a beach party he lost his keyboard player to an excessive intake of alcohol, and my sister persuaded him to let me sit in. The rest, as they say, is history. We actually became friends over Hotel California."

"We've never been to California," Mrs. Sanchez offered enthusiastically, hoping to turn this into a conversation rather than a monologue. "But Santiago has a cousin who manages a vineyard there." She glanced at her husband tentatively. "We plan to visit them some day."

"My cousin, Andres," said Mr. Sanchez chewing thoughtfully. He pointed with his knife to Geoffrey's wine glass. "This cabernet is from his winery. It is very good, no?"

Geoffrey obliged with a tiny sip. Giggling quietly, Luz's brother and sister sipped from their milk glasses, mimicking Geoffrey's hesitant gesture. Geoffrey raised his eyebrows and swallowed hard before continuing. Luz, knowing Geoffrey was not a drinker, smiled appreciatively.

"Over the next three summers, Kelly, Danny and I—*los tres amigos*," he continued, sounding anything but spontaneous, "shared a whole host of adventures. Kelly found treasure buried on the beach, and I came face to face with the Jersey Devil."

"*Chupacabra*," shouted Mr. Sanchez, glaring menacingly at his younger children while using his hands to form devil horns on either side of his head. The children screamed and ran from the table.

"Santiago, no! You frighten the children away before they have finished," admonished Mrs. Sanchez jokingly.

"Ah, if ever there were two people who were made for each other, it's Kelly and Danny," interrupted Luz, dreamily changing the subject. "They make a handsome couple and would definitely make beautiful babies."

"Hopefully they'll realize that, now that Kelly and I have taken up permanent residence here," Geoffrey responded, sincerely adding, "I'm also hoping that Mr. Koenig, the caretaker of Cedar Bridge Tavern, will agree to let me stay on as his apprentice to assist with the gardens and grounds until the county can find a more suitable replacement. In the meantime, I'm training as a re-enactor in the annual re-staging of the famous Battle of Cedar Bridge—I was hoping you all would come out to see my dress rehearsal with Luz?"

Geoffrey let this last comment hang in the air as a question rather than a statement, hoping the Sanchezes would answer affirmatively without pause. Luz sat upright in her chair, tingling with excitement. She hugged Geoffrey in anticipation.

Mr. Sanchez put down his fork and knife very deliberately and looked up into the six pair of eyes that were waiting expectantly for his answer. "Inez, this does not worry you, to have an actor so near to our daughter?"

"Oh, *Papi*," sighed Luz, the exasperation evident in her tone. "Geoffrey's not an actor; he's a re-enactor."

Mr. Sanchez shrugged while wiping his moustache with his napkin. "Same difference, no? You pretend to be somebody else."

"It's not quite the same, Mr. Sanchez," Geoffrey explained politely. "You see, I don't have any lines. It's not a speaking part."

"*Perdoname*," said Mr. Sanchez, addressing his daughter in Spanish, "but if he doesn't speak, how are we supposed to know if his acting is any good?"

Luz looked to her mother for help. Mrs. Sanchez blinked at her daughter and Geoffrey from across the table with a look of genuine confusion on her face. "Luz, honey, why will Geoffrey be wearing a dress at the rehearsal?" she asked.

4

Longboard Contest

"I don't understand," said Danny Windsor, planting his surfboard upright in the sand. Using his yellow wristband, he tied his wet, shaggy blond locks into a short, tight ponytail. "I thought you would be happy for me, Kelly. I have an opportunity to land a real job and finally make something of my life. This is a career move."

Hiding her disappointment and her sparkling emerald-green eyes behind a pair of oversized designer sunglasses, Kelly Martin absentmindedly scooped up fistfuls of grainy, crystalline beach sand and sprinkled it on her bare feet up to her ankles, until only her tan, athletic legs were visible. A blue Old Navy hooded sweatshirt covered her upper torso, denying Danny a fuller appreciation of all her assets.

Enlivened by a recent nor'easter that had skirted the coast, Brant Beach was humming with activity as surfing enthusiasts, intent on competing in the annual Alliance for a Living Ocean Longboard Classic, were taking some practice runs on the early morning Atlantic waves. Among the throng of excited spectators and the expectant vendors shilling their wares, a carnival-like atmosphere prevailed. As if on cue, the Diamondheads, a 1960s retro-guitar instrumental group, began tuning up on a makeshift stage mounted atop a sand dune.

Danny plopped down beside Kelly, admiring the long limbs that had first attracted him to the fiery, auburn-haired dynamo on another LBI beach more than seven years ago. Back then she was a fiercely competitive sixteen-year-old training to be a lifeguard, and he, barely a year older, was a hotshot instructor who got his comeuppance when a passing man-o-war decided to reach out a tentacle and say "hello." Had it not been for her quick thinking and grace under fire, Danny could have been singing Davy Jones's praises these days instead of enjoying a beautiful beach day.

"I am happy for you, Danny, really," Kelly offered, covering her outstretched legs completely in sand. "It's just that I would have preferred hearing the news from you instead of Rodney Coles," she added with a glance toward the registration table where their bald, thirty-something tattooed fellow SurfDog member was chatting it up with the young, impressionable daughter of one of the contest officials. "I had no idea you were thinking about joining the Park Service."

Actually Kelly wasn't thrilled by the idea at all. Before the summer started, she had imagined *she* would be the one breaking away from the adventurous threesome that had become a summer standard. But when she couldn't find a job in her field and Surf City Mayor Dillard Webb needed temporary office help, she was only too glad to accept. That job had placed her, her brother Geoffrey and their pal Danny in the center of an unexpected and eventful riddle that unraveled right before their eyes, one whose dire consequences they were unable to foresee or prevent.

Now that she and Geoffrey had both decided to take up permanent residence on LBI, she thought maybe she and Danny would get to spend more time together than

351

their mere summer romances had afforded them in the past. That's why she joined the SurfDogs to begin with—to keep a close eye on the one boy she had met in her life who alternately excited and infuriated her without ever trying very hard to do either. Now, Danny had pretty much driven a stake through her plans by enrolling in the NJ State Parks and Forestry Service, where he was evidently encouraged by Rodney Coles to sign up for the wildfire brigade. That meant spending a month in the Pines for training. *He might as well be going to Siberia*, she thought.

"It's not like it's the French Foreign Legion, Kelly," replied Danny, as if reading her mind. It was a bit scary, but their summer relationship had become so predictable that sometimes he felt he *could* read her mind—and she his, unfortunately. "It's the Forest Fire Service. I'll be back before you know it."

"And then what?" Kelly asked, flinging sand at a cadre of seagulls picking over the carcass of an upturned horseshoe crab.

"Whaddya mean?" he asked. To Danny, this display of caring was heartwarming but rare for Kelly. Although more than a few tender moments had passed between them over the years, the siren call for her return to school every September had always short-circuited any thoughts of a longer-lasting commitment. Danny was having difficulty adjusting to the idea that Kelly and Geoffrey were now planning to live on his home turf year round. The thought was at once exhilarating and suffocating to the freedom-loving, devil-may-care Danny Windsor.

"Where will you be off to next?" questioned Kelly. "To help poor natives in Botswana by joining the Peace Corps?"

"Whoa, slow down," Danny protested, tapping his chest. "My faint and foolish heart can't take all this sudden attention. Does this mean you're actually gonna miss me?"

"Greetings, sports fans," interrupted Rodney Coles, standing his odd-looking longboard next to Danny's. The skinny, doe-eyed official's daughter he'd been kibitzing with earlier was clinging to his arm.

"What, you don't approve of my new equipment?" Rodney joked, noticing the scowl on Kelly's face.

"Does she come equipped with a parental permission slip?" Kelly chided him as she stood up, brushing the sand off her legs with a towel.

"I'm eighteen," the young girl shot back. "Well, almost," she added under her breath, looking up at Rodney hopefully.

Danny whistled appreciatively. "What great curves," he added as he ran a hand down Rodney's surf board. It was one of those new hourglass shaped boards created by Thomas Meyerhoffer. Whereas the classic longboard was an elongated, slightly concave ovoid, the Swedish designer's board featured a curved, corset-like midsection Rodney had explained to Danny prior to purchasing it. Since longboards were ridden from front to back, Meyerhoffer reasoned he could reduce mass around the middle, making it lighter and easier to pilot while paddling for a wave. He also tapered the nose to a point so it wouldn't lose any speed going into a turn.

"Typical," thought Kelly, sharing a look of frustration with the official's daughter, to their mutual surprise.

Danny may not have been able to see through him, but Kelly was growing tired of Rodney's antics and the unwelcome innuendo he kept sending her way. From his Mr. Clean shaved head and perfect pecs, to his body tattoos and preference for young girls, it was hard to believe that this former professional diver had once considered himself a viable candidate for mayor of Surf City. Following his failure to replace Dillard Webb, who had been reinstalled by referendum at the insistence of the townsfolk, Rodney had taken up a new cause, becoming an environmental activist and getting himself elected president of the Alliance for a Living Ocean.

As the head of a fledgling organization, Rodney had hit upon the idea of a surf contest to raise awareness and funds. He expected his buddies, collectively known as the SurfDogs, of which Kelly and Danny were both neophyte members, to become the first entrants.

The rules of the contest were simple: in classic Hawaiian tradition, only vintage longboards could be used. This meant that a board had to be three feet taller than the surfer riding it, and no leashes were permitted to tether the board to the rider. Before long, the North Jersey-based Surfrider Foundation joined in, swelling the ranks. Next he petitioned LBI's mainstay surf shops, Ron Jon's and Wooden Jetty, to sponsor the event and cover the initial expenses. Suddenly there was no stopping the Rodney Coles Express.

While Rodney's appeal had greatly waned with Kelly after the whole beach munitions/mayor-wannabe debacle earlier in the summer, she had noticed that his stature still seemed to be growing in Danny's eyes. She couldn't say for sure why it troubled her. Maybe it was all the attention he was paying Danny after she repeatedly rebuked the subtle overtures he had made in her direction. Then again, it might have something to do with Rodney taking up so much of Danny's time, which she wanted for herself; but then, she felt bad because Rodney was kind of like the older brother Danny had never had. He wasn't exactly family, but to Danny Windsor, who had lost his mother early in life and never knew his real dad, this substitute for a brother might be as close as he could get at the moment, and that worried her.

"What's the problem, Pumpkin?" asked Rodney playfully. "Rhonda here tells me you didn't sign up for today's event. Lost your competitive drive, or was the entrance fee a little too steep for your pocketbook?"

Kelly paused to watch two shirtless hot shot boys—twins from Deal with long braided black ponytails and matching red Speedos, playing beach soccer with a hacky-sack. They were adorned with identical dragonfly tattoos; one twin's on his chest, the other's on his back, paying homage to rock heroes Coheed and Cambria. Kelly remembered Rodney pointing them out to her earlier and telling her they were odds-on favorites to place second and third in the contest, *behind* him. Danny was considered a dark-horse fourth. The rest of the field after that didn't matter.

"Let's just say I've had enough of little boys comparing board lengths," she replied haughtily. "Hot dog, anyone?" she asked, moving off to the concession stand. "Good luck, Danny," she called back over her shoulder. "Watch out for jellyfish."

"What's with her?" inquired Rodney, amused but admittedly somewhat taken aback.

Danny glanced hesitantly at Rhonda, who smiled naively and seemed nonplussed by the whole conversation. "I guess she must be O.T.R.," Danny whispered snidely, grabbing his board and heading for the starting line.

"O.T.R?" asked Rhonda innocently.

"On the rag," Rodney answered for him.

5

The Anchor Lady

"**T**he Anchor Lady is at it again!"

That was one of the last things Sarah Bishop-Parsons remembered Libby Ashcroft saying to her back in May before the Tuckerton Seaport Museum Curator met her untimely and gruesome demise.

The two ladies were having their usual Wednesday luncheon fare of succulent bay scallops at The Gables, an elegant but aging Victorian inn that had been a Beach Haven fixture since its early days as a lifeguard house. Originally built in 1892, by the 1970s The Gables had become an acclaimed five-room luxury bed and breakfast and later morphed into an award-winning restaurant. Through it all, the establishment had never lost its quaint Victorian charm or its connection to the community. It was the "in" place for movers and shakers on LBI and a favorite reception hall for Island newlyweds.

The Anchor Lady, or Carole Bradshaw, as she was more formally known, got her unusual moniker completely by chance when she was led by her young daughter Amanda to a metallic ball protruding from the beach on 16th Street in Ship Bottom. The year was 1983, and the ball turned out to be the eyelet tip of the four-ton metal anchor belonging to the Sicilian cargo ship *Fortuna*, which had run aground in a January gale back in 1910. All 17 crewmembers, including the ship's captain, Giovanni Battista Adragna, his wife, and their infant daughter, Saveria Fortunata Marina—who was born on the boat en route from Barbados to New York—were saved thanks to the courageous efforts of Ship Bottom's selfless citizenry.

Removing a piece of local nautical history that had been buried in the sand for over seventy years was no easy feat. So Carole took it upon herself to enlist the aid of the fire department and a bulkhead builder to extricate the anchor from its resting place. The booster effort did not end there. Together with the Ship Bottom Civic Association, she coordinated a project leading to the restoration and permanent relocation of the anchor outside of the Ship Bottom municipal building on Long Beach Boulevard. More recently the Anchor Lady, as she became fondly known, spearheaded a campaign to raise money to commemorate the 100th anniversary of the *Fortuna's* sinking.

Both Sarah Parsons and Libby Ashcroft were intimately familiar with the story and fortunes of the *Fortuna*. During her first summer as a lifeguard, Sarah's niece, Kelly Martin, had found a Spanish medallion believed to have belonged to the court of King Philip II, and attributed by Libby through provenance of the ship's records to the *Fortuna*. The Adragna family heirloom was eventually sold to noted treasure hunter Mel Fisher, Jr. for a tidy sum.

But on that day in early May at The Gables while the two women chatted, sipped their herbal iced teas and sampled sinful desserts, the Anchor Lady had come to the restaurant on a new mission: to start a campaign to fund a search for the remains of the fragile, crystal Fresnel lens from the original Tucker's Island Lighthouse before it was washed out to sea. Believed by some to have been salvaged by the lighthouse keeper in 1927 during the perilous days immediately before the tower went under, the lens had disappeared from history, and a mystery ensued. But for the dedication of a select few, like the Anchor Lady, the precious lens would have been all but forgotten. Once again she turned to the community for help and support.

"That sounds like a waste of time and money," the intractable blue-haired Libby Ashcroft remarked when the Anchor Lady approached the two of them and laid out her plans.

"Why?" Sarah asked, intrigued by the request.

"According to Seaport records, the last lens was a fourth-order fixed lens made in Paris in 1872 by Henry LePaurte and installed in the lighthouse in 1894," replied Libby in the measured tone of the schoolroom educator she had once been. "The lens apparatus was placed in a lantern and bolted to a pedestal. The pedestal in turn was bolted to an oak clock box, which was fixed to an iron grate and fastened to the floor. The lens was truly a work of art, but the entire apparatus was a monstrous device of iron, wood, and glass that was essentially anchored to the building itself. Removing it from its base would have required several men working with special equipment over a number of days. And at that time, the approaches to the lighthouse were inaccessible due to hazardous shoaling."

"Still, the rumors linger," insisted the Anchor Lady, hell-bent on solving the mystery. "They say the lens was saved thanks to the courage and cunning of the lighthouse keeper, Arthur Rider."

"For what purpose, may I ask?" inquired Libby rather indignantly.

"Why, for posterity, of course!" the Anchor Lady replied with surprise.

Now, sitting in Madame Curator's old office, Sarah Bishop-Parsons was suddenly drawn from her dreamy recollections by the sound of scuffling feet on the planked floor in the room directly above her. She looked at her watch. It read 8:30 PM. *That's odd,* she said to herself. The Seaport had been closed for hours. The staff had all gone home for the night. She had only stayed behind to catch up on some paperwork and was about to leave to meet her husband, Noah, at The Gables for dinner. That's what had led to her musings about the last time she and Libby had lunch together. Then she remembered, with a shiver that ran the length of her spine, what Libby had said to her as the Anchor Lady left them alone to finish their tea: "No man remotely related to that 'mooncussing' crook Ryder Hayes ever risked his life to save something of value for *posterity.*"

Sarah switched off her computer. As she reached for the desk lamp, it flickered momentarily then went out. Above her the scuffling noises resumed. Sarah groped for her purse, then tripped and stumbled over the chair as she headed across the room for the door in darkness.

6
Lady in White

When Noah Parsons stopped laughing his cheeks actually ached from the effort. Tears streaked down his face.

"What's so funny?" asked Sarah, irked by her husband's prolonged outburst. The two were drawing unflattering stares from the other Thursday night dinner guests at The Gables. Sarah's heart was still racing from her spooky experience at the Tuckerton Seaport thirty minutes earlier, which she had immediately recounted to Noah upon her arrival at the restaurant. She was not expecting her normally reserved, easygoing husband to react to her chilling encounter with an uncontrollable fit of laughter.

"You mean to tell me that Libby never told you about the spooky old Sea Captain's House?" asked Noah, dabbing a tear from the corner of his eye with a fine linen napkin.

"Of course she told me," replied Sarah, a little put off by her husband's insensitivity. "She told me the Andrews-Bartlett House is the oldest known private residence in Tuckerton, some say dating as far back as 1699. It's a big and drafty old Victorian mansion that the Seaport uses as its administrative building. Libby had an office on the first floor but, frankly, the place just gives me the creeps."

Noah smiled irreverently. This is where, in former days, the retired Coast Guard lieutenant who had become a volunteer docent at the Seaport would have settled back, reached for his favorite cherry wood pipe and lit up an aromatic bowl of Borkum Riff tobacco while relating a tale as old as the port itself. It was one that he had heard from his father who had learned it from his grandfather before him and so on down the line over several generations. But ever since the public ban on smoking and the promise he made to his wife when they were married a few short years ago, his long-standing habit was now but a pleasant memory. The story of the Sea Captain's House, however, remained very much alive with him.

"You're confusing the two houses on the Seaport property," Noah said patiently after the busboy had refilled their crystal water glasses. "The Andrews-Bartlett homestead is one of the oldest in South Jersey, if not the entire state—that much is true. But it is currently closed to the public. The Sea Captain's House is the one used as the Seaport's administrative building, not the Bartlett place. Libby's office, which is now your office, is in what people refer to as the Sea Captain's House."

"Come to think of it, she did try to explain it all to me once," said Sarah, re-positioning herself in her chair. "As I recall, she also made a comment about ghosts, which I obviously ignored."

"Well, I'm not surprised she mentioned it," replied Noah with a perceptible twinkle in his light brown eyes. "Because the situation there certainly unnerved her. The story actually goes all the way back … to Captain Zebulon Shourds."

"Zebulon," mused Sarah, dwelling on the antiquity of the odd-sounding name. "That doesn't ring any bells," she added with an odd twist of her face, "but that last name does sound familiar in a way. Where have I heard it before?"

"Shourds is a proud and prominent old name from around the Pine Barrens," said Noah. "Today the family is mainly known for their unparalleled craftsmanship in decoy carving."

"Like the ducks we sell in the Seaport gift shop," added Sarah knowingly. "That's where I've heard the name before."

"Most certainly," agreed Noah. "But the name can also be traced back to the origins of the Jersey Devil."

"I thought that was the Leeds family," offered Sarah. "Are you toying with me again, Noah Parsons?"

"No, dear," replied Noah, gently taking his wife's hand. "Both families are linked to the legend of the Jersey Devil. But then, a great many of the old families like to lay claim to that familiar myth. It's considered a badge of honor around these parts."

"Okay, then, but who is this Captain Shourds character? Was he some kind of demon?"

"Well ... I guess that's a matter of opinion," mused Noah vaguely. "According to tax records, Captain Shourds built the original center section of the old house soon after he acquired the property back in 1769."

"I see. Is that why people refer it as the Sea Captain's House?"

"Not exactly," said Noah with a slight pause. "Evidently a number of fishing boat captains and their families lived in the old house over the years, which is why it is simply known as the Sea Captain's House and not specifically as Captain Shourd's House."

Sarah gave her husband a skeptical look.

"I know this sounds like one of those old-fashioned yarns, Sarah, but I swear to you this is the truth—as most folks know it, anyway. Just ask any one of the old baymen around town if you don't believe me," implored Noah defensively. "And it gets even weirder."

On that note, Sarah took a sip of her whiskey sour, made especially strong to her liking by the flirtatious, dapper old bartender. Although her heart had stopped pounding inside her chest, she still felt a little uneasy, unnerved by the evening's Seaport experience and uncertain about her husband's peculiar, lighthearted reaction. And now there's this strange story. But she had no doubts about the sincerity of her husband, who had proven himself to be a man of impeccable integrity, albeit nominal levity, during their half-dozen years together. She put down her glass and met his waiting eyes with a warm, gracious smile. "I'm listening, Noah," she encouraged him. "But please, get to the point. I'm famished, and Geoffrey said Luz is in the kitchen tonight. That means this Chilean sea bass ought to be especially delicious," she added, eyeing the entrée just placed in front of her by their server.

"The point is," said Noah, tucking his napkin into his shirt collar like a bib, "the Sea Captain's House *is* haunted. I'm surprised Libby never told you the whole story, since the two of you were thick as thieves."

Sarah swallowed hard in disbelief, and for the second time that night her pulse quickened. "Do you seriously believe the place is haunted, Noah?"

"I do—by Captain Shourds and his wife, the legendary Lady in White," Noah said, cracking open an Alaskan king crab leg.

Sarah shook her head and pushed her plate to the side her hunger replaced by an intense curiosity about the people who had lived in the old building in which she was now working regularly. Being a transplant from Teaneck had its limitations when it came to Pinelands lore. She needed to know this sort of stuff for her job, especially if everyone else did.

Noah put down his crab leg and cleared his throat. "Captain Shourds and his wife had only been married a few months when he was called to pilot his cutter and crew on a daring mission against the British. It was the height of the Revolutionary War, and many of the local merchants and fishermen had become privateers on one side or the other. Shourds had cast his lot with the Patriots and his boat was often employed to smuggle goods through Tuckerton for the rebel cause.

"This particular mission was especially dangerous. News had leaked out that a British munitions' ship bound for Philadelphia was headed down the coast with no escort to speak of. Many suspected that the ship might be protected by a band of Tories from the area, and by one notorious Tory in particular—a ruthless cutthroat named Captain John Bacon. But no one knew for sure."

Noah lowered his voice and leaned in across the table toward his wife to emphasize his next point. "It has only lately become known that Bacon had in fact received Letters of Marque from the British and that he was operating legally in their employ—more or less—throughout the entire war," he said as if revealing a well-kept secret.

Sarah frowned at her husband's rather surreptitiously delivered remark, not sure why he added the drama but content to let him continue the tale.

"The night before Captain Shourds was to sail, his wife had a terrible dream—a premonition that her husband would be captured and tortured. The next morning she pleaded with him not to go out to sea, but he steadfastly refused. He was determined to carry out his duty. He had given his word, and in those days a man's word was his bond. To change his mind when it was time for action would have been perceived as an act of cowardice, and he couldn't live with that."

"Try as she might, the fair Mrs. Shourds could not dissuade her husband; nor could she shake off the terrifying vision that had come to her in her sleep. So convincing were the images that she told her husband she felt as though she were already a widow, and from that day forward she would dress only in black until he returned. Should he come home safely and prove her dream false, on the very day of his return she would dress up in her finest white lace gown and go down to the water's edge to meet his ship.

"Day after day, after he had gone, Mrs. Shourds, attired in widow's black, would walk down to the beach and wait for her husband's ship. Night after night, she would pace the halls of their lonely, empty house, unseen in the shadows, and pray for his safe passage."

Sarah had been focusing on her husband's handsome, rugged face, but now she found herself spellbound, enmeshed in his captivating story. The clatter of dishes and glassware in the busy restaurant had died away, and the distant chatter of the other diners had long faded into the velvet and wood trimmed walls. It was as if she and Noah were the only diners in the restaurant. And, on cue, the chandelier ceiling lights lowered and all Sarah heard was the sonorous sound of her husband's magical voice as he continued.

"When, after several months, Captain Shourds had not returned and no news of his fate or that of his men had reached the village, his wife began to despair. The anxious months of waiting turned into a year, then two, and still there was no news. So certain was she that her nightmare had come true that, one night, morose and overcome with grief, the would-be widow waded out into the calm water of the bay, never to be seen again."

Noah took a sip of ice water to quench his parched throat and picked up the story.

"Not long after Mrs. Shourds' disappearance, her husband returned to the village, gaunt and weary, but alive. His mission had been a total failure. It had been, in fact, a clever trap set by the notorious John Bacon to lure the foolhardy Patriots out onto the open sea, where they were ambushed and overwhelmed by combined British and Loyalist forces. Captain Shourds and his crew fought valiantly, but in the end he was captured and sent off to a squalid prison ship in New York Harbor, where he languished in the most deplorable of conditions.

"His crew was not as lucky. They were shown no mercy, given no quarter. All were hanged as traitors. Shourds was spared only because of his rank and because it was hoped that the British might effect a prisoner exchange of equal rank for him. But the arrangements fell through, and Captain Shourds lay forgotten in the bowels of the penal death ship. If not for the lingering hope of one day being reunited with his sweet young wife, he, too, would have perished from neglect.

"One day his captors opened the prison boat's hold to find several bodies—Captain Shourds' among them—to be in such a bad state that they believed all to be dead and ordered the corpses carted off and incinerated. But Shourds was alive. Using a trick he had heard Bacon himself once used, Shourds had merely feigned death and lay among the others. Under cover of night, with barely enough energy to breathe, he clawed his way out from under the death heap, only moments before the funeral pyre was set ablaze, and crawled to freedom.

"Traveling unsteadily on foot, sleeping in ditches and living from hand to mouth like a common street beggar, on the charity of strangers and generous New Jersey farmers, the Captain eventually made his way back to his native Tuckerton, only to find his house shuttered and his wife vanished without a trace."

"Mad with grief, for nights on end he would retrace his wife's desperate steps down to the water's edge and look for her among the rippling, ceaseless, unending waves. Night after night, in all kinds of weather, he would sit alone in the wet sand and look for her. Sometimes, in the dim light cast by a starry sky obscured through wispy clouds, or in the dazzling brilliance of a full moon, blinded by his own anguish and sorrow, he would see a woman dressed in a fine white lace gown emerge from the water. In the next instant, as her feet touched the shore, the ghostly apparition would be swept up into a whirling haze of white sand and sea mist and curl back into the dark water.

"Overwhelmed by his loss and the eerie vision of the ethereal woman in white, one cold and dreary December night Captain Shourds quietly crept into the master bedroom of his big, empty house and took his own life … with a single pistol shot through his temple."

During the telling of the Sea Captain's tale, Sarah had not moved a muscle. Her Chilean sea bass lay on her plate, cold and untouched, her appetite forgotten. Noah called for the waiter to reheat his wife's dinner.

"Many believe that his ghost still walks the floors of the old place, his longing to be reunited with his lost love unresolved. Libby believed it. She told me she often heard the sound of shuffling feet on the floorboards directly over her head. Perhaps that's what you heard tonight—the longing ghost of Captain Zebulon Shourds, searching for his lovely Lady in White."

When Noah ended his story, Sarah did not stir. She couldn't. It was almost like she wasn't there. Not physically, anyway. She was somewhere else in time. She blinked remotely, unconsciously, as if trying to clear from her mind a vision too unbelievable to be true. How could it be? Into the dining room strolled her dear departed friend Libby Ashcroft—only a much younger version of the old matron with her silver-blue hair a lustrous satiny black and her age-lined, mottled leather face instead creamy, angelic and wrinkle-free—sashaying toward their table. She was adorned in a flowing white linen dress trimmed in silver lace like the woman in Noah's story.

"I thought I might find you two here," the woman announced excitedly upon arriving at their table. "Creatures of habit you are. I hope I'm not interrupting," she added, taking a seat between them.

"Not at all," replied Noah politely. "We've just now finished our meals, haven't we dear?"

They both looked expectantly at Sarah, who sat transfixed with her mouth agape.

"Sarah, Sarah, honey," repeated Noah, snapping his fingers like some cheap parlor room hypnotist.

"Are you all right, Sarah?" the woman asked reaching for her arm. Sarah was staring vacantly. She seemed to be looking straight past the confused woman. Instinctively, the woman turned and looked behind her, glancing back toward the door.

"Huh?" Sarah gasped, blinking again. Then suddenly her mind began to clear. The spell was broken, and the visionary image of the youthful Libby Ashcroft as the Lady in White vanished and Adele Willoughby appeared in her place.

"You look like you've just seen a ghost," said Adele with a droll laugh as she pulled a sheaf of papers and a fountain pen from her handbag. Recently widowed, the righteous neighbor of Carole Bradshaw, the Anchor Lady, had stumbled upon the perfect cause to throw herself into, to help wind down the rest of her lonely, golden years.

"I'm fine," replied Sarah, regaining control of her senses. "I thought for a moment you were someone else." She gave Noah a reassuring smile.

"Good. Then, on to business. I'm helping Carole raise funds to search for the lost Tucker's Island Lighthouse lens. Would you two mind adding your names to the pledge sheet?"

Noah rolled his eyes upward.

7

Voice from the Past

What's a guy gotta do to get a girl's attention?

Sitting on a barstool reserved for him at the Port Hole following his victory in the longboard contest, Rodney Coles knew he wasn't the first frustrated man on the planet to ask himself that question. That didn't make the answer any less elusive. Sure, he'd read the classics: *Romeo and Juliet, Wuthering Heights*, even Eric Segal's sappy *Love Story*. In all of them the advice was the same: There are no rules.

It wasn't as if Rodney had any problem picking up girls. On the contrary, he had them at this beck and call, as witnessed by the bevy of bikini-clad beauties that had greeted him with a host of indiscreet physical and verbal overtures as he made his way through the thick and noisy crowd up to the bar, where a monstrous inflated surf board hung from the rafters in his honor. A well read, if not well bred, former Navy SEAL (with the well-defined pecs to prove it), he knew he had the brains and the brawn to attract even the fairest member of the opposite sex. To enhance his mystique and increase his allure, he had shaved his dome, added symbolic Oriental body paint, and reinvented himself as an environmental activist. The image of a compassionate, self-confident Adonis was complete—or so Coles thought.

Sure, he had the bar-hopping bimbos and the tanorexic teenyboppers eating out of his hand, but the classy, educated woman on whom he'd set his sights treated him like a Neanderthal, putting him in the same category as the dimwitted Curtis Wick a guy he knew she detested. After learning of her interest in politics, he'd made a run for mayor of Surf City, and when that failed to get her attention, he got himself elected head honcho of the reconstituted ALO, won the organization's main charity challenge —an event designed for him to win—and still she barely gave him the time of day. Downing the last of his frothy cold Yuengling Black and Tan, he didn't need to survey the room to know the object of his desire was not among the revelers. She'd made her lack of interest in the surfing contest abundantly clear when she stomped off the beach before the event had even started.

Maybe, just maybe, it wasn't his charm that was lacking. Perhaps he had overestimated his chances with her—or underestimated those of the competition. But if there was one thing Rodney Coles knew, it was how to deal with competition. He simply eliminated it.

"Barkeep," he bellowed to the friendly, walrus-mustachioed man behind the bar. "Another round for me and my buddy here, today's runner-up," he said, clamping a muscular, tattooed arm around Danny Windsor's head like a vise and giving it a playful squeeze. "Drink up, Danny boy … coz tomorrow firefighting training begins, and those woods ain't no place to be second best."

***

363

What's a girl gotta do? Kelly mused, lost in a spiral of dismal thoughts as she flipped the sign in the store window to "Closed."

The night had proven painfully slow without a single customer stopping by Crab Cove to look for a nautical keepsake or a special sea treasure to take home. Apparently, a fair number of island residents were still out celebrating the close of the day's Longboard contest. Unfortunately, that left Kelly minding a store without patrons, leaving her far too much time to stew in her own solitude. And that meant dwelling on Danny's decision to go off into the woods and play Smokey the Bear with his new BFF, Rodney Coles. The revelation of his sudden, undisclosed departure, delivered by Mr. Cool Tattoo, followed by her confrontation with Danny, had jolted her, launching an emotional wave that shook her to the core. As the day unfolded, it forced her to reassess their relationship, putting her immediate hopes for a fun-filled summer on hold and casting any future dreams of a life together in a more dim and distant light. She shuddered at the thought of Danny, the consummate blond Beach Boy, sporting a Mohawk and flashing a tattooed torso permanently imprinted with some unspeakable exotic design.

That she'd known Danny for several years and still knew precious little about him was disconcerting to the onetime high school star athlete who had built her reputation on being underestimated by her male counterparts. Her will to win, to beat the naysayers and odds makers who bet against her, was the stuff of legend. Probably owing to her competitive nature, she had never given up on Danny, but she did have a life in between their summer adventures. In truth, it wasn't much more than a few casual dates, best characterized as quasi-romantic interludes with a couple of boys she knew back at school, and somehow in those brief courtships she could never let herself go, not completely. It was as if a part of her had been programmed with an automatic off switch. At a certain point in time, whenever things started heating up, she'd cool down. Curiously, that happened every spring. At a time when other coed couples were snuggled up, cooing and courting, Kelly found herself anxiously anticipating her annual summer sabbatical to Long Beach Island, where, along with her brother Geoffrey, she and Danny would set off on some exciting adventure or find themselves engulfed in some strange, endlessly twisting mystery that made all thoughts of romance—save for the possibility with Danny Windsor—appear irrelevant and unimportant. Today, however, this erratic, endless summer love/hate romance, which had been so thrilling and titillating at sixteen, was starting to grow old and tiresome to her at twenty-three.

Clearing the cash register of the same bills she'd placed in it earlier, it dawned on her that maybe romance no longer seemed relevant to Danny. Maybe because of their amazing summers together, he had come to see her more like a sister. That was not something she was ready to accept.

With a sigh of frustration, Kelly absentmindedly lifted the paperweight she had moved earlier to make room for the latest Dan Brown thriller she was reading. The object in her hand was a strangely captivating sculpture: an icy blue, chipped-glass rendition of two bottle-nosed dolphins breaking the water from opposite directions, forming the outline of a heart above the wave where they met. It was an attractive piece with antique qualities and it had caught her eye many times before. Tonight, it somehow struck her that thie sculpture wasn't just another one of the many odd curios that lined the shelves and covered nearly every nook and cranny of her aunt's charmingly old-fashioned gift shop. This one was different. Something about it was special and it wasn't for sale. Instead it held a place of honor, front and center on the countertop, between the clunky old cash register and the plated glass case containing the very first dollar bill her Aunt Sarah had earned at Crab Cove.

That was more than eleven years ago. A few years after her beloved husband, Hugh Bishop, had passed away, Aunt Sarah, bored with her sedentary life and in desperate need of new challenges, suddenly announced that she was retiring from teaching and buying a gift shop that was for sale in Ship Bottom. The family, quite naturally at the time, thought the grieving, childless widow had finally lost her marbles, gone off the deep end. Only later, after she had turned the little store into a rousing success with summer tourists and native islanders alike, and gotten herself remarried to a kind and gentle man, to boot, did Kelly, Geoffrey, and the rest of the Martin clan come to fully appreciate the strength and foresight Sarah Bishop-Parsons had showed in uprooting her life.

Kelly held the curio in the palm of her hand, feeling the weight of the finely polished, decorative piece. It was deceptively heavy. She ran a hand over the twin dolphins arched playfully in a heart-shaped ring. They were smooth and soothing to the touch. Turning the sculpture on end, she was surprised to find something etched onto the oval wooden base. She smiled inwardly as she read the words aloud. "To my darling Sarah—May this small gift inspire you to give others the great joy you have given me. With love always, Hugh."

Tears moistened Kelly's eyes as she realized what the treasure she held in her hands represented. It must have been the motivation behind her aunt's unceremonious departure from her old life and her leap of faith into a new one. The gift shop at Crab Cove was a natural extension of her husband's heartfelt inscription.

Kelly didn't remember much about her Uncle Hugh. She was a young girl when he passed away from pancreatic cancer. But he must have loved Aunt Sarah very much. How wonderful it must be for her to have found true love, not once, but twice in a lifetime.

For a brief moment, Kelly envied her aunt's happiness. Although she was smart enough to know that it had come with a heavy price, she wondered if she would ever find someone to share that kind of deep connection. She gently set the cherished sculpture back in its rightful place and sighed.

She was about to head upstairs to her apartment atop the shop when the store phone rang. She glanced up at the leafy sea fan clock on the wall behind her. The miniature sea horses pointed to ten minutes past ten. Who could be calling at this hour, she wondered.

It was date night for Aunt Sarah and Noah. That meant a late dinner at The Gables, then drinks at the Engleside. Geoffrey planned to hang out at the Maritime Museum in Beach Haven, killing time while waiting for Luz to get off work. That left Danny. Kelly snatched up the phone on the final ring before the after hours message kicked in.

"Crab Cove," she answered enthusiastically.

"Are you the proprietor?" a raspy male voice inquired on the other end. Although his words and manner suggested a swarthy charm, there was something about his tone that was … darkly familiar. "No," replied Kelly. "I'm her niece."

"Ah, yes, the Martin girl." He said with a devious note of recognition. Her suspicions were correct. *He knew her.* And now he had the upper hand.

A wave of panic swept over Kelly as she searched vainly through the closets of her mind for the door that held the identity to the eerie voice on the other end of the line. "Do I know you?"

"When do you expect your aunt to return?" the man asked, ignoring the question.

She could sense the devilish pleasure he was taking in his evasiveness, his aloofness. She tried to remain businesslike and treat him as she would any other customer. "It's hard to say. She's been filling in at the Seaport temporarily. Is there something I can help you with?"

"I have something *she* may be interested in." His emphasis on the word "she" was obviously intended to infer a matter of great importance he wished to discuss only with Sarah Bishop-Parsons.

"If you'll give me your name and a number where you can be reached, I'll make sure she gets the message," said Kelly, struggling to stay focused and cordial.

"She's working at the Seaport, you say?" the man snarled.

Kelly hesitated. "Yes."

CLICK. The line went dead before she could say anything more.

Kelly slowly set the phone back in the cradle. She stood for a long moment in the supernatural silence, only vaguely aware of the heated gas humming in the overhead fluorescent lights. Her first instinct was to pick up the phone and call her Aunt Sarah's cell. But what would she tell her? That she'd spoken with some creepy old man who said he had something to talk to her about but wouldn't say what it was? And that she had failed to get his name and number?

An inspired thought flashed through Kelly's racing mind. Maybe she could still get the man's phone number. Using an old trick her college roommate taught her when they were getting prank calls at school from an off-campus pervert, she picked up the phone and dialed *69. A soft electronic female voice came on the line. "You have reached …"

Kelly jotted down the phone number on a notepad shaped like a sand dollar that was lying on the counter. She lay the pen aside and stared at the number she'd written down in disbelief. Her hands began to tremble. It had to be a mistake. The phone slipped from her grasp and fell to the floor with a thud, the twisted cord dangling along the edge of the counter like a hangman's noose. She recognized the number; she knew it by heart. The call had come from the Tuckerton Seaport!

8

Bamboo

Tom Banks drove his ten-year-old dust-covered F-250 slowly over the rutted dirt lane, past the rustic front porch of the old cedar shake and clapboard building. "There's certainly been a lot of activity around here lately," the noted woodsman and survival guide remarked to his passenger. Tom parked the truck on the far side of the property under the shade of a gnarled, twisted fruit tree.

Geoffrey bounded out of the passenger side with the enthusiasm of a Boy Scout about to earn a merit badge. "Yeah, it looks like someone's been doing some digging," he remarked, noticing the cordoned-off six-foot rectangular grid lining the yard in front of the tavern.

"Part of that archeological dig being sponsored by the county, I'd imagine," Tom said. "Professor McPherson is hoping they can unearth some artifacts that will help determine the exact age of the place. No one really knows for sure when it was built."

Geoffrey wandered over to the tidy hole for a closer look. He stood with his hands on his hips, surveying the site. He shuddered. It reminded him of an open grave.

Tom came up alongside him and stared up at the tavern roof. A lone two-by-four lay nailed across the roof, perpendicular to the line made by the eaves. A bundle of new cedar shingles was perched nearby. "Seems old Rudy's been doing a little repair work again," said Tom with a note of chagrin. "I swear one day he's gonna fall, and that'll be the end of him," he added with a sigh.

"We should all live so long," Geoffrey quipped.

"And so well," the older man replied with a wry smile.

Geoffrey nodded in agreement. It had been quite some time since he'd last seen Tom and he was struggling to adjust to the woodsman's curious take on things, which seemed to wax and wane with the cycles of the moon like so many of the woodland creatures he had made it his life's mission to protect. Geoffrey was having a particularly hard time getting used to Tom's new look. Banks, who had just spent six months in a remote section of the Andes on an expedition for *National Geographic*, returned sans his customary ponytail and sporting a full beard. He looked like a younger version of Grizzly Adams, Noah had remarked upon seeing him, although Geoffrey had no idea who Grizzly Adams was. As comfortable in his own skin as he was in a pair of faded blue jeans and a cotton T-shirt, Tom's new growth had been disconcerting to all who knew him. But to Geoffrey's admiring eyes, it only added to the quiet, self-assured man's nonconformist charm.

The two men followed a worn gravel path around to the back entrance of the tavern and under the vine-covered trellis archway that separated the garden from the rear of the house. It was sunny and nearly noon. The heated summer air was still but alive with every manner of flying insect from buzzing honeybees to purple dragonflies. Geoffrey watched as a colorful monarch butterfly fluttered by, landing on a giant sunflower or *girasol*, as Luz would call it, he thought wistfully—and slowly fanned its regal wings..

"That's odd," Tom said, walking past the dilapidated tool shed. "Rudy's radio's not on."

Both men knew from frequent prior visits that the blaring, incessant drone of a WPRB talk show commentator typically took the place of a comforting friend's voice for the recluse. For a hermit like Rudy Koenig, the radio had become a stand-in for human contact and conversation. It was just one of the many quirky habits the old man had developed out of necessity over decades of living alone. The decibels of the daily broadcasts rose in response to his steadily worsening hearing.

Tom rapped his knuckles on the tattered screen door and called out to the tavern's caretaker before walking inside. "Rudy?" he repeated again, louder this time, holding back the creaking door for Geoffrey as he followed him into the kitchen. Dirty dishes lay piled up next to the spotless stainless steel sink. The fresh smell of warm toast and strong coffee lingered throughout.

"Rudy!" Tom yelled a third time as they entered the dining room that contained the celebrated tavern bar. A scrapbook lay open on the aged wooden counter, surrounded by shards of pottery and some stone fragments resting on loose, dirt-soiled newspaper pages.

Tom inspected the debris. "These look very old," he said thoughtfully, dropping a flaked stone fragment into Geoffrey's palm. It was charcoal gray and resembled a crudely beveled arrowhead, but larger, and heavier, as if it was made from granite rather than slate. "Lenape?" Geoffrey guessed.

"More like Neolithic," Tom replied with an air of curiosity and surprise.

"Stone Age tools? Here at Cedar Bridge?" questioned Geoffrey. "How can that be?"

"These old woods are full of surprises, Geoffrey … and quite a few mysteries, as you well know," Tom added, putting the stone fragment back in its place.

"Boy, don't I know it," Geoffrey acknowledged. He needed no reminder on that score. After all the heart-pounding adventures he'd been on in these woods with his sister and Danny, nothing should surprise him. The Pine Barrens were sacred to the Native Americans. He knew that much from Tom's training. And now it seemed their history reached back even farther in time to the ancestors of the Lenape, maybe even to the first humans.

"At least we know what they've been digging up outside," Geoffrey said, moving to the window. He parted the faded curtain and scanned the property.

"What were you expecting them to dig up, a body?" Tom kidded him good-naturedly.

"Frankly, human skeletal remains here wouldn't surprise me, Tom," Geoffrey replied without hesitation. "I've been reading up on the pirates who made the Pine Barrens their home. They were a blood-thirsty lot, not at all opposed to leaving a corpse or two lying around."

"Right now my only concern is finding a live person, not a corpse," said Tom, the alarm in his voice raising just a notch. "Rudy rarely leaves the premises, and he certainly wouldn't have gone far without locking up first, now that he gets a constant flow of uninvited visitors. Why don't you search the grounds, Geoffrey, while I take a gander upstairs? He may just be taking an afternoon siesta."

Geoffrey didn't need to be asked twice. He was, by schooling, a learned man of science like his father, and the concept of ghosts and similar otherworldly apparitions wasn't part of his empirical belief system, but this old place gave him the creeps just the same. In preparation for his service in the annual reenactment, he had studied up on the battle that took place here at the end of the Revolutionary War, and read of the nefarious deeds associated with the cutthroat Captain John Bacon. Spirits or no spirits, he was out the door before Tom reached the stairs.

Once outside, Geoffrey immediately felt more at ease. Rudy's magnificent garden was a magical place, a botanical wonderland, with rows and rows of all sorts of native New Jersey plants nurtured and cultivated with tender loving care. During his previous visits Rudy had shown him how to plant squash and tie up tomatoes. "God asked man to tend His garden," Rudy told him, quoting the Book of Genesis. "That's all I've done. It's been my life's work."

Following an introduction by Noah and several subsequent visits, a bond formed between Rudy and Geoffrey, not unlike the one Geoffrey had forged with Tom Banks and Noah Parsons—the ever-eager apprentice only too willing to learn. Rudy encouraged Geoffrey to pick his own produce right from the vine and eat it immediately. He enjoyed berries of all types, sweet and natural. Despite an occasional parasitic infestation, Rudy never used herbicides, which was a good thing when picking and eating crops on the spot. Luz sometimes accompanied Geoffrey on his visits to Rudy's place, where she would select fresh Jersey fruits and succulent ripe vegetables to spice up the tasty dishes she served at The Gables restaurant, where her "eat local, drink global" reputation was growing steadily.

Geoffrey went down one row of edible plants and up the next, checking for Rudy and calling out his name. When he reached the rear of the garden, he hesitated. Although the property continued on for several acres, this was as far as he had ever ventured with Rudy. It was like some kind of unseen boundary; across a narrow ravine, the property widened into an open field. About two hundred yards beyond the field, a row of tall white cedar and pine trees made a formidable wall that signaled the start of dense woodlands that seemed to roll on forever. Geoffrey spotted a boot print in the mud on the far side of the ravine. The heel was worn down on the outside edge, typical of Rudy's gait. Rudy might be in trouble. Perhaps he'd slipped and fallen and needed help. Geoffrey decided to follow the print at least as far as the tree line.

As he approached the trees, he could see a narrow path cut through the center of a thicket, wide enough for a single person to walk through. He called out Rudy's name and waited. Was that a voice he heard in response to his summons, or just his imagination? He cast a wary eye back toward the tavern to see if it might have been Tom calling out to him. Over the distance, the old building seemed like it was in another county. He decided to throw caution to the wind and stepped into the thicket.

Inside, it reminded him of Fangorn Forest from *Lord of the Rings*—mossy grass under foot, layered in places with slick, sticky leaves and crunchy, fallen branches. Sunlight slotted in through holes in the canopy of green pine needles. At any moment he half expected the old trees to come alive and speak to him, or laugh at him, like old Treebeard.

Another boot print led him further in until he came to a sudden clearing. At the end of the clearing was a stand of strange-looking, green, tree-like ferns that appeared to be trembling in the wind, beckoning him closer. *That's odd*, he thought. *When did the wind come up?*

By now his scientific curiosity had gotten the better of him. What were those swaying stalks? They were too tall and thin to be corn, too thick to be bull rushes. Were they plants or were they trees? As he drew closer, he knew. They were bamboo stalks. He was at the entrance to a tightly packed bamboo grove. What in the world was a bamboo grove doing in the middle of the Pines, he wondered. Weren't they indigenous to Asia? Then, before he knew it, he was slipping in between the stalks and into the heart of the grove.

Once inside, the breeze suddenly ceased, and the opening closed behind him. What followed was an uncanny silence. It was as if he had been swallowed up by the plants, taken prisoner and put behind spiny, stalk-like bars. Each stalk was about the diameter of a broomstick, and they grew so close together that he couldn't distinguish one from another. He could not see in, out, or around the plants.

The bamboo formed an impenetrable wall. Although it was midday, the tall, slender stalks shut out all light from the outside, yet there was a strange glow shimmering from within. Instead of the inky, black darkness he would have expected, he found himself in a green, radiant jungle. It was suffocating and liberating at the same time, totally intoxicating. If he went one way he found himself expecting to be stopped but wasn't. If he went another way, invariably it led back to the spot he'd left behind. He was in a maze and yet oddly he felt no fear of being lost. He was completely calm and at peace within the dense bamboo forest.

The plants were vibrating, resonating with life, talking to him. They were pliable and giving, so light and flexible that he felt he could pass through them rather than walk around them. He came to a sudden realization that they meant him no harm. Their nature was friendly, not frenzied or fearful. He simply needed to learn their language, to listen. That's what Tom had taught him about the woods, about nature. *Silence your mind. Listen with your heart. Listen to the sounds of nature. Hear her voice. Hear the song of the plants, the trees; listen to the spirit of the bamboo.*

He closed his eyes and let the tranquility of the sacred place pour over him like droplets of rain water, full of peace and harmony. He felt the pulse of his surroundings.

It was one with the pulse of the earth, reeling through space on its endless journey through the cosmos. He was like the bamboo, rooted here in one place, walling out indifference and fear, and at the same time bending in the wind, reaching out into space, moving through the heavens. He was alone, just one stalk, and yet he was many. He was connected to all things at that same moment, at peace with himself and one with the world.

A bony hand grabbed Geoffrey's shoulder from behind. As he spun around his eyes flew open wide, nearly popping out of their sockets from behind his thick spectacles.

"Find what you were looking for?" Rudy Koenig asked with a sly grin. Geoffrey stood mute, unable to find a voice with which to answer the wily old man. Rudy seemed amused, enjoying the young man's particular confusion.

"You're alive!" blurted Geoffrey excitedly in a voice that did not sound like his own. He grabbed hold of the old man and hugged him with all his might.

"Well, of course I'm alive, unless you plan to squeeze the life out of me."

Geoffrey released his grip. "Sorry," he said, his voice quivering, overcome with emotion. "It's just that I'm surprised to see you ... out here, I mean. I thought maybe you were hurt or lost."

"Lost? In my own backyard? Don't be silly." The old man gave him a reproachful look. "From where I stand, I don't seem to be the one who is lost."

"Right, of course this is your backyard," Geoffrey said apologetically, still reeling from the effects of the surrealistic assault on his mind and senses he'd just experienced. In his rational mind he was having trouble sorting things out and coming to terms with it all.

"Well then, lad, you're certainly welcome to stay out here and figure it all out," Rudy said, smiling warmly. "But I say it's time for lunch," he added, leading Geoffrey through the bamboo like it wasn't there and out into the clearing. "And at my age, you can't afford to miss a meal. You never know if there's gonna be another!"

Speechless, Geoffrey followed the old man, dazed and lost in his own thoughts.

9

"Welcome to Hell"

"**A**ccording to some guy named Boyd, the greatest threat to the Pinelands is 'fragmentation'—the loss of the interrelationships of the natural processes of the Pines," said Danny, flipping through his training manual. He was still pumped up at having passed the Rangers' written exam. It had worried him because of the amount of math required to answer a number of the questions. That was not his strong suit and, unlike the physical exam, which was a cakewalk for him, he barely eked by on the written part, but he did pass. "I would have guessed it was forest fires."

"Uh, huh," replied Rodney lazily, as he stretched out with his arms folded behind his head, resting against his gear in a last-ditch effort to get some added shuteye. They were on a decommissioned military troop transport with eighteen other trainees stripped to their waists in rubberized overalls, heading into the Pines to a destination as yet unknown for their first day of field training.

Danny ignored his friend's lack of enthusiasm. "Says here forest fires are pretty common in the Pines and a major cause for concern and vigilance. About fifteen hundred wildfires are set each year, requiring an army of some two thousand trained part-time firefighters. On average, nearly seven thousand acres are destroyed annually. Fires will flare up naturally when the weather has been hot and dry for an extended period of time, and the underbrush gets brittle. But ninety-nine percent are started by humans through neglect, carelessness, and arson."

Rodney stirred uneasily. He opened one eye and glared at Danny, whose face remained buried in his book.

"The Browns Mills blaze in May of this year was allegedly started by two drunks who failed to put out their campfire in Country Lakes," Danny continued aloud. "Nearly five hundred acres burned. Before that in March around the Heritage Hills section of Barnegat another five hundred and forty acres were scorched. Arson is suspected in that one. And just this past June, the Cedar Bridge fire destroyed eight hundred and ninety acres."

"All right, that's enough, Danny," shouted Rodney, sitting upright. The rest of the sleepy recruits stirred angrily from their thoughts and early morning slumber. "Give it a rest, will ya?"

"Hey, what's with you?"

"What's the book say about the Warren Grove fire in May of 2007, huh?" Rodney shot back. "Does that little book go into detail about how an F-16 military jet on maneuvers fired a flare and touched off a firestorm consuming seventeen *thousand* acres in two counties?"

Danny gave Rodney a blank stare.

"I didn't think so," said Rodney, answering the question himself. "Just another example of a government whitewash. *They* control the facts that *they* release."

Rodney folded his arms across his chest, hiding his hands in his armpits. "Enough with this fire talk. I'm starting to think this whole thing was a bad idea. "

"Something bugging you?" Danny inquired quietly.

Rodney repositioned himself closer to Danny and lowered his voice. "Playing with fire can be deadly, Danny. It's no joke. I used to be a member of the pyrotechnics crew that operated on LBI," he said evenly. "We staged Fourth of July fireworks displays all over the place. I got seriously burned in the Harvey Cedars fiasco of '98."

"I remember that one," said Danny. "The barge exploded. It rained ash and soot down on the spectators lined up along the dock and drifted as far away as Long Beach Boulevard."

"That was my swan song," said Rodney, the pain of the experience evident in his voice. "At the last minute the wind shifted and knocked over a lit canister from the rack. I grabbed for it but it fell and ignited. Suddenly it was all fire and brimstone everywhere. I landed in the bay, and I was one of the lucky ones. One guy lost an eye; another guy lost a couple of fingers; I lost hearing, but that was only temporary."

"That's a shame," Danny said with genuine concern for his friend. "I guess accidents like that are bound to happen."

Rodney exhaled heavily. "It wasn't an accident, if you ask me. Yeah, sure, the wind changed suddenly. But I had some moron working on the barge with me that night. It was his first event. That clod couldn't light a match with a blow torch. I'm sure he tipped over that canister. Or tripped over it. I didn't see it until it was too late."

"Do you remember his name?" asked Danny.

"No, but he reminds me a lot of your pal, Curtis Wicks."

Now it was Danny's turn to be indignant. "Bulldog Wicks is no friend of mine," he said, sitting up. "He tried to make a play for Kelly one time. She gave him a taste of sweet chin music he'll never forget."

"Sounds like my kind of girl." Cole grew circumspect. "So tell me, what's the story with you and Kelly?" He asked hesitantly, opening a topic he'd been thinking about a lot lately. He wasn't really sure he wanted to go down this path, but he felt the need to steer the conversation away from himself, and Danny had given him the perfect opening. "You gonna marry that girl or what?"

"I'm not sure Kelly Martin sees me as the marrying kind," answered Danny, laughing. Then he turned thoughtful. "Why the sudden interest in my love life?"

Rodney was feeling exposed and needed another quick out. He blurted out the first thing that came to his mind. "I can get you a good deal on a Cape May diamond."

The pronouncement caught Danny completely off guard. "What do I want a diamond for?"

"Not just any diamond," replied Rodney defensively. "A *Cape May* Diamond."

The look on Danny's face showed that he clearly had no idea what Rodney was talking about.

"You're kidding me, right? You mean to tell me you've never heard of Cape May diamonds?" Rodney inquired with mock surprise and obvious pleasure.

Danny shook his head. "Should I have?"

"And you call yourself a Piney!" Rodney scoffed. "Don't tell me you've never taken a girl to Sunset Beach."

"In Harvey Cedars?"

"In Cape May."

"No," Danny replied reluctantly.

"Then you and some lucky miss are in for a treat when you do go. You see, Danny, Cape May diamonds are the next best thing to real diamonds. And women love 'em."

"You mean they're fake diamonds?" asked Danny, now thoroughly confused.

"Not fake," replied Rodney without hesitation, "they're natural stones, all right … just not diamonds as you know them."

"Huh?"

"They're quartz crystals, loosened from the mountains that rim the Delaware Water Gap. The stones fall into the river. Over time, they make their way downstream and out into the bay. There they are diverted by this sunken concrete ship called the *Atlantus* that lies submerged a few hundred feet offshore, and when the tide is right they get washed ashore onto Sunset Beach."

Rodney paused and chuckled. "The *Atlantus* was towed there and intentionally sunk to break the water and protect the Cape point. But storms have pushed the ship into its current position in the shallows. Its location has been a boon for diamond hunters and beach lovers alike."

Danny found Rodney's little story interesting and was always impressed by his wealth of knowledge on a wide range of subjects. But, truthfully, all this talk about women and diamonds struck him as out of character and previously off-limits in their many conversations. "That's pretty incredible," he said a bit uneasily, wondering what Coles was up to.

"Isn't it?" Rodney exhaled in relief. "I mean it's really an unbelievable journey when you think about it. Scientists say the stones travel a distance of about two hundred miles and that it takes a thousand years to get there. That's some trip. Cleaned and polished, these gems can easily pass for the real deal to the untrained eye. And think of it—at a fraction of the price. Why, half the fun is finding that special stone for your very own special someone."

"Rodney, why are you telling me all this? Kelly would never go for a fake diamond. She's not that kind of girl. And not really *my* girl … not in the way you think, anyway."

"I was only trying to help you out, buddy," said Rodney, patting Danny on the shoulder. "I know you're a little short on cash right now."

"That's why I took this job," Danny said. "To prove that I can make something of myself."

"Yeah," laughed Rodney as the transport came to a stop. "It seems we're in a fine mess, you and me. You've got something to prove and I've got nothing to lose."

"We're here," shouted the driver from the front of the truck.

"Where's *here*?" Danny called back innocently.

"Welcome to Hell!" Rodney said with a sinister grin, grabbing his gear, pushing past Danny, and jumping off the tailgate.

10

Polaroid Prints

"**W**hat do you make of this?" Aunt Sarah asked her niece as Kelly strode through her Seaport office doorway holding two Styrofoam cups of coffee in her outstretched hands. "I found it in a sealed manila envelope shoved under my door when I came in this morning."

Kelly handed her aunt one of the steaming cups and, careful not to spill a drop, placed the other down on the only clear spot on a corner of her Sarah's disorderly desk. She wiped her hands on her jeans before taking the picture from her aunt.

Her brow furrowed as she studied the blurry 3-1/2" x 4-1/2" photograph and saw what appeared to be a tarnished bronze lantern propped up on the floor of an old wooden shed. Neatly stacked panes of beveled, smoke-stained amber glass lay on either side of the decorative lamp. Aunt Sarah sipped her coffee slowly and waited for her niece's reaction.

Kelly removed the news article clipped to the photograph. She flipped the picture over. Scrawled in smudged lead pencil was an address: *20 W. Singleton Lane, Little Egg Harbor.* Kelly looked at her aunt then back at the picture. "Read the clipping," Aunt Sarah suggested, raising her eyebrows and nodding her head slowly.

Kelly laid the photograph next to her coffee cup. Squinting at the small font, she saw the clipping was an advertisement from the Personals section of this week's *SandPaper* and read aloud. *Reward: $500 for any information leading to the whereabouts of the lost Tucker's Island Light. Contact: Friends of Tucker's Lighthouse: Carole Bradshaw, Adele Willoughby and Sarah Bishop-Parsons, Acting Director of the Tuckerton Seaport Museum.* Phone numbers and email addresses were provided for each name.

"Adele insisted my name be included," said Aunt Sarah, striking a slightly defensive note. "Noah wasn't keen on the idea, but Carole and Adele both thought that adding the name of the Tuckerton Museum Director to the contact list—even if it's just a temporary position—would lend the notice an air of legitimacy. I've never felt comfortable stepping into Libby's shoes, but Noah was able to persuade me and convince the Seaport Board that my background as a high school history teacher and gift shop owner somehow qualified me as a specialist in antiques."

Kelly chuckled at her aunt's self-deprecating nature, knowing all too well it was sincere. She was acutely aware of Sarah's modesty after having spent so much time with her in recent summers. "Where did you get the money for a reward?" she inquired curiously.

"It's from the funds the ladies have been collecting for the cause." Aunt Sarah grew pensive as she turned to gaze out the office window. "Kelly, do you think this might have anything to do with that mysterious phone call you got at the shop the other night?"

"I don't know," replied Kelly. "I couldn't get anything out of the man. He insisted on speaking with you, and you only."

"Very curious," mused Aunt Sarah, retrieving the photo and turning it over in her hand repeatedly before setting it back on the desk.

"What is?" questioned Kelly, sitting down and taking hold of her coffee cup.

"The photograph. It's a Polaroid."

Kelly made a strange face, indicating that she didn't understand. "What's that mean?"

"It means it's either intentionally low-tech or it's old. They don't make Polaroid cameras any more." Sarah twirled her hair between her fingers as she contemplated her own words.

"Is that why the picture is so blurred looking? Because it's old?'

"Possibly." Sarah frowned as she picked up the photo and clipping once more. "Polaroid prints were meant to provide instant snapshots. That was before the age of digital cameras and cell phone photography."

"Okay, but what about the address? Why isn't there a name or telephone number included?"

"I don't know. But I do know where West Singleton Lane is." Sarah picked up the office phone and started dialing. "That's in Mystic Island, not far from here."

Kelly sipped her coffee pensively. "Who are you calling?"

"Adele Willoughby. She has a brother who lives on West Thames, one street over from Singleton—just across the lagoon." After a moment, she slammed the phone back into the cradle. "Darn, it's busy."

"Sheesh, you're surprised?" goaded Kelly. "There's three ways to get news on the Island—telephone, television, and tell Adele," she laughed.

"Kelly, may I borrow your car?" asked Sarah, ignoring the quip. "I've got to check this out before Adele gets wind of it."

"Oh, no," groaned Kelly, setting down her cup.

"It should take me a half-hour, tops," said Sarah, grabbing her purse. "I'll be back before the Seaport opens."

Kelly tossed her aunt the car keys. "What should I do if someone comes in while you're gone?"

"Just pretend you're busy," replied Sarah, exiting through the door. "It always works for me."

11

Double Trouble

"Hell," much to Danny Windsor's relief, turned out to be more like a slice of paradise just off Exit 77 of the Garden State Parkway, having the colorful moniker Double Trouble State Park. The two-hundred-acre partially restored lumber and cranberry village located in Berkeley Township forms part of a larger eight-thousand-acre wildlife preserve. Local legends suggest several accounts leading to the area's lighthearted name, with the most likely dating back to the 1770s and credited to a man named Thomas Potter. Potter allegedly coined the phrase when heavy rains damaged an earthen mill pond dam twice in one season. Perhaps in a twist of that twice-told tale, a late nineteenth-century newspaper attributed the name to the washout of the old dam and the simultaneous destruction of the operating sawmill. Regardless of its origins, Danny, having prepared himself for the worst, was overjoyed to see trappings of civilization, however rustic and unattended, as he jumped off the back of the troop transport.

"Settle down, everyone," bellowed an amiable, portly black man whom Danny recognized from their examination proceedings as the veteran fire spotter Bill Hogan. "Let me have your attention, please."

A tall, helmeted figure with a hawkish nose and deep-set dark eyes quietly joined Bill as the disorderly recruits assembled lazily in front of them. Harris proudly introduced Park Ranger Chief Roger Kincaid to the group. Although he had a commanding presence, several of the sleepy men stood before him yawning and stretching, still trying to shake free from the effects of their early, pre-dawn rise. Nevertheless, the no-nonsense chief pressed on with the agenda.

"All right, kiddies, I'm only going to say this once, so listen up," barked Kincaid. "Until your training is completed, you are here as guests of the Division of Parks and Forestry. So keep your noses clean and stay out of trouble." The mention of the word "trouble" garnered a few chuckles from those awake enough to be aware of the campsite's name.

"And those of you who think this week will be nothing but fun and games better think twice." Again sporadic chuckles rippled through the ranks as Kincaid's play on words, whether intentional or not, resonated with several of them, including Danny Windsor and Rodney Coles.

"In addition to your firefighting and forestry skills training, you'll be asked to earn your keep. First up, you'll clean out the bunkhouse, the bathhouse, and the outhouse before you get to use them, since they've been shut up for quite some time. You can stow your gear in the packinghouse until the camp is made ready." On cue, Bill handed each recruit a hand-drawn map of the village and the surrounding grounds with the various buildings, nature trails, and cranberry bogs labeled for identification purposes. Like a carelessly untied ribbon, the aptly named Cedar Creek threaded through the village's western perimeter.

"You'll work in teams," said Kincaid, dividing the trainees into three groups of six, leaving the only two women in the group temporarily unassigned. He handed one member of each six-man team a placard with a design stenciled on it: a bed for the bunkhouse, a shower stall for the bathhouse, and a commode for the outhouse. When Danny's group got handed the latrine duty card, Rodney jumped lines, shoving a smaller, slightly dazed recruit into his place when Kincaid wasn't looking.

"Any questions?" Kincaid shouted.

"Yeah, when do we eat?" Rodney piped up with a snicker.

Bill gave the Chief a sly wink. "Right after you and Windsor clean out the Cook's House and scramble us all up some eggs," he deadpanned, shuffling the two women—a heavyset, boyish blonde named Heidi and a pretzel-thin brunette with a pixie haircut and pencil-thin nose named Roxanne—into their respective places in line. The Park Ranger grinned at the exchange.

Following that inauspicious start, the rest of the morning was spent tidying up the sprawling campsite and getting familiar with the accommodations. In the afternoon, the recruits were treated to an array of outdoor nature talks and other lessons beginning with Tree and Plant Identification 101, in which they learned to spot various friendly or medicinal plants such as mountain laurel, Virginia creeper, and sassafras, and to avoid plants like catbriar and poison ivy. Getting familiar with the primary tree classifications of the Pinelands was also essential to their training. In these sessions they learned about the growth habits and uses of red maples, gray birch, scrub oaks, and Atlantic white cedars. Their instruction also included a class to help them distinguish tree types from among the various evergreens such as Virginia pines, pitch pines, and dwarf pines.

The first day's training concluded with a crash course on a new menace that had recently started to ravage the fabled South Jersey forests: the tiny southern pine beetle. These tree chewing insects are attracted to stressed trees, forests, and ecosystems already troubled by years of over-development, pollution, fragmentation, foreign bugs, plants and pathogens, or healthy trees weakened by drought or extremely wet conditions. Boring deep to lay their eggs, these tiny creatures can kill a tree in a matter of three to four weeks, leaving a significant fire hazard in their wake. They also carry a blue stain fungus which clogs the vascular system of a pine tree. The killer fungus acts in concert with the beetle, suppressing the pitch or sticky sap a pine tree naturally emits to thwart an insect assault. Recently it was discovered that the beetles outnumbered their predators and, without the use of pesticides to control these little devils, forest fires may become more prevalent. That wasn't exactly what the green recruits wanted to hear.

After a long and exhausting day, Danny was mighty glad to hit the rack. He had calluses on his hands from gripping a broom and sweeping away years of dust, cobwebs, and dirt that had accumulated in the unused minor buildings of the dormant village. Begun in the 1700s and operating into the early 1900s, the town had long since passed its prime. In its heyday, Double Trouble Village harnessed hydroelectric power from the surrounding Cedar Creek watershed to power a sawmill used exclusively to turn the area's abundant Atlantic white cedar into lumber. Cedar wood made excellent decking, roofing, siding, and furniture.

As the timber gradually disappeared, vast swaths of land opened up. Sinking down into the marshy soil, these bogs were quickly populated by indigenous plants. One of these was then known as the "craneberry" due to the crane-like appearance of the mature red fruit when it dangled from the vine, similar to the bird's long neck. In a bit of irony, cranberry harvesting soon replaced lumbering as the dominant business at Double Trouble Village, and migrant workers replaced skilled lumberjacks and millers as water needed for the hydroelectric power to run the mill was dammed and redirected for the annual flooding of the several burgeoning cranberry bogs.

The old sawmill and packing plant were still open for tours, but by the time Danny and the forest ranger trainees arrived, the rest of the village, including the one room schoolhouse, general store, and power plant had fallen into disuse. It was Chief Kincaid's bright idea to use the village and surrounding grounds as a staging area for forestry training while at the same time tapping the manpower to help restore the unused buildings. "A two-fer," Kincaid called his strategy for maximizing state funds in a struggling fiscal year.

"I think the two girls are into me," Rodney whispered as Danny undressed in the darkness and slipped into his sleeping bag on the bunkhouse floor.

"Is that why you were hanging around while they showered today?" Danny smirked. "Gee, and I thought you just wanted to borrow their shampoo."

"Don't give me that crap, dude, I saw the way you were checking out the skinny one."

"I couldn't help it. She reminds me of Tinkerbell with that short haircut and pointy nose. I can't see her blowing out her own birthday candles, let alone putting out a forest fire. "

"I tell you there is something exciting about them," replied Rodney, getting to his feet. He was still fully clothed. "Did you notice how they do everything together?"

"Duh, maybe that's because they're the only two women within twenty miles of Fort Blister here?" said Danny, yawning drowsily into his puffy palms.

"Well, I don't know about you, but I'm going to see if they want company," said Rodney, slinking off into the night.

"Knock yourself out," muttered Danny, closing his eyes contentedly.

***

As the first rays of new light were just beginning to stream through the open windows into the dusty room full of slumbering men and their cacophonous snoring, when Rodney crept back into the bunkhouse. Awakened by the sudden commotion, Danny opened one eye grudgingly. Rodney plopped down crossed-legged in front of Danny. Fatigue showed in his tired movements but his face was aglow.

"They were *amazing*," he said, continuing the conversation where they had left off hours earlier. "Heidi and Roxanne are my kind of girls!"

"Whoopee," exclaimed Danny sarcastically, idly rolling onto his side.

"I was certainly right about them," Rodney added, shedding his clothes and slipping into his bedroll.

"How's that?" asked Danny, half listening.

"They do everything together. And I do mean *everything*!"

12

Un-Dress Rehearsal

"**I** just *love* a man in uniform," said Luz, poking her head in the doorway of Geoffrey's bedroom.

Geoffrey stopped preening himself in the mirror and turned to face her. He was dressed in the crisply tailored uniform of a Continental soldier: dark blue topcoat trimmed in crimson at the collar and sleeves, with a matching lining, sporting a row of aged brass buttons. Creamy white woolen breeches with white cotton leggings and highly polished black boots completed his attire.

"No one was downstairs in the shop, so I just thought I'd wander up here and see where everyone was," said Luz with a mischievous smile. She stepped inside the room and tossed a rolled up magazine onto the unmade bed.

Geoffrey blushed scarlet, matching the trim of his coat. He felt dumb. Not because of the uniform he was wearing. It made him look good and feel important, and he was certainly glad that Luz had taken notice. But she had startled him, catching him off guard while he was admiring himself in the mirror.

He smiled awkwardly. "Kelly drove Aunt Sarah to the office this morning," he offered sheepishly, still feeling a little foolish. This wasn't the first time he and Luz were up in his bedroom together. But suddenly it was the only time he could remember that they were so completely alone.

Luz smiled knowingly and stepped toward him. She lifted the black felt tri-corner hat from the bedpost and set it atop his head playfully.

Geoffrey rolled his eyes upward, looking at the angled brim of the hat. Suddenly, Luz's lips were pressed against his, kissing him lightly, tenderly. The sweet scent of her delicate perfume swept through his open nostrils like the mist after a morning rain. She smelled exquisitely of jasmine and lilac, and her wet, moist lips tasted like heaven. She stopped abruptly and took a step back.

All of Geoffrey's senses burst wide open. Having been anesthetized by her intoxicating scent, his eyes finally saw what his mind had failed to take in when she first stood in the doorway. Only now was he fully aware of what she was wearing and the immediate effect of her thin fuchsia halter top stretched against her dark, tanned skin, and her short, tight white skirt, which accentuated the smooth, bronze flesh of her toned, shapely legs.

Luz felt no compulsion to reign in her own long-pent-up urgings. She reached up and removed Geoffrey's glasses, folding the arms gingerly and setting them down on the nightstand. Before he was even aware of her calculated movements, Luz had removed his hat and coat, laying them carefully across the only chair in his cramped and cluttered room.

Geoffrey felt no inclination to resist, nor did he. In a strange way he felt like he wasn't even there; it was almost as if he was watching a movie. Luz seized the moment and stepped forward, pressing the full length of her body against his. Groping and pawing at each other wildly, they fell together onto the untidy bed and scrambled to get under the covers.

13

Return of the Mooncusser

The gaunt, arthritic, foul-mouthed, foul-smelling sixty-something ex-convict who waited for Sarah Parsons at 20 West Singleton Lane in Little Egg Harbor was the antithesis of Rudy Koenig. No one could pinpoint the precise moment when he crossed the line from being someone who displayed "deviant behavioral tendencies" to someone who was certifiably, pathologically evil. And it didn't matter to him.

Surely if analyzed by any credible professional he would be classified as criminally insane. Nothing would have pleased him more than being labeled *anything* unacceptable by a society to which he was a social outcast most of his life. But it didn't start out that way.

He was born on VE Day, May 8, 1945, one of seven siblings belonging to Abner and Eliza of New Gretna, New Jersey. His father was the pastor of the town's small Episcopal church, whose tight-knit congregation consisted mostly of old seafaring families having unbroken ties to the area and roots in the church dating back to the Revolutionary War.

In fact, the Episcopal Church was organized shortly after the American Revolution, when the church was forced to separate from the Church of England. Because Anglican clergy were required to swear allegiance to the British monarchy, the War for Independence split apart the members of the Church of England in America. Patriots saw the Church of England as synonymous with "Tory" and "redcoat" because it embraced symbols of the unwanted British presence, including both the Cross of Saint George and the Cross of Saint Andrew on its coat of arms. Recent historians have estimated that nearly eighty percent of the Church of England clergy in the northeastern colonies were diehard Loyalists. Is it any wonder, then, that during the height of the Second World War it was often said that his father, the pastor, found serving the Lord conveniently rewarding since it enabled him to avoid serving his country?

Biting remarks such as these stung an impressionable young man deeply as he was growing up—apparently more so than they did his brothers and sisters. It didn't help that his father chose never to deny the accusations or that he sometimes praised the exploits of Loyalists like Captain John Bacon during his Sunday sermons.

Nonetheless, early life was idyllic for this son of a preacher, and why not? His playground was Great Bay and all that it offered—swimming, boating, fishing, crabbing, and more. His earliest dream was to become a pirate like Bacon, perhaps owing to a natural desire for more of his father's attention in such a large family. Of course, since that was not possible in post-war America—or so he thought at the time—treasure hunting seemed the next best thing.

At the age of eight, he would run down to the docks after school and wait for the fishermen to come in with the day's catch. For a penny a load, he would help them haul their fish ashore, clean them, pack them in ice, and get them ready for market. All the while he would listen to their tall tales and wild stories of the sea.

By the time he was twelve, he had become quite proficient with a fillet knife, wielding it as a surgeon would a scalpel, and he could tie a bowman's knot as good as that of any experienced seaman. At fourteen, while other kids were doing homework, he was working as a first mate on an all-night tuna charter called the Blue Fin, where he was often called upon to pilot the boat back to port when the captain got too drunk to hold the wheel.

When he turned sixteen, the pastor's son began working at a fish factory to earn enough money to buy his own boat. That's when fate stepped in and changed his plans. His father passed away, leaving his mother to care for the children alone, with nothing but a pile of debt to show for her long hard years of laboring beside him. The pastor's wife, however, had no intention of holding the family together, because in reality they were not a family at all. Absent the stern hold of her husband, the long-held "family" secrets all tumbled out.

Eliza had agreed to marry Abner in order to help him win over the parish vestry and get him elected to serve as rector of the New Gretna Episcopal Church. She was sixteen and he was twenty-one. Although he had been a priest for only a very short time, the vestry or bishop's committee knew Abner to be a young man of promise. His zeal from the pulpit was earning him a reputation as a man of influence and action. His charm and charisma were as magnetic as his ambition was large, but he was young. By marrying and starting a family, he would prove to the bishops that he could provide for those he loved and was therefore ready and able to provide for his church family as well. At the time, the small church was in a bind. Their latest pastor, proving to be weak of faith, had run off to Arizona with a deacon's daughter. Thus the timing was right for Abner, and, following a brief courtship and hurried wedding ceremony, he was married one day and elected church rector the next.

When children didn't start flowing from Eliza's womb like honey from a jug, rumors began to circulate that Abner was incapable of fathering a child. Believing that in the eyes of his congregation a man unable to father a child was a priest incapable of presiding over his flock, the audacious young rector conspired with his wife on a secret plan. Eliza would fake her pregnancies and they would adopt newborns from out-of-town orphanages. And not one, not two, but seven—the holy number in the Bible. The charade worked and life went on. Eventually Eliza grew unhappy with the life she had saddled herself with, and from the moment he realized his wife could not conceive, Abner treated Eliza differently, coldly and cruelly. All of this was kept from the children, their relatives, neighbors, and friends, lest they reveal the truth and topple the pastor from his vaunted position.

When her cruel master died, Eliza could not hold it all inside any longer. The shame and guilt had worn her down, making her physically ill, until finally she unburdened her conscience and let it all out.

Not surprisingly, what she had to say did not sit well with the community. The children were, of course, crushed. The pastor's son, who now waited in Little Egg

Harbor, was particularly devastated to learn he was adopted because he had also thought himself related to the last lighthouse keeper of Tucker's Island who shared his surname. Distraught, he changed the spelling of his first name to distance himself from another falsehood his parents had perpetrated.

Eliza had always felt the children should be told the truth. Abner did not agree. When he passed away that obstacle was removed. The children were old enough, she thought, but she was not prepared for the backlash. The scorn of her neighbors and friends and the hatred of the children she had raised were too much for her to bear.

He vowed never to see his mother again. And he didn't. He also lost touch with his brothers and sisters. Shame and embarrassment scattered them to the four corners. For his part, he quit school and moved to Tuckerton to work full time at the fish factory on Crab Island, one of seven islands jutting into Great Bay—one for each of the pastor's separated children, he often mused—and slowly tried to rebuild his life.

With that sad stage of his life behind him, he was ready to start over and strike out on his own, alone. But he did not fare much better in this new phase of his life. By the time he was twenty years of age, the menhaden fish factory, the last of four that had operated on the sod banks of Little Egg Harbor since the late 1800s, was in sharp decline.

Menhaden, or moss bunker as it was sometimes called, was an oily fish, far too oily for American tastes, but not for Russian palettes, to whom the product was largely sold. Closer to home, the fish oil had for generations been used in oil lamps, especially when whale oil became scarce and before the advent of electricity. After the oil was squeezed from the fish flesh, the carcass was left to dry in the sun, and a second product was produced—fertilizer. The residue made excellent compost, but the smell was horrendous. When in 1965 the factory burned to the ground, all that remained were the rusting twisted steel girders that formed the skeletal framework of the processing plant and the stench. To this day, locals refer to the lifeless scab of sand as Stink Island.

With the demise of the fish factory, he found himself out of work and on the street. Over the next forty years, he eked out a living doing whatever he had to do to make a buck, when it meant turning to petty crime to make ends meet. Harkening back to his childhood days of pirate dreams, he relied on his wiles and embraced Captain John Bacon and the mooncussers as his role models.

All of these thoughts ran through his mind as he waited, alone in the darkness of the vacant rancher at 20 West Singleton Lane. The past was past. What mattered now was the present, and that meant getting what he could out of the stupidity of others. It was a gift he had, and right now his eyes were set on a big prize.

He watched covertly from behind the faded, dusty Venetian blinds as a late-model black and gray Mini Cooper pulled up to the curb in front of the house. It was a car he did not recognize, but there was no mistaking the well groomed middle-aged businesswoman who got out of it. He smiled inwardly, taking notice that she was alone.

He knew Libby Ashcroft's replacement well—had, in fact, been stalking her—and, although she didn't know it, he was the "ghost" that walked the floors above her, haunting her evenings whenever she worked alone in her office at the Seaport after hours. He'd been living there for weeks, relying on an old superstition that kept the curious at bay and away from discovering his hideout. It was a far cry from the ten-by-ten prison cell in Rahway he had become accustomed to, though not by choice. His incarceration had been the result of an unfortunate run-in several years ago with this woman's teenage relatives and a misunderstanding they had had over an old medallion and a set of worthless maps.

So, now the trap was set. The fly was coming to the spider. Soon she would be ensnared in his web. The elation was coursing through his whole body and difficult to keep in check. She had taken the bait. The photograph he had slipped under her door was the lure, a lure too good to be true. And it was. For the dismantled Fresnel lens pictured in the Polaroid was not the one she sought—the one from the fabled Tucker's Island Lighthouse—but rather the disassembled Barnegat Light *sister* lens that lay in the attic of the Barnegat Light Museum. From such a poor photo, even an expert would have had difficulty telling the difference between the two lenses.

What would he do if she didn't bring the money with her, the $500 bounty posted for information leading to the whereabouts of the "lost" Tucker's Island Light? His mind raced, considering the possibilities now. That was a mere tease. What he was really after was the tidy sum he would get for the ransom of Noah Parsons's wife.

She was coming up the the steps now. The "booty" was almost within his grasp. As she knocked on the door, to focus on the task ahead of him he let his mind drift back to Abner and Eliza. What would his evangelical father say if he could see his adopted "son" now? Instinctively, he recalled a story from scripture his father was fond of reading aloud after the family meal. It was the story of the infant Moses, placed in a reed basket by his mother in order to protect him from the Pharaoh's decree to slaughter all first-born non-Egyptian males, only to have him float down the Nile and into the loving arms of the Pharaoh's barren sister, who in turn raised him as her own. A perverse joke creeped into his sinister mind, that he and Moses were not all that different. He laughed to himself. Ryder Hayes and Moses were both basket cases.

14
Trouble in Paradise

Sitting behind Aunt Sarah's big desk at the Seaport, Kelly was just about to launch an investigation via Google, Facebook, Bing, and whatever else it might take to connect with what she was sure was a vibrant young business community, when she spotted the sculpture that had launched her aunt's little enterprise in the first place. Evidently, Aunt Sarah had decided the keepsake needed a new home, or maybe she simply felt she needed it with her as a daily reminder of how she came to be where she was. As Kelly picked up the dolphins and held them in her hands, her thoughts turned to crazy, romantic notions and the one boy who just might be able to help her find the same kind of love and determination that her aunt had found in life. As difficult as their past had been, she felt fairly certain it was meant to make them stronger.

The morning may have started out with a faded Polaroid, but the bigger picture was getting clearer for Kelly every day, and it was built upon a series of memories shared with Danny that she wouldn't have traded for anything.

Despite her interest in politics and the study of international law, she could actually see herself in a commercial endeavor one day—maybe even running a small shop like Crab Cove, or something more practical, like an athletic apparel store on LBI. Purpose was needed, not porpoises, she reminded herself with a laugh and realized how nice it would be to have someone to share it with. Someone to come home to and grow old with. Someone like Danny Windsor. Was that out of the question?

With this thought in mind, Kelly felt the need to check her cell phone. It had been nearly a week, why hadn't he called or texted or tweeted? They were both upset when he left the day following the Longboard Classic, perhaps she more than he. It didn't stop him from going out with Rodney Coles and celebrating the night before. *It's all Rodney's fault*, she thought, and the thought of the man sent a shiver up her back. He was so full of himself. Hadn't Danny noticed how his friend had been coming on to her lately, how every time she was in their company he would undress her with his eyes? It was humiliating. She tried to avoid him whenever possible and couldn't stand to be alone with him. But obviously Danny took no notice. And why should he? Rodney had two faces. He was like a two-sided coin. Was it just coincidence that on the morning of the Longboard Classic he was the one who told her of their sudden Forest Service plans? Was he really trying to help Danny find himself, or was he purposely trying to keep them separated?

Nothing, she sighed as she checked her messages and missed calls. And then suddenly, mysteriously, an eerie sensation swept over her. She knew something was wrong. She didn't know how she knew it, but Danny was in trouble.

She glanced at the time illuminated on her cell phone. Aunt Sarah should have been back by now. She scrolled the phone directory until she came to the first S and clicked "send." After ten rings, the call went to voice mail. "Something's not right," she said aloud.

***

As Danny expected, Rodney was a no-show for breakfast. Not surprisingly, so were Heidi and Roxanne. Try as he might, Danny could not rouse Rodney from his lingering slumber. Following his late night frolics with what Danny thought of as the female equivalent of Laurel and Hardy, he couldn't blame him. Despite his prodding, Rodney just rolled over and tuned Danny out. "I'll catch up with you later," he said, his voice muffled by the pillow over his head. So Danny took his bowl of corn flakes and his cup of coffee and ate breakfast alone on the rear porch of the old packing plant that overlooked the presently dry Gowdy Cranberry Bog. The morning sun was just beginning to peek over the tall pines, and the view was absolutely breathtaking.

It wasn't that Danny was purposefully trying to be antisocial. He could never be accused of that. In fact, he made friends easily, had even been able to draw surly, superior Rodney Coles into some moments of camaraderie with the other trainees.

But right now Danny wanted a little quiet time so he could make that long overdue phone call to Kelly. He felt badly about having left without a proper goodbye, and he also felt guilty that she had learned about his signup with the Forestry Service from Rodney, rather than directly from him. The realization surprised him, but after less than a week away, he could honestly say he missed her—her sunny smile, her easy laughter, and how effortless he found it to be around her. In Kelly's company, he never felt the need to be someone else; he could even be himself when she disagreed with him or with the hare-brained things he sometimes did.

The fact that she didn't care for Rodney was pretty obvious. Although he wasn't sure why, in the weeks following the whole beach-closing bomb scare in Surf City, he could sense her opinion of the big man plummeting from the warm glow of their affiliation with the SurfDogs to something more akin to icy Arctic waters. At the same time, Danny had sensed a shift in Rodney's appreciation of Kelly's virtues, but in the opposite direction. Go figure. Perhaps it was all just a figment of his overblown imagination, which, out in these woods, was gradually growing more outrageous every day. He tried her cell number again. Evidently the satellite system was unable to pick up and hold a signal because his calls were repeatedly dropped each time without making a connection.

Not having expected to be near anything that remotely qualified as civilization, Danny had hadn't bothered to pack his cell phone charger with him or his laptop. Technology was lost on him. Kelly and Geoffrey couldn't even convince him to friend them on Facebook. Unwilling to waste his dwindling battery life on further futile attempts to assuage his guilt, he powered down his phone and stuffed it back in his pocket.

A big black crow perched low in a nearby tree limb let out a condescending caw. "My sentiments exactly," Danny said to the bird.

"Women," he sighed. "Any pearls of wisdom you can share on that subject would be greatly appreciated." As he shook of his head, the bird cawed again, as if in response, then took flight.

It was not until the trainees were about halfway through their five-mile endurance run that Rodney finally caught up with Danny. The group had to pull off the trail to let a team of huskies from the Jersey Sands Sled Dog Racing Association and their driver pass coming from the other direction. Before Heidi and Roxanne could reach out to pet the dogs, Bill Hogan sternly cautioned the recruits against it. "These are racing dogs," he bellowed. "Not pets!"

"About time," said Danny as Rodney pulled up alongside him and exhaled deeply. He was sweating profusely, but it did not hide the devilish smirk he wore on his face, just daring Danny to inquire. "Well, I hope it was worth it. You're gonna pay at the end of this run for missing breakfast."

Rodney didn't answer. He was bent over, gulping down air and straining to listen to the conversation between Kincaid and the female sled driver. "That's the Chief's wife, Muriel," Bill whispered, trying not to appear too obvious. "She's training for the upcoming race. Normally, they train in the Byrne State Forest, but the Chief arranged for her to run the dogs here. There's no waiting in line on these trails."

"Rank has its privilege," Rodney gasped. "I learned that a long time ago."

Danny was impressed by the eight-dog team with their thick white, gray, and tan coats, white bellies, and black noses. All of them had the same general build, standing about two feet tall and weighing maybe forty to fifty pounds. "Are they Siberian huskies?" he asked.

"Yes, they are," Bill said. "The same breed that runs the Iditarod, in Alaska."

Rodney arched his back upright and gave Bill a questioning glance.

"Hey, you can learn a lot from sharing a bottle of hooch with the boss out here in the woods," Bill responded to Rodney's glance, explaining his unusual knowledge of dog sled racing in the Jersey Pines. "Huskies were bred centuries ago by the Chukchi, an Indian tribe from Siberia, and brought to Alaska in 1908 for sport. They're known for their powerful legs and incredible endurance."

Danny couldn't help but notice that the harnessed dogs stood by quietly as their master chatted with her husband. Some of the dogs let out an occasional low howl, sort of a guttural moaning *woo-woo* sound, but none barked. The eyes of each dog were either blue or brown, except one. Positioned at the head of the team, he had one blue and one brown eye. *The David Bowie of huskies*, thought Danny with an inward chuckle as the finely-tuned animal stared back at him and sniffed about as if trying to discern his scent.

"That's the leader, Chance," said Harris following Danny's gaze. "The dogs train, race and run as a unit in partnership with the driver. If the sled driver doesn't earn the team's trust, the dogs will elect one of their own to lead. When that happens, the team devolves into a pack. Lucky for us, Muriel has their respect and keeps them under her control at all times."

As Danny stood admiring the playfulness among the queued dogs, he noticed Chief Kincaid out of the corner of his eye, a cell phone to his ear. The call was brief. Slipping the phone back into his belt holder, he said something to his wife in a low, hushed tone. Immediately, she and the dogs moved out in a hurry. As they passed, Kincaid beckoned to Bill Hogan.

"Uh, oh," Bill muttered, recognizing the urgency in the fire chief's gesture. "This can't be good."

***

While Geoffrey was lying in bed, looking up at the ceiling with a satisfied grin on his face, Luz slipped out from under the balled-up sheets, stark naked, and bent down to pick up the magazine she had brought to show him.

"Just so you know, I didn't come here with the intention of seducing you, Geoffrey," she said, holding up the latest edition of *Edible New Jersey*. He blinked twice, and she retrieved his thick wire-rimmed glasses from the floor and put them on her own face. "How do you see *anything* with these?" she said, looking around the room.

"Oh, I can see just fine, thank you," he replied, feeling a new and exciting urge as he took in the sight of at the lovely nude Luz Sanchez leaning over him.

Luz blushed and hurriedly wrapped a sheet around her body. She sat down beside Geoffrey, handing him his glasses and the magazine.

"What's this?" he asked.

"Edible New Jersey published my Thai Surprise recipe," she said, proudly pointing to the page. "The Gables is going to feature the dish on the menu next week."

Geoffrey scanned the recipe and the accompanying article quickly. "What's the surprise?" he inquired with genuine curiosity.

"The Asian grouper is sautéed with fresh local cranberries and stuffed with tender bamboo shoots," she half-shouted in her exuberance.

At the mention of the word "bamboo" Geoffrey's mind was suddenly transported back to his recent experience in the magical grove behind Cedar Bridge Tavern.

"Oh, shit," he announced, throwing off the sheets and jumping out of bed, buck naked. "We've got to hurry or I'm going to miss the reenactment."

"Hold your horses, soldier," she giggled. "We've still got time, and I just might want to surrender again."

15

Burning Desire

If I can't have her, no one will.

Some people can't take no for an answer, and eventually their past catches up with them. While Rodney Coles, Danny Windsor, and their fellow trainees were learning how to face the frightening reality of forest fires, one of them was thinking about an event that had taken place years ago and far away and shaped his life forever.

The wedding was set for the next day, Sunday, at a lovely, rustic banquet hall, hand-picked by the bride for its décor and out-of-the-way location. The place had a long and checkered past. Secluded deep in the woods just outside the sleepy village of Pleasant Mills on the navigable waters of the Mullica River, Sweetwater Casino had gotten its name during Prohibition, earning a reputation as a first-rate speakeasy and gambling joint. With a dock adjacent to the restaurant, the location was ideal for loading and unloading contraband liquor bound for Atlantic City to the east and Philadelphia to the west. Sweetwater, as its name implied, was a tasty and convenient watering hole situated safely between the two—a quiet place where rumrunners could mingle with locals without fear of the long arm of the law.

He knew the place well. He'd been working there as a cook for just over a year while trying to figure out what he wanted to do with the rest of his life. That's where they met. She was the rhinestone-studded singer and occasional fiddle player in a hot country band that had a regular gig at the restaurant on steamy Saturday nights during that fateful summer. During breaks from his kitchen duties, he would watch her onstage with her band. Standing there in the back, under the dim house lights, leaning up against the wall with his hands stuffed deep into his pockets, he would listen closely and watch intently as she shook the tousled, shoulder-length brown hair that framed her glistening almond-colored eyes while she poured her heart out in song.

He noticed how those eyes would moisten whenever she sang the Willie Nelson standard, "You Were Always on My Mind," and the way they widened wickedly when she belted out the Linda Ronstadt favorite, "When Will I Be Loved," and when she fiddled and danced her way through Charlie Daniels's "The Devil Went Down to Georgia." He saw it all … and wanted her all for himself.

Night after night, he would watch her from the shadows, and afterward when she would eat with the owners, he would serve her meal and accept her compliments graciously. And then it happened, late one night. The band was still packing up and the owners were off somewhere else. She was alone and invited him to join her. Grimy apron and greasy hair, he sat with her reluctantly. They talked hesitantly. Hers was a casual manner, all sweetness and smiles, coming from someone who enjoys every moment a charmed life has to offer. His demeanor was dark and brooding at first, curt and unrefined, but she persevered. They talked about the meaning of life and music. Not that he was an expert, but he knew what he liked. And he liked everything she did.

Eventually, he let the barriers come down. They had been built high and solid to wall off a hellish childhood and an aimless, nomadic life, thanks to the distant love of an alcoholic mother and the misplaced ambitions of a career military father—ambitions he had tried and failed to emulate; a medical discharge for schizophrenia had not made his life any easier.

The cook and the country singer found their common ground in music. He was a big fan, not merely a casual listener. He knew all the tunes. Music of all kinds became joyful, inspirational, and he was obsessed with it. It made him hopeful and kept the flame alive that someday he might find and follow his own dream and that an unguarded moment, he told her he was still searching for a dream, and that in her eyes and her voice he had found new hope and vision. She laughed at his foolishness and his painful honesty, yet was both flattered and impressed with his musical knowledge. That was the sweetest thing she'd ever heard, she said, trying to ease the sting of her initial reaction.

She told him she was dating the lead guitar player. It was not a serious relationship, she assured him. An obstacle, but not an insurmountable one, he deluded himself into thinking. And so, there in the dining hall, amid the leafy, snake-like grapevine wallpaper and the miniature white lights that always made it feel like Christmas, even in July, he fell madly in love with her.

But he was alone in his feelings, leading to a grievous mistake with enormous consequences. He was hopelessly smitten and had gone so far as to buy her a cheap diamond engagement ring, one he could afford on his meager cook's wages until he could save up for a better one. A real one.

That was before he found out she was playing both him and the fair-haired guitarist for fools. Her true main squeeze turned out to be the spoiled son of an Atlantic City circuit court judge. While cooling the guitarist's ardor and igniting the kitchen help's lust, the hot-to-trot fiddle-playing mama spent her extracurricular time cruising the inter-coastal between gigs with her latest flame on his daddy's big yacht.

It was only when the new couple suddenly announced their wedding plans that the cook was mortally crushed and became wildly enraged. Now it was payback time. *If I can't have her, no one will.* The night before the wedding, he discreetly torched the reception hall; the next morning he stood gleefully beside the stunned and cheerless crowd that had come out to see the smoking and charred rubble of what was once the Sweetwater Casino.

The wedding was called off indefinitely, and a full investigation into the blaze was conducted. Such was his skill and painstaking planning that to this day the cause of the fire remains unknown, leaving the insurance company in the position of refusing to pay. Without the insurance money, plans to rebuild the grand rustic lodge have languished, unfulfilled.

In due course, true to her flighty nature and bewitching ways, the torch singer fiddled around once more, moving on from the poor jilted judge's son. But the betrayed cook had learned a valuable lesson.

He decided to stop running, to stop hiding. He would reinvent himself as someone *he* could live with, even if no one else could. He shaved his head as a sign of his independence, never again to follow the norm set by others. He had his body elaborately tatooed to disguise the old self which had let other people make choices for him, and dove headfirst into a job for Laval Marine Works, doing beach excavation. He embraced environmentalism as both a cause to celebrate and a means to attract young women for brief and meaningless sex. But then he found himself falling in love again, and his past caught up with him.

16
Bizarre Behavior

"You did the right thing calling me," said Noah. They were sitting in his pickup truck waiting to exit the Tuckerton Seaport parking lot. "Sarah isn't answering my calls, either. You say she was headed for Little Egg Harbor?"

"Yes, I'm sure of it," Kelly said, the worry showing on her face. "She found this faded photograph of the lens shoved under her door this morning with a strange note attached. 20 West Singleton Lane."

Noah made a left onto Route 9, then another left onto Great Bay Boulevard. Thankfully the traffic was light. Turning right onto Radio Road, Kelly spotted her own Mini Cooper coming toward them from the opposite direction.

"There she is!" Kelly screamed joyfully, pointing through the windshield.

Noah slowed and gave a friendly toot on his horn. As the Mini Cooper approached them, he stopped and rolled down his window, waving his arm to flag her down, but the car kept right on going.

"She didn't see us," cried Kelly.

"How could she miss us?" Noah wondered aloud. "She didn't even look over. Not so much as a glance." Without hesitating he made a sudden U-turn, stopping traffic in both directions.

In pursuit, two cars separated them. Noah flashed his truck's high beams. The car in front of them stopped suddenly. Noah slammed on his brakes, narrowly avoiding a rear-end collision. Kelly was thrown back against her seat. "Not you, you idiot," barked Noah, waving to the driver to keep moving.

"Where's she going?" asked Kelly when the Mini Cooper passed the Seaport entrance without turning in. Noah got caught at a traffic light and had to stop. They watched as the Mini Cooper sped up, traveling north on Route 9.

"Try her cell phone again," Noah instructed.

Kelly pulled out her phone and dialed. "She's still not answering."

"Then call 911," he commanded.

"Shouldn't we wait?" she said, her own panic mounting.

Noah pounded his fist on the wheel. He turned to look at Kelly. Anger flashed in his bright gray-green eyes, but she knew it was not directed toward her. He was really worried. They both were. Lately her aunt seemed consumed, even obsessed with the idea of finding the Tucker's Island Light. Perhaps it was her way of being accepted into the sisterhood once ruled by Libby Ashcroft, Kelly thought.

Regaining control of his emotions, Noah said, "This is bizarre behavior even for your Aunt Sarah. She knows my truck. She's supposed to be at work and she knows she left you stranded."

Kelly knew he was right. She held up her phone. "What should I tell them?"

"Give them the make and model of your car. And tell them it's been stolen."

***

Ryder Hayes could feel the Mini Cooper slowing down. "Why are you stopping?" he asked in a terse, gruff voice. He was hunched down behind the driver's seat, his right arm wrapped around the headrest, holding a razor-sharp fillet knife to Sarah's throat.

"It's my husband. He's coming toward us in the other lane," she choked out, happy to see him but fearing the worst.

"Don't stop," Hayes hissed.

"Where are we going?" she sobbed softly, tears streaking her face.

"I'll tell you when we get there," he replied pressing the flat of the knife against the skin of her neck.

"What do you want from me?"

"I want you to shut up and drive," he said coldly.

Sarah's cell phone chirped again from inside her purse on the passenger seat beside her. She heard the muffled first few bars of Pink Floyd's classic "Dark Side of the Moon" that Geoffrey had programmed for her. It made her think of Noah, whom she had just passed on Radio Road without stopping. He detested the song though it was her favorite, but he never asked her to change it. What a guy. She wondered what he was thinking about her now.

"You don't have the light, do you?" she asked trying to make conversation with the man she assumed to be the villainous Ryder Hayes, based on Libby's description and his dossier of deceit. She cursed her own stupidity.

"Figured that out, didya?" Hayes snarled, toying with her.

"You won't get away with it."

"That was never my plan."

"Kidnapping? That was your plan? What do you expect to get? We have no money."

"You have friends with money."

"They'll never pay."

"Then you'll die."

Sarah shuddered at the thought of Noah and the kids fishing her body from the briny waters of Barnegat Bay or finding her dismembered corpse in some illegal dump site deep in the middle of the Pines.

Hayes leaned forward and pulled back Sarah's hair. He put his cracked, weathered lips up to her ear. "Oh, I wouldn't worry Mrs. Parsons," he whispered sinisterly. His foul breath made Sarah gag. "We know the Ladies of the Light would never let *that* happen."

***

The urgent call Roger Kincaid received on his cell phone was from central dispatch. A single engine Cessna, piloted by an Exelon executive, disappeared shortly after takeoff from the Oyster Creek Nuclear Power Plant, located on the outskirts of Forked

River. His last known position was somewhere northwest of Pinewald-Keswick Road, between the Brendan T. Byrne State Forest and Double Trouble State Park. Because of their proximity to the probable crash site, Kincaid's raw rangers were being commandeered to join in the search party on the ground for the downed plane and missing executive.

Kincaid accepted the orders with his usual "roger that" public demeanor, but as an individual who lived in the nearby community of Waretown he was emotionally ambivalent about the task. Personally he had no great love for the aging power plant—the oldest in the country—the out-of-state corporation that owned it, or its high-falootin', overpaid executives. Like many of his family and friends in the neighboring communities, he had long been at odds with the operation of a power plant so close to their homes and schools. They lived with the unshakeable nightmares of a dire nuclear accident and the irrevocable impact the plant was having on the surrounding environment. In addition to several recent and well documented radioactive tritium leaks, the plant's current cooling towers, which drew 1.4 billion gallons of water a day from Barnegat Bay, were blamed for killing millions of shrimp, fish, crabs, and clams each year.

Kincaid was elated when he learned that the power company had decided to close the facility in 2019 rather than build safer and more energy-efficient cooling towers, which—after years of pressure from environmental groups—the state was now demanding. Exelon estimated it would cost $800 million to build the new closed-cycle towers, an expense company officials said exceeded the value of the facility. "Good riddance," was Kincaid's reaction when his wife read the news aloud from the local paper.

But there was another side to the unfolding drama that the Chief could not turn away from. A downed plane in the heart of Pinelands spelled untold disaster for the beloved forest he was sworn to protect. In the heat of the summertime, with the drought-like conditions they'd been experiencing, a catastrophe was a mere breeze away.

It would be dark before they returned and because the terrain to be covered would be treacherous, Kincaid did not wish to put more raw personnel at risk than was absolutely necessary in order to get the job done. He knew the area where they were going was mostly marshland surrounded by dense woodlands. That would be problematic with a large group, especially at night. These budding rangers were his responsibility and the way he saw it not all of them would make the final cut, so why put them or himself through hell over it. Instead, he selected six of the ablest trainees, Danny and Rodney among them, and sent the remainder of the group, including Heidi and Roxanne, back to the village campsite with Bill Hogan.

The two women protested vigorously but Kincaid would not be dissuaded. Rodney lent a voice for the ladies' side in a questionable show of support. When Danny gave him a quizzical look, Rodney whispered half-jokingly that he just couldn't resist the idea of seeing the two women mud-wrestling in the woods.

An hour into the hike, well off the beaten path, trudging through thick underbrush, being slapped and scraped by catbriar and poison ivy in search of a lost pilot, Danny reflected on the life of another crashed aviator, Captain Emilio Carranza, whom he had the privilege of portraying in an ill-fated film produced by a "friend" several years back. Brave and resourceful to a fault, the twenty-two year old Carranza had perished alone in the Pines far from his Mexican homeland, trying to prove something to others or perhaps just to himself. Playing the role of the young, impetuous Carranza turned into a highly self-indulgent experience for Danny Windsor, but it changed nothing for him except his name and hair color. When at last he came down off his fences and returned to his senses, there was Kelly Martin, as constant as the clear night sky and as bright as the new morning sun, waiting for him.

So what on Earth was he doing out here in the woods playing forest ranger, when a girl like that waited for him back home? Yes, home! There, he said it. Thinking about Kelly was like thinking about home: safe, warm, secure. A home like he had never had in his entire life. A place of comfort and joy where he could rest his weary bones and enjoy the company of someone he could confide in. A home his own mother and father, plagued by hang-ups and insecurities, had never been able to provide. While so many other people came in and out of his life and he went in and out of theirs, Kelly had remained his one constant. She was the one person who cared for him, maybe even loved him, for who he was—when even *he* had no idea who he was. What was he doing, spending so much time away from her and in the company of someone like Rodney Coles, who treated women as mere objects for his amusement? And there in the middle of the Pines, far from the life Danny had imagined for himself, something inside him clicked as truly as if a light were turned on inside that dull brain of his, and he knew what he had to do. As soon the night was over and the job was done, so was he. He was going home again. This time to stay.

As he reached for his cell phone to try Kelly again, a cry went out that Kincaid had located the plane. It was partially hidden under a canopy of trees, submerged in a swamp with one wing completely under water. The semi-conscious pilot was still strapped into the cockpit and had to be extricated with extreme care. Upon examination, Rodney, who had trained as a field EMT during his stint with the SEALs, reported that the man's left leg was broken in two places. Additionally, he had multiple lacerations to the head and face and probable internal bleeding. On the whole, however, Rodney said he was confident that the injuries were not life threatening.

Kincaid took out his cell phone. He notified the authorities that the pilot had been found, gave a brief account of his injuries and pronounced his condition stable enough that he could be taken out on foot. He requested a medevac chopper stand by at Double Trouble Village, ready to airlift the patient to Southern Ocean County Hospital for medical attention.

After he finished his call, Kincaid checked the fuselage of the wreckage to see if it was leaking fuel. In the growing darkness, it was difficult to tell and the Chief had to rely on his sense of taste and smell. Based on the ramblings of the pilot, a man in his early fifties with minimal flight experience, and Kincaid's cursory examination of the plane, it appeared the crash may have been caused by a mechanical or electrical malfunction. A full investigation would come later. Satisfied that the craft was not an urgent safety risk, Kincaid left his cell phone in the cockpit to allow its GPS signal to guide the removal team to the crash site , just in case the black box could not be located.

This is what happens when you fly solo, it occurred to Danny as he watched the proceedings unfold. *You end up all alone and needing help.*

The Chief assisted Rodney with the cleaning and wrapping of the executive's head wounds, using iodine and gauze from the plane's first aid kit. Next, Rodney snapped the leg back into alignment and braced it between two stout pieces of brushwood for support during the transport out. The pain from the force of the action was intense. The pilot let out a blood-curdling scream that reverberated in the wilderness before he passed out. "Just as well," Rodney said. "Without pain medication he's better off unconscious while we drag him through the woods."

In an impromptu lesson even Tom Banks would have appreciated, the Chief instructed Danny and the other recruits in the construction of a makeshift stretcher from tree limbs and dried leaves. As the last rays of sun were setting in the west behind the tall white cedars of New Jersey's primordial forest, Kincaid and the trainees started back to the village, single-file, each man walking no more than ten feet behind the one ahead of him.

"Stay close and keep alert," Kincaid said as he took the lead, followed by two brush blockers, two stretcher bearers, and Rodney and Danny pulling up the rear.

17
Deadly Dilemma

His original plan was simple, if not elegant: *Get the reward money and run before anyone catches on to the lighthouse lens switcheroo.* He had made his living preying on naïve, well-intentioned people who were all too willing to believe their good fortune and wouldn't recognize a fraud if one kicked them in the head.

When Sarah Bishop-Parsons joined the budding sorority of the Ladies of the Light, that upped the ante some, and Hayes was only too glad to change his initial plan to *get the money and slice the bitch's throat.* After all, he had an old score to settle with her meddling niece and nephew and their witless friend, who had put him behind bars for the past five years.

But when his prey showed up at his temporary lodgings without the tip money he was forced to amend his plan yet again, this time to something akin to *forget the money, grab the bitch, and up the price for her safe return.* That's where he thought things stood until the nosy neighbors from across the lagoon spotted the Mini Cooper in front of the vacant, rundown house at 20 West Singleton Lane and came snooping to see if the old tenants had returned or if new residents had purchased the dump. Either way, it was time to vacate the temporary digs and ditch the wheels. But, where to go?

He knew he couldn't go back to the Sea Captain's House. One unexpected ghost upstairs was fine, but two would never do. Nor could he go "home" to his houseboat at Skinner's Dock, since it had been auctioned off at a sheriff's sale during his incarceration, purchased by an anonymous buyer and donated to the Tuckerton Seaport. *There just ain't no justice in this world*, his father would have said.

To make matters worse, he knew they had been spotted by Noah Parsons, of all people, cruising down Radio Road on their unplanned escape. He was fairly certain that Noah couldn't have seen him hunkered down in the back seat. Nor was it likely he'd seen the knife held dangerously close to his precious wife's pretty white throat. But he wasn't going to risk letting her stop. That was out of the question. She'd crack, sure as hell. Her face was already wet with tears. She would have been a dead giveaway. So he told her not to slow down, or even so much as look at him, or he'd kill her. She listened and continued to play like the obedient hostage. But that may have been a mistake, because not waving to Noah as they passed had prompted suspicion and now the chase was on.

He needed a place to hide out for awhile and think up a new plan. He knew plenty of out-of-the-way places deep in the Pines, places no man would ever find, if only he could get to one of them fast enough. But Parsons was tight on his tail and as they turned onto Route 72 heading west he could see the cherry tops of several cop cars stopping traffic at the light where Routes 72 and 539 met. He was trapped just like his hero John Bacon. And with that thought, inspiration suddenly came to him in the form of a childhood memory: the place of Captain Bacon's most magnificent escape.

Hayes ordered his victim, visibly shaking with fright at his shrill command, to pull off the road to the left and take the narrow sandy gravel lane known to the locals as Old Halfway Road, and make for the Cedar Bridge Tavern.

***

As he hiked back toward the village in silence, listening to the sound of the ground crunching under foot and keeping an eye on the cattail torch Chief Kincaid had lighted, Danny debated whether he should say anything to Rodney about his plan to leave the training program in the morning. He wasn't quite sure how his friend would react, but in a way he felt he owed it to him. Rodney had been instrumental in finding the job posting and encouraging Danny to try out for the Forest Service with him. It would be "a howl," as Rodney had put it, for them to complete the training together.

Thinking back on it now, Danny reflected on how odd it was for Rodney to want, let alone suggest, companionship on his newest adventure. He was his own man to be sure. He didn't have many friends— make that male friends, Danny corrected himself with an inward chuckle. For that matter, his countless female cohorts seemed more like flighty acquaintances than true friends.

Danny supposed his relationship with Rodney might appear unusual to someone looking at it from the outside—someone like Kelly, for instance, who saw it as an example of Danny's need for a father figure in his life. Of course, she would have preferred that figure to have been Noah Parsons or Tom Banks. Moss Greenberg had filled the role for quite awhile, Danny reflected.

Even after spending an entire summer with Rodney surfing LBI and now traipsing through the Pine Barrens, Danny had to admit that he remained something of a mystery. He was a showman around women—that much was certain—and, to judge by his appearance, an exhibitionist. An alpha male if there ever was one. Yet he guarded his privacy religiously, and at times it was almost as if he were two different people.

Recently, Danny was beginning to view Rodney more from Kelly's perspective. Had he been seeing him through rose-colored glasses? Here was a man who came from a military background, served as a SEAL, worked as a diver for a marine outfit until it clashed with his environmental sensibilities, organized the first Longboard Classic, and ran for mayor of Surf City. Yet, even with all that known about him, he somehow still managed to remain an enigma. He seemed to have gone to great pains to downplay his military experience and hide his true self. His distrust of the government, or any form of authority, was patently obvious—but why? In his travels, Rodney had acquired so much knowledge, accumulated so many skills, and yet he wasn't able to hold down a job—or was it just that he didn't want to? Danny didn't like the shabby way he treated women, and could easily see why Kelly kept her distance from him. So what was his beef? What was he trying to prove? Who or what was he hiding from? Danny wondered as he moved through the woods.

"Rodney, I need to tell you something," Danny called out to the shadowy outline of Rodney's form about ten feet ahead of him. "I'm quitting the program."

The hulking figure in front of him stopped. So did Danny. Rodney turned and walked slowly back toward him until they stood face-to-face. "What made you decide that?"

"This just isn't me," Danny blurted out. "It isn't who I am."

"Well, then who are you, dude? The endless surfer, or the subservient puppy dog?"

"I don't follow."

"Don't you? It's written all over your face. You've been itching to run back to your girlfriend ever since we got here."

Danny stood his ground. "Maybe. What's it to you?"

"To me? Nothing, dude. But to you, all I can say is … you'll be sorry."

"I'm not like you, Rodney. I thought I wanted to be, but I'm not. I'm not cut out to be a jack-of-all-trades, master-of-none kind of guy. I need stability. I need a rock in my life."

"You mean an anchor, man. That's what women are—they weigh you down."

"How can you say that? I've never seen you with the same girl twice."

"Haven't you?"

"What? No." Danny was sure he hadn't.

"Think back, Danny. Rhinestones and fiddles? A certain little country singer?"

"Shawna James? What's she got to do with anything?"

"Everything."

"Rodney, you're not making any sense. I haven't seen Shawna in ages. Not since the band broke up. It's Kelly I need to see. I think I love her."

"If I can't have her, no one will," said Rodney, pushing Danny up against a tree. The unexpected move caught the younger man totally by surprise. Rodney's powerful arms held him in check.

"Dammit, Rodney!" Danny shouted. "What's this all about?"

"I've waited a long time for this, Windsor."

"Waited for what?" Danny said, shoving back with all his strength. The two men fell to the ground, arms flaying and fists jabbing at each other, rolling as they went, each one taking turns getting on top of the other only to be knocked off in the next instant.

They continued to struggle, taking swings at each other like two brothers fighting for supremacy over nothing, until they rolled down an incline and into a shadowy gorge. A large boulder separated them when it broke Rodney's fall, two-thirds of the way down. Danny was not as lucky. His head hit the edge of the boulder, knocking him out cold. Unconscious, he plunged the rest of the way down the dark ravine and into the swift-flowing, tea-colored water of Cedar Creek.

Rodney repositioned himself on the rock and looked down the steep hill in the direction of the gurgling water. He listened with detachment but heard no call for help. It only took a moment for him to decide what to do. Careful not to slip, he began climbing back up the slope.

Kincaid and his ranger recruits were oblivious to the commotion. They had not heard the men's conversation and were not aware they had even stopped. By now they were a couple of hundred yards from the action, out of earshot and moving farther away. No one heard the scuffle, and nobody looked back to check that they were all still together. To a man, they had nothing on their minds other than getting back to the village where a shower and some hot chow was waiting.

At one point, Roger Kincaid glanced behind him to see how the pilot was holding up. He was still unconscious and both stretcher bearers assured the Chief that neither of them was too fatigued to carry on. In truth, they were dog tired, but both men saw it as an opportunity to impress the boss so they kept going.

Seeing movement some distance behind the stretcher, Kincaid did not stop to take a head count. He assumed all could see his torch and were moving along in double time to get to their destination. He had purposely placed Coles and Windsor in the rear, having acknowledged them as more savvy and skillful than the other trainees. A former SEAL and a smart, tough kid with lifesaving experience. Piece of cake, Kincaid figured.

18

Battle Lines

Geoffrey stood at attention in front of the rustic Cedar Bridge Tavern along with a dozen other men, similarly outfitted in either buckskin or the blue and white uniform of the New Jersey Continental militia. Luz snapped photographs of the assemblage and encouraged Geoffrey to smile for the camera.

In the hazy late August afternoon, about thirty people had gathered to watch the dress rehearsal for the reenactment of the Battle of Cedar Bridge, including Luz's parents, who, at the moment, were chatting amiably with Rudy Koenig on the rickety front porch. Playing host for the occasion, Koenig ladled out free lemonade to the thirsty visitors, and, with a nod or a wink, added a splash of hooch to the refreshing beverage for those who came asking.

"To arms!" called out Geoffrey at the sight of a band of redcoats marching over the bridge to the east of the tavern. With that battle cry, the reenactors of the Continental militia broke formation, running up the dirt road leading from the tavern. There they reassembled, loaded their muskets and began firing on the enemy.

The enemy, led by Professor McPherson dressed as a pirate and portraying Captain John Bacon, used their munitions wagon and assorted hay bales to barricade the bridge over Cedar Creek. From behind the barricade, they returned fire. Plumes of acrid smoke hung in the still air over the bridge and along the road.

From somewhere behind the clouds of smoke, a car horn honked incessantly. In the next instant, a number of the enemy began to break rank and flee from the bridge.

"Charge!" shouted a Continental officer with his saber raised. Several soldiers followed him, rushing the bridge, only to be repulsed by a Mini Cooper that had come up the lane, rammed through the wagon barricade and veered off into the meandering creek. A dusty green pickup truck sped up the lane and stopped just short of the bridge.

"That definitely wasn't in the script," Geoffrey said aloud, shaking his head. A man and a young woman Geoffrey recognized immediately bounded out of the pickup and waded into the creek.

***

Danny was only vaguely aware that he was alive. His head pounded, and there was a huge gash on his forehead. The current had taken him far downstream. His sole lifeline had been a large log, which had snared him as he floated by. Both log and man came to rest in a calm eddy.

He tried several times to rise but fell back exhausted and in searing pain. Never in his life had he felt more abandoned and alone. He tried to keep awake, hoping against hope that someone—Rodney Coles, Chief, Kincaid, anyone—would find him.

The fight with Rodney remained inexplicable, a nightmare he relived over and over in his head to stop himself from drifting back into unconsciousness. It was almost as if Rodney was possessed ... as if the Jersey Devil himself had taken control of his body and mind. Where had he gone?

He managed to remove the cell phone from his pocket, only to find it waterlogged and useless. The agonizing minutes turned into hours. as he waited in the darkness to be found.

As he drifted in and out of consciousness, Danny thought he heard the reassuring voice of another human being and the bark of man's best friend. Perhaps it was simply delirium, but the very thought of it gave him a sense of hope. Was he dreaming?

He tried willing his eyes open but they were caked shut with dried blood, and the strain was too much for him. He was about to slip into the inky abyss when he suddenly realized that a panting, wet-nosed Siberian husky was licking his face.

19

The End of Summer

"I've never been on the beach after Labor Day," said Kelly, sitting upright on a big blanket, her knees tucked under her chin and her arms folded around them. The towering silhouette of Barnegat Light loomed over her shoulder. "Just the smell of the salt air and the cool sand under my feet makes me feel so alive."

"I never want to leave," agreed her brother, stretched out on a faded patchwork quilt across from her. He stared up into Luz's beautiful face, illuminated by the glow of a roaring bonfire, celebrating the relighting of the famous red and white lighthouse. Luz leaned over him and bestowed a sweet kiss.

"September is the best time to be on the beach," Danny added, smiling at Kelly and taking a seat next to her. His head was wrapped in a tight white bandage, but otherwise he showed no ill effect from his recent ordeal in the woods. "The summer tourists have gone, but the sun, sand, and surf are all still here and ours to reclaim," he said as he tuned his acoustic guitar.

"All the restaurants are still open, too, and there are no crowds to fight," offered Luz. "It's heavenly."

"So peaceful," cooed Kelly, slipping an arm around Danny's waist as he strummed a gentle C-minor ninth and let it sustain against the quiet night.

"That's what makes this place so weird to me," said Geoffrey, gazing up at the canopy of stars overhead. "Think about it. This may have been the very spot where, two-hundred-some-odd years ago, on a night just like this, the Butcher of Barnegat slaughtered thirty people in their sleep. They have a plaque about it over there," he said, pointing toward the park entrance.

"Thanks for reminding me," Luz chimed in. "You weren't planning on sleeping here, were you?"

"I'll tell you what scares me. Even though I know he's in jail again, that modern-day pirate Ryder Hayes gives me the creeps," said Kelly. "If I didn't know better, I'd swear he and Captain Bacon were related."

"How do you know they're not?" asked Danny. "I'll bet they share some of that mooncusser blood."

"So ye thinks we should have run Hayes through, do ye?" joked Geoffrey, the actor in rare form, playfully thrusting an imaginary sword at Danny. "Just like they did when they finally nabbed old Captain Bacon: fill his gullet with demon rum, toss his corpse onto the back of a cart, parade him up and down Long Beach Island, then bury his body in the middle of the road, *arrr*, at them crossroads, matey, if'n ye catch m'drift."

Geoffrey's pirate antics broke everyone up with peals of belly-shaking laughter.

Danny reached for his bandaged head.

"Does it hurt much?" Kelly reached up and gently touched the bandage.

"Only when I laugh," Danny said with typical bravado.

"I'm sure your Aunt Sarah is glad the Spirits of Cedar Bridge have finally been laid to rest," said Luz.

"Poor Aunt Sarah. That had to be quite traumatic for her, being kidnapped by Ryder Hayes," said Geoffrey, sitting up. "She looked like a drowned rat when you and Noah fished her out of Cedar Creek."

"That's why Noah took her on a nice long vacation to the Virgin Islands."

"Where there probably aren't many virgins left, I might add," laughed Danny, letting himself join in the levity of the group.

"Do you have to be a virgin to go there?" inquired Luz in all seriousness.

"I'm fairly sure that would leave Aunt Sarah out," replied Geoffrey with a broad grin.

"Enough about Aunt Sarah," said Kelly defensively. "She feels awful about being duped so easily. She quit her job at the Seaport she was so embarrassed."

"I think she feels worse about your car, Kelly," said Geoffrey, laughing. "How does she plan to pay for it?"

"We worked out a deal. She made me a full partner in the gift shop. I get fifty percent of whatever we sell until I have enough to fix it or buy a new car."

"And then what?" asked Danny. "Things revert back to the way they were?"

"Nope. Then we branch out. We're going to open a new wing, 'Kelly's Corner,' where we'll sell beachwear and athletic apparel of my own personal design."

Geoffrey was impressed. "Cool—my sister, the entrepreneur."

"What about you, Danny?" asked Luz. "Now that you're no longer playing forest ranger, what are your plans?"

"Correction: I'm no longer playing the *Lone* Ranger." He gave Kelly a gentle hug.

"Which reminds me, did you ever find out what got into your buddy Rodney Coles?" Kelly asked sarcastically.

"You mean why he flipped out on me in the woods? It was as if he became a different person."

"You mean like a split personality," questioned Geoffrey.

Kelly sighed. "Yeah, like Jekyll and Hyde. What was that all about?"

"I guess we'll never know. He kind of fell off the face of the earth. Never went back to the village that night. I don't know if he got lost in the woods or just walked away."

"Maybe he just lost it?" ventured Geoffrey.

"Or maybe he's dead," said Kelly hopefully.

"Oh, he's not dead," Danny said briskly.

"What makes you so sure?" asked Luz.

"Because I got this in the mail last week." He pulled a diamond engagement ring from his pants pocket.

Kelly's eyes lit up. "A diamond ring? How does that figure in with Rodney's disappearing act?"

"Not just any diamond ring. It's a Cape May diamond ring," he said, handing it to her. She beamed, staring at the ring in disbelief as she slipped it on her finger. "I had it checked out," he added.

"A fake diamond?" questioned Geoffrey. "I don't get it."

Kelly pulled the ring off and threw it back at Danny. She folded her arms across her chest and gave him a glare. "You're not getting away that cheap, buster," she said in a huff.

Danny smiled and put it back in his jeans pocket for safekeeping. "I think Rodney was trying to tell me something on the ride over to Double Trouble. For some reason, he knew an awful lot about Cape May diamonds."

Kelly frowned as she tried to sort out this latest piece of the puzzle that was Rodney Coles. "So you really think this ring is from him?

"Oh, I'm sure of it."

"But what does it mean?" Luz asked excitedly.

"It's a peace offering."

"Couldn't he just buy you a beer?" Kelly laughed at the strange gesture.

"Or say 'I'm sorry'?" offered Luz, even more confused.

"That's not his style." Danny mused.

"That's because he has no style," said Kelly emphatically.

"I still can't believe you're not pissed off at him for leaving you to drown in the river," said Geoffrey, shaking his head.

Danny paused to ponder the question. He looked around at all the warm, friendly faces and shrugged. "Why should I be? Everything turned out okay."

"You could have died!" Kelly pointed out.

"But I didn't. I survived and learned something very important about myself. It's like I had some kind of an awakening. I don't know how to explain it. I just knew I needed to come home ... to you," he said, draping an arm around Kelly.

"Hey Danny, just how *did* those dogs find you?" Luz wanted to know.

"Damned if I know." Danny grew circumspect as he recalled his rescue. "Their sled master said I must have bonded with the leader, a dog she calls Chance. Funny, I remember staring at him when we pulled over to let the sled go by during our training run. I'll never forget those eyes, one blue and one brown. They reminded me of David Bowie's eyes—you know, each one a different color." He fingered his guitar and strummed the opening chords to "Space Oddity," before continuing.

"Kincaid's wife thinks Chance must've marked my scent when we met that day. On the morning they found me, it was Chance who suddenly halted the other dogs during a practice run. Bill Hogan told me huskies have evolved to the point where they are thought of only as sport dogs, but they still have this innate pack instinct. They can sense when another animal is in trouble from the pheromones the wounded animal—or human being, in this case—gives off. In earlier times, it would have guided the pack to prey. Chance picked up my scent and probably sensed the danger

I was in. Believe me, my pheromones must have been firing big time, because I was scared shitless."

Kelly stood and casually brushed the sand from her shorts. "I think I know just what those firing pheromones need," she said, coyly offering Danny a hand up and pulling him toward her. Their eyes met, and nothing more needed to be said. Danny grabbed his guitar. Kelly grabbed the blanket. With fireworks cascading in the night sky overhead, they turned, hand in hand, and disappeared over the dunes.

"Looks like they're finally going to take a 'Chance' on love," Geoffrey punned, pulling Luz to him. "Care to see that new light inside Old Barney up close?" he asked, although he already knew the answer.

"They don't call me Luz for nothing," she said with a sly smile.

***

Kelly and Danny took a slight detour off the nature trail inside Barnegat Light State Park and found a secluded spot among a grove of Eastern Red Cedars. It was almost closing time and they hoped to remain in the park unseen.

"Ah, alone at last," said Danny, spreading the beach blanket. He knelt down beside Kelly and pleaded with her to close her eyes. As she lay back on the soft sand, he reached into his pocket and confessed in a breathless whisper, "I have a surprise for you."

Kelly's deep sigh revealed that she was finally relaxed and ready for the pleasure she had long imagined she would find in his arms.

"What kind of surprise?" she asked in her most sultry voice.

Danny didn't hear the question. A blow to the back of his head produced an instantaneous ring of stars, clustered before his eyes. His mind went blank as he slumped to the ground.

"The unexpected kind," said a familiar male voice from the shadows. Before Kelly could react, a dark hooded figure had pinned her down, torn off a strip of duct tape and stretched it across her mouth.

She fought back fiercely but was no match for her assailant's strength. He overpowered her quickly, binding her wrists and ankles tightly with the tape. Kelly's eyes grew wide with fear. She watched in shock and horror as the attacker removed his hood, revealing the strange and eerie smiling face of Rodney Coles.

Rodney bent down and shoved his smirking face to within a hair's breadth of hers. "Bet you thought you'd seen the last of me, hey, baby? Well you're all mine now," he added with a sinister laugh.

Kelly couldn't do anything but watch as Rodney rolled Danny over and started rummaging through his pants pockets. "So nice of Danny Boy to bring along my little memento," he said, placing the ring on Kelly's finger. "I knew this would come in handy again someday."

Rodney's intentions repulsed her. *He must have lost his mind! Is this some kind of sick joke*? She squirmed and shook her hands, trying to loosen the ring from her finger, but it was no use. She couldn't lift her arms high enough or even swing them side to side with any force.

"If I can't have you, no one will," Rodney said gleefully, rolling Danny's body to the side. "I lost one woman to this loser and I don't intend to lose another."

As genuinely frightened as she was, Kelly wouldn't let herself panic. She quickly assessed the situation. She had no idea how badly Danny was hurt, and the park was closed by now, so all of the visitors, including Geoffrey and Luz, had gone. The park rangers might make one last round, but what were the chances they would come across them so far off the beaten path? Rodney was dangerous, but she wouldn't give him the satisfaction of showing any fear. She had been taught to believe in herself, to trust in her own abilities and have faith that she would survive. Even though she put on a brave face, she wasn't very comforted by her thoughts at the moment.

Rodney stood up and surveyed the surroundings. When he was certain that no one was watching, he bent down and started to wrap Kelly up, using the beach blanket to fashion a tight carpet-like bundle. She kicked and protested to no avail as he hoisted her over his shoulder and slowly walked down to the water's edge.

Rodney gently laid his prize down on the wet sand and hurriedly began to dig out a kayak he had hidden earlier in the brush. He waded out into the surf waist-deep with the kayak to wash it off, then scampered back to shore to pick up his unwilling companion. As he placed his captive across the open seat, She managed to get one hand free and used the unwelcome ring on her finger to scratch his arm as hard as she could. Rodney pushed her back down into the kayak with a violent thrust and was about to shove off when something struck him hard from behind, leaving a discordant twang lingering in his ears. Coles's knees buckled and he fell, face-down into the water.

Kelly felt the kayak being pulled back and beached. She struggled to tear off the duct tape and the rest of her bindings and came face-to-face with her rescuer. "Danny!" she screamed with joy, jumping into his arms. She kissed and hugged him so hard he practically had to beg her to stop. He was standing unsteadily with the remains of his guitar in one hand, watching the body of Rodney Coles bobbing on the water. He rubbed the knot on the back of his head.

"Are you all right?" he asked, taking a step back to examine her.

Looking at the now-bloody ring Rodney had forcefully placed on her finger, Kelly yanked it off and flung it as far as she could into the ocean.

"I am now," she said, relieved, and hugged him hard again.

A wave of panic swept over Danny as he numbly processed Kelly's strange action. He reached into his pocket and felt the box holding the Cape May diamond he had shown her earlier. Then he reached into his other pocket. The small box holding the real diamond engagement "surprise" that he had purchased for the occasion was missing.

"Bummer," he said with a depleted shrug.

"Danny, what is it? You just saved my life, but you look like you lost your best friend."

He only debated it for a minute. He knew she would be devastated to hear that the engagement ring he had bought with the money he got from pawning his most prized possessions—his lucky surfboard, his electric guitar, and the Bose sound system from his Jeep—now lay at the bottom of the Atlantic Ocean. So Danny did what any red-blooded American boy in love would do under the circumstances. He lied.

"This was my favorite guitar," he said, holding up his broken Ovation.

꧁꧂

Storm Warnings

1

Day 1

BULLETIN
TROPICAL DEPRESSION EIGHTEEN ADVISORY NUMBER 1
NWS NATIONAL HURRICANE CENTER MIAMI FL   AL182012
1100 AM EDT MON OCT 22 2012

TROPICAL DEPRESSION FORMING OVER THE SOUTHWESTERN CARIBBEAN
SEA...A TROPICAL STORM WATCH IS IN EFFECT FOR...JAMAICA.

INTERESTS IN EASTERN CUBA...HISPANIOLA...AND THE BAHAMAS
SHOULD MONITOR THE PROGRESS OF THIS SYSTEM.

Paul Decker had little interest in Cuba, Hispaniola, or the Bahamas, but he was going to monitor the progress of this system anyway. After forty years of sifting through daily weather reports for the National Oceanic and Atmospheric Administration (NOAA) in the National Weather Service's Mt. Holly, New Jersey, substation, the veteran meteorologist knew what to expect. A Tropical Storm Watch meant that certain conditions were definitely possible in the watch area, generally within forty-eight hours. If the sustained winds generated by the depression intensified, even marginally, they would issue a Storm Warning or a Hurricane Watch next.

He reread the bulletin from the Hurricane Center in Miami one more time, then pressed "Send" to distribute it to the local weather stations. They might be interested in reporting these latest developments in the Caribbean, since they could eventually impact the residents and properties along New Jersey's Atlantic coastline. Their safety was his job and he took it seriously.

His health was a different matter and he didn't pay much attention to it. When he was outside of the office, there was an ever present cigarette in his mouth. When he inhaled there was a slight rattle in his chest. When he exhaled, through a slightly bent though still patrician nose, it released a faint whistle. The bend could be attributed to a deviated septum earned in a barroom brawl when he was in the service, many years ago. The rattle was the result of a pack-a-day habit spanning more years than this Marlboro man and lifelong bachelor cared to think about.

He glanced down at the Staples desk calendar that doubled as an ink blotter on his cluttered workstation. He still took notes the old fashioned way and had his suspicions that everything he wrote on a computer was being catalogued, analyzed, red-flagged and compiled to use against him just in case he ever got too close to something the NSA, CIA, or some other covert agency preferred to keep hidden. It was already October and hurricane season should be drawing to a close, but Mother Nature had gotten a lot less predictable lately. The thought of a big blow developing this late in the season was disturbing to him and his mind raced to murky places he didn't want to go. Luckily, the phone rang to distract him. It was Noah Parsons.

"Sure, Noah, I'll set it up for today," Decker said after hearing his old friend out. "Have the kid meet me there around noon. If he's as gung-ho about the woods as you say he is, this'll blow him away."

2

"Prince Charming and Cinderella"

You can tell a lot about a woman by the way she walks.

Nicholas Weber had picked up this little nugget of wisdom in a conversation with a prosthetic leg salesman seated on a barstool next to him in Houston a few years back. The young lady walking into his view at the moment was telling him plenty. Her new ombre hairstyle with golden highlights was right off the cover of *Cosmo* and she had a face worthy of high fashion, too, but the Urban Outfitter's sundress brought her back down to earth.

It was the way she walked that impressed him the most, though. Head up, eyes forward, her lithe, athletic body seemed to glide effortlessly in long, confident strides. *Determined* was the first word that popped into his head as he studied her graceful movements. A *volleyball player* he ventured from the toned tan legs. *No, make that* beach *volleyball*, he decided, pleased with his perceptiveness.

As she approached, seemingly unaware of his lingering leer, he wondered what a girl with a degree in Political Science from Georgetown was doing working as a temp at an insurance agency in Stafford, New Jersey. Shouldn't she be in DC, or at the U.N.?

He had to know more about this lovely creature.

"Miss Martin, have you picked out your costume yet?" He was leaning on the desk outside his office as Kelly came within speaking distance. His secretary had just gone to the restroom to "powder her nose," as she did every morning around this time.

Startled by the overture, Kelly hit the brakes. Although she'd been introduced to Nick Weber—Regional Claims VP for Maine Line Insurance, as well as the firm's Ocean County Branch Manager—during her job interview three weeks earlier, they hadn't spoken since beyond a passing "good morning" or "hello." In fact, Kelly assumed office protocol made chitchat with the big boss off limits.

"Costume?" she asked, taking a deep breath.

"For our annual Halloween Party—at the Seaport?" Weber replied nonchalantly. "You are going, aren't you? It's Rita's baby, you know, and I'm sure she's counting on you to join in the festivities."

Rita was Rita Zenger, Kelly's floor supervisor in the claims unit. Tough as nails during loss settlement negotiations, Rita had a reputation for being a no-nonsense boss with a truck driver's vocabulary. Most of the agents quaked in their boots when called into her module for a pending file consultation. Nick actually delighted in her reputation with the staff, which had always helped insulate him from personnel issues he had no patience for. If "Hatchet Man" was a term coined to describe the guy who did the boss's dirty work, Rita Zenger was Nick Weber's "Axe Maiden," and it left him free to play the Good Cop. Kelly had heard that opposing Rita meant a one-way ticket to the unemployment line, and assumed the Halloween ball was mandatory if she wanted to keep her job.

"Sure, I'll be there," she said nervously. "My boyfriend and I are thinking of coming as Super Heroes—a Dynamic Duo."

The reference to her boyfriend was not lost on Nick, who absorbed it as information but not as a deterrent. For her part, Kelly had hoped the comment would derail the unwelcome advance she sensed would be coming. She was already feeling self-conscious and uncomfortable standing in front of the boss's office making small talk. The fact that he was darkly handsome and charismatic was also disconcerting. She looked around to see if anyone was watching, half expecting to find Rita peering over the top of her cubicle. Fortunately, there was still some time before the start of the workday and most of the early arrivals were gathered around the kitchen Keurig, tanking up on free high-test before launching into the day's work.

"Batman and Robin?" Nick suggested with a practiced smile.

"Kind of," she replied hesitantly. "Only a little more ..." she stared at her charming forty-something boss, carefully searching for a word that wouldn't offend him ... "contemporary?"

"Ah, you mean *hip*," Nick responded, feigning a wound.

"No ... no," she stammered. "I mean, as in *current*."

Weber laughed confidently, toying with her. "Well, if you ask me, you and your boyfriend are over-thinking it. You should just come as yourselves."

Kelly cocked her head, trying to decipher his offbeat remark. "What's that supposed to mean?" she inquired as the staff began filtering into the room. Rita's pointed glance struck her as a mix of disapproval and disdain.

Nick got up slowly, enjoying her anxious attention. "All I'm suggesting is that you come as the perfect couple you are," he said over his shoulder as he reached for the door to his office. "Cinderella and her Prince Charming."

3
Where's the Fire?

When Geoffrey Martin arrived there were two other vehicles parked in the clearing at the foot of the so-called "Cedar Bridge" fire tower off Route 539 near Barnegat, about a quarter mile west of the intersection with Route 72. There wasn't enough room left for a bicycle to squeeze in after he pulled alongside Paul Decker's army green El Camino and a lifted red GMC Jimmy with oversized tires. Decker leaned against the hood of his vehicle stirring a cup of coffee with his index finger.

"If you're Geoffrey Martin, you're late," he remarked blowing into his cup. "I owe Noah Parsons a few favors but wet-nursing a kid that can't be punctual ain't part of it. I had to pull some strings to get you this bird's-eye view, don't screw it up."

"I'm really sorry, Mr. Decker," Geoffrey replied sheepishly. "My GPS couldn't seem to locate the tower."

"Didn't Noah give you directions?"

"He did, but I figured my GPS would find it faster."

Decker took a sip of coffee and shook his head. "You figured wrong," he added looking skyward.

Geoffrey followed the grizzled old man's gaze up an orange and white metal-framed tower, more than six stories high, to a cabin-like observatory at the top. It reminded him of something you might build with a giant erector set. A series of alternating metal steps like fire escape rungs were welded into place and rose up the inside of the tapered skeletal frame all the way to the observation room.

"Cloudless sky," remarked Decker indifferently. "Might be able to see Cape May," he added still looking up. "Had lunch yet?"

"Yes, sir," Geoffrey responded.

"In that case I'll go first. Try to keep it down." Decker drained his coffee, crushed the white Styrofoam cup, and tossed it into the bed of his El Camino. "Time to wake up Ranger Rick," he said, ducking under a crossbeam and moving toward the metal stairway.

Geoffrey cast a wary glance skyward. He took a deep breath, exhaling slowly.

"Afraid of heights?"

"Not that I'm aware of," Geoffrey lied. "Airplanes don't seem to bother me."

"How about Ferris wheels?"

"Can't remember ever being on one."

Decker gave Geoffrey a suspicious look. "Well, this might jog your memory." He stepped onto the first rung. "Just follow me—and whatever you do, don't look down."

The sun was high in the sky, but a slight breeze was blowing out of the southwest. The going was slow and neither man spoke as they climbed toward the top. Geoffrey was wondering how the small observatory could hold more than one grown person at a time when a gust of wind kicked up. He could feel the trestle beneath him shake and rattle in the breeze. Nearly midway up, his sandy soled sneaker slipped off a metal rung. He hesitated as a sudden wave of panic washed over him.

Decker stopped climbing and looked down. Geoffrey's face was ashen. He clung, white knuckled to the metal framing like he was fused to it.

"This is why the Good Lord invented hooch," exclaimed Decker removing a small flask from his hip pocket. "Steadies the nerves," he added taking a nip. He handed the bottle down to Geoffrey.

"No thanks," Geoffrey said closing his eyes, trying to calm himself by blanking out the aerial image of his surroundings.

Decker scanned the horizon noting the sea of gently swaying evergreens before him. They seemed to roll on for miles where the progress of civilization had yet to intervene. "One day when that carrot top of yours turns completely gray, you'll wish you had made the climb to the top," he said forcefully enough to penetrate the din of Geoffrey's crippling anxiety.

Decker took a long pull then started to re-screw the cap.

"Wait a minute," Geoffrey said slowly, pushing his glasses back up the bridge of his nose. He braced his body hard against the railing hoping to reinforce his fleeting courage. He was no quitter, he told himself. This was too important to him. Anyway, he'd come too far to turn back. A warbler sang encouragement from her nest on the branch of a tall pine below them.

Decker extended the flask again. One of Geoffrey's arms was clamped around the railing like a vice, so he grabbed the flask with his free hand and took a quick gulp all in the same motion. The warm liquid slid down his throat easily, warming him instantly. He took a second, longer sip and savored it.

"Now that's more like it," encouraged Decker as he retrieved the flask and tucked it back where it belonged.

When Geoffrey reached the opening to the observatory, a powerful arm pulled him the rest of the way up. Once safely inside, that same arm—which Geoffrey could now see was attached to a middle-aged man in a dark green Park Ranger's uniform—lowered the hatch door back into its closed position.

"Welcome to the Eagle's Nest," the man greeted him with a broad grin. "I'm Richard McGuiness, though my friends just call me Ranger Rick."

"Geoffrey Martin," said Geoffrey, planting his feet firmly on the wood flooring and taking a deep breath. "Thank you for having me up here, sir," he added formally.

"No problem, son. You'll find that Noah Parsons's name opens a lot of doors in these parts—even up here where the air is clear. Ain't that right, Deck?"

The older man silently nodded his agreement.

As Geoffrey's pulse returned to normal, he took stock of the cramped quarters. Three grown men left hardly enough room to stand, let alone walk around. He smiled, thinking he finally understood the adage about a room so small that a person had to go outside just to change his mind.

Framed by four double thick plate glass windows, one on each side, the observatory provided a spectacular view of New Jersey's majestic Pine Barrens. Because the tower was located well above the tree line, there was an unobstructed, panoramic view that extended as far as the eye could see. "Wow!" Geoffrey exclaimed. "I am so glad I took your advice and climbed the rest of the way." He turned and gave Paul Decker an appreciative smile.

"I've got to hand it to you, Deck," chuckled McGuiness, "he's a little green in the gills but that hooch of yours gets 'em up here every time."

Decker laughed and offered the flask to McGuiness. The ranger declined with a wave of his hand.

"Anything going on today?" Decker asked.

"All quiet on the Western Front," kidded McGuiness as an old short wave radio cackled with static on a makeshift shelf in one corner. "Eastern, southern, and northern sectors, too, but I'm grateful for the company. It breaks the monotony."

McGuiness looked directly at Geoffrey. "Truth is, we fire spotters are a dying breed. This is one of the few remaining towers still in operation in the Pinelands. Damn satellites have made us practically obsolete. These days, we're just here to confirm the details of what they spot first."

"There are still some things that can't be captured accurately from space," Decker explained to Geoffrey.

"Like what?" he asked Geoffrey, his interest piqued.

"Like how a fire got started," Decker said.

"Now Deck, don't get start—"

"You can tell how a fire got started from up here?" Geoffrey cut in excitedly.

"Not exactly," McGuiness said.

"But you *can* tell which way the wind is blowing and how soon the flames will cross a road and reach a residence," Decker added firmly.

McGuiness nodded to Decker and smiled. "He's just trying to make me feel useful. Weathermen are the real magicians nowadays. With their satellite images and computer models these guys can predict where and when a storm will hit and how hard the impact will be. That kind of forecasting can save lives. Lots of them."

Decker shrugged. "We're watching one now—a front's trying to form near Jamaica. Probably nothing." He grew pensive. "We can't predict everything, especially when we can't trust our own science. There are things we can see from space that we're not supposed to see."

Geoffrey perked up. "What things? You mean like UFOs … they're for real, aren't they?"

"I don't think there's any doubt about it," Decker grinned. "The only question is, when will the government tell us the truth?"

"Don't pay any attention to him, Geoffrey, or this guy will have you believing that Big Brother controls everything—what we think, what we do, and what we say. Even our sex drives are controlled by a cabal in Washington, ain't that right, Deck?"

"Go ahead, laugh all you want. But when the truth finally comes out, you'll see I was right."

"What truth?" Geoffrey asked hopefully. "What's it all about?"

"Don't trouble yourself over it, son—it's just Paul Decker growing old and senile and letting his imagination run away with him. I keep telling him he needs to get out more often." McGuiness winked. "Find himself a lady friend and let her take care of business, if you know what I mean."

"That's our cue to leave, Geoffrey," Decker said a bit irritably. "You're not gonna learn anything of value with your head up your ass, up here with Ranger Rick."

"At least I know the difference between a rain cloud and a moon shadow."

The conversation halted abruptly as the three men listened intently to the drone of an airplane engine off in the distance. McGuiness lifted the binoculars dangling around his neck. Moving to the window, he peered west toward the Warren Grove bombing range.

"Crop duster?" Decker asked skeptically.

McGuiness turned to the tiny work desk and scrolled down the computer monitor. "Not according to today's flight register."

"Maybe it's an unscheduled flight from McGuire," offered Geoffrey, recalling his brief stint at the nearby Air Force Base, helping out a troubled friend in the PX.

"Plane's flying too high to be taking off or landing at Dix–McGuire," McGuiness said as he scanned the horizon. "Could be a commercial jet a tad off course, on its way to Philly. There it is," he exclaimed as the aircraft came into view. "She's up a good 30,000 feet."

As they watched, a plume of dark blue smoke suddenly poured out of the plane, trailing behind it in a thick stream.

"Fire tanker?" Decker suggested.

"Strange if it is," said McGuiness, still peering through the binoculars. "Most tankers don't fly that high and the water comes out in white streams. When it's tinted with ferric oxide to mark the ground cover, it'll look reddish-brown, but I've never seen *blue* contrails before."

Decker took the binoculars that the ranger was offering him and quickly scanned the forest in all directions. "I don't see any sign of smoke from the woods," he rasped. "Where's the fire?"

McGuiness looked back at the monitor and shrugged. "There doesn't seem to be one."

4
The Perfect Couple

When Kelly got home from work, she found Danny right where she had left him that morning. In the garage, below the apartment they shared in Ship Bottom, working on a boat he'd bought at a rummage sale in West Creek.

It was an old 350-pound fiberglass Van Duyne surfboat in really bad shape. Some of the decking had rotted away and there were holes in the bottom, the largest of which was about the size of a silver dollar. To add insult to injury, a family of squirrels had nested in the hull for some time and gnawed away at the bow, splintering it in several places.

Working on the craft was a slow and agonizing job that had begun to consume Danny Windsor day and night. If he wasn't working on it, he was talking about it down at the docks and in the shipyards with anyone who could give him advice. *What's the best wood filler for fiberglass? Where can I get a new rudder for cheap? What marine varnish should I use on the coated planks?*

Exactly what he had in mind for the boat Kelly didn't know, and she didn't think he knew, either. What she *did* know was that he had paid too much for it, tapping into their joint savings. It wasn't just that money was tight and the purchase frivolous in her mind; what annoyed her most was that he'd neglected to consult with her until *after* he brought the boat home. By that time it was too late. No refunds. She felt he had violated the trust between them. The timing couldn't have been worse and the fight that followed was epic. They didn't speak for days after that.

Danny was spending a lot of time in the garage focused on the boat repairs, mainly because he felt ashamed of himself around her lately. He knew he hadn't been pulling his weight. He'd tried the State Forestry Service in earnest, but the work of a park ranger wasn't for him; turned out he wasn't the woodsman he thought he was and it kept him away from the two things he loved most, Kelly and the ocean. Salt water was in Danny's veins, and if he had a calling it would have to be on or near the sea.

After a brush with death deep in the forest at the hands of a friend turned nemesis, he saw the light. He threw himself into a fully committed relationship with Kelly, convinced that everything would be eternal bliss. He bought the boat thinking it was a symbolic investment in a new life by the sea with the woman of his dreams. But when the shore economy tanked, so did Crab Cove, the nautical-themed gift shop Kelly was helping her Aunt Sarah run. With the writing on the wall, Kelly stepped away voluntarily, shelving her dream of opening a boutique of her own.

Aunt Sarah and her husband, Noah, felt badly about Kelly's situation and offered to help financially, but she couldn't accept a handout from them and she sure as hell wasn't going to ask her parents for assistance. That was out of the question. She'd declared her independence from them a long time ago, when she and Geoffrey first came to LBI for the summer, staying with Aunt Sarah and working their way through college.

Within a few months of giving up the job, Kelly's savings were running low, and Danny had never been one to put money aside. She took a temp job at Maine Line Insurance to tide them over until she could figure out her next move. Meantime, the surfboat had become a painful sticking point in their relationship. Whenever an argument flared up, which was often lately, she could count on finding Danny working on it in the garage. That was where she found him now.

"Did you look for work today?" she asked from the doorway.

Danny put down the sander and removed his goggles, but didn't answer. She repeated the question, more firmly this time.

"I *have* work," he said with a wide sweep of his hand over the 22-foot boat, which rested hull-side up across a couple of sawhorses.

She frowned. "And just what do you intend to do with it when you're done? Go fishing?"

Danny removed his work gloves slowly, wiping the sweat from his brow as he did. "Maybe I'll ask Moss Greenberg if he'll let me lifeguard again. How can he refuse when I'll bring my own boat?" he said attempting to make light of the situation.

She grew indignant. "That's your plan? You know how poorly guarding pays, and it's seasonal. How are we supposed to get through the winter?"

Exasperated, he sat down on an overturned paint bucket and ran a weary hand through his thick blond hair.

Kelly took a measured step forward. She was now fully inside his sanctuary, and in her present mood it was about as far in as she dared go. "If you want my opinion, I think you should sell it back to the beach patrol once the repairs are finished. Take whatever you can get for it and walk away. Then go find yourself a real job!"

This was not the first time Kelly had expressed this opinion. In fact, Danny thought she was beginning to sound like a broken record. She repeated it every time the subject came up, and it was really starting to grate on him.

"What's for dinner?" he asked, hoping to change the subject.

"We'll find something," she answered with a forced smile before turning to leave.

"Kelly, wait," he said, walking over to her. "I'm sorry. I don't know what else to say. You know me. I don't own a suit, I wouldn't make a good salesman, and Burger King isn't hiring. What am I supposed to do?"

"Maybe Luz can get you a job waiting tables at the Engleside."

He reached for her hand. "That's not for me, either."

She stiffened, letting his hand drop. "Sometimes you have to make compromises, Danny. Do you think I enjoy putting on a smile and going into that office every day to be harassed by the high-and-mighty Rita Zenger? Oh, and by the way, I was just informed that we have to attend the company Halloween party this weekend."

"We? As in you and me?"

"Yes, and that means shelling out money for costumes we can't afford."

"You can wear whatever you want," he corrected her forcefully. "I'm not going."

Kelly's green eyes flashed red. "Oh, no, you don't, Danny. You're not getting out of this one. If I have to go to that haunted hell for an evening, so do you. You can't bail on me this time."

"What's the big deal if I don't go?"

"The big deal is that the big boss is expecting us. *Both* of us!"

5

Day 2

```
BULLETIN
TROPICAL STORM SANDY ADVISORY NUMBER 5
NWS NATIONAL HURRICANE CENTER MIAMI FL        AL182012
1100 AM EDT TUE OCT 23 2012


HURRICANE WARNING ISSUED FOR JAMAICA


THE CENTER OF SANDY WILL MOVE NEAR OR OVER JAMAICA ON
WEDNESDAY...AND APPROACH EASTERN CUBA WEDNESDAY NIGHT.
ADDITIONAL STRENGTHENING IS FORECAST. DURING THE NEXT 36
TO 48 HOURS...INTENSITY MODELS BRING SANDY TO HURRICANE
STRENGTH WHEN IT APPROACHES JAMAICA ON WEDNESDAY.
```

"I know the difference between contrails and chemtrails, Noah, and believe me, these were chemtrails. But don't take my word for it—Rick and your boy, Geoffrey, saw them, too." Paul Decker shrugged. "I've asked Rick to gather some soil samples from the area and send them to Rutgers for analysis."

"All well and good, Deck, but at the moment I'm more interested in the latest weather advisory you mentioned. What's the latest out of Miami?"

It was lunchtime, and the two men were sitting at Irv's in downtown Mount Holly. The bar was on Route 38, in a run-down strip mall in which there were more vacant and boarded-up buildings than occupied ones. The view through the window was of tall, brown weeds growing up through chunks of cracked and uneven concrete in a neglected parking lot.

Decker glanced over his shoulder before responding. "It's been upgraded to a tropical storm and named 'Sandy,' and I don't like it, Noah—she's on track to become a full-fledged hurricane over the next 36 hours."

Noah shifted in his seat. "Have you talked to the station chief … what's his name—Harris?"

"He doesn't listen to me, that twit. Whatever comes out of Miami is gospel according to Harris."

"But that's not good enough for you?"

"I know, I know. It's too early to predict the path of this storm with any certainty, but the pinheads down south pay zero attention to the European models. A number of simulators show that at some point this baby is going to make a left turn."

"When and where?" Noah asked, leaning in closer to keep out of earshot of the bartender. He was the gossipy type.

"And at what wind speed?" Decker repositioned himself on his stool as he contemplated his own question. "There's no doubt this is going to become a hurricane. The only question is, what level? Cat 1, maybe 2?"

"That's the difference between 75 and 90 mile-an-hour sustained winds."

"Noah, you know what kind of difference that can make here in Jersey, with our heavily populated coastline."

"What about the Coriolis Effect?" Noah asked, recalling his Oceanic Studies as a young Coast Guard cadet.

Decker gave him a wry smile. "I see you haven't lost your touch, Professor Parsons. The clockwise spin of your typical hurricane combined with the prevailing westerlies should help keep it out at sea—or so the theory goes."

"Our cold North Atlantic water should suck some energy out of her," added Noah.

"Except that the water temperature is 5 degrees above normal this season—enough to make a hell of a difference in the weather."

Noah looked perplexed. "What's causing the higher temperature?"

Decker snickered. "Global warming ... climate change—if you buy what we're being sold."

"You're not convinced?" Noah asked rhetorically.

"I have my own theory, Noah," Decker said, looking away momentarily as if searching for something just beyond his reach. "But nobody wants to hear it. They think I'm nuts. I won't burden you with it until I have more proof, but I suspect that the plane we saw yesterday has something to do with it."

"Suit yourself," said Noah with curious resignation, adding, "but any information of possible interest to the Coast Guard that you want to share with me is always appreciated. They need to keep ahead of the curve, obviously."

Decker smiled knowingly. "That's why I come to you, Noah. You listen, and take action when it's necessary."

"When it's *prudent*," clarified Noah, "but I think we're getting ahead of ourselves. This storm could go out to sea, or make landfall before it gets this far north."

"The Outer Banks have saved our asses many a time."

"You got that right," Noah mused. "We owe a lot to North Carolina."

"But that doesn't mean we're hurricane proof. Jersey's had big blows before and it's only a matter of time till the next one."

With that, Decker downed his shot of Jack Daniels. He stuck a stick of gum in his mouth and stood to leave. "Thanks for the drink, Noah, and rest assured—I'll be keeping a close eye on this baby."

6

Rollercoaster Ride

"**H**andles well, doesn't she?" the driver said over the roar of his engine as he took Exit 82 off the Garden State Parkway on two wheels. "I know it's a little extravagant, but I lease it back to the company and we write it off as an operating expense." At the end of the exit he turned east on Route 37.

Sitting in the passenger seat of Nick Weber's sleek black Porsche 911 Turbo, Kelly was at a loss for words. She already knew he was handsome. Now she was getting a sense that he might be a little dangerous, too.

When Rita informed her she'd be accompanying the big boss on a "field trip" to assess a client site in Seaside Heights, she couldn't help but wonder why she'd been chosen. As they got closer, Nick explained that her role would be to pay attention and take good notes. He described it as a good opportunity for her to consider her suitability for a career in the insurance industry, keeping the conversation professional while expressing just the slightest hint of personal interest. She was flattered, just as he'd intended.

Ordinarily, a licensed structural engineer would have accompanied the office manager on an assignment like this, but the way Nick saw it, he'd been on enough client assessment tours to do the job without the expense of bringing an engineer down from Connecticut. What's more, he was able to convince the home office folks he could handle it.

If anyone ever bothered to ask Nick why he brought Kelly along, he'd explain it as an opportunity to evaluate a potential new team member. Of course, he hadn't bothered clearing it with either the home office or the temp agency, just in case she turned out to be more interested in him than the job. He was going to enjoy himself, and no matter how today turned out it was already a win-win: fast car, hot girl, day out of the office. He couldn't lose. When she hinted that there might be the slightest rift between her and "Prince Charming" over the Halloween party, he was careful not to press for an advantage and scare her off.

"So, what do you drive?" he asked, even though he had relished watching her climb out of her Mini Cooper many a morning.

"It's a Mini Cooper," she replied. "A black and white one—like a checkerboard."

"That's *your* car?" he said, sounding impressed. "I was wondering who owned that cool little bugger. It really makes a statement."

Kelly sensed a little deception in his banter. She wasn't sure what to make of it, but would be sure to keep her guard up.

He parked the Porsche diagonally in a small lot on the corner of Sherman and Ocean Terrace. "This is the place," he said as they ascended the wooden steps onto Casino Pier.

She was genuinely impressed. "You mean to tell me that these amusement vendors are all insured with Maine Line?"

"Well, maybe not *all* of them," he said with a self-serving grin. "Only the ones who actually paid the premiums. We have a lot of clients at Fun Pier in Seaside Park, too. I sold the policies—General Liability, Worker's Comp, Business Interruption, Property Coverage … the whole shebang."

"How did you manage that?" Now she was the one pretending to be interested.

"Connections," he replied smugly.

"Family or mob?" she shot back playfully.

His face tightened. "Look, when you're in sales you have to make your share of cold calls, and if you bang on enough doors you're bound to meet people. Knock long and hard enough and doors will open for you, too."

She laughed.

"What's so funny?"

"You seem more like the country club type for meeting people."

"The Deal Golf and Country Club to be precise," he bragged.

She decided to steer the conversation away from Nick Weber's charms and accomplishments. "This storm everyone's talking about … I know it's a long way off, but is the company worried about it?"

"Nah."

"Any particular reason?"

"For one, we don't provide the flood insurance. The Federal Government issues the policies and subsidizes the coverage. All we do at Maine Line is sell the policies and grab the commissions. We don't have to settle the claims. We don't really have any skin in the game when it comes to flood losses."

Other than a pair of young joggers, the boardwalk was abandoned. Most of the buildings were boarded up with plywood, buttressed with two-by-fours. Huddled under overcast skies the once lively summer arcade rides smelling of popcorn and cotton candy were nothing more than a pleasant memory for an insurance appraiser and his lovely, if temporary, sidekick.

Strolling past the Bumper Cars, Tilt-a-Whirl, and other rides, Kelly entered the notes Nick dictated as he checked the soundness of each seasonal structure.

When they came to the Dr. Floyd L. Moreland 1910 Dentzel/Looff Carousel, he took an inordinate amount of time going over the winter-readiness of the antique Merry-Go-Round.

"Make a note to have a small wall of sand bags brought in and piled up around the circumference of the base," he said to Kelly. "We want to make certain no water penetrates the flooring."

"I thought you said Maine Line doesn't provide the flood insurance?"

"We don't. But if the flooring gets compromised it could jeopardize the integrity of the rest of the structure, leaving it open to wind and rain damage. We could be on the hook for that."

"Is this your favorite attraction?" she asked after making the notation.

"It's probably our most valuable one," he said without emotion while carefully running his hand over the plywood sheathing, testing its strength. "The Moreland carousel has been in Seaside since 1932, but it's actually over 100 years old. I take it you've never ridden it?"

She shook her head. "My family's spent so much time on LBI that I can't remember going anywhere else."

"Too bad," he explained. "This one ride has 58 painted animals including lions, camels, and 35 hand-carved moving horses that have been painstakingly restored. It's one of only two surviving classic carousels in the state."

"Very impressive," she offered sincerely. "I had no idea we still had relics like this operating at the Shore."

"Hey, are you referring to my age again?" he said, walking over to her and standing close enough that she could smell his breath mint. His slate gray eyes pored over her slowly and purposely, almost taking her breath away. "You know, when you get right down to it I'm not really *that* much older than you, Kelly. Think of the difference in terms of experience, not age."

"What about the rollercoaster?" she asked, turning away from him to point down the pier and break the trancelike moment. His eyes followed her gesture.

"Just a heap of metal," he said disparagingly. "Fun to ride, I guess, but not particularly costly to replace. My personal favorite is the Ferris Wheel." He turned her around gently and pointed in the opposite direction.

She followed his gaze. "Why's that?"

"It reminds me of my first girlfriend," Nick said, taking her by the arm and leading her back down the boardwalk. "We had a memorable time here on our eighth grade trip." It surprised Kelly to realize that his boyish charms were starting to get to her.

As they wandered under the faded sign of Leo's famous boardwalk eatery, he suddenly said, "Hey, are you hungry?"

"I don't think they're open," she laughed as she gazed up at the once colorful sign.

"Leo's cheesesteaks aren't bad, but I was thinking of Brando's in Asbury Park. They've got a peasant shrimp dish with risotto that'll blow you away." He shrugged his shoulders and raised his dark eyebrows flirtatiously, tilting his head as if to say "Why not?" and that was how she answered.

On the way, he learned that she rented in Ship Bottom. She, in turn, discovered that he owned a place on the bay in Barnegat Township, with a hot tub and deck for entertaining—not to mention a private beach entrance that he described, somewhat suggestively, as perfect for late-night skinny dipping.

As they ate, she tried to keep the conversation away from her personal life, doing her best to keep him from gaining any advantage, but she found herself enjoying the food, the mood, and the attention more than she'd have expected. When he dabbed a little white wine sauce from the corner of her mouth with his linen napkin, an audible sigh escaped her.

Practiced at the art of seduction, but not sure whether he wanted to bed her first or train her to be the killer salesperson he thought she had the potential to become, Nick acted the perfect gentleman all the way back to the office. Pulling up to her Mini Cooper, he got out and opened the door, reminding her to think about a career in the insurance business.

"I think you're a natural," he said as they parted, "but I'm reserving my final judgment until I see what you wear to the party."

7
Reputations

"A in't much call for a replacement Van Duyne in the rescue business," said Ned Skinner stuffing his hands into his overalls. "Their surfboats are practically indestructible."

Also *unsinkable*, thought Danny, recalling a story he'd heard as a rookie lifeguard. In 1955 the legendary Atlantic City guard Richard 'Boomer' Blair rowed a Van Duyne into a hurricane on a bet. The boat flooded, but it didn't sink, and Boomer lived to tell the tale.

Danny knew the Van Duyne brothers' reputation and he'd expected this response from the elderly owner of the marina, but still couldn't hide his disappointment. The Van Duyne was lighter than traditional wooden boats, with special flotation pockets built into the fiberglass. Its curved shear let it cut through and climb over waves while always landing flat. It was the fastest *and* safest surfboat available, in his opinion.

And that's why he'd bought the boat in the first place—it was a sound investment. These boats not only held their value but the manufacturer stood behind them, offering a lifetime warrantee on one purchased new. Admittedly, he didn't know anything about economics—including the law of supply and demand—but he'd been absolutely certain of the boat's resale value. Now he was being forced to second guess himself.

Skinner spat a tarlike wad of tobacco onto the gravel lot. "You might wanna try Baker's on Dock Road. They could be looking for a few extra rowboats to rent out next season. Them eco-tourists they get over there won't use a gasoline engine on the bay."

Danny glanced around at the marina's half empty lot. He theorized that more boats would be pulled out of the water over the next couple weeks to be winterized, filling up the apparent vacancies.

"Can you use any help around here?" he asked the old man, changing tack. If there was one thing he'd learned from his surfing days, it was that you had to paddle your own board if you were going to catch a wave.

Skinner rubbed the white stubble on his chin thoughtfully. "You know anything about Johnsons or Evinrudes?"

Danny hesitated. Part of him wanted to say yes, in the worst way. He was a fast learner, and if he could at least land the job he'd get up to speed quickly through a little on-the-job training. Get your foot in the door and the rest will fall into place, he told himself. That'll get Kelly off your back about the boat—you might even be able to keep it, without the guilt trip. There'd be peace in the valley again. Amen!

But something stopped him. Maybe it was the Van Duyne's reputation or maybe it was his own moral compass, but if he lied and got the job the jubilation could be short lived. He might be found out on his very first day. If he got the job but lost Skinner's respect and confidence, what would he have gained?

"Not a damned thing," he admitted with a sad and ironic smile.

The old timer eyed the young man thoughtfully. It was not the reply he'd expected and yet it was refreshing to hear the truth.

"Tell you what," he said. "Next week is November 1, and that's when the boating season more or less comes to an end. Owners will be calling me night and day to come help them take their playthings out of the water for the winter. It could get a little crazy around here short term, but I might be able to use an extra hand lifting and hauling." He handed Danny a card. "Why don't you give me a call next week?"

8

The Engleside Inn

"**W**hat do you call this?" Geoffrey asked as he chowed down on a plate of leafy greens.

"A salad, of course," said Luz Sanchez with a girlish laugh, sliding into the chair beside him. She was still dressed in her white kitchen smock and chef's hat. It was 11:30 PM and they were one of just two couples dining in the Leeward Room of the Engleside Inn, an elegant, half-century old hotel and restaurant in Beach Haven.

"No, no. I mean what kind of salad is it?"

"It's my version of a Tuscan salad. Mixed greens with grilled chicken, cannellini beans, sun-dried tomatoes, and fiddlehead ferns."

"What about the dressing?" Geoffrey asked in between bites.

"What about it?"

"It's tasty. I like the sweetness." He munched happily.

Luz smiled appreciatively. "Why thank you, Geoffrey. It's a raspberry vinaigrette; my own concoction." Removing her cap she tousled her jet black locks revealing a stylish cut that was slightly spiked yet very chic. She picked up her cocktail and took a refined sip.

"And what's that?" he asked, pointing to her chilled martini glass. When he met her he was basically a hamburger and French fries kind of guy, but over the past few years she'd exposed him to the culinary world and, true to his scientific nature, he was always inspired to learn new and interesting things.

"It's called a Crissy, short for Chrysanthemum. Want a taste?"

"Sounds a little prissy, this Crissy," he quipped, shaking his head and reaching for his ice water instead. "Not for me, thanks, but it's a fascinating color. What's in it?"

"Benedictine, dry vermouth, an orange peel, and absinthe."

"Absinthe? You mean the stuff that made Van Gogh go mad?"

"Yep." She smiled Zen-like as she took another sip. "A friend from culinary school showed me how to make it. She used to tend bar at Vinus & Marc on the Upper East Side. That's where I had my first."

Geoffrey gave his girlfriend a look of mock disapproval.

"I allow myself *one* after a really hard night in the kitchen," she explained.

"Nice place, by the way," he said, looking around at the paneled walls and dimmed ceiling lights. "Any regrets about leaving the Gazebo?" He moved his empty salad plate aside.

"None whatsoever. This place is awesome. It's open year-round and we have our own generator. Do you have any idea how often the power goes out on the island? And, of course, we have a fabulous new sushi bar," she added, waving to the Japanese chef who was cleaning up.

"Not everyone in town shares your enthusiasm for the sushi bar," whispered Geoffrey. "Noah said I shouldn't say anything to Paul Decker about your working here unless I was prepared for a nasty harangue about how it ruined the quaintness of the old Engleside."

Luz seemed genuinely amused. "Well, it has brought in a more upscale clientele."

"And cut the drinking bar in half."

She laughed. "Decker … he's that weatherman you climbed the fire tower with, right? Noah's friend?"

"Right. What a strange guy he is, Luz."

"How do you mean?"

"He has very strong opinions, and some of the things he says are … well, a little wacky. I guess he's a conspiracy theorist."

"I'll bet he lives alone."

"He's not married, I know that much. What's your point?"

"That you'll end up just like him if you don't marry me, Geoffrey Martin—an intelligent, but strange and lonely old man."

Geoffrey knew better than to overreact to the marriage reference. The topic seemed to come up whenever they visited her family, and she'd been spending a lot of time with them lately. The two had been dating for two years, and in the traditional Latino mating manual that constituted an eternity, but they both knew they weren't ready to take the plunge. She had just changed jobs from the Gazebo to the Engleside, and his own ambitions were in a state of flux. Since graduating from Princeton with a degree in biochemistry, he found it more challenging and satisfying to continue his apprenticeship in private ecological-environmental endeavors with his mentors, Noah Parsons and Tom Banks, than to pursue a career in the academic or corporate research sectors. The post-graduate degree his mother had wished for him and the pharmaceutical future his father had paved for him were fading away with each passing day.

"We'll know when the time is right, Luz," he said at last, holding her hand to acknowledge they were in it together. "I was going to suggest we live together first, but after seeing how far off track Kelly and Danny seem to be lately, I think they might have been happier when they were apart and pining for one another than they are now."

"First of all, you're not Danny and I'm not Kelly. They'll have to figure out their own relationship. As for ours, my parents would probably kill us both if you even suggested living together without getting married. I guess we'll just have to keep sneaking around until you decide to make an honest woman of me."

He gave her a reassuring hug and kiss. She took it as a sign to change the conversation.

"Now, before they toss us out of here, tell me what your trip to that fire tower was all about."

Geoffrey went there eagerly. "It's pretty obvious that Noah and Tom see me as someone they can pass the torch to, and this was another way to see the Pine Barrens. The view from the top is incredible—you really get a feel for how special the Pinelands are, and their scope. Noah says he wants to schedule a flyover so I can see it from the air. That'll be amazing."

"Okay, I get it, you're an environmentalist. I'm pretty excited about the farm-to-table movement myself, but I really don't see what's so special about the New Jersey Pine Barrens. To me it's just a lot of trees, brush, and sand."

"In a way that's exactly what it is—over a million acres of forest situated in the most densely populated state in the union. The Pinelands sits on top of one of the largest freshwater aquifers on the East Coast and supports many species of flora and fauna that are found nowhere else on the planet."

Luz loved hearing Geoffrey talk passionately about one of his favorite subjects, and she rewarded him with a crooked smile. "And I thought it was just home to the Jersey Devil," she said with her sexiest wink.

"There's a reason that legend has persisted for over three hundred years. Did you know the Jersey Devil is mentioned in Lenape lore? You have to ask yourself why."

Luz shook her head and gave him a skeptical look, feeling the effects of the drink and the long workday behind her.

"Just think about it for a minute, Luz. In virtually every fairytale, myth, or legend, something of great value—a priceless treasure or a beautiful princess—is guarded by a beast. An ogre or a dragon, for instance."

"Go on," she said, picturing herself as a maiden in distress.

"Well, in our New Jersey tale, the precious water below the sugar sand and the rare plant and animal species above it are the treasure. 'As above, so below.' "

She thought she was hearing things. "Geoffrey, did you just quote Scripture?"

"No, Babylonian astrology. Mythological references can be found in every culture."

"So, what you're saying is that the Jersey Devil is a mythological beast, like a dragon …?"

"Not quite. What I'm saying is that the Jersey Devil is a benevolent spirit that manifests itself in malevolent form in order to protect the ecological well-being of the Pine Barrens from human destruction."

She raised her carefully sculpted eyebrows as she polished off her drink. "That's quite profound, Geoffrey. Did you come up with it on your own?"

"I wish I could take credit for it, Luz, but I really can't. I've had some great teachers. It's taken awhile, but I think it's finally beginning to sink in."

9

Day 3

```
BULLETIN
HURRICANE SANDY ADVISORY NUMBER 9
NWS NATIONAL HURRICANE CENTER MIAMI FL          AL182012
1100 AM EDT WED OCT 24 2012


SANDY REACHES HURRICANE STRENGTH...CONDITIONS DETERIORATING
IN JAMAICA

SANDY IS A CATEGORY ONE HURRICANE ON THE SAFFIR-SIMPSON
HURRICANE WIND SCALE. THE CENTER OF SANDY IS EXPECTED TO
MOVE NEAR OR OVER EASTERN JAMAICA THIS AFTERNOON AND THIS
EVENING...OVER EASTERN CUBA TONIGHT AND THURSDAY MORNING...
AND APPROACH THE CENTRAL BAHAMAS ON THURSDAY. TROPICAL
STORM CONDITIONS ARE POSSIBLE IN THE WATCH AREA ALONG THE
EAST COAST OF FLORIDA ON FRIDAY.
```

"I take it you've seen the latest advisory from Miami?" Paul Decker was saying as he strode into the contemporary-looking, minimally furnished office. The dour-faced secretary who'd admitted Decker pulled the door shut behind him.

"I have," replied the impeccably dressed, prematurely gray man at the glass and chrome desk. Ted Harris put down his cell phone and pressed a button on a black remote control device. The giant flat-screen on the wall behind him switched from a colorful swirling satellite image of the United States to a muted CNN newscast.

Decker took a seat in a padded polychrome chair on the other side of the desk from his NOAA Sub-Station Bureau Chief. Meeting with Ted Harris always brought to mind water cooler talk to the effect that the Penn State graduate in Atmospheric Sciences and Meteorology would make a better Weather Channel anchorman than a station boss. He certainly had the looks for the television role, but in Decker's opinion he was sorely lacking in character, balls, and personality. Harris wasn't one to think for himself, but he took orders well and that made him an ideal mid-level bureaucrat. Unfortunately, he'd been unable to earn the trust and respect of his peers and staff, especially the old-school weathermen like Decker.

"Then you realize Sandy's wreaking havoc in the Caribbean and is a serious threat to the Atlantic coast."

"That's one possible scenario, of course," Harris said casually, leaning back in his chair.

"You don't seem to be taking it very seriously."

"Paul, our job is to follow the weather as it develops," Harris said, "not sensationalize it. That's for the Al Rokers of the world. NOAA can't afford to spread hypotheticals that might cause widespread hysteria."

"But you're not getting out the complete picture," Decker said adamantly.

"What *is* the complete picture, Paul?" Harris asked, his irritation showing. "That the effects of global warming are causing Earth's temperatures to rise steadily and produce irregular weather patterns? Everybody knows that."

"Is that what you think Sandy is, Ted? An irregular weather pattern? We're talking about a Halloween hurricane in the same climate zone that was paralyzed by an ice storm a year ago. Or by *irregular* do you mean the cold front advancing from the north that nobody's talking about?"

Harris hesitated, surprised the old man had this information that Weather Central in Miami hadn't yet disseminated through channels. "What are you getting at, Paul?"

Decker slammed his fist down on the arm of his chair. "You know *exactly* what I'm getting at."

Forcing himself to remain calm, Harris gave Decker a half smile. "I assume you mean the polar vortex that's impacting the Midwest."

Decker shook his head in pained disbelief. "*Polar vortex*? Is that what we're blaming anomalies on these days? I've been forecasting weather for forty years and I've never heard anyone scapegoat a polar vortex until just now!"

"In that case you might want to start planning an exit strategy, Paul, because time and technology are obviously passing you by. If I were you, I'd make my move before someone posts your liquid lunch habits on social media. Now, if you don't mind, some of us have real work to do."

He pressed the intercom and asked his secretary to show Paul Decker the door.

10

Cap'n Crunch

Rick McGuiness hung up the phone and rejoined his family at the breakfast table. The puzzled look in those honest, pale blue eyes of his caught his frazzled, petite wife's attention.

"Who was that?" Jackie McGuiness inquired as she poured her husband a second cup of coffee.

"Long Beach Township Dispatch."

"Why are they calling you? Is there a fire? You're just a volunteer. You can't go in today. You've got to go to work." She was building to a fever pitch.

"Calm down, Jackie. There's no fire. The call was just to inform me of a meeting tomorrow at Municipal Hall."

"About what?" she asked, emptying a box of Cap'n Crunch into a bowl for their ten-year-old son, Billy, who was sitting across from her reading a comic. "Eat slowly, Billy," she said. "You've got some time before the bus gets here."

"Emergency CAT evacuation procedures for the island." Rick got up and turned on the 19-inch TV that was perched on the kitchen counter across from him. Keeping the volume low, he switched on the local news channel. A commercial for Bounty paper towels—"the quicker picker upper"—filled the screen. Jackie tore off two sheets of her own and wiped the spilled milk from under Billy's bowl.

With his attention on the screen, Rick took a sip of his coffee and added, "It's about that hurricane brewing in the Bahamas. Apparently some weather models show it heading our way."

"A hurricane, here?" Jackie huffed as she tied a bib around baby Caitlyn's neck. The floral bib was spotless, but the high chair she sat in and her mother's white robe wore the remnants of her Gerber's all natural applesauce like a Jackson Pollock painting. "This late in the season? You've got to be kidding." She brushed aside the applesauce and put a baby bottle in Caitlyn's mouth. "When is it supposed to reach us?"

"Don't know yet, and of course it may pass us by altogether. But the State wants us to be prepared, just in case."

"What about my costume, Dad?" whined Billy, pausing from his loud chomping long enough to shout out his question. "You promised to help me go Trick or Treating as Captain John Bacon, the pirate we read about in school."

"I will, son, don't worry. Halloween is still a week away." He turned to his wife and said, "You should probably gas up your car today or tomorrow, honey, just in case the weather gets ugly."

Rick missed Jackie's brief glare that said, "Do you take me for an idiot?", as she wiped some baby food from her brow with the back of her hand and held her tongue.

"Hopefully the storm will never make it this far north," he added, "but I'm going to gas up the generator, just in case."

***

"I don't know how you got a table at Peter Luger's on such short notice, but this is certainly a pleasant surprise," said Larry Sessions. Drink in hand, and fashionably attired in his fitted Hugo Boss suit, Sessions looked every bit the successful Wall Street broker he was. "Nobody does a steak like these guys. I still don't understand why we had to meet in person, but I'm always up for this place."

"I didn't want to risk a phone trade," said Nick Weber as he took the seat across from Sessions, "and an email or online transaction from the office was out of the question. This deal is too important." As if the venerable steakhouse wasn't a dead giveaway, Nick mused. If you're out to impress a woman you take her to Il Mulino. If you want to impress a Wall Street guy you take him to Luger's. Period. End of story.

"I'm all ears." The broker took a healthy sip of his drink.

"Larry," said Weber, circling cautiously, "how far back do we go?"

Sessions raised his glass, "Here's to Saint Rose of Belmar, where the priests and nuns taught us everything we needed to know, Nick—and here's to the fact that we forgot everything they taught us in a hurry."

Nick's face broke into a grin. "I've made a lot of money for you over the years haven't I, Larry? Commissions, fees, and a few stock tips thrown in every now and then, right?"

"I guess I've done all right by you, too," opined the financial advisor, clinking glasses with his childhood friend and long-time business associate.

"Right. So what I need most from you now is not to ask any questions. I need your word on this, and your absolute discretion." Weber had lowered his voice and piqued his friend's interest at the same time. Sessions knew this guy didn't gamble unless the stakes were high enough to net a serious windfall.

Sessions gave him a hard stare. "You're not going to ask me to do anything illegal are you, Nick? I really don't need the SEC breathing down my neck right now."

"Nothing illegal, Larry. Not for you, anyway." Nick paused. "Immoral, maybe, but that depends on your point of view." He leaned in and filled his old school chum in on the basics of his plan.

Both men laughed like co-conspirators. Back in college they had charged underclassmen twenty bucks apiece to enter parties that cost them less than a buck a head to put together.

"This sounds pretty bold, even for you," Sessions said, downing his drink and signaling the waiter for another. "You wouldn't be doing all this just to impress a babe, would you, Nick?"

"You know me better than that," Weber sneered. "I lost count of all the smoke shows we took down in our prime and not one of them ever made me sweat, isn't that so?"

"You are the man!" Sessions bellowed. "It'll be just like the old days at Rider, Nick. We were the best roommates ever—lazy, unethical, and completely disreputable. You just keep a tab open for me at Lugers and I'll get the dollars rolling in."

"I don't trust you *that* much, Larry," Nick said, only half joking. "But if we do pull this thing off, we might be able to get ourselves a table next to the high rollers."

"Hell, if we pull this one off, Nick, we'll *be* the high rollers!"

11
Fortune Cookies

The playful crustacean on the faded driftwood sign above the front door needed some touch up paint and the bay window display case could use a good cleaning, but other than these minor signs of benign neglect, Crab Cove looked as good as it had in the days when Kelly helped her Aunt Sarah run the nautical-themed arts and crafts boutique. Those were long workdays, she recalled—sometimes twelve hours or more, including weekends—but they were happy times that made Kelly feel alive with purpose.

Just seeing the lavender clapboard building again after the last few difficult months brought a flood of warm nostalgia that made Kelly's eyes moisten as she parked her Mini Cooper curbside. Many a happy summer was spent with Geoffrey and their beloved aunt, rummaging through the curio shop and sharing the spacious living quarters above it. Throughout high school and college, Kelly's life had spun around LBI, providing the lion's share of her fondest memories. She'd found the love of her life lying face down and unconscious in the surf at Ship Bottom, just a quarter mile away, though lately she wondered if her act of resuscitating him so many years ago had cemented a bond between them or imposed a debt that could never be repaid.

She bounded up the creaky wooden steps and the miniature ship's bell tinkled overhead as she pushed the front door open. "Hello? Aunt Sarah? It's me—it's Kelly …"

The gift shop appeared empty. It was off-season, of course, and that meant her aunt would normally close the store around five. She looked up at the leafy sea fan clock hanging on the wall behind the counter and realized it was almost 5:30—where had the day gone? Through the side shop window she could see the crimson sun setting over the bay.

She hadn't expected to find any customers here at this time of day, but she was a little surprised to find the front door unlocked and the shop seemingly unattended. Another wave of nostalgia swept over her as she slowly glanced around the charming novelty shop crammed cheerfully with Jersey Shore keepsakes, souvenirs, and bric-a-brac of every variety.

Sliding over to the cash register she noticed it had been rung out and cleared. She gently picked up the aquamarine quartz figurine of two kissing dolphins and thought back to the first time she'd handled it. She turned it over and read once more the inscription that Sarah's deceased first husband, Hugh Bishop, had engraved on the bottom of the wooden base: *To my darling Sarah—May this small gift inspire you to give others the great joy you have given me. With love always, Hugh.*

Reading it again reminded Kelly of her dream to open a boutique specializing in surf and aquatic wear. Unfortunately, that dream seemed to be drifting ever further out to sea.

"You startled me, Kelly!" said Sarah Bishop-Parsons pulling back the beaded curtain at the rear of the shop. She was wearing her famous "get crabby with me" shop smock. "I didn't hear the bell."

"Is everything all right?" Kelly asked, somewhat alarmed.

"Oh, yes, dear. I was just sitting out back watching a beautiful sunset. It's so peaceful and tranquil here. It got me thinking about those poor people in the Bahamas who are getting socked by that terrible hurricane."

"You mean Sandy," Kelly said, coming over to give her aunt a kiss on the cheek.

"I don't know what we'll do if Sandy makes it up this far. We've been through a lot of storms mind you—mostly Nor'easters. Then there was what's-her-name ... 'Irene' last year. She ended up doing nothing here despite our governor cussing at us to 'get the hell off the beach.' The nerve of that blowhard, as if he could care less about us."

"Now, Aunt Sarah, there you go letting your politics show again," Kelly teased good-naturedly.

Sarah pooh-poohed her and the two ladies sat down on the padded stools behind the counter. "What does Noah think about Sandy?"

"He says it could be a humdinger of a storm. He and one of his cronies have been tracking it for several days."

"Our office is watching, too," Kelly sighed, a hint of resignation evident in her voice. "They're asking staff to be prepared to come in over the weekend." She took her aunt's hand. "You do have insurance, don't you?" she asked, then let out a laugh. "That's funny—in all the time I spent here I never thought to ask you that until now!"

Sarah averted her niece's eyes momentarily. "To tell you the truth, Kelly, I'm not really sure. I can't remember if I paid the premium for this year or not. I don't have to tell you how difficult our finances have been."

Kelly leapt from her stool. "C'mon, I'll help you look for the policy."

Aunt Sarah put a hand on her arm. "Don't you worry about that right now, dear. I'll have Noah look with me later. I'd rather know what brings you here tonight—you must've come straight from work."

"Danny went to see his old mentor, Moss Greenberg," Kelly said, reclaiming her seat. "You know, the lifeguard who trained us ...? They're having dinner together, so I thought I'd swing by and see if you were up for Chinese take-out."

"It's not like you and Danny to eat dinner apart," Sarah said, stroking her niece's long auburn hair. "Is everything all right?"

Kelly let out a deep sigh and plunged in. "Not really. We're like strangers lately, and it seems like when we're together all we do is fight. I think he's having second thoughts about living together."

"And what about you, dear? Are you having second thoughts?"

She hesitated. "I don't know ... I mean, yes, I guess I am. I've been trying to work things out with Danny since I was sixteen. It seems like he's all I ever wanted."

"And now?" Sarah prodded.

"I'm not sure *what* I want anymore. Maybe it was just a young girl's fantasy, the idea of being with such a cute blond beach boy. I never even considered seeing anyone else."

"Now that you mention it, he does sort of remind me of a young Dennis Wilson," Aunt Sarah said with a giggle. She was referring to the original drummer for the Beach Boys and hoping to evoke a smile from her distraught niece.

When the smile didn't appear, Sarah took Kelly gently by both arms and turned her to look directly into her consoling sea green eyes. Sarah was taller and thinner than Margaret, her younger sister and Kelly's mother, and but for her sun-streaked strawberry blonde hair, pulled back in a scrunchy behind the nape of her neck, she could have easily passed for an older version of her niece.

"You're no longer a sixteen-year-old girl, Kelly. You're an intelligent, educated woman, and it's quite possible you've outgrown Danny, as hard as that might be for you to admit."

Kelly didn't respond immediately. Sure, she'd thought about it, but hearing her aunt say it seemed to give it more validity.

"Is there someone else?" her aunt asked shrewdly, trying to read her niece's thoughts. "Someone you've met at work, perhaps?"

"No, not really, although my boss has been encouraging me to consider a career in the insurance business. Our relationship has been strictly professional, but there's some flirting going on, too."

Sarah offered a brief warning about workplace romances, and in the next breath wanted to know if her boss was good looking.

"Oh God, he's gorgeous. Is it wrong to think I might have rushed into things with Danny, Aunt Sarah? That I haven't given myself a chance to explore my options?"

Sarah patted Kelly's hand then stood and reached for the antique wall phone. "It sounds like we've got a lot to talk about. I think it's time to order the Chinese food."

Kelly smiled appreciatively. "Don't forget the fortune cookies."

12

Gum Drops

Rita Zenger watched with concern as her eighty-nine-year-old father fiddled with his nose clip and tugged at the tubing tethered to an oxygen tank strapped to the side of his wheelchair. It was obvious he didn't want any part of it. Left to his own devices, the equipment would be on the floor in a New York minute.

"Leave it be, Pop," Rita said firmly yanking his hand away from his face. "The doctor said you need to keep it on for at least an hour before bedtime so you'll sleep through the night."

"I sleep just fine," the old man hissed dryly. "With all the pills he pushes down my throat it's a wonder I can keep my eyes open at all."

Even at his advanced age and in declining health, Helmut Zenger, a former foreman at Dinger Brothers Iron and Fence Works in Trenton, was as hardheaded as his given name might suggest. In fact, Rita considered stubbornness the defining characteristic of a man she had come to admire and detest in almost equal measure during a lifetime devoted to care and concern for him. It remained their mutual heartache that Rita's mother, the sainted and long-suffering Helga Ulrich Zenger, had died of a cerebral hemorrhage moments after giving birth to her, ending the happy couple's short-lived union.

Celebrated for Prussian precision in both his work and his childrearing technique, Helmut Zenger had earned considerable notoriety for his artistry with wrought iron railings and hand-woven garden fences. His ornate designs were highly prized by wealthy corporate and residential clients seeking to make a statement about deterrence while gaining points for good taste. But it was grueling work, and forty-three years of forging and welding cast iron and molten steel in a grimy, dust-filled machine shop on Genesee Street, eventually took its toll on the big man. Decades of inhaling sulfur and acetylene fumes has its consequences, chronic emphysema being chief among them.

Besides raising his daughter, the only thing outside of work that gave Helmut Zenger any joy was saltwater fishing. Banding together with a group of men he knew from the shop and his favorite Chambersburg watering holes, Helmut found his way to LBI most weekends from April through November—with or without his little princess, depending on the availability of their neighbor, the kindly Mrs. Marinaro, for sitting duty.

It was during one of these excursions, while fishing the Beach Haven Inlet near the Edwin G. Forsyth Wildlife Preserve, that Helmut discovered the Long Beach Island Trailer Park in Holgate. Located at the island's southern tip, the park had been built in the early 1950s by the Muroff family, Russian immigrants who were investing heavily in Jersey shore real estate at the time. In the six decades since, an eclectic mix of poets, painters, professors, performers, firemen, builders, and surfers, among others, had come to call it home.

For Helmut, the rustic community of nonconformists struck an immediate chord. In 2001, shortly after retiring from Dinger Brothers, and with his daughter safely if not happily married to the doctor of her dreams, he bought his little piece of paradise, consigning himself to a routine of sunny skies, salt air, and fishing for the rest of his days.

Helmut stopped fussing with the breathing apparatus and looked up at his daughter. "How's work?" he asked in his coarse, raspy voice.

"The same," sighed Rita. "I move piles of paper around and crack the whip for Nick Weber so he doesn't have to soil his hands. Then I go home, eat cold pizza, watch Seinfeld re-runs, and go to bed."

"Not much of a life," he mused sadly.

"Neither was yours," she answered honestly.

The elder Zenger smiled. "At least I had you."

"Ditto, Pops, and thanks to you I can still out-fish any man alive on a party boat. I think that's what scares them off."

"Still not dating? Isn't it time you jumped in again?"

"At my age the pool's a little shallow for diving head first."

Helmut cracked another grin. "Where does that leave me?" He paused. "I don't suppose you've heard from your ex-husband?"

"Oh yeah, just last week I got a post card from Maui," she replied with contempt. "He's there at the national podiatry meeting with his new flavor of the week."

Helmut was well acquainted with his daughter's sarcasm. It had been her preferred means of coping since her husband had suddenly left her. She was a bitter woman. "Another receptionist? Hasn't he finished with that box of gumdrops yet? Christ, what flavor's left?"

"I think he's trying to have one of every race, creed, color, shape, and size."

"What a waste of time. He had the best, now there's only the rest." Helmut coughed dryly as the disease choked the air passages in his lungs. He inhaled deeply several times, savoring the cool, mist-like oxygen.

"That's sweet, Pop, but you're just saying that because you're my father." Rita offered her father a glass of water, which he waved aside graciously.

"I worry about you, Rita. I'm not made of iron, you know. Before I skip off to meet my maker it would be nice to know you have someone to share the rest of your life with."

She glanced down at the sleepy sheepdog lying on the floor beside her father's wheelchair. "There's always Max."

At the sound of his name, the shaggy-haired old boy got up, padded over and nuzzled her. She gave him a good scratch behind his ears. "You'll never leave me will you, Maxie?" She looked back at her father. "Besides, I *am* made of metal. I came from you, didn't I? Or are you going to tell me at this late date that I was adopted?"

The old man chuckled, snorting through his nose clip. "I only hope I didn't let you or your mother down." He started to tear up.

Rita bit her lip. "That's my line, Pop. Besides, it's not fair. You worked hard all those years to keep me fed, clothed, and educated, and now that it's finally time for you to enjoy the good life you've earned, you're too damned slowed down by disease to enjoy it. It's just not fair."

"Rita, honey, I don't know if it's fair or not, but I do know that it's probably a good thing to be old and sick when it's time to go."

She looked puzzled. "What do you mean?"

"If living with these pocket poets and surfboard philosophers has taught me anything, it's that this planet is just a brief stop along the way to a far better place, be it heaven or Nirvana or whatever you want to call it. So it's okay for us to be old and even sick when it's our time to go. If we stayed youthful and healthy forever, no one would ever want to leave!"

Max barked his concurrence.

Rita stood to go, but hesitated. "I really wish you and Max would reconsider staying at my place for a few days. I don't like the way this storm is shaping up and this trailer park is terribly exposed."

"Rita, this is my home. These are my friends. We all help each other out. That's the way it is and that's the way it should be. Besides, how bad can this storm be? They named it after a woman, didn't they?"

"Sandy can be either male or female, and you're a chauvinist pig," she chided her father tenderly. "That's the problem with you old timers—women just don't get any respect."

13

Day 4

```
BULLETIN
HURRICANE SANDY ADVISORY NUMBER 13
NWS NATIONAL HURRICANE CENTER MIAMI FL          AL182012
1100 AM EDT THU OCT 25 2012


SANDY APPROACHING CENTRAL BAHAMAS


A TROPICAL STORM WARNING IS IN EFFECT FOR...FLORIDA EAST
COAST FROM OCEAN REEF TO FLAGLER BEACH...LAKE OKEECHOBEE...
THE REMAINDER OF THE SOUTHEASTERN BAHAMAS.


A TROPICAL STORM WATCH IS IN EFFECT FOR...FLORIDA UPPER KEYS
FROM OCEAN REEF TO CRAIG KEY...INTERESTS ELSEWHERE ALONG
THE EAST COAST OF THE UNITED STATES SHOULD MONITOR THE
PROGRESS OF SANDY.


SANDY IS A CATEGORY TWO HURRICANE ON THE SAFFIR-SIMPSON
HURRICANE WIND SCALE. MAXIMUM SUSTAINED WINDS REMAIN NEAR
105 MPH...165 KM/H WITH HIGHER GUSTS. PREPARATIONS TO PROTECT
LIFE AND PROPERTY SHOULD BE RUSHED TO COMPLETION.
```

The introduction was short and sweet as fire, police, EMT, and other first responders from the six LBI municipalities gathered in the packed municipal hall along with a range of government employees and political appointees. Acting as moderator, Long Beach Township's mayor explained that they were about to be briefed on the storm's latest activities by Paul Decker, a senior meteorologist from Mt. Holly who was a veteran forty-year weatherman. As Decker came to the podium and tapped the mic, the room fell silent.

Even in their usual state of readiness, many in attendance neglected to process Decker's opening disclaimer that he was there at the invitation of Noah Parsons and members of the township council, and *not* in an official capacity representing his employer, the U.S. Weather Service. Among those assembled were Noah, Geoffrey Martin, and "Ranger Rick" McGuiness. The latter had just entered the room after chatting with a few of his former surfing buddies about rough surf and rip currents, and what he described as an ominous, darkening line on the horizon this morning.

"Four days ago," Decker said slowly in a rehearsed monotone, "when it quietly hitched a ride on the jet stream between the Windward Islands and Jamaica, this storm was not much more than a low pressure tropical wave designated rather innocuously as 99L. Yesterday, the storm we now know as Sandy made a direct hit on the islands of Jamaica and Haiti as a Category 1 hurricane. In Haiti alone it was responsible for the deaths of fifty-four people."

In spite of Decker's bland delivery style, intended to keep everyone calm, his words were greeted by several muffled gasps, fueling his emotion as he continued.

"After Jamaica and Haiti, Sandy became more organized, picking up steam from the deep warm water along the Cayman Trench. At approximately 1:00 AM this morning, the storm slammed into Cuba as a Category 3 hurricane. Sustained wind speeds were measured at 115 miles per hour with isolated gusts topping out at 150 miles per hour. Based on very early reports, there have been at least eleven deaths and over 17,000 homes destroyed in Cuba."

With that pronouncement the air seemed to have been sucked out of the room. A moment of stunned silence was followed immediately by loud and animated chatter throughout the hall.

"Mr. Decker, in your experience, have you ever seen anything like this before?" shouted an elderly councilwoman from the front row.

Decker cleared his throat. "The last time we saw a storm with this kind of potential was in 1991."

"Can you clarify what you mean by 'this kind of potential?'" a uniformed patrolman standing near the doorway wanted to know. Decker looked over and saw that the officer was flanked by two unsmiling men in dark suits, sporting equally dark sunglasses in spite of the poor lighting in the room.

He glanced at Noah, who took a quick look at the two men before nodding for him to continue. He took a deep breath as he reminded himself that few in the room would fully grasp the ramifications of the forecast he was about to share.

"It's still a little too early to say with any degree of certainty, but this storm has the potential to morph into a hybrid like the one immortalized in Sebastian Junger's book, *The Perfect Storm*. Many of you may be more familiar with the George Clooney–Mark Wahlberg movie based on the book. In that 1991 storm, the remnants of Hurricane Grace combined with a powerful Nor'easter. Although the storm stayed out at sea, producing the rogue wave that allegedly capsized the *Andrea Gail*, the East Coast experienced extensive flooding from the storm surge—particularly in Massachusetts, where some coastal areas were hit by thirty-foot waves."

"Those movie folks came here and hired out one of our long-liners, the *Lorelei*, as a stand in for the *Andrea Gail*," a woman seated near the front of the hall said loudly. "It was a shame what happened to that poor fishing boat and her crew."

"What everyone here really wants to know is, what can we expect on LBI and neighboring communities?" interrupted the mayor, summarizing boldly for his constituents.

"It's not in my nature to be an alarmist," Decker began, causing both Noah and Geoffrey to chuckle quietly, "but there is a cold front moving down through the

Ohio Valley as we speak. If the extremities from that low-pressure system mix with the warm core at the center of the hurricane, we could have the makings of a gigantic wind generator, a couple hundred miles wide, putting the entire Eastern Seaboard within her reach. When you also factor in the maximum tidal surge expected during a full moon this weekend, the devastation from the combined wind, wave, and flooding actions of a storm of this magnitude would be severe."

"That's assuming the storm makes landfall in New Jersey," a council member clarified. "Past experience suggests that this hurricane, like Irene last year and so many others, might just leave us with some wind, rain, and rough surf as it moves out to sea."

Decker bit his lip. This fool was advocating the ostrich-head-in-the-sand scenario at the worst possible time. *Didn't he hear what I said? With or without a New Jersey landfall, this storm is going to be huge. It doesn't have to be close. Not by a long shot.*

"Nevertheless," the mayor interjected as he saw a seething, icy stare steal over the aged weatherman's face, "we need to be prepared. According to other reports we've received, and taking Mr. Decker's expert commentary into account, the next twenty-four hours will be critical. With that in mind, I am recommending that until we receive further instructions from the Governor's Office or the Federal Emergency Management folks, we start setting up a string of emergency sites similar to what we put in place last year in advance of Irene, with north and south command centers at Harvey Cedars and Beach Haven, respectively."

14

Shop Talk

Nick Weber heard a sharp rap on his open office door. Before he even had time to put down the $1200 platinum-plated Montblanc he was using to sign a pile of documents on his desk, Rita Zenger was seated in front of him with the door closed.

"We need to talk," she said firmly, pulling her long, dark hair into a tight braid as she crossed her shapely legs slowly and purposefully to get his undivided attention. Now in her early fifties, Rita was an attractive woman with a terrific figure—somewhere between an Oktoberfest fantasy and a prison guard dominatrix, Nick had decided under the effect of vast amounts of alcohol when they first met.

He often thanked his lucky stars that he'd kept his libido in check with Rita over the years, fighting the occasional urge, as she'd proven to be an exceptional assistant and he would never want to compromise their professional relationship. Despite her infamously severe attitude, he had developed a genuine fondness for her, and enjoyed her company on those rare occasions when she allowed herself to relax and let some warmth and light show in her eyes. He could see this wasn't going to be one of those moments.

"Can it wait, Rita?" he said without looking up. "I have a stack of contracts to finish and I'm way behind schedule." He wasn't making it up. He'd been out of the office more than usual lately, and work had begun to pile up.

She held her ground. "No, Nick, it can't."

He marked his place on the page in front of him and carefully put his expensive pen aside. He pushed a pile of papers out of the way and folded his hands in front of him like a priest about to hear a confession he really wasn't looking forward to. "So, what's on your mind?"

"The weather report for this weekend isn't very promising," she said, dancing around her intended topic. "Given the anxiety over what's coming, I'm thinking about canceling the Halloween party on Saturday."

He rolled his eyes. "It's your party Rita, you make the call."

"I'd like your opinion," she insisted.

"You mean you want me to make the decision for you," he said, guessing at her real motive.

"What does it matter to you? You never come anyway."

"I was planning to come this year."

She sat up straight. "I'm not surprised."

"What's that supposed to mean?" he asked, focusing on Rita's legs as she re-crossed them, without forethought this time.

"Isn't it obvious?"

"Not to me."

"It is to everyone else. It's all over the office."

Nick sat back in his chair and sighed. "Okay, Rita, what's this all about?"

"Don't play games with me, Nick. You know damn well what it's about. The entire staff is buzzing about the attention you're paying to the Martin girl."

"Is it *really* the entire staff, Rita, or just you?" He leaned forward with a flirtatious grin.

"What's the difference?" She had to stifle a laugh before recovering, "Christ, Nick, she's a *temp*, for heaven's sake."

"She still deserves encouragement and training, doesn't she?"

"I can't believe it—*that's* your rationale?" Rita arched her eyebrows, challenging him to come clean.

"Rita, this girl has more gray matter between her ears than any temp I've ever seen," he said forcefully.

"Then why do I get the feeling you're mainly interested in what's between her legs?"

"Don't bring your own personal issues into this!" he shot back defensively.

She held her ground. "Then show me it's different this time, Nick. For once, just walk away."

"I won't have to. In a month the temp assignment ends and it won't be an issue any longer. In the meantime, deal with it. That's what you get paid to do."

Nick reached for his paperwork, signaling that the conversation was over. Rita had crossed a line that only she could get away with, and she knew it. She also knew he would only put up with so much, even from her.

As she stood to leave she couldn't resist a parting comment. "I'm not paid to turn a blind eye to this sort of thing, Nick. You don't pay me enough for that."

"Fine, so cancel the goddamn party!" he said throwing up his hands. "Nobody will have to worry about drinking and driving in a hurricane." As Rita reached the door, he called out for her to wait. "Since it's already budgeted, schedule a Happy Hour for the whole staff at Finnegan's tomorrow night instead—we'll toast the impending storm. I think the employees will appreciate it."

Rita considered his idea. "What are you trying to do, buy them off?"

"No, liquor them up. Give them something else to wag their tongues about. It could be a long weekend."

15

Riot in Aisle 5

C-R-A-S-H!

A thunderous boom reverberated through the Home Depot on Route 72 just across the causeway from LBI, but most of the late afternoon shoppers were too busy gathering what they needed for the storm to even notice.

"What the hell was that?" Geoffrey turned to ask his companion, but Danny was already moving in the direction of the disturbance. "Aisle 5," he called back over his shoulder. "Lumber."

A heavy-set, bearded construction worker in a sweaty T-shirt was yelling at a beleaguered teenaged sales clerk. A jumble of latticed fence partitions and two-by-fours lay scattered on the floor in front of them.

"What do you mean you're out of plywood?" the contractor shouted. "How the *bleep* can that happen?"

"We should be getting a shipment in on Tuesday," the clerk said meekly.

"That won't do," the man bellowed. "I've got a schedule to keep and employees to pay!"

Several other angry patrons began chiming in, directing their rants over the inconvenience at the cowering clerk. A few raised their fists in the air to emphasize their rising discontent.

"Have you tried Tuckerton Lumber?" the clerk suggested.

"I just came from there, you moron," said the incensed contractor, poking his finger in the boy's chest. "They sent me here!"

"What's going on?" Danny asked another floor clerk, a middle-aged African American woman who had just radioed the store manager from a safe distance. The scene in Aisle 5 was growing uglier by the second as other outraged shoppers joined in the tirade against the lad in the orange smock. She didn't seem eager to step into the fray but was clearly worried about her coworker as he tried to head toward the front of the store, pursued by disgruntled customers.

"Haven't you heard?" she responded with surprise. "There's a hurricane headed our way and people are starting to panic. We're out of gas cans, flashlights, batteries, bottled water, generators, and now plywood. I've got two kids in daycare and I work the night shift at a nursing home to meet my bills. This job isn't worth getting beat up over," she said without taking a breath.

"Well, I'm just here for some marine paint," Danny said.

"Aisle 13, left side, bottom shelf," the clerk said without taking her eyes off the fracas.

"I'll get it," said Geoffrey snatching the shopping list from Danny and hustling back down the main aisle.

"C'mon Stephen," the female clerk yelled out to the young man who'd been taking all the abuse as she took a few tentative steps toward the building materials scattered on the cement floor. "I'll help you put this stuff back."

"Hey, where do you think you're going?" the contractor said extending an arm to block the young man's path as he turned to walk back. "I want to talk to the manager."

"He's on his way," the female clerk said sharply, rushing over to push the man's arm aside. "Now you leave this boy alone."

Several more customers were now crowding around the two clerks, moving in on them from all sides. As the mob started pushing and shoving, the young man was thrown to the floor. Danny jumped in to defend the female clerk and all hell broke loose. He tried to separate the burly contractor from the enraged woman and in the process took a left hook to the chin from someone unseen. His head rocked backward. Pulling himself together, he threw a right cross that hit the contractor on the side of the head, dazing him long enough for Danny to land a swift left jab to his jaw and bring the big man down.

As the contractor lay on the floor, the female clerk kicked him in the gut for good measure. The angry crowd started closing ranks again until a loud clanging of metal on metal brought the melee to a sudden halt.

The balding store manager banged the shovelhead on the metal shelf one more time to make sure he had everyone's attention. A stern-faced security guard stood beside him, club and mace can at the ready. The mob scattered, leaving Danny, the downed contractor, and the two store clerks to sort things out with store security.

"Here's the paint you wanted," said Geoffrey, strolling up to his friend with can in hand. As he took in the scene his jaw dropped. "Umm, I guess I missed all the … excitement?"

16

Hoagie Haven

"**Y**ou're lucky the contractor decided not to press charges," said Kelly with a judgmental scowl after Danny and Geoffrey had recounted the story of the barely averted "Riot in Aisle 5" at Home Depot.

The three of them were sitting around the kitchen table having dinner in Kelly and Danny's apartment. Danny had sprung for hoagies from the local WAWA, along with three Snapple iced teas—raspberry flavored for himself, lemon for Geoffrey, and unsweetened for Kelly. Considering the look on her face he wished he had gotten her the sweetened. He'd intended the food to serve as a peace offering in the event she reacted badly to the riot story, but he wasn't sure it was working. Lately he had no idea how she'd react to *anything* he said or did.

"He's the one who started it," he said defensively.

Kelly turned to her brother. "Is that how it happened, Geoffrey?"

"Well, the big guy threw some lumber on the floor then got all up in the clerk's face," he said in Danny's defense before qualifying, "but I was getting the paint in another aisle when the fighting started."

"Somebody sucker punched me." Danny pointed to his chin.

Kelly leaned over for a quick inspection. "I see," she said. In truth, she saw nothing and was convinced that this was just another example of Danny getting into trouble because he had nothing better to do.

"The kid and that nice lady were about to be torn to shreds," Danny insisted. "What was I supposed to do?"

"Okay, Sir Galahad," Kelly relented, hoping to cut it short. "You made your point. Let's just eat."

"Right, let's eat," echoed Geoffrey, who wasted no time launching into his Italian sub with extra-thin sliced Prosciutto di Parma and provolone.

The three ate quietly until Kelly broke the silence with a seemingly innocent question for Geoffrey. "What is Luz going to do about the hurricane this weekend?"

"She's staying put," her brother said between bites. "Her family is staying with relatives on the mainland, but she agreed to keep her shift at the Engleside and help out anyway she can—the hotel has been designated the island's southern command post, you know."

"Most people think it's going to be a non-event again," ventured Danny. "Just like Irene."

Kelly would have liked to ignore the remark but she couldn't let it go unchallenged. "Apparently that doesn't include the mob you ran into at Home Depot."

Danny bit his tongue as she turned her attention back to Geoffrey. "And what about you? What are you doing?"

"I'm staying with Luz. I don't want any of those pumped-up first responders pawing all over her when the lights go out."

"What's your Aunt Sarah planning to do?" Danny asked Kelly.

She stared at him briefly, measuring the sincerity of his question; or at least so it appeared to him.

"She and Noah are planning to stay with Paul Decker," Geoffrey cut in, catching them both off guard.

"Who's Paul Decker?" Kelly asked.

"He's a meteorologist with the National Weather Service—goes way back with Noah. The two of them have been following Sandy since it was just a tropical storm over Jamaica and they're expecting the worst. Decker lives in Hainesport, or maybe it's Lumberton—far enough west to keep safe, anyway."

Kelly turned back to her boyfriend. "What are your plans, Danny?"

"Don't you mean what are *our* plans?"

"I told you before, but I guess you weren't listening," she sighed. "I've got to work all weekend. We're already getting claim calls from Florida."

"But you'll be coming home after work, right?"

"As long as they don't close the causeway, and I can get on and off the island."

"They won't close the causeway." He rolled his eyes and looked to Geoffrey for support.

"They closed it during Irene and that was nothing, according to you." Irritation had crept into Kelly's voice.

"If they have to close it, you'll stay home and skip work," Danny said firmly, leaning back in his chair and folding his arms across his chest. Geoffrey's head swiveled from one to the other as if he was watching a tennis match.

"What if I'm already *at* the office and can't get back?" she said argumentatively.

"Then you'll have to get a hotel room," he responded, trying to keep calm.

"We can't *afford* a hotel room, Danny," she said, her tone equal parts anger and embarrassment.

"The company ought to cover it," he said raising his voice to match hers. "Since they're requiring you to work during a major storm."

"What if they refuse?" she shot back, refusing to give any ground.

"You can ask about it tomorrow. But seriously, Kelly, if they're not willing to pay for a room then you're staying right here with me." As soon as he said it, he realized it had come out more forcefully than he'd intended.

She put down her hoagie and pushed herself away from the table. "Excuse me," she said through clenched teeth as she stood to leave.

"Where are you going?" Danny asked, softening his tone.

"I'm taking a walk."

"What about your dinner?"

"I've lost my appetite."

17

Day 5

```
BULLETIN
HURRICANE SANDY ADVISORY NUMBER 17
NWS NATIONAL HURRICANE CENTER MIAMI FL          AL182012
1100 AM EDT FRI OCT 26 2012

SANDY MOVING SLOWLY NORTHWARD

SANDY IS MOVING TOWARD THE NORTH NEAR 6 MPH...9 KM/H...AND
A GENERAL NORTHWARD MOTION IS EXPECTED TO CONTINUE TODAY
AND TONIGHT...FOLLOWED BY A TURN TOWARD THE NORTH-NORTHEAST
WITH AN INCREASE IN FORWARD SPEED ON SATURDAY...AND A TURN
TOWARD THE NORTHEAST ON SUNDAY.

HURRICANE CONDITIONS WILL CONTINUE OVER THE NORTHWESTERN
BAHAMAS FOR THE NEXT SEVERAL HOURS. TROPICAL STORM CONDITIONS
ARE EXPECTED TO CONTINUE TO SPREAD NORTHWARD ALONG THE EAST
COAST OF FLORIDA TODAY AND TONIGHT...TROPICAL STORM CONDITIONS
ARE POSSIBLE IN THE CAROLINAS SATURDAY AND SATURDAY NIGHT.
```

Paul Decker was on his way to see Ted Harris when his cell phone rang.

"Hello, Paul," said a sultry female voice on the other end.

"Lucy?"

"Ah, you haven't forgotten. It's been a long time."

Not long enough, he was tempted to say, but didn't. "Let me guess, you've got the results on those soil samples from McGuiness?"

"That's right," she replied, adopting a more business-like tone.

"He told you they were from me?"

"Of course."

Decker chuckled under his breath. "And you still tested them?"

"For my usual fee, of course."

He could hear the smile in her voice as she said it. He liked the way it made him feel. "Guess they're not keeping you all that busy at the State?"

"I only work on *special* projects," she said, teasing him.

"You mean for special *people*," he replied, enjoying the banter but knowing it would not last. Nothing between them ever did.

"Surprised? You shouldn't be. You really are unforgettable, Paul."

"After all these years, I wish I could believe that."

"What will it take to convince you?"

"The test results," he said, dropping the pretense.

"You're not going to tell me what you want them for, are you?"

"No, I am not."

The caller on the other end hesitated briefly. "The soil is your run-of-the-mill granulated silicon dioxide … Pine Barrens sand, except …" she hesitated again, "except for a high concentration of heavy metals, particularly aluminum."

"Aluminum?" he questioned. "Can you tell me what that means?"

"Well, we're seeing it more and more lately. Aluminum doesn't exist freely in nature, yet it's popping up all over the planet."

"And?"

"And it's been linked to Alzheimer's and certain types of birth defects, including autism. Studies have also shown a strong correlation between aluminum and some forms of cancer."

"Okay, so how does aluminum get into the soil?"

"How do *any* of these metals get into the soil?' she sighed. "Industrial runoff from rivers and lakes."

"That's your analysis?"

"Unless there's some additional information you want to share with me."

There was long pause.

"Paul," she said breaking the silence, "you're not going to tell me, are you?" He could hear the desperation in her voice.

"What would be the point? You wouldn't believe me." His eyes moistened as the faded memories flooded back. "Thank you, Lucy. Take care of yourself." He hung up before she had a chance to protest, and continued on his way.

He was surprised to find the hallway leading to Harris's postmodern office deserted. It was a little early for lunch, so he was especially surprised that Harris's guard dog of a secretary was absent from her post.

He was, of course, fully aware that office protocol required him to arrange in advance for face time with the station chief, rather than simply showing up at his door expecting to be let in. But following protocol wasn't his style and old habits die hard.

What *was* important was the latest bulletin out of Miami showing that Sandy had begun her northerly crawl up the U.S. Atlantic coast. She was making her presence felt in a big way along the eastern coast of South Florida. Tropical Storm alerts had been issued as far north as the Carolinas, making it more than probable that New Jersey lay within the storm's path.

All of this meant that it was time to switch over to a twenty-four hour weather watch for the Garden State. Decker was prepared to take his place on the watch team as always, in spite of his disagreements with Harris regarding the dissemination of information over the past week. Noah had let him know that LBI and a growing number of other Jersey shore municipalities were now issuing voluntary evacuation orders. Action plans were in motion, and Decker intended to be at the forefront when the storm rolled into the region this weekend.

He knocked on the closed office door. When he didn't get an immediate answer, he knocked again a little more forcefully, pushing the door open and entering at the same time.

Motion sensors turned the bright LED track lighting on, but Decker was the only one in the room. An ultra-modern desk lamp illuminated a stack of papers piled neatly in Harris's outbox, suggesting that some work had been attended to earlier that day, while a half-filled coffee cup on one corner of the desk made him think the station chief was still in the building.

In the middle of the massive desk, a slender black laptop lay open with its screensaver in a perpetual loop of images from National Geographic. Decker stepped closer for a better look, surprised to learn that Harris apparently shared his love of nature photography.

Compelled by curiosity, Decker tapped the space bar. Two videos immediately popped up in split-screen fashion on the laptop, simultaneously booting up on the large flat screen monitor mounted on the wall behind Harris's desk. The left side projected a grainy video image of a volcano labeled "Popocatepetl, Central Mexico" and bearing a dateline of October 25, 2012. Three days ago. The video repeatedly showed a cigar shaped silver disk hovering over, then disappearing into the cone of the dormant volcano. Meantime, the screen on the right displayed an infrared radar satellite image of the Western Hemisphere with what looked like a Faberge egg pulsating from the area of the volcano in Central Mexico where the UFO video was allegedly shot. Simultaneously, that radar image was also tracking Hurricane Sandy as the storm proceeded up the East Coast of the United States. The right side image was date stamped October 27, 2012—today—

and credited to NOAA.

Is this some kind of joke? Decker thought to himself. *Someone's childish prank? Intended for whom?*

Another keystroke replaced the baffling split screen images with that of a giant map of the continental United States. It appeared that various weather systems were being tracked in real time, via satellite relay, using oscillating color-coded cloud-like swirls, all but one of which Decker was able to instantly identify: The familiar red, orange, white, gray, and green were there on the grid as expected, but the dark blue hue on the fringe of a system moving into the Ohio Valley appeared out of place to him. Typically, darker shades of blue were not used to delineate the composition of an air mass because of the potential for confusion with lakes, oceans, and other bodies of water. Lighter blues were often selected to reflect precipitation within a system, with purple or violet used to designate thunderstorm activity. Decker wondered if the dark blue might be suggestive of some unexplained weather anomaly.

"What are you doing in here?"

Startled, Decker turned around from the big monitor to see Ted Harris standing in the doorway. His hands were tightly clenched at his sides.

"Looking for you," Decker said with a sheepish grin.

"I was in a meeting," snapped Harris. "Where's Ms. Henderson?"

"Your secretary must have stepped away for a moment," offered Decker, feeling awkward and embarrassed. "When no one answered the door, I let myself in to make sure everything was all right."

Harris glanced up at the images projected on the wall. He was livid. "You have no right to be in here," he bellowed. "You are trespassing!"

Decker stood his ground. "I'm not trespassing, I work here."

"Not any more, you don't. You're fired."

Harris dialed a code into his cell phone and raised it to his lips. "This is Harris. There's an intruder in my office."

"You can't fire me!" Decker said angrily.

"I just did," barked Harris, checking his desk to see if anything else had been disturbed.

Decker held fast. "I have seniority, and the right to appeal this idiotic decision."

"We'll see about that."

In the next instant, two men entered the room—plainclothes security guards, Decker quickly surmised.

"That's him." Harris nodded toward the older man.

As Decker instinctively backed away from the men, he realized he'd seen them before. They were on him in a heartbeat. One of them slammed him against the wall, pinning him with a right forearm across the windpipe. At his age, Decker was no match for the man's strength as the second man drew a syringe from his jacket pocket and, in one fluid movement, stuck it into Decker's neck and pressed the plunger home.

The lights in the room began to spin, and just before he lost consciousness Decker remembered where he had seen these men. Dressed in black, they had stood in the doorway during his LBI briefing yesterday, observing in stony silence through impenetrable black shades.

18

Lines

"**H**i, Honey. I'm just calling to let you know that I'll be late. Very late."

There was a long pause on his side of the conversation as Rick McGuiness was chastised by his agitated wife. She eventually got around to asking him if everything was all right.

"Everything's fine," he said as cheerfully as he could under the circumstances. "I left the latest emergency management meeting about an hour ago. Yes. That's right. They're expecting Sandy to arrive sometime over the weekend. Yes, an order's been issued for voluntary evacuation of the island."

He listened again as she changed the subject.

"No, I haven't forgotten, dear. I'll pick up some milk for the kids on the way home. I'm just not sure when that will be."

McGuiness could hear his son Billy moaning in the background about the possibility of Halloween being postponed. Holding the phone to his chin he put his truck in park and stepped out.

"Yes, I know, honey, but at the moment I'm a little bogged down. The exodus has begun. I'm waiting to get gas at Chet's Sunoco on 72 West—the line is backed up to the causeway."

He slipped back into his truck and rested his head on the steering wheel while his wife described her exhausting day with the kids at length and in great detail.

The car behind him tooted his horn, and when McGuiness looked up he saw that the car in front of him had moved forward about a car length. He put his pickup in gear and dutifully inched forward.

"Yes, we're making progress," he replied into the phone. "Slowly, but surely. The station's in view now, anyway."

Rick watched as a silver Maserati sped by on the shoulder of the road and squeezed in line up ahead in a gap between a late model Honda and an eighteen wheeler who couldn't get his rig in gear fast enough to close the opening. Dozens of vehicles honked their displeasure. A few drivers got out of the cars and made obscene gestures. The driver behind the tinted windows of the Maserati simply ignored them.

"No, dear. I don't think it's wise to look for another gas station at this point. There aren't that many once you pass the strip malls on 72. Yes, I need it now—I'm on call this weekend and I don't know when I'll get another chance to fill up. Uh, huh. I just hope they don't run out of gas."

He turned off his phone and switched on the radio. Something told him the fun was just getting started. He thought briefly about phoning Paul Decker as he waited in the gas line; he was curious to know if Lucy had phoned the test results of his Warren Grove soil samples directly to Decker, as she'd said she would. Won't he be surprised to hear from *her*, McGuiness mused, given their history. He decided to wait to hear from Decker rather than calling him.

19

Happy Hour

When Nick Weber's smartphone rang for the fourteenth time that day, he was standing at the front entrance to Finnegan's in Manahawkin. Through the thick, beaded glass doors he could see the distorted faces of several of his staff members mingling at the bar. He had closed the office early for the benefit of the emergency crew that was coming in to work over the weekend. Having personally hand-picked the team for this special shift, he mandated that all of them meet at the bar immediately after work for additional instructions and a well-deserved TGIF send-off drink. Rita Zenger was far from thrilled with one of the people he'd chosen for the assignment, but after a drink or two Nick hoped she would let it drop.

His cell rang again.

"Talk to me."

"All the bases are covered," said a snappy male voice that Nick recognized instantly. "I can still get you out under the wire. What do you want me to do?"

Nick hesitated for less than a half a beat, making sure he understood the implications completely. It was now or never. "Sell," he said, disconnecting and pushing through the heavy glass doors into the rowdy bar.

A lively round of applause greeted him as he entered the room. He signaled the bartender for another round of drinks and spotted Kelly at the far end of the bar, alone and looking a bit uncomfortable, to his secret delight. He wasted no time heading in her direction, but Rita intercepted him.

"Try not to make a fool of yourself," she cautioned him in a half whisper.

"Yes, mother," he grinned as he walked around and past her. "You just remember to keep all the other kiddies in line."

He found Kelly ignoring a glass of sangria while sorting through her phone messages. She gave him a forced smile as he leaned in next to her and ordered a double dry Sapphire Martini with extra olives.

"You and Prince Charming got off the hook on the party," he said, meeting her gaze head on, "but I'm afraid you won't have much time to lounge around the castle this weekend, since you and I have work to do."

His cocky smile told her he had taken immense pleasure in saying those words.

"Do I have you or Rita to thank for the honor?" Kelly reached for her glass.

"That depends on whether you view it as an opportunity or a chore."

Kelly glanced around at the happy faces of her co-workers. "They all seem to think it's a pretty big deal."

"That's because weekends pay double time," Nick said with a toothsome grin.

"Sounds good to me," she admitted with a restrained laugh. "We can sure use the money."

"Hard times for the enchanted couple?" he queried cleverly.

"It is when only one of us is working." No sooner had the words left her lips than she regretted saying them. Maybe it was the wine talking. Or maybe her hostility and resentment toward Danny had simply reached the boiling point. Either way, the words had come out and she couldn't take them back.

Nick studied her slightly blushing face slowly, contemplating his next move with great care. However inadvertent her remark may have been, he knew he'd just been given the opening he was waiting for. But he also knew she was smarter than hell, and wary of him. He would have to be careful in leveraging his new knowledge.

"Want to talk about it?" he asked in a relaxed, almost brotherly manner. "You'll find that among my many other charming qualities I am quite a good listener."

She responded to his self-deprecating manner with a genuine smile. He definitely had a way with women. She knew he could still be playing her, but he was pretty good at making her feel comfortable.

"There's nothing much to tell," she said. "We've just kind of hit a bump in the road."

"Small bump? Or more of a rut?" he probed gently, planting a seed while downplaying the intensity of his interest.

"More like a crossroads," she replied honestly. "We seem to be headed in opposite directions."

He stirred his martini idly. "Listen Kelly, it's none of my business but I'm concerned about you."

The hairs on the back of her neck stood up. "Why should you concern yourself with me, Nick?"

"Well, to be honest, it's work related," he said, throwing her a curveball.

"I think I've been doing a pretty good job." She sat upright on her stool. "That *is* why I was picked for the work detail this weekend, isn't it?"

"Well, yes, of course," Nick stammered. "That's not what I meant."

He took a slow, calculated sip of his cocktail, considering how to best navigate the delicate terrain around a rather brazen idea.

"I'm just worried that it might be difficult for you to get home over the weekend. A volunteer evacuation order is already in place for LBI and it could end up being mandatory. If you can't get back on the island you'll need a place to stay."

She stifled a laugh. Since arguing with Danny about it the other night, she had been giving the situation a lot of thought. She'd come here tonight hoping to get some answers, but she wasn't very comfortable asking about a company-paid hotel room. Now it appeared she wouldn't have to ask—the boss himself had brought it up.

"What's so funny?" he asked.

"Well, I expect that kind of concern from my boyfriend, but not necessarily from my boss. You surprised me, but thanks for bringing it up. I guess I might end up needing a room on this side of the causeway."

"No problem. Consider it done. And while you're at it, Kelly, please try to think of me as a friend, not just as a boss—a friend who is inviting you to stay at his place in Barnegat for the weekend so that you're safe and out of harm's way."

The comment caught her completely off guard, at once flattering and mortifying her. "Are you saying you want me to stay at *your* place?" she asked, looking at him with wide eyes.

"Sure, why not?" he said as casually as he could.

She glanced around the room, expecting to see all eyes on her. There were a few, including Rita Zenger's piercing gaze. "Why not just put everyone in a hotel?" she said, turning back to him.

"Because there aren't any decent ones in the area, and as far as I know you are the *only* emergency crew member who lives on the island."

He could see from the look on her face that although she was skeptical, she hadn't quite slammed the door on the idea. He continued. "Listen, it's no trouble. I've got plenty of room and it's a great place to unwind after a hard day at the office. You'll have your privacy, not to mention a hot tub, full bar, great sound system, sundeck—I can even grill us some nice steaks. Think about it?"

She didn't know what to say. It was as if she'd found herself swimming in an unfamiliar ocean. Part of her wanted to run; another part wanted to hide. She took a long sip of her drink, trying to bide time and compose her thoughts. "You make it sound so … inviting," she said at last.

"You'll be safe and it won't cost you a dime," he persisted.

"Safe with a wolf like you on the loose?" she heard herself say jokingly.

"I promise to be on my best behavior." He made the sign of the cross. "Cross my heart."

She took a deep breath. *Was he being sincere, or was there an ulterior motive? He'd been coming on to her from the beginning, after all. On the other hand, how do you say "no" to the boss? You don't. At least not right away.* She thought about Danny. She thought about the extra money she'd be making over the weekend.

"I'll think it over," she promised.

"Fair enough."

His phone pinged with a text message and he glanced at it hurriedly.

"Sorry, Kelly—I've got to run," he said, standing to down what was left of his martini.

"What about the meeting?"

"Rita will handle it." He pulled his Montblanc pen from the breast pocket of his suit jacket and jotted something down on the back of his coaster.

"Here's my cell number," he said handing it to her. "Let me know your decision." He reached for her hand. "Remember, it's just until the storm passes." He patted her hand reassuringly as he turned to go. "Call me."

He shot a quick glance Rita's way. Then, without a word to anyone, he strolled out the door, scanning the stock indexes on his phone as he did.

Kelly finished her sangria and was about to leave when Rita slipped onto the stool that Nick had just vacated.

"I thought you were a lot smarter than that, Kelly."

"Excuse me?"

"Georgetown grad … magna cum laude, no less. I didn't expect to see you give in so easily to our charming boss."

"Who said I have?"

"It certainly looked that way from where I was sitting."

"Oh, I get it. You fell for him and got hurt, so now you want to save me from making the same mistake, right?"

Rita let out a laugh. "You got that wrong, honey. Not me—I know better. And this is just a word to the wise, by the way. It's not my job to protect you."

"I can take care of myself, thanks."

Rita picked up the coaster lying on the bar in front of Kelly and turned it over. "I can see that," she said as she studied the phone number in Nick's scrawl. "Do yourself a favor: leave this for the barmaid or toss it." She spun the coaster like a top on the bar.

Kelly looked up to see the entire team watching them. The coaster stopped spinning and landed number side up.

"Should I consider this a warning from my supervisor?"

"Consider it a little friendly advice."

20

Day 6

```
BULLETIN
HURRICANE SANDY ADVISORY NUMBER 21
NWS NATIONAL HURRICANE CENTER MIAMI FL        AL182012
1100 AM EDT SAT OCT 27 2012


A TROPICAL STORM WARNING IS IN EFFECT FOR...SOUTH SANTEE
RIVER SOUTH CAROLINA TO DUCK NORTH CAROLINA. INTERESTS
THROUGHOUT THE MID-ATLANTIC STATES AND NEW ENGLAND SHOULD
MONITOR THE PROGRESS OF SANDY.


HURRICANE FORCE WINDS EXTEND OUTWARD UP TO 105 MILES...165 KM
FROM THE CENTER...TROPICAL STORM FORCE WINDS EXTEND OUTWARD
UP TO 450 MILES...725 KM...MAXIMUM SUSTAINED GUSTS ARE NEAR
75 MPH...120 KM/H. GALE FORCE WINDS ARE EXPECTED TO ARRIVE
ALONG PORTIONS OF THE MID-ATLANTIC COAST BY LATE SUNDAY OR
SUNDAY NIGHT.
```

"**W**here am I?" Paul Decker demanded to know as his eyes began adjusting to a sudden, intense light. He was strapped to a sturdy wooden chair in the middle of an empty room that smelled damp and musty. The cinderblock walls gave the impression of an unfinished basement. Facing him, leaning back comfortably in a plush leather chair, was Ted Harris. To Decker, Harris's attitude suggested a man with a pipe in a smoking jacket, which seemed more than slightly incongruous given their inelegant surroundings.

"Somewhere safe, where you won't be a bother to anyone," Harris said with no hint of emotion in his voice.

Decker twisted in his chair. He was desperate for a cigarette and a drink but he wouldn't give Harris the satisfaction of knowing it. "You won't get away with this," he said pulling at his bindings. "People will be looking for me."

"I doubt that very much," laughed Harris condescendingly. "It's been twenty-four hours and I'm not aware of anyone asking about you yet."

Had it really been that long? Decker glanced at his watch. So he'd been held hostage, unconscious and out of sight, for an entire day. But where? This could be the basement of any one of thousands of vacant buildings in and around southern New Jersey—if he hadn't been taken even further afield. As to who might be concerned enough about his disappearance to look into it, Noah Parsons was his only candidate. He and his wife were planning to ride out the storm as his houseguests over the weekend. From where Decker sat, Noah's innate curiosity and friendship were his best hope for being found.

"That's because it's Saturday," Decker challenged, knowing full well it didn't matter. "The office is closed."

"Not this Saturday," Harris reacted with amusement. "Haven't you heard? There's a hurricane headed our way—a real *Frankenstorm*," he added, using the buzzword coined in anticipation of Sandy's arrival around Halloween. He raised his arms in a gesture of mock fright. "By the look of things, it's going to get quite messy around here." His broad smile betrayed how much he was enjoying himself.

"Right, because the public is ill-prepared," Decker lamented in a weak, raspy voice. "Because you haven't been honest with them. What I want to know is, what's your game?" With nothing to lose, he let his conspiracy theories tumble out, hoping Harris's reaction would point to the truth.

"Bravo! Listen to *you*," Harris said smugly, clapping his hands after Decker had laid out several scenarios. The station chief added grimly, "as if anyone ever will."

"Then humor me," Decker seized the opening. "What am I missing?"

"Now *that's* rich—the leading authority on anything and everything weather-related asking *me* to enlighten him! Well, fasten your seat belt, old man, because you won't believe it when you hear it." Harris stood up and began pacing the room, as if considering where to start.

"About the only thing you had right over the years is that people are more concerned about their local weather than any long-term, global issues and goals. You can't convince them to reduce carbon footprints when they're addicted to riding in air-conditioned cars and tossing their Styrofoam Big Mac boxes along the roadside for the lower classes dressed in orange jumpsuits to pick up and dispose of in landfills no one wants in their backyard."

"We both know that if the government was serious about greenhouse gases they would have instituted a carbon tax by now," Decker said hoarsely. His throat was parched and he was growing desperate for a cool drink.

As if reading his mind, Harris poured a glass of ice water from a pitcher by his chair. He smirked, adding a generous splash from the flask he had pilfered from Decker's jacket before putting it back in his own pocket.

"That's probably the first thing you've said that I can agree with, Paul. China and the U.S. are by far the biggest abusers in terms of carbon dioxide emissions. China is responsible for 29% all by itself! The idea that the United Nations will ever reach a consensus on CO_2 is pure folly, and that's why a group of concerned philanthropic *realists* have taken matters into their own hands."

He walked over to Decker and held the glass to the old man's lips, letting him drink greedily until he'd drained every last drop. He set the empty glass down on the concrete floor, then circled behind his captive to check his bindings.

"You mean wealthy industrialists, don't you?" Decker countered, now able to speak more forcefully. "Top one-percenters lining their pockets under the guise of philanthropy?"

Harris's shrug was unapologetic. "I don't suppose you and I will ever see eye-to-eye on this. You can go ahead and rant on behalf of *everyman,* but as you've probably gathered by now, I decided a long time ago to align myself with the Powers That Be, rather than fight them. They pay much better, and all I have to do is look the other way."

"Right," Decker snickered, "and invent colorful codenames to conceal the increasing number and intensity of weather aberrations that are popping up on the satellite screens." He shook his head. "Like your polar vortexes. So how long have you been covering for them?"

"I'm actually sorry you saw what you did in my office, Paul. Ordinarily, there is software in place to filter out those things and keep anyone from seeing what we don't want them to see, including nosey weathermen."

"Your software won't work for squat when the blue snow starts falling. What are you going to tell the public then?"

Harris stopped and hovered in front of him. "You still don't get it, do you, old timer? As William Randolph Hearst once said, 'Truth is the first casualty of war.' And this is most definitely a war. A war for the survival of the planet and of our species."

Decker lifted his aching head. "There are laws to stop you and the people you work for. Laws to prevent you from seeding the clouds with your poison."

"Seeding the clouds?" Harris let out a haughty laugh. "I had no idea you were so far behind the times, Paul. What's being done here goes way beyond cloud seeding. Let me be clear: We're not simply trying to make it rain. Of course we can impact regional weather, but with geo-climate engineering we are actually strengthening our solar shield."

"For what purpose?" Decker scoffed. "Nature keeps us humans humble."

Harris began pacing again as he spoke. "We're trying to do what fragmented governments obsessed with their Gross National Product *can't* do. We're going to protect the planet from extinction and ensure humanity's future."

Harris was now strutting confidently around the room. As he spoke, the certainty of his words came flowing from his lips to match his strides.

"You said it yourself, Paul. Greenhouse gases are not going away, and no one can agree on what should be done about it. No nation wants to give up its industries. Certainly not emerging third world countries! Self-imposed limits and disorganized summits have failed. What's needed is a bolder plan. Modifying the Earth's climate to offset the effects of global warming is the right call. We can reduce the amount of solar energy reaching Earth through an artificial filtering technique, comparable to the effect of ash released into the atmosphere during a volcanic eruption. Such bold action will deliver far more reliable and immediate results than planting trees, don't you agree?"

"It's insane!" Decker shouted. "You're talking about playing God—and all to protect wealthy capitalists and their investments."

Harris stepped around to face Decker again. He leaned in close, placing his hands on the arms of the older man's chair. "Perhaps, Paul, but the beauty of what we're doing is that there are no laws, no international authority, and no single jurisdiction that can stop us." He stood and backed away slowly as he continued. "We're doing governments around the world a favor by performing a service *they* should be providing!"

Decker stared at Harris intently. "You say this is for the good of humanity, Harris, but surely you must realize the danger from fallout. Earlier this week, I saw some unusual high altitude dispersal going on over Warren Grove—it made me suspicious, so I had soil samples collected and tested."

"Yes, I know all about it," Harris said irritably. "We've had you under surveillance for some time." He pulled Decker's car keys from his jacket pocket and dangled them in front of him. "That banged-up green El Camino is a most conspicuous mode of transportation."

Decker ignored the slight and plowed ahead. "Then you also know the test results, which showed the soil was tainted with aluminum. I'm sure you're aware of the link between aluminum ingestion and birth defects, not to mention cancer."

"Yes, so I'm told," Harris said. "And they're working on it. Delsanto Chemicals is developing fruit and vegetable strains that are resistant to aluminum particulates."

"Sounds like another Agent Orange waiting to happen," Decker said angrily.

"That couldn't be helped, but important lessons were learned. It's only a matter of time before the new technology filters down to independent New Jersey cranberry farmers and everyone gets on board." Harris's increasingly shrill tone suggested that Decker's accusations were getting under his skin.

In spite of being tightly bound, Decker managed to stand, awkwardly, by leaning forward then pulling the chair up behind him. "*Farmers*? Christ, Harris, are you completely brain-dead? This stuff's in the air we breathe, the water we drink. Right now it's being ingested up and down the food chain. Is that the legacy you want to leave your children and grandchildren? For God's sake, man, you're killing them!"

He lunged headfirst at the station chief, chair and all, but the younger man sidestepped him, watching in amusement as the old weatherman crashed into the wall and collapsed to the floor.

Defeated, Decker looked up in disgust at his former boss. A wave of pity washed over him as he considered the man's corruption by a system that had led him to sell out his professional integrity.

"Why tell me all of this?" he said wearily, his voice cracking.

"I see no harm in letting you know what you're up against, Paul. Besides, nobody's going to listen to a discredited old drunk like you."

21

Headin' for Stormageddon

Whether it's the roar of crashing surf at the water's edge, a fishing boat engine humming on the horizon, or a seagull cawing overhead, sounds at the shore seem to travel a long way. Perhaps it has something to do with the salt air, a theory favored by Danny Windsor, or maybe it's simply the lack of tall buildings—nothing around to block the path of radiating sound waves. Whatever it is, the fact remains that sound travels at the shore, and on this particular Saturday the echo of thundering hammers could be heard for miles.

Although the streets were largely deserted, hundreds of LBI's year-round residents were busy battening down the hatches in anticipation of a 100-year storm. Fear and worry were the watchwords of the day, with the prevailing sentiment summed up on the spray-painted particle board covering a Long Beach Boulevard storefront:

SANDY KEEP AWAY!

A horde of nonresidents with summer homes and seasonal businesses had arrived on the island early and were attending to similar tasks. The monotonous sound of hammers pounding nails into plywood sheets over windows and two-by-fours across sliding glass doors had begun at the crack of dawn and continued incessantly ever since.

With Kelly at work, Danny had some time on his hands. His surfboat project was as complete as his depleted bank account would allow. In any case, the boat was seaworthy, and any remaining touches would be cosmetic. That left him free to make something of the day, and when Geoffrey called to ask if he'd help him and Noah board up the Crab Cove shop, he was happy to do it. Breakfast on Noah at the LBI Pancake House provided extra incentive.

"I just don't get it," Noah was saying as he and Sarah emerged from the shop. "He's not answering his cell phone and the receptionist in Mt. Holly says he isn't at work today."

"Have you've checked the local *establishments* he tends to frequent?" questioned Sarah, raising an eyebrow.

"He hasn't been to Irv's Bar since we were there mid-week."

"Are there any others he might have stopped at?"

"A few, but not with a hurricane heading this way. Whatever else people may say about Paul Decker, he takes his job very seriously."

Noah kissed his wife and turned his attention to Danny and Geoffrey, who were securing the last of three large pieces of plywood over the shop window. "Boys, I'll have to leave it to you to finish up here. I should be back before nightfall."

"Where are you going?" Geoffrey asked.

"Off to find a missing meteorologist," Noah said. "Paul Decker seems to have fallen off the radar, and we'd been talking about riding this monster out at his place."

"Mr. Decker said that what makes Sandy unique is its size," said Geoffrey, recalling the weather briefing at Long Beach. "It's nearly a thousand miles in diameter."

"What does that actually mean?" asked Danny.

"It means this one isn't all hype, like Irene," Noah said. "Combine a hurricane with a stalled low pressure system and you've got the recipe for a mega-storm. We may well see cyclonic disturbances from the Carolinas to Canada."

"The media is calling it Stormageddon," noted Geoffrey.

"I get it, like in the Bible," Danny said. "We're headin' for Stormageddon."

"Makes you wonder if this isn't the shape of things to come," said Sarah. "My first husband, God rest his soul, used to say that the weather turned strange as soon as we started sending men into space."

"No slight to Hugh, but I sincerely doubt there's any connection," declared Noah with a glance toward the kids.

"Do you mind if I tag along?" Geoffrey set his hammer down on the porch steps.

"Ordinarily I would love to have your company, Geoffrey. But with this storm coming I think it's best for you two to finish up here and get moving. You are planning to leave, right?"

"Sure," said Geoffrey.

"Of course," agreed Danny.

Sarah kept her thoughts to herself. She'd seen no evidence of their imminent departure, and, to be honest, she wouldn't be leaving either if Noah hadn't been so insistent.

"Good," said Noah. "I'm afraid this one's for real, and Ground Zero is expected to be somewhere between here and Atlantic City."

"It has to be taken seriously," affirmed Danny.

"You've got that right," Noah said emphatically. "Thanks to technology we've had plenty of time to prepare, but all the advance notice in the world won't do any good if we don't take advantage of it."

He turned to give Sarah another tender kiss. "Get your things together, sweetheart. I'll be back for you as soon as possible."

22

Risky Business

Kelly had come home late and a bit tipsy from Finnegan's last night, setting off another argument with Danny. She hadn't gotten much sleep, though no amount of rest would have prepared her for the workday from hell that was now mercifully drawing to a close. She shut down her computer and rubbed her eyes, feeling totally spent.

It had been a grueling shift of endless phone calls as harried claimants from the Southern Atlantic States related their woeful tales of Sandy's devastation, many in tears as they described losing *everything*—homes, cars, boats, treasured family photos and keepsakes.

Then they waited on the line, expecting her to wave a magic wand and end their misery; to vanquish the nightmare, ease their pain, and make them whole again. Her heart bled for them as she heard their gut-wrenching stories, but all she could do was "hold their hands," as Rita was fond of saying. "Listen patiently, write down every important piece of information … but promise them nothing."

That was the exhausting part, the demanding part. That was the part that left Kelly feeling empty and inadequate. All she could do, over and over again, was write up an initial report of loss, take down a telephone number where the insured could be contacted—assuming they had one to give—then repeat the standard line that "Someone will be in touch."

As she was packing up her few personal items the phone rang for perhaps the 50th time that day. She debated what to do. Should she take it? It could keep her here for another half-hour or more. She glanced at the clock on the wall. 5:10 PM She was officially off duty and could simply walk away, but compassion got the better of her. She picked up the phone.

"Maine Line Insurance, Kelly speaking."

It was Nick Weber. She relaxed momentarily, but stiffened when he said he wanted to see her in his office before she left.

As she replaced the receiver, grabbed her purse, and stood to go, she found Rita standing by her desk.

"Tough day, Kelly?" her supervisor asked sympathetically.

"It's heartbreaking," she said, glancing nervously in the direction of Nick's office. "Some of these people lost everything."

"It gets easier, trust me," Rita said. "Meantime, I suggest you go home, get a good night's sleep, and come back fresh tomorrow. I guarantee it will be nuts all over again." She raised an eyebrow. "You *are* coming in tomorrow, aren't you?"

"That's my plan," Kelly said. "Why do you ask?"

"Some of the crew have expressed concern about the storm, and their own safety. There's some family pressure, obviously. We may be short-handed."

She was right about that, Kelly thought. She'd heard a number of agents discussing the situation, though much of the talk centered on a possible state of emergency, which so far the Governor hadn't declared. Even if he did, they were all aware that Maine Line's emergency claims staff was considered "essential personnel"—they'd even been issued special passes in the event of a driving ban.

Rita watched as the wheels spun inside Kelly's head. She felt a pang of empathy, allowing in that weakened moment for her maternal instinct to surface.

"Look, Kelly, I need to be on LBI early in the morning to look in on my dad, in Holgate. If you like, I can swing by and pick you up."

Kelly studied Rita's stoic face. Did she know about Nick's offer to put her up? "That's very kind of you, Rita," she said, "but I'll be all right. If necessary my boyfriend, Danny will drive me—he's got an SUV and time on his hands."

If Rita took any offense to Kelly's mild rejection, she didn't let it show. "Suit yourself, Kelly. See you tomorrow."

Kelly waited until Rita had walked out with a couple of the agents before heading across the room and down the corridor toward Nick's office. She'd done everything she could to avoid contact with him today, arriving early and immersing herself in Rita's training session to avoid running into him. To her relief, at lunchtime when the pizza he ordered for the staff arrived, he stayed in his office with the door closed. Later, the pace quickened and the phones never stopped ringing. Through it all, she was hoping he'd forgotten about the offer he made at Finnegan's, or would at least let it drop. There was no way to avoid him now.

The door was ajar when she reached his office. She took a deep breath, then pushed it open and stood undecided in the doorway. He appeared to be crunching numbers on his calculator. He looked up and motioned for her to come in. She stepped inside.

"Rough day?" he asked with a grin.

"You might say that," she said, slowly walking over to his desk.

"Don't let the bastards grind you down," he said waving her into a chair.

There were three chairs to choose from. She took the one furthest from him and closest to the window. "What was that?" she asked with a puzzled look.

"Just something my Irish grandmother used to say."

"I didn't know you were Irish."

"Then you haven't seen me drink," he replied with a playful smile.

The comment and the smile put her a bit at ease, though she still felt her heart pounding in her chest. She smiled back and leaned back in the chair.

"Don't get *too* comfortable," he said slyly. "It's gonna get worse before it gets better. New Jersey should get its first dose of Sandy tomorrow. If she stays at hurricane strength and makes landfall *anywhere* in the state, all hell will break loose here. Especially when confused homeowners are confronted with the rather sizeable wind deductibles that will come into play. We'll all need therapy after that."

She took a deep breath. "It's hard to imagine what's coming, looking out the window right now." The blinds were barely open but she gazed through the gaps as night was falling over the lighted parking lot. "It's almost eerily calm."

"Kelly, I know this job isn't what you expected," he said, slipping out of his corporate shoes and into his patented "time to be a friend mode." He was eager to find some common ground from which to approach the elephant in the room. She was obviously trying to avoid the subject and he was uncharacteristically hesitant to bring it up. He couldn't afford to press too hard. If she didn't come to the decision to stay at his place on her own, and he forced the issue, it could be misconstrued as harassment.

"It's obviously not the right job for you," he continued. "Hell, I don't think it's the right job for me anymore, either, which is why I was working on my exit strategy just now."

She gave him a quizzical look. "I don't understand. Are you thinking about leaving Maine Line? Why? Where would you go?"

"No, I'm not leaving—not yet, but someday soon. My goal is to retire early and see the world while I'm still young. "

"Isn't that everybody's dream?"

"I suppose so, but I'm actually in a position to make it happen, through the right investments."

There was an awkward moment of silence and he tried shifting gears. "What do you know about the stock market?"

"What's to know?" She laughed. "Buy low, sell high!"

"Exactly," he said with intensity. "It's all about timing. There are investment opportunities around us every day—even during a hurricane. You just have to know what to buy, what to sell, and when to do it."

"Sorry, Nick, but you've already lost me," she smiled shyly. "I barely made it through Economics 101."

He was not opposed to showing off his acumen when the situation called for it, especially where the prize was worth the risk. At this moment, he could hear Larry Sessions in his other ear counseling against it: *Boasting about making money is never a good play, not even with an attractive young woman.* But at this point, he was willing to use any weapon in his arsenal to get this one into the sack with him.

"That's okay," he said with mock sincerity. "I can teach you."

Kelly was amazed by his circumlocutions. She had no idea where he was going with this, but as long as it staved off an uncomfortable discussion about "shelter from the storm" in a hot tub at his place, she was okay with it.

"I warn you, you might want to rethink *that* proposition," she said, thinking about the money problems she and Danny had been fighting about lately. Even if she had the money to invest she didn't know anything about the options. "Teaching me about high finance will be no easy feat."

"Let me worry about that. You'll see. I can make it easy and even fun." *But first you have to ditch that useless boyfriend*, he thought to himself.

"Lesson number one," he continued. "There are a number of ways to make money during and after a hurricane: through insurance risks, gas rationing, and building repairs, to name a few."

"Should I be writing this down?" she asked half-jokingly.

"Only if you want to remember it."

She took out her iPad.

"Put that damned thing away," he commanded, and he meant it. "Here's what you need to know: If you own stock in an insurance company, short-term losses will eventually turn into long-term rate increases. Sell before the storm hits and the stock nosedives. Buy it back after, when the stock price is low and premiums are on the rise."

Kelly nodded her understanding.

He continued. "With gasoline, buy long-term futures. Period. After a storm, when supplies are cut due to damaged refineries and way-laid tankers, prices will soar."

"Does that also apply to building supply retailers like Home Depot?" Kelly asked remembering Danny's recent unpleasant encounter.

Nick appeared impressed. "Right! Another case of simple supply and demand. And believe me, the demand for building materials will be huge with this storm if it turns out to be anything like what they're predicting."

"Got it," said Kelly, anxious to wrap up her first and hopefully last investment lesson with her boss and high-tail it home while the going was good. She assumed she had stroked his ego long enough, so she stood ready to leave. "If it's that simple, why doesn't everyone do it?"

"Because not everyone's got the balls that I do." He stared at her long and intensely, realizing she was ready to bolt. He knew he had just one chance, so he decided to attack a weakness he'd perceived and challenge her. He stood up and walked around his desk. He came close beside her and put one arm around her waist, feeling how nervous she was. He started guiding her slowly and gently toward the door, without taking his hand off the small of her back. Even though the connection was physical, and she felt it, she was surprised that he appeared to be sending her away rather pulling her to him. It confused her, just as he'd planned.

"Kelly, I can tell you have mixed emotions. Welcome to the real world. There are incredible opportunities for an intelligent, beautiful young woman like you. You can have anything you want in life."

He stayed close to her, resisting the urge to touch her face while sending the message that they were sharing an intimate moment nevertheless.

"Lesson number two will be given at my place, tomorrow after work. You won't get another chance. Be there, unless you're afraid to take what you know you want."

23
Day 7

```
BULLETIN
HURRICANE SANDY ADVISORY NUMBER 25
NWS NATIONAL HURRICANE CENTER MIAMI FL          AL182012
1100 AM EDT SUN OCT 28 2012
```

```
SANDY EXPECTED TO BRING LIFE-THREATENING STORM SURGE FLOODING
TO THE MID-ATLANTIC COAST...INCLUDING LONG ISLAND SOUND AND
NEW YORK HARBOR...WINDS EXPECTED TO BE NEAR HURRICANE FORCE
AT LANDFALL...THE CENTER OF SANDY IS EXPECTED TO BE NEAR THE
COAST MONDAY NIGHT.


MAXIMUM SUSTAINED WINDS ARE NEAR 75 MPH...120 KM/H...WITH
HIGHER GUSTS. SANDY IS EXPECTED TO TRANSITION INTO A FRONTAL
OR WINTERTIME LOW PRESSURE SYSTEM PRIOR TO LANDFALL HOWEVER,
THIS TRANSITION WILL NOT BE ACCOMPANIED BY A WEAKENING OF
THE SYSTEM. IN FACT A LITTLE STRENGTHENING IS POSSIBLE
DURING THIS PROCESS.
```

Trapped between random moments of disturbed, restless sleep and nightmarish wakefulness, Paul Decker knew he would never get out of this makeshift prison cell alive. He wasn't someone who could be trusted to keep secrets, and now he knew too much for Harris and his handlers—whoever they were—to let him live.

He laughed to himself, taking stock of his life and thinking that Harris was right about no one taking him seriously. He had a certain reputation, earned through countless missteps and a long history of behaving in a paranoid and uncooperative manner.

It seemed that the highs and lows of his life could be traced back to 1974, when he found the love of his life. Lucy Neville was a fun-loving naturalist, nine years his junior. When they met on a kayaking trip down the Mullica River, she was studying agriculture at Rutgers and he was an up-and-coming meteorologist with an ABC affiliate in Philadelphia.

It was not a case of love at first sight—far from it—but they did share a passion for wine and the great outdoors, which led to a serious relationship. Unfortunately, Paul was prone to severe mood swings in the days before bi-polar disorder was clearly understood let alone effectively treated. His medication of choice was alcohol, which he used with increasing frequency and in large doses as his moods dictated.

Lucy wanted to get married, raise a family, and operate a vineyard, which as a result of recent legislation was on the cusp of becoming a booming industry in the Garden

State. Her parents supported her dream and were more than willing to help her finance it, but the idea of her sharing a winery, let alone her *life* with a temperamental drinker like Paul Decker would never earn their blessing.

After graduation, Lucy fell in with the budding campaign to protect and preserve New Jersey's Pine Barrens, which ultimately begat the Pinelands Protection Act and cemented her reputation for tenacity and integrity. From there, she parlayed a life-long desire to tend the soil into a job with the state, eventually becoming acquisitions director for the Farmland Preservation Program. In that position she maintained strong ties with the School of Agriculture at her alma mater, where she regularly taught and conducted research.

While Lucy was gaining broad recognition for her preservation efforts, Paul's career as a TV weatherman slipped into sharp decline. He managed to move over to the public sector, taking a desk job as a meteorologist with the National Weather Service in Mount Holly, but it felt like a big step down. Depression followed him and unchecked paranoia came along for the ride. As the manic depressive episodes worsened and increased, along with his alcoholism, Paul began to see unexplained lights in the night sky and shadowy figures lurking on every street corner. To make matters worse, he openly described these encounters to anyone willing to listen. While the changes in his behavior scared the hell out of Lucy, it wasn't until he began to see her career success as a potential threat to his that she put an end to their relationship.

Shortly after she left him, he hit bottom, and found a pharmacist willing to fill forged prescriptions. He put himself on a daily dose of lithium, cut his alcohol intake, and dedicated himself to the public service aspects of his work. By this time, however, it was too late to salvage his relationship with Lucy. There were still strong feelings on both sides, and they kept tabs on each another through mutual friends like Rick McGuiness.

As Decker's life continued to flash before him, he suddenly wished he had given Lucy the benefit of the doubt in their last phone conversation. If he had only trusted her enough to tell her why he wanted the samples tested, she might have someday realized that he wasn't crazy after all.

24

Fall from Grace

Rick McGuiness had left home in a hurry. As he motored south on Route 539 toward Route 72 and LBI, he realized that somewhere in between Jackie's nervous nagging, Billy's worried whining, and Caitlyn's ceaseless crying he had forgotten to pack a first aid kit. Chalk it up to the joys of domestic life, he chuckled, thinking he wouldn't have it any other way. Anyway, he kept a kit at the fire tower, and since it was on his way he'd stop and grab it.

It was early, it was Sunday, and bad weather was coming, but Rick was still surprised by how few cars were on the road. He was even more surprised when he pulled into the clearing near the tower to find Paul Decker's El Camino parked there.

An eerie silence greeted him when he climbed out of his truck. A chill in the misty morning air told him something was wrong even before he spotted the rumpled figure lying at the base of the tower. Instinctively, he glanced up at the observatory, reappraising the distance to the ground. A turkey buzzard circled overhead.

His heart was beating as fast as his feet were running as he rushed over to the body. His worst fears were immediately realized. He fell to his knees, his face coming within inches of Decker's own contorted face, staring back at him through the one open eye the buzzard hadn't pecked out yet. There was no need to check his pulse. A hip flask lay on the ground beside the broken, bloodied corpse.

***

Noah got Rick's call around 9:00 AM as he was heading back to LBI to pick up Sarah. His unsuccessful search for the weatherman the day before had been such a long and exhausting ordeal that it forced him to change his plans at the last minute and crash for the night at his friend Johnny Longfeather's place in Cedar Run. Before leaving a day earlier to help with the Sandy relief effort in his native Jamaica, Johnny had called Noah to ask him to check on his boat if he had a chance, and to remind him he kept a key under the doormat. Though she tried to strike an understanding tone, Sarah was none too happy when Noah phoned her late in the evening rather than coming home as he'd promised.

In his search for Paul Decker, Noah had spent a couple of hours waiting around the weatherman's house in Hainesport, and may have fallen asleep in his car for part of that time. Next he went door-to-door to see if the neighbors knew anything, but it turned out that most of them had no idea who Decker was, let alone where he might be. He drove to the Mt. Holly Weather Station where he had brief conversations with a couple of Decker's coworkers before finally getting in to see his boss. Ted Harris was able to shed at least a little light on the situation.

According to Harris, he had summoned Decker to his office two days earlier with the unpleasant task of firing him for insubordination and drinking on the job. Security had escorted him off the premises after that meeting, and no one had seen or heard from him since.

Decker was gruff and combative by nature, and he'd never made a secret of his lack of respect for the station chief, so the insubordination charge didn't surprise Noah. However, in the thirty years of their acquaintance he'd never known Decker to drink during work hours other than his traditional shot of whiskey at Irv's with lunch, which was public knowledge. Certainly, Decker never demonstrated any physical or mental impairment from that shot of Jack Daniels, and Noah surmised that "insubordination" had been his downfall. "Drinking on the job," he suspected, was no more than a persuasive extra strike against him in the event of an appeal.

For Noah, the news of Decker's firing made his death not only more understandable but infinitely sadder, as he imagined his friend's state of mind in the final hours. His work had been his life; he truly had nothing else, Noah reflected. According to McGuiness, the coroner had described the wounds, which included a broken neck, as consistent with a fall from the tower. Decker had evidently been dead for several hours before Rick stumbled upon the body.

The autopsy might reveal more, but Decker's body reeked of alcohol, suggesting that he either slipped and fell from the tower in a state of inebriation, or jumped. No suicide note was found at the scene.

After Rick related the tragic news to Noah, he shared some nagging questions. Where had Decker been for the last 48 hours? What was he doing at the fire tower? Although remarkably spry for his age, and a frequent visitor there, why would he attempt to climb the tower in the dark?

Noah listened, then added a question of his own. If Decker wanted to commit suicide, why would he take such a theatrical and uncertain approach when he had easy access to any number of prescription drugs? Unquestionably, their friend suffered from severe bouts of depression, but he was an innately private man who had always managed to keep a low profile.

"I have to agree with you on that," said McGuiness. "The whole damn thing makes no sense. Climbing that tower in the dark, let alone jumping from it, sounds too crazy even for Paul Decker. Impossible, I'd say, if he was drunk."

"Could he have been after something in the eagle's nest?" asked Noah.

"Nothing I can think of," admitted Ranger Rick. "There's not much there to begin with."

"And how would he get in?" inquired Noah. "The observatory is kept locked when it's not in use, isn't it?"

"Always," replied Rick.

"Had he broken in?" asked Noah expectantly.

"Doesn't look like it. The padlock was still on and nothing was out of place."

"That's even more confusing," Noah said, struck by the number of loose ends.

"It certainly is, but we have a more immediate problem," McGuiness said with a heavy sigh.

"What's that?" Noah gave him his undivided attention.

"Somebody has to notify his next of kin."

Noah had an idea where Rick was heading with this, but waited for him to continue.

"I can't stick around, Noah," Rick said. "I have to get to LBI for my EMT shift. The water's rising."

"And I've got to get Sarah out of there before they close the bridge," Noah said. "Isn't it the police's job to notify the relatives?"

"I suppose so, but they don't know of any. Do you?"

Noah thought for a minute. In all the years he'd known Paul Decker he'd never heard him talk about family. "Jesus, Rick, if he had any living relatives he sure kept it to himself."

"I can only think of one person he ever talked about," McGuiness said.

Noah didn't need the name. "That's sad, Rick, if she was all he had." He quickly added, "Under the circumstances."

"She never stopped caring about him, Noah. She tried to keep in touch, but he didn't make it easy; she asked me about him frequently. I think they may have spoken recently about some soil samples he wanted analyzed."

Noah straightened in his chair. "Okay ... I remember something about soil samples—from Warren Grove, after some unusual aerial spraying, right? Do you know the test results?"

"No, he asked me to send her the samples, and that was the last I heard of it," Rick said. "She was planning to phone him with the results—another good reason to call her ...?" He left the question hanging.

"I'd better go see her in person," Noah said.

"Thanks, Noah, and good luck."

***

As she showered that morning, Kelly agonized over whether or not to pack for an overnight stay. Before she got dressed for work, she pulled a small duffle bag out of her closet and threw in clean underwear, jeans, sneakers, a sweatshirt, and a few toiletries. She told herself the packing had nothing to do with Nick Weber. It was just a precaution in case she couldn't get back on the island after work. She needed to be prepared for the worst.

"Going on a trip?" Danny asked pointedly, staring at the duffle bag from the doorway.

She turned around slowly and looked him in the eyes, but she couldn't answer right away. She didn't quite know what to say. The kitchen phone rang, breaking their staring contest and putting a confrontation on hold. He left to answer it and returned a couple of minutes later, a different person.

"Before either of us says something we might regret, that was your Aunt Sarah," he said. "She's got water coming into the shop and Noah hasn't gotten back yet. She didn't want you to worry, and I guess she didn't want you to hear her crying because she didn't ask to speak with you. You do whatever you have to and we can sort things out later, but I've got to get over there." He started for the door without waiting for a response.

"Wait!" Kelly shouted, running after him. "I'm going with you!"

25

Stranded

The floodwaters arrived well before the gale force winds. On LBI, waves began climbing onto beaches and plowing through the inlets, even though the storm had yet to reach the shore. The back bays swelled to capacity with the rising tide. Held there by the advancing winds, the water did not flow out again.

As the bays were overwhelmed, Barnegat Bay and the Little Egg Harbor crested from Barnegat Inlet to the north and the Beach Haven Inlet to the south, sending wave after wave over bulkheads, down streets, across parking lots, and onto shorefront properties. The structural integrity of the Manahawkin Causeway—the only roadway connecting LBI to the mainland—became a major cause for concern as rising floodwaters and swift currents built up pressure underneath it. The Governor issued a mandatory evacuation order, giving the island's roughly ten thousand inhabitants until 4:00 PM to get out.

This was the state of things as Rita Zenger arrived on the island Sunday morning to make one last attempt to pry her father out of his home. Her backup plan consisted of two bags of groceries, dog food, and bottled water, in case the stubborn old man refused to leave. She steeled herself for a battle as she drove south toward Holgate.

When she got to the trailer park, it appeared that most if not all of the residents had evacuated. Helmut and Max were nowhere to be found. She knocked on a half-dozen nearby doors before she found someone home. Flo Sweeney was an elderly woman attending to a litter of four Yorkie pups she would never dream of leaving behind. Flo said she'd spoken to Helmut that morning and believed he was planning to ride out the storm.

"Try the beach, sweetie," she said blithely. "He probably took Max for a walk." With a big smile for Rita she added, "While you're at it, please see if you can find my Bessie—the mother of this brood. She and Max are great friends … if I didn't know better, I'd swear he sired these adorable pups."

Rita looked out at the slate gray sky. Rain had begun falling, driven by intermittent gusts of wind, full of stinging sand. "Do you really think they'd have gone for a walk on the beach in *this*?"

"Some dogs need to be walked to do their business," Flo said cheerfully. "And don't let these little Yorkies fool you," she beamed. "What they lack in size they make up for with their big personalities."

Rita thanked the old woman and headed for the beach, or what was left of it. She found her father sitting on a bench staring out at the churning ocean, wrapped in a worn patchwork quilt as the wind whipped around him and waves crashed thunderously on the shore. She couldn't recall ever seeing the water line so high.

"Hey, Pop!" she shouted at the top of her lungs as she put a hand on his shoulder. "What are you doing here?" She glanced around. "Where's Max?"

"I've lost him," the old man said sadly, his words punctuated by several dry coughs.

"What do you mean you've lost him?" She took a seat beside him, wrapping an arm around him.

"He's run off."

Rita pulled the quilt a little tighter around his fragile form. "Okay, why don't you start from the beginning."

"We came out here this morning to watch the surfers," he said, gazing blindly out to sea. "The surf was too rough. They had to call it quits."

He gulped a breath of air before continuing. "Then that little bitch Bessie shows up—old Flo Sweeney lets her run loose, you know. Max took off after her and I haven't seen him since." His eyes misted over.

"Did the other dog come back?"

"No," he said, coughing raggedly.

"How long ago did this happen?"

"I don't know, maybe ..." He didn't finish the thought.

"Pop, have you used your oxygen today?"

"Today?"

"Come on, Pop. Let's get you back to the trailer and out of this wind." She helped him to his feet. "We've got to get off the island."

"I'm not leaving without Max," he said, standing his ground.

"I know, Pop, and don't worry. I'm going to find him, but first we need to get you into some warm clothes and hook you up with a little oxygen." She put her arm around him and guided him gently but firmly back toward his trailer.

Twenty minutes later, after calling into the wind for Max until she was hoarse, Rita made a difficult decision and called Nick. He was pissed, but he'd have to get over it she told herself as she ended the call. She'd covered for him far too many times to beat herself up in this situation, though she was genuinely sorry to hear that half the emergency crew had called out. Apparently even Kelly Martin, his pet project, was a no show. Sure, he was pissed, but when it came to choosing between her job and her dad's safety it was no contest.

Rita knew what a hurricane could do to a sardine can like the trailer her father called home, but if she couldn't get him off the island, so be it. They'd look for Max together, and she'd stay with him to the bitter end.

***

It was late afternoon by the time Noah made it to Route 72 on his way home from the Rutgers lab in New Brunswick. Between breaking the news about Paul Decker to Lucy Neville and discussing the results of her soil analysis, the trip had taken much longer than expected. He was convinced that the test results were part of a much larger puzzle, but he'd have to start connecting the pieces later. He had more pressing matters to deal with at the moment.

His call to Sarah an hour earlier had him worried. The first floor of the shop was flooded, and although Danny and Kelly were there helping her move some of the more expensive items to the second floor apartment, the water level was still rising. He was afraid that in their efforts to save Sarah's inventory they may have missed the opportunity to evacuate. He kept a heavy foot on the pedal as he imagined the three of them trapped in the building, in danger even before the full force of the storm came ashore.

As he passed the exit for Route 9 he could see a line of eastbound cars making U-turns and heading back his way via the westbound lanes. A uniformed group of New Jersey State Troopers, supported by an armed contingent of National Guardsmen, stood in front of the barricade blocking the entrance to the causeway in both directions.

He glanced at his watch. He knew from Sarah that there was a mandatory evacuation order for 4:00 PM. It was already 5 o'clock now. He was going to have to try and talk his way across.

"Halt!" said a young trooper putting up his hand. He waited for Noah to roll down his window. "The causeway's closed."

Standing straight as an arrow, Noah guessed the young trooper was about Geoffrey's age and no doubt fresh out of the academy. The peak of his cap was pulled low over his forehead, covering his eyebrows in order to create an authoritative appearance.

"My wife is on the island and I'm on my way to get her."

"I'm afraid you're too late, sir. If she hasn't left by now she's stuck there with about 2,000 other residents who chose not to leave."

"She didn't *choose* to stay." Noah was emphatic. "She's been waiting for me to come for her. We only have the one car." He wracked his brain for a more persuasive angle.

"I'm sorry, sir, I can't let you through," the trooper said firmly.

Trying to remain calm, Noah said, "Listen, officer, my name is Noah Parsons. My wife is Sarah Bishop. She owns the Crab Cove Gift Shop—"

"Please turn your car around *now*, sir," the young man said in a loud voice. "You're blocking the roadway."

Noah tried a different tactic. "If you'll just call Mayor Huelsenbeck in Ship Bottom, he'll vouch for me." Picking up his phone, he clicked on his contacts and handed it to the officer with the mayor's name and telephone number on the screen.

"Are you a council member?"

"I work very closely with the council," Noah said, stretching things a bit.

The trooper glanced at the rearview mirror bracket through the windshield. "I don't see your hang tag. Were you given an official hang tag?"

"Hang tag? Well, no," the older man admitted.

"Then you'll have to move along. Now."

Noah felt the panic rising in him as his face flushed red. "Who is your commanding officer? I demand to speak with him *now*!"

The trooper put his hand on his gun holster and immediately several armed National Guardsmen were standing behind him, weapons cocked and ready.

"This is your last warning, sir," the trooper said, his tone brooking no further argument. "Turn your vehicle around now or you will be placed under arrest."

In a fury, Noah pulled his truck out of line, made a sharp K-turn and sped off, kicking up gravel in his wake.

26

Captain Courageous

As a U.S. Coast Guard veteran, Noah knew better than anyone that what he was about to do was beyond dangerous, it was absolute madness. Even for an experienced seaman like himself, crossing Manahawkin Bay in a small boat just ahead of a forecast hurricane was nothing short of a suicide mission. Perhaps he could be forgiven for not thinking straight given the stress and emotion of the past 24 hours, not to mention his mounting concern for the safety of his wife, niece, and nephew.

He'd promised he'd come back for Sarah and bring her to safety, and that was all he could think about now. As irrational as the idea might have seemed to him at any other time, he knew that if he couldn't get her off the island he would at least make sure they were together when the storm hit.

Johnny Longfeather hadn't had time to pull his Boston Whaler, *Clewless*, out of the water before leaving on his goodwill mission to Jamaica, and Noah didn't give a second thought to borrowing it. He rationalized that if Johnny were here, he'd be with him all the way on the rescue mission across the bay.

After gassing up the engine, Noah looked up at the darkening sky, wet an index finger and thrust it into the air. The wind was roaring out of the southeast at 15–20 knots with even stronger gusts. Sandy was on her way with a vengeance.

He donned a rain slicker and a life preserver, then started the engine. It coughed to life in a guttural rumble. Running from stern to bow he untethered the boat from its moorings and pushed her away from the dock, hopping on at the last minute.

The Whaler was seaworthy to a fault, and Noah told himself he couldn't have selected a better transport for the rough waters ahead. Famous for its flat bottom, wide girth, and durability, what this craft lacked in comfort it easily made up for in speed and stability. Johnny had boasted that *Clewless* could run in a foot of water, and to cross the shallow bay waters Noah was counting on it.

He'd traversed this narrow bay many times, aboard many different boats as both pilot and passenger. He was familiar with the ebb and flow of its seasonal tides, and with the eelgrass and sedge islands that dotted the shoals just below the surface, often fouling the propellers of unsuspecting boaters. Tonight, he could see that wouldn't be a problem. It was high tide, and Manahawkin Bay was full and angry, her surface whipped into a frenzy.

It was practically a straight shot east across the bay from Johnny's place in Cedar Run to Ship Bottom, but there was a powerful headwind to contend with. Noah knew his only option was to make slow, steady progress while keeping the causeway on his port side. He chugged past Cedar Bonnet Island just in time to watch the last vestiges of the iconic hunter's shack fall away. A relic from bygone days, the shack had become a kind of welcome marker to a generation of LBI vacationers. It saddened Noah to see it crumble into the marsh.

He checked the depth finder. Ordinarily that might have been a problem with the course he set outside the channel markers, but the bay was flush with whitecaps and overrun with choppy waves and rolling swells, so the real challenge was to keep the boat afloat and on course. Capsizing would spell the end for both ship and captain.

The chop was even worse than Noah had anticipated. The *Clewless* rode up and over one huge swell after another, her hull striking the water like a sledgehammer on each descent. Noah felt the impact in his clenched teeth every time as he churned forward across the dark, turbulent waters. Drenched to the bone from the spray, the deck was so slippery he could barely stand. Twice he lost his grip on the wheel, slipping and sliding across the deck until he could find his footing and make his way back to the console. More than once he tasted bile as the jostling motion brought a breakfast he didn't remember eating back up from his stomach.

To avoid losing control again, he lashed himself to the wheel with the towline. Peering around and over the rain splattered windshield in an effort to get his bearings, he wondered if he'd gone off course. He knew the bay like the back of his hand, but tonight it was barely recognizable. Channel markers and buoys appeared in one instant and disappeared in the next, bobbing up, down, and sideways as the whitecaps passed over them.

Squinting across the bay he saw what he believed to be the lights of Ship Bottom, his destination, but there were so few lights that he couldn't be certain of hitting his target. Scanning the horizon, his eyes latched on to the township water tower, in particular the distinctive halo of red lights that girded it. With the causeway lights off to conserve power, those red lights were his beacon now.

He cut the engine and pulled out his cell phone, pressing the quick dial number for Sarah's device. He couldn't hear well enough to be sure it was she who answered, but he shouted out anyway for her to look out the back door of the shop. He was on course for the pier that butted up against the shop's rear deck, but he couldn't see either the top of the pier or the deck.

Noah's heart soared as a light came on in the shop's second story window and vague faces appeared in the rain-splattered panes. At that moment the *Clewless* struck something solid, head on and with tremendous force. Noah's forehead met the ship's solid mahogany wheel with a thud and the lights went out.

27

Day 8

```
BULLETIN
HURRICANE SANDY ADVISORY NUMBER 29
NWS NATIONAL HURRICANE CENTER MIAMI FL        AL182012
1100 AM EDT MON OCT 29 2012
```

```
SANDY EXPECTED TO BRING LIFE-THREATENING STORM SURGE AND
COASTAL HURRICANE WINDS PLUS HEAVY APPALACHIAN SNOWS.


THE CENTER OF SANDY IS EXPECTED TO MAKE LANDFALL ALONG OR
JUST SOUTH OF THE SOUTHERN NEW JERSEY COAST THIS EVENING
OR TONIGHT. REPORTS FROM AN AIR FORCE HURRICANE HUNTER
AIRCRAFT INDICATE THAT THE MAXIMUM SUSTAINED WINDS HAVE
INCREASED TO NEAR 90 MPH...150 KM/H...WITH HIGHER GUSTS.


SURGE-RELATED FLOODING DEPENDS ON THE RELATIVE TIMING OF
THE SURGE AND THE TIDAL CYCLE...GIVEN THE LARGE WIND FIELD
ASSOCIATED WITH SANDY ELEVATED WATER LEVELS COULD SPAN
MULTIPLE TIDE CYCLES RESULTING IN REPEATED AND EXTENDED
PERIODS OF COASTAL AND BAYSIDE FLOODING.
```

Helmut Zenger's condition worsened through the night. He came down with the chills and began running a low-grade fever, but he refused to leave the trailer park without his beloved sheepdog, Max.

Rita thought it was probably too late to attempt an escape anyway, so she tried to get him into bed and then keep him there—no easy feat. His breathing was labored, so she kept his oxygen connected all night, switching him to a spare tank in the early morning hours when the first one ran out. When he finally fell asleep, she seized the opportunity to call 911 and request an ambulance, but was told that all available EMT personnel were dealing with other emergencies. Demanding to know *when* they could expect help, the operator explained that all of LBI's ambulances had been moved to the mainland just after the curfew, for their own protection so they'd be available once Sandy passed. Rita knew the hefty price tag these vehicles carried, and suspected that the real reason they'd been moved was to avoid the high cost of repair or replacement. She silently cursed the insurance industry.

With the causeway flooded, no one could leave LBI other than by troop transport, which was under the jurisdiction of the New Jersey National Guard. If Rita had a four-wheel-drive pickup or SUV she would have attempted the short trip to the Engleside Command Center in Beach Haven, from which a troop truck could take them off-island to Southern Ocean County Hospital. Unfortunately, the rising waters were already topping the wheels of her Toyota Avalon.

She stared out the window as she contemplated her next move. Other than herself, her father, and neighbor Flo Sweeney, the trailer park was a flooded ghost town. Looking across the lot at Flo's place, Rita couldn't tell where the bay ended and the street began. Several of the makeshift cinder block foundations under the mobile homes showed signs of giving way, and more than one unit had broken windows and other visible damage from the force of the wind and water. She took her cell out to dial 911 again. As the dispatcher answered, the phone went dead.

***

Noah awoke to find a pair of pale green eyes gazing down at him with tender concern. He reached for the ice pack resting on his throbbing forehead.

"Easy," said the owner of those beautiful eyes, gently removing his hand from his bandaged head. "You've got a nasty bump and a small laceration, but it doesn't appear you'll be needing stitches."

Noah smiled weakly at Sarah.

"You gave us quite a scare last night, mister," she scolded him gently.

"Johnny's boat?" he asked, attempting to sit up as the final moments of his trek across the bay streamed back into his consciousness.

"Listing badly, I'm afraid," she said, easing him back onto the bed. "Along with dozens if not hundreds of other boats left in the water—and you'd be in Davy Jones's Locker right now, Noah Parsons, if Danny and Kelly hadn't been here to pull you out of that one. What on *Earth* were you thinking?"

"You," he said, smiling at her. He glanced around the room. "Where are the kids?"

"They went back to their place to get a few things. They'll be by later to take us to the Engleside to meet up with Geoffrey and Luz. Apparently we can board a truck there for the mainland, courtesy of the National Guard."

He let out a low moan at the mention of the National Guard, recalling his confrontation with the young state trooper that had at least indirectly led to his near-fatal trip across the bay.

"I'm sorry, Sarah. I should have stayed with you instead of traipsing all over creation looking for a man with a questionable grasp on reality. I don't know if Paul killed himself or not. Something isn't adding up, but the fact is, he's dead, and we need to take care of the living right now."

"He was your friend, Noah, and you did right by him. I'm just glad you're safe."

"I'm so relieved that you and the kids are okay," he said, overjoyed to be back with the one he loved. Even in the eye of a storm.

***

Rick McGuiness was on patrol in Beach Haven, cruising Long Beach Boulevard in his GMC Jimmy, when he spotted her. Floating vertically, clinging to the driver's side door handle of a parked Volkswagen Passat, the young woman was helpless against the swift currents surging past The Chicken or the Egg.

He parked the raised Jimmy with its oversized tires at the curb, several yards in front of the woman's disabled car, facing it. He yelled to her not to panic—help was on the way. As he opened his door and climbed out, he was nearly swept away in the deluge that was formerly a street. He struggled to grab the front bumper of the Jimmy and pull himself to his feet.

From around his shoulder he uncoiled a 75-foot orange extension cord. Tying one end around the bumper and the other around his waist, he tested it to be sure it was secure.

"Hold on!" he shouted to the woman as he took a first tentative step forward in the thigh-high water. "Just hold on—I'm coming!" he yelled again, though he doubted she could hear anything but the sound of rushing water.

Like a tethered mountaineer crossing a precarious canyon gorge, Rick painstakingly made his way toward the frightened woman, pummeled by all manner of flotsam and jetsam as he closed the gap between them.

In addition to trash cans, lawn furniture, and other fast-moving debris, some of which he couldn't see let alone avoid, the sheer power of the current made for slow going. The wind-driven rain felt like pellets being fired at his face and hands. It flashed across his mind that if he lost his footing he'd likely be dragged underwater and sucked into a storm drain. He put the grim thought aside to focus on the task at hand.

When he finally reached the woman at the Passat, he untied the cord from his waist and fastened it around hers. Her back was to him as he helped her get to her feet, all the while screaming incomprehensibly and pounding her free hand against the car window. He tried to pry her other hand from the door handle, but she refused to let it go. Turning an ear toward her, at last he understood. "My baby!" she cried. "My baby!"

Wiping the condensation from one of the car's rain-streaked windows, he could make out what appeared to be a toddler strapped into a baby seat on the passenger side. Holding on to the exhausted woman with one arm, he used the other hand to try the door handle. It wasn't locked, but the pressure of the water outside the vehicle made it impossible for him to pull the door open. Looking into the car again, he saw that the water had risen nearly to the top of the console. It was a highly perilous situation, and he knew he'd have to take care of the panicked mother first to have any chance of saving the child.

He turned the young woman's tearful face toward his own, forcing her to look directly in his eyes. "I'll come back for your baby," he shouted. "Trust me!"

Moving away from the vehicle, the two began their slow, arduous journey against the current. Rick had her walk in front of him as he pulled the cord, arm over arm, inching them closer and closer to the Jimmy. The fatigued woman slipped and fell several times, submerging briefly then resurfacing as he pulled her up by the cord that bound them together.

When at last they'd reached the idling Jimmy, Rick opened the passenger side door and lifted her up and onto the seat. He unfastened the cord from her waist and again secured it around his own. "Stay in the truck," he said firmly. "I'm going to get your baby. Don't worry—I'll be right back."

"Hurry!" she cried. "Please *hurry*!"

As he worked his way back to the Volkswagen, Rick thought about his own kids, remembering how cute they looked as he was getting ready to leave home that morning; Caitlyn sitting in her high chair splashing applesauce on her mom's spotted bathrobe, Billy spooning away at his Cap'n Crunch as he watched cartoons on the small TV in the kitchen. These thoughts served to increase his determination and he quickened his pace. As he neared the Passat he saw it move, slightly, but unmistakably.

Jesus, the current is moving it, he thought in horror. He quickly closed the final yard that separated him from the vehicle and dove toward the passenger side door. The water was now up to the lower edge of the window. He yanked on the handle only to find that this one was locked. *Damn these VW's and their automatic childproof locks!* He cursed under his breath.

He reached around and grabbed the heavy-duty flashlight clipped to his belt. He lifted it above his head and brought the butt end down against the window, instantly turning the safety glass into a web of conjoined fragments. Applying firm pressure with his hand he forced the crumbling glass out of the frame, reached inside, and released the lock. Grabbing the door handle in one hand, he was able to pull the door open with the other, all the while bracing himself against the car to keep from losing his footing as the floodwaters surged waste high around him.

The baby was bawling uncontrollably as Rick tugged at the buckle holding the car seat in place. It wouldn't give. He reached into his pants pocket, removed a utility knife and cut the seatbelt strap. Grabbing the car seat, baby and all, he yanked it free of the car, falling backward into the murky water just as the VW gave a lurch and, lifted by the powerful current, was swept away down Long Beach Boulevard.

Watching through the windshield from inside the Jimmy, the young mother screamed at the top of her lungs at the sight of her car sailing down the street. It crashed into a nearby utility pole. The pole splintered, snapping in half and sending a nest of hissing, sparking wires cascading toward the flooded street. The wires caught, hanging suspended just inches above the rushing water.

McGuiness rose unsteadily to his feet, holding the baby seat and its tiny passenger tightly in his grip. Standing sideways in the current, he managed to quickly loop and thread the extension cord through the car seat and around his waist. As he was about to start moving back toward the Jimmy, something drew his attention and he looked up. Less than 10 yards away, a jumble of live wires was suspended just above the water line, crackling as it spat sparks in every direction. He recognized the danger instantly:

if an exposed high tension wire touched the water it would send an electric charge rippling through the flooded street. By now the water had risen well above the level where he'd first come in, almost to chest height, and as he pulled on the cord with all his might he couldn't seem to make any forward progress.

Watching from the inside the Jimmy, the rescued mom suddenly realized that the water was too deep and the current too strong for the man carrying her little girl to make it back to the vehicle. As McGuiness continued to struggle, she clambered over the console into the driver's seat, threw the Jimmy in gear, jumped the curb, and landed the SUV within inches of man and child. Rick yanked open the passenger side door and climbed in, the car seat with baby on board held tightly in his arms. He used his knife to cut the extension cord then tossed it aside, shouting "Go! Go! Go!" as he pulled the door shut.

She punched the accelerator and the oversized ties spun, then caught. The Jimmy lurched forward and rocketed down the street, as a snaking power line fell sizzling into the rushing floodwaters.

28

The Love Boat

Heading south on Long Beach Boulevard Danny struggled to keep his Jeep positioned over the centerline separating the north and southbound lanes. Between the lashing rain, the flooded roadway, and his panicky passengers, his concentration was being taxed to the max.

"Keep to the middle of the road," instructed Noah from the back seat. "It's the highest point."

Sarah gave her husband a soft elbow jab. "Let him be, he's doing fine."

Danny thought he had it under control, but being blown down the boulevard sideways by storm force winds was nerve wracking, no matter what he told himself. Combined with the havoc they saw Sandy wreaking on the island properties they passed, this was a bad trip and he was eager to put it behind him. He was happy that Kelly had stayed with him after all, but there were issues between them that he knew they'd have to face eventually. At the moment, the storm was more than enough to deal with.

He turned and glanced at Kelly sitting beside him in the passenger seat. She had her window rolled down and was snapping photographs with her smartphone, quickly downloading them on her iPad and tapping in a string of notes.

"What exactly are you doing?" he asked, no longer able to contain his curiosity.

"My job," she replied matter-of-factly. "Maine Line insures a lot of these properties and it may be helpful to have a record of the losses as they occur. How often does that opportunity come along?" she added, obviously impressed with her idea.

"My guess is, never," answered Danny.

"Exactly," she said. "It's like watching a robbery in progress."

"How will it help in an insurance settlement?"

"Simple," she responded confidently. "If there's a dispute surrounding the proximate cause of the loss, which can arise in multi-peril situations like this when wind, rain, flooding, and falling tree limbs all seem to happen at the same time, then a real-time record of events could shed light on the sequence of events."

"So you're like the roving reporter for Action News," he said admiringly.

"More like the mobile adjustor for Maine Line Insurance Associates," she smiled as she invented the title.

Just then the Jeep hit a pothole, and the weighty cargo Danny had lashed to the roof lurched sideways.

"Danny, tell me again why you brought your surfboat," Noah said.

"It seemed like a good idea at the time," Danny said. "Look around. All I see is water. If we get stuck we can always row ourselves to safety."

A typical Danny response, thought Kelly, his clear and concise explanation impressing her as much as her idea had just impressed him. They shared a quick glance and a smile, confirming that opposites still attract.

"In this mess that almost makes sense," Noah said. "Smart thinking."

When the Jeep pulled up to the Engleside, they found the parking lot bustling with what looked like paramilitary activity. Olive canvassed troop transports were coming and going like clockwork, and service men and women in fatigues were ushering frightened, rain-soaked residents in and out of the hotel, bracing themselves against the wind and hard driving rain.

Night was beginning to fall and although the surrounding area was without power, the hotel was lit up like a Christmas tree. A loud gas powered generator could be heard above the howling wind. After the Storm of '62 nearly wiped them out, the hotel owners had the good sense to install it, along with a 12-foot cement seawall to protect them from breaches in the beachfront dunes.

Geoffrey took a break from assisting the guardsman and hotel staff when he saw Danny's Jeep pull up. He ran over to greet them.

"How's it going?" Noah had to shout to be heard above the rain as Geoffrey pulled open the back door.

"Incredible!" Geoffrey beamed. "The hotel only has accommodations for 75 but we've got about 200 hundred guests on hand right now and we'll be able to billet a hundred more if necessary. I've been working out the logistics, with a little help from the National Guard."

"Have you seen Ranger Rick?" Noah asked as he climbed out of the car with Sarah right behind him.

"I think he's still out on patrol," replied Geoffrey. "I sure wish he *was* here—all our first responders are out on calls." He shook his head and continued as if he'd been a dispatcher all his life. "It's been one of those nights, and we just got another 911 call from Holgate. Some people are stranded at the trailer park, including an old man with emphysema. From the sound of it, that area is going to be completely under water by morning."

"I know the trailer park," Danny interjected. "I'll go get them."

"Be careful, Danny," Noah cautioned. "That part of the island is very low—they always get the worst of it."

"I'm going with you!" Kelly shouted above the din. The rain was coming down in sheets now.

Danny appeared stunned. "You don't need to do this, Kelly."

"Neither do you," she said. "But we work better as a team."

Sarah started to protest, but stopped abruptly when she met Kelly's determined gaze. "It's your life, sweetheart, and you're old enough to make your own decisions, but please be careful!"

"I'll send backup as soon as possible," Geoffrey shouted after Kelly and Danny as they climbed back into the Jeep and waved their goodbyes.

"How's Luz holding up?" Sarah inquired as Geoffrey led the couple out of the rain and into the crowded hotel lobby.

"She's in the kitchen, cranking out hot meals with whatever ingredients she can lay her hands on," Geoffrey said with a grin. "I think we should let her know you guys are here, and get you something hot to eat while we're at it." Looking at Noah closely, he noticed the bumps and bruises on his head for the first time. "What happened to you?"

"It's a long story, Geoffrey," Noah responded, putting an arm around this young man he was so fond of. "But don't worry—it's not nearly as bad as it looks."

"Still, I'm going to find out when the next transport leaves and see about getting you on it. You should see a doctor."

"I appreciate it, Geoffrey, but we're in no hurry now," Noah said as he took out his handkerchief and wiped the rain from his face.

"Maybe we can give Luz a hand in the kitchen," Sarah suggested, eager to pitch in and help with the relief effort—and forget her own fears and worries, for a little while.

***

As Danny and Kelly sloshed down Long Beach Boulevard in the Jeep, they couldn't help but notice the signs that the storm was intensifying. Fried transformers were popping and smoldering in the wind, while downed power lines and cascading debris made the going slow and hazardous. There was a reason they were the only recreational vehicle on the road, and it didn't take them long to run into trouble.

South of Merivale Avenue the ocean and bay met in the middle of the Boulevard, turning what used to be a road into a river. Kelly peered out the window ahead of them, trying to gauge the water's depth, but all she could honestly report to Danny was that it appeared bottomless. And ugly.

"Looks like the end of the line," she said dispiritedly.

"For the Jeep it is," Danny agreed. "From here, we take the Van Duyne."

He got out and waded to the back of the Jeep, untying the surfboat from the rear bumper before repeating the action at the front end.

"Danny, we must be twenty blocks away from the trailer park," she said as she climbed out of the vehicle. "Is this a crazy idea, or what?"

"Right," he said inscrutably as he freed the bow and dropped the boat into the flooded street. "We better get started." He grabbed the oars and placed them in the boat, then handed Kelly a flashlight and a pail. "I'll row, you bail," he said as he helped her climb in. "Try to keep the light steady, okay?"

"What's with the bailing action?" She flashed him a coy smile. "I thought you said this old scow would float!"

He laughed and offered, "We'll find out soon enough."

As the boat began to move down the street, Kelly flashed briefly on Venice, Italy, then decided that the only thing romantic about *this* gondola ride was that she and Danny were together. *For better or worse,* she thought to herself, realizing how very appropriate the catch phrase was at this moment—at least the "worst" part. Here she was … cold, wet, hungry, and scared, sitting in a small boat in three feet of water that was rushing down what used to be the main street of an over-developed barrier island, with a life-threatening hurricane ready to hit at any time … yet, as they moved forward, a sense of serenity came over her that was unlike anything she'd felt before.

"I love you, Danny Windsor!" she shouted over her shoulder.

He felt extremely lucky as his eyes took in the sight of his girl—his woman—lighting the way from the bow. "And I love *you*, Kelly Martin!" he shouted back.

Danny was like a new man as he steered the lifeboat he'd worked so hard to restore through the surging floodwaters, navigating around all manner of objects and obstacles, with the woman he loved doing yeoman's service. Time almost seemed to stand still as a familiar sign came into view just ahead. He set down his oars and announced, "We're here!"

The trailer park was a disaster area. A number of the units had come off their foundations and were floating in dirty water, bumping into one another aimlessly. Carports had collapsed and awnings had been torn from roofs. Rising seawater had turned the development into an island unto itself.

"Which one is it?" Kelly called out.

"I don't know," answered Danny. "Wait! What's that?" he shouted, pointing to something moving in the water.

Kelly trained the light just ahead of them.

"It's a dog!" she exclaimed. "He's heading directly for the unit with the coral pink shutters—he may be leading us to someone."

As they reached the trailer, they saw the smiling face of an elderly woman in an open window. "You've found Bessie and Max!" she said happily, pointing to the wet sheepdog. Max stood on the trailer stairs, just above the waterline, a tiny Yorkshire Terrier held gently in his mouth for safekeeping.

Danny pulled the boat up alongside the window and urged the old woman to climb out. She disappeared for a moment before returning to toss a suitcase down to him. "Be careful with that!" she exhorted him as she worked her way slowly over the sill and out the window. Dressed in an old-fashioned housecoat, Flo Sweeney could have stepped out of a 1940s movie, right down to her abundant makeup. She extracted her little dog from the mouth of the larger one before tumbling into the boat.

"He's a good boy, that Max—we'll have to take him with us," she informed Danny.

He glanced over at Kelly, who just shrugged. Guiding Max off the steps and into the boat, Danny was rewarded for his effort with a spray of cold seawater as the sopping wet sheepdog shook out his coat.

Mrs. Sweeney opened her suitcase on the floor of the Van Duyne and four tiny balls of fur popped their heads out. She set Bessie in the case with her pups and a joyful reunion ensued.

"We were told there were two residents in need of help," Kelly said as she leaned in for a closer at the puppies. "A father and daughter?"

"Yes, of course—over there," Mrs. Sweeney said, pointing to a blue-shuttered trailer. The unit had come off its foundation and was tilting precariously as it floated, heaving up and down in the wind-blown water. The waterline was above the bottom of the door.

After making sure his passengers were seated and secure, Danny rowed the boat over to the trailer and pulled up to the bay window. It was dark inside, and he couldn't see a thing. Kelly shone the flashlight beam into the house, putting it on strobe in an effort to catch the attention of anyone inside. When she held the beam solid again, a woman's blanched face appeared in the window like some ghostly apparition. She waved at them, either annoyed or excited, and Kelly redirected the light away from her face.

A second later the woman smashed the picture window with an empty oxygen tank. As Kelly held the boat steady against the loosened, bent siding, Danny assisted the woman in lowering an old man, wrapped in a worn patchwork quilt, gently into the boat. The man was wheezing and his breathing was labored, but as his dog came over to nuzzle him, he called out Max's name joyfully.

With surprising agility, the woman in a tan skirt, black stockings, sensible heels, and a black jacket followed, climbing through the window and into the boat unassisted.

"Don't be upset," Flo said as Rita took a seat beside her. "I called 911."

"Upset? Mrs. Sweeney, you saved our lives!" Rita enthused. "And you found Max!"

"Actually, Max found us," Kelly said, turning toward Rita and removing her hood. He led us right to you."

"Kelly?" shouted Rita as she realized who she was looking at. "Kelly Martin?"

Kelly was wide-eyed in surprise. "Oh … my … God! Rita!"

"You're my savior, Kelly—my Joan of the Ark!" Rita said, tears of joy streaming down her face as she leaned over to give her temp a grateful hug. Turning to Danny, she added, "And you must be Noah!"

"Danny. Danny Windsor. And this is The Little Boat That Could," he added proudly.

Danny returned to his duties as Master and Commander, and soon had the Little Boat That Could on its slow trek back toward civilization. Despite the Van Duyne's reputation as "unsinkable," between the five adults and assorted dogs it was well over the recommended load limit and Danny knew they weren't out of the woods yet. She was sitting extremely low in the water, and a sudden movement by any one of the occupants could easily cause her to capsize. He didn't even want to think about where that would end, so he concentrated on rowing slowly and steadily, keeping a close eye on his passengers—including an unpredictable old woman and one large, rambunctious sheepdog.

"Look!" Kelly shouted excitedly, pointing up the street to the headlights of an approaching Humvee. "Geoffrey did it!"

29

Day 9

NO BULLETIN ISSUED
HURRICANE SANDY ADVISORY
NWS NATIONAL HURRICANE CENTER MIAMI FL
TUES OCT 30 2012

The morning sun made a welcome appearance over the receding Atlantic Ocean, and none were more appreciative in greeting the new day than Danny, Kelly, Noah, and Sarah. Standing on the second floor balcony of the Engleside Hotel, they were enjoying the relative calm and brilliant blue sky when they were joined by Rick McGuiness, who was counting his own blessings.

"How's your father doing?" Kelly called down to Rita Zenger as she came walking up from the beach.

"Much better, thanks. The EMTs stabilized him enough to have him airlifted to the medical center." She turned and pointed to a helicopter, which was quickly becoming a tiny dot on the horizon.

"According to the pilot, LBI looks like a bomb was dropped on it," she continued. "More than half the island is still underwater and a lot of homes were destroyed. There's sand, water, and muck everywhere, and boats all over the place—in backyards, on top of cars and houses. Unbelievable."

"It's going to take years to recover from this mess," Noah said with an arm around his wife. "But we'll get through it. The Jersey Shore is resilient and so are its people."

"I couldn't agree more," said Ranger Rick. "Nothing can keep us down … not for long, anyway."

"Why didn't you go with your dad in the chopper?" Danny asked Rita.

"I wasn't ready to go, and they had to clear the airspace—Obama and Christie are coming to tour the Jersey Shore together." Rita chuckled. "Talk about an odd couple!"

"No wonder it feels like the end of the world," joked Sarah just as Danny's cell phone rang.

After a conversation comprised mostly of pithy affirmatives from Danny, he pumped both fists in the air and let out a wild yell. "Yeah!" he bellowed. He gave Kelly a big kiss and a bear hug that took her breath away.

"What's this all about?" she demanded.

"That was Ned Skinner," he said, almost giddy with joy. "The phone at the marina has been ringing off the hook. People are calling him like mad begging him to bring their boats in for repairs and salvage. He's got more work than he'll ever be able to finish, and he offered me a full time job. I can start right away!"

Kelly pulled her to him and kissed him passionately. When she finally broke away she enthused, "Now *that's* my Prince Charming!" in a voice loud enough for Rita to hear.

"Hey—Cinderella," Rita yelled up with a sly smile, "I talked with the Home Office earlier to let them know what happened here yesterday. I told them about the photographs and notes you showed me of the damage, and they were really impressed. Those photos should give Maine Line a big advantage in settling the claims fast and fair."

"*Fast and Fair* sounds like a great slogan for an insurance company," Geoffrey said as he and Luz joined the group on the balcony. "Way to go, Sis!" he said and a wave of high fives ensued. Then his tone turned serious. "Has everybody seen this?" He held up the *Star Ledger*, its front page photo showing the twisted wreckage of the Seaside Park rollercoaster, rising out of the Atlantic where Sandy had unceremoniously deposited it.

"Holy crap!" exclaimed Danny. "I guess we can be glad we weren't any further north."

"I was there last week with my boss," Kelly shook her head. "There was no way he was expecting *that* kind of damage."

"I'm glad you mentioned that," Rita said as she joined the gang on the balcony. She looked directly at Kelly. "The main office called this morning to advise that Nick Weber has been put on unpaid leave until further notice."

"Why? What did he do?' Kelly exclaimed, her words escaping before she could stop them.

"Who's Nick Weber?" Noah asked.

"My boss," replied Kelly.

"Your *former* boss, it looks like," Rita said. To Noah she added, "Our Regional Vice President."

"So, what did he do?" asked Luz.

Rita turned back to Kelly. "Apparently he submitted an engineering report about the Seaside Park Pier that left out an awful lot of information."

"That doesn't sound like sufficient cause for a suspension without pay," Rick offered. "Especially for a VP."

"You're right. It wouldn't be …" replied Rita, looking to Kelly for some sign of compassion, regret, or even complicity, "if that's all there was to it."

"So there's more?" interjected Sarah, nudging Noah. "Honey, I think he's the young man who sold me the policy on Crab Cove. Maine Line is the carrier."

"I don't like the sound of that," Noah muttered under his breath.

"So *this* is the guy you've been working for, Kelly?" Danny said. "Did you have any idea what he was up to?"

Rather than answer, Kelly turned back to Rita. "What else did he do?"

"It's almost like he knew some of the pier structures wouldn't hold up under the intensity of the storm, but he accredited them anyway."

"Why would he do that?" asked Geoffrey expressing the confusion everyone else was thinking.

"He may have had a financial motive," Rita said. "Apparently the SEC is investigating Nick Weber for investment irregularities."

"That doesn't sound good," nodded Geoffrey. "What sort of *irregularities* are we talking about?"

"I don't have all the details," admitted Rita. "What I know for certain is that his investment broker was censured by the SEC for trying to make transactions after the markets closed on Friday."

"Wow, sounds like some serious financial hanky-panky," Danny said. "And I thought the real storm had passed!"

"Go on, Rita," Kelly urged, anxious to get it all out on the table, and happy as hell she never went to Nick's place for lesson number two.

"Well, the most damning fact is that Nick unloaded most of his Maine Line stock three days before the hurricane."

"That's not against the law, is it?" Danny asked.

"I'm sure it's not," Noah said, "but we're talking about an executive in the insurance industry on the eve of a big storm. It certainly sounds suspicious."

"And unethical," added Ranger Rick. "Especially if he was filing questionable engineering reports. Sounds like he knew the losses would be greater than expected and intended to capitalize by selling short. It's like betting against your own house—insider trading stuff."

"So what happens now?" asked Kelly, thinking out loud. "Who replaces Nick as head of the regional office until this all gets sorted out? The claims are going to be rolling in, and the office can't operate without a leader."

"And it won't," acknowledged Rita. "The Home Office has already begun the search for a permanent replacement. They've asked me to take Nick's place in the interim."

"Rita, that's wonderful!" Kelly exclaimed. "You really deserve it … and everybody knows you run the show anyway."

"Thank you, Kelly. I appreciate the vote of confidence."

"Do I still have a job after bailing on you Sunday?"

"I guess you've forgotten that I bailed, too?"

"Of course—you had to go see your dad at the trailer park."

"My father's health and safety are more important to me than any job I'll ever have, Kelly, and frankly I won't work for a company that can't appreciate that."

"Well, you certainly made the right choice," Kelly said.

Rita smiled. "It obviously doesn't apply to my ability to pick husbands, but I've always had a particular knack for making the right choices where staff is concerned." Rita paused for a moment as if to let the comment sink in. "Maine Line wants me to reopen the Ocean County office as quickly as possible, and I'd like you to take my former position as supervisor. Interested?"

Kelly was flabbergasted. "What? *Me*? Floor supervisor? Doesn't that require Home Office approval?"

"I recommended you for the promotion, and it's already been approved. I told you how impressed they were with your initiative during the storm, Kelly, and frankly, so am I. In fact, let me just that say in the face of *all* the storms swirling around you lately, you have handled yourself admirably."

"Does that mean she gets a raise?" asked Danny, embracing Kelly and initiating another round of high fives.

"Effective immediately."

"Now, if only restoring Crab Cove were that easy," Sarah said wistfully as she put her arms around her husband's waist.

"Don't worry, honey. We'll have her pumped out, dried out, and cleaned up before you know it, won't we, Geoffrey?"

"You bet," the volunteer dispatcher agreed enthusiastically.

As Danny and Kelly celebrated some good news coming out of such a devastating storm and everyone around them agreed that they should all take this opportunity to rebuild their lives for a brighter tomorrow, Noah grew pensive, remembering that one of their own would not be part of that optimistic future.

"What is it, Noah?" his wife asked.

Watching as seagulls circled high in the deep blue sky over the newly reborn beach, he said thoughtfully, "We may never know the whole truth about what happened to Paul Decker, but I can't help thinking he was trying to tell us something, trying to warn us about something important … and not just the weather."

Epilogue

After a week of intense anxiety, heavy with anticipation, Hurricane Sandy—officially classified as a post-tropical cyclone when it swept through New Jersey—arrived pretty much as predicted.

Following some early missteps and vacillation among the weather community, they finally got it right. Unfortunately, even knowing ahead of time could not have prevented the widespread destruction Sandy left behind. On the East Coast, in the midst of plunging autumn temperatures, millions of people were left without power. Thousands became homeless overnight. In the wake of the massive flooding caused by the torrential rains and tidal storm surges, which reached a height of thirteen feet above sea level in some areas, dams burst and bridges collapsed.

Littered with debris from fallen trees, shorn limbs, ripped roofs, torn siding, and lined with hundreds of stranded and damaged vehicles, roadways became inaccessible. Mass transportation shut down. Businesses closed. The relatively few gas stations that could operate on auxiliary power were sold out within hours. The cost in dollars ran into the billions. The cost in lives totaled a few hundred; almost everyone agreed it could have been much worse.

In the aftermath, stories of heroism and self-sacrifice abounded. Those who had lost everything bravely began picking up the pieces and starting over. Hundreds of thousands of Americans from all over the country reacted with charity and compassion, giving what they could of their time, money, and material goods in support of the victims.

Drawing on lessons learned from Katrina and Irene, federal and state government agencies acted quickly, if not seamlessly, providing important relief through emergency management expertise, monetary aid, food, housing, transportation, and medical supplies. Over-burdened insurance, banking, and financial institutions—all operating in crisis modes themselves—responded in an orderly if not always empathetic manner to settle claims and resolve disputes.

Did the system operate perfectly? No. Was everyone completely satisfied? Of course not. The world is not perfect and some people will never be satisfied, but the system worked. Neither the country nor its economy collapsed. The afflicted communities and states rebounded, as did the nation as a whole.

And what to make of Sandy? Had Mother Nature simply flexed her muscles, reminding us how insignificant and helpless we arrogant human beings really are? Or was it the result of something far more sinister and foreboding? Could the storm have been accelerated or even triggered by climate change? Was greed and ignorance to blame?

Whatever the cause, a tantalizing question remains ...

Will we be ready when it happens again?